A KING IN COBWEBS

TOR BOOKS BY DAVID KECK

In the Eye of Heaven
In a Time of Treason
A King in Cobwebs

A KING IN COBWEBS

David Keck

TOR

A Tom Doherty Associates Book
New York

A KING IN COBWEBS

Copyright © 2018 by David Keck

A Tor Book
Published by Tom Doherty Associates
175 Fifth Avenue
New York, NY 10010

www.tor-forge.com

Tor® is a registered trademark of Macmillan Publishing Group, LLC.

The Library of Congress Cataloging-in-Publication Data is available
upon request.

ISBN 978-0-7653-1322-5 (trade paperback)
ISBN 978-1-250-30397-4 (hardcover)
ISBN 978-1-4299-8834-6 (ebook)

Our books may be purchased in bulk for promotional, educational, or business use.
Please contact your local bookseller or the Macmillan Corporate and Premium
Sales Department at 1-800-221-7945, extension 5442, or by email at
MacmillanSpecialMarkets@macmillan.com.

First Edition: December 2018

Printed in the United States of America

0 9 8 7 6 5 4 3 2 1

FOR AMY

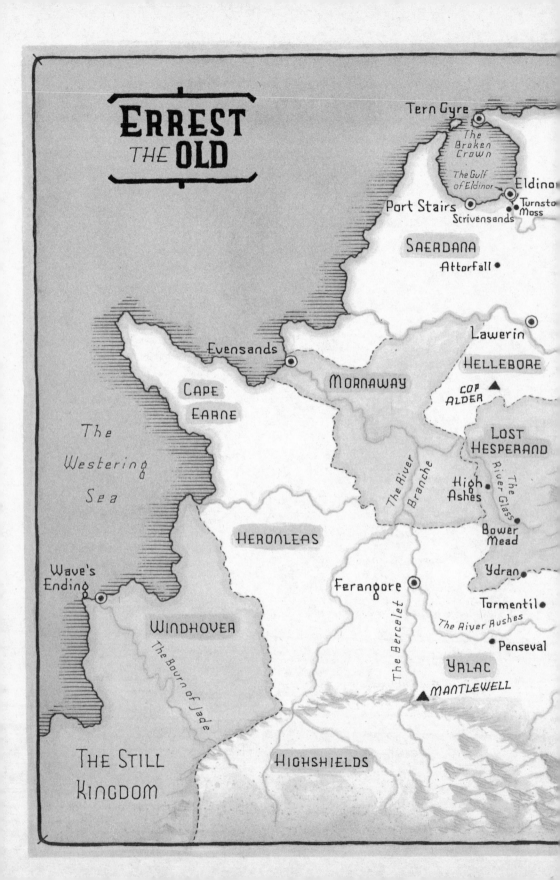

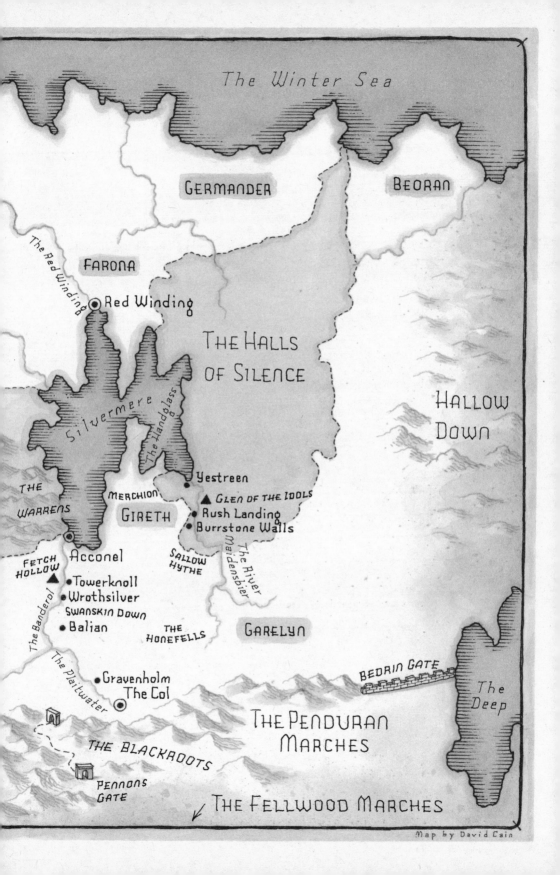

A KING IN COBWEBS

1

A Feast of Life and Death

Kieren the Fox leaned back from the high table. "In the old stories, these feasts are always the start of something."

Durand looked down on the little knight from his spot over old Duke Abravanal's shoulder.

"I need no such looks from you, Durand Col," said Kieren. "How long have I known you? Man and boy, it must be twenty years. You were rolling on the rushes there like a puppy when I first saw you.

"And you may make a skeptical face, but what I say about stories is true: it's always this feast or that feast. They were gathered for the Feast of the Ascension when. . . . They all start that way. You check with that minstrel friend of yours, next time you see him. Heremund?"

"I've not seen the skald in years." There had been no new tales for many winters.

Sir Kieren glanced up and down the high table, winking at young Lady Almora where she sat by her ancient father a few spots down. "The hall was crowded; throughout Creation the Sons of Atthi feasted the Ascension of the Eye of Heaven over darkness and the beginning of Spring. And so half the fractious barons of Gireth and Yrlac, ten years sulkily united under Abravanal's rule, muttered under green garlands in that black hall, their ladies in gowns of emerald while knives winked, wine sloshed, and greyhounds roiled in the rushes like fat eels."

Almora laughed, tucking her chin a bit. She was the only cheerful thing in the hall.

"Where do all the dogs come from, anyway?" Kieren wondered. One of the brutes was nuzzling its way past their knees even now, its coat as coarse as brown oakum. Kieren slipped the dog a scrap and was lucky to keep his fingers.

"Now I've got lost. Ah yes. The greyhounds. All under the lowering eye of the duke's champion, Durand Col, who stood like a black-bearded idol at the duke's shoulder, forever watchful, forever loyal, and forever lowering at me though I've known him since he was a pup and I his master. You could stop lowering, Durand."

This got another bright laugh from the girl.

It was enough to draw a cautioning frown from Almora's lady-in-waiting, Lady Deorwen.

Sir Kieren pursed his lips behind his great mustaches, and made sure he was out of Deorwen's earshot. "Worse than usual?"

Almora ducked her dark eyes. "The dreams again," she said.

"Ah," said Kieren. "You'd think she'd have laid the last of the old ghosts to rest by now."

"They still come to her," said Almora. "She is often abroad at night."

"Running errands for the Lost." He clucked his tongue. "Ten years since Radomor of Yrlac put this place under siege, and still the dead are not done with us."

Kieren set his hand on Almora's shoulder and she smiled, wistfully now.

Just then, something drew Durand's attention from the girl, his old friend, and Deorwen. There'd been a word misspoken, and a shushing—too loud.

Durand Col, Champion of Gireth, scratched his beard and shot a glance down the long tables, where he spied a bald fighting man struggling with his companions.

"Let me speak, you hissing pack of fishwives!" The bald fighting man waved a boar's rib in the air as he shrugged off his companions. He wasn't one of the usual men who came to Abravanal's board. The dullard had a shapeless face, a bit like a pig's bladder.

Kieren frowned. "It's that Euric boy, idiot brother to the Baron of Swanskin Down."

"I only asked why the old man hasn't married the girl off," Sir Euric said. A ring flashed on his finger. "What harm is there in asking?"

"What did he say?" old Abravanal quavered, scarcely more than whisper.

"Nothing, Your Grace. He's drunk, most likely," Kieren said, but Euric had ventured onto dangerous ground.

Lady Deorwen took Almora's elbow and shot Durand a cautioning look. The woman was half his size, but her dark eyes still nudged him off balance, though long years had passed since he'd set a finger upon her.

"In the autumn, the king's messengers show up here in Acconel," Euric continued. "They tell us, 'Ride over the mountains. Get to Fellwood.

Quiet that rabble down there.' A land that's nought to do with Gireth or Yrlac—not much to do with Errest the Old, some might say. Leave half a rebellion behind to go haring off to the Fellwood Marches. But the snows come early and the high passes are choked. And that gives us a winter here at home to settle things with the barons in Yrlac. It's a gift from the Powers of Heaven, sure enough.

"But what did we do? It is Ascension time now, and some of our friends from Yrlac are hopping over the river every other night. . . . A winter wasted, and Yrlac still not sorted. They need a sign over there. While there is still time!"

Only then did Euric seem to notice that the eyes of the high table were upon him, and that his tirade was in the ears of his masters.

Abravanal rose unsteadily to his feet.

Euric straightened, patting the air with one greasy hand. "With respect, Your Grace. With respect. But you must show the lords of Yrlac your mind! We have lost one winter since the king's message, but there have been ten long *years* since Radomor of Yrlac rebelled against the king. Ten years since we vanquished him. Ten years since you have held the traitor's lands. Are the native lords in Yrlac free or conquered? They must know where they stand. King Ragnal has business of his own, worrying that them forest lords in Fellwood do not heed him, I suppose. And what cares he which of his lords plays duke in Yrlac? The king will send word now that Spring is here: over the mountains to Fellwood and show them they're not forgot!"

There were lords of Yrlac in the room, shifting on their benches, but the drunkard began counting options on his fingers: "Marry the girl off to that Lord Leovere of theirs, if you must; bind his house to yours. Or, if you won't give them the girl, *crush* them, and think on marrying the girl to one of your own barons here. Drop the gate on the devils in Yrlac! They must know your mind, Your Grace—*you* must know your mind. And it must be now!"

Duke Abravanal trembled in every limb. "Must? *Must?*" He could hardly choke out a syllable, so full of rage was he. "Who are you to speak this way, to tell me that I *must* give up my daughter?"

"Father . . ." Almora gave the old man a beseeching whisper, then shot a pointed look at Kieren.

Kieren the Fox, Abravanal's Steward in Gireth, was already on his feet. "Lord Euric, for your late father's sake, I hope you'll spare a moment to remember where you are. You've a right to your own mind, but we're in our liege lord's hall just now."

It was a noble attempt and had to be made, but Euric only blinked stupidly.

"That's just it, Sir Kieren. Maybe His Grace *needs* a word," Euric said. "It's our future he's fumbling with." He jabbed his rib bone at his duke. "I know he's got plenty of reason to hang on to the child with all his others dead. But locking her up in here in Acconel? The king will send us all over the mountains any day now, and Acconel will be left with hardly a fighting man to defend it. What if Lord Leovere or any of the rest of his Yrlaci friends choose to make trouble? Is Abravanal with us here in Gireth or them in Yrlac?"

A few hands in the hall shaped the Eye of Heaven to ward off evil. The man's words were treason.

"Almora is my own affair, you stupid fucking boy," rasped Abravanal. "As is how I govern the lands my late sons wrested from the rebel Duke of Yrlac. And my dead children. God! As if I do not remember them. As if they ever leave my mind!"

Euric looked up into the garlands crowding the soot-blackened vaults of the Painted Hall. Lady Deorwen was gathering up Almora to get her from the hall. Almora's hair bobbed like sable as she snarled in Deorwen's ear. She was no infant to be sheltered from harsh words; it would be something like that she was telling poor Deorwen.

And Deorwen was not quite quick enough.

"Your Grace. She's like a dove in this black old tomb." Euric's hand swept expansively over the girl and the high table. "Is she fifteen now? A girl her age should be out on her own, not cooped up here with her old father. I know a great lord on the border who's of an age to marry. That would be a message sent." Durand wondered if the man referred to himself. "I mean . . . is there something amiss with the girl? Something wrong with her?"

A big hollow rage filled Durand's head. There was not wine enough in Creation! She was a little girl. . . .

Almora had nearly reached the door. Deorwen had been too slow.

"What's that you say?" the duke breathed.

"I only wondered if there might be something—" The boar's rib dangled in silence.

"Durand Col!" spluttered the duke.

Durand stepped from the gloom behind the old duke, drawing every eye.

"The fool's in his cups. He's brother to Swanskin Down," Kieren whispered, but the old man would not hear—could not hear. To bring up

marriage. To offer the Yrlaci's favorite, Leovere of Penseval. To question Abravanal in his own hall. To say that something might be wrong with Almora. And all in a hall full of headstrong lords from the two lands of Abravanal's domain. Durand was the Champion of Gireth, oath-bound to defend the duke and his daughter. And Euric had one way back.

Chinless Euric's expression hardened like a stubborn child's. "I've said what I meant."

"Then you must unsay it," said Durand.

"But there *must* be a reason—"

"Oh Host Above . . ." said Kieren, despairing. Kieren and Coensar had been trying to arrange for a marriage with Yrlac for a year or more.

Durand, with a flat smack of his hand, set twenty goblets wobbling. Wet blooms of wine spread over the table linen. "Sir Euric, you've slandered the kin of our liege lord, sworn and rightful. You will not recant. A hundred noblemen of Errest are witness."

The man stared back, the little bobble of his chin glistening with grease.

"Get a horse," said Durand. "I'll meet you in the yard and prove her ladyship's honor on your bones!"

Abravanal's eyes bulged and Kieren put his face in his hands. Lady Deorwen had managed to get Almora from the hall.

DURAND WALKED HIS shaggy black giant of a warhorse, Shriker, into the inner yard where knights and lordlings shuffled in the cool brightness of a spring afternoon. Most were a little the worse for the wine. Some would have known Euric—page, shield-bearer, and baron's brat—since he was a boy. A ruddy banner of silken cloud rippled above the battlements where guardsmen weighed the odds, wagering their pennies. Durand remembered fighting a siege in this place, ten years before.

Taking a man to the yard was a mortal business. Durand was already muffled to the eyes in straps and iron. He winced at the stink of the stained, rag-stuffed old gambeson under his hauberk and coat of plates. He jabbed a brace of lances into the turf.

He scrutinized Shriker's gear, fighting the brute's black trappings to get his fingers on double girths and broad breast band. The monster shifted—a quick tramp meant to slice Durand's foot off, no doubt. But Durand knew the animal.

Sir Kieren stalked across the grass and bent perilously close to Shriker's flank. The little man's drooping mustaches bobbed at Durand's ear.

"Euric's kin have been bound to the Dukes of Gireth since old Duke Gunderic was a nipper. They've held that Swanskin Down for the Dukes of Gireth time out of mind, Durand. You remember his poor father. Looked like a baker. And now Euric's brother is the baron, of course."

"Catch hold of his bridle a moment, Sir Kieren," said Durand mildly. Shriker was nodding. "The devil bites when he's cross." And Durand tugged a girth tighter. "I take it you've spoken to Abravanal then? He won't listen?" If Abravanal had relented, Kieren would already have his peace.

Kieren's mustache jumped as its owner grimaced. "Swanskin's an important man. The Down is right on the blasted border with Yrlac, not a league from Leovere's seat at Penseval. Things are ticklish out there."

"Ticklish, aye. So Euric said. But I gather Duke Abravanal is adamant," said Durand gently. "So Euric must be taught a lesson."

"His Grace has had a hard time, Durand. You must make allowances for that. And it's Ascension Day. Think on it. In an hour we'll all be stood in the high sanctuary with the cedar and the balsam and the Eye of Heaven. Is this the time to shed the blood of the Sons of Atthi? What can the King of Heaven think of such a thing? It is his day, after all."

"You ask the King of Heaven. I'm Abravanal's man. And if Abravanal won't be talked around, that's an end to it."

Kieren grunted. "If Euric had spent more time in Acconel, he'd have known better than to open his gob about the girl. His Grace will no more marry her away to some lord of Yrlac than slit her throat. We've been trying to bring him round to Leovere for two years. To him, all the men of Yrlac are traitors and murderers and only the Host Below knows what else. Me? With Yrlac and Gireth bound in blood and kinship, I'd dance at the wedding. And this drunkard thinks he can fix it up by shouting down the high table? Maybe I should have you give him a knock or two on my behalf, once you've settled his account with His Grace.

"Still, a man might wonder why his brother sent him. That new baron, Vadir, is not the simpleton Euric is. Was Vadir trying to press his own suit? God, he can hardly have thought Euric could woo her!

"But it doesn't matter. The poor girl won't see a betrothal until the old man's gone." Fighting the infernal Radomor of Yrlac had taken both of Abravanal's sons, and dark-haired Alwen had died while wife to Radomor. Durand had seen Alwen in her tower while Radomor smoldered and their infant child howled. Three children dead over Yrlac. The duke would not allow his last surviving child to leave his sight. Giving Almora to yet another lord of Yrlac was unthinkable.

In the daylight, Durand noticed that the Fox's long mustaches were more silver than red. The poor man had been managing Abravanal's affairs for more winters than Durand could guess.

"You might speak to Euric himself," Durand suggested. "I cannot, but there's nothing barring you from having a word."

"Have I not done so? But it's a rare baron's brother who has the courage for contrition."

"And our Euric is not the exception," Durand concluded.

Just then, high-strung Shriker tossed his big head, screaming up between the walls: Somewhere down the yard, Euric would have led out his warhorse, and Shriker was not pleased to scent another stallion. "Here's our baron's brother now," said Durand, and indeed Sir Euric had appeared, stomping into the yard, still wrestling with his battle gear—and with an entourage of agitated friends. The slab-sided brown stallion who had so offended Shriker permitted Euric's friends to catch hold of his bridle.

"Here it is. Doom has come among us," said Kieren. "I'd better get to His Grace. You'd best take care of yourself."

Euric, clad in green and gold, was shaking off his comrades and leaping into the saddle, a bare blade wobbling in the air.

Durand climbed soberly onto Shriker's back. He lifted his helm and slid the riveted barrel down over iron links and hair-stuffed canvas, grateful as the closed helm resolved the confusion of Creation into one narrow gash. He could hear his oft-broken nose whistle. A quick-whispered prayer hissed and rattled like the splash of water on a skillet.

Abravanal and his family looked on, the duke under a heap of blankets. Tiny Deorwen's disapproval was enormous. She had an arm around Almora, once again ready to hustle her away.

Durand found the hilt of the old sword-of-war he carried: a gift he bore but never used. It had belonged to a comrade and there were tangled feelings. No. For fighting, he used a chained flail. With its rough links and nasty blacksmith's ball of filed nails, it did the job. He thumbed the tines for a moment, then let his eye settle on his opponent.

Already, Sir Euric had spurred his charger into neutral ground, letting the animal's hooves lash at Heaven. He bellowed, "Black Durand! Old Hunchback! You're a canker on a sickly court, and Gireth wastes away with you at its heart! And it is past time that someone cut you out!"

Durand blinked. He resented "hunchback." His shoulder gave him trouble since Radomor and the siege, but hunchback was unjust. Iron links of mail crunched as he worked his jaw.

Euric seemed unhappy with Durand's silence and waved his brass-pommeled sword vigorously.

"Bloody old cripple! My plowmen will have that patchwork head of yours for a football. What say you to that, vile ogre?"

Durand hauled in a deep breath. "You may yet be reconciled with your duke, Sir Euric. Recant and have done." Kieren the Fox deserved that much, and a scar or two did not make a patchwork. His beard hid a lot.

"The old man does not know his enemies, Black Durand," Euric snarled. He snatched a lance from a stone-faced shield-bearer. What a master that boy had.

"So be it," said Durand. He roughly reseated his helm, wrenched one lance from the ground, and managed a quick salute to the duke and his daughter.

Euric had already lashed his mount into a full gallop.

Durand prodded Shriker on, even as Euric's pell-mell rush gobbled up the ground between them. Durand felt the straps of his shield creak in his iron mitt. And, finally, he gave Shriker the spurs and chose a spot amid the riot of green charging toward him. He lowered the point, tensing—

And there was nothing. Nothing but the rushing thunder of hooves and flying canvas.

Drunken Euric had slipped in his saddle. Just enough to duck the lance: a drunkard's luck.

"Who'd believe it," Durand muttered as an irksome smattering of applause broke out among the duke's liegemen. There was even a laugh or two as Durand swiveled and caught his breath.

"I'm the man in green, hunchback!" shouted Euric, helm in his hands. He had to probe a minute to get his right foot in the stirrup, but he was smiling. "This way! You can hardly miss me."

Durand hauled Shriker around, and the big brute wheeled hard enough to fling hanks of turf at the gawkers. Euric made a great show of hurrying his helm back in place.

Durand tore down the yard, the nobles along the walls flashing past his visor. Euric leapt to match the charge, and, in twenty surging strides, the two knights collided. There was no mistake this time. Durand's lance cracked like dry lightning, and the shock of impact nearly wrenched him from his saddle. His point had bitten hard.

Astonishingly, Sir Euric trotted, apparently unhurt, toward his incredulous friends. His shield must have caught everything.

"Impossible," Durand muttered. The man had survived a second pass. And it occurred to Durand that Euric had the kind of luck that got other men killed.

Stiffly, Durand rode for his remaining lance; old wounds had him breathing short. But he would not be beaten easily.

He tore the second lance from the ground and faced his man.

The two knights hung in pendulum's stillness an easy stone's throw apart. The wind over the yard danced for a moment with the green trapper round the legs of Euric's horse. The filed edge of Euric's lance-head glinted. Durand ran his tongue along the old broken edges among his teeth.

This time he meant to stake Euric to the turf.

He spurred big Shriker, his lance floating free of Shriker's jolting stride. Euric's storm of green and steel swelled in the slits of Durand's helm, and he aimed for the heart of the man's shield with a remorseless determination to teach Euric his lesson at last.

Then, at the instant of contact—just as it all ought to have come clear— Euric's lance twitched. Quick as a wasp, the heavy point was at Durand's jaw. The thunderclap of its touch put Durand in the sky with torn rivets shrieking through his skull.

He spun under the roaring Heavens.

And slammed to the face of Creation in what might have been an-other age.

The moments that followed were scrambled and elastic. There was a smell like hot copper reeking in his head, and he could hardly remem-ber where he was. Everything was blood.

He pawed at his face, trying to see while the castle yard pitched. There was a fight; he'd be butchered if he couldn't move. Was the other man alive? Dead? Was he walking upright then, with a sword in his fist, mea-suring Durand's neck? Or was he lying with a lance in his ribs?

He forced his eyes wide.

And found another impossibility. It seemed that the afternoon grass brimmed with uncanny shadows, all trembling like wine on a taproom table. They shivered, real and alive. And, even flat on his face, he remem-bered seeing such things before. Long ago with his onetime captain, Coensar. These were the Lost. For now, Durand squeezed his lips tight against a bulge of nausea and levered his face from the spinning field.

Across a few paces of grass, he spotted the man in green, flat on the turf; they were like two drunkards waking on the same inn floor. The pig's-bladder face was bare and pale. The impossible shadows swelled in the grass where the knight struggled. There were mouths. Durand saw the hollow ring of an empty eye.

They were the Lost, the souls of the dead. Thirsty for blood, and wary of the Eye of Heaven.

But Euric lived. Suddenly, the man was up and looming taller than Gunderic's Tower. There could only be instants. Durand rolled to his knees and, with a wrenching effort, stumbled onto his feet, even as the shadows stirred round him like silt in ditch water. They lapped at the blood on his face. He breathed them.

And he faced Euric, shield in hand.

The two men reeled. The tip of Euric's blade flashed in the grass, but his green shield was gone, and the arm that had held it now hung at a nasty angle. One good thing, anyway.

Durand forced himself though the lapping shadows, weaving at the man in green. Only at the last did he realize that he'd no weapon in his hand; the chained flail he'd brought was still slung on his belt. But Euric didn't wait. In a baffling clap of iron and splinters, Durand's shield exploded from his fist and he was left with nothing. Euric had tottered past, striking, though Durand never saw him swing.

"I have you, hunchback," the man said, his voice slurred. "You're mine!"

Durand threw himself out of reach, struggling to haul the rattling flail from his belt; his left arm was still caught up in a mess of straps and splinters.

Euric launched another hammer blow.

This time Durand lurched close, swatting the man's blade wide and managing a brawler's butt over the man's nose. Euric tottered around, blinking and gawping, but then he hoisted his blade and threw the flashing sword into an utterly baffling loop of flashes. A blow cracked down on Durand's shoulder, its rebound nicking his ear. Euric followed with a flurry of blunted prods that bent Durand double, till he was bowing like a traitor before the headsman. Like a traitor before Gunderic's Sword.

Euric staggered back to swing his blade down from the Heavens, and there was nothing left for Durand to do. Against sense and training, he caught the blade in his fist.

Here, the Lord of Dooms set his mark on the day.

By rights, Durand's fingers should have tumbled free like so many raw sausages, but Euric's luck had abandoned him. Mail and leather held.

And so, Durand gripped Euric's blade, clamped in a vise of muscle and mail. And, for just an instant, Euric's sword arm was stretched stiff. Durand took that moment to finally wrench the flail from his belt, lashed the iron head down over Euric's shoulder, then yanked it whistling round and—with a dizzy spin before the hissing crowd—switched the ball of tines across Euric's jaw.

The force of the blow nearly landed Durand on his backside.

For an instant, the flail's head was nailed there, fixed like a burr on a couple of black spikes, but Durand's stagger jerked the thing free. Even Durand had to wince. Once, he'd had the same treatment.

Kieren the Fox put a crabbed hand up to ward his eyes as droplets splattered, and a few onlookers made the fist-and-fingers Eye of Heaven sign.

Durand felt a greasy caul of blood over his own face.

Euric, meanwhile, tottered a pace or two across the turf until, finally, he collapsed in a pool of shadows. The Lost lapped hungrily.

Durand caught a few swallows of air; it was in his head that he shouldn't look winded—a notion that soon had his head spinning. A dozen paces away, Abravanal stood, looking for all the world like an outcast grandmother in a rug beside him. The duke's vindicated daughter clung to Lady Deorwen. The two women gave Durand a look he could not decipher before turning back into the castle. He guessed they did not approve.

But Durand had a more immediate concern, for the yard teemed with slithering shadows like the spawning of dark eels under the skin of a brook, even as men came to gather up the stricken Euric. Soft tongues slid over his boots and the backs of his hands. And, as Durand wavered there, he remembered seeing the Lost before in that place: ten years or more. He'd been sitting with Coensar—hero, friend, and traitor. A botched tourney had left a friend dead. And the Lost had been sad and forlorn and hungry as flies.

Either Euric's lance had cracked Durand's head, or he was seeing the things in truth. Had they been with him all along?

Before he could decide, a commotion started among the courtiers, and he looked up to see Sir Coensar, Abravanal's Steward of Yrlac, ride through.

Even bloody and calf-deep in dead men, Durand smiled.

2
A Rite of Fire

Gray-cloaked Coensar rode at the head of a dozen armed men, gaunt as a wolf. Once, he had been Durand's captain, the chief knight in Lord Lamoric's Red Knight tourney band. Now, Durand's old captain was called "steward" and "lordship"—and stood second only to Abravanal himself in Gireth and Yrlac.

All this—all of these grand titles—had come to the man after he had nearly killed Durand and the duke's son. The memory was knotted in Durand's bones. In the midst of that wicked siege, Radomor the rebel had trapped Lord Lamoric beyond the walls. Durand had got the young lord free, and they had been flying over the market cobbles with the castle gates before them. But Coensar? Coensar had lashed out and—oh so very nearly—destroyed them all.

Durand had not understood the fear and rage of a landless, aging fighting man watching a younger man take his place.

Still, Durand had agreed to bite his tongue. So many had died. So much had been burned. People had seen such terrors. Gireth had needed a great man to lead them out of the disaster of Radomor's war. And Coensar had been a hero—as far as most men knew.

In the yard, Coensar stopped short. Here were Durand and half the barons of the two dukedoms. He blinked at bloody Durand, standing with the chained flail dangling in his fist and the wreck of Sir Euric sprawled before him. It was an ugly thing to be struck in the face with a chained flail. The tines. Durand could still feel the shape of Coensar's flail when he touched the bones of his own brow and jaw.

"The dullard spoke of Almora," explained Kieren. Most of the gathered nobles found something fascinating to look at on the tops of their boots. "Now we will have to find a quiet room for him. And a surgeon, I think. A baron's brother!"

Abravanal tottered forward in his heavy robes, the only one grinning. "My steward! You have arrived in time for the Ascension. We have had our feast, but perhaps the kitchens can yet manage something. . . ."

"Ascension," said Coensar. The man had forgotten. "That explains the greenery. But, no, Your Grace, I've come to say that the high passes'll be clear any day now. The king will expect us to run this Fellwood errand soon. If we're to take care of our own problems in Yrlac, we haven't much time."

"King Ragnal is young still. He *has* time."

"'Before the first snows,' was his word, Your Grace. And more than one man carried that word. And yet we did not move. But King Ragnal wants the Host of Gireth over the mountains and settling whatever's stirring in the Fellwood Marches. I hear he is busy arguing with his brother in Windhover." Another rebellion. "Already, the Sowing Moon has waned. Your Grace, it's bad in Yrlac. Bad on your border. We *must* get our house in order before we set out for Fellwood." As Steward of Yrlac, Coensar would have much to discuss.

"Well," said Abravanal, tugging his cloak tighter, "we cannot leave before Ascension, no matter what the condition of your high passes. Let us do our duty to the Creator, then we may do our duty to the king. The Eye of Heaven will not wait."

"Yes, Your Grace," said Coensar.

Durand left the yard and its ghosts behind.

"WHAT DO YOU think you are doing?" Deorwen demanded.

Durand's chamber was a stone room up in Gunderic's Tower, a foot or so longer than a grave. He had a pallet, a trunk, an arrow-slit, and a basin.

Deorwen stood in the narrow doorway. Too near. Durand dripped and stank. He glanced from her face. He was stupidly conscious of her shape. "Lady Deorwen," he managed.

"Ah. You will insist on politeness, I see. Well, I must ask, regardless: What is in your fool head? Kieren is trying to keep this place together and you're in the yard murdering your master's liegemen."

"I am the duke's champion. I've sworn to defend his honor and to protect Almora."

"A fine answer, but you do *neither* of these things playing headsman to every lout who cannot mind his tongue."

"Deorwen, there's no time." They required a much longer conversation, but hadn't managed it in ten years—and a quick look at the arrow-slit showed that the Eye of Heaven was very low. The priests could not hold the sunset for a pair of laggards. "We must be in the high sanctuary. The last hour has come." He peeled the mail and padding from his scalp, wincing at his stiff neck and thick ear. And caught Deorwen looking at the blood and bruises with a shiver in her eyes.

She raised her gaze. "And Euric's laid out in one of the bedchambers with the physicians. A fine Ascension Day. Honestly, Durand, how is Kieren meant to manage with a hall full of ladies, hawks, hounds, and barons—half from Yrlac and half from Gireth, all bickering and snarling—with Abravanal as he is? This whole little world of ours depends on him." With Radomor dead and Almora unmarried, Abravanal held much of the kingdom in his old hands.

"Deorwen, it was *treason*."

But Deorwen gave him a long, tired look—the like of which he'd seen many times. "And Creation might have come to an end for such a treason?" she said after a cold few moments, leaving him.

Durand reached to shut the door, but Almora popped her head around the corner, startlingly close. He wondered what she'd heard. "Fear not, Sir Durand. It's only that she's had another of her dreams last night."

"Not another." She saw the dead: the Lost. How many hundred such visions had Deorwen dreamt since the siege? Each vision the last memory of some Lost soul who'd died in the flames and fighting of those fatal days. "Until she finds the body and gives the poor thing rest, she never gets much rest herself."

"No." She would search, sometimes alone, sometimes with the wise women of the town, hunting through the new city for the bodies of the Lost. And the burden of it pulled her away.

"You mustn't worry too much," Almora said, and then she too vanished from the door, chasing Deorwen down the passageway.

Durand shoved the door shut and blinked for an instant in the red light of the coming dusk. He peeled off sticky layers of mail and plates and canvas and tossed them into a heap in the corner. He scrubbed at the worst of the gore on his face with a rag from the basin. And then, to make certain, he fished a looking glass from the bottom of his trunk. As he raised the thing, something moved behind him.

Durand spun. "Who is there? Deorwen?" he demanded, but the door remained closed. He looked around at the blood-tinged basin, trunk, door, bed . . . and saw nothing at all.

Finally, he lifted the hand glass once more—and only then caught a glimpse of something reflected in the murky lens.

"Host Below!"

Pearl-dead eyes shivered in the shadow of his old bed, full of fever and incomprehension. And there were more. Durand gripped the mirror as he realized the freakish shapes crowded the dark chamber all around him, visible as dustings of soot and shimmerings of ash beyond the reach of any mortal light. A pair of long wings shivered with clinging moths.

A white giant stood against the wall, its blank face as wide as the moon. Near Durand's bloody basin, cracked nails scrabbled hungrily at the flagstones. The Lost. He had not left them in the yard; they had followed him, or they'd curled up in the cozy dark of his skull.

He got hold of his courage and turned. And there they were before his wide, naked eyes, more than figments of the looking glass. Mottled shapes. Shoulders, wrists, uncomprehending faces.

"*Begone,*" Durand breathed. "What do you want with me? I've done nothing. Begone by the King of Heaven!"

At the Creator's name the things exploded away, scuttling with more than the haste of vermin—shapes as big as men chittering down into the cracks of the floor.

Snatching up a clean tunic, Durand bolted from the room.

The last he saw as he shut the door was the pale bulk of the moon-faced giant.

DURAND RAN DOWN the steps of Gunderic's Tower like a terrified child, but, though the last to reach the courtyard, he took an instant to check his pace before stepping out. The company was gathered at the gates to march out in the procession, with Almora and Abravanal in the lead. Still belting on his sword—a knight must wear a sword—he leapt aboard a skittish little saddle horse and barged into the crowd. Even rattled as he was, Durand couldn't let Almora or her father ride unguarded, not when so much of Yrlac was up in arms.

Before Durand could bully his restive mount closer, a fanfare brayed over the city and the ducal procession was off, plunging into the fairground streets of Acconel without him. Durand spotted the duke riding under the gates—riding through a curtain of crimson banners and into a sea of bright faces. Then, he spied young Almora trotting behind and spurred the anxious rouncy cruelly, catching the girl—and very nearly riding over a scowling Lady Deorwen.

The crowd in the streets out-shouted the trumpets as the highborn wallowed into Acconel. Every window overhead fountained greenery with boughs and bunting and swags of flowers. Up front, crowned Abravanal teetered in his saddle like a parading icon while the crowd threw their garlands. He raised Gunderic's Sword of Judgment, and the people sang paeans of joy. Almora's eyes flashed. "Sir Durand! There are so many people. More than ever, since the war."

Flowers tumbled down on the beaming girl.

"It may be, Ladyship," Durand gasped, blinking at the rain of blossoms.

"There can't be a posy left for leagues." But he felt as awkward as a bull-dog in ribbons with the petals heaping on his black gear.

Almora reached out to him, touching his cheek an instant. "I am glad you survived, Sir Durand. And I think Lady Deorwen was pleased as well." Though Durand wondered what was left in Deorwen's heart for him.

"Lady Almora!" said Deorwen, confirming his fears. "I'll do my thinking for myself."

The girl smiled. "And *I* wouldn't have missed Durand in daffodils." She took in the crowd, smiling as Durand gave her the grimace she wanted. "It is grand to see so many people. It's wonderful that they wait for us to pass before going on to the high sanctuary!"

"It is a fine custom, Ladyship," said Durand. Light flashed from the old Sword of Gunderic as the Eye of Heaven sank.

Behind them, the gabbling ocean of humanity surged shut, forcefully cutting them off from the safety of the castle. All around, arms and oily faces crowded close, groping in from above and below while the duke's banners passed near enough for servants and housewives to reach out from upper floors and loop wreaths around their stark lances.

"It has been a long winter," said Almora. "And always a crowd at the gates for handouts. Now, they all seem so alive."

Meanwhile, the crowd cheered the duke and his daughter. And they cheered Coensar, the silver-haired hero of the siege of Acconel. Almora laughed, actually clapping her hands as one maiden leapt up to the aging steward, daring to plant a kiss on his cheek.

"There you are, Sir Coensar!" exclaimed Almora, and Coensar scowled like a drover in a downpour.

Despite the crowd's obvious good humor, Durand could not help but see danger in all the tumult. How simple would it be for some Yrlaci villain to slip near?

As he watched the crowd with visions of Yrlaci knives in his head, he caught sight of a man moving along a row of shops: a large man, bulling his way toward Almora or Abravanal, churning forward even though the crowd had him nearly pinned to the collarbones. And so Durand gave his skittish rouncy the spurs again and surged into the mob, wincing at the shrieks of pain and panic. Within a wallowing lurch or two, Durand was on top of the man, hauling his flail from his belt just as the fellow lifted his hands—to reveal only a garland of wildflowers.

Thankfully, the unflappable Almora took the proffered garland and set it on her brow. Her charming flourish saved the good cheer of the crowd in a single smiling moment. Behind Durand, folk were already picking their fellows up from the road. Some laughing. Most smiling up at the girl and none worse than bruised. "Flowers, Sir Durand," she said. "Flowers."

"Ladyship," said Durand, his face burning. "Very nice." He nodded to the man whose face was contorted with the conflicting emotions of having got so close to Her Ladyship and nearly being felled by her champion. "You have my apologies." The man bowed low, but Deorwen looked none too pleased.

Thankfully, just then Sir Kieren called out. "Lady Almora, we had best press on!" And he pointed up at the high sanctuary, just then coming into view between the rooftops. The new stone was bright as fresh snow.

"Oh, it's *so* beautiful!" Almora said.

The construction stood complete from the Dawn Altar down half the length of its old foundations, soaring some twenty fathoms above the highest roofs nearby, all built since Radomor's rebellion and the siege. Where the unfinished aisle might have gaped open to the weather, the priests had hung a vast black cloth like a giant's curtained door. "They will have bought every bolt of black canvas in Errest the Old," said Almora. "What will you do for surcoats now, Black Durand? Shall we dress you in gold?"

"I have black enough to last," said Durand. He'd worn the color since Lamoric had died in Radomor's little war. Always black. He ran his thumb over the handle of his flail.

The procession mounted the sanctuary steps into the ruined nave, jingling among the sheds, limekilns, and timber of the builders that was spread across the floor. Funerary effigies stood open to the Heavens. Almora marveled at it all.

"These seem so strange in the weather and the sawdust," Almora said, looking down on the alabaster faces.

"Aye," Durand agreed. He saw chips over white bodies.

"We will soon have them back under the shelter of the sanctuary once more, do not worry," the duke whispered. "The masons said they could not build it in *sixty* years, but I was adamant. Though it takes every piece of silver from our treasury, your brother and his comrades will not wait so long." His wide blue eyes flickered at the high curtain in its frame of white finials. "Already the high sanctuary is greater than it ever was."

The wonder in the girl's wide eyes ebbed away. Acconel's high sanctuary was the resting place of the heroes of the Siege of Ferangore, including her brother, Lord Lamoric.

As the duke reached the curtain, the black wings sprang wide, freeing clouds of beeswax and rowan smoke to billow high into the evening. Priests bowed while battalions of kettledrums and trumpets thundered from the corners of the sanctuary. The horses shied and snorted, doubly alarmed when their hooves struck the paving stones. In the midst of it all, Father Oredgar, the fearsome Patriarch of Acconel, stood tall, bedecked in gold and fire.

"The Ascension is at hand," announced the Patriarch.

The duke raised Gunderic's old sword. "We are come in full thankfulness, and have brought with us our sworn men."

The Patriarch's eyes sparked like those of some barbaric chieftain of another age. "Enter then under the Eye of Heaven."

Dismounting, Abravanal and his company shuffled to a canopied stall set aside for them. "Your Grace," said Coensar. "We must be off the moment this is over. By morning, if it can be managed. Ragnal wants us over the mountains, but we've trouble that won't wait."

"Yrlac," was Abravanal's answer.

Durand's forehead ruffled a silk fringe as he took his position behind the duke. Dubiously, he fingered the crimson linen of the stall's back panel, thinking that a few ugly pine boards might have stood a better chance of stopping a dagger.

Lady Deorwen took her position beside him, very close.

Meanwhile, the highborn of Gireth shuffled to the facing rows of benches along the sanctuary. A completed sanctuary might have admitted more of the citizens, but soon the vast curtain had to be shut on the multitudes to allow darkness to take the sanctuary; this was key to the Ascension rite.

And Durand could feel Deorwen, the heat of her body, almost touching him in the dark stall, where she stood behind Almora's chair. He closed his eyes. His ear throbbed. One eye was swelling shut. His neck hurt whenever he dared to turn his head. Still, it was better to stay far from Deorwen, even after all these years.

Somewhere up front, Coensar leaned close to Abravanal, whispering, "Your Grace, Yrlac is on the point of war. We may have defeated Duke Radomor, but the native lords who survive cannot abide our hold over them."

"What would Radomor have done to us?" Abravanal growled.

"He'd have snapped Gireth up without a thought. You'll get no argument from me. But in their own feasting halls when no one can hear, what do you think these native lords are saying? Every slight is recounted. Every wrong recorded. And now, the men of Yrlac won't rest till Yrlac has a duke of its own. Those are the whispers, and you must know it."

"You are speaking of that Leovere."

"He's the last man with any of the old blood in him. And every knight and baron of Yrlac has been wheedling and cajoling and driving him for ten winters. Every whisper of discontent ends up in Leovere's ear. Every crime of a Gireth-man on the soil of Yrlac is brought before him in Penseval. It is a place of rage and tears."

Abravanal's answer was like a blade's hiss upon a whetstone: "*I* did not wish that war. It was Radomor who pulled down Penseval. The sanctuaries. The Well of the Spring Maid. The Red Hall of that boy's ancestors, curse them. He tore it all down just to deny his enemies food and water."

A shrill of bells drew the attention of the congregation, and every soul turned to the Dawn Altar, where ancient Oredgar stood, apparently balanced on the heels of his own reflection upon the deep polish of the sanctuary floor. Durand remembered bodies lying in the same scent of beeswax and balsam. It was an unwelcome image. And here he was caught between Coensar and Deorwen, Lamoric's widow. A breeze on the curtains let a fiery seam of light slip down the aisle and blood-redden the faces of knights. As one, the people winced. Durand wanted out.

"We did not ask for war," said Coensar. "No one doubts that. But the native lords of Yrlac have grown bold." And bolder as Abravanal grew old. "They would have a duke of their own blood, and think it is time for Lord Leovere of Penseval."

"But I do not, Coensar! He's the man who *surrendered* at Ferangore, the ranking peer in that street of fire. I'm sure he choked on that. And he has not once been to my hall in all the years since. That man has sworn no oaths to me at all."

"He has not. But he's faithful enough when he gives his word. The man has brought us a hundred petitions from his people in Yrlac."

"*His* people."

"Lands stolen. Rights violated. Custom ignored."

"Leovere knows our numbers. Our men have turned him down and turned him down, but he will not stop. Once, a steward of yours clapped him in irons for impertinence. He has rebuilt the Red Hall of his forebears, but he will not be silent, though he has never had the power to resist us. No, Yrlac is vanquished, its lands forfeit. He is fortunate to have his hide intact. It is more mercy than Radomor showed my children."

"Aye," said Coensar. "But now there's a change. The barons of the king's Great Council have grown jealous of your two dukedoms, Your Grace. They're grumbling. And that might mean money, men, and arms for a rebel in Yrlac. Given the power to break our hold, Leovere might move from his Red Hall. The native lords might give him no choice."

"Then we will move first! We will strike into Yrlac. We will root out these rebels and see just what Leovere has to say for himself!"

"We might forestall him, Your Grace. He is enraged, but I think he will talk. We might still wring a peace out of him."

"It isn't peace he wants." The old man looked to Almora. "When we return from the sanctuary, make ready. Call up our host. It is too long since the lords of Yrlac have seen our numbers."

"Your Grace. Send for Leovere. What harm is there in hearing him?"

"What harm? I know what you intend, Coensar. You would give him my daughter!" The old man's voice rang loud in the sanctuary. "Leovere would be heir to Gireth *and* Yrlac. He would have my daughter while I live, and rule in my hall when I am gone!"

Coensar subsided. "Well, whatever is done, it must be before Ragnal sends a messenger we cannot ignore."

OUTSIDE, THE MULTITUDES intoned the ancient litanies, the reverberation bulging against the beeswax silence of the sanctuary until, slowly, the harmonies seemed to mingle, to merge. And the living air took on uncanny weight, swelling against Durand's ears and the bruises around his eyes. The Gates of Heaven were open, and the Powers had come into Errest the Old.

"The moment is upon us," spoke the Patriarch, and the congregation answered in a deep rumble: "Thanks be to the King of Heaven and His Host. Now, His Eye must reach even unto the darkest places of His sanctuary."

And so, throughout the black sanctuary, acolytes threw doors wide. The great valves of the crypt groaned open. And, for reasons Durand could not fathom, his own jaded heart began to hammer. All across the Atthias, it would be the same.

Chains rattled high in the clerestory above the Dawn Altar as they would in Penseval and Evensands and Eldinor with the king himself. Novices at the rail held an enormous censer: a fire basket on a long chain fixed to the vaults above and glinting like a knot of brazen swords.

"The King of Heaven is Triumphant. Winter is ended. Over the Host of Darkness, the power of light is ascendant. Praise the Host of Heaven!"

And, with a roar of "Praise the Silent King!" the novices above the altar kindled the fire within the bladed censer. It blazed like a bonfire in its cage of brass, and the young men sent the censer down from the heights above the altar toward the tiles before the duke's stall. Its long arc brought it flashing low right before Almora, then carried it high toward the great curtain. Priests hauled the canvas apart. There was a flood of ruddy twilight, and a moan rose from the city. The brazen pendulum flashed like a star—like the Eye of Heaven rekindled.

And, of course, the censer returned. Bells rang across the city. People sang. The censer flashed above the Dawn Altar and swung back toward the city. This was the end of another grim winter in a city still rebuilding after Radomor of Yrlac cast it down, a new city thriving where the old had burned, where the streets still smelled of sawdust.

These thoughts had scarcely entered Durand's mind when an odd flicker from the light outside drew his attention. It might have been something as small as a crow darting past the curtain, but that was not what Durand saw. Priests scrambled at the foot of one of the huge curtains. They had lost their hold on the acres of cloth. At the same time, the chained bonfire was making its glorious return. As the huge black wing broke free of its handlers, it swung down on a spinning welter of brass blades and naked flame. Embers flew over the assembled company as seams of fire darted up the curtain. It was all aflame.

Durand shot to his feet, despite the day's hoard of bruises. Already, priests and noblemen had rushed toward the sudden blaze. Some tried to get hold of the hurtling censer as it swung back. There was a mighty crash, and a man spun with his cloak in flames. The masses sprang to life.

"Your Grace, Your Ladyship, you'd best get up now," said Durand. At the same time, he caught hold of Coensar's shoulder, saying, *"Coen, that's the entrance on fire. It'll be like horses in a stable fire when they realize. We've got to get the family out."*

Coensar stood. Deorwen met his eyes.

"There's a doorway to the yard," said Coensar. "This way. Quiet. We'll want a head start."

Durand followed Coensar's glance and slipped into the crowd. Already, people were running; they would have the duke's canopied stall collapsing in moments. "God no," the duke was saying. "God no." He clung to his daughter. Deorwen caught Durand's hand. She caught his hand! He would not think.

The curtains bellied out. They billowed, full of fire. Some devil of the Hells opening its wings. Durand's glimpse beyond showed scaffolds, outbuildings all kindled now. Thatch soared in the furnace torrents of the air like a rain of fire. They would be lucky to save even half the city.

Durand would let nothing happen to Deorwen or the girl. He would get them safe.

IT WAS LONG past midnight when Durand finally shuffled up the black entrance stair and back into the Painted Hall. The duke's people, transfigured by soot and nightmare, climbed beside him. They had seen loss, salvation, and a thousand buckets slopped down the crazed and firelit alleys around the high sanctuary. They had seen a street festooned with flowers, black and in flames. With hooks and ropes, they had pulled down building after building to starve the fire. Durand recalled carrying a dead child; he remembered the weight of it in his arms. He remembered Deorwen serving as captain of nurses in the street. In the end, they all watched the fire bring down the ceiling of Abravanal's sanctuary—the thing plunging like a burning ship from the black Heavens, laden with sparks. And every eye stung.

As Durand hauled himself up the stairs, he wanted nothing more than to find his chamber and drop into a dreamless sleep. But what he got was a different matter.

As the company mounted the steps, a torrent of dark birds—hundreds or more—flooded the staircase from the Painted Hall, throwing everyone against the walls in astonishment. For several heartbeats, wings battered the company.

When they staggered into the hall itself, spluttering and smearing feathers from their faces, Durand saw a stranger standing alone in the midst of the hall, near the great, open hearth. The man was as pale as plaster, and taller, by far, than any knight in Abravanal's household. The last embers of the afternoon's feast had him glowing like a specter.

"Your Grace," Durand managed, "we've guests." And Abravanal's men drew swords.

It was Abravanal himself who stepped forward to meet the stranger, raising a cautioning hand to Durand and the rest.

The figure had made no move throughout.

"Friend," said Abravanal, "I fear you will have had a meager welcome this night. I am master of this place, but much has gone on this evening. I hope you will understand."

The stranger seemed to gather himself. Durand glimpsed a chalk-pale face. He held what Durand took for a traveler's staff, but as the man faced them, the firelight slithered over what seemed to be silver, not wood. This was a herald's trumpet. The tall figure executed a courtly bow.

"Your Grace, Duke of Gireth, I carry the word of His Royal Highness, Ragnal, by the Grace of far Heaven, King of Errest the Old, realm of the *Cradle*'s Landing."

Here was no mere messenger. Instead, Ragnal had sent the Herald of Errest himself. This was a man who had served ten kings over three hundred long winters. He had passed the Gates of Heaven and blown the Crusader Horn beyond the Sea of Darkness. Durand's memory took him back over ten winters, to the day when Lamoric fought before the king at Tern Gyre. He had seen the Herald then. The Powers had worked a strange Doom upon Kandemar in return for his passage through the Heavens: The man had not, in nearly four centuries, spoken a word except his king's—not since he walked the Halls of Heaven to carry word of Errest's Lost Princes to its bereaved king. *Life for silence, was his bargain.*

Now, Kandemar the Herald lifted his chin. "Thus says your king, Duke Abravanal: To our vassal in Gireth say that we are surprised that our messenger finds a liegeman of ours in his own hall when our royal command has compelled him to travel south over the passes of the Pennons Gate and to quell what unrest he might find there among our subjects in the Fellwood Marches. We ask how we are to accord this great delay with this vassal's avowed loyalty. You are meant to be elsewhere."

Abravanal blinked. "His Highness must understand that the snows came hard upon the heels of his messengers, barring the passes to every man under Heaven."

"To this our king has bade me say: Winter has ended, Abravanal of Gireth. The feast of the Ascension is past. We have been mindful of your service to us, but since the days of Radomor your house has profited from our patience. The peculiar fate of Yrlac and the trade concessions you won from Mornaway are much discussed among the councils of the great. They chatter while your grateful monarch stands by you, our servant. Can it be that you repay our faith with indolence?"

Ordinarily, a monarch's threats in the mouth of a deathless Herald would hold Durand's attention. But, as the man spoke, Durand became conscious of movement in the darkest shadows. Sinuous shapes slipped through the cracks between the stones and soon the whole room seemed to writhe before Durand's eyes. Durand twitched too quick for his twisted neck. Smoke-ring mouths gaped and eyes rolled like peeled eggs in a tub of ink. Near the door to the living chambers glowed the pale disk of the moon-faced giant from Durand's cell. It seemed that the Lost had found him again.

At the center of the hall, the Herald tugged his mantle tighter across his lean shoulders. "To you His Highness says: Our messengers are abroad with tidings of the great journey you are about to undertake, Abravanal. In the autumn, a tour of the forest barons might have sufficed to demonstrate our mastery. Now, it will no longer answer. And so we grant you royal license to host and hold a grand tournament beyond the Blackroots at the Lindenhall in Fellwood. You will be lavish with the proceeds of your conquests and alliances. While we settle the rebellion of my brother, Windhover, you, our vassal and ally, will prove to the restless lords in the Fellwood Marches that our power extends beyond the Blackroots and that, even in the Marches, none but Ragnal is king."

The groping Lost made their way over the straw and reeds. Durand almost jumped when Abravanal spoke: "The high passes, they might yet be shut against us."

Almora had taken her ancient father's elbow.

"To this Ragnal bade me say: Go to the pass, Duke of Gireth. By your oaths to us, if you find that it remains snowbound and shut to mortal men, wade thou to thy waist, and cry aloud, 'I lament that I have lived so long that my weakness prevents me from fulfilling my duty to my king, but on the morrow I will find greater strength.' And do so again each day until you find that you may walk farther. Gather your men and set forth before noontide tomorrow, or we will number you among our enemies, Abravanal of Gireth, and you will be beyond our protection with no safe place for you or yours between the mountains and the sea. We have sent Kandemar the Herald to accompany your party so that your deeds, good or ill, may ring throughout the realm.

"So saith Ragnal, by the Grace of far Heaven, King of Errest."

"By the Grace of far Heaven," whispered Kieren in that gloomy hall. "Very far indeed, some nights, it seems." Ragnal's threats and imprecations sounded far from heavenly, especially when leveled at a frail old man. Durand found himself clenching his fists, as if he might answer the king's insult.

Whatever the affront, Coensar's plans for Yrlac were finished. There could be no timely talks with Leovere to avert disaster. Ragnal would not be put off. Not by an hour. And Abravanal could not go to war against an entire kingdom to force the issue.

LADY DEORWEN TOOK charge in Gunderic's Tower, as she so often did. With stern glances, she persuaded Almora to seek her bedroom. At the same time, she caused a room to be cleared for Kandemar while gently badgering the deathless herald into a nodding agreement that he must be tired, so that Abravanal's advisors could argue over Ragnal's commands.

There was a crowd now in Castle Acconel, thicker than before the sanctuary fire, as several banner knights had lost their lodgings in the city. The servants danced to Deorwen's commands, unearthing pallets and ancient rugs from the darkest storerooms. Hot wine steamed. The Painted Hall filled with sprawled bodies, and the Lost retreated before the crowd, slipping back into the cracks and black passages of the tower.

At the high table, Durand sat with Kieren and Coensar long into the night. The two old commanders debated endlessly, hoping to find a means of keeping Abravanal's lands secure while every knight in Gireth rode for the mountains. But it must be exile or expedition, and no quantity of disputation could make a bit of difference.

Durand yawned.

Kieren laughed at him, his fox mustaches twitching. "I had a dog who yawned like that, once upon a time. A big brute he was." He grinned at Coensar. "One of those short-muzzled butcher's beasts. Stiff neck. Thick as a barrel. White as a bone with a big black eye. You're the living spit, after your bout with Euric." He bobbed his eyebrows. "That dog scared me to death."

Even Coensar smiled—something Durand had rarely seen in the last ten winters.

"You may as well let us gnaw at this one, Durand." Kieren hugged himself and shivered. "We'll never find our way out, but sometimes the inevitable needs a bit of talking. Out of respect, I think. Go on, get to bed. We'll be up at cockcrow if we're to pack this household up by noontide."

Unfolding stiff limbs, Durand made to leave, but found the black mouth of the chamber passage a source of stupid, childish dread. Serving men and handmaidens had been walking in and out all night, but the black mouth of the thing looked to him as though the darkness visibly brimmed and bulged with living shadows. Still, he saw no way around it.

"Goodnight," he said. "We shall see what the morrow brings, I suppose."

And, with a painful nod to his onetime mentors, Durand stalked into the doorway, pushing through shadows that were a bit too much like cobwebs. But the Lost were harmless, or nearly so, and housemaids had been bounding through them all night. So Durand pawed his way up the dark passages of Gunderic's Tower till he found his own door.

Standing in the black little room, he took a few deep breaths to master himself. Finally, he shot the bolt and lowered himself into his bunk, shadows be damned.

HE TRIED TO sleep, and, for a time, the pell-mell violence of the day dragged him deep.

But there were eyes upon him, and, as each furtive watcher added its scruple of dread, he soon feared to lie in the teeming, intimate darkness.

Figures surrounded him like mourners round a sickbed. There were empty-faced men. There were things cobbled together from nightmares. And each of them seemed far more solid now than they had been in daylight. Real as curtains round the bed, these were no filmy shadows, but beings with weight enough to stop the feeble moonlight. He could hear tongues and spines and talons move. Some were squatting over his basin. A pair of pale men held his surcoat between them, sucking absently at the black broadcloth where they must surely have found blood. Beyond them all was the moon-faced giant, standing by the door. They watched him impassively.

Durand stared back. Coensar's shadows he could endure, but these were altogether different. Madmen in the streets ranted about the spirits teeming in Creation, but was this what they saw? Had he *always* been surrounded by these things? Were they sent from the Host Below to collect him? Had the knock from Euric's lance driven him mad? Was he dead already?

Durand took hold of himself. He could not be dead, not with his fool heart beating fit to crack his ribs. The rap on the head had likely rattled something loose. It must be that. He was not mad, and he would not go haring off down the castle halls screaming about the spirits in his bedchamber. If they had always been there, then Creation was as it had always been, and he must become accustomed to the sight of these things.

"What do you want of me? Why do you plague me, of all men?" The words rasped between clenched teeth, but the things looked on without an answer.

He pressed his eyes shut for an instant while his heart galloped. And he heard a step from the passage beyond his door, an impossibly ordinary sound: Deorwen's step. She would have dreamed of some Lost soul, and now she was off to search the streets. Durand felt a prodigious urge to call out, more like a child than a man.

One of the dusky things leaned a little closer.

And Deorwen's footfalls were gone.

The leaning thing peered into Durand's eye. Its skin was as white and real in the moonlight as runny cheese. And its eye was a fish-scale ball of black and blue and silver.

Durand thought, for a moment, that he recognized the face. It had only one eye and there was something about its fat throat. . . . But he could not quite remember.

Choosing a spot on the ceiling, Durand waited for cockcrow, willing the madness away, and trying to ignore the shapes crawling the walls.

3
Familiar Spirits

The next morning, Gunderic's Tower bustled like a great black ant-hill, with the Herald standing motionless in its midst. Messengers charged out. The yards filled with workmen and clouds of sawdust. And, inside the tower, serving men scurried in torrents down every passage-way, catching up every object from candles to coats of mail and depositing them all in the yard.

Of mortal men, only Euric's comrades—a few dozen knights of Swan-skin Down—were still. They sat a grim vigil on the benches of the Painted Hall.

All of this, Durand had seen with his own eyes. Since before cock-crow, he had been hard at work; he much preferred hauling baggage and the occasional brush with a Swanskin knight to snuggling up with Lost souls in his bedchamber—though he soon learned that the devils were plentiful enough even in the Painted Hall. They chittered in dim corners and gaped at the goings-on among the living with a vacant species of curiosity.

Durand fetched and carried like a serving man to occupy his mind.

Kieren called across the crowd as Durand lugged one half of some knight's trunk toward the entry stair. "Durand! See if you can't ford this cataract of baggage and get over here. His Grace will need a word with you in a moment."

At the head of the Painted Hall, the duke and his two stewards clung to the high table. The table on its dais might have been a raft in a flood as Durand approached.

"This early in the year we'll be short of victuals, no matter what we do," Kieren was saying. "There hasn't been a good harvest since Durand here was in diapers— Good morrow to you, Sir Durand. Have a glass of beer. You look thirsty, boy." A jug bobbled toward him. "And the larder won't have the salt pork we'll need. You can't kill a beast and pickle him the same morning." Kieren's mustache bounced as he worked at a bit of bread. "Still, we won't need so many barrels if we've nothing to put in them, so that's a blessing."

"And what of those birds?" demanded Abravanal, blue eyes clouded. He lowered his voice with a glance to the Herald. "There he appears, the Herald, like one of the Powers of Heaven, and my Painted Hall is full of birds. It was the middle of the night. What were they?"

Kieren munched. "The birds, Your Grace? Starlings, perhaps. Durand, have you eaten?" The man passed Durand a hunk of bread.

"We will bring a strong company," said Coensar, "and keep most of the men in mail coats right through to the Lindenhall. If we can't bring an army, we'll make sure every man is ready for whatever comes. I didn't like what I saw on the roads. Bad winters breed wolves." This last was an old saying among the Sons of Atthi.

"The devils flew in one window and down the stairs right past us," continued the duke, fixated. "Must have been a thousand! Is there an omen attached to starlings then?"

"None I can think of, Your Grace," said Kieren. "Though I knew a woman once who taught one of the little devils to speak like a very Son of Atthi. I hear they have a talent for it. Mimicry. And they've a filthy tendency to come in great stinking mobs."

Coensar was shaking his head. "This ride to Fellwood will cost us dear, I reckon. I wouldn't leave Yrlac behind now, not without a royal command."

"And the Herald of Errest standing guard with his hourglass?" Kieren added, nodding his head toward the Herald and his curious vigil. "We shall leave the city as full of soldiers as we may."

"Another week and we might have brought Leovere to the table."

"Leovere!" said Abravanal. "A bandit. Bring him to the table indeed. You would dine with wolves and wild dogs?"

"Now, both of you," said Kieren, punctuating with the heel of his bit of bread. "We've talked enough of Yrlac. How well we know our troubles there! But we have the Fellwood in front of us—a great ocean of trees and darkness stretching from the mouth of Pennons Gate to beyond the ken of living men, while our halfwit countrymen are dabbling in its shallows. The Fellwood will require thinking about."

"Men go where there is land to be had, and three hundred winters have passed since the Solantine Knights still watching the Pennons Gate have seen the Enemy. Once, the Sons of Heshtar held all the southlands. In these days, the maragrim thralls. The turnskins. Gone beyond the inner seas, as like as not. It's no surprise our countrymen have brought their broad axes to those empty lands."

At the far end of the high table, someone approached the foot of the dais.

From Durand's spot on the floor, he couldn't make out the man's face. The table stood between them.

Durand took the man for a messenger, but not a soul at the table took notice.

"Here's my trouble," said Kieren. "Men in Fellwood are too free with their axes. In Errest the Old, the wise women know what haunts the trees and ponds and rivers. In Fellwood, there are men cutting timber on land that the Sons of Atthi have not commanded since—since I don't know when." The work of guessing screwed up his face. "It must be the days of the High Kingdom, anyway. Say twenty, thirty lives of men?

"And so, when King Ragnal hears of trouble down in the Fellwood Marches, does he imagine we'll find only rascal knights and runaway plowmen? A scattering of upstarts needing a strong hand to remind them of their duty? I will be glad indeed if it's nothing but a few headstrong settlers."

While Kieren spoke, Durand's mysterious messenger abruptly climbed right up onto the dais by the high table. Kieren and Coensar made no move, though the fellow was likely close enough to touch the duke's cloak.

"Well, Almora is not going," the duke was saying. "Not to Fellwood. Not over the mountains." The duke registered Durand's presence. "Durand? Good. Yes. You will remain here with her, watch over things. She must be safe at all costs."

As Durand shifted to catch a look at the stranger's face, he hardly heard Abravanal's command, and it was only when all three lords had turned his way that he realized that his assent was required: "Yes, Your Grace."

The stranger must have swayed a convenient inch or two, for just then, Durand got a look. Brown spots crusted a broad bandage round the man's forehead. His face was white as lard and slack as a pig's bladder. Why had his appearance caused no alarm?

"Euric?" Durand murmured.

In the hall, Euric's countrymen ignored the battered lord completely.

Still, Euric stared with eyes like boiled eggs, his mouth agape. The poor devil had clearly escaped his sickbed in the commotion.

"What?" said Kieren. "What was that, Durand?" Euric had set one hand on the table linens while the others waited for Durand's answer.

Then, abruptly, the pale bladder of his face twitched toward the chamber stair.

"Durand, what were you saying?" Kieren began.

But shouting rang from the stairway—men's and women's voices both. Euric's slack face quivered. And a young man—one of Acconel's serving boys—stumbled from the doorway.

"Host of Heaven," he said, and remained half-bowed before the Duke of Gireth.

"What is it, boy?" said Coensar.

"A messenger," gasped the boy. "A man from Swanskin Down. He's come to join Sir Euric, bearing messages. He is Euric's shield-bearer."

"Unfortunate," said Kieren, adding kindly, "But I suppose Euric could do with a visitor."

"*No*, Lordship." The serving boy twisted his tunic in his fists.

"No?" said Kieren, surprised.

Footfalls resounded on the chamber stair. "Host of Heaven! Someone should have stopped him. We could, at least, have warned him," quailed the serving boy as a shield-bearer tramped from the stair: a sturdy young man with his hair cut square; he was splashed with clay from a hard ride down the Wrothsilver Road.

The shield-bearer might almost have been drunk as his dark glance flashed over the room. "Dead," he gasped, as if puzzling at the problem. "The baron's brother."

There was something half-familiar about the young man's face.

"This is Ailric, Your Grace, Your Lordships," the horrified serving boy stammered. "Lord Euric's shield-bearer. Or he was."

The duke rose. "Ailric. It was Ailric? I do not understand you," he said, leaning across the table. The men of Swanskin Down were on their feet.

Ailric faced the high table, even managing a stiff bow. "Your Grace . . . I came bearing tidings for Sir Euric: word from Milord Vadir, Baron of Swanskin Down for Sir Euric. Sir Euric and I had recently been separated. A death in my family." He glanced back to the chamber stair.

"My condolences, boy. Surely, he had a shield-bearer yesterday? God. It was only yesterday, wasn't it?"

"A borrowed man, I expect," said Ailric.

"I'm sure. Yes. And Euric's injuries? Had you heard?" asked the duke.

For just a moment, Ailric's mouth was an empty slot. "Your man took me up, Your Grace, and admitted me. Sir Euric was dead of his wounds."

Durand glanced to slack-jawed Lord Euric there beside him—and, in an instant, Durand understood the man's strange and gaping stare. Euric looked no more human than the day's catch on a fishmonger's slab. The Lost lord's pallid hand splayed on the tablecloth near Coensar's.

Out on the floor, the men of Swanskin Down were shaking their heads and raising the fist-and-fingers sign.

"It was a question of honor," said Coensar while the thing that had been Euric stared. "He fought bravely. No man could be ashamed."

Ailric straightened. "Your Grace."

"Young man," said the duke, "we are sorry and sorely embarrassed. You should never have found your master thus. We have only just heard ourselves. It is a great shame. But you came in some haste, I think. And though we must not ask you to divulge anything you had in confidence from Baron Vadir, if the matter is of great consequence, you must decide whether or not you must speak."

The shield-bearer frowned a moment while his late master gawped past his ear.

"I should say that my tidings were meant for Your Grace, in the end. Baron Vadir of Swanskin Down says: Two nights past, raiders forded the River Banderol from Yrlac and struck three holdings. Two of these were the personal lands of Baron Vadir. There was great damage to property: a shrine, two mills, and a manor house belonging to Sir Euric. They were put to the torch."

"*Leovere,*" Abravanal growled. There were snarls among the Swanskin men as well.

Ailric nodded sharply. "Your Grace. It may be."

"And he wishes my daughter's hand," said the duke, glancing to Coensar. "Why do I suffer him to keep his seat in Penseval when he will not swear fealty? I've had a bellyful of that devil. What say you, Durand, my champion?"

Durand blinked. "Of Leovere?"

Coensar shot him a warning look, but Durand was more than distracted: Euric gaped right by his shield-bearer's side. "These raids. Men are dead. Men sworn to you. But he will not swear, though he holds your lands. Yrlac rallies round him, and there is no peace."

"You see?" said Abravanal, stabbing a finger at Durand. "You see! Here is honest counsel. Leovere will not take my hand! Yrlac will not rest. He is a thorn in my rump! A knife at my throat! It is past bearing. It is too much. Fat lands would I give the man who finally put an end to this devilry!"

More than a few ears pricked at the duke's tirade, and the rivers of baggage were still for a moment.

Coensar stood, giving Durand a stiff glance.

"Ailric, our riders are on the road to Vadir as we speak," said Coensar. "The duke rides south for the high passes and the Fellwood beyond. We will see Vadir in two days' time, but only on the way to Fellwood."

Ailric blinked. "Fellwood." When there was open fighting in Gireth itself. The Baron of Swanskin Down was certain to be astonished. "I see, Lordship."

The young man spent a sober moment looking straight into Durand's face.

Kieren spoke next. "The duke thanks you for your tidings, Ailric. We will see to your accommodations while you recuperate from your journey." As Kieren stepped from the dais, he passed close-as-kissing to Euric's revenant. The thing tottered nearer to Durand.

"Host of Hell," Coensar said. "We are thick with omens once more."

Kieren was walking the shield-bearer away. "You spoke of a death in your family. I hope I am not pressing too far if I inquire?"

"My father," said the young man. "Priest-arbiter to the Baron of the Col. He was not young."

"The Col?" said Kieren. "That is the home of Sir Durand's kin. Had you met Durand?"

"Yes," said the young man. "In the Col, once. On the head of Merchion, later."

And Durand was taken back to a moment, more than ten years ago, when he'd chased one of the Powers of Heaven down a well in his father's keep. He remembered the boy's flinty stare at the top of a well in the Col. The boy had thrown a wish of folded lead down the old well, and its hard corner had struck Durand by mistake. Durand's own father had found this boy a place with Swanskin Down. He might otherwise have become a priest.

Durand's knuckle had drifted up to the spot where the lead prayer had cut his brow. Many scars had followed that one.

Dead Euric shuffled closer, gaping like a boiled calf.

"I remember," said Durand.

HE MARCHED OUT. Dead Euric. Live Ailric. It had been too much.

He nearly collided with Almora in the chamber stair.

"Isn't it exciting!" she exclaimed.

It took him a moment to comprehend the girl.

"Exciting. Yes, Almora." A little more excitement and he'd join the Lost. "It must seem so," he allowed.

"You are fully as sour as they say, Sir Durand. Gulping like an old carp."

"Aye, well. Yes, Ladyship. There's excitement enough, I'll warrant. So many packing so quick, and riders charging off in every direction." He swallowed, trying, for the moment to forget dead men. "Sure that's excitement."

She hugged herself. "I never imagined that this old castle could come to life again! It's like finding that a mountain can shake off the dust and march away. There have been nothing but whispers here for so long, Durand."

Durand ventured a nod. To him, this live and chirping girl seemed more impossible than a range of marching mountains. "The castle will seem all the more empty when they've gone, I suppose," was all he could manage.

Almora stiffened at his words, her head suddenly a-tilt.

"You say, 'they,' Durand? When 'they' have gone?"

"Aye," Durand said. Oh, he was dull that day. Only then did he mark all the traveling clothes bundled in the girl's arms: a waterproof cloak she'd brought in from the stables, a pair of strong boots. Only too late did he realize that she had been packing her possessions with her heart set on getting free of the old place, of leaving the castle and the city.

"Oh. Almora. The mountains and Heaven knows what awaits us in Fellwood. These are the wild places of Creation. Your father won't have a soul along but armed men."

"He will never let me leave this place," Almora said, her words as dead as the Lost.

"Your father thinks of nothing but your safety."

"It is the custom, I think, to wait for a woman to die before walling her up in her tomb. But he would have all of us entombed: both of his sons, and both his daughters."

Deorwen had been in the girl's room. At this moment, she stepped into the corridor, then shoved past Almora and slammed the door, leaving her startled charge on the wrong side. The bang startled a leathery snap and rustle from a pair of birds silhouetted in a passage window: black birds with dagger beaks and bald faces. The things must have been there all the while.

Deorwen rounded on Durand.

"What have you said, Durand Col?"

"I only told her that she's not to come."

"Of course she's not to come! His Grace would hardly take his daughter through rebels and mountains to the haunted Fellwood, now would he? And it was to be the work of hours, I thought, to talk her around to seeing it her father's way. But you found a hastier method."

"I didn't see that she was packing."

"No, you would not. You say you protect her. You watch over her—men have died over it—but I find that you know precious little about her. Here you are, year in and year out, and yet you scarcely know the first thing about the girl!"

One of the birds in the windows cawed. There was no glass in the window, and so the strangely human sound racketed around the passageway. He'd seen too many carrion birds with Radomor and his Rooks.

"What's the matter with you?" said Deorwen.

She was too near. His head spun with memories.

First, rooks in the windows of Acconel—just like in Radomor's war. And now, Deorwen. They'd done such terrible things. In the fear and despair of Radomor's siege, they had lain with each other, night after night, though she was his master's wife—his friend's wife. And now, these long years later, they lived on with Lamoric in his tomb. He should have put leagues between them, but he had not. And so, in ten years, he'd come to know a thousand forms of shame.

But it was like drowning, still, to stand near her.

"I didn't think," Durand managed.

"Haw!" said the rooks.

And Durand got free of her—of all of it—abandoning the woman at Almora's door so that she might manage the feat of persuading the girl to open up and to stay behind in Acconel.

"Durand?" Deorwen called. "Durand!"

But he shambled down the passageway, the birds harrying him. He heard their laughing racket at the windows, following sill to sill, goading him on.

Just for a moment, he wanted free of it all: the Lost, damned Deor-wen, himself—and now Radomor's Rooks.

He had killed the Rooks up in Ferangore: Radomor's necromancers. Killed them. But he was sure he heard a whisper: *"Durand Col?"* It scratched and tumbled round his skull, and he clapped his hands to his head.

He found a corner.

But then, very suddenly, he found himself face-to-face with a solemn young stranger. It was Ailric, late Euric's shield-bearer. At the very moment of their meeting, an eerie metallic note chimed through the old castle.

"Well, sir," said Durand, finally. "If you would speak, you'd best do it." Man or spirit, Durand would hear.

"Sir Kieren wishes a word, sir."

"His Lordship is in the Painted Hall?"

"Not quite, sir. He's here," the young man answered.

And Kieren puffed into the passageway, climbing the last steps from the Painted Hall.

"My thanks," Durand said to the stern young man.

"Durand," said Kieren. "Coensar will certainly be pleased to have your thoughtful answers to His Grace's questions. You've plopped a fox among the poor man's pigeons, but perhaps it is in the best interest of a knight to make sure there is a ready supply of battles? In any case, I've come about our Ailric here. You remember? Your father sent that priest's boy to the old Baron of Swanskin Down? Bound the boy as page up there?"

As Kieren spoke, the two black rooks peered through an arrow loop some few paces down the passage beyond Ailric, and Durand heard the metallic ring once more. And so it took an effort of will for Durand to turn to the boy, taking a good hard look. His eyes were like black beads in his square face.

"He's been Euric's shield-bearer," said Kieren. "Haven't you, man?"

"I was sorry to hear about your father," said Durand. Durand hadn't known the old priest-arbiter, but it must have been hard.

Ailric nodded.

Now the two carrion birds lolloped into the passage itself, staying up-right on the stone floor only with an awkward effort of their wings. And there was another metallic chime beyond walls. *Clink.*

"You were with the barons back during the siege, were you not?" said

Durand. "I'd just swum across the bay searching for them. You were there."

"He was," said Kieren, nodding for the shield-bearer. "He's been page and shield-bearer for old Swanskin Down since before the war. Capable, by all accounts. Though I cannot speak to the quality of his most recent master; we must not speak ill of the dead, after all. In any case, now, Durand, Ailric's a masterless man." As, once, Durand had been.

Ailric had waved from the gate of the Col as Durand rode out to fight and find his way.

As Durand looked into the half-stranger's face, a sourceless whisper reached him: *"Poor Durand, he can hardly leave the lad behind now, can he? What choice has he got, brother?"* And the words skittered through Durand's skull like a shower of earwigs and spiders.

He was sure he flinched.

He began to see shapes on the stairs. The moon-faced man. Creeping things. Twitching claws. Pale against the gloom, bladder-faced Euric came lurching up, step by step.

Ailric lifted his chin, wary.

Kieren raised his palms. "Now, I suppose I might send him down to the Swanskin knights, but it was your father sent him there, won him a place. And I thought I had better acquaint you with the situation."

The Lost now surrounded Kieren, earning not a single glance despite their grotesque appearances—though a wary crease stitched Ailric's forehead as the boy stared. He was no fool, and Durand was no great actor. Something was wrong.

Kieren scowled at the black birds. "Cheeky devils."

"My gratitude to you, Sir Kieren," managed Durand. There was nothing for it. He must be haunted by grave Ailric and dead Euric both. "Ailric," said Durand. "It seems I have a shield-bearer."

The crows—the Rooks, Durand was certain—hopped a lame caper.

And then, with the dead rising all around Kieren and this new shield-bearer, another metal chime trembled in the air. *Ting.* It came from the stairs. The black eyes of Moon Face twitched like a falcon's, and Euric's face was as empty as a skin bag.

Durand gave his head a firm shake. "Yes. Ailric. To begin." He blinked. "There is work in the hall. The Painted Hall. They will need every hand."

Ailric nodded slowly, and departed.

"Ah, excellent," said Kieren. "I was not sure what you might say, but I am happy to hear that young Ailric will not be cast out upon the roads. Are you well, Durand?"

"And a shield-bearer for the gallant champion. Brother, was it not the cruelest oversight to deprive our poor champion of such a stalwart aid? But what is this? Our hero falters?"

Indeed, as the Rooks filled his head with their scurrying whispers and the dead loomed closer, Durand tottered a half step. He saw Kieren peering up. "Durand?" asked the Fox. "Are you well?"

"It's nothing," Durand managed. "I must see to something. You will excuse me, I hope."

And, with nothing else but a sort of flinching nod, Durand stepped past Kieren and Euric and plunged through the spiderweb throng of the Lost and down the stairs.

"Oh, where the stalwart hero of yesteryear?" the Rooks lamented as he made his retreat.

But, half-stumbling down the stair, Durand decided that he would find the source of the ringing. He was not simply escaping Kieren, or the dead, or the Rooks, or Deorwen, or the boy who conjured memories of a father's hall long ago. And so Durand descended through the fortress, flashing past the light and noise of the Painted Hall and finally leaving even the Rooks' whispers behind as he descended into the clammy stillness of the castle's depths. Through living rock, he descended after the shimmering note, like a diver after a tumbling silver coin until the chill gloom swallowed him.

Ting.

Blind in the ultimate depths of the tower, Durand stumbled upon an impossible chamber. The empty dark rang with voices, but he could feel the walls pressing close. There could not be space enough for so many living beings so deep in the earth.

After a moment's dread, Durand made out a patch of light in the middle of the room, as well as traces of a hole in the vaulted ceiling and a matching hole in the floor. This was the well chamber, and every floor of the tower echoed down. Durand damned himself for a fool, hearing a bench groan over a stone floor, a cleaver struck deep in some butcher's block, a door rattled on its hinges. And Durand remembered the last time he'd come to this room.

Ten winters had passed since he had been confronted by the Powers of Heaven, but this was the very spot.

No sooner had this realization dawned upon him than a sudden note clanged in the empty room—*clink*—only a few paces away. Durand snapped straight.

Somewhere beyond the wellhead, soles rasped on gritty flagstones.

"You have returned," came the enormous whisper. Now, a towering figure unfolded itself from the gloom beyond the well, a broad hat brushed the ceiling three fathoms above Durand's prickling scalp.

"Host Below," Durand said. He knew this thing of bones and rags and knots. There was a long, forked staff in the giant's hand, its brass heel winking at the well's edge.

"Traveler," Durand said.

The Power lifted its chin, allowing the feeble light of the well shaft to play in its wild beard of knotted grass and the plowshare planes of its face. A coin glinted in one eye.

"You have returned, Durand Col."

"Have I?" said Durand. The Traveler was the Power of roads, of crossroads: places fit for madmen, beggars, and gibbets. And Durand was as tired as if he'd fought for a year and a day.

But the Power simply passed its dry hand over the room in a gesture like a slow shrug. Not a soul alive could mistake the bone and twine thing that stared down upon Durand for a living man.

"You have stepped upon the road once more."

"Long years have passed since first we met," Durand said. He could not forget. He had been promised a great deal then: land and love and position. But now here he was, mad, haunted, and useless.

"Are you not your liege-lord's champion?"

Durand opened his hands, peering up into the shadows of the old Power's face. "Champion? Yes, I am that." Durand rubbed his face, going further. "Lord, I am content. Ten years have passed." He meant to tell the thing that he'd had enough.

"'Content.'" The face turned a degree, like an insect, a mantis. *"I am Lord of Ways. Warder at Crossroads. Prince of Mazes. He whom the lost alone may find. And you have returned to my Kingdom."*

"Lord." He had never felt more beaten. "I am not the man I was."

The Power raised its staff, like a gibbet swinging high. The staff hung poised over the wellhead. Durand remembered another well where the Traveler had swung its staff, striking prophecy from deep water.

"No," said Durand. "No prophecy."

But he found nothing in the idiot blackness of the Power's old-penny eye. The giant settled like some shabby dragon on its haunches. Its skeleton jaw opened—a wide, death's-head leer over its beard of knots. Slowly, with no change of his expression, the Power tipped the outsized head of its staff down toward the mouth of the well.

"Please," Durand said.

"*Everything you desire.*"

"Please. Lord, I am content. It is enough."

But the Power thrust the forked staff, striking the wellspring of Acconel, every road and trail and river ringing to this blow of its ancient master.

"*Now* I *tell* you '*no,*'" said the Power, "*for again I see the place you crave. And again, glory.*"

"No."

"*And a true beauty.*"

As Durand stood, eyes upon the wellhead, the Power's words loomed before his mind's eye. He felt the Traveler rising, mounting slowly like some midnight storm. "*She is there. It is* all *there once more. You have only to find it.*" There followed a sound like a warship gathering sail, like ropes and rigging, and the Traveler receded from the light. But Durand did not raise his eyes until the gloom had drowned every tooth and knuckle of this Prince of Heaven.

Durand drew a breath in the empty room. His doom was laid before him once more.

4

Lord in All but Name

Hardly a moment passed before the living and the dead crowded back on Durand. First, voices poured down the well shaft from Gunderic's Tower, then the lolling and creeping dead tumbled from the stairs.

Durand faced the Lost and, in a moment of bloody-mindedness, bulled straight through the heart of them, climbing stair after stair, seeking the sky, gritting his teeth as the things groped and clung. He wanted open air. Finally, a small door let him into the light and noise of the crowded castle yard. With Heaven's Eye burning bright above, Durand tumbled free and left the dead behind.

The duke's whole column of carts and horses was packed in the yard, tight as an adder in its shell, as the duke's people struggled to be ready before noon. Durand slammed the door on Lost souls and dove into the easy chaos of wheels and barrels and hooves like an otter dives into a stream. With a little luck, he'd get Abravanal's train through the gates in time to beat the Herald's deadline.

And so, though Durand still felt the effects of a night's missed sleep, he was wearing an honest smile—and levering half a ton of loaded cart out of a tangle—when Kieren peeked around a nodding mule. "Durand, is this what called you away so suddenly? I hadn't known you were a muleteer. In any case, there have been developments since we spoke. You will be pleased to hear that I will stay behind when His Grace leaves us. The business of government cannot cease. And, as I explained to His Grace, our Sir Coensar has always been a man for the tournaments."

The cart Durand was levering shifted ominously, threatening to drop its entire cargo—furniture, it looked like—on Durand's back. "We will be happy to have you, Sir Kieren, I'm sure," he said as he forced the cart back on its wheels.

"Do not rejoice prematurely, Durand, for I will not be loitering in Acconel. With all this trouble over the border, I will travel west with a strong party into the lion's den itself!"

"Yrlac?" Durand said.

"Yes, Yrlac. I thought 'lion's den' was clear enough. Ferangore itself, I think—the very capital of the place. No sense giving the rebels the space and time to move, with Coensar away."

Durand pictured Ferangore with its high sanctuary full of Rooks and horrors, Lamoric dead before the gates, and Radomor seething upon his throne like some Power of the Hells. Durand scrubbed sweat from his forehead. "You do not plan to bring Almora there?" Durand said.

"Not quite the dullard you pretend to be, I see. You bring me to my point. Perhaps you have already been wondering why I sought you out here among the carts and asses. I am not only passing the time till the duke departs. Which he must do before long." Kieren shot a glance at the Herald, who stood amid the confusion, fixed like the needle of some giant sundial, marking the seconds. "No. I need a loyal man to take command of the city and garrison of Acconel itself, someone not caught up in this bit of idiot minstrelsy. And I'd rather it was someone with at least a grain of good judgment." Kieren's mustache gave a wry twitch. "I am afraid it will need to be you, Durand. We'll need to be sure the city is prepared should the Thorn in His Grace's Backside, Lord Leovere, or any of his compatriots come calling. You'll need to reinforce the garrison and keep your eye on the watch."

Durand blinked at the man. "Me, Commander?"

"Oh, Heavens, Durand. Close your mouth. You'll have me thinking again."

"It is an honor," said Durand.

"Heaven help me. It's a job, not an honor. Someone must take charge while I'm in Ferangore. You'll need to keep your wits about you. As for the stores, stables, taxes, feast days, docks, serving men, candles, bedstraw, beggars, widows, orphans, and fish in old Silvermere, Lady Deorwen knows the daily running of Castle Acconel. Any man would interfere with her at his peril, I think."

Durand glanced back at the narrow doorway where he'd left the Lost and the Powers. He could feel himself on the Traveler's crossroad.

Kieren was smiling around that big mustache. "That is, if you're willing to play more than Almora's nursemaid-in-chief."

"Honored, Sir Kieren."

"Again. Honored beyond deserving, I'm sure. But what else? Oh. The fire. By rights, that's the Patriarch's business, but you'll have to sit with our treasurer. Maybe the silver for the quarrying could be turned to demolition. The burghers could be squeezed. The duke didn't set the fire, after all.

"Be that as it may, Yrlac must be foremost in our minds," Kieren said. "When I reach their capital, I mean to fill the roads with our men, calling every loyal lord up to Ferangore, one after another. They'll just happen to come fully armed, marching slow with herds of household knights along for company—trooping past the gates of every old Yrlaci lord. Perhaps with the duke's bull banner flying, should there be anyone who misunderstands."

Durand found himself grinning. Yrlac was a riddle that a man might solve. Even if it came to fighting, it would be the honest work of blades under the Eye of Heaven. "There are knights enough in Gireth to watch that border. Riders up and down the River Banderol. A man or two to watch the fords and bridges. They're eager to do it, is my guess. There will be hundreds of men, ours for the asking."

"Ah, Durand. Perhaps you are more than a nursemaid after all." Kieren clapped Durand on the shoulder.

A new clamor erupted at the tower door.

"That'll be His Grace," said Kieren.

At the outer gates, the warders took up the slack in the portcullis chains. The big chains clattered taut around the windlass upstairs.

"Here they go," said Kieren. He glanced at the stern Herald of Errest. The Eye of Heaven was climbing the last degree toward its zenith as the duke took Durand's oath.

With Coensar urging him away, the old man hesitated with one foot in the stirrup. "Where is Almora?" he said, and when the girl found her way to his side, "I know you wished to travel with us, but you must see.

You are the last of our line, my daughter. When Lamoric lived. And poor Alwen. And Landast. And Landast's wife. . . . She might almost have been your mother. I wonder, do you remember her?"

"I do, Father."

"Too many have died, Almora. It is too much. You must stay."

Before he could say more, the girl gave her father a quick kiss, as poised as a princess all the while. And Abravanal's tears tumbled down his face.

"Your Grace," said Coensar. "It must be now." The Herald was watching.

And so Abravanal climbed into the saddle and rode out with Coensar and the watching Herald at his side—and half the peers of Gireth behind. Half the contents of the castle followed, under high tarpaulins. An astonished serving girl commented that even the duke's bed was somewhere among the teetering mountains lurching under the low gate. And off they went to the Pennons Gate, Fellwood, and the tournament at the distant Lindenhall.

A black bird croaked and fluttered on the battlements.

Kieren stepped out in front of Durand and the rest. "Now," he said, "it is my turn." And a party of forty knights cantered round the old keep, every man grinning like a brigand.

Durand had to marvel. "Sir Kieren, where did you find all these men?"

"One must be resourceful, Sir Durand. And I'd be happier, all things considered, if the highborn of Yrlac found me in Ferangore before they had word that His Grace is larking off for the Fellwood."

Durand shook his head, smiling. "Amazing."

"A journey is so much more enjoyable when one brings a companion or two." This inspired more fierce grins among Kieren's armed escort. No one knew how many of Yrlac's old liegemen might rise against Gireth, given the chance.

Just then, a large party of town burghers appeared from the gates, the tallest puffing like a bellows in his hurry to reach them. Each man pulled off either hat or hood, taking a knee if he could bend so far.

Kieren gave them only a frozen, sidelong look.

The tallest look up from his bow. "Sir Kieren. Ah! It is as we heard. You are departing. We hastened to the castle to learn your mind about making safe the fire damage and clearing the ruined structures—as well as settling the matter of responsibility, of course. It began with the carelessness of the priests at the high sanctuary, as we all saw."

"Indeed," said Kieren. But, with a broad fixed smile, the aging Fox turned to Durand. "Sir Durand, I am very much afraid that I must leave you. Hospitality is arranged on the road, and we cannot keep our hosts waiting. Farewell to you." Kieren nodded a bow to the burghers. "And to you as well. You must take these things up with Sir Durand, my friends. We must go!"

With that, Kieren swung himself aboard a spry bay gelding and led his laughing companions through the gates.

DURAND SENT THE burghers to the Painted Hall, reasoning that the walls must come before shops and sanctuaries. He had no intention of losing the city to some surprise raid and spent the afternoon marching back and forth across the city, kicking sentries awake and peering into barrels of arrows. There were no men in half the city's towers. And, though some captains spoke of means by which he might get hold of more men, he knew that if Leovere mounted an attack, disaster must follow.

He tramped back through the gates of Castle Acconel, as footsore and begrimed as if he'd come from a battlefield, only to find the solemn Ailric stepping out to greet him.

It took Durand a moment to recognize his new shield-bearer.

"They're complaining, Sir Durand," said Ailric. "According to the treasurer, the strongboxes have been emptied to supply Abravanal's cavalcade. There isn't a penny left for the high sanctuary, fire or no. Patriarch Oredgar waited two hours from noontide and vows to return."

"The Patriarch was waiting for me and left, you say? There will be a reckoning for that."

"He grew impatient with the burghers."

"'Impatient,'" Durand said. "Patriarch Oredgar, with his sanctuary still smoldering, was impatient with them. I'm surprised they're alive. Perhaps it's just as well I missed him."

A dozen Rooks croaked their scorn from the battlements as Durand climbed into the cool gloom of the entry stair.

In the hall, the living townsmen were far outnumbered by the Lost souls who stalked haltingly through the room like cloaked men who had only just forgotten why they had come.

"They have been waiting some time, Sir Durand," whispered Ailric. And it took a moment for Durand to realize that the youth referred to the living and not the dead—and that Durand had stopped on the threshold while fifty anxious men waited.

"A moment," said Durand. "You'll get nothing badgering me in the doorway. I'll have a seat and listen." And, without a flinch at the horrors peering in, Durand walked down the hall and took a place by the duke's throne, one usually reserved for Kieren or Coensar. He was alone but for Ailric at his elbow.

"Where are their ladyships, Ailric?" Durand asked.

"The chamber block. They will not be disturbed."

"Will they not?" Durand said. He would be needing Deorwen.

"Adamant."

"Right," said Durand. "Almora has been pushed hard enough today. She may stay where she likes."

Serving men brought bread while Durand sat alone before the delegations.

A round man twisted his hat in both hands. "Sir Durand, we'll need to work out some way of making this good."

A yellow-bearded companion interjected. "It was the priests' fire."

The first man gave a sidelong nod. "I'm sure we're all brave enough now that His Grace the Patriarch has left us, but something must be done. Many will be without homes."

"And we won't see a clipped penny from Oredgar."

Durand nodded gravely. "It will be put right. Somehow we will do it," he said, though he did not have a penny to offer.

He was distracted too, for the Lost souls wandered among the townsmen and servants. They tugged at the hems of living men. They probed like herons in shallow water. They knelt among the floor rushes to let their tongues flicker at spilt wine.

Durand closed his eyes.

"There could be a levy from the householders of the neighboring streets," said the round man. "They benefited most from the houses which were pulled down."

"And the Patriarch could pay for the houses that burned," his comrade added.

When Durand opened his eyes, a bloody face was blinking into his own—someone he had crushed under the gates of this very fortress, long ago. At his elbow stood a man that he'd killed in the lists. A bloated white figure in a bondman's blue surcoat scrabbled at the tablecloth. Water pattered from the skirts of his garment. With astonishment, Durand recalled throwing the man from a bridge over the River Glass years and leagues away. And there was Euric, of course, fumbling and shambling.

More of the townsmen felt brave enough to speak. There were raised voices.

The dead gathered at the high table, soon filling every seat.

"Something will be arranged. No one will sleep in the street," Durand said.

But there were dead men all around him, and he could not think. They leered on every side.

"I did nothing, you devils," Durand muttered. "Nothing but what had to be done. The gates. The siege. The river. All to defend my lord and my people. To the Hells with you all." But the dead remained.

"Sir Durand?" asked Ailric. Some of the arguing townsmen might have noticed.

And then Durand heard a scrabbling at the narrow window behind him. Silhouetted against the panes, Durand saw black and shaggy wings, half-flattened against the leaded glass.

He clenched his cracked teeth.

"And so he is duke, or nearly," said an uncanny, but familiar, whisper. *"I wonder how he enjoys it? A man might develop a taste for such things."*

"And find means to indulge such tastes, brother."

Durand felt like some fairground bear, prodded past exhaustion by the dead, the living, and now by the whispering Rooks.

"What do you want with me?" Durand rasped. As ever, the Rooks' words circled and circled in his head, their echoes never quite dying.

"Oh, brother, he speaks to us—and in the company of others." The castle's folk were too busy eating to notice, Durand hoped. *"Does he draw glances? No? Well. You see how the common herd passes oblivious through life, noticing nothing but the bread before them."*

Durand tried to keep the alarm from his face. "What do *you* wish of me?"

"Sir Durand?" asked Ailric, a line stitching his forehead.

"Sorry. Thinking aloud." A serving man set wine before him and Durand poured a cup for his shield-bearer. A few drops landed on the cloth, spreading.

"Oh, Durand, can a ghost no longer haunt his slayer without interrogation? Where is custom gone in these dark times? You become impatient with us, but we are only curious, Your Grace. Yes. Only curious."

"But you ought to be . . . *elsewhere.*" The Hells should have snapped up two creatures such as these.

"Oh yes. 'Elsewhere.' I suppose. But we do so enjoy your company, Durand of the Col. And curiosity has always been our vice. How would the spider look without his legs? How will you deal with this man

*Leovere, for example? With his people only just across the bridge and
this castle surely full of his men?"*

"Oh, brother. You don't mean spies, do you?"

"Spies in Acconel?"

"Or assassins, brother."

"How delicious!"

*"Think of it? Do you imagine that anyone took the time to count the
serving men who accompanied the cavalcade? Might there not have been
room for a man or two to slip away? To carry news? The duke is on the
road! The city is leaderless! And, well. . . Heaven knows."*

Durand turned to Ailric who waited at his elbow. "Ailric, are any of
the serving men missing since the duke took to the road?"

"Three men, maybe. The ushers are cursing it. But the place is in a
muddle. They may simply have gone along with His Grace."

"Check the stables," Durand began, but stopped himself. "No. After
this morning, who could say whether one horse more or less was
missing?"

As Durand tried to think, he found Euric's halfwit ghost bending over
the tablecloth. It had found the spilled wine, and a gray and gleaming
tongue slid from the monster's slack face, very near Durand's own goblet.

"Hells," said Durand. He snatched the goblet out of harm's way, though
the wine sloshed and Ailric had to be nimble.

"I could try it, sir. If you wish." A dozen dead men looked up, dazedly
startled by Ailric's sudden preparation to stand.

"No. No."

Durand himself was standing. He looked across the Painted Hall. The
dead tottered and slunk and prowled in every corner. The huge moon-
faced giant bobbled mere inches from his side. At close quarters, Durand
made out a jutting beard. And it stirred a memory. There had been fight
at a mill. Durand and Radomor's man, Gol, caught a Valduran. Fulk,
Durand remembered. Was he the first man who'd died on Durand's account? Was that what this was? Was it the blood on his hands?

Euric seemed happier with claret.

The delegation of townsmen stood staring at him, looking as pale and
gape-mouthed as a basket of fish. What had he said? What had they seen
him do?

Durand couldn't go on as he was, but neither could he run into the
yard to play duke by daylight and avoid the Lost. He must find an escape. Deorwen had long dealt with her own plague of Lost souls. She
dreamt of them, then helped them to peace with shoe leather and a few

wise woman's tricks. And, though he was loathe to throw himself on Deorwen's mercy, she might be the one to bring him peace as well. He would find her now.

Durand spread both hands in the air between himself and the townsmen. "Let me see what can be done," he said, and he left them.

DEORWEN SAT ON a stool before Almora's door.

"Deorwen," Durand began. The Lost filed in behind him: a procession of dead men. The things filled the staircase at his back. Still, something about Deorwen's attitude stopped him. "Why do you sit here? In the passageway?"

"Durand." She stood, small and straight, gathering herself with a quick tug of her gown. "You might as well know. The fool girl has been locked in her chamber since her father left, and she won't answer."

"She won't answer you?" Durand could not imagine anyone holding a door against Deorwen.

"Would I be waiting here otherwise? There are nothing but tears from inside. It's not like her."

Durand heard a choked sob from beyond the girl's door. Half-turning, Deorwen called: "It's no good hiding in there!"

The sobbing came sharper.

"Girl!" said Deorwen to the closed door. She could not quite shout; the Painted Hall was not far away. "You're too old to play such games. This door will open if you will it or not."

The girl shrieked.

Durand put a hand over his face. The dead were all around; he would not be rid of them. And now the girl was playing up. With a sigh of resolution, he took hold of the door's iron handle, turning the latch, hoping that a firm shove might get him inside.

The door did not move, and the crying was redoubled.

"You've no key?" he asked.

"Once again, Durand, if I had a key, do you suppose that would I be still waiting on Her Ladyship?"

Durand swallowed. "Let me see what I can do." And, with a snarl of frustration, he threw his good shoulder into the door. The thing smacked wide. And Durand was staggering in the midst of Almora's bedchamber. A maidservant cowered behind the bed, face streaming, but there was no sign of Almora. The girl was gone.

Black wings left the window. "Haw, haw!" he heard.

Durand remembered the missing serving men.

"Deorwen, there are men missing since the duke departed." His thoughts rabbited off with devil-plots—the maid, the runaways, the girl, and ransom or worse.

Deorwen looked at the maid. "This witless child has not conspired with kidnappers."

The serving girl threw herself to her knees. "Oh, mistress, we meant no harm. Only Almora did so wish to get out of this old place."

"You find no excuse that satisfies me for even a moment, girl," said Deorwen.

Durand had no interest in the serving girl's doom, whatever it might be. "When did Almora go?" he demanded, but the girl dissolved again into wild sobs.

Deorwen intervened. "I have not seen Almora since the cavalcade left the gates, I am ashamed to confess."

"And I was fighting with patriarchs and burghers," Durand said.

"There was much to do. She will have kissed her father good-bye, I think, and darted back to the stables, bold as you like. All it would take is an old cloak if she chose her moment. Why should the warders keep anyone in? Acconel Castle is not a prison."

"Except for Her Ladyship, it seems," said Durand. The Rooks scrabbled at the windowsill, more like pigeons than gallows birds, and much to Durand's surprise, Deorwen stalked toward the window, flapping her arms and driving them off. "Dirty creatures."

There was a chuckle in Durand's skull; the two Rooks, at least, were enjoying themselves. The Lost had slipped into the girl's chamber now, aimlessly probing corners.

Some noise from the doorway caused Durand to flinch around, too quickly for his stiff neck. Ailric had appeared in the wreckage. He seemed to be everywhere. Durand's head pounded from his thick ear to the base of his skull.

"All right, Ailric. The stables now. Find Almora's palfrey. A gray. Sugar white. She would not leave the animal. And not a word to anyone—on your life, boy! If the girl is alone on the road, Leovere cannot learn of it."

Ailric nodded and vanished.

"Even if she has simply chased after her fool of a father, she's defenseless," said Durand. "Abravanal's heir alone, and Leovere hungry for any chance to force the old man's hand!"

"She is not safe."

"No, she's not safe!"

He would fill the roads with horsemen. He would send word to every baron in Gireth. And then everyone would know. The moment he spoke, his words would reach the Red Hall of bloody Leovere by a hundred roads. Durand thought of his oath to protect the girl. He thought of the promises he had made to watch Gireth as Kieren set out for Ferangore. He had sworn to protect Acconel. The duchy had been put in his hands.

But there was only one thing for it.

"I'll call Sir Kieren back. He's gone hours, only. And this girl." The tears. The wild eyes. The secret might have been plastered on her forehead. "Get her out of sight, by Heaven. And someone will have to do something about this bloody door."

Durand nodded to Deorwen. "We'll get her back."

AILRIC HAD THE door rehung before a soul had noticed, and still he managed to scout the stables: The girl's gray was not in the stalls. And, without a word from Durand, the youth had found Shriker; Brand, Durand's hunter; and a rouncy.

"They said the stallion was yours," Ailric explained.

Durand looked over big Shriker. "Aye, he is." The brute was treacherous with strangers; Ailric was lucky not to have been bitten purple. "And the dun rouncy too." The lad had everything ready. "I trust you gave them a story?"

"Aye, yes." He nodded. "I'm the new man, and maybe I'm eager to put my stamp on things. I found fault with the shoeing, the stalls, and the condition of their coats. I'm marching them straight to fresh stables in the city. The groom's boy has cause to expect a beating," Ailric explained.

"So he won't be wondering where we're going," said Durand with a shake of his head.

"I wouldn't think so. The boy seemed quite rattled, Sir Durand."

"That'll do, then. Now, we must hope the girl's on her father's trail. They'll be no finding her if she's done ought else."

Ailric seemed watchful.

"Hells," said Durand, "I've a mind to turn the city upside-down and send a hundred men haring into the countryside after her, but she'd make a fine hostage for any man of Yrlac. A whisper in the wrong quarter could kill her."

He took Ailric by the shoulder, giving him a hard look. "Ailric of the Col, much depends on this secret. You must be my man in this."

"I am, Sir Durand. We must get the girl. Every moment that passes is too many."

"Good," said Durand. He let the boy go.

With that, they were on their way. The Eye of Heaven blazed low, making black canyons of the streets. He led Ailric through the dark city and slipped by the gatekeepers at the Harper's Gate only moments before curfew bell.

JUST BEYOND THE big stone barrel vault and the iron-bound gates, they nearly trampled Deorwen. She'd known what Durand intended.

The men in the gates pushed the big valves shut and dropped the bars.

Toads shrilled from the Mere.

Deorwen's eyes were as steady as stone.

DURAND SET AS quick a pace as Brand, his thickset blood-bay hunter, could manage in the mud; the brute was as coarse-boned as a plowman's ox, but tireless and laudably cool. The road followed the valley of the Banderol. A kingfisher flashed blue over the ripples, vanishing into the creaking of the frogs and the boom of a bittern somewhere off among the reeds. It was an eerie evening beyond the wet clop of the horse's hooves.

From the far bank, Yrlac glowered. Plowman's houses and sanctuary towers stood out there in the damp gloom and, in unshuttered windows, fires glowed. Durand rubbed a knot in his bad shoulder and imagined Leovere's men peering out from one of the hovels on that far bank. A single unlucky glance from any of those windows might have sent Leovere's men splashing over the river for Almora.

Just then, a strange, half-human voice called across the reed beds, causing Durand to squint again at the valley walls.

"It's lambing time," Deorwen supplied.

"Hells," said Durand. "What a sound." Pure anguish.

"Those'll be *lost* lambs, I shouldn't wonder," she added.

"Lost lambs . . ." repeated Durand.

"It can't be more than a few hours since she rode out. And she'll keep to the road. I should have broken that door myself. Who knows where she's got to?"

He let that pass. "I wonder what they're thinking in Acconel," said Durand. "No duke, no steward, no champion, no Almora, no Lady Deorwen. That will give them a shock."

"If we can catch her in the next hour or two, we'll be able to stare them down come the morrow. Otherwise, well, it doesn't bear thinking about. . . ."

"She'll put her head down. We'll catch her and be back by dawn," said Durand.

"If we find her, it must be sooner than that. You forget the night, Durand Col."

"The night? Ascension? There is nothing ominous about the days after."

"You are thinking only of Heaven's Eye. But we are in the province of the moons out here. The Sowing Moon has passed, and the Farrow Moon will not rise tonight. Through all the Atthias, every village has folk standing watch. There will be no moon, and the Banished will be free with Heaven's Queen gone."

"It is Calends," Durand breathed. The girl gone, and this the night for hags and worse to creep from their dens. "Of all nights."

"We've an hour before Last Twilight. We'll find her, or we will hope she's found shelter—and find shelter ourselves."

They rode on as the heavens darkened. Durand found himself watching the shape of every stray plowman on the misty Yrlaci side. He'd been so intent on the far bank that he started when a Rook croaked from the branches of a crooked blackthorn closer at hand.

"I wonder if it's all connected, brother," said a scrabbling whisper in Durand's skull.

"What, exactly, is connected to what, brother?" The blackthorn rustled as the Rooks teetered among its naked spines.

"Leovere and this girl and the fire in the high sanctuary and King Ragnal issuing mad commandments that bully men into the trees."

"There is no way of knowing, I am sure."

"And there are strange things abroad this night."

"A disquiet is upon the land."

Durand was about to spur Brand at the Rooks' thorn when Ailric called out from the rear. "Sir Durand!" And, as the chuckling Rooks flapped and tumbled upriver, the young man's blade hissed from its scabbard. "Up the river," he said. "Among those trees."

The track curved toward a riverbank copse of willows. Maybe there was a crossroads. After a moment's scrutiny of the trees, Durand began to pick out mute figures among the branches.

There were, perhaps, a dozen silent men between the trunks. Beggars or bandits, they must be. "I'll flush them," Durand murmured, "and we'll be on our way."

The Rooks had circled round to settle in the high, bare branches.

Durand had unshipped his flail and prepared to set his spurs when a west wind breathed across the Banderol and set the willows dancing.

Suddenly, another hundred watchful human forms were clear among the dancing branches, suddenly obvious in their huddled stillness not more twenty paces from Brand's twitching nostrils. The Rooks laughed their reedy "Haw! Haw!" from the branches.

Durand set a hand on Brand's neck. "Easy."

Faces turned, hollow-cheeked below wide, mad eyes; there would be no scattering a hundred such men.

"What is this?" whispered Deorwen.

Durand shook out his flail's chain, eyeing the crowd. "Outcasts. Madmen. There's nothing odd about a beggar or two beyond the city walls."

"'A beggar or two.' I'd imagined you could count, Durand," said Deorwen.

But Durand was making different calculations. The roadbed where they'd stopped was a heavy clay muck. No good. The verges were fatally steep. A trench. And there was nothing but mud on the hillsides.

Durand and his party could only back away, hoping to find another road.

But the beggars had not been still. As Durand eyed the ground, the creatures slunk for better vantage points, shifting only inches. Among them numbered men and women both, smeared with mud and some naked to the patches of hair between their legs. "Host of Heaven," he said. It was too cold.

A few of the mob were dead already, hanging low and crook-necked from the branches where the living stood. An idle corner of Durand's mind wondered whether the beggars had gathered to strip the rags from the swinging corpses—or to do worse. The end of winter was a hungry season.

"I did not know that things had come to such a pass in the countryside," murmured Deorwen. "We have been sheltered in the city."

"What are they wearing on their heads?" wondered Ailric. It looked as though every man and woman wore a raven's nest of sticks.

More figures rose from the reeds and ferns below the trees. Others appeared by a low roadside wall—too many, too near. Durand could see the ivory pegs of their teeth.

"How will Almora have got through?" asked Deorwen.

"Who knows when these creatures came to this place?" said Durand. "We must worry about ourselves for now. We'll give them their privacy. Back, and we'll find another way." He stole a tighter grip on the reins even as the figures in the trees heaved deep breaths, snarling prayers and obscenities.

It was suddenly clear to Durand that the bird's-nest garlands were crowns. Willow. Bleeding hawthorn in ragged flower.

"Ailric . . ." Durand warned.

And the entire throng rushed.

In a giddy instant, Durand knew there could be no escape, not for all of them. Deorwen could have only one hope. He saw it all, and understood.

"Ride!" Durand shouted. Deorwen must not argue. Durand spurred his poor hunter at the crowd, and the levelheaded cob jolted forward like a warhorse. Durand and the boy would buy Deorwen a moment to break free. Brand wallowed into the devils while Durand swung his flail, kicking and cursing at each bounding shape that surged past him. But it was like battling the sea. A fist got Durand's belt. A bearded man swarmed up, grappling for Durand's flail. Poor Brand kicked and wheeled, panicked now. And the wild bearded face scrabbled close by Durand's ear, the thorny crown in his eyes.

"Traitor!" the man hissed. A dozen other hands tore Durand from the saddle, and Durand hit the clay, twisting under waves of fists and feet—an engulfing violence, swallowing him under thorn-crowned, twisted faces.

Deorwen *must* be free.

It was his last thought, the last impulse of his heart.

Then one powerful blow smacked his chin into the muck, and he was lost to Creation.

5
A Keeper of the Dead

Durand came to his senses in the belly of a trench or ravine, his face half-frozen to the muck. Alive.

A canopy of willows shut out the Heavens where some trace of the twilight still remained over the ditch. He half-remembered the beggars hauling him on their shoulders. Now, it looked as though they'd discarded him.

He must learn what had happened to Deorwen and the girl.

As he prepared to move, a strange hiss reached his ears. A few paces away, a hill of huddled stones bulged from the dark. The muddy stones might have been a nest of serpents—but louder. Then one of the huddled boulders twitched—an arm slid past a pallid knee—and Durand understood that he lay three feet from a hundred round backs, all packed as tight as corpses in a grave.

They spoke.

"The Queen," said a hundred crowned madmen. *"She watches. Forever peering from the tail of my eye. And well she might, for my every breath thwarts her ambition. Her ambition for her child. For herself! But I will not die easily. I will not climb down."* A hundred voices popped with venomous spittle; hands clutching at shoulders in vain spasms of self-comfort. *"I could manage her—and handily, if it were not for this plague of whispers. But I cannot think for whispers. Who would have a crown at such a price?"*

Durand marveled. Was this some cabal of traitors?

"My people?" said the voices. *"They starve. They sicken. They throw their gripes at my feet. But do I command the rains? Do I call fishes to their nets? Am I wet-nurse to their beasts? Why must they plague me?"*

Durand began to understand. In Errest the Old, the king was bound to his people. Life to life. Pain to pain. It was priestcraft of the eldest sort that knotted the king's life into the soul of the kingdom. For three days, every king must lie under the high sanctuary in Eldinor. Three days under stone. Three days there among the tombs of his forbearers. Durand had seen the place as he fled with Lamoric through the tunnels under Eldinor.

It seemed that this could only be some strange echo of the king's mind.

A mind tortured.

But Durand could not picture the fearsome king of Errest the Old nattering like these mad things. Not Ragnal with his warrior's sword and his robes as jeweled as the Book of Moons.

But it did no good to wonder—not there in the bottom of a pit where he could do nothing. He must get free; he must find Deorwen. Almora was lost and abroad on the Eve of Calends.

The hint of twilight remaining between the branches told him that the beggars had not taken him far—there had been no time for it—and so the ravine had to be some flaw in the valley of the Banderol. It should lead to the river and back to the Wrothsilver Road. And so Durand resolved to put madness and omens from his mind and creep downhill.

Without another thought, he set off along the black foot of the ravine wall—never more than a pace from the nearest rocking spine. He crawled on his belly, trembling with cold and fatigue. Soon, however, a bulge in the wall narrowed the passage and forced Durand near to the mob. He clung to the slime, not touching, moving as soundlessly as a living man could manage.

Finally, though, the walls shoved him too near, and one of the whisperers rose from the muck. It was the graybeard maniac who'd led the attack back on the road. The man must have felt Durand's breath on his neck.

"I can feel their eyes upon me," the madman was saying under his jittering hawthorn crown. *"The same smirk on the face of every groom and serving man when my head is turning, as though every devil in the palace shares the same bloody joke. It is past bearing! Oh, and there are signs upon my son as well. Slow to answer. Watchful. Poisoned against me. Devils! I have lost them all, but they will not have me!"*

The madman did not see, and Durand had no time to think of faraway kings. As he inched around, he winced at the graybeard's every sudden motion. Then, there came a snap of wings over the mob and two black and ragged shapes tumbled against the Heavens, perching on the brink.

One cocked its head. *"Ah, here he is, brother."*

Durand closed his eyes, as still as one of the roots in the mud. He dared not breathe. The madmen had stopped their rocking. It seemed that they listened.

"Indeed, yes. That is him. But he seems to have come down in the world somewhat since noontide."

"I should say so. How like worms in the earth these creatures look. Is this a grave trench, do you think?"

"No, no. You see? They are moving. Hello! Do you suppose they can understand our speech, brother? See how they jump."

"Now, where has Durand got to?" said a Rook.

The mob came uncoiled, craning and gaping, dashing themselves to the muck. Durand was accustomed to the devilish whispers, but for these creatures in the ditch it must have been a new shape to madness. And so the ravine filled with flying heels and hands and elbows—until the graybeard mashed a clawed hand onto Durand's face.

"Oh, my brother, that's no good. I fear we've rather put him in it now."

In an instant, all the churning coiled tight, clutching Durand like a fist.

The mad beggar held Durand eye to eye under the bloody brow of the hawthorn crown. "What is this? What is this!"

Behind him, the mob twisted, flexing like a single worm of thronging limbs, piling up the wall in a heap, always with the bearded man at its heart. *"What is this?"* they echoed, the words darting from mouth to mouth.

"Your face!" the man snarled. "I know this face!"

The others were a chorus: *"Your face! Your face!"*

He grabbed Durand's collar. "The hitched lip. The beard, black as devils!" A hundred eyes blinked down on Durand—the faces mashed together like cells in a wasp's nest. The bearded man crushed Durand's hated face into the slime.

It was incomprehensible.

"Wild and wretched! Red as beefsteak. With the crown, spinning and ringing empty on the stones." His eyes rolled as free as marbles in their sockets. "A bursting, burning face! And it is a fire I would put out!"

Distantly, Durand heard the Rooks take flight as fifty clawed hands caught his limbs. He plunged for freedom, but the hooked nails of a hundred fiends held him. It was all he could do to wrestle his knees up, to twist from the claws at his eyes. Nails shredded his skin. He would be torn to pieces, dying beyond the knowledge of men.

Until, with an impossible suddenness, the whole thrashing multitude stopped, frozen as stiff as branches.

Durand hung in two dozen rigid hands like a bird impaled upon a thornbush. Only the heaving of the beggars' lungs showed that they had not been struck dead.

"Hells," said Durand.

First came the dull light. Through the puzzle of their contorted limbs, Durand made out a round white shape, like a chamber pot in the twilight. There was the pale glow of his moon-faced giant, and beyond it, the empty stare of old Euric, his jaw slack while the rest of his company were limping and slinking in. The sudden stillness was not a reprieve, Durand realized. In this nameless ravine above the banks of the Banderol, the Lost souls of Acconel Castle had found him.

Perhaps this was why they'd gathered all along. This was the reason they had sought him out in Acconel. This was the moment of his doom and Durand's victims had come to bear witness.

"Damn me," said Durand. "Damn this all!" He must get loose. In a moment, the beggar crowd would wake and turn upon him.

Durand pulled his collar free of the graybeard's fist.

The man's eyes snapped around, seeing Durand—and his inexplicably hateful face.

Then, just before the crowd could fall upon him, there was a third arrival.

A shriek shot from the dark upper reaches of the ravine, and every living being spun. An explosive racket battered the stones of the streambed, charging nearer. There were chains in the sound, and the scream returned, louder still, and closer. The mob convulsed. And a vast black shape rampaged into the very heart of the madmen's lair.

But Durand knew this monster—he'd picked every one of the fiend's hoofs a thousand times. It was Shriker.

Durand leapt from the mud and the reeling mob onto Shriker's back, seizing on to the stallion as it bulled through specters and madmen and out into the blackness. Hands caught at them. The accursed graybeard maniac threatened to haul him down—snarling, ranting, and leaving nothing for Durand to do but kick as they lurched toward the black river. The horse must surely break a leg.

The madman clung; he caught Shriker's mane. Shriker swung for the riverbank, careering past uncounted invisible trees in the failing light. In a moment, both riders would tumble off and Durand would be dead against some tree stump, or back among the mob. He stamped down with the force of desperation.

His heel struck the graybeard's brow at a moment of fatal ill-fortune for the old devil—the bole of some great tree was just then flashing past. One instant, the man's face snarled up at Durand; the next, the man was dead, smashed past recognition with a jolt that nearly took Durand's leg.

And, just as he careened around the corner for the upriver road, Shriker now at full wild gallop, he found Deorwen in the track.

The beggar's tumbling corpse rolled to a halt between them.

DEORWEN WAS WAITING on her own mare, with Brand's bridle in her hand, and there was a commotion as Shriker came roaring up. Durand nearly hurtled over the brute's neck.

The horses jostled them very close.

"Durand! Thank Heaven." She looked to the horse. "We're lucky he hasn't broken a leg already. He will have picked up thorns, at the very least." She was already turning. "Ailric is meant to be here by now. I've been careless with that boy's life in all this. Host of Heaven, it's dark."

He felt her hand awkwardly grip his arm. The night breezes sent her dark hair to lick his jaw, and he blinked stupidly at memories of past closeness.

"You're alive," Deorwen said.

There was a moment that she leaned close, but then there came a sound from the crossroads and willows, and Ailric was darting into the trail, swarming nimbly onto Brand's back.

"I met a man or two on the way back," was all Ailric said by way of explanation—all he said about fighting madmen in the dark. For Durand, these two had nearly got themselves killed.

"There is no time," said Deorwen.

Durand's Lost companions were already tumbling into the roadway.

"Almora is out here somewhere," Durand said. He closed his eyes for an instant, wondering how long it would be before he was as mad as the graybeard beggar king.

There were cries among the trees: the beggars were gathering themselves.

"If she hasn't had the sense to seek shelter, Durand, it is too late for her by now," Deorwen said. "There is no moon tonight, and Last Twilight is upon us. Every spirit of well and stone is stirring by now. If we do not take care, there will be no one to rescue the girl. It will be dark as a mine before we can cover half a league. Hurry. There will be a village somewhere beyond these trees and hedgerows. Host of Heaven, we should not be abroad. It is already too late."

Ailric had one foot in the stirrup.

"Get the dead man," said Durand. Only the Hells knew what would happen to a murdered corpse on Calends.

THE ANIMALS SLIPPED and jostled between the ruts as the flowers faded among the thorns. Bonfires glittered down the black valley of the Banderol. These would be hagfires, kindled by the wise women and priests of village after village. In this night between moons, the Queen of Heaven gave way to the Hag, consort of the Son of Morning and mother to monsters. To Durand's bleary eye, the hagfire lights seemed to pull the starry Heavens down around them.

Ailric scouted just ahead of the little party, nimbly slipping on and off Durand's packhorse whenever there were signs in the trail. Maybe he was a little more eager with the dead man over his saddlebow.

Durand's train of dead men brought up the rear.

Finally, Ailric was calling out with good news. "There is a track. Well-trodden, I think. But small."

"We've no time," said Deorwen.

A deep and hedge-crowded track opened like a black door in the ghostly hawthorns. The track was narrower than Durand liked. Anything that crouched among the thorns would be a step from Deorwen's throat.

"It will be a village," Durand said, though he could not be certain. "I will lead."

He slipped down, taking a only single step, his hand on Shriker's bridle, when the whole empty track exploded into silent motion. Shapes boiled off in a thousand directions. And Shriker nearly jerked Durand's arm from its socket.

Durand held on as the gray shapes swarmed away like cobblestones come to life. As quick as they came, the strange shapes drained away into the tangled hedges.

"Host Below," Durand hissed. He'd got the flail out. "What in—"

"*Rabbits!*" said Deorwen.

Durand jammed the flail back in his belt, puffing, "Host Below." The things had been invisible until they burst into motion. "Hells."

Deorwen had no patience. "The champion and his fearsome charger. Rabbits. Get a move on! It'll be worse than rabbits in a moment."

In a hundred fumbling paces, the hedge gave way, and they entered a cool place as dank as the old ravine. The air was thick with growing things, rotting thatch, and the manure of penned animals. Somewhere a big dog was growling, tied to some plowman's doorpost, though Durand could not say where. Not a soul was moving.

"There," whispered Ailric, and Durand spotted a dark shape against the stars. "That'll be the sanctuary. The tower's too narrow to defend." The merest trace of a bell tower could be seen above them, and Durand thought he could make out a low wall, enclosing the whole thing.

"We'd best set your friend down in the sanctuary yard," said Deorwen. "He'll trouble no one."

Ailric answered: "The priest will curse us."

"On Calends, the body's best on sacred ground," said Deorwen. "In the morning I'll need a word with the village women. Maybe we'd best try to get into the sanctuary ourselves. Quick."

Durand gathered the beggar's corpse in his arms, mounted a low bank, and made to hoist the body over the wall. Somewhere the dog kept up its low growl, putting the horses on edge, even Shriker. Durand found the top of the wall and lifted. Over the devil went.

"Stop!" ordered a voice.

A fire blazed up with a rush of heat that had the horses rearing.

"Go no further!"

As Durand turned, flames were still climbing a great heap of dry pine boughs. There must have been plenty of grease and dry kindling in the stack.

A squat and ancient woman stood in the crazed light. She was bald to the top of her head, and an open sore wept where her nose ought to have been.

Deorwen strode out. "Have you been waiting in the dark all this time to spring that on someone?"

The old woman knotted both hands on the head of a walking stick. From her puckered expression, Durand guessed that she had no teeth in her upper jaw. "It is the hagfire!" the woman announced.

"The hagfire? Only now? Old woman, nightfall is long past. Where have you been until now?"

"Two may play at posing questions, I think." She sucked a breath with a smack of her lips. "Why do we find you skulking about on Calends?" And, over fences and berms, from sheds and hovels, every plowman in the village now appeared to glower in a great ring—a mattock, a bill-hook, or an axe clamped in his fists. "What's your business here this ill-omened night?"

Deorwen looked into the vault of Heaven. "We've been caught on the road. Any fool can see we're no spirits, surely."

"Aye. 'Surely.' But there's something about you three. The tall one with the scars: He's been using his fists, I reckon. Black with mud. Red with blood." She was almost sniffing at the air then, searching for the other something—Durand's ghosts, perhaps. "And we've found more devils than just the Hag's brood on the roads these last weeks."

"Do you imagine that we were part of that naked mob at the river? Is that what you're thinking?" Deorwen said. "That we've just popped on a few clothes for an evening in the village after a few week's living in a ditch by the Wrothsilver Road? Or do you imagine we're a troop of raiders from Yrlac, the three of us?"

The old woman grunted. "No, you're no riders from Yrlac, young woman. And you're right that we're late with our hagfire. Today, His bloody Lordship commanded every soul into the fallow fields. Every acre must be under the plow. But I've told His Lordship: He may seed a thousand fields, but he'll have no harvest. The end *is* nearly upon us. Soon, we shall choke on nightmare. I've dreamt it all! But His Lordship will not heed me."

The villagers pulled uneasy faces, uncertain where to look.

"And so the hagfire was late . . . ?" said Deorwen.

"And so the hagfire was late, girl! And so madmen pack the roads! And though His bloody Lordship hangs a hundred beggars at the cross-roads, the fool will not turn back the end."

There was a moment of muffled conversation from high above, followed by a flash of torchlight and cursing. From his spot by the sanctuary wall, Durand heard the sound of a door slamming. He made out torch-

light on a hillock and the flank of a tower. Finally, there was a man snuffling his way through the crowd, accompanied by a wake of villagers
muttering, "His Lordship!" the man broke through the ring of villagers
and stepped into the light.

The lord of the place was homely as a fighting dog and naked except
for a blanket, a stout crossbow in his hands.

A knuckly crook of a nose gave the man's face the look of a blunt axe.
"So who are you, then?" His eyes could have been two black studs. "Out
with it. You've got the whole village out of their beds."

Deorwen sighed.

"I am Deorwen, Lady-in-Waiting to Her Ladyship Almora, the daughter
of His Grace, Duke Abravanal of Gireth." She nodded toward Durand.
"At the wall is Sir Durand Col, the Duke's champion."

The man's mouth opened and shut. The blanket did little to cover his
hairy limbs. "Blast," the man grunted. "You'd best come along."

He bandied through the ring of bondmen toward a stout, half-timbered
hall below the tower, but not before shouting to the old woman: "Mother,
you'd best come as well. I'll wager this has you all riled up again."

While Durand gaped, the old woman grunted, following along.

"I AM TUROLD, Lord of Towerknoll, and you are welcome," said the grizzled man. "For poor Mother, I apologize." He favored Deorwen with a
backward glance as he tramped inside. "She loves when I call her
'Mother,' don't you, Mother?"

The old woman gave a wet grunt.

"That's love," he said. "It's all kisses and cuddles with us two!"

Durand burned to know what they had seen of Almora, but he was
loathe to trust such creatures as these even with the questions. He was the
champion. If he described the duke's daughter, they would know his
errand. Durand snarled like the bondman's cur.

Servants hurried through the barn-like hall while the rustic lord ushered his guests to a stair on the plastered back wall. All through the hall,
armed men were hitching themselves up on elbows, watching like long
cats with still eyes. There were plenty of blades.

"You must have a groom see to the horses," murmured Durand.

"I've got a good man," said the country lord, but he was on to other
business before they reached the top of the stair: "Wife. Here! Throw
me a tunic and drawers. We've got bloody guests! *And* your mother's
been at them."

The man showed Durand a row of yellow teeth. "Has it been the choking on nightmares again? The choking on nightmares is an especial favorite of mine."

With a wincing shrug, the man led the bedraggled party to a door at the creaking top landing. In the lamplight was a bed and blankets. Handing the naked lord his breeches was a stout woman, just past her middle years, with a coverlet pulled to her chins.

"In you come," the man said. He jabbed one paw toward the bed. "Sit down. You too, Mother, why not? It'll be nice and cozy, won't it?"

Deorwen followed the old woman to join the row on the edge of the bed, but Durand stopped on the threshold, and Ailric did not come even that far.

"What brings you to the bedchamber of Lord Turold of Towerknoll in the midst of a moonless night, then, exactly, eh?"

"Good evening, Lord Turold. The duke travels south," Deorwen said, carefully omitting Almora's escape.

Towerknoll squinted at this, nodding along. "The duke. Aye. My reeve watched that crowd on the Acconel Road." He found Durand in the gloom at the door. "I took it for a good sign—gave my man a skin of my best claret when he told me. He said there was a vanguard of Swanskin men up front, making good time. Do they mean to cross at Wrothsilver? Leovere's Penseval is not far from Wrothsilver if memory serves, just over the river and up the hills. Is that what he's up to, our old Coensar? Taking a few boys to knock on our Leovere's door? Maybe ask him to settle down?"

"There is to be a tournament in the Fellwood Marches," said Deorwen.

Towerknoll squinted. "Fellwood?"

"There have been messengers," said Deorwen. "They will meet at the Lindenhall. Over the Pennons Gate."

Towerknoll threw up his hands. "Your messengers must have missed old Towerknoll. . . . So Abravanal means to leave Leovere and Penseval and all of Yrlac behind him. All those men are headed to Fellwood."

"He is the Duke of Gireth. He does as he sees fit," Durand said.

Towerknoll managed a few quick nods. "So he is . . . and so he does. He knows of the raiders? Men from Yrlac? All along the river, there are barns and mills in ashes. We're seeing riders in the daylight now."

"It is no secret," said Durand.

"And he's having himself a tourney over the mountains." Towerknoll gave an odd little pant, his eyes darting. "And you find yourselves separated from the rest, I suppose?"

"We do," said Deorwen, warily explaining nothing. "I wonder what else your vigilant reeve saw on the Acconel Road?"

"He has orders to watch for raiders. That's what he's looking for, my reeve. More worried about that drove of naked beggars down at the landing. Willow Hythe, they call that place. A few of their kind you expect near the city, but not here. The duke's party flushed them, but they settled right back. I had a few hung—making a point, you understand. Riled them up, no doubt. But I wonder what you're driving at. Not them, surely."

Durand decided that the man had heard nothing of Almora.

"We met one or two of your beggars," said Durand. He heard the men down in the hall behind him.

"Yes. I saw one in your baggage, I think." Towerknoll quirked a bitter smile. "But they're nothing to do with you or Leovere, I think. More likely to be something in my dear mother's line. Eh, Mother?"

The old woman's face crumpled around her half-eaten nose, and she said not a word.

"This plan. It'll keep the duke on the road till, what, the Reaper's Moon? What do you think will remain when the old man gets back?"

"That must be in the hands of the Powers," said Durand.

"Yrlaci boys have been poling back and forth across old Banderol. Setting fires. Stealing cattle, sheep. Making the duke look a fool and weakling. Killing. I could run a ferry and make a pretty penny, but I've put new floors in the old tower and swept the owls out. My hayward and reeve are keeping men on watch. Every blade is sharp. Every window full of archers."

He winced an eye shut. "*Some* of us are lucky we didn't find ourselves full of arrows, the way we came roving in, I might say."

"His lordship's tricks—" began the old woman.

Turold twisted. "Don't start with your nightmares, Mother. Leovere's men will find my little tower a devilish tough nut to crack. I'll not give up without a fight."

Turold stuck his chin in the air for an instant, gathering himself, and went on. "I saw you in the streets of Ferangore. I was in that street with the fire and the arrows, when there you was with Moryn of Mornaway on your back, half on fire with that hitch in your shoulder and the twist in your lip. I've never seen the like of it. Not in forty years' biting and scratching in one fight or another. No one has. After Radomor was done, Abravanal gave me Maudy, here—or Kieren did—as a sort of prize. She was a widow, you see." Turold's wife choked back a sob. "And I got my fists on good Gireth land. Put my hands in old Abravanal's and knelt on his pavers to swear my oaths for it."

"What of it, Turold Towerknoll?" said Deorwen.

"What of it? Leovere's coming. They had him surrender at Ferangore, but now it's been ten odd winters and his people are never quiet."

"So you say," Durand said.

The old knight rocked. He fixed Durand with a despairing look. "Come on, lad. With Abravanal and the rest over the mountains, Leovere will not wait. You know it, though you're too stiff necked to speak against the old man. I can see it in your eyes as I saw you in Ferangore. On fire. Bleeding. Abravanal will heed you. Turn him west for Yrlac. Some of those men who fought in Ferangore have land out there without even a river between them and Leovere's boys. Why not stretch a few necks and show them? Tell him that the tourney's madness, or Leovere will snatch Yrlac and make a pyre of Gireth. A man like you could make him see."

"You might watch what you suggest, Turold Towerknoll," said Deorwen.

But Durand stopped her. "No," he said, for he understood this man. He'd won Towerknoll with blood and pain and, though the place no great prize, it was all he had. And now he'd gone to ground in this tower. "I won't keep the truth from this man." Not all of it.

"There will be no turning Duke Abravanal, Turold Towerknoll," Durand said. "This thing is the king's will, not some notion of the old man's. Ragnal wants the men of Fellwood to know the reach of their king. And all of that business in Ferangore was a long time ago. His Grace must ride south."

Towerknoll kept his eyes on Durand's for a long moment. If Yrlac crossed the river in force, places like Towerknoll would be the first to fall. "I see," he said. "The king. Raise the banners of Errest over Fellwood, and make great Abravanal jump. That explains much. But then it is me and my wits, here in Towerknoll."

The man's mother-in-law pulled a great wheezing breath through her ulcerated nose. "Your tricks will avail you nothing, Your Lordship. For soon Errest the Old will—"

"Be choking on nightmares. Aye, Mother." He slipped a hand under his bed, very deftly, and dragged out a bright-honed axe. "They must come if they choose."

And this was how things were on the border.

* * *

WHEN DURAND SET his head on his arm and stretched out on the rushes of Towerknoll's hall, he expected to sleep, but he had forgotten the dead.

The first he saw was his moon-faced giant. The thing had ducked near, pale and as close as a lover above him.

But soon there were many more tottering, slinking, or skittering in pointless circles among the sleepers in Towerknoll's hall.

So Durand lay awake on the rushes. The breathing of mercenaries and serving men sighed about him like stagnant waves. The blood knotted thick in the wool and linen of his gear drew the Lost closer even than before.

Men shivered without knowing why.

Durand set his teeth and lay there, desperately tired but enduring it, waiting for morning, picturing Almora vanishing like a pearl in a black ocean while the tongues of dead men found blood on his skin and clothing. Cold as slugs and eels.

Hours must have passed in this horror when, suddenly, the pack of dead things froze all at once, every slack face jerking toward the door. Durand seized the moment to break away. He struggled to his feet, following their gaze to where the door of the hall waited.

In a fit of something like anger or courage, Durand lurched up and blundered to the door, throwing the thing wide on the dark village. He saw the sanctuary in the faltering light of the hagfire, and made out a gangling figure just visible by the sanctuary yard. Its head swung back and forth, back and forth, back and forth—like the rhythm of a loom. Durand set one bare foot on the step. In the gloom of Calends, he could see little but the stranger.

"Sir Durand?" a voice said, close by.

Ailric had found the door—and a good dozen dead men had joined him, packed tight like a basket of rotten pears. The boy looked cold.

"Find what rest you can," Durand croaked. He stepped outside, more than half certain that he'd lost his mind.

Out in the yard, the vault of Heaven was full of stars and otherworldly mists. Only the figure by the tower was visible. Durand felt his way across the unfamiliar ground with the soles of his feet. Somewhere that big village watchdog they'd heard as they arrived was still growling.

Durand fumbled his way through the ruts and tussocks toward the stranger.

"What do you want of me?" he said. "It's me you're after, isn't it?"

The stranger turned, and Durand knew the graybeard madman at once. His face was like a few brushstrokes of white grease on the black night, and there were missing angles where the tree trunk had clopped home.

"Why do you pursue me?" Durand asked. "*You* leapt upon me. You would have taken people I care about. A man has a right to fight for his own life."

The thing lurched off along the wall of the sanctuary yard, and Durand wove after it, his footfalls swishing through wet grass where the beggar was silent.

Then the shade stopped, turning to face the yard. And Durand recognized the spot: they had fetched up where Durand had tipped the corpse over.

"Is it this? Is it your carcass that's bothering you? Let me get it for you!" In a stride, Durand was past the specter and swinging his leg over the wall into the sanctuary yard. He reached into wet grass and darkness, scrabbling for the dead man's corpse. Finally, he caught hold of stiff flesh: the beard and the crook of a rigid armpit. "Is this what you're after?"

There was a monumental snarl. Creation itself seemed to shudder.

In the sanctuary yard stood a dog.

Enormous.

Moving and not moving.

Without a step, the spirit flickered between trunks and hummocks, more massive than a bear. Its eyes were bowls of green glass, and a slithering flame crawled over a black pelt.

In the road, Deorwen screamed his name.

But the vast darkness of the monster loomed over him now, its eyes spilling green light over the grass and the dead man. He felt blind in the face of it, seeing in flashes like the squeeze of fingers at black eyelids. There was a muzzle, packed with dagger teeth. One snap of the thing's jaws would take Durand's head and both shoulders.

"Slowly backward, Durand. Slowly back." He could hear Deorwen's footfalls on the grass and then on the stiff muck of the road. The darkness spun with the green slither of the dog's fire.

"That's a good lad," he said, "Good lad," as if the thing were someone's ill-tempered lapdog. And he took his hands from the corpse and eased back toward the wall.

A sickening flame spun in the globes of the dog's eyes.

Durand had edged a foot closer to the wall, almost ready to throw himself over, when, finally, the monster seemed to apprehend his intentions.

In a sudden snapping lunge, the teeth flashed. Durand moved. And, with a twist of every muscle in his frame, he threw himself over the wall.

When he landed, winded, at the foot of the wall—alive—Deorwen stood over him. A single bound should have brought the dog down on her.

But it was not Deorwen who spoke. "They say it is guilt that binds them." Towerknoll's mother-in-law was mostly a voice. He could not see her out there with her cane in the dark. "But the boneyard's as far as the grim may go."

Durand set his back on the stones. "Host of Heaven," he said, though the beast's growl rumbled on.

The woman chuckled. "You might choose to leave Heaven out of it," she said. "Such a grim as this is priestcraft, after all."

"Priestcraft?" The thing had seemed more devilish than heavenly.

"As old as Gunderic's Sword, no mistaking."

"Durand, what were you doing in the yard?" Deorwen asked. She stood a pace or two from him. "What is happening with you?"

Durand hadn't slept an hour since Euric died. At least twice, he'd been thrown from a horse. He'd been battered first by Euric and then by the crossroad beggars. He'd faced one of the Powers of Heaven. And the Lost were coming nearer. Even now, the things had left Towerknoll's hall and were tottering across the hummocked yard.

The moon-faced giant stood in the doorway of Towerknoll's hall.

"Durand?" said Deorwen, her voice aching.

The old woman clicked her tongue. "It's no strange thing, for a fighting man to see the Lost. But that's not all with you, is it?"

Dead Euric half-floated past her, his face more pale and shapeless than ever. Durand held his tongue.

"You were going to fetch the body," breathed Deorwen.

Durand must have glanced—maybe shown confusion—for the old woman snorted. "Ach, you dullard! She's not peering into your head. You growled nearly that much when you hopped over the wall."

The dead had drawn up in a great crowd now, like a knot of gawpers around an overturned cart.

"You must tell me what afflicts you," Deorwen pressed.

The old woman shivered in her place among the dead. "Trying to appease the dead man, were you? Not daft, that. But the boneyard is no place for a man when the Eye has set. Our old grim, he nearly had you. The nights'll be long, for him. Sleepless, I expect, watching among the dead. Waiting for the next to die. He'll be eager."

It was all Durand could do to think. Mangled shades from the gates of Acconel loomed all around. A man who's been caught in the teeth of a portcullis is no pretty sight. "This devil lives in the middle of your village? What sort of priest allows such things?" Durand said.

"Are you a child, Durand Col? There's many a boneyard has its grim in Errest the Old, though the patriarchs might wrinkle their noses now. The dead needed keeping, in the old days. And our grim, he's a watch-dog, or nearly so. Some poor priest will have bound the grim in Towerknoll when the land was wild hereabouts. And a quick and bloody binding must have been easier than staking out the hallowed ground and calling Heaven down. Or maybe the Wards of the Ancient Patriarchs had yet to be woven. But you will find them here and there. Your priest slays a dog under the cornerstone, plays his priestly games, and there is our grim for two thousand winters." She gestured to the sanctuary. "Keeps the de-parted safe in their graves." He thought the woman winked. "But you've seen that much, have you not?"

The dead shuffled, peering uncomfortably here and there, closer.

Durand shut his eyes. "A dog," he said. "Even pickled for a thousand winters . . ." He felt like a blind man.

The woman snorted. "The dog's nothing. The shape of the first bur-ied: dog, goat, sheep. Men sometimes. It don't much matter. And the dog's shape is little more than the cloak of the watchman. The priestcraft be-gins with some black boarhound and a young priest's knife, but the shape of the dog or goat or sheep or man is worn by the latest to be buried in that yard. Watch after watch, down the long winters. Each watching for those who went before, soul after soul in turn. There must be a sin or two weighing the poor devil down, but, so long as there is a pang of guilt to catch hold of, the dead must take their watch. They're caught and they serve till the next one comes."

Deorwen was shaking her head. "It is an abominable practice—to die only to wake in the burial ground, surrounded by the fiends of the night."

The woman gave Deorwen a noncommittal grunt. "Priestcraft. Not the best sort. Makeshift." Then she turned on Durand, stumping near to bend low above him. "But you, Durand the Champion. . . ." She squinted, her eyes glinting in her broad shadowed face like chips of glass. "What was this beggarman to you that you leapt into the grim's jaws? Hmm? Someone slain by your hand? Was that the blood?"

"The blood was mine, like as not," said Durand.

She grunted. "So. How many are they? A shadow's no easy thing to count on Calends night, but they're here, ain't they? This moment?"

Deorwen took a step backward, stumbling into the Lost crowd. "Durand?" she said.

"They are," said Durand.

The stout woman cast about, scenting the air like a sow. "All about, I reckon. And you've slain more than one. Are you a haunted man, Durand Col, as fierce as you are? Is that it?"

The gathering of specters thickened until the beggar king was just one more among the great throng at the graveyard wall, with the grim rumbling just out of reach. And there were the old woman and Deorwen standing among them. Durand wondered how many men he had slain. How many could there be?

Beyond sanctuary and tower, Durand thought he could make out the first blue traces of dawn.

6

His Grace's Shadow

When dawn took hold in the east, they scrambled back onto the road. They found the marks of laden carts and hooves enough to make them sure that the duke had come that way. There was no sign of the girl, but they rode as though hope was certainty.

When they were hungry, they tore at hunks of Towerknoll bread and cheese. Never did they dare leave the saddle. They took no time to speak. The girl might be around the next bend.

Soon the Blackroot Mountains hung like a blue smudge of cloud beyond the lowland hills. In Gireth, a man could always find the mountains. From high places near Acconel, you might see faint traces, but now the Blackroots stretched across the whole of the southern horizon. This was where Abravanal's column was bound, and soon this blue image would tower as large as a shipwrecked moon. It was hard to imagine that a man might climb the vast face of such a smudge, dwarfed by every crack and tumbled pebble. Durand had grown up at the foot of the Blackroots.

They rode hard, hoping to overtake the girl.

Before Noontide Lauds, every print in the roadbed clay seemed so fresh and sharp that Durand was certain that they must have been cut within the hour. As he lifted his fingers from one clean print, Deorwen loomed over him.

"Perhaps you will tell me how many Lost souls are haunting you," suggested Deorwen. She had managed to nudge her mare into the track beside Durand.

Durand closed his eyes. "I do not count them, Deorwen. They are many; the old woman said as much. But none now."

"Not in daylight."

"No, not in daylight. In shadows, maybe. You're better off worrying about the girl."

Up the track, Ailric had dropped from his saddle to peer into the road's steep bank. There were trees near the road. "Here," said Durand, "what's this?"

"Where the oaks stand close by the track, someone has climbed the bank and gone up into the trees. Someone was watching, I think."

Durand narrowed one eye. "There will have been men emptying bladders and bowels since Acconel, Ailric."

"They climbed the bank on horseback. I cannot tell their number. The ground they've chosen is full of roots and stones. And the duke's horses obliterated their marks when they rode through."

Durand eyed the hills above the river where they stood, thinking that a shrewd captain would have no trouble hiding a conroi in the dells and basins there, leaving a few picked men by the road to count heads.

"Ailric, if that is where they went up, let's see if you can tell me where they came down again."

The young man nodded. He spotted something fifty paces down the road, where the small stand of roadside oaks gave out. Durand kept his eyes on the trees as they rode to the place.

"They rode down here. Not worried about covering tracks now." Gashes shredded the sopping gray turf. "It's hard to be sure how many, but they followed His Grace, that's clear. The signs are very fresh."

"So they slipped out of the road before Abravanal came, and the duke's men trampled all signs of them in the road. But when the duke had passed, they dropped back into the track," Durand concluded.

"It's respect. They heard Duke Abravanal and the king's herald and the whole retinue overtaking them. They took themselves out of the road. They were making way," offered Ailric. "Standing aside while the duke overtook them."

"You tell a fine tale, and I might take comfort in it, if we hadn't all seen the wagons and carts and oxen in the duke's train. Abravanal and his company could not overtake a plow team. No one nimble enough to mount that bank would need to step aside. They waited. They heard him coming. And they follow him now."

As Durand peered down over Brand's shoulder, he saw slash after slash in the bank, scattered up and down the road. "Ailric," said Durand, "how many do you see?"

"More than one. Twenty? The road is unreadable."

"You'll count better in the woods, Ailric, please," said Deorwen. Her mare had quietly caught them up. And Ailric answered with a curt nod, mounting the bank himself and disappearing among the trees.

Deorwen stroked her mare's neck. "Who would follow the duke's party?"

"Anyone," said Durand.

She was becoming frustrated. "Men of Yrlac?"

Durand nodded once.

"Durand, is the duke's party in danger?"

"Abravanal has the better part of two of armed squadrons at his back," Durand said. "It would take a very strong party to trouble them." But he did not know how many blades Leovere could call upon. Durand might have said more if Ailric had not reappeared.

When Ailric trotted back, he said, "Ladyship, I can't know for certain, but there must be more than twenty. Big men, mostly. Good boots when they climb down. They might be wearing mail." Deep marks, then.

"Not enough to give battle to the duke's squadrons," said Deorwen.

"No, Ladyship. Not enough for that." Ailric had taken the rouncy's bridle, but now he glanced to the ground.

"Ailric, what is it? If I'm being a fool, you'd best say so."

Durand was looking up the valley. Milky-pale water stood in the ruts and hoofprints. A conroi of armed men rode just ahead of them. It could be very bad.

"If they are shadowing His Grace, we will have to go through them to reach Abravanal," supplied Durand. "And twenty Yrlaci horsemen would be more than a match for the boy and I."

"And where do we think Almora is in all this?" Deorwen asked.

"It would be far better if Her Ladyship had already overtaken the duke," said Durand.

"It would be better if she'd never left Acconel." Deorwen's tone was muted. "But it is done. There is nothing for it. We cannot turn back. We'll have to go on and see what comes."

"They may not mean the duke any harm," offered Ailric.

If Leovere's men got hold of Almora, a great deal might change in Gireth and Yrlac.

* * *

THEY RODE CAREFULLY.

Ailric played outrider; Durand kept his eyes moving, thinking only that some useful advantage must come to hand at the last moment. He considered ordering Deorwen back to Acconel with Ailric, but knew she would take no order from him. Or anyone else.

The country broke into choppy hills, and the Banderol writhed restlessly between them while Ailric roved ahead as they watched for signs.

At one bit of high ground, crows reeled into the air just over the rise. At another, Deorwen heard a horse cry out. But, for an hour, they met no one.

Then, on a fencepost near the road, Durand spotted the Rooks once more. The two birds tussled, flapping for space. *"What we really want to know is the end of the story. We were called."*

The uncanny sound made Durand flinch despite himself.

"There were whispers."

"Dreams, brother."

"And then Radomor and power and sanctuaries aflame, with King Ragnal going mad in Eldinor."

"Fine days, brother."

"But who was our Whisperer? Who summoned us to this northern land? Who wished us here, making trouble? Was it coincidence that the high sanctuaries burned or fell in? And the Wards of the Ancient Patriarchs grew thinner and thinner so we could play our little games?"

"Fine days, indeed."

Durand passed near the fencepost and saw the birds struggling with flies. Nipping them from each other's quills. Flapping at a cloud of the things. He feared that Deorwen must notice. It was no natural sight.

"But someone called us, Durand Col. Someone sent their whispers through the long nights to find us. And we wonder now, who they were. Could we leave in ignorance? And where are they now?"

"And we think you may be the key, Durand Col."

Durand remembered the days when he'd first met the Rooks, and the murders and battles that followed. They had all served Radomor, at least for a time. He remembered Ferangore's high sanctuary heaped with skulls like toadstools, as black birds carried souls from the roasting streets of the city under siege.

"We think this may be the time, and that you may be the key."

Just ahead, Ailric had halted upon a wooded rise. And Durand left the Rooks to their mad muttering. They had come upon a village.

A jumble of low, mossy farmsteads slumped in a basin below the hill. The scar of the trampled roadway lay like the mark of a lash across the back of the place. "Millstrand," said Ailric. "Part of Swanskin Down's domains."

They could see no one abroad in the place. Not even the smoke of a hearth fire.

"I think we take a moment to bang on a few doors. Find someone. Learn what they've seen."

As they jounced into the village, still trying to get a sense of the place, all of the doors around them flew wide. Armed men swarmed over the village's bermes and hedges, trapping Durand's party in a thicket of blades. Durand had a glimpse of grim-faced men leveling crossbows, but the shock was more than Brand could stand. The animal reared and plunged, positively spinning while Durand got his flail loose. There was a snap and vicious hiss.

The bolt caught him in the collarbone before he knew it had been shot. And it would have been buried there in the sinews, veins, and bulging windpipe, except that he'd worn his mail coat. He felt the thing nick the point of his jaw as it glanced from the iron links.

"Wait! All of you. Have you no eyes in your bloody heads?" And Durand knew Coensar's voice. "Another bolt, and you'll have me to answer to!"

And Durand rounded on the crowd, seething. Anything might have happened. Deorwen was right behind him.

Weapons were lowered—at first only a fraction, but already the call was traveling the line. "Durand Col! Lady Deorwen!"

Coensar strode out to meet them.

"We thought there was someone following."

"There was. They should have been between us."

"Durand." Coensar took in Deorwen's face. He saw Ailric. "Why have you come?"

DURAND WAS ON his knees in the wet turf.

"My daughter!" howled the duke. The girl was not there. She was lost—lost, they feared, beyond all hope.

The duke's company sprawled across the road and into the reeds and fields all around. And everything stopped at the sound of his voice. Every drover and laundress was still.

Abravanal tottered on a camp stool with Coensar and the Herald of

Errest on either side. Deorwen stood behind him. "In the turmoil as the column rode out, Your Grace, she slipped away," Durand answered. "We prayed that she'd reached you."

"You prayed that she had reached me? A girl alone? In this land of traitors? You prayed that she had *reached me*?"

Durand lowered his face.

"You were meant to guard her!" Abravanal said.

Durand bent as low as he could. "Yes, Your Grace."

The man struck him and struck him again. "Where is Almora? That is the only answer I would have of you. Damn the king! Damn Ragnal, the devil! I should have been at her side!"

The old man thrust a finger at Deorwen. "You are foresworn! You are both foresworn. Oath-bound to watch over her! These long years have I placed my trust in you! My daughter. My only child. The last. Where is my life now? You are meant to have been her companion!"

Deorwen bowed low. There was no answer to give.

"It is treason, this. You have foresworn yourselves. Both of you . . ." He was muttering these things, but no one in Errest the Old would stay the old man's hand if he went farther. Gunderic's Sword, that great remedy of traitors, was somewhere in the man's baggage even now. Or it could be the rope, if he wished. Even Durand could not gainsay him.

Durand took a breath to say "The fault is mine alone," or something like it, when he felt an impossible tug at his sleeve; there was Ailric in the midst of all this. He had been standing a respectful pace behind. Now, Ailric gestured into the crowd where a young woman stood, head low: a laundress presumably, barefoot in a hairy blue cloak, standing among Abravanal's lords with the Herald of Errest at her side. She wore a married woman's sack-like wimple over her head and shoulders, but now she threw it off.

"Father!" she said.

Abravanal had fallen to his knees by then, looking up into the girl's face. "Almora?"

Here was Almora: alive, cold, and pale.

A soft rain fell.

THEY TOOK SHELTER from the drizzle in the greatest of the bondmen's meager cottages—a place that steamed like something plucked from a cauldron when the fires were lit within. There was an hour of affection, of relief and joy. Durand was there. Somehow the old man had half forgiven him. He'd been made to stand by the fire, steaming some of the damp from his clothes.

Abruptly, though, the duke seemed to realize where they were and a dread took hold of him.

Now, the old man looked into Durand's face, ashen. "You must take her back," he said.

Little gales of rain spun through the smoke holes at either end of the blackened roof. Coensar, Abravanal, and Deorwen surrounded the girl.

There was mud to Almora's knees. It looked to Durand as though she'd fallen more than once, and, not for the first time, Durand cursed himself for letting the girl get away from him. Where was her horse?

The duke smiled. "She will be back in Acconel before noontide tomorrow." And Durand wished that it were so. He could go to the Patriarch with his damned Lost souls. He could lock the girl in a good stout tower, and he could rest. The thought alone loosened the knots in Durand's shoulders. Maybe Durand would sleep in the sanctuary. That would keep the dead from bothering him.

"Your Grace," said Coensar, "it is not safe. I cannot say where they've got to, but there was a pack of Yrlaci raiders shadowing this column, moving pretty freely. They'll have her as soon as she's out of sight. There are a score or more back there."

Coensar was right.

"We will send a squadron of knights with her. Two!" argued Abravanal.

"Your Grace," said Coensar, "we've only got two squads. That lot behind us might well have fifty men. And fifty is more than we'd have left if you sent even one squadron back. We did not bring an army. We cannot divide our strength with the enemy on our heels."

The duke was shaking his head, but Coensar was right and even the duke could see it.

Again, Ailric tugged at Durand's sleeve. "Wrothsilver," he said.

Durand winced; grimaced really. Wrothsilver was the last place he wanted to go: It was the chief town of the Barons of Swanskin Down. And the baron would likely have questions about his brother, Euric. Still, Durand's discomfort didn't count for much, even in his own reckoning. And the Acconel Road led them straight to Wrothsilver. He filled his lungs, stepping forward.

"We'll take her to Wrothsilver," said Durand. "We can get the girl shut behind iron gates and stone walls in an hour or two." With the girl in Wrothsilver, Durand could ride for Acconel, or he might just stay with the girl, keeping her from slipping away again if the baron would allow Durand to sleep under his roof.

Ailric nodded. The town wasn't far off.

"She'd be safer there than on the road," said Coensar. "It would take more than a few raiders to break the walls of Wrothsilver."

The old man set his faltering hand possessively upon his daughter's shoulder. "She should be in Acconel. . . ."

Durand scowled, arms crossed over his chest. The old man was being peevish, and he likely knew it.

"There's no better way, Your Grace," said Coensar. "We can put her well beyond danger. It can be over and done by nightfall."

The duke's blue eyes bulged accusingly toward his daughter, but he only waved his hands. "So be it."

IN A LITTLE more than two hours, the duke's party had wallowed to a point where they could see Wrothsilver. The white town gleamed on a high green hill over the valley of the Banderol. Despite the wet afternoon, the place looked good. Durand judged that Almora would be safe there. He guessed that he could soon ride back for Acconel. He wondered whether he'd leave Deorwen behind to watch over the girl. It seemed wise.

Then, he heard the Rooks laugh. They erupted from the branches of a roadside thornbush, their racket causing horses to shy before they arrowed off through the drizzle.

Coensar was cursing at Durand's side; he'd nearly been thrown.

He checked his horse sharply. "Damnable beast," he muttered as the Rooks tumbled high under the clouds, banking toward the leaping spans of the White Bridge where it crossed the Banderol into Yrlac, west or southwest. Planters in the fields made the Eye of Heaven. Sheep took flight on the valley walls.

"Wrothsilver," said Ailric. "Seat of the Barons of Swanskin Down." This had been the shield-bearer's home for ten winters or more, and they had been good winters for the town: Wrothsilver commanded the best crossing of the Banderol, and it flourished while Yrlac and Gireth remained under one rule.

"His Lordship sends riders." The boy drew Durand's eye to a road that led up to the town. And, sure enough, a double file of knights was already rumbling down through the drizzle, trappers flying. "That's the Swanskin blue and gold," said Ailric.

Coensar nodded. "Sure. But why so many? That's fifty men. Vadir's brought a little army. What's in the man's head, I wonder?"

Quietly, Coensar stiffened the vanguard, put a man or two on the shoulder of the road, and made sure that the duke and his daughter were locked up tight. It paid to be careful.

Vadir's men pulled up twenty paces short of Abravanal's company. Not before Durand's hand found the handle of his flail. Their straight-backed baron brought his charger stepping forward. He came in full battle gear and he looked nothing at all like bladder-faced Euric—and even less like the old baron. You might have mistaken old Swanskin for a village baker, with his paunch and white mustaches. Euric was a wineskin. But Baron Vadir was wolf-quick, with an impractical sweep of brown hair.

Old Swanskin was the man who'd ordered Durand to bite his tongue about Coensar's treason for the general good. Now Durand had killed one of the old man's sons. He did not leap forward to shake Vadir's hand.

"Your Grace," said the baron, "I have summoned every knight-at-arms who could reach the White Bridge in time, but the attack must already be underway. Your force left in a desperate hurry, stopping only to beg a change of mounts."

"Force?" demanded Coensar. The rest were dumbstruck.

Vadir acknowledged Coensar. "I wish you'd told us what you intended instead of playing bloody games! And what's this about my brother? What's happened to him? They are saying he was injured."

Durand wasn't ten feet from the man. Like as not, he had Euric's blood still under his nails.

"Your brother must wait," said Coensar, and Durand thanked the Host of Heaven for that. "I need to know about these riders," Coensar pressed.

Vadir blinked once, but looked at Coensar squarely. "Knights of Swanskin Down, mostly. Some men from lands along the Banderol, Sir Coensar. I knew half of them by sight. A pack of them charged in on blown horses right on the heels of the galloper who'd brought us word of Ragnal's tournament rubbish. I sent every boy in Wrothsilver pelting into the country to call up my liegemen in time. We'll fall in with your column. Leovere's Penseval is no great distance beyond the White Bridge, but we should leave these carts of yours or we're sure to be too late."

Now, Abravanal was quavering. "What is he on about?"

Vadir spread his sword hand wide, as though calling upon the Host of Heaven. "Lord Leovere, Your Grace! You ordered that the traitor be rooted out. Your men were riding hard for Penseval before he could mount a defense. What has been going on in Acconel?"

A cold horror of recognition flashed over Durand. Towerknoll had spoken of a vanguard, of men riding hard toward Wrothsilver. Now, Durand understood: The fools meant to attack Leovere at Penseval.

"Damn them!" snarled Coensar. "Leave the carts behind! We must hurry." The reckless idiots would have been sitting at the Feast of the Ascension. While Durand was goggling at dead Euric, they'd taken the halfwit's ill-considered counsel—and old Abravanal's ranting about fat lands and thorns in his backside—and now they would pitch the whole of Abravanal's domains into war just as the duke rode into the Fellwood. They must be stopped.

"His Grace sent no one to kill Leovere," barked Coensar. "We'll have to ride them down before they reach Penseval, or it will be war!"

"These men crossed the Banderol several hours ago," Vadir said. "You will never recall them in time."

"We cannot have war, Baron!" said Coensar. "Not now."

Already, he'd pulled a dozen of the best riders from the column. But, as Coensar made to set his spurs, the wind switched, shifting like a drawn breath and taking the rain with it. It was as sudden as sorcery, and every man squinted. "Host of Hell."

Durand remembered the laughter of the Rooks. He remembered their sudden flight across the White Bridge, west or southwest. His stomach heaved, hollow.

There was a long note on the wind: the call of a horn, clear beyond explanation, riding the air from beyond the White Bridge, west or southwest.

"That was Penseval," said Ailric. "I don't understand."

Next, the Herald of Errest, who had been as still as a sanctuary icon since Acconel, rose in his stirrups, taller than any of them. He peered south toward the blue smudge of the mountains, his pale features grim. In his fists, he held the long horn of silver and ivory that he had winded at the gates of the Burning City three hundred years ago, across the Sea of Storms, long as a sorcerer's staff: an heirloom of the people of Errest. Faintly, it could be heard to moan, taking up the call from Penseval.

But there was something else.

Knights and lords swiveled in their saddles. Then, the grass whispered. In the distant pastures, the wind had come alive, its rush swelling until it broke over the road, picking up mantles, manes, and trappers, throwing them like flags.

Vadir's mount was stepping high. "This is something new again."

And a new sound throbbed over Creation, blatting out like a battle horn as though the Blackroots themselves brayed in outrage. The rattling groan arose from the whole of the southern horizon: an answer to the call from Penseval, grotesque and vast beyond understanding. Durand had never heard the like of it. No one could have.

"Now what?" demanded Coensar.

Bondmen all down the valley took to their knees, and Durand clenched his broken teeth as a great drove of sheep swept down from their hillside pasture like a flight of birds. Ailric had his hands full not getting himself clubbed senseless by his dun rouncy's nodding head. The sheep stormed through the roadway, tumbling into the track and out again, further unnerving every man and beast in the column. Vadir's charger spun. Animals reared. Men made the Eye of Heaven, hissing charms against evil.

It was Ailric who spoke next.

"Smoke," he said. And, almost, it broke the spell of the uncanny note from the mountains. He sprang into his saddle—a vantage point. West or southwest, beyond the Banderol and into the hills of Yrlac, a trace of smoke hung like a smutty feather on the horizon. "Leagues away, but near enough. That will be Penseval burning," said Ailric.

"No!" said Coensar. Durand rumbled the same word.

Vadir had mastered his charger once more. "An omen!" He waved a hand over the whole of Creation. "An omen. A call to battle!" He pitched his voice so that every man in the ranks of knights could hear as well. "We must send a strong party to Penseval." The tall baron's eyes flashed. "If Leovere is slain, the traitor lords are leaderless. If Leovere lives, then the traitor lords of Yrlac will rally as they have not done these ten years, and they will come to us for blood! We must be sure."

Vadir turned to Duke Abravanal, where the old man clung to the reins of a gray palfrey. "Here, Your Grace, we have the heart of an army to strike them down. Now that our first blow has landed. We must finish what began with the devil Radomor. Summon the Host of Gireth to Wrothsilver, and we shall cross as one!"

The duke hardly moved, though his cheeks burned bitterly, for the Herald of Errest sat tall and mute beside him. Every man in Abravanal's column wanted nothing more than to charge over the river. But the mere sight of the Herald was a silent reminder that they could not turn, even to avert a rebellion.

Coensar's voice was a crumpled thing. "Do you know the pass called Pennons Gate?"

Vadir looked to the duke. "Your Grace? What is this about?"

"The pass, it is open?" pressed Coensar.

"There has been some trade—not many go by that road. It is an ancient route. In these times, most men take the lowland road by Bedrin Gate."

"So the pass is open," Coensar concluded.

"Sir Coensar, I do not understand."

"We must leave your White Bridge behind us, Baron. Penseval is burning. There's nothing to be done. Leovere lives or does not." Durand swallowed at a knot of something uncomfortably like shame or horror.

The wind tugged at the astonished Vadir's long, storm-blue mantle. "You would leave now?"

"The *king* commands it, Baron," Coensar growled, his voice rising. "His Grace is *bound*. If His Grace *turns,* it's treason. If he *tarries,* it's treason. If he does ought but ride south to that pass, he's defied Ragnal's writ and it's treason and his kin must be exiles, his lands forfeit, and all of us must war with every lord in Errest to hold a damned thing!"

Vadir said nothing, at first, to Coensar's tirade; his men were silent. Few men harangued a baron before his vassals, but Vadir was grave. "Then you must go," he said, carefully.

Coensar subsided, even putting his face in his hands for a moment to recover himself. "'Must' is the word, Baron Vadir. There is no escaping it. If we turn aside, the duke must lose Yrlac and Gireth both. Riding on, we *may* lose Yrlac, but we may still keep Gireth, at least."

"Men will bleed for this pettiness of the king's. But we will make ready here. If the duke cannot ride into Yrlac, we must look to defend our people."

"We will send riders to Kieren in Ferangore," said Coensar. "And Durand must get back to Acconel. The defenses must be made ready. If Leovere comes, there is no telling how many men he may bring." He shook his head. "Only days ago, we were near to peace." He looked to the pale Herald, to Almora, and back to the baron.

"Baron, you asked about your brother. You are owed an answer."

This, of course, put Vadir on his guard—and Durand as well, sitting in a saddle at Coensar's hip. There must be hells like this.

"Your brother, Euric, he was rash at the Ascension feast," said Coensar. "There were highborn men all around to hear him. Strangers. Liegemen. There was drink, and allowances were made, but he would not recant. Kieren spoke with him. But your Euric fought."

"The duke's champion?" said Vadir. He quickly spotted Durand in his black gear. And for the first time, the man seemed to notice Ailric—Sir Euric's onetime shield-bearer—at Durand's side. Durand did not look from the man.

"What are you saying?" Vadir said.

"Euric died of his wounds the following morning. Yesterday." To Durand, it seemed as if a year had passed.

"'Yesterday' . . ." Vadir repeated, the word a hollow thing in his mouth. "Sir Coensar, why? What could he have said?"

Coensar struggled to fashion a reply. How did one tell a man that his brother had made a drunken pig of himself and slandered his liege lord's daughter? How did a man say such a thing before the girl herself? The duke's face was stiff, and Durand watched a confusion—anger, even—flash over the baron's face as he waited. And then Almora spoke from the rear of the ducal party.

"He spoke of me, Baron," said the girl. "They rushed me out, but he was speaking about me."

Vadir turned to Almora. From the shock on his face, he hadn't even seen the girl among Abravanal's people. "Ladyship!" Durand guessed it was as near as this polished lord ever came to stammering. "I did not expect to find His Grace's family with him here."

"That is a story in itself," said Almora.

"Lady Almora, I apologize on behalf of my kinsman." Vadir shook his head. "I remember you, a child playing with her dolls. You had a brass Power, did you not? A marvel. Little wings like a locust's. I remember it buzzing high through the Painted Hall."

Almora had ducked her head, but looked up at him with bright eyes. Her white fingers found the slender chain at her bosom. "I still have it, milord."

"It is a marvel," Vadir affirmed.

"She should not be here at all," muttered Abravanal. He would not meet the baron's eye.

"But there are not soldiers enough to spare to protect her on the return journey," said Vadir. "Not with Leovere's men on the roads. Not with every eye in two duchies watching."

"The devil."

"Your Grace, leave the girl with us. For my brother's fault, I will make amends. There below, we have our White Bridge, narrow enough that twenty chosen men could thwart an army. Above, my Wrothsilver has her hill and stout walls. If Leovere lives, if he rallies the native lords of Yrlac, then Wrothsilver and the men of Swanskin Down will make a stout shield for all of Gireth until Sir Kieren brings your host to relieve us." He seemed to remember something; he looked toward the white town above them. "My father's tomb was built on the hill's flank, the first of my kin to face Yrlac. You can see the tomb from this place, if you look with care. Just there." The white face of a rock-cut shrine was barely visible on the green hill, overlooking the Banderol. "Perhaps he saw this day coming."

"My daughter?" said Abravanal, clearly hearing little else.

Tall Vadir drew himself up.

"If His Grace should entrust Her Ladyship to our care, here, it would say a great deal to your people. It would be a sign of your faith. And the valiant Lady Almora would kindle a new fire in the heart of every loyal man." The baron's smile flashed in Almora's dazzled eyes; they might be heroes here together.

But Abravanal's lip trembled. His eye darted. "No," he said. "No, it cannot be. At your side. It cannot be. We must keep her with us. She will be safest with us." He glanced to his grim commander. "Coensar, we must press on."

Coensar opened his mouth.

"Coensar, you are my man." Whether it was the thought of Wrothsilver, first to face the rebels of Yrlac, or of handsome Vadir himself, Abravanal could not leave his daughter. "The king has ordered us south. We cannot retreat. Durand will ride with us. He will watch her."

Durand gaped. In an instant, here was Acconel snatched away, the defense of the city in another's hands. But he could not say a word. He owed the old man. He'd been lucky with Almora. He had been sure that he would find the girl dead on the road.

Coensar was watching him and he answered with a nod.

Coensar frowned.

"I am sorry, Baron," said Coensar. "It must be as the duke says. We will move quickly and be away at once. Get word to Kieren. He must return to Acconel and summon the Host of Gireth. I am sorry about your brother."

"I see. Sir Coensar, Your Grace, Your Ladyships. I understand. You have the right of it. Wrothsilver may not be safe for long. We will listen for word of Leovere and make certain that Sir Kieren hears. Meanwhile, allow me to reinforce your column with a few of my own men."

He turned to a red-headed lordling. "Here, you, Raimer. Bring your conroi."

The startled Raimer quickly cut ten startled knights from the baron's squadron.

"My man, Raimer, will see you through to the Fellwood," said Vadir.

Sir Raimer recovered himself well enough to bow in his saddle.

Durand sat, numbed, as apologies and well-wishes continued. The baron's high-flown nonsense had neatly scuttled any chance that Durand and the duke's daughter would be stopping in Wrothsilver. Someone had found a mantle for her. It bore a collar of white fur. Durand could not put things right. He could not join the fight he'd begun. He could not strike out for Acconel or Ferangore. And the Patriarch of Acconel would not soon rid him of the Lost.

He clenched his fists.

In the high passes of the Blackroot Mountains, the great moan still rang.

7
A Test of Fire

Durand, Vadir's men, Almora, Deorwen, the Herald, and all of the duke's squadrons slept in the hovels of a tiny village a league or two beyond Wrothsilver. In the longhouse where Durand lay, the bondman's dogs and children cowered. The Lost gathered, one by one, to pack the place. Thin rays of firelight probed the chinks in the fire cover. The light glittered in the staring eyes of the living and the Lost.

ERREST THE OLD broke in its climb toward the Blackroots. The rolling downs split into rude chalk bluffs. The broad-hipped valley of the lowlands assumed the character of a narrow gorge, where the slow Banderol became a clean and darting thing. Away to the south, three sheer peaks rose from the azure wall of the mountains, blue and pale like praying hands.

Durand rode with Ailric at the head of the column—a practice which kept him clear of Deorwen's questions and let him put his unease and guilt to good use, scouring the rocks ahead for hidden enemies. From time to time, the track pushed the column between chalk banks and obliged them to straggle out in double file. Once, the ox-carts had to put a wheel in the river. The few stray travelers on the road to Pennons Gate could not help but catch the cavalcade as it picked its cumbersome way upriver, but it was no easy matter to get by them.

Durand led Ailric up a twist in the track with the Banderol foaming beside them. "Host of Heaven," Durand said as they labored up. "We'll be a bowshot or more from head to tail."

Both men knew that a raider who knew the land could fall upon the cavalcade like a cleaver on a serpent's back. The whole company was lost in the twists behind them. At that moment, Durand and Ailric seemed very much alone.

"You were Euric's man for ten winters?" Durand asked.

"I was."

"My father's gift to you?"

"It was," said Ailric. Durand peered at the boy, but saw no irony in his face. A priest's boy might follow anyone and be grateful.

"In Wrothsilver all that time?" Durand asked.

"On holy days. Some years. We were not often summoned to the baron's hall," he said carefully. Euric was not so welcome then, even among his kin, but a man did not speak ill of the dead.

"He was not his best at the Ascension feast," Durand allowed.

Up between the walls of the gorge, Durand could see the mountains. It was not unlike the foothill town of Col, where he'd grown up. But they spent little time climbing. Only great need drove a man into the wastes of the high mountains.

"I imagine we'll carry a few stragglers with us through the wilderness," said Durand. "They'll look to us for safety."

"A few hours ago, there was a group of religious brothers. Monks. Coensar had men search their hands for calluses and court brands."

Durand approved of that much at least. "That will cost him a few boils for certain," he said. "The holy men, they won't thank him for such handling."

He heard the clatter of the cavalcade now, even over the roar of the water. He nudged Brand forward and nearly blundered into an upturned cart in the midst of the trail. A tall, bent figure worked to right the thing while a mule moaned at the Heavens.

There was no room between the fool and a quick river full of broken rock.

There could be no better place to lay a trap.

Durand shot a quick look around the gorge for hidden men, then snarled down at the man. "Get that thing out of the road!"

The long-faced man strained his thin limbs against the cart, but it did not move.

To Ailric, Durand said, "Ride back. Tell them halt and expect trouble." Then Durand leapt into the road. As he landed, one boot clapped a tin pot shut. There were pots and iron-shod tools all around the upset cart. Everything not tied down was in the road. The man was a tinker, or playing one.

Impossibly tall and bent as a hoop, his head was wreathed from forehead to jaw with a rough fringe of brown hair. Durand shifted the flail in his fist.

"Get it on its wheels," said Durand. If there were any tricks, the man would die in a moment.

"I will need help," said the tinker. "It's the way it's landed."

And, though the cart was half made of willow hoops, even Durand couldn't right the thing with the uphill way it had fallen.

And now the first rank of the column was right behind him.

The tinker looked mildly over the dozen or so knights at the head of the column glowering up at him. "You will never get those carts over the pass," he said. "They're not made for this road. You'd do better with twice as many, half as big. This is just the start. Fellwood is worse."

There was just verge enough for a few of the column's hangers-on to dodge the ruts of the main road track—plodding forward to gape at the Champion of Gireth wrestling in the road. Maybe they thought they were going to get by.

Durand was in no mood for gawkers. He hooked his thumb at a gaggle of these men. "You lot, come here."

A half-dozen laborers chuckled into the roadway.

The first, a toad-faced man, knuckled his forehead. "I'm Morcar, lordship. These here are Grugan and Tosti." A pair of equally homely men nodded bows. "The others, I am not sure." He grinned.

"Right," said Durand. "I am sure we will all be friends in time, Morcar. Put a shoulder in."

A mule-faced man—either Grugan or Tosti—smiled. "Me? I'm happy to work for my passage with the wilds full of bandits and Banished spirits. Numbers are safety, milord." The man shook his head at Durand as together they put their cheeks against the cart and heaved. "I never thought to see a duke's champion work so hard for a tinker."

Durand smiled. Here he was, mucking in with laborers when he was meant to be commanding the defense of Acconel. Here, even a tinker's cart wouldn't obey him. He snorted a laugh and, together with his new comrades, threw the tinker's cart onto its wheels to a smattering of applause from the vanguard. Even young Almora managed to get a look.

The tinker was already back at the reins, urging his mule onward. And so the duke's column followed a tinker's clattering cart as it wobbled up the Banderol.

They had been lucky so far.

*   *   *

THE THREE PEAKS Durand had first sighted from the valley of the Banderol soon towered above them, but the road opened up for a time and lay broad and stony before them. Fractured hills loomed all around, bristling with resinous pine trees.

Durand led the vanguard up a broken ridge under the vast sweep of the haunted mountains. Brand tossed his big boxy head. At nearly the same time, one of the packhorses let out a screaming whinny.

Durand shortened his grip on the reins.

"Smoke again, I think," said Ailric. "Pitch and something wet—half-rotten."

"That'll be thatch and rafters," said Durand. Thin curtains passed across the tunnel of branches ahead, and Almora's horse pranced skittishly at the touch of the strange scent.

Durand heard a chiming tone: a bell tolling somewhere.

And so the pair pelted back to the column where Durand saw no choice but to speak with Coensar. The duke's whole party pricked up their ears.

"We've got smoke," said Durand. "House or barn on fire, like as not."

Abravanal peered at Coensar and Durand.

Finally, Coensar spoke. "It's a raid then? We're halfway up the mountains."

"Smells of pitched timber and old thatch," said Durand.

Vadir's man, red-headed Sir Raimer, was there. "There is a town, Broklambe, on the road to the pass. There's something of a plateau, I understand. Not far. I don't know how anyone could have got here from Yrlac ahead of us."

"You've a generous opinion of our pace, Sir Raimer, and I expect you'll find that there are more crossing places than the White Bridge," said Coensar. "We'll advance as a body. If there are raiders, let them tackle the whole lot of us. See how they like it."

Men unshipped their weapons and the company rode until the pine wood gave way. The track forded the Banderol at the side of a big stone mill. Beyond it, a village was scattered along the stream, every building burning. Crags and pine woods ringed the plow lands. There was no sign of a torch party, but Coensar had sense enough to be wary.

"All right," commanded Coensar. "Break out anything that'll hold water. Let's see what we can do but, by the Host Below, keep your eyes open!" With a few orders, he cut forty or fifty men from the column. The rest made ready to protect the duke.

Coensar, glancing over the remainder, noted Durand sitting behind the duke's household. Their eyes locked for a moment. "Sir Durand," he said, "I will need you to watch over this lot till I get back."

And the knights cantered into Broklambe, Coensar and a full squadron riding over a Banderole that exploded under their hooves.

Thus the first part of Abravanal's guard charged away.

Ailric and Durand kept near Almora, Deorwen, and the duke.

Ailric steadied his borrowed mount. "Most of Broklambe is ablaze," he said. "Scattered houses. Outbuildings that lie far from the rest."

Durand scowled. Only human hands could carry fire so far. "This will be part payment for Penseval," Durand said. He wondered, if he'd handled Euric differently, whether Broklambe would have been left in peace. Now, the fires blazed high enough that Durand guessed the raiders hadn't been gone more than an hour. "We'd best keep a sharp eye out. I'd wager they're closer than we'd like."

He saw no riders but Coensar's. After a moment, though, he spotted blotches of color moving over the plow lands. A large group had broken cover.

Ailric raised his hand. "Not soldiers," he said.

And sure enough, Durand made out a woman with hiked skirts and several men racing as fast as tilled muck would let them. Durand took it for a sign that the raiders had cleared off. Here were survivors eager to save what they could. Maybe they'd been in the field and run for shelter.

"Some of these villagers will know something useful: seen a blazon, heard a name. We might learn which of Leovere's people likes fire so much," Durand said. "Maybe we can hold someone to account for this."

Almora shifted uneasily in her saddle. No one liked standing by, and Durand's rumblings about justice did little to comfort her. "It is awful," she said. "Where will they live? They'll have nothing." Durand had no answer.

Meanwhile, the villagers reached their town. They did not stop at the first sheds and outbuildings. And soon they passed the blazing cottages themselves, never stopping to douse a fire. Not once.

"Where are they going?" wondered Durand aloud.

There was a large building ahead. It had a bell tower—almost a keep—and narrow windows; mere arrow slits. The whole building was ablaze, and the bell rang on. Again and again. Villagers tried to reach the doors, but the fires drove them back.

"It's the sanctuary," declared Ailric.

Durand watched uneasily as the villagers rushed to the blazing doors.

"There are bales of straw heaped against that door," said Ailric.

"Durand," breathed Deorwen, "the bell. Host of Heaven!"

Now, apprehension dawned upon the whole astonished household of the duke. If the sanctuary was burning from wall to wall, and the bell was still ringing. . . . Almora caught her breath, realizing. "There must be someone inside to ring it!"

Raimer, Baron Vadir's man, spoke next. "We cannot stand by! We must ride! With me, whoever will come!" And what could Durand say? In a few moments of chaos, everyone rushed away, leaving the duke and his immediate household behind with a half dozen workmen. Even the mendicants were driving their donkeys downhill. Durand had his fist in Almora's reins.

Almora's face was taut; Durand imagined he saw a little hate there.

"I'm sure Coensar and the others will save them," Deorwen said.

The last of Abravanal's guard reeled into the smoke and flames. Snatches of smoke blowing through the village blinded them to the action at the sanctuary. They could only hear the bell over the millwheel and the stream. The dozen or so of them might have been alone in Creation.

"It is terrible," said Almora.

"Coensar and the rest will do what they can," said Abravanal. "The door of a village sanctuary will not stop armed men for long."

Deorwen spoke out. "I'm not sure why we've hung back."

"The men who set the fires might yet be near," Durand said. He would be damned if he led Almora and her father charging into a blazing village when Leovere's horsemen had hardly finished with the place. Over Deorwen's head, Durand saw signs that one of the raiders had managed to loft a torch onto the mill's thatch not too long ago—and it was a good throw in Durand's judgment: two or more fathoms. They could not have gone far.

"Folk will need tending to," said Deorwen. "We'll have to see what shelter can be arranged. Water will be needed, and I'm sure we'll need more clean linen than so small a village will have at hand."

Abravanal was nodding. "As soon as Coensar sees these people safe, I will cause riders to bring help from the villages and steadings nearby." Durand feared that those riders would be galloping through the night. It was hard, upland country. "Coensar will know whose holding this is. Their lord may have resources to draw upon as well."

Durand squinted into the smoke, wondering if the bell had faltered. At any moment, he expected to see some knight or other hauling one of the villagers into the clear air. And, more than once, a trick of the twisting

smoke had him certain that a wracked plowman or a stumbling child
was about to step free.

With all of these things to draw his eye, he did not see the moment
when fifty horsemen broke from the pines behind them. And, as those
horsemen tore across the open acres, the clatter of the millwheel drowned
the thunder of their approach.

Only at the last did Durand feel the shaking of the ground. "That is
not the mill," he said, and turned.

He had been a fool. The whoreson bastards had peeled away the duke's
defenses, piece by piece.

Durand roared out, "A trap, Your Grace! Ride!"

Durand snarled and spurred his red cob close enough to swat the rump
of Almora's little palfrey—but one of the workmen jostled close. "Not so
quick," the man said, and there was the one called Morcar, sneering
broadly. There was Grugan, and who knew how many others. Men who
had helped him right the tinker's cart, all sneering. Durand could not
fight fifty men—and now half the workmen and hangers-on. Not in the
open.

"Maybe His Grace would be safer with us," said Morcar.

But Durand saw the mill. There was a fire struggling in the thatch,
but the rest looked sound.

Ailric was quick and handy with his fists: before Morcar could finish
his leer, the shield-bearer had struck the devil across the temple, and Durand had pulled Almora free.

"For the mill! The mill!"

They rode, leaping down in time for Durand to bundle the duke and
his family around the building where the millwheel pounded and a strong
door opened. Durand had a momentary glimpse of the pale Herald still
sitting his horse, sacrosanct and irrelevant. He had not followed. Fifty
horseman stormed around him as if he were a fence post.

Durand drove them on. "Inside! Inside!" But he stopped Ailric before
the man could dismount. "Ailric. We'll need the steward and anyone who
can follow!"

Durand had no time to watch. The raiders leapt down, intending to
sweep Durand aside, but there was only a narrow ledge between the door
and the river—no place for numbers to tell—and Durand braced himself as the two fools came on. The first he dashed into the stony bed of
the stream—and the churning millwheel. The second, he brained between his flail and the mill's doorframe.

Though Durand bellowed, the rest came quick.

Deorwen was screaming at him to get inside, but the mass of men was on him before he could move. They had him like a bear in a pit, but he fought, savaging them, ripping shields aside, breaking bones, and catching their clubbing blows on his mailed arms and shoulders. Bruises stabbed through iron links and padding. Deorwen was still screaming. And he knew that he must go.

After his initial ferocity, Durand suddenly gave way, pitching back to get himself behind the heavy door. They all wrestled a massive bar into its iron brackets.

Durand staggered back from the door. The mill's cogwheels drowned out the sounds of fighting. They should have been safe.

"We haven't long," said Deorwen.

It was then that Durand noticed the smoke. He glanced up and found, to his horror, that the fire he had seen struggling on the roof had taken firm root in the dry rafters. Already, the fire roiled in the hairy underbelly of the thatch. Heavy beams twisted like candle wicks. The refuge he'd meant to offer them would be their pyre.

"Ailric rode to get them back," said Durand. And he might just have got away.

A sharp report sounded from the door. And, already, Durand saw the square gleam of a felling-axe flash through the wood. They'd hardly had a moment. He whipped the spiked head of his flail around on its chain.

"Hide yourselves," he said.

As the others scrambled back, the axe flashed. Durand set his feet, swallowing against a dry mouth as he squared himself to the door. He must hold it as long as he could. They were already choking behind him. Durand brought his cloak to his face.

Then the door gave way.

In an instant, the blank oblong of a shield flashed in Durand's face, driven by the weight of a soldier. Durand crashed onto his back, with his attacker sprawling over him. The door was already lost. From the floor, he punched and pummeled with the hardwood haft of the flail. Something struck his shin. A fist hammered a cloud of blood into his head, the follow-up mule-kicking his ear. But Durand had not been made the Champion of Acconel for nothing. In fury, he wrenched himself from the floorboards, catching at men with hooked fingers, and flinging them like dolls and straw men. Smoke and embers stormed. Blades and cudgels hailed down, but he could not relent.

The room seemed full of spinning mill shafts and toothed hardwood gears. Durand's back struck the supports of the clattering wheels. Smoke bit his eyes and snatched the air from his lungs. He ducked a half-seen axe and collapsed some man's helm. A gawky creature with a flat nose charged, but found only the sudden violence of the mill's spinning teeth— whose first touch spattered the rafters with blood.

In bright rectangle of the doorway, someone was barking orders. "Get hold of the bastard! There's only one of him." Blind figures stumbled through the stinging smoke, choking—wavering. "At him! Cowards! At him!" It was Morcar's voice. The man stood in the doorway.

Durand moved first. Taking advantage of the darkness, he broke for the door. In a heartbeat, his hand came out of the smoke, his fingers hooked in the surprised commander's collar. With a fierce twist, he got one of the whoreson's arms and put the man's own sword at his throat, jerking him backward into the mill.

With the pinioned man as a shield, Durand snarled, "Get out! I'll slit this bastard's gullet! I swear it! I'll fling him into the works." Then he was seized with a coughing fit that nearly cut Morcar's throat for him.

The whole pack of raiders was bent and peering through the smoke, every eye on Durand. He had never cut a man's throat in cold blood, but he doubted the raiders would guess that. The roof timbers spoke in clicks and groans under eight tons of flaming thatch. One grizzled soldier's hands rose in the fist-and-splayed-fingers sign of Heaven's Eye. No one else moved.

"Here," said Morcar, "you'd best humor our champion. Go along while we work this out." And soon enough, every one of the devils had backed out of the door.

"Here, we're only after the duke and his kin. Getting him to safety, like. We've been watching out for you lot. Now you've thrown them all in a bonfire. Have some sense."

"Not sure I'm known for my good sense, friend," Durand said.

He gave the man's arms an extra wrench and muscled him to the doorway to get a view of the raiders outside. A ring of fifty men watched— knights, shield-bearers, and common sergeants. There was no sign of Coensar or the rest.

Behind Durand, the others were choking while the beams cracked and popped over their heads. Durand called into the smoke, "Come to the doorway, all of you. Close as you can." Abravanal and the others ducked and squinted their way to the air. Abravanal himself would have pushed straight into the clean air beyond the threshold. Every eye streamed.

Durand cursed the stone mill. In the lowlands, he'd have been able to kick through a wall, as likely as not. But in Broklambe, stone was cheap.

Across the stream, most of Morcar's men wore armor. One hardened-looking bastard—a whoreson with a boar's-bristle mustache—was matter-of-factly winding a crossbow with a hook and pulley rig. The weapon looked heavier than a miner's pick.

Durand ducked back into the boiling smoke. Already, Abravanal had buckled to the floor. Deorwen was bent over him. They would not live long, and Morcar was busy hissing the fact in Durand's ear. "The duke is not well served by this, Sir Durand." Durand felt like slitting the man's throat then and there.

"Then tell those whoresons to clear off!"

"And leave me here with you? You might lose your bloody temper, friend. I'm protecting you from yourself, aren't I?"

The smoke had Durand blind, or nearly so. He couldn't breathe, and it was damned awkward to hold a sword at a man's throat in a doorway. "Tell them."

The roof groaned like a dying thing.

And there were new hoofbeats outside. Durand could see nothing anymore. Smoke and tears snatched everything away.

"Let me go," Morcar grunted. "Mine or yours, we'll be dead before they get here!" He coughed.

Smoke billowed around Durand. Almora and the others cowered. Every breath caught in his throat. Soon he would have no choice but to burst out into the air.

"Let me run and do what you like!" Either it was Coensar's men or more of the raiders. There was no way to know. A devilish groan came from the rafters. All that thatch was coming down. Durand had to get the others out of the fire. With Morcar running, they could breathe.

Morcar broke free. There'd been no more bargain than a twitch of Durand's hand. Hands free, he caught hold of Almora. Of Deorwen. Abravanal was straggling after. And they all leapt into the Banderol as the tons of flame and timber and reed came thundering down in a welter of foundry heat and searing smoke. The water was a slashing winter cold.

Durand fetched up against the millwheel just as the twenty-foot monster was wrenched from the water by the meshing of gears and shafts and spindles. He could not find Deorwen or the others. Beyond reach, he saw Morcar stumbling toward his men. And Coensar and his knights charging in beyond the ford, his sword flashing. As Morcar reached his line of Yrlaci renegades and the flood tide of Coensar's knights swept round the walls of the mill, Durand cast about, desperate for Deorwen—for any of them.

Ailric dove into the stream, getting hold of Almora.

And there were men in the water all around. Hands caught hold of Durand, hauling him from the water, but he fought them when he saw a tumbling shape he knew: Deorwen, alive but stunned. He rolled her onto the green bank, nearly sobbing for air.

Coensar dropped from his saddle in front of him.

Nearby, a group of men huddled around Abravanal's sprawled form. The steward bent. "We are too late," he said.

"No," said Durand. Smearing soot from his eyes, he scrambled to the man's side and looked down into the old man's face while the pale mill building roared like a three-storey bonfire close enough to roast them. Knights and villagers appeared. As quick as thinking, Almora was there, her shaking hands seeking life in her father.

The duke began to cough. He lived. And there was Almora, and Deorwen. All alive.

"The sanctuary?" Durand murmured toward Coensar.

"No," was all Coensar said.

Durand nodded his hanging head.

8
The Trial of the High Passes

That evening, they camped upon a stony pasture as the day's thin heat vanished into the Heavens. By nightfall, the victims of the raid had been laid to rest in the gravel that passed for soil at Broklambe. Durand was black with the soot of hauling dead men from the sanctuary's embers. There had been a priest and some twenty villagers. In a wide and somber circle of firelight, the duke's men shared their food and fires.

Durand hunched atop a wall of rubble beyond the firelit circle, a black unmoving thing beyond the light. His people were not safe. He would not have his sight dazzled by the fires, and he would not have another man die on his account that night. Monks moved in and out of the old duke's tent. He watched and knew the old man was not well. He saw Deorwen gather Almora in, moving from villager to villager with ladles of something boiled from the duke's provisions.

All of this was retribution for Penseval. Durand thought back on Euric at the feast. If the man had been handled less roughly, would his kinsmen have gone riding for Penseval? Now Broklambe had burned. And the little sanctuary: Would they have broken through if Durand hadn't called for Coensar? If he hadn't let Abravanal's guard go haring off? If he hadn't locked them all in a burning building? Not far off, Ailric waited. It was as Durand tried to see the youth's mind in his blank gaze that he felt something move nearby.

A breath of air stirred at his neck.

And there they were in the gloom all around: Sir Euric with his swaddled skull; a bondman in a blue tunic, all the way from the River Glass; a madman with his head staved in above his searching eyes. One after another, they were making their bewildered way across the turned earth and rutted track of the village. Over by the stream, more were gathered. Trapped, for the moment, at the riverbank. But there were others now: armored men with skin like bubbling cheese brought the faint scent of seared meat. And, from their gravel beds rose black specters by the dozen. They milled, as if on the verge of speaking with one another. The moon-faced giant crouched at the stream's edge. It looked up from its own round reflection.

Durand made the Creator's sign. "Go, by the Host of Heaven," he muttered, and they flickered back, quick as minnows in a black pond, though he could still feel them watching from the crumbling darkness among the furlongs. Soon they would return. His words were a puff of breath on a stubborn flame.

Ailric watched him.

HE WOKE TO singing.

Mist steamed from the cold stones and tussocks of Broklambe. Durand lay on one frozen shoulder, stuck to the ground. Even with the dead all around him, he had slept. And, somewhere, the monks were singing the Dawn Thanksgiving in their hollow, modal harmonies under the mountains.

He blinked stiffly through the mist, peering over ruined cottages. Their timbers jutted like dead men's knees on some battlefield. The company was, for the most part, still abed in their hastily pitched gaggle of pavilions. A few shield-bearers moved through the chill half-light. Durand heard coughing.

Wincing, he spotted a stocky shape on the move. Someone was trudging briskly toward him, wrapped tight in a cloak. It was Ailric.

There was a flinch, very little like a smile. "I thought I'd see what I could make out about the raid."

"Well, what did you see?" Durand asked.

"The ground is bad for it. Stony. But they had a squad of foragers, looks like, who looted what they could from the village."

"Did they?"

"And there were more, I think, than we met at the mill. Some fraction of their number was driving stock on the way out." He pointed up the far valley wall, where the three bladelike peaks towered, blue and ghostly, into the vault of Heaven. "I found tracks of oxen. Pigs." He shrugged. "Meat on the hoof rather than on their backs. There're still some of these shabby mountain beasts wandering out there, though. They must not have been serious about reprovisioning—or they were in a hurry."

"They'd just lit the fires when we rolled up."

Ailric nodded.

Durand squinted at the trail of the village beasts and the peaks beyond. "And those mountains?"

"The Sisters, they are called. They mark the pass," said Ailric. "I've seen it. We're a league or less from the foot. We will find a waterfall where the three peaks meet: the Tresses. A thready thing. Ice. You climb switchbacks and come to the ruins of a gate or wall in a stand of pines. Sir Euric rode to Fellwood a few years ago. We traveled that way. Over the pass, through to the commandery of the Solantines beyond, and down into the forest."

The Solantine knights hardly seemed like real men to Durand. Half deathless, never sleeping. Monks and soldiers both. And the stark commandery in Pennons Gate must be the loneliest place in Creation.

"What did your man want in Fellwood?"

"He hoped to start something of his own in the Marches."

"A younger son," said Durand. Euric had never been meant to inherit Swanskin Down. This was something Durand understood. He had left his own brother in the Col to wait on their father.

"It is a wild place," Ailric said. "There are things in the trees."

Durand raised an eyebrow.

"Truly. The Fellwood Marches are not Errest the Old."

"No matter what our king says?"

"They have carved it from the deep wastes of Fellwood and men go missing. Villages."

"But a man needs no title to reign there. How long were you and Sir Euric in Fellwood?"

"Not long, Sir Durand. The moons of one summer were enough. We met the Solantines again in their commandery before the leaves fell."

"My father's gift, again?"

Ailric did not quite smile.

Together, the two men packed Durand's few possessions and set about waiting.

THEY WATCHED ABRAVANAL'S pavilion all morning. The man did not emerge. The knights and men of the column were unnaturally still.

Villagers drove strays from the thin shoots of corn in the hardscrabble fields and worked to clear the ruins in that valley below the mountains. Animals brayed and shrieked. Houses crashed. Shield-bearers beat and scrubbed the soot from the knights' gear. Almora went to her father's pavilion, and she did not come out. Monks moved in and out. By noontide, the tents were struck, rolled, and stowed in saddlebags. Every horse was saddled. But the duke's great pavilion stood, until every other tent was gone. And Durand fell from wondering about the next move of the raiders to wondering what would happen if the duke never emerged. Without him, would they march to Fellwood? Could they oppose Leovere? The duke choked and strangled. The king would hold the duke's lands and make a ward of Almora, at least until the unmarried Almora came of age. Gireth would be turned on its head. This was why dead Euric had spoken out, of course: the girl must be married off, or the doom of every soul in Gireth would rest in the hands of a bankrupt king who had never come within fifty leagues of Acconel.

Durand watched the pavilion and winced at the sound of coughing.

Coensar and other ranking knights came and went from the duke's tent, their faces grave. Then, sometime after the monks sang Noontide Lauds, the old man tottered out of the tent hung between a valet and a footman.

At a surly thrust of the old man's chin, Coensar bullied the company into motion. The villagers of Broklambe cheered as the column rode out, following the trampled trail of the stolen beasts up the vast peaks. Many of the knights scattered silver pennies over the crowd.

Only a league above the village, the icy wind brought them the smell of burnt flesh and the slaughterhouse reek of voided bowels. In the midst of a trampled plateau was the charred crater of a substantial fire. The fatty racks of half-picked carcasses lay scattered, hooves jutting into the damp air. A league was no distance at all for a fast horse. They had slept this close to death all night.

Almora huddled on the back of her palfrey under a white fur cloak and blankets. She looked at the black scar in the grass. "I met him once, on a rare journey beyond the walls of Acconel—Leovere," said Almora. "We met hunting. He was dashing, or he seemed so, and had kind words for a hen kestrel of mine. He smiled, and I was fool enough to blush, I remember. He seemed so very serious—and then the smile. My father was not pleased."

Coensar scowled as he surveyed the abandoned camp. The place was something of a crossroads. Tracks scurried off into the heather and juniper like little gullies. Ailric probed two of these lesser ways, but the matted grass and stony earth told him little. The raiders could have gone anywhere.

"Will they come again?" Almora asked.

"These men rode ahead of us this far. Now, it seems they've had their laugh and slithered into the rocks. They took a chance, and very clever they were. But they never had men enough to face us. These mountain tracks might lead anywhere. Highshields. Down to the Col. Back to Leovere in Yrlac."

He paused a moment. "Still," he said, "we will be wary."

The old man was hacking into a knotted fist.

Through the afternoon, the company climbed the face of the Blackroots. The air was cool and the track beneath them was as stony as a streambed. No one for a league could fail to hear the clatter of their hooves in that hard emptiness. The three limestone peaks called the Sisters towered above them like the frozen hands of a Power. Everywhere, vast boulders crowded the trail. Durand rode with his shield on his shoulder.

Perhaps two hours before dusk, Abravanal simply dropped from his saddle. Tons of horseflesh and cartloads of baggage were still rumbling forward as the old man's boneless form hit the road. Coensar jumped down. Durand joined him. Coensar was turning the duke over even as teamsters shouted. The stricken man's gray head lay upon the stones. Durand looked up. As quickly as they could, the column was reining in their horses. Soon, Deorwen and Almora joined them.

"He is very hot," said Deorwen.

Durand set the back of one broad hand against the old man's cheek. It felt like the skin of wax at the mouth of a just-cooling candle: slack and hot. The old man began to cough, gulping for air between brittle spams.

"The monks have done nothing for him," Durand said. "He's fevered now. As, I'll wager, he was this morning." Abravanal should never have been moved and there wouldn't be a village ahead until the Fellwood. He turned on Coensar. "Why did you let him ride?"

It was Almora who spoke: "If you seek to blame anyone, Sir Durand, you ought to accuse my father. He would not ride in a cart like an invalid. He did not want the others to see him that way."

"No," said Durand. He shouldn't have been without his guard yesterday. Durand should not have let Raimer take a single rider. "None of it should have happened." Penseval. The raid. The deadly refuge of the burning mill.

"We must get him to shelter," said Coensar. "It is too narrow on this mountain for the company to camp. We will have to send parties down. There may be another village somewhere."

Durand looked at the sheer peaks, at the implacable vastness of the range.

A cough erupted from the duke's body that seemed ready to tear the old man to pieces. Shelter, if they found it, would not be enough. At their shuffling pace, Abravanal would die before he reached help.

"No," said Durand. "We've let a sick man bounce around on the back of a mare for half a day. We're lucky the fall hasn't killed him. We do not have time to waste camping among these stones. We might reach the knights up in Pennons Gate." They would have leechcraft to match any in the Atthias.

"You'd ask me to drag the man the length of the pass. He'll be dead, and we'll still be days away," Coensar said. The others looked on.

Durand waved toward the baggage train. "We cut loose these rolling storehouses, we'll reach the Solantine commandery before dusk tomorrow."

"If we travel through the night. . . ." Coensar's eyes glinted like the honed points of awls, calculating.

"Ailric has seen the pass," said Durand.

The shield-bearer returned Durand's fierce look with something tense, considering. "Sir Coensar, I traveled to Fellwood only three years ago, accompanying Sir Euric. The journey required four days, but we were not pressing."

"There is nothing below us," said Durand. "If we climb, we reach help tomorrow at dusk. We have remounts."

Ailric nodded fractionally. "It is possible," he allowed.

Coensar stood. "We'll need a cart for His Grace. And not an oxcart."

"I have just the thing," said Durand, rising. Leaving the others behind in bewilderment, he stalked down the column and found the stooped tinker and his cart still with them. Durand stepped round the cart's big wheels and set his boot on the rung under the thing's back gate. Pots clattered.

"What're you doing there?" demanded the tinker.

There was room enough for a man to lie down, or there would be, so Durand cleared the bed, flinging pots and kettles out the back. He took hold of a narrow grindstone and made to throw it.

"Hey there! Stop!" said the tinker.

And, in an instant, the gangling man had landed among his wares.

All down the line, the grand carts were cut loose. After a few shocked protests, every horse fit to ride wore a saddle. Bags were torn apart. Every man at arms would ride with the duke and few were the serving men who would stay behind. Thus, a greater treasure than was scattered to the plowmen of ruined Broklambe was abandoned on the roadside stones.

Almora and Deorwen climbed into the tinker's cart with the duke. The girl looked very young beside her father; too young to watch him die.

"I'll get him to Pennons Gate. You have my oath," Durand said, and took the reins.

THEY SCRAMBLED UP the face of the mountains, clattering along sheer switchbacks in the angled light. Durand was now driving two mules, harnessed nose to tail for the narrow track. Below, the hills tumbled away, forests gobbled up the light, and the Banderol and far more distant Silvermere flashed like bullion spilling from the Creator's mold. Soon, Durand lost sight of the Sisters among the high walls above them. A cataract of icy water tumbled down the sheer face.

"I see the falls," said Durand. In the cart, Creation had become impossibly small. The old man's jagged breathing caught at every motion, while the cart shook with each jerk of the mules' bony backsides like a hut on an elephant's back. Every stone in the road had it heeling over.

"Good," said Deorwen rocking in the bed of the cart, "but, Durand, he cannot stand these ruts."

"Next we'd have to carry him in a litter. It would add a day or more."

"Then do your best." Durand saw her glance at Almora. "But speed may do no good if this shaking continues."

There was little point in rushing them all to Abravanal's funeral. Deorwen mopped Abravanal's brow, balancing at his side as the cart pitched and heeled. Finally, she crept forward and settled on the bench beside Durand.

"Where are these raiders now?" she said, looking up at the cliffs.

"There is a chance that they're up ahead. That could be. But, if I were them, I'd have ridden to Penseval for orders. They haven't the men to fight us, and they will never lay another trap like Broklambe. That was the devil's masterstroke. It would be hard to match."

She leaned near, but had her eyes on the mountains. "So, if they've any sense, they've gone home?"

"Aye," said Durand. "But I don't know."

She cursed and settled back at Abravanal's side.

IN AN HOUR, the spray of the Tresses misted the shadowed air. They mounted a final corner and reached the scrub of twisted pines in the shadow of the knife-sharp Sisters. Durand saw fear in the wild glances of his fellow travelers as they climbed into that crabbed glen. The skalds told tales of the vast and frigid hearts of these mountains, where thoughts dread and fickle scraped through caverns of stone. Banished spirits haunted the uncharted labyrinths of the heights. Only grudgingly would the Blackroots suffer a mortal to pass. Blocks of frost-white marble lay heaped and scattered over the ground, each with some ancient sigil deeply incised in its face. The clatter of hooves and wheels swelled in the gelid twilight.

"It is there," said Ailric, pointing into the deepest shadows where the bald track led into a narrow defile. A man could almost hear the hate creaking through the hearts of the peaks.

Durand twitched the reins, urging the tinker's stolid mules onward.

The shield-bearer cut close to the cart.

"We're not the first to reach this place," Ailric said. "There have been horses."

Deorwen came climbing forward. The cart wobbled like a basket.

"What is he saying?" she asked.

"Pennons Gate *is* a pass," Durand said. "People *will* ride here from time to time." Though it was newly opened and likely half-choked with snow.

The boy nodded. "Some prints are like those at Broklambe: a big animal with a barred shoe. One with round nails. Others."

"They're in the pass?" asked Deorwen.

Durand spat a curse, not at her. "This is what he's saying, Lady Deorwen." With his free hand, he rubbed his face. Morcar and his thugs knew where Abravanal must go. There was only Pennons Gate. The road would not fork. Abravanal's knights had the numbers, but Morcar could choose whatever ground he liked. It shouldn't be enough, but Morcar was a cold-blooded creature. The only thing that might upset whatever scheme he'd worked up was the speed of Abravanal's party. Morcar had no reason to expect a headlong dash.

"So, they'll be waiting," Deorwen said. "Trying again to snare us."

"Aye. Likely," agreed Durand.

"So we rush straight at them, hoping the Powers of Heaven will grant us some advantage at the last moment." She tugged her cloak tight.

"Such things have been known," said Durand.

"Sir Durand?" said Ailric.

"Aye, what now?"

"There is another thing. I cannot be certain, but I'd wager they've added to their number." He shrugged. "It's all stones up here."

"I suppose I was childish to imagine that there might be a shred of hope, was I?" snapped Deorwen.

Durand shook the reins. "If your wise women have any magic for the mountains, we might be glad of it soon."

HERE AND THERE, Durand saw signs of the ancient bones of the pass: tall stones jutted from the roadside, the inscribed rock aglow in the twilight. Almond-eyed Powers and serpentine beasts writhed across the stones—their tails, tongues, and tendrils hopelessly interlaced. Here in the wastelands of Creation, only the Wards of the Ancient Patriarchs kept the Banished at bay. The cavalcade crossed bridges. Balusters from broken railings high overhead lay by the trackside here and there like tusks. Impossible though it seemed in those days, pilgrims had once raced back and forth through the chill pass, muttering charms but carrying on a living trade when the Atthias were young and the Fellwood full of men. The track had been hewn from living rock straight across the mountains, and the patriarchs of the day had consecrated every stone against the haunted peaks. Now, who knew what remained of those ancient defenses?

Durand rolled past a tumbledown roadside shrine. Uncanny Powers in alabaster beamed from the interior gloom. From the flagstones grinned an idol's head, unperturbed at having been lopped from its shoulders. A black void had been opened in the floor, as though some spirit of the wilds had torn its way from some crypt below.

His thoughts tended this way as the light failed. Among the peaks far above, he could no longer tell stone from Heaven. Everyone was anxious.

"What was that?" said Almora's voice. The girl appeared at Durand's side. Her dark eyes glistened very near. He did not know how long she had been there. It surprised him how pretty she was, but she was very frightened.

"A shrine. Heaven knows," he managed. The girl looked out through the back of the cart as the company left the little ruin in its wake.

Without a further word, she settled back at her father's side.

Shadows brimmed up from the depths of every gorge. Moment by moment, they rose like the waters of some dark wellspring until, soon, the flood engulfed Creation.

DURAND SWAYED PAST twilight and on for midnight. Knights jockeyed around the cart but seemed no more solid than ash and shadows. Once, rocks tumbled from high overhead to scatter across the track as pebbles no larger than knucklebones. Men grumbled questions about what was there to knock pebbles down. But Durand was certain that no man from Yrlac could have found his way so near the black vault of Heaven. Beyond that, he dared not inquire.

Clouds that had hardly stained the sky at sunset now smothered the steely sliver of the Farrow Moon. There was only the sound of iron shoes falling, the rustling twitch of the cart roof, and the sound of the girl behind him.

She prayed, whispering at her father's ear. The old man coughed. Durand stole a glance back, but she noticed the motion before he had turned his head. In the black shiver of Almora's wide eyes, he felt like a bear creeping under a manger door. He should have known their danger at the mill and kept their guard close. He should have let Euric talk, or argued him down. Kieren might have done it. Much could turn on a moment's thought.

Now, the girl prayed—and they were rolling toward hard men in the dark.

As Durand brooded, something in the high rocks called out.

There was a moan—not the old duke, but something from invisible cliffs.

Tack jingled up and down the cavalcade.

"What in the Hells?" asked one of the knights.

"Host of Heaven," said another.

"What is it?" asked Almora. Deorwen unwound from her crouch as well. She'd found a knife.

Durand twisted on his seat, the whole cart flexing under him as he scoured the black steepness of the horizon for the source of the sound. "Wind, maybe. My father's hall stands at the head of a lesser pass a dozen leagues east of this place. Odd stones and hollow gorges can lend their voices to the wind."

"You hear strange things by the sea as well when the wind gets up," added Deorwen.

Then the moan filled the gorge once more. It bellowed out as if an ox had been butchered somewhere among the crags.

Almora's face appeared at Durand's shoulder. Her lips were open.

Durand felt that he should say something to cheer her. "This pass is much grander than little Col of the Blackroots," offered Durand. "Blessed by the Ancient Patriarchs. Kept by the Solantine Iron Knights. I remember Heremund the Skald saying that the ropes the builders used to haul the stone were woven of maidens' hair gathered from the silver combs of a thousand bowers. He said the workmen's calluses smelled of rosewater."

He tried a smile, giving her his few broken teeth, anyway.

She looked no happier for it.

Deorwen set her hand on Durand's wrist.

There was no new sound.

THE WIND VISITED them in the high places.

Durand felt the track swing upward and, with a twitch of the reins, the mules hauled them to the face of a precipice high above a great chasm. An oxcart would have toppled over the brink. And it was still so very black that the weight of a glance seemed to crumble the peaks like a bit of charcoal. Gusts tugged at the willow cart and Durand prayed for the sense and senses of the mules on the too-narrow track. From time to time, some idiot's voice would quaver out, certain he had seen *something*. Durand felt trapped, like an ox perched on the tinker's worn bench. But he resolved that his imagination would not terrorize him—until he heard a shout that even he could not deny.

It came from behind them, this time the voice of a man. It was a chilling battlefield sound: a yelp of hopeless terror. The trail was too narrow for easy passing, but riders galloped back, flickering in and out of sight. Coensar's stiff face flashed past. Durand glared back through the barrel of the cart.

Finally, Ailric popped his head round.

"Sir Waldhere, a knight, riding rear guard."

"What of him, Ailric?" said Deorwen.

"The man's gone. His comrade saw nothing."

Deorwen spluttered. "I can see nothing, even now. That moan. It might have been anything with this wind. I'll not wager on monsters yet. In this darkness, it's more likely he's followed his blind horse over the brink, poor man."

Durand could *just* see the track, but the whole white belly of the road slipped away when he tried to fix it in his eye.

Durand wondered whether this Waldhere was another on his account. It was Durand who'd bullied the cavalcade up into the pass; now the man would not come home. Durand supposed that he would soon know, assuming the Lost could catch him on this long ride.

Silence returned.

In the cart, the duke rambled, and Deorwen slipped back to his side. Almora's clear voice spoke comfort. Deorwen did sensible things, Durand was sure.

"How far do you think we've come?" she asked.

"Hard to know with the Farrow Moon a sliver and these clouds. Ailric may see something when the light returns."

As they spoke, the echoes changed.

Creation had opened wide before them, and now a burly crosswind bowled out of the dark to wrestle the wicker cart. They had lurched out onto a stone bridge, and there the wind was really blowing—a proper storm, if a man could see it—and the pale deck was no more than two carts wide, with the greedy blackness beyond the wheels devilishly close.

High on that bridge with the wind making a game of lifting the tinker's cart, the butchered-ox groan rang out once more, this time beyond doubt. The animals shied, and Durand held tight, waiting for the one bolting horse to come barreling out of the wind to knock them all into the dark. But no runaway came.

Ailric appeared from the gloom at the hip of the tinker's mule, a pale face and staring eyes. Durand flinched.

"Hells, boy," he said.

"There's something up there," was Ailric's reply, and Durand was down in an instant, the flail clattering loose in his fist. At first, Durand couldn't hear Ailric in the wind. He seemed very reluctant to shout. They rushed forward, telling every man "halt" and slipping past the few knights in the vanguard to a point where Ailric suddenly crouched low.

The wind nearly knocked Durand off his feet. Even with a load of rain and damp, his cloak flapped like he'd got an eagle by the neck.

They faced bushes and rubble on the far end of the bridge. "Here," Ailric said, whispering hard and close against the gusting wind. "I'd been riding ahead, trailing the vanguard. Not far. Saw something move."

Behind Durand, the whole of the column was invisible, the tossing head of every horse had vanished as if it had never been.

Ailric was pointing. Durand thought, maybe, he caught a bitter smell in the wind. "We should get them out of here," he said. "But we'll never turn the column on a bridge. In the dark."

Something moved, white as bleached bone against the bobbing road-side brush. In a moment of wild impulse, Durand rushed at the thing. In an instant, he'd struck, his full weight hammering a surprisingly human grunt from the shape. Durand rode the stranger to the ground. The spot where they landed stank of the shit and the sour wood-smoke reek of a man.

Durand mashed the man's jaw into the gravel. "Who are you?" But he got no answer. He twisted until the man's joints popped. "Answer me!"

"I am a crossbowman . . . Leovere's."

"Hells." It should have been impossible. Durand's thoughts scrambled over the catalog of fatal possibilities as the wind snatched at his cloak: ambushes, spies, and stealthy attempts at kidnapping. It should have been impossible. Where were Coensar's scouts? This man must be one of a party stealing back to attack them on the bridge.

"What're you doing here?"

The man managed to choke out, *"Sentry."*

"Sentry?" A sentry was no part of an ambush; Durand put a fearsome pressure on the man's shoulder.

"We're camped ahead. Lost the light. A camp! Just there," he panted.

Durand looked up, and, with a dull horror, spotted the lumpen shapes of many sleeping men only a dozen paces away, in a sort of a ring-shaped gravel plateau. They had walked right into the enemy's camp. And, with the wind knocking the bushes about, Durand thought they were all getting up. The man had just stepped off to void his bowels. With hardly a thought, Durand cracked the butt of his flail over the stranger's temple.

The camp was very close, and they could risk nothing. He had to wipe a stinging splatter from his eye. Ailric nodded.

"What's happened to Coensar's outriders?" Durand demanded.

Ailric cupped his ear, not hearing.

Behind them, Durand could see nothing of the bridge or the waiting column. An animal snorted. He heard somebody chatting. There would likely be another sentry. He winced up into the black-on-black horizon for any sign, but saw no one. Still, only a fool would leave one guard on a camp of fifty.

"Ailric, down the line. Everyone's to shut up and hold still. I'll find

Coensar," said Durand—far too loudly. But the boy heard him. They separated.

Durand met the steward at the bridgehead, appearing from the dark to catch his horse's bridle. "We just caught one sentry. He was bent over emptying his bowels right there." He jabbed his finger at the bushes. "The rest are just up that bank. You could throw a stone at them if the wind wouldn't take it."

"My lads can't have trotted right through an armed camp," Coensar said.

"Those boys are dead, or sleeping, or lost. It doesn't matter now."

"All right. We cannot go on, but we'll never turn this lot on the bridge," said Coensar. "There's no getting off."

Durand pictured a chaos of men and beasts jostling on the narrow bridge only to be struck by fifty fresh raiders just when the column had got itself most tangled. "We'd be better pitching His Grace over the bridge and saving the sweat." What could they do?

"Did you see Leovere?" Coensar asked.

"I didn't go poking around in their camp."

"No, of course." The man glanced into the hundred shades of coal and soot and ashes ahead, following the smudge of the path. "But you will. We all will. There are nothing but damned high rocks ahead; no path fit for a horse anywhere but straight through that camp. There's no other way."

"We have enough men," said Durand. "They don't know we're here. . . ." They must swarm the camp, blades in their fists. Throat after throat before a man could wake. It would be grim, but they'd sworn to keep the duke alive.

A gust caught Coensar's cloak. There was rain in the air. And the wind bowled through like a slap. "We'll muffle the horses the best we can."

"You mean to ride us through?"

"Maybe this blasted wind will help us."

"Coensar, if so much as a single man wakes, we are fighting for our lives, with the duke and his daughter right in the midst of it."

Coensar ducked close. "Durand, our men won't do what is in your mind."

"These devils are asleep. That is our chance. It's not what anyone would want, but Leovere's men would treat us no better."

"No matter what we say. Almora, Deorwen. Half the knights. They won't, if it kills us all."

The wind roared between them. "Kill us, it may." But Durand could not slit fifty throats on his own. "I'll head to this camp of theirs," Durand said, finally. "Keep your eyes on me. If they're not moving, I'll wave you on."

"Take care. We won't survive a mistake."

With a nod, Durand was off. Keeping his head low, he mounted a steep bank to reach the stony lip of the camp's plateau. Once there, he realized that he was looking at a sort of ringwork. There was a ditch and a bank studded with a broad circle of idols, like a jaw full of dull teeth. He set his hand on the pointed head of one limestone Power, toppled and half-buried in the heather. On his right, a steep mountainside brooded above the gravel circle of the camp.

There had to be scores of hips and shoulders.

A low tent or two jumped and rumbled like tethered beasts.

He saw the big, hump-backed shapes of horses across the clearing to his right, almost invisible against the mountainside. Coensar's scheme was madness.

Durand hunkered low on that windy bank, holding his cloak in fistfuls to keep it from betraying him. From time to time, one of the lumps in the ring would roll from back to shoulder. The tents jolted against their ropes.

After an age, Coensar signaled from the bridgehead, mantle lashing. And Durand could only call the column across.

It was Durand's guess that the road had once skirted the circle. In another age, that track had fallen and so, now, the track humped over the bank between the idols. Thankfully, most of Leovere's men had not chosen to bed down near the road.

As the first horse stepped out, the Rooks plopped down on the ridge at Durand's knee. It was the first he'd seen of them since Wrothsilver. They had to grab at a knot of gorse to hold on.

"*Brother, despite these tiresome winds, we have found brave Sir Durand!*"

"*And we have arrived at the very moment of decision! See how, at our hero's word, his allies creep across the raider's camp.*"

A knight led his horse up onto the rise, and, stroking the muzzle of his mount, walked the beast into the ring. From where Durand crouched, he could hear the gravel under each muffled hoof.

"*How the listener will incline his ear when, someday, the tale is told. I can see them cringe when they learn of the second sentry, blithely walking his rounds as the duke's men are helpless and—*"

Durand shot another glance over the camp, this time spotting some-one: a standing figure, on the far bank. Here was the second sentry, looking off toward Pennons Gate, far across the camp.

One of the damned Rooks opened its dagger mouth to speak, but Durand had already gone, running a tightrope between the sleeping raiders while Coensar's first fool tiptoed by. With every step, Durand was sure he would stamp his heel into someone's gut or trip over an out-flung arm. He ran with his breath caught in his teeth.

From Coensar's side, another knight crested the bank, leading yet another horse.

The sentry's eyes flashed, and Durand struck, swinging one arm around the man's head, lips smearing apart under his fingers, dagger hooking round to gash the man's throat. Together, they slipped from the bank into the camp among the sleepers, tottering, nearly stamping on hands and feet. Blood, like warm oil, pumped over Durand's fingers, but he held on, crushing the man's lips shut, swiveling to survey the camp around him. He'd fetched up in the remains of a cooking fire. The risk had been mad, but the camp remained still. He crouched low with his still-twitching victim, not daring to flinch himself.

Another horse entered the ring.

The Rooks landed right at Durand's feet. *"Oh, valiant! Oh, brave! Such decision, brother. Where the others quail at doing the necessary thing, Sir Durand throws his soul into the service of his fellows. Where is their honor, that they allow such a sacrifice from so gallant a champion?"*

Durand gritted his teeth and held the sentry tight, like some parody of a lover. He was slick with blood.

But what else could he have done? Even now, a horse's snort or man's stumble would turn the camp into a butcher's alley. Each passage gam-bled the duke's life. Coensar had done one thing right: they made no more noise than the wind. The riders that jagged across the camp passed al-most like trooping spirits. They had used every horse-thief's trick. Du-rand saw rags stuffed through the rings of bit and bridle. Hooves had been knotted in cloaks. Men shivered in shirtsleeves. And, oh, but they were praying, calling the Powers of Heaven down to that place in the roaring wilderness with every sinew.

Durand could feel the dying man struggle.

The Rooks looked on, buffeted by the wind. They commented on the passage of each knight.

After an age, the fits of the man in his arms finished and Durand could relax his grip. He lowered the sentry gingerly to the gravel where he crouched. Exertion had his hands trembling in his sticky gauntlets, but he would not move till the duke was past. And there he was, neatly trapped in the heart of the enemy camp where every man lying in that ring seemed on the verge of waking. He was certain that any motion on his part, added to the muffled scrabble from the track, would be too much. He concentrated on pulling the thin air in and out of his nostrils.

The duke's cart bobbed over the rise, with Deorwen sitting rigidly on the bench. When the wind stumbled, Durand heard the muttered syllables of a prayer from Almora. Coensar had sense enough to put them in a knot of fighting men. But to send them across so late was to risk their lives. They should have been first.

Every grunt and mumble among the raiders, Durand heard. The insides of his gauntlets were wet as fresh guts when he flexed his fingers.

Finally, the duke's cart disappeared over the far bank. Packhorses, shield-bearers, grooms, sergeants, knights and their various war-horses, donkeys, mules, and palfreys crossed. Durand teetered in his crouch.

At long last, the last of the duke's company had passed across the stone ring, and the eerie procession was finished.

"A miracle," said a Rook. "Oh, to labor in the cause of Heaven, brother, where such wonders are commonplace. One might almost regret the path one has chosen."

Durand listened, soaked in the blood of murdered men; he doubted very much that Heaven would claim his part.

"We were forever too inquisitive, brother. You know as well as I that we could never have restrained our various curiosities."

"We are, I suppose, as our Creator made us, more or less." The thing shrugged its dead-bird wings, scattering maggots.

Durand waited, not moving as the column vanished in the wind. He would not let a misstep on his part betray the girl or her father before they were free. Moonlight slipped down through slender rents in the ragged cloud. Durand watched faint patches of silver slide over the rumpled flanks of mountains.

There was a sound.

"What is this, now, brother?" said a Rook.

From the mountainside above the ring, pebbles bounded down, landing among the sleepers. High overhead, a hulking silhouette stood poised atop the cliff above the ring. The shape was rounded and knobbed—like a set of hunched shoulders and a misshapen head—but was so still that it might have stood there since the First Dawning. And far too big to be a man. Still, he could imagine it springing to life—or giving its butch-ered-ox howl to shake the world from its sleep.

"Do you remember that call from the south, brother?" said one of the Rooks. It walked a small circle. He wished they would stay still. He wished they would go to Hell.

"A voice beyond the mountains! A horn. A call, certainly. Perhaps an answer?"

"And the very sky shivered from the flames of Penseval to the depths of Fellwood. A call from Yrlac and an answer from some uncouth throat in the wastelands. It is a thrilling start, for we too once answered a call from Errest the Old, though ours was but a dreaming whisper."

"A summons of exquisite delicacy, I thought."

"Not a braying thing, not the rallying cry of vulgar hosts summoned to break a kingdom."

"But where is our Whisperer now, brother? That hidden hand? That weaver of many threads? He is still here somewhere, behind it all. Bid-ing. Baiting. Moving in the dark."

They were goading him. Hoping he'd speak up, or crumble. Instead, he watched the misshapen thing on the clifftop, daring the thing to move before he did: gargoyle versus gargoyle. Finally, as he relented—thinking that he was a fool and that a man could not outwait a mountain—the Lost reached the northern lip of the circle.

He had nearly forgotten them.

He saw bloated Euric, tottering up the bank. The moon-faced man. The thorn-crowned king. The villagers of Broklambe, black and brittle. The sliding shapes snuffling at the gravel.

"Now, where has it gone?" said a Rook, and Durand looked up. The high shelf where his hulking doppelganger had stood was empty. But, down below, the dead were already shuffling down into the sleeping camp, worrying at blankets. Men struggled against their cold touch.

Durand would stay no longer. Silent as the dead, he ghosted through the wind and away. The Rooks stayed among the sleeping men and the dead, chortling and dancing their little circles as the gale lashed them against the turf.

And Ailric was waiting for him just beyond the rise.

9
A Gate of Cloud

Dawn came, faint and cold, with much of the duke's exhausted party alive and marching. They never found Coensar's outriders, though Durand had heard rock falls and strange noises on the heights through the night, and could guess their fate.

Soon, the long blades of dawn slid up the valleys from the east, revealing the pass of Pennons Gate. Marble-gleaming spans danced through the high twilight between the peaks, and Abravanal's column rode like looters through the wreckage of palaces. Men sang the Dawn's Thanksgiving along with the old monks.

Deorwen appeared on the bench beside him, marveling at the mountains. "I've been sleeping," she said. "I can't believe it is the same place. Last night, it could have been a tomb."

She turned to Durand, who'd been about to rub his burning eyes.

"Host of Heaven," she said. "Durand!"

There was blood caked on his knuckles. He would be blood and soot from the top of his head to the soles of his feet. And, before he could stop her, she'd pulled a rag from the back of the wagon and was wiping at his face. "It is no wonder they mutter about you."

"Deorwen . . ."

"You do nothing to help yourself. The scowls and scars. These black clothes. Now blood. We were camped by a fresh stream since that fire, and there is soot still. But you wear these things like badges of shame. Or is it to shame all the rest of us? You could be the Son of Morning himself."

Durand batted her hand away. He was shaking. Tired.

She stared at him, startled, but began again: "Ailric has been looking after us through the night. He's a good man."

Durand nodded. "He is. He is."

"I saw you with the dead man," she said, "in that camp. You were stooped low, but I saw what you'd had to do."

She looked him in the eye, but whatever might have happened next was interrupted by another bout of coughing from the duke. The frail old man rocked the cart, even startling one of the stolid mules. When Durand looked back, he saw the panic in Almora's face.

He twitched the reins, willing the road shorter and the mules faster. He had sworn they would arrive at dusk. But the duke must last that long.

CLOUD SETTLED LOW.

Each valley became a stone world of its own under great vaults of mist. Time seemed to freeze in the empty air. In the column, shield-bearers and sergeants rode with the gaunt resignation of the plowman or the ox. Exhausted horses balked on rubble hillsides. Men without remounts trudged till they washed up in the column's wake, sitting on roadside stones, abandoned to Leovere's thugs and worse.

They could not gauge their progress in that forsaken place. Durand knew they must be getting nearer, but the crooks and twists of the pass seemed numberless. With every swell, he prayed to see the Solantine commandery, the fortress at Pennons Gate. Instead, each time, they found only another empty gulf, another stone cauldron under its cover of low-ering cloud.

In the end, it was the monotony of these dull hours that nearly killed them all.

They climbed the flank of a rubble hill—no beginning or end in sight. Then, without warning, the man riding before Durand's cart took a false step. In an instant, man and horse lost the trail, plunging down the steep face in a tearing skid. To Durand it was like watching a rabbit snatched by a hawk's claws. It left him numb.

But then he felt the roadbed move.

The fall had torn the guts out of the trail.

The cart slid a step or two, enough to alarm the mules. Then, before Durand could get hold of anything, the whole mountain seemed to give way beneath them. Rubble rushed from under the cart, and they were over, rolling, bodies flung the against each other, stones bounding all around. Durand had glimpses of the mules, screaming and twisting. Then, in a hundred, hurtling paces, the thunder subsided.

They had come to rest under the broken cart. In the tentative still-ness, it was all Durand could do to breathe. He had been hammered nearly witless, but he was still alive in the upturned bed of the cart. After a moment, he twisted for a look into the hollow of the upturned bed. The thing was black as a coffin. "Deorwen!" he said.

Her head appeared. "We've got to get him out this."

Durand grunted relief. She lived, as did Almora, though there was blood.

They set to work, pulling out survivors and meeting rescuers who scrambled down the slope. The fall had not been enough to kill Abravanal either, though his breath rattled in him as though he were a hollow thing. They had found a place to lay him on bedrolls and cloaks. He could not have long.

Coensar had gathered the leaders. "It's time we gave some thought to what we're doing," he said. With the slide and the long night, they would leave many dead men in the pass.

"Coensar, the duke must reach the Solantines," said Durand. "There's nothing for him between here and the Pennons Gate."

"Milord Steward," said Sir Raimer, "you'll find no man here willing to give up, but dozens are dead already. Half of the horses are dead or will surely be lame. If the men rest, we might make better time."

Coensar turned to Deorwen. "And His Grace? How long can he last?"

"You've heard," Deorwen said. She was daubing blood from his face. Almora held his hand. "He cannot get a breath. I do not know what the Solantines will do for him, but he cannot go on much longer. Even the fall did not wake him."

"Ailric," said Coensar, "by all accounts, Euric dragged you through this pass twice, there and back. You're the only one of us to have seen this road from end to end. How far have we come? Where is this damned fortress and our Knights Solantine?"

Ailric did not speak at once, and he began by shaking his head. "There are landmark peaks that travelers use to chart their passage, but . . ." He gestured at the low cloud above them.

"No peaks," Coensar said. "Nothing."

The duke succumbed to another fit—the hacking, drowning cough shaking the nerves of everyone who heard it. Almora's comforting murmur acquired a hysterical edge.

"We must stop," said Raimer. "The Blackroots cannot be crossed in one march."

"If we stop, how will it be before Leovere's men overtake us in the dark?" said Coensar. "We cannot have the light much longer."

Raimer frowned. "We passed a sort of blind glen half a league back, Lordship. Less. Off the road. We could manage that, I think. Slip back and vanish for the night. Let Leovere's raiders search how they will. I don't know how they'd find us in the dark on this stony ground. In the morning, you can make up your mind: send gallopers up the pass to fetch the Solantines; saddle the whole cavalcade."

There could be no doubt that Raimer's plan would leave Abravanal dead. "Coensar," Durand said. "The men are weary, it's true. But"— Durand dropped his voice—"the old man does not have another night. Not if he must lie with us in some cold gorge, waiting till morning for someone to ride for the Solantines. We cannot wait."

Durand stared into the steward's lined face. Raimer's exasperation was clear.

"He is right. While we can, we'll go on," said Coensar, finally. "The duke must have his chance."

They rigged a horse litter for the duke, and, with a few sharp orders, the cavalcade lurched back into motion.

OVER THE VERY next rise, they saw it.

The impossible weight of cloud overhead lifted, and, slowly, leagues of stark mountain valley opened around them. Above their heads, a massif swept a thousand fathoms into the Heavens like a second, barren world.

"Host of Heaven," murmured Coensar.

"It is here!" breathed Ailric. Moment by moment, they saw more of the vast cliff. Some great force had rent the blank face of the mountain, so that a fissure ran from the valley floor, broadening until the half-hidden peak was split.

But Ailric was not looking to the rent peaks. His eye was on something low, where the fissure began. "There!" he said. The fading mists had revealed a squat tower, sitting like a child's block at the foot of the split mountain. Where the keep stood, the fissure was narrow—only paces across—and it neatly barred the way.

"Pennons Gate," said Almora. "Just as the stories tell."

The mountain was named for the white banners that streamed from its peaks when the wind rose in the south. Even now, Durand could see the ponderous banners of fog rising into billows above the double summit, red as copper in the fading light.

They had come to the modest rear door of the Solantine fortress. It was twenty fathoms to the battlements.

Despite herself, Almora was shaking her head. Lowland men thought of a wall stretched between the peaks. What the Solantines had built was different, and here they saw behind the stage: a cavernous fissure between mountains, a backdoor keep, a clutter of ropes and landings in the high vault. "Pennons Gate. Two thousand winters barring the pass. Maedor the Greyshield. And the Solantines of old, beating back thralls like a seas of nightmare. Giant Hornbearer, driving maragrim waves against them with all of the south fallen." The girl's eyes glowed with the impossibility of it. She could not help herself. Somewhere above was the commandery of the Solantines with its rime-crusted battlements, stained in blood.

"It is a smaller fortress than I imagined," said Deorwen.

"There is more," said Ailric.

Quite abruptly, Coensar laughed. "How close you came, Sir Raimer. We nearly turned on the doorstep. It is of such accidents that a man's fame is made."

THE GATES OPENED as Durand and Ailric reached the keep, Abravanal between them. The strong hands of ugly, silent men ushered the company into the keep. There were whispers. A thickset soldier with a face of creases scowled over them.

"You'd best come," he said.

The gray soldiers ushered the company through a cavernous tunnel and into a gravel courtyard right at the heart of the keep, where they were led onto a timber platform. The thing had been moored to a stone ramp. Burly hempen cables rose from the corners. "Catch hold of something," said the creased soldier. "And be thankful: once, we had naught but nets for this work."

The dour soldier gave a nod and the men leapt to the lines, brandishing long gaffs. Hawsers creaked tight, and the barge-like platform swung between the naked walls of the mountains.

They were swayed up from derrick to derrick.

A dozen of Abravanal's people clung to the deck with Durand and the duke's family as the platform rose and the lower keep sank below them. Men on corner stays kept the thing from spinning. Durand knelt against the splintered timbers, glad that his glance found wrought-iron fittings. Ailric looked to Almora. "With Sir Euric, we climbed stairs. I lost count of the steps at five thousand."

Stage after stage, they were hauled upward. The Solantines had landings like brackets on the walls, each strung with counterweights and treadwheel cranes. It was a sailor's work to rig them. But when the party finally landed among the battery of groaning treadwheels in the high dark of the uppermost fortress, the mountains swayed below their weaving feet.

Two gray knights waited. They picked Abravanal up and made to carry him off. The knight who had admitted them even stepped in Durand's way.

"The duke alone." The man's scowl was like a clenched fist.

Durand saw Almora's lips part.

"The girl's his daughter," said Deorwen.

"We have no nursemaids to follow you about in Pennons Gate."

The girl's eyes were wide.

"He may not have long," said Deorwen. "He should not be alone."

"Then only the girl. You will not be wandering this place." With a jerk of the knight's ugly head, Abravanal and the girl were taken up into the fortress.

The homely knight remained behind. "Follow me," he said, and the rest were taken by a lower way to a near-lightless gallery. Their guide's solitary lamp smeared a slick glitter over the passage walls. His shadow bobbed in a black ring, until, finally, they were deposited in a stone chamber with neither light nor windows that Durand could perceive.

DURAND AWOKE TO the tolling of a great bell. Something masked his face, and he clawed for a foolish moment until he realized that he'd been scrabbling at the iron links of his own chain hood. Overhead were the stone ribs of a long, low dormitory vault. The place was colder than a meat-larder in midwinter, and his breath bloomed white in the air. Somewhere, the deep and trembling harmonies of Dawn Thanksgiving throbbed faintly in the frigid air.

Prisoners since the door rattled shut, they had slept.

Durand pried himself from the floor and found Deorwen stealing toward him across the disorder of pallets, bedrolls, and sleeping men. Snow had dusted both the sleepers and the bare floor between.

"All the hours of darkness have passed since those monks threw us in here. Anything might have happened. Almora is alone."

Durand nodded. Arrow loops pierced the far wall of the dormitory. "I will at least learn where we are," he said, and padded across, blinking into the brilliance. He thought he might get a look at Fellwood. Instead, he found not the wilderness where evil once held sway, but the hard road back to Errest, Gireth, and Acconel. Leagues of clear air hung between the slit and the spot where Coensar's riders had first sighted the fortress—and no sign of Leovere's raiders on the leagues of bare road.

Deorwen stood at another slit. "Arrow loops a thousand fathoms above the valley. What does this say about the minds of these men?"

"It will have been habit," Durand said. "And the air is cold. I will try the door."

The door opened onto a black passage.

Durand was surprised by a rustle of mail, close at hand. Startled, he reached for the dark shape, only to be met by metal scales and sudden motion. A weight struck his back as something hooked his ankle, pitching him to the dormitory floor.

Twisting from the flagstones, Durand jerked his dagger free. But the sight of the man in the doorway brought him up short. He was hardly more than five feet tall, and nearly square in a hauberk of dull steel scales. Under the weight of night's exhaustion, Durand had hardly registered who these gray men were. Here was one of the Iron Knights of Pennons Gate: a knight of the Solantine Order.

A dozen of the duke's men grunted and mumbled.

"I should not have laid hands on you, brother," said Durand, replacing his dagger.

The Solantine hooked his thumbs in his belt, his feet planted wide.

"We wanted a man on the door," he said.

Durand gathered himself up and smiled. "You're our jailer, are you?"

"We needed the door shut."

Just then, there was a rattle beyond the Solantine and a gleam of light. Someone had opened a door across the dark passage. And, in that momentary flash, Durand saw a face he recognized: a man with the fat jowls of a toad. Durand had last seen him running from the mill in Broklambe. Now, he was here and only across the hall.

"Morcar!" Durand said, and he started forward.

This was a mistake. The Solantine moved with the snap of a siege-engine. His hand shackled Durand's, instantly twisting his arm to the point of dislocation.

"It is sacrilege, shedding Atthian blood in Pennons Gate," the Solantine said, his eyes dull as nail-heads. "You and I? We are wrestling on holy ground. It is a perilous thing. One of us might bleed."

Morcar's door, meanwhile, had rattled shut, slamming on the raider's muffled laughter. But the Solantine waited another few strained heartbeats to relax his grip.

"There can be no bloodshed here," the monk said, "though you may go where you like in the company of my brothers—if you've good reason."

The monk—the Iron Knight—closed the door, and Durand's gaze lingered on the dark wood. At least now he knew where Leovere and his henchmen had gone. The men who'd burned and killed to get their hands on the duke and his child were just across the passage, and maybe free to wander.

"I need to see Almora," said Deorwen. From the flash of her eyes, Durand knew that Solantines and murderers would not dissuade her.

THEY SPENT AN anxious day in the cell, hearing nothing from Deorwen or Abravanal or Almora.

From the room across the hall, however, they could hear the shouts and laughter you might expect from soldiers throwing knucklebones.

"My brothers are with him," was all the monk at the door would say.

Finally, Durand gathered himself up and had the Solantine arrange his passage through to the infirmary. The knight who played guide did not hesitate or turn as they penetrated the gloomy labyrinth. Evening probed the place. And suddenly, they came upon a long, low room. The Solantine stopped at the door, saying nothing.

The room was large enough to accommodate a hundred men, but, as Durand peered through the doorway, he saw only one bed filled. Not far from the door, Abravanal lay on a narrow cot between two braziers of hot coals set out to drive the chill back into the stone. Almora knelt. Dark ellipses of melted frost bloomed over the coals.

Deorwen, who had been perched on the bed, stood.

For a moment, she seemed as small as some winter hedgerow bird in that stone place.

"Night is coming," said Durand, thinking of Morcar and his friends.

She compressed her lips. "He is no worse," she said, and, with a glance to Almora: "I will tell the rest, back at the room. I didn't like to leave them."

"Good."

He noticed that she was very close to him. Likely cold, but it was she who was suddenly saying, "Make sure you put a blanket round you, and keep one on the girl: she won't go. Maybe she will lie down. I think she's afraid that, if she looks away, she will lose the old man. There are plenty of old rugs around this place. Though the sheep and shepherds are long dust who got the wool."

They were together in the doorway. And then Deorwen nodded and was gone with one of the monkish minders.

Durand hesitated there at the threshold as the light drained from the infirmary's few arrow loops. The Solantine Brothers came and went with plasters and potions. They spoke their charms and drew the evil with wine and saltwater while Almora prayed. Bells tolled through the dim passages, marking the hours.

Durand glanced into the dark corners. His Lost friends had found him once more—though they flinched when the Septarim tolled the bells. In Pennons Gate, they were not quite the same as they had been in Acconel or the villages of Gireth. Something in Pennons Gate did not agree with them. Still, their shivering darkness brimmed in the cracks and corners, filling passage after passage behind him, they were so many.

Durand did his best not to think of them. The old man must live. Without him, the king took Almora and no one would stand in Leovere's way.

Durand set his jaw and paced.

As THE NIGHT deepened, the duke's wracking cough worsened. He thrashed and mumbled as though his soul were wrestling with the infernal Powers. Durand shivered, thinking of Lamoric, dead. And the eldest son, Landast, gone before. Alwen and her child, dead at Radomor's hands. He thought of his own part in all these things. He had been in the tower with Alwen. He'd seen Landast poisoned in spines of frost. Now, there was only Almora and her father of the whole family.

Durand abandoned the girl, for a moment, leaving her with Ailric and closing the door on the scene. Deorwen joined him. The duke's cough hammered against the door like a fist.

"She's slept a few hours on the next bed. They are scarcely softer than the floor. She's tangled all of this up with running away, as if she'd set the fire or burnt the mill."

Durand sighed, and Deorwen came close to him then—as close as that night near Towerknoll. She lifted her hand as though to touch his wrist, nothing more. And it struck Durand that there was one dead man not among the shades around him. The man he'd followed, his friend, the man he'd betrayed.

He almost wanted Lamoric to be standing behind him when he turned.

Instead, he stepped back inches, saying only, "The girl's done nothing." And stalked off through a stirring of inky shadows, seeking space to breathe. He blundered into the fortress's empty cloister where the stars were sharp as needles. The Farrow Moon was a sickle. There were crude icons under the squat arcades. Some, Durand hardly knew. One contained nine women with linked hands; another was a knight belted to a tree. He saw the twin Warders in their nail coats; their faces resembled acorns or the tapered backs of beetles. Almond-eyed kings glared above their bladed beards.

Durand stopped, turning under Heaven, thinking that, in this place, the knights and heroes of the long war must have clasped their fists and wrestled with terrors of their own. The stone had a lumpish sheen like brown wax, polished by uncounted brows and fingers.

He saw what seemed to be a bird fluttering through the cloisters. But, after an instant, he realized that few birds flew so high. And, in a moment, shadows darted all around him. Durand spun on his heel. A few paces away, an icon beat tall wings—live flesh pinned to stone. Tiny birds—little curls of rock—skittered through the dark.

Durand got out of the place. He'd had enough of the otherworld.

Reeling from the cloister, Durand stepped into a towering figure and was half-certain that he faced another Power. There was an icy beard, and a pair of eyes like lodestones in a face of leather and seams. The man stood taller than Durand and was clad to the shins in a coat of scales that shone like new silver.

"What is it that so disturbs our stone friends, Durand Col? You and your train of dead men have done little that might rouse the Powers from their sleep. Yet they see your doom, I think, and quail before it."

"What?"

"Something comes, Durand Col," said the strange knight.

And Durand left him there, that man of ice and iron.

He hadn't gone twenty paces before he encountered Ailric. "The men of Leovere's company are in the passage ahead," he said. "The Solantines have asked us to find another way."

THEY WERE SUMMONED to a feast—and, though their liege lord barely clung to life, Abravanal's people were hungry. The bulk of their own provisions had been abandoned among the carts at the foot of the mountains, and the monks ate the grim, boiled fare one might expect in a barracks with neither fields nor pastures, where every dried bean must be hoisted a thousand fathoms.

A monk led them to the refectory. The peers of the duke's retinue sat at its long table alone, squinting up at the imposing ribs of the refectory vaults and the trophies below. Steel and silk banners caught and held the flicker of each candle in their gleaming curves.

Durand put himself at Coensar's right hand; Raimer sat at the other. "I would at least hear your mind," said Raimer. He sounded anxious.

"When it's necessary," said Coensar.

"It is only that the girl will be the king's ward. He will be protector of the girl and the duchy both, if nothing changes."

Coensar's attention was fixed on the doorway where the lone Solantine stood.

Raimer leaned nearer. "And what will Ragnal do with Gireth? With you? With everything?"

"Raimer . . ."

Raimer subsided. "I know. But the man has begged and borrowed in every corner of the kingdom for a dozen years. And I fear he will not be content to pick a few apples from our orchard, but may well cut the orchard for the timber. Or burn it all to ashes."

Coensar sighed. "You are worried about orchards, Raimer?"

And the knight put his face in hands. "Coensar. Lordship. Here is our liege lord, comforted with village simples—an old man. The king might sell the girl's hand if someone does not move, and, even now, we may be too late."

Durand could not decide whether he was furious with Raimer or not. Those around the duke had allowed the old man to hesitate, too meek to force him to do what terrified him. And what would this kindness cost them?

But, before he could settle his mind, something whispered in the doorway—and there was Abravanal. With Deorwen on one side and Almora on the other, the duke made his way to their end of the vast refectory.

Durand stood. Every man in the company was on his feet.

The duke had survived, and so might his people—though he was still as gray and wobbly as a hatchling.

Durand was not the first to shout "Praise Heaven!" The men swarmed round the tottering duke until the old man had been seated at the board. He lifted his head to the assembled company.

"I am told there is to be supper. I am famished," he said.

The men erupted, crowding round the old man to clap him on the shoulders and wish him well.

Then they turned to the entrance, where the solitary representative of the Iron Knights stood, still silent.

"What of it, then, sir knight?" Raimer said.

"It is the week of the Ascension," the knight answered, with a puff of pale steam from his mouth.

"I see," said Raimer.

At this, the sound of voices issued from the room's only doorway. The Solantine stepped aside, and another knight, identical but for a pinched scar that crossed his face from lip to ear, stepped from the dark mouth. In his wake strode noblemen in rich surcoats, with arming swords belted at their hips: Leovere's men. At their head was a knight neither tall nor heavily built, but standing like a man who could run with deer. Red-gold hair flowed in waves past his shoulders. On his chest was the blazon of a round horn. This was Leovere, would-be successor to the last free duke of Yrlac.

Leovere hesitated in the doorway as his men found their seats across the long table. To Abravanal, Leovere bowed low. "Your Grace." And again, catching sight of Almora, "Your Ladyship. I am heartily glad to see you safe." There was concern and relief in his look.

Durand stepped between the girl and the traitor.

The escorting knight told Leovere to find his place.

Abruptly, from the head of the refectory came a heavy shuffling, and all movement in the room stopped as the Iron Knights of Pennons Gate made their grim entrance. They marched in two long lines, every monk in battle gear: mostly long hauberks of antique design, with horn scales and skirted cuirasses of iron splints. At every hip was a blade: arming swords, swords of war, cleaver-bladed falchions. Under each arm, a burnished casque. Every head was bare.

There was the better part of a battalion, perhaps seven-score knights.

By unspoken assent, the ragged strangers to Pennons Gate got to their feet.

The double file of gray men parted as it met the long table. And finally, when each man reached his appointed place at the board, they moved together. A drum-roll of hollow thuds pounded from down the line as the Solantine knights set helm after helm on the bare boards. Candlelight gleamed in dents and scratches.

Not a man sat then. Instead, their faces turned back to the old doorway.

A last knight appeared, but waited on the threshold. He might have been some mad ship's master. His beard was white as salt and ice, and his eyes were like lodestones. His coat shone like new-minted silver. And Durand knew him.

One of the brothers spoke in a gruff, foreigner's accent.

"Brother Maedor, called 'the Greyshield,' Constable of Pennons Gate."

This was the tall knight who'd seen the Lost and guessed at Durand's doom.

Almora touched Deorwen's hand. Maedor had been among the heroes Almora had named when they first saw Pennons Gate. How near to the Powers was he? Even the Herald of Errest was a child next to him. When the Sons of Heshtar last swarmed the walls, he had been commander.

When the Sons of Atthi threw the giant Hornbearer back into the forest with his host of thralls, he had been roaring on the battlements.

"Sit," said the Constable, and a dull thunder followed as the whole congregation subsided onto the benches—all but the Constable. The tall man stood with head thrown back and scarred arms wide.

"By our Creator," he said, "by his Queen, by the Warders of the Bright Gates, by the Champion, the Maiden, the Nine Sleepers, by the whole Court of Heaven. It is the Feast of the Horn. I greet Abravanal, Duke of Gireth and Yrlac; Leovere, Lord of Penseval; and Kandemar, Herald of Errest."

The pale Herald inclined his head, and the Greyshield answered.

"Long years have passed, Herald," he said. "Einred ruled in Errest the Old when last we met. Calamund and Heraric rode to war beyond the Dark Sea, his sons. And Heaven had not yet bound your tongue." Three hundred winters had come and gone.

"You are welcome, all of you."

Men in Solantine gray served the assembled company, lugging claret as bitter as green acorns and bowls of peas pottage tangled in threads of gray salt pork.

The company ate without comment. Who could dare complain?

Durand watched the men of Yrlac, noting that Morcar and the principal raiders were absent.

"I am pleased to see that your health has improved, Your Grace," Leovere said across the table.

The old man's wrinkled face drew itself up in disgust, and he shrugged off Almora's gentle hand.

"I hope His Grace does not believe I ordered his company waylaid," said Leovere.

"A futile hope," snapped Abravanal. "A futile hope indeed!"

Coensar narrowed one glinting eye. "We knew your men. Men from Yrlac."

"Not mine. Not on my orders."

"And this Morcar who penned us in the fire?" said Abravanal.

"He has told me that he meant to protect you, but that your man would not listen."

"Indeed? Then tell him I shall not survive his protection a second time."

Leovere subsided, and the uneasy company supped their pottage and ate a coarse rye bread, tough as rope. Until, without obvious sign, the

Solantines stopped. Every one of the men was finished. There was not a bit of bread at any bowl. And, once more, Maedor the Greyshield stood at his place, the candlelight finding the thousand facets of his hauberk's scales.

"On this night of the rolling year, it falls to me to recount the history of Uluric and the Horn." The man closed his eyes for a long moment before beginning.

There were glances exchanged among the guests. Leovere blinked at the man's words, or so it seemed to Durand.

"It was in Aubairn of the Forests, in the days when King Aidmar reigned there in peace and prosperity. They were happy days." It had been nearly six centuries. "No man foresaw that their doom was upon them. Word reached Aidmar's court of strange happenings in the south— of an army—that the Sons of Heshtar had stretched their hand across the Dark Sea once more, and that their minion thralls were swallowing up the kingdoms of the south faster than messengers could ride. The Enemy was coming. So the messengers said.

"Aidmar sent riders to every corner of his realm, summoning the war host of Aubairn to the capital. More than this, wise Aidmar chose also to send the knights of his household to keep watch over his southern marches till the host could gather.

"Uluric was well suited the task. He was foremost among the barons of the kingdom and a man of iron. A champion. The king gave to Uluric a great round horn—the battle horn of Aubairn, and no mean gift. Aidmar commanded Uluric to sound the horn if he met the Enemy. In return, Aidmar vowed that the host of Aubairn would ride at its call.

"Although Aidmar was wise, the Enemy was swift. Even as he uttered his command, the Sons of Heshtar were in the marches of Aubairn. Even as Uluric was given the battle horn, the thralls were on the River Greyroad. Uluric and the king's guard found shapes beyond naming, and numbers beyond counting, as they reached the southlands. All was lost without every man of Aubairn. And so the horn rang out.

"But, in Aubairn of the Forests, Aidmar knew fear. More news had reached him: stories of the swift terror from the sea. And when he heard the battle horn, he feared that he could not save his court and his champion both. He saw only one course: He must flee with the Host of Aubairn, with the women and children and common folk, making all speed north to Pennons Gate. And this he did, abandoning Uluric and the bravest of Aubairn.

"Soon, the horn was silent. But the folk of Aubairn were too taken up with flight to mark the sound. Thousands fled.

"It was here they came. Below these walls. Many hundreds broke from the trees below the battlements of Pennons Gate. We Solantines saw them enter the field. I myself witnessed these things. They ran through the long shadows as the Eye of Heaven failed in the west, carts and beasts and lives scattered behind. They ran with children in their arms. And we Solantines made ready to throw our Forest Gates wide. But, as the fastest came in sight, the last of the light failed. And the thralls of the Enemy rose up. Ragged forms tumbling through the sudden gloom. Hurtling devils. We could not save both the Aubairn folk and hold our gates against the Enemy. All of Errest lay behind us, unwarned, unguarded. I saw them dying. And I commanded the gates barred.

"My duty and my shame," he said.

"Under the Eye of Heaven, we searched the field of the slain. And few, indeed, did we find to bury. They had only come so far because Aidmar fought rear guard in the trees to the south. His crown was there, years after. But none of it was enough. He was as helpless as we. And, for long decades, thereafter, we ground our teeth in helpless shame and stood guard where we must, upon our Gate."

The man looked over the table.

"On this night, we feast the return of Uluric's Horn. It was nigh two centuries before the kingdoms of the Atthias drove the Enemy from our realms once more, and we ceased to see the Hornbearer in Fellwood. A man of Yrlac wrested the Horn of Uluric from among the prizes of the Enemy. Shield-bearer to Prince Calamund, he was, and he winded the horn in the face of the Enemy with the whole Host of Errest behind him and he bore the Horn from the Fellwood at war's ending. In this hall, we saw it. A defeat had been redeemed."

The Solantines bowed their heads, and Durand was sure they prayed a thanksgiving.

Nearer at hand, Abravanal muttered, "Many kingdoms, many kings, one army to break the Enemy," and he looked across the Solantines' table to Leovere.

"I know this story," said Leovere. "It was told in Yrlac, in Penseval. Leowin bore Uluric's Horn before the army of Errest and broke the Host of the Hornbearer at the side of the Lost Princes and was made Duke of Yrlac in the days of joy and grieving at war's end by Willan Blind. Duke Leowin—a kinsman of mine."

There were puffed chests among the men of Yrlac, but Abravanal made a bitter face. "From so great a tree, such piteous fruit."

Leovere stiffened. "It is my sincere wish that you had passed unmolested to this place. My banner is brandished by men with whom I have not spoken. As, I think, is yours. The attack was not my doing. I would see our two houses joined in peace."

The duke's knob-knuckled fist clamped tight around his spoon. "You say 'joined'?"

"Your Grace," Leovere began, "I—"

"How do you wish to come by this joining?" The duke coughed into his fist, wincing sharply. Almora clutched her father's shoulder, urging him to settle, but he only erupted once more, leaning across the table. "Do you know who was in that mill? Do you know?" Fury twisted the man's frame. "The very girl after whom you lust so greedily."

"It should not have happened."

"No. No! It should not. We are in agreement. Your dogs should not have set upon my family in my own lands."

"Your Grace, I cannot help what desperate men will do—"

"How can I believe you when you smile and lie to my face? What is the vow of a man foresworn?"

"Enough!" said Leovere, his eyes flashing. "Enough." From his cloak, the man drew a curving horn of hammered bronze and iron bands. He slammed the thing down.

The uncanny horn gleamed.

"What do you do here, Leovere of Penseval?" said Maedor.

"From the fire at Penseval—the fire of my father's Red Hall, only newly rebuilt. Leowin's hall, by Heaven. And we did not all escape, my kin. But, from the fire I have this horn." He let it go, lifting his hand, and Durand saw scars that matched the convolutions of the sculpted bronze, curve for curve, like a brand. "What do you say to this, Abravanal of Gireth?"

Benches groaned backward as knights on both sides stood. More than one sword whispered from its scabbard. Durand had his flail free of his belt when a great voice boomed.

"Stop!"

The ancient Constable of Pennons Gate stood, his arms spread like a man summoning devils. The candles guttered, pitching the room into a shivering darkness. "Put up that horn, Leovere of Penseval. I had not thought to see it pass this way again.

"This feud among Sons of Atthi must end. Hear me, all of you. No man may shed Atthian blood in this place, or you will find yourself cast beyond the protection of patriarchs. Outlawed. Your heirs, dispossessed. Fight here, and you will have nothing else to fight for—to win or to lose. Set your differences aside and make peace."

Standing in the dying echoes of these words, the knights, hands still on the hilts of their swords, subsided back into their places, though Durand was not first among them.

Faintly then, an aching note reached Durand's ear. Something was crying out, a moan rising from the frozen emptiness between the peaks. The Solantines touched the hilts of their weapons as their commander lifted his chin. Faintly, the horn in Leovere's fist trembled in harmony. The brass curve buzzed against the tabletop.

Finally, the sound left them.

Maedor gestured to his captains, a nod sending men to the battlements or out into the high barrens. "I would have you part ways, milords— Leovere to Penseval, and Abravanal to Acconel. Or all of you to the ends of Creation. But there is a knotted doom upon us, and the Powers must work their will.

"The feast is ended," Maedor declared.

10
The Horn of the Forest

Abravanal was not fit to walk after the excitement at Maedor's table. Pennons Gate was black as a mine. They walked long reaches with hardly a lamp or candle's flicker. Durand kept an eye on every door and passageway as the party walked the old man back to the infirmary. Though Maedor made sure they went nowhere without some grim minder, Durand had seen ruthlessness from the dogs of Yrlac and he would not forget.

Yet it was neither knights nor captain who led them. Instead, Almora marched straight-backed through the old fortress, and it was all an exhausted Abravanal could do to keep up. Deorwen shot Durand a beseeching look, but soon the girl had swept them into the sickroom and the old man capsized on the bunk.

"There you are, Father, safe and sound once more," said Almora. She brusquely smoothed a blanket. "I hope your second recovery is as swift as your first. I think I might like to see something of this place. I have heard so much about it, after all. Like as not, the Powers have heard enough from me on your behalf."

"Almora!" said Deorwen.

But Almora lifted her head and left the old man gaping from his bed as she stalked from the room. She had not left his side for days.

Durand followed, with one of the Solantine brothers right after him.

The girl climbed the winding passageways of the fortress, passing arrow slits glowing faintly with the light of dusk. Sometimes Durand followed her by the slap and hiss of her soles on flagstones, listening at the mouths of stairwells and hesitating at intersections.

Finally, she climbed a last long stair and stepped into the light at the top. Durand braced his hands on the icy walls and followed, only to confront a scene like that which must have met the Creator at the close of the first day. The dark stone world had ended; Almora had found the battlements of the fortress and climbed into the sky. She stood there awestruck, a tiny thing against that broken world.

Between two mountaintops, a valley plunged through six hundred fathoms of gloom into untold leagues of forest.

Almora just stared.

Durand let her have the room to think. Soon, Ailric and the Solantine joined him, climbing into the last twilight.

This was the Pennons Gate of the skald's tales. Here, where the fortress faced the Fellwood, Pennons Gate was a single wall whose battlements spanned the whole valley from side to side, a thousand paces. Every hundred paces or so, a stern turret jutted over the abyss. Even on that day, three hundred years after the war's ending, Iron Knights walked the wall. Clouds passed by low enough to touch.

Almora walked, and the rest stepped out onto the parapet, not far behind.

"I do not understand," said Ailric.

Durand's glance took in the forest, the mountains, the wall, and the girl. "What?" he said.

"All this." The young man lifted his spread arms. Ailric stepped to the wall, vanishing between two merlons and reappearing. "The wall is too tall to be any good to an archer, and no man living could pull the bow that reached these embrasures from below." He peered down once more. "What is it, five hundred fathoms?"

Durand nodded; it was certainly more.

"How far can an arrow fly?" said Ailric.

Durand's mind took him back to sieges in Yrlac and Gireth. He had seen arrows. "They won't get through mail past a hundred paces. Less. They'll bother horses and the like to three hundred, just falling. Cuts, if it's a broadhead. Shooting from this height, that's what you'd have."

Now, it was the turn of the Solantine. The man grunted, and Durand turned to recognize the flat nail-head eyes of his jailer from the first day.

"You've been misled, you lot. This fortress is not as you think it," he said. "It is not a wall."

"It has the look of a wall," said Durand.

"It is a cliff and a crooked road. The road climbs the cliff, each section battlemented and looking down on the one below. Each switchback is commanded by a gate. In time of war, the gates are packed with archers and difficult to approach."

"Ah," said Ailric. "No matter how large the army, the front would be measured in paces. Even the lower gates would be impassable."

"Thralls beyond number have come against us here. Pennons Gate— the wall you'll hear the skalds go on about Pennons—is naught but a keep at the end of a winding road. The last stitch of road passes below these highest battlements, or we wouldn't bother shooting. It is hardly more than twenty fathoms to the track."

"So no one ever fights from these heights."

"Arrows have been loosed from every tower. And stones flung. Even to the stones of the Gate itself, where they could be pried free by desperate hands. The Enemy has climbed every step but the last."

"Host of Heaven," said Ailric.

The man grunted. "You will see marks in the stone along the parapet." And, indeed, there were funnel-like grooves around each embrasure. "Fear-sick archers worrying at their arrowheads. The whole wall a fool's whetstone." Off where Almora walked, the wall bore thousands of scars. "I have done it."

The monk subsided back into silence, and Durand watched Almora, alone above the forest in the evening light. She had lived through more in a few days than she had in ten years, and Durand was glad to see her walk in the open air, far from the murk of the sickroom.

She had just passed one of the towers where the round flank obscured part of the wall walk when she screamed out. Durand was there in a moment, and found her standing before a pack of soldiers who'd been sheltering against the curve of the tower.

This was where Leovere's dogs had gone.

The soldiers sneered up at him. They were casting knucklebones along the parapets. He saw someone passing a wineskin: a soldier with a boar's bristle mustache. The man who turned to receive it was Morcar the Toad.

"Cold, ain't it?" said Morcar. After taking a swig of wine from the skin, he waved the thing toward Almora. "She want some, you reckon, Durand Col? Do her good."

Durand swatted the skin into the forest. It tumbled through the shadows and shadowed sentries all down the wall turned their faces.

Morcar gave Almora a leer, not giving ground.

"This one always speak for you, dear?"

"Leovere said you'd left this place. Said you acted without him knowing," Durand said.

"Here you are, lumping me in with them raiders, Sir Durand. But I took His Grace's part. I said as much on the day. There we were, Grugan and I, watching over the old man—in disguise—when suddenly there's that village aflame and unsavory horsemen on all sides. If you'd have let me get Abravanal safely away, he might have been spared a few hard nights."

Durand grimaced. "So that is the tale you're telling?"

Somewhere, a high-flying carrion bird called, "Haw! Haw!"

A sneer spread over Morcar's face, and Durand saw the great green gulf of the Fellwood through the embrasure at the man's elbow. The black shapes of two Rooks flickered over the trees. Morcar was very near the edge. In the next moment, Durand had lashed out. The heel of his hand struck Morcar's breastbone with force enough to send the toad through the nearest embrasure—and only at the very last instant did Durand drop to his belly and snag a bony ankle.

"Rash," said Durand, straining. "I understand." Fathoms below, the Rooks turned a circle, their shadows flickering over the billowing treetops, but it was more likely that Morcar would hit the road or the battlements a hundred feet below. "Haw! Haw!"

Nearer at hand, sentries swarmed in, catching hold of Ailric and Morcar's thugs.

"Now, what do you say, Morcar? Eh?"

"Let me up!"

"I should have killed you in that mill, friend. A man does not often get a second chance."

"This is sacred ground!"

"Sacred ground? I'm not sure you're on any kind of ground at all, friend."

As Morcar twisted to look down, his weight wrenched Durand's shoulder. He very nearly lost his hold.

"Best not to do that again," said Durand, panting. He thought of the Solantine who'd guided them. "How many fathoms is it, brother? Eh? Ailric, what did he say?"

"Twenty to the track," Ailric said flatly. "Five hundred to the bottom of the gorge."

Durand felt the blood bulging at his temples.

"Say what you will, Morcar. I know what you've done, and I know what was in your mind. But you will never get your hands on His Grace or his daughter, no matter what devilry you conjure. Your master has disavowed you. Knows nothing. On his oath. Keep clear of His Grace."

"Pull me up!"

Durand could see the shadowed tiers of the Pennons Gate road. Morcar had burned a sanctuary full of people. . . .

Suddenly, there was a voice at Durand's ear. The breath was hot.

"Bring him up now, or you will be carted round the Atthias in chains for the plowmen to spit on. You've had your fun, hmm?"

Durand swiveled his head and found the jailor-knight flat on his belly at Durand's side.

"It might be worth the price if my people would be safe."

The Rooks were laughing.

"I hear you, and know your mind." The monk's lips scrabbled at Durand's ear. "But let us think on this price and who would pay. You are the duke's man. How would it be if my brothers judged that old Abravanal or his daughter had ordered this man dead, hmm? Maybe now it isn't just brave Durand Col shouldering the blame. And there've been *kings* scourged over less. Poor girl, maybe. Poor old man, certainly."

Durand looked the man square in the face. On either side of a nose like a broken finger, the nail-head eyes blinked once. A man believed such a face.

Durand heaved at Morcar till the jailor-knight could get a fist on the devil's belt. The other Solantines rushed to his assistance.

Back on the walkway, Morcar's men lunged at Durand, shouting murder. Solantines seized him, and those monks not wrestling Morcar from the brink rushed to keep the others at bay.

Almora sheltered beside young Ailric, her dark eyes wide. Durand could not get free.

"Get her inside," he called to Ailric over the commotion, and watched as Ailric shepherded the girl away.

"Durand!" said Morcar.

Durand turned to see him being dragged from between the two merlons, livid and thrashing.

"I'll have your guts for this!" The man tore at his clothing, reaching for a sword or dagger despite the restraining arms of the monks.

He knew the rage of a chained bear. He should have dropped the devil. The Solantines hauled Morcar off, herding Boar's Bristles and the rest in the same direction.

The jailer-monk withdrew himself from the embrasure a moment after, and, brushing his surcoat with rough palms, turned to Durand. He smiled a brief sardonic grimace.

"You'll come with us?" said the monk.

Durand found that a good dozen Solantines remained around him. Every one looked as solid as a sack of nails.

"Fine," he said, and they led him down into the fortress.

BELOW THE BULK of the ancient citadel were galleries cut deep in the living rock by chisels and masons all long since crumbled into dust. Durand and the party of knight-monks walked through blackness in a wobbling circle of torchlight. The rasp and jingle of boots and mail scampered off through leagues of black passageways.

A hand stopped Durand.

"Here," said Durand's jailer.

In the wall of the passageway was a low door. A quick tug revealed a featureless void beyond.

"Inside."

Durand glanced round at the weathered faces in the torchlight. Pitchy smoke stung his eyes.

"What do you have planned for me?" he asked.

"You'll stay in this storeroom till your people take their leave of Pennons Gate."

It was not a bad bargain. Durand squeezed under the door, and stepped into the blackness.

"Any hope of a torch?"

"Well," said the monk with a quick grimace, "you're not having mine," and shoved the door shut.

Standing blind in his cell, Durand heard a bar scrape home and the monks make their rustling passage back up through the fortress. He laughed.

HIS PATTING FINGERTIPS found nothing so much as a stalk of straw in the frost bristling over the walls and floor. As he settled stoically against the wall, it occurred to him that a storeroom as cool as this might be very suitable indeed. The Solantines could store years of provender in the frigid heart of their mountain. He reckoned that they would have less luck keeping prisoners if alive was how they mean to keep them. With a chuckle, he pulled his cloak tight around his shoulders.

When Durand next heard movement somewhere among the leagues of passageways beyond his door, the better part of a day had passed in the featureless cell. He forced his stiffening frame to stand and crossed to the exit.

With a scrape of drawn bar, the door opened.

Durand winced into torchlight and a gust of tarry-smoke.

"I hope you've brought a blanket or two with you," Durand said.

There was a grunt.

Durand's dazzled eyes made out a wild face, mostly shadowed by the torch above and beside it: pale skin, a glitter of gray eyes, and a beard of twinkling hoarfrost framing the chin. It was Maedor Greyshield himself, and two of his knights playing torchbearer.

"The haunted man," the ancient knight rumbled.

Durand withdrew a wary step.

"They are all watching you," the Constable said. "Once more, Heaven has you in its eye." There was something in the quivering pressure of the old man's eyes.

Durand's mouth opened. "What—"

"Still, your time has almost come."

Somewhere in the fortress a door must have been opened, for a cold wind poured down the passage from beyond the Constable. The torch-flame lashed, sending tattered sparks and ashes whirling round Durand's cell. The old Constable's cloak leapt up like wings, reaching to envelop Durand.

When the gust subsided, the torch was out and the blackness was pouring in.

It was in this uneasy darkness that a peculiar light began to arise all around them. If Durand had not known of the fathoms of rock above his head, he would have believed that shutters had been opened on the blue sky. Somehow, he still believed it. The Constable was lifting his up-turned hands, fingers hooked. It was as though the Eye of Heaven had found the man.

His eyes were still fixed on Durand.

"I must say nothing more, Durand Col. I will not invite the Host Below to answer. I would not free them to move. And they are waiting. But long years have passed since I have looked upon a man of your ilk. Most would have been dead long ago. There are forces at work to oppose you."

"I do not understand."

"Heaven has you in its Eye, Durand Col. Your doom, for good or ill, is woven through many lives."

Afterward, Durand would wonder what compelled him to do it. He had seen much and slept little. The Lost were on his mind—and Deor-wen, and Almora, and so much else. But he took hold of the old man's surcoat, as though he would brace the Constable against the wall till he spoke in a straight line.

He might as well have tried to uproot the mountain. The man seemed locked to the stone, and Durand remembered who he was: Maedor Greyshield.

Durand opened his hands.

"Often, we gain most by denying ourselves," the Constable said.

Durand put his head in his hands. "Why torture me with this, Brother Constable?"

"It is my duty to every prisoner," the ancient knight said. "And, if you had not disturbed me, I might have let you be." A thought seemed to occur to him. "Did you know they are all here?"

Durand was mystified. "Who?"

"Every man who has fallen, Durand Col. Every knight and common man for uncounted black winters. They all are here. Catacombs in the living rock. From time to time, a sealing slab will fall. A niche will be laid open until one of the brothers finds it. And it is cold here, Durand. And the cold preserves them. So they say. Scores of thousands. But your Lost friends have been at work among them, drumming in the rock. Fumbling at lips and latches. It is ever the way with the Lost, to rummage among dead men's bones. And stones have fallen on your account, say my men. My brethren have found comrades long dead standing among the frozen corridors. It is no pleasant thing to find dead men abroad in the dark, Durand Col."

He turned to the knights at his side.

"Close the door on him."

* * *

IN BLACK STONE, the vibrating notes of distant bells and, more faintly, the sonorous voices of the Solantines carried word of the advancing Eye of Heaven's King. There was Last Twilight; the Midnight Invocation with its murmured litany of Powers; First Twilight; Dawn Thanksgiving; the Laud of Noontide and the Plea of Sunset once again. By the time the wheel of prayers had turned once around and started again, Durand was truly dazed by the slow, chilling effect of the stone around him.

A man might confess terrible things under such pressure, were any questions put to him. A man might well die.

Durand told himself that he had known colder nights when he'd followed Coensar and young Lamoric around the kingdom. He recalled more than one occasion when he had found his blanket frozen to the ground underneath him.

He paced to keep warm. He could manage four long strides before a wall caused him to reverse himself. The rhythm of tramp and rasping pivot kept him awake and distracted from his growing hunger. He heard strugglings in the rock: unquiet sleepers. He blunted the edge of thirst with frost scratched from the walls and licked from his fingernails.

He wondered about his jailers. The Solantines, it was said, did not sleep. They did not rest. They had willed themselves near to the Powers. Their sentries kept their watch for days beyond counting. They lived long.

He wondered whether they would expect a weaker man to do as well.

Still, until the cold finished him, he had only his thoughts for companions.

He thought of golden Leovere, the heir to Yrlac, who spent his days steeped in the grumblings of the outnumbered native lords. The man had likely been very pleased when he met young Almora. A simple marriage vow would make him lord of his Yrlac at a stroke. Moreover, he would gain Gireth as well. A lovely girl. A triumph without blood. A dukedom. Two! He would want the girl.

But that devil Morcar was another matter. The man had put innocents to the torch simply to draw off the duke's guards. Morcar clearly saw Abravanal as the key to breaking Gireth's hold on Yrlac. If Abravanal died, the king would snatch Almora for a royal ward, the dukedom would fall into chaos, and there would be Yrlac, ripe for the native lords to cut free of Gireth. Abravanal wouldn't give his daughter to any kin of Radomor of Yrlac. Knowing that, Morcar's plan was ugly, bloody, and wise.

Leovere wanted Almora's hand; Morcar wanted Abravanal's neck. And now they would have their chance without Durand. He could do nothing. He had been a fool to let Morcar goad him. He could only hope the price of his stupidity was not too high.

Bells rang and monks chanted as Durand grumbled about barons, stewards, the Constable, and monks.

Finally, there was a sound, loud as a crossbow's snap in the silence. Durand turned to the source—was the rattle coming from the stone of the mountain, or was he facing the door? For a moment, he had lost his bearings. Then a seam of fire split the darkness and light lanced through Durand's warding fingers.

There was a shadow in the doorway, an incandescent firebrand in its hand.

"Sir Durand?" asked a voice.

"Aye."

"They say you can go now." The voice was Ailric's, though Durand could not make out his face beyond the torch's glare.

"Good," Durand said, snatching the torch from the young man's hand. He thrust the flame toward the floor behind him, to save his eyes. He noticed the silvered pelt of frost covering the walls, and how it had been almost completely clawed away. There were thousands of black scars where his nails had raked up moisture.

The boy's face was clear in the glow.

"I reckoned they'd wait till Leovere's men had left this place."

"They've been gone some time."

Durand snorted. "How long have I been locked away?"

"Two days."

The number matched his tally of the monks' prayers.

"What's been going on since I gave that Morcar his little ride?"

"They've all gone. Yesterday at Dawn. Morcar and the others left with Leovere."

A question occurred to Durand. "How did they seem together?"

"Leovere and Morcar? Leovere was not talking much. He wished us all a good journey to the Lindenhall and promised to meet us all there. Maybe Morcar took liberties in Broklambe."

Durand grunted. It hardly mattered. Morcar was Leovere's dog. "What of the duke?"

"He is nearly recovered, I think. He still coughs, but the great weakness has left him."

Durand nodded.

"When do we leave?"

"The duke and the others have gone already, after Dawn Thanksgiving. It is past Noontide now."

"Ha! I should have guessed. I don't suppose you thought to bring any food down? Even their twine-and-pea pottage would tempt me."

"They said you can eat in the refectory at mealtime. You've just missed one."

Durand grunted. "These Solantines like their little jokes. We must be on our way."

THEY HURRIED TO catch the others.

Like a flea on the face of mighty Pennons Gate, Durand looked out over Fellwood—vast beyond measure and unspeakably ancient. He and Ailric passed through gatehouse after gatehouse on the switchbacking trail down, looking out on a forest as boundless as the sea. Durand was used to the arcane knots of woodland that beetled here and there throughout Errest, but Fellwood was an altogether different thing: old before there were Sons of Atthi. And as Durand and Ailric rode their stitching path between the sheer walls of the pass, they descended below the swells of the green sea and beheld the immense darkness below.

A guard in Solantine garb stood at the bottom gate—the fortress called the Forest Gate—ordering the monstrous iron portcullis hauled up. There were castles that weighed less than that grill of iron and oak. Beyond it was a mighty breathing silence of trees that loomed like a wall for giants; Rooks coughed and clattered among the remote branches.

"Be watchful," said the porter, in a familiar voice. Durand turned to see eyes like black nail-heads. "Fellwood is a demon-haunted place. You will not long be alone once you enter its precincts."

"A nice thought," said Durand.

The porter laughed.

"I have a nicer one for you, Durand Col: Do not tarry long here below the Forest Gate. Men and thralls have died in this place beyond counting. The Gorge of Pennons is a place for living men no longer."

THEY TRAVELED A forest track through halls of oak and alder that made toys of every sanctuary in Errest the Old. The cool air was heavy with vegetable decay. When breezes ran free over the canopy, sunlight pierced the high crowns in glittering waves. A man felt like some worm on the floor of the sea.

Sometimes, the two men could see for leagues, sometimes no distance

at all. Once a sound like a spinning festival ratchet clattered franti-
cally from somewhere in those treed halls and the croak of ravens
echoed.

Few men used Pennons Gate in that age, and few settlements survived
along the path. Occasionally, Ailric caught sight of some old foundation
or the humped back of a fallen shrine among the roots, but not once did
they smell a hearth fire.

As they rode past an upturned shrine or manor house, a pair of Rooks
tumbled from a broken pillar to alight in the branches above the track.
A sharp reek of carrion stung the air. It was enough to make Durand
blink.

"Ah," said a crawling whisper, "here is our man. The hero of our little
tale."

"Good, good. For a time, I thought we had lost him in that fearsome
pass."

Under his breath, Durand cursed.

"There was only ever one way out, brother."

"He might have died."

"Two then, brother."

"And I would not go among those bleak Solantines."

"Nor I, brother. They are too dour. Hardly a jot of humor in the whole
of Pennons Gate."

Durand scowled, but rode on without comment. And, of course, the
Rooks followed, lurching ahead, tree to tree among the mossy giants.

"And now to the Lindenhall, yes? I have heard of the place."

"Have you, brother?"

"Oh, indeed. Its founding brought comment throughout the Atthias."

"It escaped my notice, I fear."

"You've heard of the Lost Princes?"

"Ah, well, yes. I think. Princes of Old Errest. They died, the poor
things, as I remember it. Years back."

"Princes Calamund and Heraric, eldest sons of the Crusader King
Einred of Errest. They fought so famously over the Sea of Darkness. Both
valiant. Both lost in a day. A wound at the heart of Errest, even as the
war was won."

"What was that battle again, brother?"

"The battle? You will feel foolish if I tell you, brother."

"Then I must feel foolish; there is no help for it."

Durand cringed.

"'Lost Princes,' brother. 'Lost Princes' they call it."

"Lost Princes. You were right to warn me. Lost Princes. The poor devils."

The Rooks flapped to a new perch. Durand saw feathers and maggots tumble at the shock of their clumsy landing.

"But what has this to do with our Lindenhall? It is, unless I am very much mistaken, not beyond the Sea of Darkness. It is quite near."

"Well, when Princes Calamund and Heraric left Errest to sail into danger and to fight and to die beyond that foreign shore, they left a girl behind them."

"One girl, brother? They shared her between them, did they?"

"Hardly, brother. They contended for a while, but the eldest won the young girl's heart. Godelind she was called. Perhaps her head was turned by Calamund's being Einred's heir. And Calamund left her with a great gold ring set with a fat carbuncle, dark as heart's blood. They say it was Heraric's, but when Heraric knew that Godelind would belong to his brother, he passed on the ring."

"Very big of him."

"And this Godelind is meant to have suffered."

"When the ships returned!"

"The black sails, to tell Old Errest that they had lost their favorite sons: the dashing princes."

"I feel foolish that I didn't remember: Lost Princes. How could anyone forget such a thing?"

"I did warn you, brother."

"And so, the Lindenhall?"

"The girl, Godelind, it is she who brings the Lindenhall into the story."

"I struggle to comprehend, brother."

"You must imagine her, waiting for her prince."

"And he, Lost."

"But not knowing. And there she was in Tern Gyre when the ill-omened ship returned. Its black sails winged into harbor with its terrible news. The ship that brought the news that the Princes were Lost, you see. There was Willan, the youngest prince, who must then be king. Poor Calamund. Poor, big-hearted Heraric. Princes who would never be king. And she took it badly."

"Well, she might, brother."

"One can sympathize."

"You are no monster."

"Perhaps some would argue."

Leaves and feathers and maggots scattered as the birds lurched to another branch while every syllable the devils uttered caught and scrabbled around Durand's head like whispers down a well. It was maddening.

"*In any case, the girl,*" said one of the rotting birds.

"*The girl. Godelind.*"

"*The news drove her from her perfect mind. By all accounts, she bolted from the court of Prince Willan, slipping away when no one watched her, so stricken was she by these dark tidings.*"

"*Slipping away?*"

"*Perhaps she did not believe the news. Not truly. But she walked from the court at Tern Gyre, trending south.*"

"*Willan blinded himself, did he not?*"

"*Possibly, brother, but we are thinking of the girl now. Godelind. South and south again.*"

"*I can almost see her. They will have told her 'no' and 'it is not safe, you must not pass the mountains.'*"

"*But she followed her path south like a spirit drawn beyond her will to the Pennons Gate and then, with the warnings of the Solantines in her ears, south again into trackless Fellwood of the lost kingdoms and thralls.*"

"*No! Not alone! Fellwood was a waste and haunt of devils!*"

"*And the Solantines were the last to see her as a living woman.*"

"*As a living woman, brother? How else?*"

"*Well, there we find the Lindenhall, you see.*"

"*Now, here you have missed your guess, brother, for I do not see, in fact. Not at all.*"

"*Through the Fellwood, our girl drifts like a spirit. Lost to song. Lost to story. And finally, Lost altogether. And nigh unto three hundred winters sift their downy burdens over her resting place among the trees.*"

"*She died? Is that what you intend by this poetry, brother?*"

"*Indeed, and she must have lain undisturbed for all those sad years before a gang of hardy louts from Errest the Old made their way into the empty forest, intent on robbing land from the silence and the spirits. They found a likely place for their forest stronghold: a glade in a grove of lindens. Axes rang as they broke the soil, and they built up a fortress of timber set high upon a mound of earth.*"

"*Showing commendable prudence and industry, I'm sure, but what has this to do with our Godelind, pray tell, brother?*"

Durand hunched his shoulders as the whispers scurried around his skull like spiders or wasps or Heaven knew what. He put a hand to his head.

"I am just coming to it, brother. For, you see, it was while our stout-hearted exiles made a stockade of the lindens atop their forest mud heap that they turned up poor Godelind."

"How improbable."

"A prodigy, then, surely, brother. And they knew her by the love token twinkling upon the delicate bones of her tiny hand."

"The ring!"

"There in a shovel of muck was Calamund's ring, the better part of four centuries since the Lost Princes."

"Or Heraric's ring, four centuries and so on."

"Godelind's, anyway. The fat carbuncle like a drop of heart's blood. A sign of love, undimmed by ages. They reckon she must've swooned among the lindens, her eyes upon the southern sky with hope and life having died with her Lost Prince."

"Or she was dragged there by beasts. Wolves are a dogged breed, brother. Was the body entire?"

"Uncannily so, by all accounts."

"And the story brought men south."

"Men and women and boys and girls into the Fellwood, where the ring remains enshrined in this Lindenhall, and the pennies of pilgrims have built walls of stone for the halls of linden."

"Most enterprising. A happy end to a sad tale. But why do I feel that I know this sad history? I am sure I have not heard it, though I can almost see that poor girl. And the ring. The band is serpentine. Two twining creatures clutching the fat stone."

"Serpents and a bloody stone! We have dreamt *it, brother. Now why should that be?"*

"Here is the interesting part, I think, for—"

Durand glanced up just as a stone smashed the half-rotten bird. He turned and saw Ailric's face: wide-eyed but closed-mouthed. The man's well-aimed rock had scattered fragments of one Rook down the trail. The other hopped into the air, with its hoarse laughing call.

"I didn't like the look of the things," said Ailric carefully.

"No," said Durand, as the scuttling syllables began to file from his head. "It's a devilish place."

He tried a deep breath. But, in another step or two, Brand overtook the surviving Rook. The thing had landed among its brother's remains and was greedily jabbing its beak deep in the breast of its brother's carcass. The thing seemed to notice Ailric and Durand staring down.

"Flesh is flesh. To act otherwise is to deny the immortality of the soul. A sacrilege of sorts. And we were priests once, before curiosity became our master."

Even Ailric could not throw a stone.

11
The Marches of Fellwood

Too soon, they lost the light—and with it, any hope of reaching the Lindenhall before nightfall. By Durand's reckoning, the tourney began on the next day. They had ridden hard.

They chose a campsite on the barren floor between the giant trees. A few blankets were all they had, but they bedded down. Durand thought of the Rooks' Godelind and the Lost Princes. He thought of the Herald of Errest who'd watched the poor brothers die. And he wondered where the Rooks had gone.

"Sir Euric came for the hunting," Ailric said, in an undertone. "There is a brute like a bullock, sudden as a stag. Boar in droves. Bear. Wolf. He'd heard there might be lion."

Somewhere, a pinecone or acorn detached itself from a high limb. It struck the ground like a stone a few paces from the tent, the thud galloping off through leagues of silence. The horses shifted uneasily.

"But he did not care for the place when he saw it," Ailric said. "We lost four huntsmen before he made up his mind."

Another acorn struck the earth like a stone from a catapult.

"It is no hunting park," said Durand.

DARKNESS SWALLOWED THEM up as they lay on the floor of the ancient forest like sea-buried sailors on the bottom of a black and teeming ocean. Columns of insects whined in the fathoms and leagues of clammy darkness. A moth fluttered like eyelashes against Durand's face. And there were bats and scuttling things as well, all crowding the darkness. But these creatures were only the mundane denizens of Fellwood, and there were other beings among the trees: thralls abandoned in the Heshtarians' flight, Banished spirits of the wastelands, and the Lost of ages. Any fool could see it was no place for men. Durand could not imagine dragging plowmen here.

Twigs snapped; he could not say how near. But nothing came.

And Durand turned his back on the denizens of the dark, groping his blankets tighter.

"It came upon us with the whispers, do you recall? And now, among these devilish old trees, does it not plague you? The ring? A girl like a ghost among the lindens. A dream. A dream. A dream."

Durand woke.

"You lie if you claim to know linden from lilac, brother dear."

"True, brother, true. But why should we dream of this Godelind and her jewelry? What has it to do with our Whisperer?"

"But it could be any ring in the dream. Any girl. What makes you think it is this Godelind?"

As Durand lay in the gloom, he realized that he'd been hearing a household sound: a baby squalling in some distant room. It took a heartbeat for him to recall that he was on his back in Fellwood.

"Well, first, mad Ragnal sends our friend to the Lindenhall, of all places. And, second— Ah, wait, he's awake!"

A fog had flooded the forest, thick as new milk. Around Durand, the boles of mighty trees stood like a ring of stones—but between the trees were shadows: a second ring of human shapes.

Durand rolled up, fumbling the chained flail from his belt. The shadows could have been Leovere's raiders or devils from the Fellwood, but Durand found that he knew them. The hitches and crooks of their posture told him enough: one silhouette could only be Euric with his bloody head cocked and, there, the beggar king with hardly a head at all. Durand might have taken a strange comfort in knowing the congregation for what it was, but the child was still wailing, and there could be no live child in this company. What infant had he killed and when?

He searched the fog and shadows for the source of the cry.

A woman stood nearer than the rest of the crowd. Young, she seemed, and pale. Her hair was long and black. Her gown was soaked with water. The smell of rushes and thick streams of algae reached him. And in the woman's arms was a struggling bundle. Very small. The woman's face was tilted toward the tiny shape. And the cry sent Durand back. He remembered those days just after he left his father's hall when he'd stumbled in with Radomor's men. He remembered long hours standing guard over Duke Radomor's poor wife: Alwen, Abravanal's daughter. This was the same child. No one knew what Radomor had done with the child, but Alwen ended in the river. They said she'd made a cuckold of Radomor. He remembered Radomor sitting in his hall at Ferangore. The diabolical fury. He remembered standing at Alwen's door: the swelling dread, the shame. In that tower at Ferangore, Durand had caught hold of her arm when she'd made to leave. She'd looked up into his face, with eyes desperate and black as ink. Ten years later in that forest clearing, here she was, and her child with her. Dead. He recalled the infant quailing at the heart of Radomor's monstrous Champion, part of the Rooks' sorceries: that thing wrought of Radomor's dead kin. Of the man's poor father. Of the man's son.

Such horror. Durand had been blind. A mad child. He thought back on himself as a young shield-bearer leaving the Col, bidding farewell to Ailric, running off to join the first knights to pass. What a dangerous thing he'd been.

Alwen and her crying infant were three steps from him. He could see her shoulder, the sodden wing of hair over the infant's face. The rest of the congregation pressed closer, from the fog—bloody, maimed—drifting nearer. Each one looking on.

Guilt and shame crushed him to the earth. Alwen was turning toward him; he could not yet see her face. What could he ever do that might outweigh that moment when he'd caught the woman's arm? He had endured women, children, warriors, and blameless common men, all dead. Now, though, it was more than he could endure.

At the last instant, something twitched through the dead crowd and every eye among them suddenly darted to the same spot, fixing on something: Something beyond Durand, something in the trees. For heartbeat after heartbeat, every dead soul froze where it stood. Could it be terror he saw in their white faces? Durand was afraid to look.

He became conscious of the horses' snorts.

Then, just as he found the will to move, the Lost scattered, flashing into the fog high and low like a vast shoal of minnows.

He had seen only the merest glimpse of Alwen's black eyes, of her child's blue face. And he was left on his belly with Ailric crouched alongside.

"How many?" said Ailric. His voice was scarcely audible.

Durand turned on the young man, not sure what he had seen beyond a grown man thrashing against the earth like a madman. "What?"

"How many are they?"

"How many what? What do you mean?" Ailric could not have seen. Even Deorwen could not see them.

"The horses. When the dead come round, they pin their ears."

"The horses . . ."

"But this fog," said Ailric. "They were all around. Shapes in the air." It was hard to imagine that so many Lost souls made no mark. "We nearly lost Brand. Your Shriker half tore up the stump where I'd lashed him. And there was something else, I think."

This time, Durand nodded. "Aye. There was."

Ailric got to his feet, watching the fog. He found the place where the dead had fixed their collective gaze and he scoured the ground, staring for a space of many heartbeats. "There was a tree here. All night. I thought it was a tree." The pair both looked up into the shifting billows overhead where the Lost had vanished. They could see three fathoms before the fog smothered the sky. Durand could just imagine some devil of the Fellwood standing, still as death, under that ceiling. "It was here. The Lost had not seen it either." Even Durand could see fresh, greasy tears in the carpet of brown leaves. "It stood like a man. Hours, I think. Then it turned from the clearing. Its footprints vanish in that direction. It watched over us all night. It was brooding there while we lay in the dark." Durand had never seen Ailric rattled.

"But it is gone now, and there is nothing we can—"

Durand heard birds flapping nearby. Landing on the branches of a tree a few paces distant.

"Brother, you were speaking of Godelind and how you came to under-stand that the ring was hers."

Now Durand heard a brittle *crack-crack* somewhere ahead, sounding very near. He twisted.

"Meat," Ailric said, abruptly.

Durand twisted again, cornered. "What?"

The man was scenting the air. "Sir Durand, I think that is meat I smell. Flesh and fire."

"How did you know the ring was Godelind's?"

It was time to move. "We will get clear of this place," Durand said. "I can still see the road. Saddle the horses." In a few moments, he spurred his red cob into a canter, and within a bowshot, rode into a space where the trees were pockmarked with the white ellipses of freshly hacked branches, some thick as a man's wrist.

He realized that he stood on the verge of a substantial clearing, surrounded on all sides by stockades of mighty trees. Beyond it all stood a castle like a diadem of alabaster on a tall hill.

Ailric's rouncy plodded close, with Shriker in tow.

First, Durand spotted a line of bondmen swinging brown billhooks in the brush along the perimeter of the cleared area. A hundred paces across the green, below a reviewing stand, a great square of tables had been laid out. Diners crowded around. Durand saw the wink of silver over white cloths. A whiff of roast venison and boar passed on a smoky breeze.

Above it all stood a squat shell-keep, white as new ivory, on a twenty-fathom hill.

Ailric was shaking his head, his face pale.

"And this will be the Lindenhall," said Durand, "and here we are, just in time."

"There was a rather homely skald singing the ballad of Godelind not far from here," said a Rook, and the pair flew off above the misty green.

As DURAND AND Ailric skirted the clearing to approach the tables, they blundered into what looked like a stand of dead trees and brown leaves, but turned out to be a multitude of starlings. The things exploded in every direction, giving both men a job to keep control of the animals. Still, the commotion got the attention of the diners, and a small man bustled out to meet them. The little fellow blinked up, narrowly avoiding Brand's hooves.

"Sir Durand, let me see if I cannot find you a place at the board. It is all a bit rustic here, I'm afraid, but we are doing our best." Durand heard the sound of minstrels plucking courtly ballads.

Durand did not answer the country steward, so intent was he on getting hold of something solid to eat. It had been far too long.

"Ailric," said Durand, "picket the horses, then get back here as quick as you can. There is food left." The assembled company was already eating.

Ailric nodded sharply, with no sign of complaint or resentment.

The little steward was bowing. "This way, Sir Durand, unless you would prefer to spend a moment recuperating from your—"

"I do not think so."

"I will have a page attend you with a basin and towels."

Perhaps Durand betrayed some surprise. Perhaps the Marcher steward was alert for slights. "You will find us quite civilized, Sir Durand."

The tables in that forest clearing might have stood in some noble's hall, with crisp linen and silver all gleaming under the Eye of Heaven. Each knight wore the blazons of his lineage as clear as a banner. And there were ladies in the forest, each flashing in silk and jewels. Durand might have laughed at the whole thing, but he saw young Almora at the head of the table. Her eyes were dark and her hair as black as her drowned sister's. They were very much alike. It could have been the same girl.

Durand faltered. But it had been many hours since food had passed his lips, and there were pages already gathering up the wreckage of the feast, so he forced himself to take a place and pick some cold flesh from the bones of a young pig—congealed and badly picked over. Some dregs remained in a jug of claret. Ailric would likely starve if he didn't hurry.

Durand had placed himself beside a gray-haired man, and as Durand picked at the leftovers, the man started. "Durand?"

White hair curled from the man's nostrils, with matching bristles in his ears. And a patch of black leather nestled among the wrinkles where one eye ought to have been.

Abruptly, Durand knew who had spoken. "Berchard!"

The good eye squinted close and the wrinkled face split into a grin. "It has been ten winters since I turned my back on Gireth."

He had not seen Berchard since Radomor's war. In the aftermath, the man had been given lands in Yrlac, but there had been trouble. Berchard had been very angry.

"I am surprised to see you at Abravanal's table," said Durand. "What was it? You called His Grace an ungrateful bastard?"

"Injudicious words, I admit."

"I nearly had to meet you in the lists, I recall."

"The vacant lands Abravanal granted me in Yrlac after the war were not vacant, as you recall, their 'deceased' previous owner being alive and well and in full possession of the lands and titles and fifty armed men."

"And now you're in the Marches?"

"I did well enough—or I thought I had."

"Durand Col?" said a second voice.

Now, Durand found a pockmarked face and a nose as flat as a saddle. This was Heremund Skald, but there was no smile on the man's face. His mouth hung in hollow circle; his mandora was silent.

"By Heaven," said Berchard, "we are all here once again. Heremund Skald, is that you?"

"We are like a leaves on the wind in this life," said the skald.

"It's an odd chance to find us all in the same place once more, I suppose."

"Chance, Berchard? There is Leovere of Yrlac and Abravanal of Gireth," said Heremund. "There is the Herald of Errest." The tall, pale Herald sat at the head table by Abravanal's side. "Here are we."

"Aye, but—"

"I'm in Fellwood because of what I've heard. Strange things. And I've been sniffing round. But now here you all come trooping down. Our Herald there, he hasn't crossed the passes of the Blackroots since the Sons of Heshtar reigned in all the lands to the Pennons Gate. Since the battle of Lost Princes. And here is Leovere. He's taken the Horn of Uluric down from the wall and carried it back to Fellwood where it has not been since his people wrested it from the thralls of Heshtar. No. The trees are full of starlings—thousands of thousands, all suddenly. We've not come here to meet old friends."

"Well, I'm not here for horns and gates and signs," said Berchard, blinking hard. "I've had enough of doom. I am working for a quiet life."

"Will you fight?" asked Durand.

"Fight? No. Though I'd give these young dandies a run for their money, old as I am. But no, I'm here to ask a boon of my liege lord, and time is short. I'm hoping His Grace can manage to— Oh, now. Who's this? Yet another friend of yours?"

Durand found himself staring up into the grinning face of Leovere's pet brigand, Morcar the Toad. Worse, someone had dressed the creature in a knight's surcoat—mustard bright—and combed his lank hair. His mustachioed cur of a comrade stood at his side.

"Sir Durand," purred Morcar, his face shining with grease. "Is that surprise I see on your face? Is it my costume?"

Durand curled his lip. The linen of Morcar's surcoat was divided down the middle white and yellow—silver and gold—and charged with the heads of three black dogs.

"I'd only just begun to introduce myself before that unfortunate fit of temper of yours. I'm Morcar of Downcastle; Baron, as was my father before me."

Downcastle was a substantial holding on the far side of Yrlac, and it seemed that Morcar had stayed clear of Abravanal's court these last ten years. The thought of Morcar in command of such an honor caused Durand to laugh: a puff through his nostrils.

"And this is my cousin, Sir Baradan of Stonebeck, a kinsman and liegeman both. He fought at the Siege of Acconel, and at Ferangore."

The soldier with the boar's-bristle mustache bowed mockingly in the face of Durand's frown. "Thought we had you lot both times," the soldier said.

"Seems we let a few too many get away," Durand answered. Now it was his turn to be clever. "But all of that is long ago. We are liegemen of Duke Abravanal now. A happy family. I am surprised not to have seen a fine pair like you at court in Acconel."

"It is a great distance, you understand."

"A mercy," Durand said.

Morcar smiled. "I look forward to meeting you on the field, Black Durand, but I don't see what old Ragnal is thinking with all this. How can we cow these Marchers here when we are afraid to fight with bared steel? If you had not lost your pack train in the mountains, I hear we would have been fighting with whalebone and gilt leather. Or battering each other with brooms. These Marchers will quake with laughter, not fear."

"Blunt will be enough," said Durand.

Morcar sneered. "I will make do with what I'm given. May Heaven stand by you, Champion of Gireth."

As Morcar and his henchman strolled off, the great flock of starlings rose among the trees, storming in a vast, sinuous cloud from resting place to resting place.

"Host Below," muttered Berchard. "I don't much like the sound of your new friend, I'll tell you that for nothing."

"I nearly dropped him from Pennons Gate."

"Nearly? We all have things we regret," said Berchard.

Almost before Durand could finish, the tables were gone and the field was ready for the fight.

THE STARLINGS CHURNED in the canyons of the forest as the combatants broke into two companies on opposite ends of the great clearing below the Lindenhall. Stallions thrashed their heads in the heavy air. Grooms ran with lost gear. And the mossy trees all around the field rose like the walls of some vast arena as heralds, nobles, and five hundred Marcher men and women gathered to witness this demonstration that the King of Errest the Old was king in Gireth too—and in the Marches of Fellwood.

Durand took a place near the north corner of the vast rectangle, ignoring a pair of Rooks clattering among the branches. Ailric eyed the creatures, but he had found a half-dozen good straight lances, each with a blunt little tournament crown where the blade should be, and Durand weighed one in his fist. When he'd ridden from Acconel, tournament fighting had been the last thing on his mind, and so he was glad to have the lances—and lucky indeed that he had carried a coat of mail at all. There had been no sense in bringing the thing—not to race after a runaway girl. He'd likely been thinking of Yrlac and the raiders even then.

One of the Rooks cawed in the trees as the starling multitude swarmed past.

Durand worked his jaw with a crunch of chain links as Berchard tried to chat with Ailric. He had the boy by the wrist, but Durand paid attention only to the opposing camp. Despite a valiant effort on the part of the heralds, all of Leovere's men would ride together. But it was in the Atthian nature: cousins fought alongside cousins and liegemen under their lords. And so Leovere sat at the head of a small army of mercenaries, exiles, and Yrlaci malcontents, like the brass handle on a boiling kettle's lid. The two camps faced each other, fingering hardwood blades and blunt lances.

A commotion closer to home drew Durand's attention. Red-haired Raimer trotted into the lists, facing Durand.

The man straightened. "Sir Durand Col." And Durand nodded, unsure of the man and this sudden formality as conversation faltered among the knights around him.

"It saved the old man, pushing through the pass. And there's more than one of us would have dangled Morcar by his ankles." At Leovere's end of the clearing, Durand could see the toad, Morcar, laughing among his men even then.

"I had this among my packs," said Raimer. He produced a good steel helm: more the sort of thing used in war than in a pageant like this. Raimer turned the thing in his hands, looking into the empty face of it. "It belonged to a kinsman of mine. I had few things of his when we set out from Wrothsilver. We think he fell. In any case, you must have it."

With a lifted chin, the man tossed the helm across. Durand caught the thing at the last instant and gave Raimer a startled, solemn bow. There was a strong stirring of mutters as Raimer answered and returned to his men. Perhaps, he was not the fool Durand had thought him.

A fanfare rang out from the reviewing stand that stood where the two companies must soon collide. Durand peered down the rectangle of turf between him and the dignitaries, and saw Sir Coensar in his azure surcoat of terns.

"His Grace has asked if I'll lead you all in an oath of fellowship, and I am honored," he said. The duke raised his chin with a fierce expression. "But," Coensar continued, "I would pass this honor to another who will fight in these lists today." His eye flashed like a spear point and he turned to the Yrlaci side.

"Sir Leovere. Please."

A murmur circled the clearing. The duke's mouth opened in outrage, and Leovere's men looked from one to another. Durand had to clap his own mouth shut. But Leovere made no show of surprise. The Horn of Uluric glinted at his hip, and a breath of wind played among the high branches around as he reined in his charger.

"Well enough. Ladies. Gentlemen," he said. "It is rare that so many peers of our kingdom stand together in such a place." He waved at the gaping colonnades of shadowy giants all around. "This forest. The trees. We must pray that this day's sport may forge a bond of fellowship and goodwill between we who have gathered here, wherever we were born. We are knights. We are peers of Errest the Old, the kingdom of the *Cradle*'s Landing. May honor be shown to all and by all whatever the place of their birth! May the green shoot of a new peace be planted here in the midst of this great forest.

"And now, we will speak the oath under Heaven."

The crowd of gawkers climbed to their feet as Leovere drew his sword, followed by scores of others at both ends of the lists. The Eye of Heaven kindled the blades. "By the Host of Heaven and my sword, I swear to abide by the peace of this meeting and to bring honor to this gathering." No blades. No points. Peace, not war. "Before you all, these things, I swear!"

And the ranks thundered back, "As do we all!"

And there was Leovere, unflappable, the hero. Blades flashed on both sides of the clearing.

"Ah," said Berchard. "Here come heralds to mark out the lists."

"It is Kandemar himself," said Ailric.

"Aye, it is. More doom for Heremund Skald."

Kandemar the Herald strode into the clearing with a gaggle of local heralds trailing behind. They carried a bundle of stakes to mark the bounds of the lists, beyond which no combatant would fight. Without even a glance, the gaunt Herald snatched a stake.

"That stake will be aspen," said Berchard.

Durand glanced at Berchard. He could not tell one green stick from another.

"I spoke to the local men," Berchard explained. "I am not fighting, but the business of the markers . . . I could not let it pass."

With the local heralds crouched like acolytes about an altar to steady the stake, Kandemar held out his hand for a long-hafted maul and hammered the thing home. As the maul struck, every one of the ancient trees shivered. The Herald struck again—a thousand trees. And again—ten thousand. It was a great, rising whisper that seemed to take the air out of Creation. And with the fourth blow, the whole of the Fellwood quaked as though the trees were hissing a warning one to another.

"Aspen, for remorse," breathed Berchard. The long-legged Herald was already on the move, walking across the face of Leovere's company toward the distant southern corner of the field. "Struck four times in the west."

"Now, the south," said Berchard, and the Herald drew a knobbed stake, taking an extra flash of his knife to satisfy himself of the point. While the startled band of heralds crouched around the thing, the Herald of Errest raised the maul once more.

"Blackthorn for doom," said Berchard.

And the maul struck.

Now, the Fellwood roared. The stake struck deep, but the whisper of shaking leaves that had arisen with the aspen stake now roared with the blackthorn. A wind had taken hold of the trees, and now it battered men and horses in the field.

But the Herald paid no heed to the commotion. He turned toward the eastern corner and the men of Gireth, though the wind tore at his long cloak. The bravest of the lesser heralds chased him with a third stake, which had Berchard raising the fist and fingers sign of Heaven's Eye. "Elder! Grown in blood. The battlefield root. The poison tree. The stinking leaf. The hollow limb. Dead and living. Living and dead."

Durand looked at the old knight, but Berchard could not turn from the Herald.

Kandemar waited as his men crouched around the elder stake. The wind threw the towering Herald's mantle over his face, but the man only batted the thing away and hoisted the maul yet again, swinging against the gale with all the force of his long limbs.

And, this time, the stake burst like a rotten log. For an instant, the wave of alarm down the face of the Gireth line obscured what had happened. But when Durand could see again, he found that not only had the hollow wood snapped, but it seemed to have overflowed: a fountain of writhing complexity boiled from the broken shaft. "Spiders," said Ailric. "Thousands. More than thousands." It was as though the Herald had tapped some vast cavern of the things beneath the forest. The heralds tumbled back, swarming with the things. Choking. One man collapsed, caught in clouds of pale web, drowning on the field as the rest rolled and pounded at their tunics. Not a knight alive would enter the lists to help now.

Leaving all of this in his wake, the Herald continued his march around the bounds of the lists, this time empty-handed and alone. He walked down the line of Girethi horses, stalking toward Durand and the final corner of the lists. Berchard's eye was wide as the Herald drew closer. Durand had ridden with the Herald for so many days, he had all but forgotten that this pale man had lived many lifetimes and walked the Halls of Heaven. Now, gaunt as something from the tomb, the Herald stood at Shriker's muzzle and reached out.

As the wind roared, the Herald snatched the lance from Durand's hand. Was this to be the final stake? What could such a thing mean? But the Herald would not answer—could not answer since the day when he had passed the Gates of Heaven. He raised the thing in his two fists and drove it down, crown-head-first into the sod, almost at Shriker's feet. The shaft broke with a crack like thunder and the lance burst into splinters that struck blood from the Herald's fists. The man turned toward Durand, his hands open and full of blood. A ragged gash on his forehead bled from temple to temple like a crown of garnets.

"Your lance. Ash," said Berchard. The Herald looked on. "The spear, the axe, the warrior."

"Broken in blood," supplied Ailric, and Berchard peered up at Durand with horror. "A crown of blood."

"Aye," said Berchard, "all of that, as well."

And the wind roared on, storming over the trees, as the Herald turned once more. Upon the dais where Coensar, Abravanal, Almora, and Deorwen sat, the Battle Horn of Errest gleamed. The Herald stalked from Durand, finally taking up his horn, and waiting.

Somewhere among the trees, Durand heard the Rooks crying, "Haw! Haw! Haw!"

Durand took a moment to unbuckle the sword he carried. "Berchard, here. Hold this for me."

Berchard fumbled at the big sword. It had belonged to a friend of theirs once. The thing was tangled up in memories.

"Is this Ouen's sword that Coen gave you?"

"Hold it. They'll have my head if I forget."

There wasn't a lot of motion on that tiltyard. In the face of so many prodigies, every man felt as though he had been served up on some vast altar. But, finally, the facing companies awoke. They scrambled to dress their lines with every trapper and surcoat flapping like a living thing. A lance appeared in Durand's fist. He seated his borrowed helm and groped to find the balance of this new lance while the Herald looked out over them all and raised the horn.

Durand felt his heart hammering like the Herald's maul. Leather creaked in his fists, here where Godelind of the Lost Princes lay down to die among the lindens.

It should only have been another tournament, but the Herald sounded the horn, and its silver note leapt up to pierce the wind and thunder, so high and so sharp that every man of Atthian blood set his spurs—all shock and astonishment banished in an instant.

They thundered out, warhorses jostling at the gallop like hogs down a chute. Durand was one of few who rode without a pack of close friends all around him. But when he and Shriker struck the enemy lines, Durand's lance punched a blue-clad Yrlaci from his saddle as neatly as the hand of the Creator.

The crowds crashed and wheeled. Durand rode Shriker pell-mell, bolting among the brawling knights, forgetting himself in the fury of the thing. Men and horses pounded between the trees. Claw-headed lances tore men from saddles. But, after a second and third roaring onslaught, two hundred small battles tangled the two companies beyond unraveling. Lances snapped underfoot and the hardwood blades began their brutal work.

Blunt weapons loosened teeth and sent stars spinning through the heads of many men. Durand roved the lists, striking at anyone from Yrlac. But, far too soon, he found groups banding together to face him. A bar of blunt steel rang from his helm. Then a hardwood blade cracked over his elbow—and Durand saw Morcar the baron pointing at him across the press, face bare and sneering a wry "hello." It was a trap. The men around him were Morcar's raiders. The devils had him alone, and surrounded.

Blows hailed down, stamping him this way and that as he roared. But, though he struck back, he could not bull his way out. Lights flashed, he tasted blood, and he would have fallen but, suddenly, a sound like an avalanche of iron crashed into the men around him and Durand tumbled free. A squad of friendly horsemen had charged into Morcar's little scrum and, as the Yrlacies scattered, Durand found himself face-to-face with Raimer. The man laughed, though there was blood on his lip when he tipped back his helm. "The fight follows you, Sir Durand. Do you mind if my Swanskin lads ride with you a while?"

"You are welcome," said Durand, and he heartily meant it.

It was as handsome a rescue as a man could wish, and so Durand fought alongside Raimer's squad, battering the enemy, and forgetting all omens until Morcar took his second crack at revenge—this time with greater subtlety and force.

In the spinning fight, Durand found himself at the rear of Raimer's squad when a pack of Morcar's raiders launched itself at Raimer. Later, Durand would see that this was only the first of Morcar's moves. As the men of Raimer's squadron leapt to defend their lord—Durand included—Morcar sprang a simple trap: a second gang of raiders plowed into Raimer's squad, driving a neat wedge of men and iron between Durand and the rest of Raimer's men.

Durand was alone and surrounded before he realized. In a real battle, he would have been butchered. Shriker lunged left and right, but could not break free. Durand found himself driven far from the castle and any onlookers, back against the forest edge where stakes of fresh-cut bush jutted by their hundreds. Shriker reared. Blows stamped down, flashing in Durand's skull, thrashing him like a straw doll. Finally, he pitched out of his saddle, landing explosively on one shoulder.

Hooves stabbed all round him with Shriker plunging in terror and half a dozen knights right on top of him. Something pinned his gauntlet to the earth for an instant, then set him free. Durand crashed into the face of the hedge. White tines of thorn and hardwood dug at his face and arms. A blow against the top of his helm half choked him. There was laughing and whooping everywhere.

Durand tumbled into an open space and, wild with pain, turned on his attackers. Knights were barging through the brush on every side. Some had their helms back, exposing laughing faces. Then there was Boar's Bristles—the name was lost—beaming down, a lance held over-hand, ready to spear Durand like a beast.

But, against one of the trees, the foresters had left their tools: bill-hooks, one with a three-foot haft and a hooked cleaver-blade a foot long. Bright edges curled round the blade's brown face.

As Boar's Bristles reared back, Durand caught hold of the bill and, in one wheeling arc, whipped the thing high. The blade—suited to hacking the limbs from trees—caught its victim below the ear, half-beheading the man.

As Durand's victim toppled, the man's stunned friends gaped at Durand, certain murder in their eyes. And so Durand leapt for the dead man's horse. The frantic beast tore through the wall of branches, Durand ducking low as they exploded back into the lists.

He rode for his own people, or what he could see of them. In an instant, the tournament would change, for Leovere's men would want blood, and the Herald's cursed markers wouldn't hold them. Men would die. And they would not stop with Durand.

He angled for the reviewing stands, hoping to get Deorwen, Almora, and the duke into the Lindenhall. The place was likely built to withstand a few raiders. And, all the way, he roared, "To the castle! To the castle!" even as a matching cry of "Murderer! Murderer!" rose up from Morcar's thugs, and a wide crescent of Leovere's knights tore itself free of the fight to pursue Durand.

Heaven knows what they thought, but the knights of Gireth rode in on every side of the reviewing stand, snatching up young women and old men before careering toward the white gates of the Lindenhall. Durand watched as Raimer caught Almora and made for the gates. Sweeping through, Durand led the flight through the tents of the knights' encampment and up the steep hill to the gates of the castle. Pages and camp followers scattered. Once there, he wheeled his borrowed mount and brandished the billhook. Scores of riders passed him, rushing inside, including the duke and Almora, before he broke free himself and followed them to safety.

Durand galloped through the gateway and leapt from his saddle, trying to count the people who mattered. Coensar was barking orders. Abravanal huddled with Almora. There were men shouting at the gates. A group of Raimer's comrades had slotted the bar. For a long moment, he could not spot Deorwen—but then she found him.

"What in Heaven's name happened?" she demanded. They could still hear the ringing clash of swords on the bank below the walls.

"It was Morcar and his dogs."

She noticed the bloody hook in Durand's fists. "And what is that thing? Durand, what have you done?"

"They got me in a corner."

"Oh, Durand." She knew it for a disaster.

Coensar was looking on as Durand spoke. "I had best have a look," he said. Durand gave Deorwen a pleading look and followed the steward up a crabbed stair to the top of the gatehouse. Below, the lists and tents and reviewing stands were a wreck. A crowd of Leovere's men stormed around the gates.

Morcar the Toad was stabbing a finger in Durand's direction as his henchmen fought to keep the man from rushing the walls barehanded. "Throw him down! The murdering pig must answer for this!"

Coensar raised his hands over the crowd. "Patience!"

Some in Leovere's throng snatched up clods of earth, and these pattered down around the parapet. Morcar struggled in his comrades' arms.

"We cannot have this!" Coensar shouted down, adding aside, "You will keep your head down, Durand."

Durand found his way to an arrow loop a step or two below.

"Here is Leovere," said Coensar, quietly. The young lord rode a trotting warhorse through the crowd.

"You are Atthians," said Coensar. "Sworn to peace."

Morcar launched himself against his friends' arms. "What do you know of peace, you whoresons? What do you know of oaths?"

"Restrain yourself, Baron!" barked Leovere, pulling to the forefront. His warhorse danced before the mob. He turned to the parapet. "Black Durand Col has butchered one of my men," he said. "A man under Duke Abravanal's protection."

"Sir Durand claims provocation," said Coensar.

The crowd shouted jeers.

Leovere's hand shot up over his people. "This is a tournament of peace, and your man has murdered a peer of Yrlac with a groundskeeper's hook!"

Morcar repeated his cry. "Throw him down!"

The fearsome look Leovere flashed at Morcar stopped the man.

"We must learn the truth," said Coensar.

"Your man is a murderer," said Leovere.

"Throw him down!" shouted Morcar again. "Throw him down with a rope around his neck!"

The duke was at Coensar's side. To the old man, Coensar said, "They will want a trial."

But, looking over the ugly faces of the Yrlaci's, Durand knew it was no trial they wanted, but blood. Coensar could not have the peace without handing Durand to the mob.

With a muttered curse and a glance at the helpless duke and yammering multitude, Coensar turned to Durand, pitching his voice to carry:

"Sir Durand Col, Duke's Champion, I ask you to surrender yourself to the duke's justice."

Durand still had the billhook in his fists. He looked into Coensar's grim, almost despairing expression. Abravanal looked on. There was Deorwen and Almora. One man could not foul the wheels of so great a thing as peace between the duke and his barons.

The bill clattered from Durand's open hand.

Deorwen was shaking her head.

Coensar nodded, his steel eyes on Durand's, then turned back to the mob.

"Gather your witnesses, Leovere. We will settle this matter before nightfall."

A GUARD LED Durand to a lightless storeroom under the Lindenhall. But, before the door could close on him, he saw a second prisoner standing in the shadows. The stranger wore the torn hauberk of a fighting man. For an instant, Durand could make out the stranger's face. Then, just as the door fell shut, he spotted the ruin of a mangled skull and a mustache like a boar's bristles.

Durand cursed and the door thumped shut.

12

Judgment of the Sword

Durand huddled in the frigid silence, while the lords above arranged their trial.

From time to time, he heard the rustle of mail, very close, and felt the ghost of a frigid tongue lapping where the blood seeped from his temple. Dead man after dead man joined him in that cellar room until Durand felt the frost bristling on the stones. He wondered if Lady Alwen were there, and her baby. He could be face-to-face—her pale, drowned visage to his bruised and stubbled cheek—and never know it in the dark.

"Ah, here you are!" said a Rookish whisper. "Brother, I've found him."

As he sat, wide-eyed and numb, he wondered. Had the Host of Heaven sent old Berchard and Heremund to the Lindenhall just to witness his end?

After a glassy age in the dark, there was a "caw!" and scrabble of claws at the door just before the keys rattled in the old lock and the door blazed, banishing the Lost to the darkest corners.

"Sir Durand, you'll have to come with us. They're ready upstairs." The voice belonged to one of the fighting men from Acconel. A couple of grim-faced but familiar men led him through castle corridors. The babble of an excited crowd echoed through the little castle.

Finally, they turned a corner onto a fierce light—not the twilight of the keep's great hall—and an enormous crowd erupted. Pebbles and spittle hailed down. Durand snarled and shielded his eyes as he understood: They meant to hold a trial in the castle's paved central courtyard. Hundreds of people had crowded in, turning the yard into a round theater. Faces looked down from the battlements as the half-blind Durand was led out like a bull trussed for the slaughter.

Finally, the tugging hands left Durand's elbows and he was left to find his bearings. It seemed that the duke's box from the reviewing stands had been carted up the hill and deposited in front of him. The duke and his court stared out at Durand. Durand winced, wishing—almost—that he had not given up the peasant's chopper.

"Sir Durand Col!" Coensar's voice declared. The man stood, still dressed in his tournament blue, beside the ducal throne. Almora and all the others looked out from the shade of an awning. "You have been called before your duke, charged both with murder and violating your pledge to uphold the terms of His Grace's tournament."

There were jeers close by, but Leovere strode into the circle, glaring his people into silence. He turned to Durand with an eyebrow raised.

Durand opened and closed his fists, and he looked into the shadows of the duke's box. One fist was sore. He kneaded the bruised tendons.

"Tell us how Sir Baradan, Lord of Stonebeck, came to die," said Coensar.

"I defended myself. Stonebeck was not alone. He bore a lance."

Leovere raised his eyebrows. "Is that all that the man wishes to say?"

"Durand?" said Coensar.

"It is the truth."

"Sir Durand," said Coensar, "they've an heirloom of the Lost Princes in this place. On it, you must swear your oath."

Somewhere, they'd found a priest, and now the dusty old man stepped into the sunlight with a black pillow in his trembling hands. From the black folds glinted a small hand of ivory and gold. On one finger, a fat carbuncle gleamed like a blob of heart's blood. Durand imagined the girl

Godelind, dead so long ago, lying down among the lindens. In the sunlight, the thing was hard to look upon, flashing blotches into a man's eyes.

"*Oh,*" said a chittering whisper. Somewhere among the battlements, the Rooks were watching. "*It is the ring from our dream, brother. The very one. See how the two serpents coil around one red stone, almost as though they are contesting for it? It is very like a drop of blood. Why should we dream of this Prince's Ring? Why was it mixed among our whispers?*"

"*Brother, you are forgetting yourself. Our hero must attend to this Coensar. And it is poignant. Coensar, the old captain. Coensar, like a father. I wonder if the old captain keeps the flail with which he struck his young protégé? Even the marks of it must conjure the memory. The gallant captain sees Lord Lamoric rescued. Sees Durand riding to glory. The pang of jealousy, so unworthy in a great man. The rage and risk of the charge and swing. And then the years, every day, a reminder of shame. Oh, poor Coensar.*"

"*Now it is you who is forgetting himself, brother.*"

"*Just so.*"

"*It is not Coensar for whom we should feel sorrow. Not today.*"

Coensar spoke. "With your right hand on the Prince's Ring, swear that you have spoken truth." Durand had sworn oaths aplenty in his days upon Creation, but as he looked upon that old ring, he could feel—he could see—Creation twist around that dark and gleaming stone as though the world could scarcely bear the weight of the thing, and the sorrow and misery and hopelessness and faith that had weighed it down.

With the briefest sigh, Durand reached out for the ring regardless. And there was Deorwen at Almora's shoulder, gazing upon him. Not with admonition, but with dread: a raw and open terror that struck Durand to the heart.

Very suddenly, he wished that he might live.

Durand reached out and swore upon his soul and on all the sorrow in that old stone. For an instant, the air in that white courtyard seemed to tremble: uncountable golden motes shivering. Durand took his hand from the fat, blood-dark stone, and he felt, almost, that the crowd was a thousand leagues from him.

"Now let his accuser step forward," said Coensar.

Leovere turned to his man and Morcar tramped into the center of the court.

Coensar looked down upon the man. "Morcar, Baron of Downcastle, cousin to the dead man, what have you to say?"

Leovere thrust his chin at Morcar. "Tell him. What is your testimony?"

"Only that your Durand is a liar and coward who would not have been chased if he hadn't run, who would not have been outnumbered if one man could have brought him to ground."

They had not restrained Durand. There was nothing keeping him from Morcar's throat. He thought only of Deorwen and the long-lost girl in the wastes.

Morcar snarled in Durand's direction. "This man here is the worst sort of coward. He hacked my cousin down with a peasant's bill despite the duke's peace! The king's tournament! And there was Baradan armed with a blunted spear—a toy!"

"No," said Durand. No one could even have heard, but Morcar rounded on him.

"That lance of his you spoke of, it had no bloody point. Just like every other spear in the lists. Would the heralds have let it pass? Could he hide a sharp lance under his surcoat? I tell you, there was no one but Durand Col with a blade in his fist."

Morcar addressed the crowd. "How many of you saw us have words at the duke's table? How many saw Baradan laughing at this bastard? And now Baradan's dead." There were plenty of shouts in answer.

Durand could not remember. Had there had been a blade on the man's spear? Certainly he'd taken a beating.

Morcar pressed on. "Whether it was cunning or rage, we must put my cousin in the ground, and it was no sickness or act of war that slew him. It was murder—and here is the man who slew him!"

The men of Yrlac bellowed. The men of Gireth were grim.

From the courtyard's bear-pit thunder, Durand looked to Coensar. The steward was eyeing the crowd, his eyes swiveling gray as steel beads. "Silence!" Coensar commanded.

He brushed white hair from his eyes, and called for the priest once more.

"Morcar of Downcastle," said Coensar. "Your oath upon the Ring of the Lindenhall."

And Morcar gave his chin a defiant lift and raised his hand over the red stone.

"Enough," said Coensar. "Your oath."

Durand thought he saw a twitch in the man's jowls as his fingertips touched the stone. "I swear," he said, cowed for an instant despite himself. In a voice free of bluster, he said, "Baradan was unarmed. A toy only. Durand struck him with a peasant's bill. It's murder."

After the accused and accuser had spoken, the duke's men brought forth such evidence as there was. All the while, Durand stood in the midst of the circle like some brute beast in a pit. Out came the blunted lance, the bloody hook, and the slick wreck of Baradan's helm. Next came oath-helpers: men who would swear along with the accuser and the accused, adding the weight of their own oaths to the testimony before the court. Each of the men who had beaten him stood to lay their hand upon the ring.

Durand had no witnesses. At the last, he'd been alone. Ailric had not seen. Even he could not be sure: had there been a blade? He knew nothing.

And Coensar's face was beyond reading. The steward watched the crowd. He stared long into Durand's face. When the testimony ended, he spoke with the duke, and Abravanal stood.

"As Durand Col is my own Champion, I must allow my counselors to advise me in this." He glanced to Coensar. "My steward. Name whom you will and I will be governed by your counsel."

Coensar nodded. "Cassonel is a ranking liegeman and friend of neither accused nor accuser." And he found a few others among the throng. Banner knights, but not a man was of Coensar's standing. With a strange coldness, Durand understood that his life had been delivered into the hands of his murderer. Ten years had passed since Coensar lashed out and Durand fell. For ten years, Coensar had lorded it over Yrlac and Gireth, but always with Durand's scars to remind him.

Durand saw Deorwen among the throng, their eyes found each other just as the guardsmen took hold. Her glance was raw and rending.

As the guards hauled Durand down, the old Rooks surprised the priests of Lindenhall and snatched their ring away. "Haw! Haw!"

IN THE STOREROOM, Durand waited. He blinked as he felt Baradan's cold tongue lick at the blood on his jaw. He kneaded his bruised right hand. He could see no way out. Baradan was dead, and Morcar's faction must be appeased or halls would burn. Innocents would bleed. Coensar must hand Durand to the mob. What choice did the man have? But Durand wondered about his old captain's mind. Duty, honor, peace, and justice had tied the man's hands. But what would be in his heart? Relief? Guilt? Or a measure of both? Durand wondered what he deserved. Both Ailric and Deorwen had bothered him about how many Lost souls followed him. How many had he slain since he left his father's hall ten years ago?

In the haunted dark, Durand remembered Deorwen looking down, her gaze untainted by all the disappointments of ten foolish years. And he wished once more, despite burning halls and lapping specters, that he might live.

FINALLY, THE CELLAR door rattled wide once more. Durand blinked into the open air as the Lost fled, and he saw Coensar's face. The dusty priest was with him.

"I must tie your hands," the steward murmured. It might as easily have been, "It is death. We've decided." But Durand could only nod. He remembered the months of fighting at this man's side, besting Radomor, proving his worth to this man more than Lamoric or any of the others. He locked his hands behind his back and Coensar led him up an unfamiliar stair. Almost, he wished he had never seen Deorwen in the courtyard.

"You must prepare yourself, Sir Durand," said the priest.

As Coensar helped him from the dark, Durand became conscious of a curious shrilling on the air. The inner courtyard was bare and empty.

"We've led them out," murmured Coensar. "This way." And the steward took Durand up a narrow stair that rose from the cobbles to the battlements along the wall overhead.

The Rooks perched among the battlements. For an instant, the fat carbuncle winked in one black beak.

"You can see it in his eyes, brother. He is the sacrifice. As every new king spends his three days in the tomb before he may be crowned, cleansing himself for the kingdom."

"Three days under stone!"

"Though this will be a different sacrifice—an offering of blood for peace. A few moments in the air. This is in our man's mind. But, in his soul, perhaps he wonders whether he should have died long ago."

Durand set foot on an uneven stair.

"In the siege, brother!"

"When Coensar, his mentor, struck him down. Before so much that he loved came apart."

"A simpler life. The hero! No muddled years of guilt and misery, on and on, year after year. Betrayed. His woman grieving for her secret love, lost."

"But the king lives on after his three days in the tomb, does he not, brother?"

"True. True. Durand will be a more . . . complete sacrifice. Ah. And here is the Herald as well. I think we will give the fellow a wide berth."

Durand climbed the shadowed steps up into the red glare of sunset.

There was Abravanal. Kandemar the Herald watched like a thing of alabaster staring into Durand's soul. And the men of Yrlac roared like a tide beyond the notched ring of the battlements. Coensar was a step behind him. The whole of the tournament crowd spread below the high wall.

And somewhere, Abravanal's boys had set up a grindstone. The mysterious shrilling would be Gunderic's Sword of Judgment. They were grinding the edge of the outsized blade, sharp as razors.

Durand swallowed against a sudden knot of dread. He could hardly see the way forward in the glare, but he straightened his back and walked through the jeers toward the duke.

Deorwen was there. Where she had come from, Durand did not know. She looked wildly at him and rounded on Abravanal. "You must not do this! He has been your man his whole life!"

Abravanal blinked his blue eyes, rigid. Where he stood by the wall, the crowd would be able to see him.

Durand's tongue was thick in his throat. He wished they'd taken Deorwen below. She should not see.

"Morcar tried to kill us," she persisted. "Tried to kill you. Your daughter. How can you take his word? Is this what you want?"

"When have we ever had what we want? When?" said Abravanal. The Herald looked on.

Stiff-necked, Coensar took his place in the blazing sunset at the duke's side. The old priest joined them, looking foolish and shabby beside the stark Herald. "To be snatched by birds," the priest was muttering. "It is a thing not to be believed."

"Your Grace," said Durand. "I understand." And Deorwen gaped at him, knowing that nothing could be averted.

Coensar turned into the bloody light. "Peers. Atthians. Hear the pronouncement of your duke and liege lord under the Eye of Heaven!"

And there was Abravanal with the light gleaming in every spidery hair. "Sir Durand Col, son of Hroc. Champion of Gireth. Today, you must face your doom. We will pray for your soul." The Herald would not look from Durand's face.

The grindstone rattled to a halt. A guard took hold of Durand's hands and he was brought, roughly, to a gap in the parapet and into the red glare. Someone had thrust a platform out over the wall, like hoardings in a time of siege. "You'd best go forward," said the guard. "Out on our little scaffold. Best to go on your own two feet. Careful. It's higher than you think." The man's breath was full of onions.

Deorwen could not rush to him. He could not call to her.

He took the one tall step up into the gap and walked upon the bending planks, twenty fathoms above the crowd, on a platform the size of a
door. He caught his balance—no mean feat with his hands bound. The
naked face of the wall and steep hillside below him blazed. Somewhere
behind him, they were hustling the Sword of Judgment to Coensar's hand.
Durand could almost feel the razor edges free upon the air.

"You'll have to kneel, sir," the guard said in his ear. The rope tugged
at his wrists as Durand dropped to his knees, in full view of the multitude. Once upon a time, Durand had stood before a throng with the
Sword of Judgment in his hands. It was after Ferangore, when Moryn
Mornaway faced Abravanal's judgment. In Atthias, the killing stroke was
a downward blow. He must bend. There would be no block. The scaffold creaked and flexed under his knees, little more than a gangplank.

Then Coensar was on the scaffold too, the whole thing groaning and
struggling as though the two men were sharing a bed. Flashes of light
played over the planks as Gunderic's Sword caught the sunset.

"I do not want this," said Coensar.

"Durand!" It was Deorwen's voice.

She watched from the gap. Durand could not stand her there. She
should not see. He could not endure it with her looking on. "Get her away
from here," Durand said.

"Aye. Yes." He heard Deorwen curse them all, and the sound of her
voice nearly got him crying.

Below, red faces stared up. The downward glance also showed Durand
that his train of Lost men and women now waited for him in the shadows among the living, silent where the living roared. Soon, Durand knew,
he must join them.

Coensar balanced on the rough tongue of wood.

"You'd best duck your head," he said. Durand thought he heard the
man swallow. He was breathing hard.

Durand imagined breaking free: sending Coensar toppling from the
scaffold. Bolting back into the keep. He would find a horse. He pictured
himself hauling up the gate and charging down into the woods. But the
fantasy was like a bubble on a pond. There was no freedom.

He saw fierce Leovere. He saw Morcar jeering. The Eye of Heaven
blazed over the forest. Men swung wineskins and the Lost slavered for
the wine, crowding close even as Coensar loomed at Durand's shoulder,
Gunderic's Sword in his hands. He would make the killing blow. Coensar would swing for all he was worth, hauling the blade down from the
Heavens. It took great force to fell a man at a stroke.

Durand closed his eyes, thinking of Deorwen. Someone tried to fling a clod of earth, but it was a long throw from the skirt of that hill.

"Coensar," called the duke, "it cannot be delayed any longer." Durand glanced back for a moment, then settled himself. "Father, it is time," Abravanal said, prompting the untidy priest.

The priest scrambled up into a gap in the parapet, craning his neck. "My son, your doom is upon you, as it must come to all. Ready yourself to stand before the Keeper of the Bright Gates and bow before the Throne of far Heaven."

Durand bowed his head.

"May word of your deeds have reached the Halls of Heaven before you," concluded the priest. "Proceed, Lord Coensar."

"Yes, Father," said Coensar.

"Hell. I am sorry," he said, and he took a great gulp of air. Durand pictured Gunderic's Sword flashing high in the sunset.

But Coensar was no headsman.

And Gunderic's Sword was not Coensar's blade.

The ancient weapon was an oversized thing, too long and too broad for a fighting man.

Over the dizzying thunder of his heart, Durand heard a splintered clang. Something hard clacked from his bent head, and a confusion of bright shapes flashed and fell. They tumbled from the scaffold in a welter of blood.

A hand caught his collar.

An instant later, he would have followed the blood into the crowd.

"Not now," Coensar rasped.

Durand blinked with his nose suddenly against the rough planks and he could not understand.

Gunderic's bright blade had shattered.

But why? The grindstone may have ruined the temper of the old blade. The point might have caught the parapet on Coensar's backswing. Or a wild stroke might have caught the stone at the tail of its arc. Perhaps Coensar had deliberately smashed the thing, or it had broken over Durand's stiff neck.

He would never know more of what had happened than he did at that moment. There was a flash, and no one saw clearly.

A dazed and dripping Durand felt a grubby scrabbling at his back. He heard a knife and felt the pop of the ropes at his wrist. The hasty blade snagged a crescent from his palm. "Not for them," Coensar said. "Not for this!"

There were hundreds of wide eyes and gaping mouths.

"Get up, Durand," said Coensar.

"Justice!" cried the men of Yrlac.

Coensar was shaking his head over the gulf. "Get off this accursed scaffold, Durand!"

"The sword . . ." said Abravanal. "The sword is shattered. What have you done, Coensar?"

Barely able to master his limbs, Durand climbed back over the battlements. The Herald of Errest stared down on him as he reached safety. Durand saw Deorwen, as shattered as the old blade.

Coensar stabbed his dagger back into its sheath, his lip twisted in a snarl, and strode out upon the scaffold. "That is all the justice they will get! Drop the gates and draw the bar!"

Durand could hear Leovere. "Coensar, you are bound by the laws of Errest! You cannot find for your man. Where were his oath-helpers? What could the man prove?"

Coensar thrust his hand toward Durand and the parapet. "The man's bruises bear witness."

"And what of Baradan? What of his blood?"

"And what of that shrine? And what of that mill?"

"We see how things stand! We see what *our* people mean to *their* duke. If we had forgotten in the past, we will not forget again! Tell the old man that he has held Yrlac too long! He is no part of it. He will never be. Before the peers of both our lands, I tell you that this injustice will end. No man of Gireth will hold the land of my fathers lest he bleeds for it."

His allies roared.

Coensar stood on that narrow platform with the sunset blazing all around. "We will see who bleeds, Leovere!"

13
Kingdom of the Hornbearer

Before dawn, the castle was waking. Durand had spent an anxious night alone. He could not sleep. He could not hold still with the Lost all around. And he must have looked like another specter, stalking the halls in battered, bloody war gear. Of the living, no one but Ailric came near him, though the little keep was packed from cobbled yard to tower rooms with pages, knights, country damsels, and serving men. No one knew what to make of Gunderic's Sword, a bungled death, and a sudden war.

In any case, with Leovere raging, the men of Gireth must get Abravanal out at once and ride hard for home. Unless Coensar was a very great fool, he would run the cavalcade north too fast for Leovere to gather forces. Durand paced a back room as Ailric packed. His hand ached. His head throbbed. And bruises covered his body like spots on a leopard's pelt. But he would be ready for whatever Leovere planned.

Deorwen appeared in the chamber door.

Durand winced. "Coensar will have us leaving at once. Try to keep Leovere off balance if he's anything clever in mind."

"Durand," said Deorwen. A pointed glance sent Ailric bowing out of the room, and she closed the door neatly behind him.

"Deorwen. I am sorry." Why did he assume that she was coming to talk about travel arrangements?

"You're not coming with us."

Durand started. He spread his hands. "But I am the Duke's Champion. I've sworn to watch over his—"

"Coensar has summoned every liegeman in Fellwood. They are saying that Leovere cannot muster so many this side of Pennons Gate."

"But I've—"

She took a half-step forward, her eyes glinting in the gloom. "For now you are Champion, Durand. But you will not be accompanying the duke back into Gireth." Durand was outcast. Exiled. Banished from court. From everything he knew.

"And he has sent you to tell me?" Durand said.

"I came for Coensar. He has been tearing his hair. There will be fire and blood across Gireth despite ten years trying to make a peace."

"I did not set out to kill Baradan!"

Though Durand could hardly contain his frustration, Deorwen came nearer. Did she know he couldn't think with her so near?

"Morcar knew what you would do, that you couldn't stay your hand when his men goaded you. I am not sure they meant to lose Baradan, but now Morcar's lot have their way. There can be no peace between Leovere and the duke."

Durand shook his head. He felt heavy. It was impossible.

"Durand, it nearly killed me to watch you on that scaffold, but I do not know what to think of us any longer. What have we become after so long? It is all scars around us, I think. All guilt and grief. But I could have killed you myself when you had Coensar take me away. I am so tired. All these years in that house of sorrows. Nothing but memories. I have sent a thousand Lost souls to their rest in that old city. Night after night. But still I am haunted. They beseech me in my dreams, even here."

"I know something about that," Durand said.

"Durand. You should be dead." He could almost see the execution in her eyes. "Many times over."

He did not want to say good-bye to her.

Very nearly, she grabbed hold of him, such a fool was he. There were tears in her eyes—in his eyes too.

"You can get free, Durand. Find another life."

"But what am I now? What am I to do?" They were words he should not have uttered.

"I do not know about tomorrow, but today there is something. Here." She pulled away, and shoved the door a fraction. Beyond her, Durand saw old Berchard standing with Ailric.

She closed the door again, adding, "Berchard is another exile. He came to petition the duke for aid. But do you remember how he ended up in the Marches, Durand? After fighting for Lamoric and Coensar and Abravanal, he came away an old man with nothing."

"Aye. It was sad." The man deserved more.

"He had something here in Fellwood, and now that too is taken from him. He came to Abravanal to ask the duke to intercede." Begging favors from a man he'd insulted. "Berchard is not well, I think. You will have noticed that his eyesight has failed him."

Durand blinked. This was new, but maybe there had been signs that a wiser man might have noted. "He has been leaning on my man, Ailric. I thought he was hard of hearing, maybe."

She smiled gently. "He might be both."

"And Abravanal will not be interceding for the old man." Not with Leovere hard on his heels and war coming.

"He has nothing left, Durand. He came to the Lindenhall with a shield-bearer, but even his man has joined the duke's service for the journey back to Acconel. Do you see?

"There may be something you can do. You are Champion of Gireth, still."

"Until they think to take it."

"Until they think to take it, yes. But you have been given a reprieve, and the world is thick with omens, a chance at another way. I am tired of Abravanal's court. These people. Gireth. Yrlac. Acconel. All of it. But I won't leave the girl. I cannot. But perhaps you can step free of it all, Durand. Maybe it is time to bid farewell."

She seized him in a fierce embrace, clinging despite the stains and armor. He never remembered how small she really was.

"I will do it," he said. "Of course I will. I have been blind."

COENSAR'S CAVALCADE WAS leaving. Durand clapped his eye to an arrow loop and watched as the column lumbered from the Lindenhall. Carts and warhorses wallowed over the churned turf of the lists, setting their misty course for the track that led toward the slate-blue face of the Blackroots. Before he noticed, Ailric, Berchard, and Heremund had joined him. Durand kept his eyes fixed on the duke's people. Almora glanced backward, perhaps to see him at his peephole, dwindling with distance. Coensar, once, twisted in his saddle as if he felt Durand's stare needling his spine. Without him, they rode into the half-charted wilds.

"Durand Col, there's men watching the Lindenhall," Heremund said.

"Men?" said Durand.

Heremund jostled into the arrow loop for a squint and pointed at the forest verges with one blunt finger. "There. There. There." There were shapes in the trees. Durand saw a man with curling copper hair.

"Not the best choice for a spy, red hair," said Durand.

"Not sure they care who knows."

"Coen knows?" Durand said.

"Aye. Coen knows. But I'd wager they'll be looking for you. Your friend Morcar has put up some land as a sort of reward. It's enough to set up ten men happily enough, I think."

Berchard smiled, not bothering to crowd to the bit of light and breeze with the others. "Has he? Ten men, you say? That might suit me. Is there a comfortable hall for the lord of the manor, did you say, Heremund?"

"Don't be clever, Berchard. It seems I stung Morcar a bit," said Durand.

"It's Baradan's land, I gather," said Heremund. "I'm afraid you put an end to the line of Baradan with that hedge chopper."

Durand glanced at the Yrlaci men in the trees, thinking that he should ride out and give the devils a chance at him.

"Three men watching the castle. Every one watching for us."

"For you," said Berchard.

"For now they'll be busy counting heads, making sure Leovere's got no surprises if he wants to take the duke on the road. After that, they'll look after themselves and come looking for you."

"Let Leovere count. His men can count off every nag and shield-bearer. It won't do him any good. He can't take Coen on the road."

As he spoke, however, another thought occurred to him. "At this moment, Leovere's men have got their eyes on Coensar's column."

"Every man, I'd wager," said Heremund. "What are you thinking?"

At that moment, one of the castle's men was rushing past. It was the fellow who had helped Durand out onto the scaffold. "Here," said Durand.

Blind Berchard did better, catching the man by the arm and bringing him up with a jerk. "Here, friend. Is there a sally port? A door somewhere? Something we could get a horse through?"

The man hesitated a moment, astonished. Maybe leery of Durand's temper. "Aye, Lordship. There is, Lordship. Would you care to see it, maybe?"

The three men were smiling. "Aye," said Durand. "We would."

And before Coensar could cram the rest of his column through the front door, Durand's band had tumbled out the back. Jouncing with loose gear in their hands, they hared off into the forest and were soon a league from the pretty Lindenhall and all its spies and tournament grounds.

THEY LED THEIR horses between giant trees, knowing that even one glimpse from the men at the Lindenhall might have put fifty soldiers on their trail. They struck thickets of thorn and leathery acres of open ground without warning, and listened hard, cringing at the uncanny echoes of every hoofbeat and rattle of tack under the green vaults. Sometimes they were certain they heard others on the move, beyond the gray trunks.

Sooner or later, someone must know they'd gone. Soon or later, someone would come looking.

Finally, without a word, the four men swung themselves into their saddles.

At first, they rode south into the forest wastes to get clear of the Lindenhall, then they swung west and came upon a luminous region where clouds of bluebells billowed over the forest floor. Even Berchard's jaw dropped as they plodded through the lavender mists.

"So, what is the story?" said Heremund. "I'd like to know why I'm riding into the West Marches."

"Aye, well," said Berchard, "Abravanal left me landless in Yrlac. He had his own problems, I suppose. Too much on his mind to make sure his loyal men didn't starve on the road."

"You threatened His Grace, didn't you?" said Heremund.

Berchard grunted. "And so there I was with nothing but my few bits and pieces. A blade. Friendless. And I took up with these Fellwood boys and found a place at the table of one of these forest lords in the West Marches: one of old Baron Hardred's liegemen—thank Heaven he didn't know how blind I was. But the poor man died and left his widow with the lands and hall. Avina. And she needed someone around the place with some sense, who'd listen. I tell you, though, she was a fine girl. Could have been my daughter, I suppose, but a fine-looking girl with a smiling, open way about her."

"I thought *you* were the one going blind," said Heremund.

Berchard only smiled. "I've never known another girl like her. We were wed when the snows melted a year ago."

He paused, then added, "There was fever last winter," like a man confessing.

In that mad place of bluebells and gray forest giants, Durand thought of Deorwen riding north, and the girl, Almora. Heremund was saying something about it being a shame.

"It was my doom to lose her before a year was out. She would read to me. I never minded what. But I buried her under the Sowing Moon." He swallowed. "And under the Sowing Moon, Avina's damnable cousin came crashing into her hall. I could go hang. It would be his land. And I was out again with just my few bits and pieces and just my shield-bearer to keep me from losing my way to God knows where." Blind and alone. "But Baron Hardred's holding his Springtide Court at Leerspoole—in two days' time, now—it's his land to grant or not. Hardred holds most of his land from Abravanal. And so I groped my way back to that devil Abravanal, hoping someone there would speak up for me with Hardred. That is meant to be my chance. If he hears me, there might yet be justice."

He hesitated, overcoming rage and shame. "Avina's cousin? His people? They came for me with swords. It was midnight. Past midnight. I can see well enough for that, at least. My man had to fumble for my things in the road."

There was mud on some of his gear, even then.

"Leerspoole," Durand vowed.

"Yes," said Berchard.

"My word on it," said Durand.

But, in the next instant, they rode into a riot of fresh tracks through the bluebells. Brand tossed his big head, shying. Someone else had come this way.

Ailric was off his dun rouncy and down in the track like a scent-hound. "Horses. Not sure how many. Last night, maybe. Fresh anyway. Heading south."

"South?" said Berchard, shaking the anger and shame of the moment before. "There's nothing south of here, boy. I'd be surprised to hear of a charcoal burner's hut south of here. The land's not settled. It's half mad to ride *this* far."

Durand squinted back through the trees, remembering what he could of the lay of the land. "They will have come from the Lindenhall or nearly. Maybe on the Leerspoole Road."

Heremund scrubbed his chin. "Quickly west, and then sharply south. What else can you tell of them, son?"

Ailric shook his head. "It's Leovere, I think."

Berchard laughed. "Well, you are a wonder or a liar, boy. That's certain."

"The ground here is very good. Clay more than anything. The smith at the Lindenhall makes his shoes on his own pattern. Narrow. Heavy bar stock. Leovere was on that fine-boned gray of his. Toe-in, a little. The animal threw a shoe in the excitement yesterday. I saw his man having it reshod. Just the right forefoot. This is the same animal. Or one very like it."

"Damn me, but you would make a fine huntsman," marveled Berchard.

But this news puzzled Durand. "He should be riding north. He'll want to make the pass before Coensar, if he can. Could he be hunting us?"

"Well, he's missed us, if that was in his mind. And there's nothing south of here but trees and dead men," said Heremund. "The Glade of Crowned Bones is down that way. The Solantines say it is the place where Aidmar of Aubairn fell in his flight from the Enemy after Uluric blew his horn."

"Uluric's Horn again," said Durand.

"That's where he and his men turned on their pursuers, thinking to hold them while his people ran for Pennons Gate. As the Solantines tell it, they found a neat heap of their skulls with Aidmar's crown glinting on the top. I'm told they left it, centuries now. Nobody got through."

"They closed the gates," said Durand, remembering the words of Maedor Greyshield. "There's no settlement at Crowned Bones?"

"Are you mad?" said Berchard. "Who but the meanest half-wit would hang about in such a place?"

"I would say that the whole of Leovere's party has gone to Crowned Bones. They left last night. They rode swiftly. Recklessly so," said Ailric.

"He brings the Horn of Uluric to the Crowned Bones once more. He is enraged."

"Host of Heaven," Durand mumbled. "We would be better off if he's sent his men for me."

"You're no favorite of those Yrlac boys," Berchard allowed.

"Whatever Leovere is up to, we cannot afford to stop here scratching our heads. Leerspoole grows no closer."

THEY GROPED THROUGH Fellwood, clambering over muscle-bound roots. From the empty acres at their backs, branches snapped and stones clattered without explanation. Once, Durand wheeled Brand around and charged into the silence, only to flush a boar from its nest in the thorns.

The forest was an uncanny place no matter what Leovere had chosen to do.

They saw impossible beasts. An elk larger than a warhorse watched them pass, his coat rain-beaded and dark as the earth. Wolves and ragged bulls prowled the distant shadows. More and more, they felt that the sounds of stealthy pursuit dogged their steps.

"Perhaps we are in luck," said Berchard. "I'm sure there is someone behind us. Killers likely. Leovere's vengeance flashing on a dozen blades. Luck of a troublesome breed, but luck nonetheless."

Durand grunted a laugh.

Soon, the Eye of Heaven hung low before them, pricking the walls of beech and oak with blazing needles. Ailric was sure he heard running water somewhere ahead.

"We shall soon lose the light," Ailric said.

Heremund nodded. "We will have to set up camp."

"Leovere's men will see a fire," said Ailric, "if it is them."

"Or smell it, aye," said Durand. He did not say what he thought of lying out among the Lost without even a few embers to see by. He had done it before.

"Heaven save me from a cold camp in these bedeviled woods. There must be a few hours left to us," said Berchard. "Maybe there is a kindly crofter somewhere out here who's a bed for a few stalwart strangers."

"I shouldn't think so, Sir Berchard," Ailric said.

"'I shouldn't think so.' A man's allowed some hope, ain't he?

"I would be happier if we raised Leerspoole tomorrow," he continued, "but here we are. This wood is riddled with bogs and streams and ravines. While the meanest roads might miss or bridge them, we'll be sure to blunder into every last one." A branch pawed at the man's face. "These trees! We'll miss Leerspoole altogether, like as not."

"You're better off than you were yesterday, aren't you?" said Durand.

Berchard snorted. "At least you lot are as blind as I am. There is that. But I suppose I'm the guide, ain't I? Heremund doesn't know these woods as well, Heaven help us!"

Durand couldn't help a grin, even in that damp and haunted wasteland.

"Now don't you laugh at me," Berchard said. "I can hear. Let's have a think."

The man clapped the palm of a hand over his eyes. "Here now, what was it the boy said, that he heard running water? Well, boy, was there water? And don't just nod."

"Aye, Sir Berchard."

"'Aye, Sir Berchard' it is, then. Let us bring hope to bear on the problem. It may be that Ailric has heard the River Keen. It runs through these woods. And Leerspoole stands on the River Keen, so it will make a road for us. When we strike the river, we will be on its doorstep, or near enough."

The forest was very dark. Only a few coppery rays reached them.

Durand heard Rooks caw above the canopy, laughing.

Durand said, "This Hardred is meant to be Abravanal's man. I think I'd have been happier if he'd come to the Lindenhall and saved us all the journey."

"Old Hardred? No. Hardred will not be moved. He has seen eighty winters. Ninety, though he's as fearsome a creature as draws breath. He's held a Springtide Court at Leerspoole at the turning of the Farrow Moon for sixty years. Neither daft king nor mad old duke will pry him away. These Marcher barons are little kings down here."

"I have seen him only once," said Heremund. "Cold and wild as a hawk he was. Crabbed hands locked on his throne. He came to Fellwood early, did Hardred. When the trees belonged to no man."

Just then, something cracked in the trees, louder by far than any man's imagination.

The Rooks called out, "Haw! Haw!"

"Right, that's enough," said Durand. A legion of bone-gray trunks stood behind him, washed in red where the light struck them. "Whoever follows, there cannot be many of them. And if we don't deal with them, it won't matter where we go. Leovere will have us long before we reach Leerspoole."

"We might lose him in the dark. We could find some stony ground. Make it difficult," said Heremund.

Ailric was looking back into the coppery trees. "This one is too close."

And, of course, Ailric was right. Their pursuer would not need to see tracks to follow five iron-shod beasts on stony ground in this echoing place. Durand stroked his bearded jaw.

"Ailric, we will lie in wait as the others press on. Berchard and Heremund, keep moving. Lead the rest of the horses, and we will catch you up."

After a few curt nods, and a disapproving shake of Heremund's head, the horses clattered on while Durand and his shield-bearer doubled back and hid themselves where their party had plowed through a patch of bracken and holly.

They waited as the echoes of their party muttered into the distance, and within a few minutes Durand and his man might have been alone in Creation. The spy could not be allowed to escape. Leovere's men were sure to be nearby, and a word could bring them. Durand resolved that he would be quick. There was little point putting the man to the question. With the spy gone, they would change course and vanish onto stony ground for a time. Disappear. Durand worked his fingers on his flail's handle. Amber needles of light probed Durand's hiding place.

And something screamed. A wet, wild, butchering gibber of a thing, very near.

Without a thought, Durand was on his feet, bulling through the sopping brush. Ailric was running too. There was a dip and twist in the terrain. And they blinked into the sudden gloom of the place, for a moment, seeing nothing.

Then there was a splash. Something spattered Durand's face, his hands.

Streaming, steaming. Bowels lay in a great gleaming slop over the roots of a beech tree. Overhead, Durand saw someone hanging. It was the red-headed spy from the Lindenhall. Leovere had sent one man at least. He'd been split, gutted. Ankles knotted around a branch three fathoms over Durand's head.

Durand spotted the silhouettes of the Rooks leering down, a pair of inky glyphs among the branches.

"What could do such a thing?" began Ailric.

But Durand thought he saw something split from a tree: a towering shape. They should not have left the light.

"Run!" Durand said.

The two men tore back uphill into the warm blush of the Eye of Heaven, all the while conscious of a figure—like a man made of ship's masts—scissoring between the shadows of the trees, striding in the gloom of that low place, seemingly trapped by the blades of sunlight. High among the branches, the thing's head swung like the root ball of some storm-slain tree: an incomprehensible tangle of hair and horns, a mask of mad dispassion.

Ailric had a blade in his fist, his eyes flashing wide.

"There's no fighting it," said Durand. "We must get to the others, to the horses. Before we lose the Eye of Heaven. Run!"

In a wild rush of stumbles and flashing branches, they overtook the rest of their party. "A thing in the trees! A giant," said Durand.

"Ride for water! A river!" said Heremund. "Our only hope!"

And, more by instinct than reason, Durand spurred into the Eye of Heaven, slashing headlong to the high ground, urging Brand through hollows and valleys. Everywhere where the night pooled. It clung to the trees, to their very backs. Durand felt the vast being behind them. Beeches cracked and fell. The thing lunged from shadow to shadow, long-legged. The darkness stretched; the thing drew nearer.

But Ailric had heard water.

The Eye of Heaven was already caught in the reaching branches ahead. Timber crashed under the monster's hands. "There!" said Ailric.

Durand shouted, "Go!" and spurred Brand between the gray trunks.

And then they saw it: Not the stream, but a wall—a pale rectangle against the darkness of the forest. Durand cut toward it, abandoning the river, if river there was. He drove for the white shape, baring his broken teeth as a bondman's longhouse swelled from the gloom. He saw stout timbers and a mountain of gray thatch.

Durand leapt from Brand's saddle at the last instant to wrench the low door wide and throw his comrades through. He slammed the door in the horned face of the forest devil. Durand had seen a bar, and this he rammed home in the same instant that the great specter beat a deafening thunder from the door. The blows loosened Durand's bones, but they soon stopped. Then, the thing was at the roof, and the old beams shook, raining debris into the cottage. Then again. And then nothing.

The cottage creaked, settling in the inexplicable stillness.

For a hundred heartbeats, they waited in the gloom of the longhouse, breathing damp air thick with the crumbling stink of pigeons or swallows by the thousand.

"What is this place?" said Berchard.

"Must be someone's hunting lodge. Empty. A bit much for some hermit, and I saw no sign of a farm. Hard to be sure in the dark," said Heremund. "I would be happier on the other side of a river. I'm sure there was something ahead. You could smell the reeds."

Durand found a shuttered window near the low door and peered out. Outside, the giant moved indistinctly against the branches, dark as beetles. Had there been a wind, it might have been another tree swaying.

"That thing could have the door off in a moment," said Durand. "The roof!"

Heremund answered. "The Banished won't cross a threshold, some of them. The Strangers neither, depending. Some houses are armed with all manner of toys. Iron at the windows. Burials at the cornerstone. Shoes in the smoke hole. Pots of pins and piss under the doorstep. Curses and charms and all that."

"I'd do that and more if I were building a house in this place," said Berchard.

"Well," said Durand, "something's kept the devil off."

"It's cold in this old place and it stinks," said Berchard. "Someone see if there's anything to start a fire." And Ailric began to scuffle in the dark.

"What did you see of this thing, Durand?" said Heremund.

"It is tall. Very tall," said Durand. "As long-limbed as a spider. Its head is a mess of tusks or horns or God-knows. Narrow and stooped like a long corpse in a short grave."

"What about *on* its head. Did you see anything?"

"I don't know." There hadn't been time.

"It might be the one they call the Hornbearer."

"Impossible," said Durand. The Hornbearer was something from Maedor's day. From Pennons Gate and the Lost Princes. It was a monster from children's stories. "People would say if they'd seen that. There'd be no one in Fellwood at all, if it were here."

"Fellwood is deep. These forest barons have only dabbled at its margins. The Host of Errest may have broken the Enemy's hold on the north, but the Hornbearer was not slain. It sneered at the men of Atthia with a battle horn, in mockery of Uluric's Horn, and a crown to match the crown of Aidmar of Aubairn."

"You asked about what was on its head," said Durand.

"If you see a crown on its head and a great curved horn round its neck, you will have seen the Hornbearer. It was called, in mockery, the Crowned Hog. And, if the Hornbearer is here, he is not alone."

Durand turned his eye back on the window, peering out. He could not be sure of crown or horn, but the monster was there. Still, now, and a few dozen paces into the forest. "What is it waiting for? What do we know of these maragrim?" It would not take such a giant long to snap the roof beams. They must have a plan.

Berchard chimed in. "Things from nightmares, thrown up to destroy living men. Drinkers of souls. We should have taken the road."

"They are souls lost in battle, swept up by the Enemy in blood and guilt before they could rise to Heaven—maybe. Or the fallen turned against their own. Enthralled by the Enemy, anyway. There was talk of hags—the Beldame Weavers, our side called them—sweeping the air over the battlefields with nets or bags. I was never clear. The Enemy had many creatures. These, the Sons of Heshtar used by the battalion. There is a great deal that a man might know of such things, Durand."

"They must hide from the Eye of Heaven," said Ailric. He was working low, striking sparks at what Durand guessed to be a hearthstone in the middle of the floor. "You said they don't like rivers."

"No," said Heremund. "Nor fire, I think. There is something about the curse that binds them. A bit of bone or tooth or hair somewhere. But I may be inventing what I do not know."

Berchard grunted. "The Fellwood is one of their haunts, that's sure, but not so far north. In the south. In the west, maybe. Not many survive in the settled Marches."

"Well," said Durand, "this one's right outside." He hardly dared to breathe the words. It was only a few paces from the door, soot on the coal-sack of the trees.

"None alive knows their number," said Heremund. "Your heroic ancestors left many behind in their rush to drive the Enemy over the sea. But this is not one of the general multitude. A great man, he would have been. A hero, fallen. A great man cast down and bound." What shame could bind so fearsome a soul?

"Five hundred winters," said Berchard. "Lost and bound. More! What will become of us? I've fixed it for us all now."

It was hard to hear Berchard talk this way. Thankfully, then there was a flash as fire bloomed between Ailric's palms.

"I cannot believe this door will keep such a thing at bay till— *Host of Heaven*." Durand took his eye from the shutters, turning with the others to warm his hands, and saw the room for the first time—along with the things that shared its narrow confines.

"Why has everyone shut up?" said Berchard. "What is it?"

Everywhere, misshapen beings crowded the longhouse, groping at the few sticks of furniture, crouching in the cottage corners: abominations thrown together in mockery of beasts and men and worse. These were the maragrim of legend, the drinkers of souls. One mad thing leered through a monk's cowl, and there was a man's outsized head sporting the limbs of a crab. The things roiled in tangles. They rocked and slavered. And, as the fire caught, they began to murmur.

"Durand?" Berchard hissed. "What is that?"

But Durand did not answer. He had seen a rafter of slack faces, and, beyond the monstrous things, bones—thousands of bones. The mad will of the maragrim had wrenched apart the bones of hundreds of men and driven each thigh and rib into the thatch. Ribs swirled in flat fans, pinwheels. Bands of long bones spiraled around grinning skull after skull. A man might empty the charnel houses of a city without finding so many bones.

He heard a rising moan: the maragrim in greed or despair, trapped between life and death. The maragrim would drink their souls. The house was their snare.

"Durand, by the Host of Heaven, what is it?" Berchard said as talons and toes and fingers reached him.

"We must leave!" Durand answered. "We must risk the thing outside!"

With a nod from Ailric and cursing agreement from the others, the four shoved their way out the door, tearing a path through the groping appendages of a hundred maragrim and into the clearing beyond.

Durand imagined that he might hold the giant thing, stopping it long enough to let the others run or ride, but in a few heartbeats he knew that they were not alone. The forest seethed with fiends. Chittering, rocking abominations crowded the bushes. A glance took in bare skulls. Cowls. Animal limbs. Empty visages. And the pulsing carapaces of vermin. He saw Berchard's horse broken up like a roast among a dozen fiends. The horses thrashed in jumbled talons. And the things from the longhouse tumbled into the clearing around Durand's men as the giant stared down on the scene, fathoms high and as black, narrow, and still as a long-limbed spider stretched in its web. Durand could see the crown glint high in its hackles, now; a dark horn of bronze curled round its shoulder.

In the face of all this, Durand might have died then without a murmur, but—only a few steps away—the bastards had Brand. And maybe it was the sight of the red horse wallowing in the hands of the maragrim that woke Durand, but he moved. He caught Ailric by the surcoat. "That river of yours!" Shriker was still standing. Brand was alive. They would ride downhill and hope to hit water before they were overcome. He threw the shield-bearer at old Berchard. "Ride!"

Durand took a tearing stride and flung himself on Brand's neck, snatching Heremund up behind him and howling back to Ailric: "Ride! Ride or be lost!" And Brand was away, bursting through the ring of fiends as Durand snarled and swung the iron head of his flail through the bones and scales and God-knows of the maragrim. Brand tore free.

The trees flashed past, pale as specters but hard as marble. But Durand clung to Brand's bull-neck as the animal plunged into holes and thrashed on. They were still alive. He twisted in his saddle, spotting Ailric and Berchard jouncing on Shriker's back.

Durand rode to open the distance. There had to be a river. It had to appear before a branch or hole threw them all to the maragrim, but he hardly knew where to find it, and the devils were all claws and bounding speed behind him. Durand broke into a clearing of tall grass and saw the Hornbearer, the Crowned Hog, stalking from the black forest, its shins like ships' prows, striding nearer and nearer with a maragrim flood boiling round its ankles. What hope had mortal men against a thing such as this? It would be easier to outrun the wind or wrestle the bones of Creation. They needed the river.

Before Durand's horrified eyes, the forest giant hauled the horn from its shoulders and swung the thing round to its tangled face. But Durand saw Ailric—hardly a pace from the giant's grasp—sheering away.

"The river! The river!" the shield-bearer was screaming. He pointed. A way through! Durand wrenched Brand's head round, vaulting a cataract of fiends to match Ailric's course. And the giant sounded its horn. The roar of it stamped a hurricane of leaves into the air. It resounded in Durand's bones. He could not breathe. But, before Durand could pitch from the saddle, the ground tipped away. They hit the running stream and spun and crashed.

Through glassy blackness, Durand fought to the air and thrashed for the far bank. Brand's hooves threatened to batter him to death, then the horse was gone, tumbling in the current. Durand fetched up against something solid in the dark: the slime of a piling. There was some sort of pier or landing. Durand groped past the thing in the current and soon felt mud and reeds under his fingernails. He clawed his way up the far slope.

Their horses had tumbled off into the night—Durand felt a little horror at that. But all four human fugitives had survived the crossing and now lay sprawled among the reeds and willows, unable to do anything more than pant in the dank air. But Durand could not leave the maragrim unwatched for long. He levered himself from the turf and peered through a screen of leaves, noting first the uncanny silence. He could hear nothing but running water and the wind in the high branches.

But, as he squinted into the dark forest, Durand spotted a glint among the trees. Eyes blinked. And soon he made out dozens, hundreds—thousands—more obsidian eyes winking. And he knew that a host watched him. They were high and low, hanging in the trees and hunkering low like a shield-wall at the water's edge. This was the war-host of the Hornbearer. And, as Durand watched the silent, insectile eyes, something enormous stirred and the Hornbearer himself strode to the riverbank. Its black eyes were lost in the broad mask of a face rimmed in tusks and horns. In a single step, it might have crossed the narrow waterway, but it did not follow.

"The river," said Heremund. "Running water. Thank Heaven. You hear these things, but I don't know. How can you trust a bit of cold water to keep a thing like that at bay?"

As Heremund spoke, Durand heard a hollow, comical little splash from somewhere near the maragrim bank.

"It makes a man wonder," said Heremund, "what good were these maragrim to the Enemy when the merest trickle could hold them?"

And then a stone plopped somewhere up the stream.

"I will confess to doubts," said Heremund. "How can they hold the fastnesses of the Fellwood? The old forest is veined with nameless streams and bogs and ponds, but here we are." The skald smeared mud from his forehead. Durand got to his feet.

Another stone splashed into the river. And another. "We must go," Durand said. In an instant, a rolling hail of stones poured into the river. And there were bared teeth glinting now from the far bank. How had the things marched the thousand leagues from the Sea of Darkness over land veined with rivers? How had the things crossed this Fellwood with its uncounted streams? A tree—roots and all—crashed into the river, throwing spray over them all.

The Hornbearer tilted his crowned head.

"Here!" Durand shouted. "Quick!"

The giant bent and plunged its spidery hand into the earth, uprooting a great boulder. Durand looked up into the splayed, flat, featureless face. The tusks and horns. The Hornbearer was as still as an oak. Then, with a sudden twist, the giant flung the stone over the river. Clay and water exploded at the riverbank, spattering Durand and his comrades. In another instant, a second long-limbed fling had buried another boulder in the bank. The Hornbearer tilted its head.

"Run," said Durand.

The men scrambled into the forest, colliding with barricades of thick undergrowth as they thrashed and climbed away from the things at the river. Durand pitched between facing hillsides, careering along a rugged track that rose from the landing at the water's edge. He fought uphill, clawing when he stumbled, catching at the hands of Berchard and Heremund when they fell.

And he stumbled into a broad clearing—and fifty wild-eyed soldiers.

A body of armed men crouched in a ragged crescent with a campsite at their backs. They must have been shaken from their cooking fires by the giant's horn. Now, every man gripped a spear or sword or axe. There was a paddock of fierce war-horses. Tents bulked in the gloom.

As Durand wavered on the edge of their clearing with Heremund and Ailric and Berchard bowling in behind, a familiar figure pushed through the line of warriors. And there was the damnable Morcar, mouthing the air like a frog. He had found a spear somewhere and he shook his head, eyes bulging. "Black Durand," he said. "The Devil of Gireth himself, delivered into our hands!" The man seemed to remember the spear in his fist and let the thing fly. Before Durand could slip the thing, its blade had gashed his hip. And Morcar was screaming: "A barony to the man who takes him!"

The knights of Yrlac rushed Durand, swarming after him or sprinting for the horses.

Wild, Durand shot a glance at the impenetrable branches and high hillsides. There was only the black ravine behind him as the spears surged forward—no way but back to the maragrim. But, as Durand pictured the downhill charge, he saw one desperate chance and seized it. "Follow me!" he roared and was off again, bolting past a gaping Ailric and Berchard and into the ravine.

He pelted back for the river and its devils as Heremund howled after him: "Durand are you mad?"

"Keep up!" Durand replied.

After a few lashing heartbeats, the black flash of the river swung into view. Somewhere, the maragrim thronged in the shadows. But on Durand's heels, the Yrlaci horses tore through the branches. In a moment, he must leap into the water with the horses tumbling after him. The horsemen must sense it. But, at the very last, Durand spotted the planks of the landing. There was just time. "Now!" he roared and threw himself down, rolling into the slime and reeds below the landing.

They slipped under cover just as the Yrlaci horses thundered overhead, blind with an evening by the campfires. The rotten boards shuddered an inch from Durand's face. The ever-canny Ailric had Berchard pinioned in the mud, and they lay as still as crayfish on their bellies. Horses struck the stream. Some balked. Some collided with bone-snapping force. Men thrashed. Men tumbled downstream. Durand could see a slot of open water under the dock. The whole thing might have been a fine joke between fugitive and hunter had it not been for the maragrim.

With the river full of thrashing, cursing men of Yrlac, the maragrim wailed in the darkness. Durand did not look away. The Powers had given him little choice. But this was his doing. Long limbs snatched men from horseback. Pouncing shapes ripped men from the water and carried them back into the talons of the multitude. In moments, the surge of nameless creatures swarmed forward, carrying men and horses like a spinning tide. Yrlacies on the far bank had little hope. Some in the water thrashed toward the safer bank.

Durand clung to one greasy piling, knowing that this carnage had been his wish.

Ailric slipped to Durand's side, whispering, "Look." He pointed at something shimmering at the surface of the water, and, after a moment, Durand understood what he was seeing. Where there had been deep water, now the river brimmed with pebbles. Durand nearly drifted from cover, for here was the maragrim causeway, finished. And, as Ailric pointed, Durand heard stealthy movement through the tangled branches all around the dubious shelter of the landing's deck. Durand felt his stomach lurch. The maragrim had already crossed the river. Durand risked a look around the deck and saw shapes moving among trees until finally the Hornbearer itself stepped from the trees, tall as towers. And here they were lying at its feet with no way to escape.

The Hornbearer strode forward, instantly overhead and swinging down. Durand writhed back under the dock, but the thing's taloned hand snapped wide, catching the deck with sudden force and pulling until the pilings ripped from the slime like rotten teeth.

The monster's face hung over the four men, blank as a saddle and bearded with tusks. The four comrades shrank against the slime. The Hornbearer reared back.

Then there was a sound from the far bank. It ran through the trees and the terrible Hornbearer stopped. Its great horn-shaggy head turned, raining earth and debris onto Durand's bare face.

The sound was the long hollow note of a hunting horn, moaning out from another time, and it was the perfect match for the thing round the Hornbearer's neck.

"From the south," Ailric gasped. "South and east."

"Leovere! He and his horn are at the Crowned Bones," said Berchard.

"He calls the Hornbearer," said Durand.

In an instant, the maragrim were gone.

14

A Road of Stone and Spirits

The men crawled and tumbled downriver in the blackness, finally coming up against a bank of reeds and slime and willows. Durand sloshed out of the current and hauled the rest out by their sopping clothes. None of them could speak. And, when something huge loomed out of the dark at Durand's shoulder, spluttering its hot breath into his ear, Durand gave himself up for dead—until the monstrous creature nosed him and closed its horse teeth on his shoulder. Here was Brand, washed up alive.

In the end, they found three of the animals alive: Brand, Heremund's mule, and Shriker. Nothing could kill Shriker.

No sooner had they corralled the animals than the four men heard voices through the dark. They heard first one call, and then two. Heremund was saying, "This is a lucky thing, finally. I've had the mule eight winters," when Durand clamped his fist over the skald's mouth. How many of Morcar's squadron had survived, Durand could not guess, but he didn't dare risk a fight, not with boys and old men in his charge and a wilderness of maragrim doing Heaven knew what. It was time to get away.

"Leerspoole," Durand said. It was a town and must have priests and walls and fighting men. "We must go." And they left.

The night was a delirium of trees and clawing thorns. They led the horses when the forest closed in, and when the trees soared like temple columns in the vast silences of the wilderness, they scurried like insects over the empty places, starting at every sound, knowing that the snap of a twig could herald an onslaught of horrors beyond counting. It was dawn before any of them dared to speak.

"Host Below, where is this place?" said Berchard.

"I wonder. Was that river the Keen?" Heremund said. They had reached a clearing of high bracken. There was no horizon but trees.

"Another night like that, I cannot stand," said Berchard, and, indeed, he looked very old. His skin was white as a smear of lard.

"That horn!" gasped Heremund. "There we were, like grubs, when that Hornbearer ripped up that dock, writhing against the slime. That face!"

"I begin to think there is something to be said for blindness," said Berchard.

"We may yet regret that trumpet blast," said Heremund, "moaning out through the trees. So like the Hornbearer's groaning cry, and from Crowned Bones." Ailric nodded: south and east, where Leovere's trail had been leading. Where old King Aidmar had fallen to the maragrim after leaving Uluric to die. Where the Solantines had found the dead king's crown: Crowned Bones. A man might profit from knowing how those things were connected.

"Uluric's Horn in Fellwood," said Heremund. "He should have left it in Penseval."

"The duke's men burned Penseval," observed Ailric.

Heremund gaped for a moment. "That's twice. Radomor burned it before that. Poor fool Leovere, but what is he doing?" Leovere came to Fellwood full of rage and vengeance, meaning to give Abravanal one last chance, but carrying the forest horn in his bag.

Durand saw a pair of black birds arrow overhead. Ailric had seen them too. The Rooks settled in the branches of a dead elm.

"What *has* the man done?" said Durand.

Ailric looked back from the ill-omened birds. "The Hornbearer has answered," he said. It was unlike him to play at guesswork. "That is what I think. We heard a call from Penseval, and an answer from the Crowned Bones."

"Now, here is the Hornbearer and his Host." Heremund was shaking his head.

"I like nothing about this," said Durand. "I will not be able to keep clear of Abravanal, after all. We must tell them of this."

Berchard grunted. "Durand, you are a dutiful type, no one would deny it, but I fear we're not in the best shape for riding messenger, lost in Fellwood with all the maragrim from here to the Sea of Storms on our heels."

Heremund's eyes darted. "What strange doom is this that has drawn us to this place, together? What Powers are meddling here?"

The Rooks laughed. The company was riding near their gray perch.

"I am muddled as to direction," said Berchard. "We ran from the river last night. What of it, Ailric? Are we to spend our last day wandering the forest without hope?"

Ailric had found a stone and was eyeing the Rooks. "We've been working north and west," he said. "We've crossed no real river since Last Twilight."

"I say we've yet to meet the Keen. The Keen is deeper than that trickle last night, even below Leerspoole. Below the falls."

"It is true," said Heremund. "We might reach Leerspoole yet."

"You see, Durand? The river cannot be far, and then we need to know upstream or down. Is there a great green cliff? Old Baron Hardred built Leerspoole atop that cliff and dammed the river to keep the forest devils off the island. And for good measure, he's stuck his keep on the top of the island in back of a sixty-foot wall of hundred-year pines."

They all looked to Durand then.

Berchard said, "If we push our way north and take the first tracks toward Pennons Gate, even Heaven could not tell how far we'll get in these trees. We'll be caught on the road. We need to get under cover." And Durand could see the grim certainty of the thing.

"Then we'll find the river. We'll head up and make for Leerspoole." There was no choice.

"The Powers look on," declared Heremund.

"A town in a river with a strong lord, a stone island, a keep, and bridges," said Durand.

"And a sanctuary," said Berchard. "And a priest. There's even an idol in the market square. But we must reach it by nightfall."

Heremund took Durand's sleeve a moment. "From Leerspoole, Hardred has made a good road to the Pennons Gate. The baron might send riders. A warning might still reach Coensar."

The Rooks, right over their heads now, laughed and laughed. But Ailric snapped the stone up into the branches, and one Rook fell, landing between Durand's boots. A ring fell from the thing's mouth. A fat red gemstone winked.

"Hells," said Heremund.

Durand plucked the thing from the leaves.

AILRIC DID HIS best to blaze a trail through tangled acres of branches. They led the horses, laboring over ravines and through clots and knots of thorn. Every sweating league took hours, and there was no way to know how far they had come—or where the town lay. At one point, Ailric stumbled over a stone head, crowned and bearded in an ancient style. After this, the party blundered among building stones and low walls for a time.

"A city," said Heremund. "They built it up. They paved its streets. They stood tall, never guessing that it might end. I could not even tell you its name." They struggled on, knowing only that Leerspoole must appear before dusk.

At noon, they found the River Keen running down a deep cut in the mossy forest floor. The four men stood panting among their animals. They had all been catching sleep in the saddle.

Heremund was working his tongue in the slot where his front teeth should have been. He wiped his face and peered into the half-grotto where the river ran. "Now. Upstream or down? We go the wrong way and we'll have a long walk."

"Till the maragrim catch us. Then it'll be running," jibed Berchard.

"And not much thereafter," said Heremund.

Durand put a hand on Ailric's shoulder. "What say you?"

"Sir Berchard spoke of a cliff below Leerspoole," said Ailric. "It is possible that we've missed it."

"It's thirty fathoms top to bottom!" said Berchard.

"I don't think we can have climbed such a height of land."

"Upstream then, it must be," said Durand. "Are we agreed?"

"Aye, it's the better bet. We might even see Leerspoole before we lose the Eye."

Berchard grimaced. "We'll know when we hear the falls. We might yet have five leagues before us. More, if we are unlucky. Our midnight ramble took us leagues through the trees."

Five leagues might be too far; more would be worse. But Durand only nodded. "We've spent half the day getting here. Dusk will be upon us before we like. We'll water the horses the first time these high banks give way."

THEY PRESSED ON, dogging the River Keen's writhing course through waterlogged leagues of reeds, willow, and alder. Soon, however, the shadows pooled in the low places and seemed to drown the forest in a clammy chill. Durand saw the Eye of Heaven now only when a low beam slipped between the trees, and he cursed every false turn and hesitation, for dusk was coming—and in his mind's eye, Durand saw observers in the green depths beyond the river.

Darkness was settling over the forest.

Ailric was scouting on foot when he stopped still. And, without a word, he bounded onto the inclined trunk of an alder that leaned out over the river.

"What is it?" demanded Berchard. "What's going on?" But Durand only shook his head, watching as the youth peered up the river. Finally, Durand spurred Shriker to the riverbank. It was only as he reached the open air over the stream that he heard the low thunder of the falls.

He called out to the boy. "Can you see it?" They had so little time. It had to be close or there was no use.

"I can!"

Berchard grumped, "It's been the trees, or we must have heard it ages ago."

Durand swung himself down. Even a splendid view of the falls wouldn't help if they were more than half a league distant. But as he bounded out onto the shaking trunk beside the boy, the falls came into view, hanging like a white veil down the face of a green cliff that loomed over their heads some thirty fathoms high. It was nearly close enough. Already, the mist from the thundering water reached them on the breeze.

"I think I see a trail," said Ailric. And Durand saw it too: a switch-backing track stitched its way up the mossy wall.

An eerie call reached Durand from the forest acres behind them. The maragrim had awakened, and now clung to the black trunks of every tree where the failing light could not touch them.

"Still, we might do it," said Durand. "Come!"

Durand and Ailric scrambled from the alder and leapt onto horseback. The company careered through the trees, ducking low boughs and leaping bushes, Berchard clamped behind Ailric on Brand's back.

The maragrim strained like hounds at the sight of their quarry breaking cover; they bayed and howled from their hiding places as Heaven's Eye burned low. Soon the green bulk of the cliff was directly overhead. A track swept away to the left, as rough as a streambed full of tumbled stones, but it carried them up, swinging through misty gulps of flying spray and back into the Eye of Heaven. They pushed the poor horses like devils, for the trees below the river were now full of wild sounds. Screams, sobs, laughter, and bestial brays and howls rang through the gloom. Countless times, Shriker came within inches of tumbling off, his broad hooves flinging stones to clatter among the trees below.

Finally, Durand tore round a last corner and up into the open air—and a clean view of Leerspoole. They'd crested a dike at the cliff top.

And the town stood in a churning black lake like a giant-flung stone. Near at hand, the Keen roiled and heaved against the dam.

Above it all, the Blackroots filled the northern horizon, their peaks glowing golden. But, nearer the cauldron lake and stone isle, the Eye of Heaven was nearly gone, needling through the cool shadows between tree roots and reeds.

And Durand saw the bridge.

They rode, Durand urging Shriker to leap the last paces, where half the bridge was under the flood. And so they barreled into the streets of Leerspoole well before Durand understood that the town was a ruin.

What he had taken for buildings in the red, slanting light were scorched beams.

He reined in amid the blackened timbers.

"What is it now, then? Why's no one talking, eh? Where is everyone?" said Berchard. "What is that smell? Wood smoke?"

Durand surveyed the place. Once, Leerspoole had stood on its tall stone island like bristles on a hog's back. Now the town's houses, shops, and sheds were all in ruins. Gone were the thousand citizens and every soul who'd come for Baron Hardred's Springtide Court.

"Gone," said Durand. "Leerspoole is gone." There were bodies in the wreckage. All teeth and rigid, twists of limbs.

In horror, the four men circled the island, Berchard harrying them with questions. He could not fathom it.

"Hardred's keep will still be standing," said Berchard. "It would take an army two years to pry him out." He gestured to the hilltop, where Durand could see the charred remains of a fearsome palisade and ring fort. It had all burned. The island must have blazed like a bonfire. Now only ash and cinders remained.

"The sanctuary then," said Berchard. "At the market. All the way round the east side. It's stone."

They had to be wary of cellars and wells.

Durand rode into the market before the stark shell of the sanctuary. Stone walls had not saved the place, just as a palisade and moat had not saved the town. In this pyre of a thousand souls, Durand and his comrades would find no refuge. He stopped by the outsized statue of a barefaced knight: the Champion belted to his standing lance tall as a ship's mast. A breeze stirred the ashes.

And something moved, very near.

Durand had his chained flail whistling in the air before he found a desperate visage atop the idol's shoulder. A long-limbed man clung to the neck of the marble Champion like a rat at a man's throat. "Wait! Wait!" He was all over soot and bloody scratches. His clothes were charred tatters.

"What in Heaven? Who is that now?" demanded Berchard.

The climber cast an anxious glance over the market ground, his eyes bulging white in a face of black streaks. *They're all around!*

Durand gave the place a hard look, but saw nothing. Ailric shrugged.

"They are still here! In the shadows," the stranger said. "There!" The madman's finger snaked out with a force that nearly unhooked him from the Champion's neck.

This time, however, Durand saw movement too. A long shape scissored in the shadow of a wall, like the dark forelimbs of a water scorpion.

"The place is full," said the stranger. "They clutch. They cling to the shadows."

"Who *is* that?" said Berchard. "I know that voice."

"Are you real?" The hollow-eyed survivor reached for Durand, poised like an ape. "Through the wall they came. We were at the Bells." The man glanced to the ruined foundation of an inn or tavern. "Old Hardred had no room on the hill. And this thing . . . It crashed through the wall. They'd already made the island crossing, the maragrim—a host. And there was smoke by then. Someone said Hardred had fired the storehouses where the devils came ashore. They don't like fire, they say. But Hardred was too late and there the maragrim were, in the streets."

"Come down," said Durand; to his comrades, he added: "Maybe the road?"

The stranger leaned into Durand, swinging precariously. "I fetched up in the market square, you understand. I saw men pulled down. I heard screams, howls everywhere. I felt clawed hands upon me—but the Champion was there! And they would not touch him." A spark flashed in the man's eye. "Oh, but the fire! There was no one to stop it, and the devils only ran and stormed like bats in their hordes as the blaze leapt the housetops. I thought that all of Leerspoole had been dropped into a hell of fire and fiends and screaming, with me clinging here as it all raged around me." He twitched back to Durand. "But they dared not touch the idol."

With every word the mad survivor spoke, the shadows spread. Beings crabbed over the cinders. They swarmed. They were losing the Eye of Heaven.

"We'll run for it," said Durand. "Now."

"I know that damned voice!" said Berchard.

The maragrim rose up, unfolding, tumbling, and stretching their crooked limbs in every alley and ruin. They leered and grimaced and chattered and stared, trembling like greyhounds at their ropes' end.

"Ride!" commanded Durand.

And the stillness snapped. Brand bolted. The madman sprang. And the leering wall of devils slammed shut like a tangled sea.

Durand drove big Shriker, hooking around the shadowed isle for the West Bridge. But in a hundred strides, they met a wall of maragrim. Durand kicked and cursed until he tore loose from the fiends, then threw every ounce of the towering warhorse into a slashing charge for the river, drawing old Brand and Heremund's stalwart mule behind. The maragrim shot through the ruins, tumbling over themselves, airborne in the fury of their pursuit.

Suddenly, the riverbank was under Shriker's hooves and there was no stopping. Men and beasts together crashed into the water, spinning in the searing shock of the Keen's mountain chill.

Heremund tumbled past, and Durand roared, "Catch hold of the saddle," clapping the skald's hand on the saddlebow as Shriker thrashed.

With the waves at his chin, Durand strained to see. A thousand horrors crowded the Leerspoole bank, but they were behind him now. He was caught in the huge black current churning around Leerspoole, far stronger than he'd feared. The maragrim would have filled the eastern channel to reach the island, and so the West Bridge was half awash and the whole torrent roared round the western flank.

And then, of course, there was the falls.

"Make for the dam!" Durand called. "We'll be carried over!" He churned ahead, snatching Shriker's bridle from the lashing chaos of the animal's hooves as the water bowled them along like a whole team of horses. They could only strike out across the current and try to catch hold of the dam before they were pulled into the spillway and over the top.

He could see water high against the dam, exploding as it struggled through the spillway. Durand heaved Shriker's bridle, half-leading and half-hauling the big horse. He clenched his teeth against the roar of the falls. For every yard he struggled, they flew a hundred downstream, rushing for the spillway and the kicking gulf below. In a heartbeat, the spray fountained in Durand's face. The black water of the spillway surge caught his legs—but he struck the dam and hauled for all he was worth, finally wrenching himself free. Shriker was already lurching up from the water, tearing deep furrows in anything that got under his hooves—mud or men. And the rest were behind him in the thundering water, beating against pilings or scrabbling at the earthen dam. Durand caught Brand's bridle, giving the old hunter a tug to help him get purchase on the bank. Ailric wrangled Heremund ashore; Berchard came up on his own; Heremund's mule was lost.

For a moment, Durand could not find the man from Leerspoole.

Finally, Durand saw the gawky figure thrashing against the water, his long-fingered hands clawing the mossy pilings that guarded the spillway against the river. No one could long endure against that rolling weight of water. Durand ran for the stranger's hand. But, as he took his first stride, the dam lurched under his feet—tons of turf and timber flexing like a living thing. Durand sprawled, pitching to the very brink before his fingers hooked the sod. Then the pilings were giving way before the flood, uprooting the foundation of the whole broad embankment. And the dam was still heaving. Durand felt the thing shift, rolling like some vast beast. There was no point clinging with Creation turning on its head. He scrambled, first climbing, then hurling himself clear as the whole bank gave way, plunging over the precipice in a mighty torrent of earth and water.

From the ragged brink of the ruined dam, Durand dared a backward glance: there was the survivor, still fighting to hold the sole upright timber. Durand met the man's imploring eyes just as the force of the flood ripped the piling loose. He saw the poor devil fall, his arms extended even as he plunged into the spray and stones. But that was not the end for the Leerspoole man, for a dark hand shot from the trees and he was snatched like a doll from the falling water.

Durand saw the tusk-maned head of the Crowned Hog of Fellwood. The thing leaned out like a dark mantis from the branches. After regarding its writhing prize, the giant turned its blank face up. Water beaded on flat surfaces and hidden eyes. Maybe it was a wry look. Maybe there was rage or disappointment. Durand could not know. The giant simply paused a moment, staring up.

And then tore its victim in two.

THIS TIME IT was Durand who felt friendly hands upon him, hauling him from the crumbling brink, muscling him into the saddle. The last he'd seen of the Hornbearer, the thing had been climbing the Leerspoole cliff in long fluid strides.

The four men tore across the muck, vaulting willow hurdles and balks of turf until the trees swallowed them up and the wreck of Leerspoole was behind them.

DURAND WOKE TO the tap of water on his forehead. He snorted a lungful of cold air and twisted into a crouch—in a stand of dripping pines. Thrushes and blackbirds sang. He took a deep breath of mountain air and felt the needles crunch under his hands. Dew twinkled in spiderwebs.

They'd stopped after a wild black hour of crashing down benighted trails. Durand had meant only to rest the horses. He had intended to keep watch; now it was morning.

Ailric crouched close, offering a wineskin as Durand sat up and peered at the clearing.

"They did not kill us," Durand said.

"I heard nothing all night. A fox yapped nearby and an owl was hunting."

"Foxes and owls may have their fill of hunting so long as the maragrim keep their distance."

Berchard and the skald were grumbling hummocks in the pine needles, and Durand put off waking them. The horses needed a look. The two surviving animals stood under dewy rugs and Durand felt a sharp pang of guilt. They had not been well treated.

"We're killing the horses," he said.

"I've hung their saddles and had a good look for thorns and cuts."

Durand ran his hand down the arch of Brand's neck. "There will have been one or two."

"The thorns are out. The wounds are as clean of earth and sand as they can be made. I found blankets and linens enough in our packs to bandage the forelegs to the knees and Shriker's right hind leg. Brand especially is troubled with saddle-galls, but there's not much to be done."

"Did you sleep?"

"No."

He wanted to tell Ailric to rest. He wanted to find a village and get the horses cleaned up. "Coensar will have them in the pass by now," was what he said.

"He might."

He wanted to warn Coensar, to get himself between Deorwen and harm. He shook his head. "This madness with the maragrim, I can make no sense of it. What use are the maragrim to Leovere? His men alone might have taken Almora on the road, and these fiends will do him no good in Yrlac. The Solantines watch the pass and the Wards of the

Ancient Patriarchs bar the thralls of the Enemy from Errest the Old. For this, the Powers will shut the Bright Gates of Heaven against him. What sort of fool is he?"

Ailric set his hand on Brand's shoulder. "Maybe he needs men. Coensar could ask every forest liegeman who came to the Lindenhall to ride round the old man all the way to the pass. What is left for Leovere? If he throws his few rebels against the duke's swords, he gains nothing and loses more men than he can afford. If he calls the Hornbearer and hurls these maragrim upon his enemy . . ."

"Without warning. A host of maragrim out of the dark," said Durand.

Ailric shrugged. "As you say."

"But we had the Hornbearer with us in bloody Leerspoole last night. Coensar will have made Pennons Gate, or nearly. There was never time for both. It must be leagues," said Durand.

"I am not sure what part of Creation that Hornbearer could cover between dusk and dawn."

"But he has been with his Host. Half of them are lurching, halting things. It is all dark to me. But there is rage in Leovere of Penseval. He would hazard much. I think we must get to Abravanal." And Deorwen, and the girl. "There is something wrong in all this."

Ailric nodded with a blink of his dark eyes.

Durand shook his head heavily. "Our people will soon be in Pennons Gate. Coensar will have them in the pass in an hour or two."

Just then, a voice croaked from the forest floor. "Do not speak in certainties," said Heremund. "The Powers must not be tempted. They are near, I think. Watching."

With that, Berchard popped up, his beard bristling with needles, his good eye blinking wide. "I've got it! The voice! That Leerspoole man. It was my Avina's bloody cousin! The last man in Leerspoole was Avina's damnable cousin come to see Hardred about stealing a blind man's hall. If he hadn't died, I'd have throttled him! The old Hornbearer's done me a good turn."

Durand turned to Ailric. "There's nothing for it. We must get to Pennons Gate and see for ourselves. We're some leagues west along the Blackroots. I wonder whether we're any further from the Gate than Lindenhall? What say you?"

Ailric opened his hands.

There was no way of knowing whether they could reach Pennons Gate before nightfall.

"It is in the hands of the Powers," Durand said.

*　*　*

WITH MUTTERS AND groans, they climbed out of the pine grove and rode onto the rubble-strewn high ground under the Blackroots, doing their best to save the horses as they covered the uncertain leagues to Pennons Gate. It was a barren place and cold. The hard clack and rattle of every falling stone clattered from horizon to horizon.

The Fellwood stood below them: a sea full of monsters.

A league or less from their camp, Durand led the company across a knife-cold stream with banks of white sand. The far side was full of ruts. Durand, Ailric, and Heremund crouched at the water's edge to read the signs. The maragrim had been in that place.

Heremund spread his hand over the track of a naked foot with bent toes. Each toe was as long as a woman's arm. He shuddered. Durand found the deep splayed socket of a boar's split hoof and dew claws, but the hole was as broad as a butter churn. There were drag marks. He could not guess what they were. "Last night," said Heremund. "Moving so fast, even on these uplands."

"Only two or three," said Ailric. "It is hard to be sure. And not bound for Pennons Gate."

"Not the host at Leerspoole, then," declared Berchard. "Is that what you're saying? Where are these fellows headed?"

Durand looked at the soot-streaked massif above them. "North," he said. "The Blackroots. They might be following this stream." There was a glint of falling water and a narrow defile in the mountain wall half a league uphill, though the way might be hopelessly steep and lead the devils nowhere. Still, it was clear: the fiends were trying to pass the mountains.

THEY SCRAMBLED EAST over fields and valleys of rubble under a lowering sky.

Again and again, Ailric saw signs of maragrim thralls. The things traveled in small bands, never more than twenty. And always, the tracks tended north. Durand watched the vault of Heaven, counting the hours until finally the clouds swallowed the Eye.

In the hours after Noontide, a pitiless rain fell. A hiss rose from the naked acres of stone.

"There is something horrible about their tracks," muttered Berchard under his hood. He had touched one at their last stopping place, and now sat on big Shriker's back while Durand walked. "I remember the first of the things that I saw. Years ago. A woodcock's long bill peering from a monk's cowl. A heron's legs naked under its robe. In its hand, it had a hook for fishing meat, I remember, like a cook in a big kitchen. We spotted it in the trees along a trail, shuddering fit to shake itself apart and staring without a peep. A thing like that should not be something you can touch. But here they have flesh and bones.

"Always, they were alone. Like finding an adder in your barn. A man could deal with it. Sometimes, there would be a nest of them. You would hear of a man clearing forest, finding a knot of the devils. Like that longhouse we ran across." A shudder. "A dozen. A score."

"We must have seen traces of a thousand," Heremund breathed. Durand had never seen the man cowed, but now Heremund looked like his own ghost.

"Where is the Eye?" asked Berchard, twisting and giving the sky a pointless squint. The vault of Heaven was a welter of gray rain.

"Lost," said Heremund. "The clouds have got it."

"Have we seen Pennons Gate yet?"

On their left hand, the peaks stood under the clouds like teeth in a shark's jaw.

"Maybe," said Heremund. "We cannot know. One mountain looks much like another with this sky."

Berchard pulled his cloak tighter and asked no more. They needed to find the pass. And so, yet again, they raced the shadows.

Durand, walking and slipping on the stones at Shriker's bridle, stared up as though he might glare a hole through the mountains. There had been no town, no refuge—nothing but Pennons Gate.

And the rain swung over Creation in measureless veils.

TRAMPING OVER STONES is no good for a man's boots.

Durand still led Berchard on old Shriker. The others were behind, traveling a ridge above of a wall of midnight pines, like thieves skirting a watchful city.

"Host of Heaven, we're losing the light again, aren't we?" said Berchard.

"The Gate can't be far."

The light ebbed from the clouded Heavens as they clung to the high ground. They could see when they stayed on the high bright stones. But, time and again, the rugged land shouldered them down to the very eaves of the forest. They struggled to avoid the branches, as anxious as children. And Durand was not the least craven of the company.

As they drifted down for the hundredth time, Durand shot a glance into the trees—and saw that the forest was not empty, but crowded.

"What is it, Durand?" said Berchard.

Still forms watched from among the trunks. After the shock of fear—he was certain the maragrim had returned—he saw that the figures standing among the trees were too regular. He knew these faces. He saw bloated Euric; the thorn-crowned king with the bloody wreck of his head; there was the moon-faced giant; there, Baradan and his boar's bristles; there, the charred villagers. All of these were still, or nearly. Some lolled against trunks, some stood like stocks of marble, but only one was moving: she wore a long gown, trailing dark with the weight of the river that had drowned her. She carried an infant in her blue-pale hands.

"When a blind man says a thing like that, you have to answer. You really do," said Berchard.

"Nothing," said Durand.

"My arse," Berchard growled.

Durand pulled Shriker scrambling uphill, climbing up the broken stone and freeing himself from the Lost for a moment. But, with the next rise, a great arm of pine forest spread before the party and Durand found himself tramping back among the trees and the Lost. They stirred at his ankles as dark and slick as minnows. Their pale faces hung against the gloom like silver masks.

And, abruptly, they were gone.

Now, Durand froze.

A glance showed big Shriker's eyes wide. "We've stopped," said Berchard. "It's cold. Hells, Durand, you need to say something."

The pines stood empty now. And the light was gone.

Something came free of the forest. It swarmed behind Brand—a hulk of copper and clicking swarming limbs. For an instant, Durand could not move. Here was the round dome of an upturned cauldron—no crone's hut was larger. And under the cauldron, all the limbs of a black-legged wolf spider were crammed tight. Writhing.

Durand rang the spiked head of his flail off the copper dome. The thing balked, rearing long enough for Brand take flight.

A score of maragrim erupted from behind the copper hulk: a headless ogre in a thresherman's breeches; a priest with a fox's mad eyes; a hybrid thing that was both a naked man and the stunted devil which had swallowed him to the hips.

They had lost the Eye of Heaven.

Durand sprang behind Berchard as Brand tore past them. He saw Ailric hunkered at Heremund's back. But behind them, the band of maragrim galloped on a tide of inhuman groans. The track rose, treacherous with stone, but they could not stumble. They could not slow. They crested the rise ahead of the devils and found an open gulf before them. The trail plunged from this undulating high country of rubble and ditches into a gaping valley of stone. A mountain soared against the high clouds, a single blade of stone, splitting only a thousand fathoms above the valley. There were the switchbacked battlements of the Solantines. There were the countless gates. This was Pennons Gate and its Gorge of Pennons. They had nearly reached safety.

They bolted into the long curve of a ravine that swung down into the gulf, the maragrim bounding and lurching after them. Durand kicked a running horror off balance, but there were hands and claws and worse snatching at his tunic and trying to catch Shriker's surging legs. They were like a stag caught by a pack of dogs. The fastest would drag them down. The rest would tear them to pieces.

The track swung into the belly of the gorge, where they met a sudden boiling fog. Clouds flashed past, and then Creation was snatched away. Durand clung to Berchard's back in the mounting cloud. This was the Gorge of Pennons. Durand could hear the slobbering groans of the maragrim. The Gate was ahead. Something lolloped out of the fog in front of him, eager and stupid as a hound, but looking more like a leg-less ogre swinging on two long arms. It grinned wide.

Durand felt a sudden hand upon his arm.

And there was a blond man turning to him, his eyelashes white in the red light. "It is the Gorge of Pennons! Heaven be praised!"

Durand had never seen the man before that moment.

But Durand was no longer in the same Creation.

He found himself lurching in a vast drove of humanity, every soul hurrying through the trees. His memory was failing. He could feel the fear of the people all around.

A woman near him had a half-grown child wrapped around her. An old man rumbled in a wheelbarrow. Eyes were hollow, faces blank. In a glance, Durand could see a thousand people. Someone dropped a rucksack. He saw others slip out of pack straps. One sack clattered like a bag of silver plates. Above, Durand saw the face of Pennons Gate. The long shadows of sunset sharpened every battlement. The trees gave way and a naked plain of silt and stones lay before them. The road led straight to a great gate of oak, iron, and stone.

Another figure, a stout woman this time, smiled at Durand. One of her front teeth was missing. She gasped, "Our Aidmar's shown them now, Heaven help him. He's left Uluric, but he's got us free."

Durand faltered a smile, looking back over the multitude. How far had they come from Aubairn? How many leagues had they left behind them? The king was in the forest, holding the Host behind them. How many died in the forest march?

Just then, the maragrim thralls broke from the forest—bestial shapes, deformed figures: impossibilities, impossibly close. He glanced to Pennons Gate. It was nearly within their reach. Like a single animal, the refugees surged forward, every possession abandoned now. Durand hurdled the old man; his wheelbarrow crashed sideways. There were shrieks from the forest edge. The woman could not run with her child clinging; Durand snatched the boy from her arms. The maragrim were in the crowd now. Durand saw a man carried down, the maragrim grappling for his face, his mouth. Every attack sent shocks through the fleeing mob.

Over the child's head, Durand saw the stalwart Forest Gate loom above them. If they reached the fortress, if the Solantines took them in, they would still survive, even now. He saw Solantines in the huge gatehouse. They were scrambling. He could not imagine the trees that made up the huge square teeth of the portcullis that hung in the shadows above them.

On the battlements of the Forest Gate, Durand made out a tall figure in Solantine gray. His beard was white as ice. He wore an open helm and leaned over the onrushing crowd like the master of a ship, staring into the teeth of a great storm.

The dark hollow of the enormous entry gaped above them.

And the portcullis thundered down.

The onrushing crowd flagged. One man dashed himself against the portcullis, howling outrage. "Women and children! Babes here! You cannot!" Almost, some could squeeze between the square timbers, but the gaunt-eyed men in the Forest Gate were already moving, and a pair of iron doors was swinging now, shutting out all hope. Durand watched as the last thread of freedom vanished between those doors. He heard a bar rumble home.

There were sobs, but Durand only turned, quiet now. Men had already lined up to face the multitudes. Durand saw Ettin thralls stalking in the ranks of the enemy, twisted and maddened and chained. Soon they would test the Forest Gate. He saw also coy ogres, tittering one to the other. They would be the Beldame Weavers, and they measured reams of gossamer web, chattering like washerwomen. How many days had it been since life had ended?

The maragrim seethed in thickening ranks, drawing up before the small crowd of refugees. This was a chase no longer. Durand heard the piping cry of an infant; he set the boy down with a nod to its mother. Durand had only bare hands to face the maragrim, but he was walking to find a place in the line when the Host of the Enemy came down.

ABRUPTLY, DURAND FELT a heavy hand across his jaw.

He was again in the Gorge of Pennons, though now there was fog. The air was damp and shockingly cold. His boots had frozen to the sod. Frost stood in needles. His heart hammered a useless din against his ribs. And a Solantine knight had him by the jaw. The man stared with eyes like brown nail-heads. He knew the man's face.

"I told you," the knight growled.

15

The Mercy of Iron

The Solantine guard had a troop of friends. The whole lot scowled down from gray horses.

"No place to be after dark," said the Solantine. "We'll get inside now."

Durand's comrades had their eyes on him; he could do little but wonder what they'd seen.

They walked into a space of clear air below the Forest Gate. Durand peered up, noting the outsized portcullis. And, high above, he saw Maedor the Greyshield on the parapet as though he had not abandoned his vigil since the fall of Aubairn.

The jailor knight led them up the face of the wall through fearsome ranks of Solantines. They tottered sideways as men rolled heavy barrels down the stone track. Ailric and Durand exchanged glances: the knights were making ready for more company from Fellwood.

"They know the maragrim are on the move," said Ailric. "They would not have been so ready to ride for us."

"We are fortunate that they did not close the gate," said Durand.

This got a glance from a few of the hard-faced Solantines.

Durand exhaled. "Ailric, what did you see?"

"The maragrim were on us, and we were surrounded. Then they stepped from the fog. Shadows."

"Not maragrim?"

"No. Shadows. Beyond counting."

He had seen more than shadows.

"The maragrim did not like it and backed away."

"Even that spidery brute?"

"Even the worst of them. The frost knit in the air. And, as the maragrim left us, one of the shadows reached out. Quick as a flame."

"A shadow?"

"You were not breathing," Ailric said. "The Solantines came then, I think to break up the maragrim. But when they found the Lost, it sobered them. But the Lost gave way. I don't know what would have happened otherwise."

The party climbed the battlements and found Maedor the Greyshield watching still, armed and in the pale mantle of the Constable of Pennons Gate. He watched from the battlements below a substantial gatehouse that glowed like a carved lantern. The tall man turned and led them inside.

"My brothers are barracked here to relieve the garrison on the Forest Gate, should the maragrim try it," he said. "There are braziers for the men to work by. You will warm yourselves. And something must be done for these horses." Then he rounded on Durand. "What did you see, Durand Col?"

"They were before the gates. The people of Aubairn. Hundreds."

The man's white brow hopped. "Thousands, though they are uncounted—uncounted and unburied. The Forest Gate fell thereafter. And my brethren retreated twice more before the host." The old man closed his eyes briefly, then regarded Durand again. "You have been fortunate. Many have died who came to the Gorge by night. The dead are jealous. They do not know when or where they are, and they are stronger than they know." He touched Durand's shoulder. "But you know much of the Lost, and these of Pennons Gate are mine, not yours."

Durand inclined his head, and the ancient knight continued. "You have come unlooked-for from the east with the maragrim close behind. . . ."

"I was not traveling with His Grace."

"Yes, we have heard of the tourney at the Lindenhall and of the oaths sworn on the Prince's Ring there." Durand touched the pouch on his belt, where the ring lay, half-forgotten. "The Sword of Gunderic broken— along with all hope of peace between Lord Leovere and your duke."

Durand was cowed. "I'd meant to warn him. We have seen a great deal."

"You will not find your people here. Your Coensar took his company into the pass at dawn; they will be encamped in the high country by now. He had a force with him that was twice what went south." Durand could imagine them in the towering darkness somewhere, camped in the wind. It would not take long to overtake them.

"You should know what we have seen," said Durand. "The maragrim are on the move."

Berchard was nodding along. "Leovere took his horn to the Crowned Bones, near as we can guess. Leerspoole is in ruins. We saw signs of hundreds in the foothills. Thousands."

"First, the call from Penseval. Now at Crowned Bones. He will have called that devil to parley," said Maedor.

"It certainly called him. We were on the trail to Leerspoole," said Berchard. "The maragrim came in battalions. The Hornbearer slew a man who'd been stalking us, and soon there were a multitude. But we heard that horn and we'd seen Leovere's trail heading off that way. That horn, it drew off the Hornbearer—though a river, and our own stalwart cowardice helped as well."

"The Hornbearer has been seen near the gate."

Durand nodded. "It found us on the road to the Lindenhall, but did nothing, watching only and stealing away. And we might have seen something in the high passes before. We heard something like his groaning horn."

"He was with the force at Leerspoole," said Berchard. "His company waited for us there at nightfall. We fled with the river at our backs. But I'd guess the maragrim scattered then, fanning out and coming north to meet us tonight."

The ancient knight bowed his head. "Durand Col. Once more, you have come to Pennons Gate. The dead pursue you, and the signs and portents rise like dust at your step. Now, the Hornbearer seeks you."

Durand might have spoken, but the knight raised a forestalling hand. "He found you in the mountains, on the Lindenhall Road, and then Leerspoole. Where is coincidence? Where chance? The Hornbearer has you in his eye. You, the haunted man, are more than the broken knight you appear. The Powers have their hands upon you. Where there had been a balance, you leave ruin."

Durand marked subtle shifts among the Solantines around as the wind battered the flames low in their fire baskets. What did the Greyshield intend?

"You would pass this wall with your portents and your strange dooms

and the Hornbearer following? You would carry all of this into Errest
the Old?"

"Speak plainly," said Durand. He clenched his fists. "I can do nothing
about the Hornbearer. I am only a man."

The big knight's head swiveled. "The Powers have placed you in my
hands. They have placed you in my hands, and I will act. Once more will
I close the gate. And we shall see. Brother Sigeric, his friends may stay
or go and be welcome. Durand will remain here with us."

The Solantines stepped close, slipping in a moment from saviors to
jailors.

The jailer knight, Sigeric it seemed, took Durand and the others up.

TWO FILES OF Solantines formed their silent escort, and Sigeric led
the way.

"It is outrageous," said Berchard. "You are no more dangerous a man
than I. Maedor has more to fear from Heremund and the boy. I don't
sleep well knowing Heremund's abroad, but I am not Constable of Pennons Gate."

Heremund nodded a bow to Berchard.

"We must work out what to do next," said Durand, but the Solantines
gave them no time to think or breathe.

They climbed for an hour or more through the wind and dark, passing gate after gate. Finally, the gates of the uppermost fortress stood before them. Durand looked over the Gorge of Pennons and the great
dark suggestion of the Fellwood beyond, and was surprised not to see
ranked armies standing by bonfires and torches. This was what Leovere
had summoned. This was the Host of the Hornbearer. But still, the Fellwood was empty and the forest night uninterrupted by even a single
flame.

As the last gate rose, the company clattered into the dark commandery,
dismounting in a jingle and scrape that echoed in the silent place. The
galleries were largely dark, with so many men far below. Sigeric said, "Your
horses will be taken care of," and accepted a torch from the men on the
gate before leading the company into the warrens of the fortress. They
penetrated deep, passing the refectory and infirmaries until they entered
a passage where the wind piped at a row of arrow loops. Durand remembered Deorwen mocking at these. Arrow loops half a league above the
valley floor threatened no one below.

It was black outside.

"Sigeric," said Durand, "will it be the storeroom again?"

Sigeric turned, the torch blazing above his face. "The others to the guest halls. But, aye, you're for the storeroom. We need a strong door, I think, and you found no way out the last time." There was a door at the man's side and, without fanfare, he gave the thing a push. "We will make your companions comfortable here and then take you down."

As Durand hesitated, he saw the darkness move, suddenly full of shadows. Faces surfaced from the gloom: Euric, Baradan, Alwen . . .

Berchard was speaking, standing tall. "We will wait. We'll have words with Maedor. He will not shut you up in this place forever. We are all Sons of Atthi."

One of the Solantines at the doorway put his hand on Berchard's arm, and Berchard's sudden twist shot the knight into the doorframe.

"You cannot hold a man," said Berchard. "You are no king or court!"

And there was a great wrenching mêlée where Solantines seized Berchard and his comrades while Berchard roared against his restraints. Sigeric held the torch, stiff, above the grapplers until, suddenly, the floor trembled.

"What was that?" said Ailric.

The Lost stood at the arrow loops. Every one.

Ailric stepped out of his attackers' hands and moved to one of the deep, narrow windows, sharing it with Euric and the mad king.

"This is the Errest side. This is the pass," he said.

"Aye, it is," said Sigeric.

"Listen," said Ailric. "There."

And now they heard what their grunts and snarls had drowned a moment before. Echoing out over the moon-glinting peaks came a long, empty note: the maragrim horn. It groaned in the air, trembling in their lungs, shaking mortar from the ceiling and conjuring an uncanny moan from the hollow mouths the commandery bells.

Durand pushed through the viscous frigidity of the Lost and thrust his eye against the nearest loop. "The devil is in the pass. The Hornbearer," he said. It was out there with Deorwen and Almora and Abravanal. He had not been imagining the sounds in the mountains all those days ago. "They must be warned." At any price, he must reach them.

"Brother Constable has made himself plain. I did not mistake his meaning."

"And I did not bring the fiend into the pass. It has gone before me while you led me to this cell. I am the sworn man of Duke Abravanal. Leovere has summoned this devil, and together they will strike at my liege lord while you hold me here beyond any hope of aiding him."

The sound ebbed away and the men dusted mortar from their heads. Berchard was the last to his feet.

"The Constable has spoken," said Sigeric. He looked to the man who'd fought with Berchard, and another man supporting him. "Brothers, take word to Maedor that the Hornbearer is in the pass." And the men left with hardly a nod.

When their footfalls had left the passage, Sigeric turned to his remaining brothers. "Does anyone else need an errand? I've a list if it's wanted." A few of the men gave their chins a prideful lift, but none spoke. "Down we go, then. For, after that bit of excitement, I think all of our guests will need to spend the night below."

"Send to Maedor, Brother Sigeric," said Durand. "Get me loose."

"You have seen Brother Maedor. You have seen him watching from the Forest Gate. He stands watch, fair and foul, forever. He had walked those battlements when the Gorge of the Pennons stood empty. He looked down upon the trees before Aidmar was king in Aubairn. There is little bend in our Maedor. Little bend in any in this cold place, if I'm honest."

"And you," he said to Berchard. "If you think to try your tricks again, you will pay a price. You will not fool us twice with your blind dotard game."

"It's no game," said Heremund. "He's just an ornery old fool."

"Come a step closer, dear skald. I cannot hear you," said Berchard.

One of the Solantines growled.

They descended further, finding a spiral stair and following the flame of Sigeric's torch into utter darkness. The Lost filled the vaulted ceilings in skittering droves that rolled from archway to archway. And every living man raised his collar against the unnatural chill whether they could see the things or not.

Finally, Sigeric found an iron handle in the dark. "Here we are then," he said, and yanked the door open.

Durand thought hard of breaking away. Ailric would back him and the Solantines would likely avoid blades. But the knights were many and powerful, and he was deep in their stronghold with no means of escape. Still, he thought hard, and the bridled fury had his fingers curling when Sigeric bowed at the door.

Durand ducked through, feeling like some chained and toothless bear, ready to round on the Solantines, to see how they fared against a Champion of Gireth in the blackness of his fury.

But he was in no cell, and the hinges echoed in clear air.

A thousand peaks glowered at Durand from a vast mountain night, sullen giants crowding the horizon. Sigeric had led them to the rearmost hall of the fortress where men and goods were lifted from the valley below. Here, they had arrived with Abravanal, as the old man fought the lung fever. Huge landing stages stood against the abyss, and cranes hulked under the dark vaults, stooped over the brink like squat shorebirds of iron and timber.

"We'll take you down," Sigeric said.

Durand turned. He felt almost dizzy as the spent rage tumbled in his blood. This was what he'd wanted.

"What does this mean?" he said. "Do you go against Maedor in this?"

"Let's not give anyone time to find sense," said Sigeric. "Come."

What ancient and terrible oaths were breaking now? And with hardly a word spoken?

Sigeric led them under the jib arm of a crane like a siege engine and aboard one of the heavy wooden platforms. The thing shifted like a ship's deck under the creak of its heavy cable.

Heremund must have looked dismayed.

"Fear not, skald," Sigeric was saying. "We dump one now and again, but with six hundred fathoms to fall, a man does not suffer long."

Ailric put Berchard's hand on one of the lines that skirted the deck while a pair of the Solantines picked up long gaffs with hooks and points. Another grinned as he casually kicked away the locks and lines that held the platform. With a hop, he left the deck and took hold of a worn wooden lever as long as a ship's tiller. They could feel the platform slew and drift underfoot. Durand saw the Lost spilling into the room, questing after him. Seeking this way and that, and always coming nearer.

"What Brother Sigeric says is true. Them what don't hold on don't suffer," the grinning man said. "But they do bounce. It's a sight. The truth." He winked as he wrenched the long lever—and the platform dropped away, leaving him behind.

Pulleys shrieked as the man grinned down and the rope spooled out.

"Devil!" shouted Heremund.

The man upstairs put a little more weight into his brake lever and the plunge slowed to a steadier descent. The cavernous space opened above them as they plunged toward the next landing. Somewhere, a counterweight was rushing upward.

"I'll be sick before long," said Berchard, through clenched jaws.

"You'll have a moment to catch your breath," Sigeric was saying. "There is a limit to ropes and to men. The descent must be done in stages, or there is no rope long or strong enough. Before a load rises, our men on the cranes must walk and walk the treadwheels while the cables moan and tighten. Unloading can be a problem. Think what it's like to snap a bowstring. Lively. And the ropes will weep if there's been rain."

"Oh, you *are* a comfort, Brother Sigeric," declared Berchard.

The other Iron Knight on the deck laughed. He held a long gaff, quite idly, as though no one had broken oaths, and no one was spinning hundreds of fathoms high.

Sigeric peered down where the next landing stage jutted into the gulf. And, despite a slow rotation, the Solantines brought the platform neatly home with a few practiced thrusts of their gaffs.

"A moment now," said Sigeric, and the knights were moving as deftly as sailors or builders, locking off the platform, swinging out the next jib arm, and shackling on the next hemp cable. The cavern groaned and creaked with the work of the ropes and pulleys. "This they call the King's Seat, for once it carried a King of Errest the Old." And, with another man left behind on the brake lever, down they went.

After the third such stop, they had dropped the height of many towers. Durand looked off into the faintly moonlit valley below, thinking of Leovere and Abravanal and Deorwen and the Hornbearer all together in the high passes. Here he was with a blind man, a minstrel, and a boy, coming to save them all.

He said to Sigeric, "Sigeric, do the thralls often pass your gate?"

"Aye, yes, Durand Col. But not in numbers. One or two, only. Now and again. The Blackroots are a devilish haunted place, and have been since long before there were knights in Pennons Gate. But you will find maragrim here and there, mad in blind ravines, and a thing like the Hornbearer is long-limbed and strong. You cannot bar the high wastes to them completely. For such reasons, the ancients set shrines and wards upon the pass. And countless more shrines and wards and sanctuaries knotting tight the lands beyond. The maragrim are sorely bound in Errest the Old. They keep to the wilds. They steal along borders and crossroads."

"I have not seen them."

"Yet they are there, traveling crabwise where the wards are weakest—bound as the Strangers are, but there nonetheless, like vermin in the walls."

"It is so, Durand," said Heremund. "They are there in their odd corners. It has long been so."

In Durand's eyes, all the distant stones in the world beyond the fortress could now harbor watching shapes. Things like the wolf spider in its snug cauldron or the Hornbearer striding the ravines. The mountains could be teeming.

Just then, the Hornbearer's Horn stabbed across the mountains, moaning with all the force of that mad thing's lungs till the great cables buzzed with the sound. The Iron Knights caught hold of the rigging. The deck throbbed like the belly of a skald's viol. Durand felt every inch of the three hundred fathoms below them.

Debris sleeted past, shaken loose by the sound.

Sigeric began: "It is not good. The hoists are not built for such a pounding. Not since the wars have we heard such—"

Then something struck from the dark. Durand smacked the deck, but the platform dropped beneath him like a trapdoor. Smashed. They were sliding. Durand plunged till his fingers snagged a line. Only at the last possible instant did he see Berchard rolling past and catch the man's collar.

A block of masonry tumbled into the abyss with one of the Iron Knights falling after, end over end. All of the others hung on.

The platform hung in two halves, the stone having snapped it neatly in two. The main cable still held and the men hung wherever they found a stray line. With one fist locked on a line and the other in Berchard's collar, Durand's arms were wrenched wide. He could scarcely draw breath. He felt the rope squirming in his fist. Sigeric swung close, spattered with blood. "Brother Hulstan," he said. "The stone struck him." It must have been Hulstan who fell. "Here." He stretched to get hold of Berchard's forearm. Heremund and Ailric were reaching down. Together, Durand and the Solantine hauled Berchard to the relative safety of his friends on the dangling wreck.

A second stone. The thing missed by moments as the platform made a slow revolution, and the slim light of the Farrow Moon revealed little of the fortress above. But two or three more blocks shot past like a giant's fistful of stones.

"This is no good," said Sigeric, spidering round. "We must—"

Another huge block plunged by. "It will take out a landing stage! Ours, maybe!"

The cable jerked, nearly shaking the clinging men. And, sixty fathoms over their heads, the brakeman knight let go. Durand felt them plunge, but he held on, not even able to shout. The limb-thick cable wailed through its block.

They were falling toward the landing stage below. Its crane jutted into their path. But, before the stricken platform could crash down on it all, something snagged in the works. The platform slewed and then jolted to a halt two fathoms below the landing. The counterweight must have struck the crane or landing stage above.

"Get clear. For your lives!" snarled Sigeric, and so, with shouts and clutching hands, they fled, scrambling over wreckage and onto the stone landing just as the stage above finally let go. Durand watched, for an instant, as the cable whistled by, then a tower's worth of masonry and timber exploded before his eyes.

As quick as blinking, a centuries-old crane vanished.

"Here," roared Sigeric. And he shepherded the survivors through a door cut in the mountainside.

THREE THOUSAND STEPS awaited them, all as black as a mine. Every shuffling moment in the long twisted chimney of the stairs, Durand's head flashed with visions of Leovere and his Hornbearer falling on Coensar's defenses. He felt the clammy walls with his hands.

"Have a care when you touch the walls," Sigeric cautioned. "The old ones have writ a thousand prayers thereon. A hiss of skin over the glyphs is as good as whispering."

Durand heard the others breathing around him, stumbling. In his mind's eye, he saw Almora; he saw Deorwen.

Finally, the company staggered into the keep in the pass below.

The knights on the north gate had already sent runners to learn what had happened. They had heard the horn, and suffered as tons of wreckage thundered down in the lift yard and upon the rooftops of their stronghold.

Sigeric came away from these men, scowling. "You will go now. None died on the ground, but there were two above. My men. One with us, the other from the third landing stage." It was a terrible price for haste, and Durand did not know whether to lay the blame on Leovere or to shoulder it himself. Sigeric took Durand by the arm, leading him through the fortress to the great barrel-vaulted passage that led between the lifts and the gates. Behind them, Durand saw Solantines at work upon the wreckage. But they approached the outer gates, reaching a range of familiar-smelling halls that could only be stables. "You will have horses. Your own were not fit to travel further without much rest." He shook his head. "These are sound enough, and the groom will tell you what you must know." The man looked from Durand to the wreckage with his dull, dark eyes. "The mark of the Powers are upon this, good or ill. The horn, the fall. . . . It may be that Brother Maedor sees better than I what price we'll pay for your passing this way, but there is danger in holding a man against the will of the Powers—and you did not lead the Hornbearer."

Durand nodded as the Solantines produced four horses, and he climbed aboard a strong, pig-eyed gray with the battered cadre of traitor-Solantines looking on. He bowed his thanks, his dread growing.

"Durand Col," continued Sigeric. "Be warned. These things, they will tear out the wards. Every hour they are free in Errest the Old will lend them strength. They will break up the realm like roots break a road. Every day they will be harder to shift, till there is nothing any man may do. Maybe we will be guarding our pass from both sides now."

"Thank you for what you have done," said Durand, and the old knight bowed low.

They crossed the stark valley and mounted the wandering track, climbing into the higher passes with the old fortress at their backs, lost from one turning to the next. While the Farrow Moon gleamed, they could see. When the black rags of cloud caught the moon, Creation vanished into darkness. More than once, Durand was forced to rein in, not knowing whether he was leading them over a cliff or into some hopeless canyon. He heard mysterious noises under the tattered sky. Stones clattered, once skittering out in the track before him. And, deep in the night, a storm dropped upon them, raging over the high places with a terrible power that finally drove even Durand under cover.

The duke's party could not be far. Coensar could not have gone much further before nightfall, and they would surely be sharing the same wind and rain. Durand tallied the leagues and hours between them, knowing that the cavalcade had left at dawn, that it would have ridden ten or twelve hours, and that it could not travel with the speed of a driven man on a fresh horse.

They did not stay long in shelter. Before the storm had tired of the mountaintops, Durand forced his companions back onto the trail, groping his way downward, leading the horses and his comrades, fearing that they must already be too late, that Leovere was out there too, and closer.

As they rode, the storm vanished into the night once more and they pushed on until the Eye of Heaven cast light upon the peaks. They had reached a valley that Durand had only passed in the dark. The road was good, though a shallow stream joined them along the way, running like a thin coat of glass over the paving stones. They splashed in the water as the track slipped between two stone idols: the Warders in their Nail Coats, tall as spires. No sign had they seen of Abravanal the duke, or

Leovere his enemy, though Durand spurred his borrowed gray to the top of every rise and cursed at each empty valley.

"Where are they?" he said to Ailric, riding alongside.

"Coensar must have pushed on past sunset."

Berchard called forward. "They'll have heard that damned horn, same as we did. They'll have been settling down—wondering how to kindle their cooking fires with only stones as tinder—when that great braying thing interrupted. What would you have done? I'd be riding till I hit the Sea of Ice."

A shadow passed.

"Look there: an eagle flies before us," said Heremund. Everyone looked.

"White tail?" asked Berchard. And, when they confirmed his guess, he continued. "The Erne." The huge bird flew onward down the valley, looping low between the idols on the trail. Then it flinched and staggered under the assaults of a hail of smaller birds—starlings—that shot by the company on every side. "Emblem of kings, harried," finished a wincing Berchard. He could see a starling if it flew close enough to strike him.

"It is bound for Gireth," said Heremund.

"Or Eldinor beyond, if it holds its northward bearing," amended Berchard.

"Let be! We've had omens enough for ten lifetimes!" said Durand.

Just then, the stone head of one grim idol—disturbed by the violent passage of the birds—toppled into the stream, and the splash soaked Durand to the thigh.

16

Dark Homecomings

That will be the valley of the Tresses," said Ailric. Before them were the three blade-like Sisters that towered over the northern mouth of Pennons Gate. The young man extended his hand toward the Eye of Heaven, marking distance between the Eye and the likely horizon as another man might measure a colt. "It must be the ninth hour. We have made good time."

In the empty sweep of plain below them, Durand saw the stream and ruins and stand of pines they had passed only a few days before; Deorwen and the others were nowhere to be seen. Durand rubbed his chin.

"Coensar has driven them hard. But it is just as well, for we have yet to overtake Leovere and his men." Neither had they found the scattering of corpses Durand had feared.

And so they followed the track through valley of the Tresses and down the switchbacks of barren mountain road that stretched from Pennons Gate. At Broklambe, they found some sign that the villagers had begun rebuilding—sawdust on the air, a heap of cut timber twenty paces away— but there wasn't a soul visible from the road.

"No animals," said Ailric.

"Nothing," Durand agreed.

"It could be that they've thought better of rebuilding," said Berchard. "It is high stony ground. The growing season will be short. With their stores burnt, they may have fled to Wrothsilver." The old man scratched his beard with both hands. "Who is their liege lord, do you think?"

No one knew; Baron Vadir in Wrothsilver might be the man.

"If we had an hour to spare, we would turn the town over." As it was, Durand urged his borrowed gray downhill.

An hour later, they passed a forest hamlet under a column of crows. Durand eyed the circling birds as their hoarse calls rang between the trees. Down the gloomy village lane, he saw the humped corpses of cattle and the black rectangles of open doors. Here and there, bodies lay, marked by lost-laundry shocks of color against the grass. Nothing moved but ravens and crows.

"Another empty village. Men and beasts lie where they fell," said Heremund. "Broklambe will have been the same. What has Leovere done?"

"It is not worth thinking of," said Durand. Deorwen and Almora were out there, with only Coensar's few swords between them and whatever Leovere had managed to slip through the wards. He wanted to ravel up the distance. He felt a fury of desperation building.

In half a league, they found another ruin. Durand cursed. There were blackened timbers. Here, there had been fire. Bodies hung from the trees, men and beasts both. What could hang an ox? Durand clenched his cracked teeth.

"Let us think," he said. "Of Coensar, we've seen no sign." Neither had they seen a massacre on the Wrothsilver Road. "They must be ahead of us still." Just out of reach. His fists clenched and opened like a heart's beating. "But this will be Leovere, or Leovere and the Hornbearer's minions. And they have wasted time with this devilry, for if they mean to overtake our people, Coensar will not have dawdled on his way to safety." Durand stood in his stirrup irons, shooting a futile look down the empty

Wrothsilver Road, thinking they would find village after village like this with only Leovere and his maragrim at the end. To reach Abravanal's column, they must sidestep the rebel lord. And night was coming on.

"To the Hells with the Wrothsilver Road," he said. "Let Leovere squat in the track; we are not in the mountains now. There are a hundred farmsteads and hamlets in these hills. We will find our own way by back roads!" They had a skald in their party, and such men had traveled every village track. "Yes. By the plowmen's paths we will slip Leovere, and still know where Abravanal has gone. Quick!" He gave the gray the spurs and they leapt from the river road to the crooked tracks of the forests. A thousand tracks bound farmstead to farmstead in that high, rough country.

They passed clotted circles of carrion birds and myriad dark and silent ways. Durand's eye was always on the next crossroads, grilling Ailric or Heremund to get some word when the way was unclear. He had to overtake Coensar.

By this means, they blundered into a long village that sprawled either side of their forest track with dark fields opening like a rib cage round a naked spine of hovels. Here too, there were crows, though here there were survivors moving. In the long shadows of evening, Durand saw the deep mounds of new graves. He saw broken buildings cleared. He saw exhausted villagers still at work. The Solantine horses pricked their ears at this place, their heads high.

In the midst of the village stood a very tall, very narrow, crooked tower. He had never seen the like.

"Benewith," said Heremund.

"What was that?" said Berchard.

"They call that the Benewith Tower," said Heremund. "It is the dwelling place of the Lady of the Tower."

"It is in Gireth? I have not heard of this woman."

"Benewith ain't near the usual ways. Only our crow's-flight run down from the pass has brought us here. Most men? They'd never travel thus."

Berchard was squinting up. "It is a tower, you say? It looks like a twist of smoke." The tower must have topped twenty-five fathoms, and, though it was as tall any keep in Errest, it looked too narrow to stand; indeed, from base to battlements, it looked more like a rope than a tower.

"Her Ladyship's no great stonemason, whatever else she may be," said Heremund.

"Who is this woman?" asked Durand. "We might have fresh horses from her. Or word of the duke."

"I would not wager on it. They say the Lady of the Tower has this land since Willan Blind," said Heremund. "Never stepping from her tower." The pile looked like it was held up by moss and creepers. Some of the stones seemed to belong elsewhere.

"A hundred years!" said Berchard.

"More than that, Berchard. More than two hundred! Willan was younger brother to Heraric and Calamund, the Lost Princes, dead over the Sea of Darkness when Einred led the armies south. That is no hundred years."

They all peered up at the twisted tower, brown as burnt sugar against the gloomy Heaven. "As you say, skald," said Berchard. "I'm not fool enough to argue a lady's age where she might hear, but it has been a long time since Willan's day."

"It has," said Heremund. "But she will not come down, so we shall know nothing more."

Durand thought he perceived a narrow window very high in the tower, not broad enough for a man's shoulders. He edged his gray into the village, and soon enough a barrel-chested plowman left the crowd of exhausted laborers. Here was their first witness to Leovere's raids.

"You needn't ask to see his lady," said Heremund. "No man living has."

The bearish peasant nodded a quick bow, brushing his hands. He wore nothing but grime, clogs, and breeches, but said, "Lordship," clearly enough.

From his saddle, Durand said, "I am Durand Col, a liegeman of Duke Abravanal. Can you tell me what's happened in this place?"

The man narrowed an eye. "You were the Duke's Champion."

"It may still be so."

"I am Aed, bailiff here. This is Benewith village." He waved a heavy arm quickly over the ruins of his town. "Devils in the night. We met them in the road here and, thanks to the Powers of Heaven, fought them off."

"Fought them off!" said Berchard.

The plowman-bailiff turned and nodded to Berchard. "Lordship."

"How?" said Berchard.

"We had what mauls and axes and tools came to hand. The things came from the night. The trees. I don't know, Lordship. Her Ladyship gave us word. Sent us warning. Nigh too late, but a man hears little from Her Ladyship."

There was that narrow window near the top of the tower.

"You did well if you're still here," declared Berchard. "We've seen this elsewhere. You are the first who could speak sense about what he saw."

The man winced at the compliment. "Lordship. My sons here stood with me." He indicated two similarly broad bondmen nodding sternly nearby.

"Bailiff Aed, I will have to tell the duke what I can. What did you see? As exactly as you can remember it."

The man rubbed a forehead as broad as an ox's brow. "All manner of things. Hard to put in words. The devils ran out of our Burnt Oak Wood there away north, the way you've come. And they were already at our Bera's longhouse before anyone raised the alarm. Bera had three boys," the man added solemnly. "Then there were nightjars and owls in every house, storming round our ears as we slept. That'll have been Her Ladyship, we think. Half the village stumbled out and heard the howling up at Bera's place. His oxen, most like, but there's no way of knowing, for all of them were caught inside: Bera, his boys, the beasts. We burnt the place ourselves come morning."

"Were there men among these things?"

"Not what I would call men, Lordship, no."

"And a tall thing. A giant. Dark. With a face full of horns?"

The bailiff shook his head slowly. "No, Lordship. Not that. But others."

"And you defeated them?" This was the real mystery. This could be something important. "Had you a priest?"

"No, Her Ladyship does not hold with priests. Never has. And the nearest shrine's half a league off. We fought the devils in the road there." The man pointed. "We buried ten of our people, along with everyone at Bera's, but they could not stand the Eye. When dawn came, they folded into the earth, like. Cowering down. Into the Hells, we reckoned. 'Twas dawn that saved us."

The whole of Durand's party had been listening intently, but now Heremund looked up.

"Into the ground, you say? When dawn came?"

Ailric's head had already swiveled round, searching the western Heavens. And Durand saw it too: It was evening, and, sure enough, the Eye of Heaven had nearly gone. Durand prayed that the bondmen's courage had bought them more than a single day of pointless labor.

"Get them out of the fields. Get everyone together. Is there a door in that tower?"

The man was shaking his head, eyes wide. "No. No door."

"And no water. No running water."

"In the tower?"

"Anywhere!"

The man shook his head. "A well, only." He pointed out among the longhouses of the village.

Durand cast his eye over the thatched half-timbered houses, all low and nothing of stone. A man could kick through such walls. But, then he spotted a dark track. An alley between two overgrown hedges. The gnarled walls of thorn were two fathoms high.

Durand swung down from the saddle. "The maragrim are still among us, like wolves in the high grass. They will rise where they fell when the dawn struck them. I reckon we'll make our stand between the hedgerows. You have no time."

The bailiff blinked for a moment, but then turned to his people and roared.

Everyone ran. They called to their families.

Durand stalked into the damp warren between the hawthorns. There were flowers. Two dozen survivors—men and women—hunkered down in the narrow track. A gaggle of little children huddled, white with terror. They had all reached the tunnel of thorns, crowding close into the gloom with the Solantine horses.

"What was this path for?" said Berchard, eyeing the devilish thorns crowding close on both sides.

"It's the Marlepit Field track. It goes up to Marlepit Field, yonder. Plowlands. Hedging the crofts and that."

"That's everything explained, then," said Berchard. He had his patterned blade in his lap.

The last needle of daylight winked out between the thorns and horses and children. Every soul in Benewith had gone to ground.

Ailric pointed down into the village from the mouth of their dark lane. Already, misshapen things were moving, rising from the ruts, blinking where the fight had taken place twelve long spring hours before. Durand was conscious of the children huddled in the shadows behind him. A handful were very, very young. He tried to make sense of the uncanny shapes of the maragrim. There were little brutes, skittering sidelong. Something like a hooded man stooped under the weight of a massive swinging head. There was another thing that carried the wrong number of limbs. The man, Aed, was murmuring reassurances to the children. Durand thought of Almora and Deorwen and Coensar. How flimsy a thing the future was and how easily and often it was snatched away. There was Heremund the skald with a stout walking stick. There was blind Berchard, dandling his blade. And here now was Aed and these few children behind him. He must fight here and learn what steel could do against the maragrim. A man's schemes counted for little in the face of doom.

They huddled, whispering in the mouth of the alleyway as the maragrim moved, seemingly heedless. "They are the same," said Aed. Only the fighting men could hear him. "All the bloodshed last night and they are just the same. Not one gone."

"Here," said Berchard, louder. He fumbled a moment and found the bailiff's wrist. "We're with you now, eh? Take heart. I've tickled more than a few surly devils with this old broadsword of mine. An heirloom blade, it is. And we've toyed with a few of these fellows in Fellwood, between us."

Durand nodded along, but was more concerned with the new movement he saw in the sunken roadway. Like a swarm of silverfish, the impish things had suddenly slipped away, losing themselves among the bushes and banks. The bigger brutes remained.

"Aed," said Durand, "get a couple of your people behind us. Anything that tries to go around should have a fight." Whispers were passed through the crouched clot of villagers. "Those boys of yours look handy." There was a scuttling shuffle as men changed places. Durand must have taken his eyes from the maragrim in that moment, for the bigger maragrim had vanished from the road when he turned back.

He had lost them.

Out in the village, laughter echoed like a dog's barking. Durand could see nothing, but he listened with the rest as screams rang, frantic. They heard a cackle and shriek of hens. A few more of the stunted maragrim swept past the alleyway, not ten paces away. Durand wore no armor, but he had hauled the shield from his packs and now the leather straps creaked in his fist.

Then there was the huge startled bellowing of an ox. He heard the shipboard creak and groan of ropes hauling hard, and remembered seeing beasts hanged in another village that day. Beasts howled out all around Benewith—shrieks of weird horror.

"They are taking their time," said Berchard. "Working their way around the village, plucking the low fruit. I've had heard that it's fear they hunger for, terror. They are mad by now. All of them. Dead so long."

And, suddenly, the maragrim were there.

Something flashed in the mouth of the alley, broad and dark as a barn door. Durand swung, lashing down with the urchin head of the flail. Then Berchard got a blow in, his antique broadsword flashing up like a blade of fire.

The creature staggered back, and in a flash of the Farrow Moon, Durand saw an outsized human form split three ways—three faces, three shoulders, three huge ropey arms. Eyes bulging in distorted terror along with its gaping, howling mouth. Every one of the three faces was straining as if to pull away from the others. Berchard's blow had half severed one forearm.

Now, Aed bulled forward. He had a broad woodcutter's axe, and he leapt into the three-armed brute, heaving mighty blows as it gibbered and howled back at him. Durand darted out, protecting the bailiff's flank, joining the man with wild looping swings from his flail that cracked bone and knocked long teeth from several mouths until, finally, a second blow from Berchard's old sword fell on the thing's knee, and the brute dropped onto the tangle of its half-severed thigh. It did not take long for the village axemen to leave the thing a twitching heap of butcher's meat.

They stopped, out of breath, stupid with victory and spattered with blood.

Durand managed a look at Aed, about to say something: a word of praise. But, in an instant, the stocky villager was snatched away as a pale enormity from the gloom snaked a long hand around the man's wrist.

Astonished, Durand tried to catch a hand, but the man was gone. And, suddenly, Durand realized just how many other things were out there in the dark.

With his eyes open, he saw huge shapes swing and lurch, rolling like bears, shrieking.

"Back, back!" Durand cried. "It is too late! Back to the thorns. We will do no good surrounded." And the panting villagers stuttered back.

Berchard got hold of Durand's elbow, groping till he found his hand. "Durand, what are you doing with that damned flail? You won't put these brutes to sleep with a tap on the head. Have you still got that sword? Ouen's sword?" Durand had almost forgot Ouen's sword. It had been a gift from Coensar. The outsized weapon was more full of memory than the flail could ever be. "I don't know what demons are worrying you, but it is time for a very large blade, I think."

Durand ground his teeth. The maragrim had the bailiff now. "No one steps beyond the thorns. Keep your wits about you. More could have gone that way."

Durand heard something howl behind them; one of the fiends must have met Aed's boys at the back of the party. In the same moment, the enormous mass of a giant dropped into the alley mouth. Big as two bulls and pale as a gob of suet, the thing bent, groping forward, its stolid face as closed and blind as a fist. One hand dragged a club of enormous thorns. It heaved close, then stopped, lifting the huge block of its face as a thousand slits over its moist skin burst. Pustular eyes erupted in every crease and wrinkle, each one rolling with its own mad terror.

Durand forced himself at the creature. He hauled Ouen's huge sword into the air, chopping and stabbing, digging more than fighting, with fists on hilt and blade. But the brute shoved forward. A mass of writhing eyes blinked against Durand's jaw as the thing drove Durand stumbling backward into the screaming children. The giant's face dragged in the thorns overhead, slashed and pierced and bleeding, while its manifold eyes blinked in shimmering waves; the club snagged in the high branches. Half in revolt, Durand thrust his sword out—a foot of steel vanishing into the ogre's breast. A waste, it should have been, stabbing where no heart beat. But the ogre caught at Durand's blade with both hands, every eye popping wide.

Something spread from the point of Durand's blade, wet and black but running like flame over dry leaves. The thing was coming apart. Stones, beetles, wet glop, roots like hair. In a few moments, the slab-like head had pitched into the reeking collapse, and the rest was a writhing mess: running vermin, rotten matter, flying things, bits of stone. And a sharp reek.

Durand's sword had skewered a bit of bone—a fragment of jaw and two yellow teeth stitched all around with hooked script. He had seen such a thing years ago, in Acconel, when poor Ouen had been sent by the Rooks. When he killed the sending. A sorcerer could bind a man's soul to a bit of the dead man's body.

But Durand had only a moment to notice it, for over the corpse of the giant leapt a cowled snipe, and a man of barbed iron cages. Shrieks came from the rear, and the dwarfish maragrim rattled in the branches overhead. There was no time to draw breath. The maragrim had them from every side.

Then Durand saw the horses. "The horses must go!" he roared. "Stand clear!" With luck, they would bowl a way through the closing ranks of the maragrim. Some of the women had hold of bridles and reins, but now they let go. Durand rushed among the horses, roaring as wildly as the maragrim while Ailric and the villagers slapped the animals' flanks. The beasts surged toward the mouth of the tunnel and the wild shapes there, but one solid shoulder knocked Durand against the hedge. And, when he stumbled, he struck a hollow place—a spot where the branches were few—and saw a chance of escape. The maragrim would set upon on the horses, expecting the villagers to follow in their wake, but they would not follow. "Follow me!" Raising his shield, Durand rammed through the branches.

At first, he struck the face of a whitewashed wall, but he could not stop, so he threw his elbow against the willow lath and plastered clay to land in a bondman's longhouse between the man's startled oxen.

Before Durand found his feet, Ailric was already handing child after child through into the dark house. Durand thought of cellars and lofts— places where a child might be hidden—but he had no time to search. The trick had gained them only heartbeats. Already, he heard fiends on the thatch. And then, the maragrim appeared at the breach.

Durand fought in the gap, striking limbs and beaks and eerie human faces. Berchard and Ailric swung too. Abruptly, a hand shot through and one of the oxen was snatched through the breach, the wall and bones breaking.

In the next instant, an incomprehensible thing had seized two of the corner posts that held the roof. Limbs of all kinds. Faceless or many-faced. The longhouse shook like a wicker cage. The villagers had to get out. To Durand, the tower was the only option. At least there, they could have stone at their backs. "Get the children through! Rally at the tower!" Durand said. He leapt at the thing, striking relentlessly at insect limbs and fish's flesh even as it tried to pry open his lips, to catch his throat, to haul him in, to drink the life and fear from him.

The light shifted.

Heremund had found the hearthstone, and the skald was flinging coals into the thatch as the monstrous maragrim struggled through the house. Maybe the place would burn.

Durand ran.

The survivors poured through the bondman's yard, dodging sheds and troughs and sties and stumbling out a gate where the crooked tower seemed a hundred leagues away. But they ran, tangled with their pursuers. Behind them, the longhouse bucked like a flaming bed on a man's back. The thing within bellowed in agony.

Durand slapped down dwarfish obscenities to buy the villagers time for their desperate retreat while the ragged pack of stumbling men and half-carried children sprinted for the tower. Ailric and Heremund dragged Berchard. And, finally, they piled up against the pillar-narrow tower's base, trapped and scrambling to make their final stand as the maragrim bounded straight into their ragged line.

Durand yanked the huge sword around in fatal loops, splitting a bearded head on spider's limbs and hacking to the wishbone in a rotten man. But, before he could wrench his blade from the rotting shape, an enormous figure in a priest's cassock caught his shoulder with dead fingers.

Above the collar, the priest's head was utterly lost in the maw of a living woodlouse that swung over the huge man's back like a bulging grain-sack. All the louse's limbs and mouthparts worked in running blood. Stronger than carthorses, the thing heaved Durand from the ground, belly to belly, crowding him close to the hideous face.

The woodlouse swung like a pendulous hood and there wasn't room for an entire human head in the thing. Blood and bile was in Durand's eyes.

Berchard struck, but the thing might well have been made of brass. Durand's heels were kicking three feet from the ground.

He could not work his blade around. He could not free his arms. There, in the open, the thing would go through him and all the rest. He could not stop it.

It was at his face, pawing with its gray limbs, mouthparts jabbing like writhing fingers . . .

And then it exploded, and Durand hit the ground in a spray of chitin and bile.

Choking and fighting for air, he still twisted to see what could have struck the maragrim. At the top of the tower, he saw a face vanish from the window.

This was very nearly the end of the maragrim at Benewith. The survivors slew a moth-thing with a maiden's face and another two of the smallest fiends. And then they were alone, swaying with exhaustion and terror under the tower. Children sniffled. Durand looked over the pale gaggle of survivors. The bailiff was gone, along with one of his sons and, perhaps, three of the other men. All the rest had survived.

"It nearly killed me," said Durand. "I could do nothing."

"Did you see?" said Berchard. "The woman in the tower? The stone? Didn't miss you by a handspan." Berchard pointed at a substantial block of masonry that had appeared in the midst of the gore at the bottom of the tower. This, then, had exploded the maragrim.

The nearest of the villagers were making the Eye of Heaven, and a few glanced at the top of the tower. And, indeed, something moved, though it was not at the top of the tower. Something slithered along the masonry. At first Durand could not understand what he saw, but, after a moment, he knew. It was rope—rope of a gray and patchwork sort, but rope. Inch by inch, it descended from the window until the tail of the thing brushed the ground.

Durand looked to Aed's son, but the startled blank of the man's expression told him that this had never happened before—not in their memory at least. The villagers departed, bent and furtive, unwilling to look up. Most touched Durand's arm. Some gave his hand a squeeze. Finally, Aed's son gave Durand a nod and backed away with the rest.

Durand and his companions were alone in the firelight.

The rope hung in the midst of the silent company like a question. Finally, a face appeared high overhead. A pale, perfect oval, shining like the full moon.

Berchard shifted his weight, foot to foot. "Do you notice that the base of this tower is littered with dollies? Cloth mostly. Rag. Twists of willow. There are hundreds, I think."

They stood upon a low mound. Here and there, it was sod. Always it had a forest-floor give. Things cracked.

"Some of the things are in wedding garlands," said Heremund. "And are those wounds on some? Signs of sickness?" Heremund bent. "Here. This is the skull of a lamb." He looked to Durand. "They have been leaving their bits and pieces here for many lives of men."

Still, the rope dangled.

Ailric met Durand's glance, but gave no counsel.

"She dropped the stone," offered Berchard.

And Durand nodded. "I will climb."

"Be careful," said Heremund.

"How can a man be careful in these times?"

Durand climbed, feet against the tower and its mortarless patchwork stones. Hand over hand, he pulled, with his forearms searing and his boots sliding in the ivy. It was not curiosity that compelled him. He felt that the rope and the Lady were a doom of sorts, and the Book of Moons counseled that a man must face his doom. When such a door opens, a man must step through or dread the day he stands before the Bright Gates of Heaven.

High overhead, he was unsurprised to see two black birds teetering in a lopsided gyre above the uncanny tower.

"Where is he going, our hero? Our precious spider so far from the ground? Does he know?"

"We know little enough."

"The Atthias are so full of oddities. Every hill is a barrow mound of knocking kings and silver coffins. Does it not seem so?"

"What has come to this place on the straight road from Pennons Gate? What relic survives here that these villagers make their humble offerings and leave their little prayers? Their menfolk will all have tried the climb."

"Oh, of course."

"What youth could resist it? A question standing in their midst and the answer awaiting the first one to climb. Curiosity has long been the downfall of humankind."

"And of ourselves, brother."

"Indeed."

"But still, they know nothing."

"No one has made the climb."

"Or none have survived to tell of what they've seen, brother."

Before long, the suffocating effort of the climb squeezed all thought from his skull—even the rattling whispers of the Rooks. His back and shoulders burned. Twenty fathoms below him, the village might have been a scattering of drab toys, but Durand saw nothing to do but press on. He squinted at the dark socket of the window above as his soles slithered over the masonry, and a chaos of birds flew out of that dark stone mouth.

Finally, Durand levered his elbows onto the narrow broken sill of that high window to blink into a tiny room little larger than a sentry box. A pale light glowed in the room, as though moonlight penetrated the chamber through a flaw in the roof.

There sat a woman, young and slender.

She worked at an embroidered hanging on a tall stretcher. Her cheek was pressed against the broad drum skin of fabric like a maid listening at a door. Her dark and gleaming eyes were elsewhere—far away indeed.

Then the eyes twitched and he was caught.

"You are not he," she said.

And, after an instant of stillness, the girl was at his side. He had not yet got his legs over the windowsill.

"No," she said. "But I thought . . . There is something."

Her lips swept very near his jaw and a cool scent stirred in Durand's nostrils: green leaves and dark earth, rain and rotting things.

"Fellwood," she said.

"I—"

"But you have been in the glade. I waited so long."

The lady slipped back from Durand's cheek. And the wholesome living glow of her dimmed like a passing shadow, giving Durand a glimpse of the same woman drawn in shades of ice: clear over black depths, the scratches of frost over blue darkness.

"Hells," said Durand. He had climbed twenty-five fathoms. I have ghosts enough of my own, he thought, but held his tongue.

She wafted back to her embroidery and now Durand saw the scene depicted there: two princes, two warriors of the Atthias with antique arms, on each brow a diadem. The taller prince bore the eagle of the royal heir, a blond warrior in gold and russet. The other bore the Windhover blazon of a younger prince, and was picked out in the blues and grays of the thrush's egg and the heron's wing.

This dead woman pressed her high cheek to the golden prince—the prince who must be Calamund, lost to Einred, lost to Godelind to whom he gave the twining serpent ring. The ring upon which Durand had taken his oath.

"I have lost my ring," she said.

Durand remembered the pouch at his belt.

The woman was at Durand's cheek once more. She was a thing of faint bones, a pale tracery of ice, delicate as the bones of a pike. And frost grew upon the walls of her bower, bristling like needles while she spoke, confidingly, in Durand's ear. "I left it, you know." Her voice was the same, though now its childlike softness was conjured from the air and the Otherworld. "He came from the forest, south, where I knew he must come, stumbling toward my reaching arms. I thought he was my Calamund, my love, my life. And I could not help but follow. Follow him north, back into Errest the Old. Back even to Eldinor. So wounded, so lost was he. But he knew me not. He could not see or understand, and he was much changed."

Her voice tore at him, and Durand shuddered.

"It was long before I understood that he was not my love returned to me, but another. Another who knew me of old. Near to me, but not my love. But I am waiting. For perhaps he will follow, over the mountains and down as I came. The king, he gave me this place, and bid me rest and say no more. So I wait in my tower, the tower I built, stone by stone. And at my needlework, I press my ear so that he will not pass without me."

She stood, and the chamber shivered to a flicker of eerie light, like a flash of distant lightning. "But how will he know me without our ring?" And as the specter turned, her pale gown floating upon the air, the neat room was a bare tower, hollow and stark. "We have been parted long and I fear that I, too, am much changed." The girl's breastbone rose and fell, and blades and fans of frost sprang from the masonry with her every gasp.

Where had the thing tied the rope? Durand wondered. Upon what tissue of dust and cobwebs had he trusted his life?

"What if he should never come? What if I am to be alone here for all time?"

The blue-black light flashed once more, and Durand saw the well below the girl, the empty shaft fathoms down to a white nest of broken bones. Here was every fool who'd ever climbed the tower and joined this mad girl in her tower cell. She had slain them all. Every one had fallen to leave their bones. But there was more. Beyond the tower walls, a throng had gathered, mobbing the base of the tower. Durand nearly grinned, for these were his own Lost comrades, come once more over mountains to find him.

The mad, dead girl was still speaking.

"But *you*," she said. Between one glance and the next, the little room was restored. Godelind seemed a very mortal woman. Her skin glowed like white petals in the moonlight as she came near. Her eyes were wide and soft. But the frost bristled between Durand's fingers, and a bone-splitting ache worked in his bones. "You have seen the ring," she said. "You have touched it, I think." Her face blazed, black and hollow and empty as the night at the top of Creation. "Where is it?"

He had touched the ring. It was true. He had it now. But could he give her the ring? Would it free him? He knew little more than that the Rooks had seen it in their dreams. Why had the Rooks seen it? Where did it figure in this business of kings and war and maragrim thralls?

The blazing face darted nearer. "What have you done with my ring?" she howled.

Durand shoved himself back, scrabbling from her reach, catching hold of the barrel of the tower by the cracks and outcroppings of the stones. Some were loose. His feet slithered till his toes found purchase. But Godelind was howling with the madness of lifetimes alone, lifetimes under the earth in the Lindenhall, lifetimes high here among these mad villagers who had not driven her out or summoned priests enough to lay her down.

"Let me go!" shouted Durand. "It's been three hundred years! They've gone, your princes!"

The tower shook. Jagged rents like thunderbolts shot the length of the thing, and the mad spirit howled. All around, the death-light blazed, full of ice and agony. It snatched the air from Durand's lungs as he climbed. Could a man argue with the howling dead? He scrambled for handholds with aching fingers and bloody nails. Blades of the death-light shot between the fractured stones. He caught the phantom rope and swung ten fathoms, then grabbed again at the tower as the rope gave way. Then there was nothing to do but creep downward, stretched to the snapping of sinews, stabbing with the soggy toes of his boots.

The Rooks darted past, laughing aloud. *"She seems unhappy."*

"Is a wooer not meant to descend upon knotted bedclothes?"

"Perhaps all did not go well in the bower."

Durand struggled, hooking his fingers in the raw gaps between stones. *"She seems quite preoccupied with that old ring."*

"This mad girl and the dreams that called us over the sea. It is strange."

Durand climbed by his fingertips, dodging Rooks and the shafts of uncanny light, cursing the witch in the tower and the Rooks and Creation itself. Then he put a hand wrong, and there was no way to keep hold of the icy tower.

He fell.

The earth punched his lungs empty and left him stupid, gasping.

He blinked up into a circle of terrified friends and the Lost. The beggar king was already stooping, its tongue slithering for a gash of blood in Durand's beard.

Two hundred years of rag dolls and moldering bones had broken his fall.

The instant he could lever himself up onto his feet, Durand led the others a reeling few hundred paces up a crooked lane and out over the fields. The madwoman was still in her tower. He wondered if the old ring might have calmed her. But he wasn't sure. And still, it was too late.

He settled on his haunches and sent Ailric to learn the doom of the Solantine horses. "Be quick," he said. "And careful, by Heaven!"

They hunkered down behind a berm. Durand could see the dead woman's death-light darting through the chinks of her tower as she chased around from the frail heights to hollow bottom. He closed his eyes. Beyond his few friends, the dead were gathering now. And in the baleful lightning flashes of the tower, Berchard and Heremund looked no better.

He tried to think.

"We cannot meet more of these devils," he said. "We must get to Coensar now."

"Agreed," said Berchard. "I am more tired than I've been in my life.

But there's no rest, not with these maragrim thralls loose in the land. It is madness. Where are the Ancient Patriarchs, eh? Not what they once were, these wards of theirs."

"Benewith has no shrine, no sanctuary," said Heremund. "It will have long been one of the maragrim's crooked ways between the wards. They will have come this way time and again, though never in numbers like these. The shrine at Broklambe burned. I wonder, would we find that other shrines had fallen in recent days?"

Durand shivered as he recalled his last days in Abravanal's court. "The high sanctuary has burned," he said. "In Acconel."

Heremund grimaced. "Once the land was bound in a web of priest-craft. During Radomor's war, there were high sanctuaries in ruins through all of Errest the Old, and remember what we saw then? It seems there've been rats gnawing at the wards."

"We are none of us priests," Durand said. "Coensar will have been driving the duke's party hard. Let us say he has reached Wrothsilver by this time."

"It is a fortress town on a high hill," said Berchard.

"And as full as any with priests and soldiers and idols," added Heremund. "They will find no place as strong on their road."

"They might have come so far," said Berchard. "Coensar is crafty, and his men brave."

"Wrothsilver it is, then. If they are dead in the road, we cannot help them. If they are alive, they must be in Wrothsilver. Agreed?"

Berchard nodded.

There were noises off in the village. "I should not have sent Ailric," said Durand. "How is he meant to find horses in the dark?"

Heremund was watching the eerie tower. "What did you see in that place?" he said. "Who is she?"

"The woman from Fellwood. From Lindenhall."

"I thought they had her in a reliquary, all neat and tidy."

Durand had an eye on the tower, still. "Quietly, skald. The woman is Lost. She has followed something, abandoned her vigil. Come this far. She wanted this." He pulled the fat carbuncle ring from his belt pouch; then, at another howl from the tower, he stuffed it back among his few coins.

"And you had other plans for it, did you?" asked Heremund.

"I don't know. She is mad. How did these villagers put up with a dead woman all these years?" Durand wondered.

"It will be the tax," declared Berchard. "A living master demands a thousand taxes. A dead woman will ask none. And be a better master than many for it."

"Now she waits, sure that her man will follow the same track into Errest," said Durand.

"If the poor woman had proper friends, they would have taken her aside long ago," said Berchard. "No prince, live or dead, could be worth all this."

Light slithered between the courses of stone, like an eye at a peep-hole.

"We should be gone from this place," said Heremund. "Ah. Here's Ailric."

Ailric was lugging a coat of mail and a few packs. He was alone.

"How are they, these horses of the Solantines?" called Berchard in a long-reaching whisper.

The young man shook his head. "There is nothing alive in Benewith but the few villagers who rallied at the tower, and they are taking their belongings to another town." The man's face was pale. Durand wondered when any of them had slept last. His eyes burned and a thousand pains assailed him. The boy stood under a mountain of gear.

Durand reached for the iron coat—and found the thing blood-greasy under his fingertips. "This is mine. I will carry it. But anything that can be left behind, we must leave—and count on reaching Wrothsilver before anyone is hungry."

Durand led them, leaving the trembling tower and its howling denizen behind.

17
An Ill-Suited Hero

In the chill of the Dawn Twilight, a patrol of Vadir's mounted sergeants rumbled down on Durand and his companions, bristling with lances and terror. The wide-eyed horsemen knew nothing of Abravanal or the rest—or at least they knew enough not to speak when put to the question by a pack of gaunt, blood-caked strangers.

Ailric knew two of the men. Had he not, Durand's wild quest to reach the Duke of Gireth would have ended in the gatehouse cells, or a ditch outside the city. As it was, the riders rushed them up to Wrothsilver Hall and the seat of the barons of Swanskin Down.

Wrothsilver had always been limewashed from top to bottom. Durand and the others followed their guides through pale and shadowed lanes while the uppermost stories of the citadel blushed in the morning's touch. Finally, a pair of astonished guards ushered them into the polished gates of Wrothsilver Hall.

Berchard chuckled. "We are making many friends here. You'd think they had never let four reeking scoundrels into the baron's hall before now." His whisper was the only sound in the place.

The hall was abandoned.

Perhaps Vadir had ridden for Yrlac, or the maragrim had taken the castle and left it barren and cold.

But instead, as the hall door opened, Durand looked into the faces of a hundred people. They filled the feasting boards before Vadir's high table. Every soul stopped to stare at the four battered interlopers.

On a dais at the hall's farthest end stood the high table. Vadir, Abravanal, and Coensar sat with Kandemar the Herald. Every face was somber.

"You had better come," said Vadir. He did not even need to raise his voice.

The four men entered the hall, passing between long feasting boards till they could bow before the high table: an eerie march.

It was only as Durand made to speak that he saw Deorwen. Her eyes were so full of despair that he nearly forgot the maragrim and the Hornbearer both. What had happened when he'd been in Fellwood? What had they walked into?

There was Abravanal, broken. There was Coensar, his fist a sudden coil on the tablecloth. Many men from the Lindenhall tourney were absent. Raimer, for one, ought to have been at the high table.

"Lordship. Your Grace. Sir Coensar," he began. "We had meant to bring word that Leovere had summoned the Hornbearer, that his host was on the move in the Fellwood and Errest . . . but I can see you know much of this already. What has come to pass?"

No one spoke.

Deorwen met his glance, and he half forgot the throng behind him as he noticed an absence more important than any hundred tourney knights.

"Where is Almora?" he grated.

"Lost," said Deorwen. The rest, Durand could hardly hear over the rushing of blood in his skull. "A thing from the night, in the high passes. . . . Terrible noise. . . . Raimer left, and half the fighting men with him. No word. . . . No sound from the pass at all." He thought Heremund caught hold of his arm, but he shook the man loose.

Durand looked up and down the table, the hollow of his chest thundering like a drum. He wanted to rail against them for failing to search, but what would anyone have done? Could Coensar let old Abravanal scour the mountains, wild with grief, his lungs still raddled with the sickness, and Gireth and Yrlac all tied up with him? They could not remain in the pass with the mountains full of maragrim.

But Durand knew that he would be in the mountains still, tearing at the cliffs with his teeth and nails, had he been with them. Images of the girl danced like flame before his mind's eye. He remembered her as a toddling thing, chased around the Painted Hall. He remembered the siege of Acconel, when she had kept a starving mob from despair.

Somehow, he should have been there: a better man would have contrived it.

He had looked, unthinkingly, to Coensar, but found that he recognized the memory, regret, and disbelief storming behind the old knight's eyes. None of them should be in Wrothsilver.

A bird flapped the length of the hall, its small, dark wings snapping.

"How did it happen?" said Durand.

Coensar blinked. "In the night. A giant, its face full of horns, quick as a spider from the dark. It threw the men off like rats. Blades made no mark upon it. Then it was gone into the black again."

Durand's mind was a millrace of accusations. He had seen the thing in Fellwood. Had it tracked him? Could he have slain it if he'd had the wit? Where were Coensar's sentries? How could Coensar be here and alive and obscenely breathing if the girl was taken? How could they break their fast in Wrothsilver Hall with the girl in the mountains, alone with that thing?

Or dead and frozen like a rag on some mountainside.

This last image seemed very clear in his mind's eye.

What would they do now?

"She is the world," Abravanal said, speaking for the first time. "And she is gone."

It seemed that he was right.

DURAND WAS STILL standing there like a man who had been knocked senseless when a boy darted to Vadir's side, crouching low with a message.

Vadir straightened. "From the gate. A delegation. From the king, they say."

And another bird shot down the length of the hall, bothering the high table.

Durand wheeled in time to see the wings pouring into Wrothsilver Hall. Dark birds tumbled through smoke holes and louvers, starlings all. Men and women crouched low, warding their faces, and Durand drew Ouen's long war sword.

In the doorway stood a stout and grinning man. He wore the black robes of a court functionary and bobbed an awkward bow.

"Hod!" said Heremund, astonished. "It is old Hod, alive and in the flesh." But he faltered. "The man should be dead, Durand. The way he slipped us out of Eldinor and away from those creatures of the king. He was sure they'd have him. He was sure!"

The stout man bobbed his way up the central aisle, skirting the haw-thorn flowers in the big hearth and casting sheepish glances at the birds. Prattling as he came: "Odd. Most odd. Shoo. Shoo. Yes. Excuse me. Do excuse me."

Finally, he bowed himself between Durand and his friends, wincing up at the high table.

"Baron Vadir. A pleasure. Oh yes. And Your Grace! I am the most fortunate of messengers, I see. I had not hoped to find you so far advanced on your journey, but here you are, and much riding have I been saved. Oh, yes."

Heremund stared at this strange figure with his mouth slack. The man, Hod—who had tutored Ragnal and Eodan, the rebel, and even Lost Prince Biedin in their youths—had behaved nothing like this prating fool.

Abravanal seemed to perceive only that the strange man was speaking to him. Coensar interrupted.

"You have come from Ragnal?"

The man squinted. He was always wincing and squinting. Glancing at the east windows. "Oh yes. Yes. Well. No, I should say, I suppose. His Highness has called the Great Council while you've been. . . . Where was it? Lindenhall. Oh, yes. The Lindenhall."

"You say that he has called the Council?" said Coensar.

"Oh, yes. And they are in Acconel. Your Painted Hall, in fact, waiting for His Grace. And the talk concerned you, Your Grace. This business of two duchies and one duke, and whom the rightful heir might be—of Yrlac, not Gireth." The creature grinned with oily condescension, clearly looking to find favor with Almora. "Where is her young ladyship, by the way? There's been some talk of her as well, I must confess."

The thing with Hod's face looked at Durand, who stood in blood and tatters with a bare blade in his fist. Durand stared back. Could this be the man who spirited Durand and Lamoric and Deorwen from the Mount of Eagles in Eldinor?

"Has there been some unpleasantness here?" said the thing that wore Hod's face.

Durand made no answer, and, after a querying moment, the thing turned back to Abravanal.

"Regardless, we must have you in Acconel. Oh, yes. At once, I should say. It is time. A homecoming of sorts. His Highness has sent an escort, these times being what they are." The man fumbled among his robes a moment. "Yes. It is three hundred knights, Your Grace. A strong party." A battalion. "Strong enough to keep the peace, oh, yes. His Highness wishes you in Acconel, and there is time for nothing else."

"When?" said Coensar, drawing Hod's attention.

"I should think that you might finish your meal. Yes. But Acconel is not around the next corner. Your king calls. He deliberates. Will you tarry over your courses in Wrothsilver? In any case, I will leave you to your decisions and rejoin your escort. They will water the horses, that sort of thing. Each man knows his own conscience best." With that, the thing that could not be Hod bowed and departed, wincing and shrinking into the morning light, hauling a deep hood over his face.

"Three hundred," said Coensar.

"It is no escort," said Deorwen. "We have been taken prisoner."

"I cannot leave," said Abravanal.

Coensar stood. "Baron Vadir, we will need fresh horses."

"We have already come too far from the pass," said Abravanal, his voice faltering. "You told me Wrothsilver. We cannot go farther."

Coensar set his teeth, not looking at the duke. "Baron, as many as you can spare. We leave at once. The king has commanded, and we are bound hand and foot."

THE KNIGHTS OF the Great Council had been wise enough not to wait beyond the gates. There would be no siege. The armed men of Hod's escort filled the streets.

Durand saw all this from the arrow loops of Vadir's castle.

In the castle yard, he watched grooms and shield-bearers checking cinches and loading gear with grim alacrity. The men who'd ridden north with Abravanal made ready with the tense haste of a squadron preparing for war.

Durand cursed the king's name as the full scope of his plan came clear. That madness at the Lindenhall had been a lever to prize Abravanal from his capital. Now, the king and the grasping barons of his Great Council held the city. Abravanal, in the midst of his grief, would be fighting for his every land and title.

Baron Vadir had joined the duke's party, unwilling to let the old man ride into this obvious snare alone, and Durand could not fault the baron in this.

But Durand would not be there. He too was making ready, bundling up what provisions he could carry and slipping away. With a few gruff words, he'd convinced one of Vadir's grooms to bring a pair of stout horses to a small gate in the rear of Wrothsilver Castle.

Durand was bound for the mountains.

He lugged the packs, avoiding the press in yard. There was no sense in what he was doing. What fool could believe that the girl still lived? He had seen the Hornbearer; he knew what it was. The girl was dead. The brute had dashed her brains in, had crushed her, had torn her asunder—all in an instant, and all in that same night. It was certain. But Durand could not let it be.

Still, he would undertake his fool's quest alone.

Vadir's groom should now be waiting at the small gate, but it had taken too long to get the few supplies together. And a dozen little things might yet go wrong: the groom might be intercepted, questioned about horses and back doors. The man might begin to wonder why Durand had chosen that odd door at all. Durand hurried onward.

Yet as he swung around a castle corner, he ran into Abravanal himself. For a moment, Durand wondered if the man had died, joining Durand's train of Lost souls, but the man's crabbed hand caught Durand's surcoat. Somehow the duke had evaded his nursemaids. He had been waiting.

"I saw you with Vadir's man, Durand Col. I knew what you would do." The duke sucked a deep breath through his nose. "I'm not always the fool you think me." He shot a glance down the castle passageway toward the chaos of packing. "I know she must be dead, but it is not enough. Lamoric, Landast, Alwen . . . and now Almora? I cannot allow it; it is too much. I cannot think of mountains and dooms and horrors and strong men who have given all, and the king's men coming now like the coils of a serpent. But you know that, too. You must take her back!"

He stopped a moment, his eyes on Durand's chest. "The things we've done to you. All the things I have let be done to you. . . ."

"There is no need."

He gripped Durand with shaking hands, as frail as a bird. "And yet I ask. Do what I cannot. Ride from all this, and damn the king! I am the wandering, grief-addled dotard. In a moment, they will come for me, to coo and stroke my head and bundle me in blankets."

"I will take her back," Durand promised.

"What I have to give is yours, but there is nothing that can aid you. And every moment I spend here brings my minders nearer. The king's men might have something to say about my Champion riding off. And they will have men on the road." He twitched a sour frown as he heard a call from the passageway behind him.

"They are coming for me. So take her. From death or doom or Heaven, I do not care. They cannot have her. Go!" And, with a nod, the duke tottered into the path of the stream of handlers and henchmen, allowing himself to be caught up again in the tide that would soon have him mounted and riding to hollow, empty Acconel. And Durand was free to make his way down to the rear door.

But where he expected to meet Vadir's man, he found Ailric. The shield-bearer waited in the alcove by the sally port, his hands on the bridles of two sturdy horses. Berchard and Heremund grinned in the shadows.

"I see I can have no secrets," said Durand.

Berchard's smile broadened. "Is it a secret that the hammer falls when the hand is opened?"

Durand smiled. "I am riding for the pass. We have two horses."

Heremund nodded, giving Durand a square look. "It is not the pass for me. They have taken Hod. They have the king of Errest bound in knots and snares."

"Hod was a good man," said Durand.

"These devils have woven their net around the king. Whatever Ragnal might have been, there is little left of him but blindness and venom. The maragrim thralls pour down the high passes, and the King of Errest the Old lays snares for old men.

"In Windhover, the kingdom is broken. You've heard of the fighting there? Prince Eodan, the king's own brother, holds his Windhover title in defiance of the king. The king, with his debts, has been at odds with the Great Council these many years. Yet now, he joins the Council and turns on his most loyal men.

"With Yrlac and Eodan and a hundred smaller struggles, we have heard more of rebellion and backbiting in these last dozen years than in the fifty years before. Someone is behind these webs and snares and nets. Something tugs the strings and unravels the kingdom, and I will learn nothing more by following you into the mountains." Heremund would follow the duke, to learn what had become of Hod. And his curiosity would have him gnawing at that knot until someone slew him.

Berchard laughed. "I have no such high-minded purposes. And I hope a blind old man has all the excuses he needs. The mountains are no place for me. I will follow Heremund, here. But search for the girl, Durand. She was a fine little thing at Acconel when Yrlac's men were all around and the castle was like a pot on the fire. She deserves better."

Durand caught each man in a quick clinch. Though he would miss them, he could move faster without the skald and the old man. "Farewell."

Durand and Ailric slipped from the sally port of Wrothsilver Castle down into the streets of the town, quickly losing themselves in the whitewashed alleyways. Ailric led them, by a hundred swift turnings, out of the Wrothsilver and, unseen, onto the shaded green shoulder of the hill.

The air was dank with wet grass, but they could see across the leagues to the high blue massif of the Blackroots. A farmer's track led over the hip of the promontory down toward the Pennons Gate Road. It seemed so easy, but he knew the long leagues to the pass and the mighty climb to the ring where the duke had camped. And he knew the blood-drenched fiends that roamed each track. The girl was far away.

Ailric's blade hissed from its scabbard. *"Behind us, Sir Durand."*

Durand turned, but knew the newcomer at once. For the second time, Deorwen had found him as he left to search for Almora. She led a bay mare down from the gate, her eyes glinting dark and wild.

"No," said Durand.

"I was there when the Hornbearer descended upon the camp," she said. "We lay side by side. Her hand clutched mine as the thing tore her away. I have as much right as you."

"The maragrim are loose in the foothills. They will come for us at nightfall. I do not know how many."

"Still I must come."

Durand made no argument.

* * *

THEY RODE LIKE fools toward the Banderol Road, quickly taking the measure of their borrowed horses. Durand's roan was a rolling thickset bruiser with a coat like snow on black slate. As they bowled down from the citadel, Durand was relieved at the horse's courage, for they waded into droves of refugees—haunted survivors from outlying villages scrambling to reach Wrothsilver before night fell once again. The crowds were thick for an hour or more as they rode south. And, even from the saddle, a man could see the waking nightmares still shimmering in their wide, hollow eyes. There was no one foolish enough to ride toward the Blackroots now.

When they broke free of the multitudes and were riding only among the stragglers, Deorwen said, "It is all very well our following you, Durand, but how do you mean to go about this?"

Durand checked his pace a bit and faced the others. He had only the rudest fragments of a plan in his mind, and it took him a moment to speak. "We must get into the pass. You will know where this thing came down. We will turn our Ailric loose in the place of the attack, and maybe he will find something when he reads the ground. I would pit Ailric against any of the duke's party as huntsman and tracker. The thrall will have left some sign of its passage."

Deorwen pulled her mantle close. "Cause for hope, then. And, of course, I doubt there is another man alive as bullheaded as Durand Col."

"I will not leave her up there."

"I know, Durand. Now, what of these maragrim?"

"If we reach Pennons Gate by nightfall, then we must put our faith in the wards upon the high passes." Deorwen held her tongue, but Coensar had surely trusted to those selfsame wards, and it had done them no good. "There is no other choice."

"If we would not risk the mountains, we should not have set out. I agree. But are you sure that we can reach the mountains by eventide?" It was a perilously long journey, and the grim days and nights of the last week lay heavily upon them.

"The pass is a great distance. We must trust that the Powers of Heaven will throw some shrine or sanctuary in our path." He glanced to Ailric.

"There are hamlets and shrines in Errest the Old, beyond counting," said Ailric, though there was little comfort in his eyes. Few were the places of refuge in the high country of Gireth—and fewer still on the road to Pennons Gate. This, they all knew.

"Then if this is our plan, we had better ride!" said Deorwen.

*   *   *

BY NOONTIDE, THE road was empty, and the vacant track made space for memory. Durand thought of the bright, damnable girl running away, riding her sugar-white palfrey away from Acconel. . . .

The road dipped and something caught the attention of Durand's big blue roan. Ahead, the track twisted around a towering old oak tree. And, as Durand watched, he saw something in the high branches, large and secretive. "Here, stop," Durand said, raising his hand. He pulled old Ouen's blade. The flail had been worthless against the maragrim.

"I will look," he said. "It may be nothing." He shot a grim glance back at both of them. "Stay together." And he drove the blue roan bowling toward the oak, hauling up to peer into the crown of the tree. A few crows scattered, churning above the branches. There was movement in the high shadows: an awkward shape larger than a man. With a quick twist, Durand unshipped his shield, but reminded himself that the Eye of Heaven was still high and the maragrim must cling to shadows. He let the roan dance a step or two and tried to make sense of what he saw. There was something knocking and swinging. The light fell on a heavy wheel. He saw the blunt horns of oxen and the dangling hooves. "Hells," Durand muttered. Something had slung an oxcart into the branches. The thing was five fathoms high. And he thought he made out other dangling shapes higher in the branches. Another cart lay broken over the roots of the giant oak.

As his companions caught up, Durand heard the harsh chuckle of carrion birds over his head. They would be perched on every dangling carcass.

"This will be the maragrim," said Deorwen, as she reached him.

"We should get past this place. There's nothing to be done." He wanted to get a half-dozen leagues behind them before they hunkered down for the night.

"It is sobering," Deorwen said. "How many have died? Is anyone left in Gireth?" One of the swinging burdens in the tree creaked and groaned, and Durand heard the birds hop and chortle. "There has not been so much as a plowman. Not for an hour or more."

Ailric had been giving the wreckage a scholarly eye. He now frowned at the Banderol Road. "Ladyship, Wrothsilver is now too distant for a man on foot. A man still on the road at this hour could not reach the sanctuary before Twilight. The roads will be empty now, even of living men."

There was another croaking snigger from the tree. Durand squinted up. He saw beaked shapes sidling along the horn of one piebald ox. He saw their heads quirk.

"We must hope you are right," agreed Deorwen. "We must hope that they live and are more clever than we think."

The Rooks' rough laughter echoed over the road.

"She is charming! After all she's seen, brother, I had not expected hope."

"Not in the face of these mute witnesses. What grandeur these mara-grim possess. To imagine that the common folk could face them? And what sorcery! To bind a man's soul for so long."

"We should expect some to have survived," Ailric was saying. "I do not know how many maragrim the Hornbearer commands, but they did not seem to be marching as one. I should think that many will have escaped, especially once they realized that the Eye of Heaven could protect them."

"What a power had the Enemy. These thralls. It is like finding that a child's top is still spinning two hundred winters after the child's hand last touched it."

"And such variety of expression!"

"Beasts, men, things from the sea, horrors of every combination, an-imal and mineral."

"Man and nightmare."

"And all bound with such gossamer thread: fear and shame and guilt and dread."

Durand shook his head impatiently. The words of the Rooks had begun their insect scurrying through his skull.

They were under the tree.

It was Deorwen speaking now. "The people are strong. And they are no fools. The priests and wise women will have remembered something of these maragrim. By now, they will be taking every advantage of the streams and holy places. We must do likewise if we are to reach the mountains."

"Shame is no gossamer, brother. Guilt no mere thread."

"You say not, dear brother?"

"I flatter myself that I have made a little study of it. An example: Guilt can drag a man from safety through a haunted land into the hands of a very devil, brother."

"Are you alluding to our hero and his friend? What guilt should they feel?"

"Poor Durand knows little but remorse, brother. You must specify."

"Over this wayward girl, then?"

"His charge, brother? Lost? Neglected?"

"I see. It is that simple?"

"Damn you," said Durand. He had the sense that the others were looking his way now.

"I would not say simple! Think on it a moment, brother. The girl's father was Durand's lord from childhood. The young Durand grew up in that hall. He was trusted. There were oaths, indeed. Add into this Lamoric. And Lamoric's wife. The betrayals. How can he discharge such a debt? Such shame."

Durand pitched, catching the saddlebow for an instant. Every hiss the Rooks uttered had a life of its own, chattering in spirals through his head. Somewhere near the fallen cart, Durand dropped to the road, his jaw smacking hard against a tree root. He heard the others calling out. He heard his name, but it was all he could do to breathe.

"It is too much, brother. The girl is not her father. She is certainly not the cuckold Lamoric."

"But these ties—though they seem less than a breath of air—are real to a stanch fellow such as our Durand, and strong as chain: he is oath bound. He must watch the girl. His debt he pays with vigilance, with loyalty. And the girl, she slips away. It is the beginning."

Durand groped the roadbed, knowing that he should have held on to the saddlebow. He had endured these devils before, but by what right did they cackle over the business of a man's soul? "Shut up!" he cried. "Shut up!"

"A thousands steps led the girl to that pass. Could our hero have turned a key on her in Acconel? Could he have sent her back at Wrothsilver when Vadir smiled too broadly?"

Durand snarled. The fall had knocked him stupid. The Rooks' mutters were running round and round, filling his head like the boiling tide at Gulf of Eldinor that had nearly drowned him so long ago. He saw the gray beams of the wrecked cart standing before him in odd angles, saw something moving below the cart. Durand screaming: a distant, alien thing.

"If our hero had checked his temper at the Lindenhall, he might have been at her side, blade bare to defend her. It is the same for the woman."

There were hands clutching at him, but Durand saw a face. Under the cart it was, and soot-blackened with wide blue terrified eyes. He lifted his hand, stretching out.

"He can be made to do most anything when the ropes of guilt are tightened round him. How can he refuse a fellow sufferer? Shame is the

leash that makes men tame. It can make a man do anything. It can make him die. Look here at Durand—"

The whispers exploded. They burst like flies from his head with a force that threw him from the cringing shape under the cart.

Durand rolled, gasping onto his back. And saw Ailric, white-faced and armed with a stone—a second stone. Black feathers and maggots tumbled down, landing on the man's hair.

Deorwen's fist was in his collar, her weight on his lungs.

"You were reaching for that thing under the cart," she said. "Cursing and twitching. We couldn't pull you away." She crawled off.

Durand stood, shaking his head and giving Ailric a good hard look.

There was, indeed, something under the cart. He could see it moving in the shadow of the planks.

"What is it, Durand? What is going on?"

Durand stooped, seizing a cart shaft. The thing cowering underneath twitched like a broad spider. And, with a glance at the Eye of Heaven, Durand flipped the cart over. Underneath were two identical horrors, each larger than a man. Each slate-black thing bore four taloned arms. Below their sapphire eyes was a tongue like a wicked blade. They spun, backing into the earth—into the cracks in the ground, lashing the roots and road with wild desperation until only the glint of blue eyes remained in the shadowed crevice.

"What was that about, Durand? What is happening?" said Deorwen. "The horses will be half a league down the road." But Durand had no words. They had nearly killed him, the Rooks. If not for Ailric's stone, Deorwen would have watched him die. The Champion of Gireth caught like a miller's hand between the grindstones.

Deorwen deserved more. Deserved better.

"We must get away from here," he said, finally.

Feeling like a fool, he stalked after the runaway horses, fighting not to weave between the banks as he staggered toward the mountains.

ON AND ON they rode, until dusk returned to the high ground above Errest the Old. Once more, Durand had his eye on the ruddy western horizon. His small company had pounded the hills higher and higher since the maragrim oak, pushing the horses as hard as Durand dared. And now, though the blue wall of the Blackroots filled the southern Heavens, Durand knew that they would not reach the Sisters before nightfall.

Every crack and shadow seemed to quiver with the maragrim. At first, they pointed out each horror. Soon, however, the things became too commonplace to mention. They needed to find a shrine or a sanctuary soon, or they would never reach the pass.

Durand remembered a nameless hamlet on the way down from Broklambe. "Ailric, there was a hamlet not far from this place." It had been littered with the dead, but it would have had a sanctuary.

Ailric looked at him in surprise. Durand imagined that the young man's eyes were full of the carrion birds and dead men they had seen. It seemed a vain hope.

"There's nothing else till Broklambe," said Durand.

"And nothing in Brokelamb would stop the maragrim," said Deorwen. "We must chance this village, I think."

18
Whispers in the Lonely Places

They soon found the village: a clutch of low buildings huddled among broken pinnacles on a bare shelf of gravel. Where Durand had expected to see bodies and carrion birds, he found an empty hamlet and an empty sky. Without thinking, Durand had reined in.

"Why do you stop?" said Deorwen.

"There were bodies here, yesterday. A good many. Broklambe was empty. This hamlet was strewn with corpses."

There were a dozen buildings clustered in a space little larger than a castle yard, every wall fashioned of the same stones on which the huts and sheds stood.

Deorwen urged her mount forward and onto the narrow plateau. "Where are they now, I wonder?" She passed within arm's reach of the damp stone walls. Every corner and barrel looked like it might conceal monsters.

"Buried," said Ailric. "Some, anyway," he added, pointing toward a place of mounded stones. He hopped from his saddle and scrambled to the heaps, peering close before calling. "Yes. The stones are a jumble. Earth on top. Dry lichen under. Fresh laid."

"And many stones," said Durand. There were ten or more mounds and the builders had done a proper job. "They did it today and they wanted the dead to stay buried: this will have been a long day's work, even for a dozen men—and there can't have been many survivors." He eyed the few buildings. Not one of the thickset hovels could be mistaken for a sanctuary.

"We must find shelter," said Deorwen. Already, the western crags were slicing long shadows from Heaven's Eye.

Durand considered. It was a small village and there were so many graves. "These people had little time to travel after such a task. They must be nearby."

"Are there cellars, perhaps?" asked Deorwen.

Durand winced. "A man in a cellar might drown in the things. We saw whole horrors folded into a crack in the ground. What would a cellar be like?" He eyed the foundations of the nearest huts.

"All right, Durand. Enough. So we can't sit down and wait for the maragrim here. There's Broklambe still. We might reach it, though I don't fancy digging through the ashes of that old sanctuary again." They all remembered the curled cinders of the dead villagers. "We've no way of knowing whether the maragrim would shy from anything left in that doomed place."

Ailric, who had been doing some grubbing of his own, stood abruptly, for all the world like a hunting dog who'd stumbled over a scent.

"Ailric, what is it?" said Deorwen.

"It is hard, reading the stones, but there is a path here." He gestured uphill, where a gravel trail led into the broken hills to the east. "Men have passed this way. It has not been long."

Durand thought of the empty road behind them and the burned shrine ahead. "It is the only way," he said. The Eye of Heaven was low and the mountains cast long shadows before them. "We must pray they were not going far. An hour will be too long."

They followed the unknown path, riding as the track twisted between bare stone crags, sometimes as close as columns in a castle hall. Already, the blazing pinnacles were mantled in swags of shadow, and furtive shapes stirred in the darkest gullies, and fluting calls echoed among the stones.

"They will not wait for nightfall," said Deorwen.

Durand made out crouched shapes lying in wait. Eyes jittered in the deepest places.

They scrambled up between grim hills with the Eye on their backs. Soon, it was clear that the ravines teemed with a confusion of horrors. From one ditch, spears and glaives jutted like reeds. Great spidery shapes groped the valleys, pressing close. And Durand began to wonder if he had killed them all, dragging them into the highlands.

Soon, the glow of the empty Heavens would fail and the maragrim would have them. They were already unfolding. He heard a hiss like cicadas rising and falling around them.

At this last moment, a strange pinnacle blazed before them. Someone had hewn a shrine from the living rock and a last ribbon of sunlight lay upon its face. This must be their refuge.

It stood across a meadow of boulders and tangled grasses. Durand made out the square sockets of dark windows and the lean-to peak of a roof.

And then that light was gone.

"That is the sunset, Sir Durand," said Ailric.

And into the gloom rushed a sea of hisses and clicks and screeches, and the maragrim were on the move.

"Ride now!" said Durand, and they bolted over the rough grasses as fiends rose from the tussocks, flexing their claws. The devils lashed from every side as the three charged for the strange stone shrine.

There were people crowding the windows—living men and women who could not help but call encouragement as Durand and his companions galloped the last hundred paces. Durand saw a door flung open four fathoms above their heads.

"You must climb!" said a voice. "You cannot save the horses. Climb!"

Durand threw himself down, catching at bridles to slow the others as they dismounted at the cliff bottom—in the face of a galloping phalanx of thralls. There were hands waving down from the high door and traces of footholds on the way up the rock wall. Durand shoved Deorwen as high as he could and got Ailric climbing as well. And he, himself, only scarcely managed to pull his boots from the talons of the mob.

Refugees and maragrim howled above and below as Durand climbed. Skull-sized stones whooshed past as the villagers drove the maragrim back. A black hand caught Durand's shin in a grip to grind bones, only to be dashed away by a block of granite from above.

Then Durand felt friendly hands catch hold of him, hauling him into the snug, crowded darkness of the shrine.

"Thank Heaven," said Deorwen. The pale oval of her face was very close. "I thought you were lost."

The maragrim screamed a mix of glee and rage over the wild, gabbling shrieks of the poor horses. In his mind, Durand could see the beasts brought down, kicking and lunging, by the teeth and talons of the mob. It was not quick.

"Here," said a woman's voice. "As far from the door as you can. There was nothing for it. An hour with ropes could not have got your horses safe up here, and there is no room."

Durand made out the lined face of an old woman. She slapped a pair of strong hands together; it had been her stone that saved Durand, he had no doubt. "And I wasn't about to leave any man to those things. We are all that's left of Gowlins. Four men, three women, and my boy. We have seen what those things are, and you will be safe enough. They did not dare to enter the shrine last night. And though they tried their tricks with torches and burning straw to drive us out, it's all stone. You should have—"

Abruptly, a pale youth stopped the woman. Wisps of beard darkened the hollows of his neck and cheeks. He poured whispers into the old woman's ear, his eyes fixed on Durand.

"Here," she replied. "Take your hand from my shoulder and I will ask him."

She ducked her chin in Durand's direction, saying, by way of introduction, "This here is the hermit. A young one." The staring youth gripped the lady's shoulder again. "Here! What did I tell you?"

"We've had a hermit on the rock for ages," she said. "And it's good luck we care for 'em, what with them expecting the birds to pluck the juniper in the autumn and to live on air or God knows the rest of the year. This one is new to us, or nearly so. Three winters. The last one came up in my grandmother's day."

The hermit ducked, hissing at the woman's ear.

"I know, I know." She looked at Durand. "He says he's seen you. He wants to know who you are."

Durand grunted. He should have said something before now. "I am Durand Col, this is Lady Deorwen, and this my shield-bearer, Ailric. He might have seen me in Acconel."

The feverish stare continued and there were more hissing words.

"He says 'no.' And 'shield-bearer' has him agitated, the silly thing. I fancy he means a dream, Durand Col. He will be thinking it's the future, and he looks none too pleased about it, I must say."

Durand looked at the wild eyes for a long, exhausted moment.

Finally, the hermit burst with frustration. "This hollow little place, it is like a bell. It rings with memories and dreams. I have heard the Horn of Uluric resound from the vault of Heaven, and the Hornbearer's devilish horn making mock of it."

Durand looked into the mad face, feeling every step of the leagues and leagues behind him. "We have all heard."

"But there is more, Durand Col. Do you know where you have come? Who climbed this rock and died upon it, Durand Col? And who built this cell? This shrine?"

"I am weary beyond measure," said Durand.

"Then will it wake you to know that a Lord of Penseval caused this place to be built upon this stone? Duke Leowin, who carried the Horn of Uluric before the Host of Errest."

"I do not understand."

"Leowin built it to shelter a man, Durand Col: a man who would not descend into Errest the Old, who could not quite return."

"What?" said Durand.

"It is no wonder that you vowed silence, hermit," said the old woman, exasperated. "The whole thing is back to front. Here. What he's trying to tell you is that there was a crusader came back over the mountains and couldn't go no further, though whether it was guilt or gratitude that held him, I couldn't say. And the crusader was one of the men with the Lost Princes and Leowin of the Horn. In fact, they say he was Heraric's shield-bearer. And sure Leowin would have known him. And would have wanted a roof over the poor man's head when he sat here by the track. That's all. A fine story."

The hermit stared. "Theoric, shield-bearer. Theoric, who rode with the Lost Princes, who fought the Host of Thralls. Theoric, who lost his Prince to the Sons of Heshtar and stood astride his master with bared blade, battling back the darkness. This place of shame and thankfulness."

The old woman frowned. "That's what I've said, boy. If you must speak, you shouldn't waste words by repeating your elders."

Deorwen was very near. Very warm. There was no room in the hermit's cell.

"This place rings with dreams and memories," the boy-hermit repeated. "I have heard their voices, those crusaders calling in pain and victory. And there is a voice on the wind, even now. A whisper. A voice that niggles at the memory. Few remember Theoric, but he fought with the Lost Princes and grieved their passing here."

Durand tried to imagine someone from that long-ago time curled up in that same stony darkness. The man might have known the Herald. He might have seen Godelind in Eldinor. He might have sat with the Knights of Iron in Pennons Gate. But here, he stopped.

"I think that his people should have come to get him," he said, "but it is our good fortune that they did not." Durand's eyes were heavy. Even with Deorwen and the hermit and the cries of the maragrim all around him, exhaustion hauled him down.

"The voice. It whispers, Durand Col," the hermit was saying, but sleep took him.

DURAND WOKE COLD and stiff in that crowded hermit's cell, with Deorwen huddled against his back, small as a dove. In the doorway, Ailric stood watch over the hills. Durand shifted away and joined his man, looking out where the predawn mist swirled over the meadow.

"There," said Ailric.

A thing like a half-butchered man was hobbling and sobbing through the mist below the hermitage toward a gap in jostling hills to the north.

"That is the last of them," said Ailric.

"The last?"

Ailric nodded. "The first took his leave around midnight. It was not easy to make out, at first; they left in ones and twos. But soon the crowd grew thin." The young man squinted into the northern mist. "Always north."

"Gireth."

Ailric nodded.

Within the hour, the three searchers bid good-bye to the folk of Gowlins, with the old woman chuckling about how they would all be praying for juniper berries before long. The haggard hermit boy never ceased his staring.

It would be a long climb on foot, but the horses were gone except for a few cracked bones. Worse, there was nothing but scraps and tatters left of their packs and provisions—though Durand's old hauberk survived, hanging high on a thornbush. He expected that the devils had licked each link for the flavor of old blood.

It was an eerie, empty Creation through which they climbed. At deserted Broklambe, they mounted a search for anything that might keep them alive in the mountains. There were a few sacks in a shed near the mill, a few leather bottles here and there—and plenty of water in the stream—but there was little food after refugees and raiders and thralls had passed.

Yet if they were hungry, how hungry must Almora be in the high passes? And if they were cold, how cold must Almora be in the mountains alone?

The voice of doubt nagged that Almora was likely far colder than they, and far less hungry, but Durand could not stop until he knew, and neither one argued.

"I spoke to the old woman after you slept," said Deorwen. "The hermit rambled on about the Horn of Uluric and the Hornbearer's mocking trumpet, and about these whispers he hears. They come at night, though I doubt the boy knows what they say. These hermits, one after another, alone with the echoes of past days, and caught between the mountains and the kingdom below. It's a wonder any of them are sane."

Durand scowled. "What sights would those men have known, brawling with the Enemy in his own nation? It is not to be thought of. Yet perhaps they only see what we dare not."

THE WHITE BLADES of the Sisters soared against the vault of Heaven and, after noon, they felt the distant spray of the Tresses upon the high chill air.

At long last, they came to the high pass and the campsite ring where Leovere's men had sheltered, the place where they had crossed in the storm. It was now scattered with abandoned pavilions.

"It is here," said Deorwen, "where Almora was taken."

"Why did you not tell me?"

"I did not wish to be left behind, Durand. It seemed a neat way to force your hand."

She had not needed such a trick. "But why in this place?" wondered Durand.

"Everyone was tired, and it was a league to the next place that suited. Leovere's men had left nothing behind." Neither dead men nor blood, Durand thought.

Two of the tents had survived the nights since Coensar had left the pass, and now the slack canvas flapped in the cold and aimless wind. Ailric and Durand slipped across the tangled grass and wreckage, checking each tent behind the points of their swords.

Deorwen stepped out into the ring. There were shocks of color against the grass: tents, trappers, surcoats, packs. "We'd pitched tents on the level ground with men standing guard. I think Coensar made certain that no one could steal up on us. He remembered how Leovere's sentries fared."

Coensar was no fool, not in such matters. "He would have been careful. Men on the track north and south. More than one or two. But he would have been thinking of Leovere and his rebels."

Durand took in the desolation of the place, laid bare under a clouded sky. Here, the land showed a man how small he was. How could Almora, alone, have survived this? Why had he believed, even for an instant, that he would find anything but a little corpse, dead and frozen like some shattered bird.

A little corpse.

Durand remembered crouching in the sentry's blood while something watched from the high stones. He had not been sure what he saw.

Deorwen moved between the fire pits and canvas, her hands fluttering. Durand could almost see the fires and shadows shimmering in her eyes. Then she knelt, setting her hand in the ruin. "This was our tent." It was torn. In places, twisted into the earth. "I woke with the thing right on us. Maybe staggering in torn canvas. The face was horns all around. And then it had Almora. It leapt like a spider, out of the firelight and out of the world."

She blinked, freeing herself from the memory. "I think it went—" She stopped, looking about herself at the cold camp. "We have been fools. Wishing cannot scratch out what is already written." The ruins were all around them. Durand had brought them here, and they would be hungry before long. And all for nothing.

Ailric, meanwhile, was grubbing over the earth once more. Durand had become used to the shield-bearer's constant searching. Now, however, the young man stopped, looking up the wall of the cliff that towered over the camp.

"Something moving," he said. "There, at the cliff edge. I cannot say what."

Durand, too, saw a small motion against the pearl vault of the clouds. Something was there, fathoms overhead, flirting with the edge of the cliff. "I see it!" he said. The maragrim could not be abroad in daylight. Without a word, Durand was in motion.

"That is where I saw the thing on the night we first passed this way. We'd heard that ox-groan in the blackness," Durand said. He let the others scramble after him as he stalked across the camp, eyes fixed on the cliff top. "Right there! I let myself think it was some knob of rock, but I knew that something had us in its eye." He strode over the knotted grass and out of the ring, seeking some way to attack the cliff. He had done nothing before, and look what it had cost them.

"Durand?" said Deorwen. "What do you mean to do?"

"We will see what is watching us this time."

A hundred paces north, he found a rubble-choked breach in the cliff wall leading to a soaring fissure that rose before him like a ruined stair. He threw himself into this alley of stone and climbed, sometimes grappling up between the high, facing walls. He had been chased and thrown and treed and mauled since Acconel. Now, he had a chance to do some chasing of his own. He did not rest or slow until he crested the final rise.

A gust at the cliff top met him like a bullock's shoulder, and he winced into the eternal gale that boiled over the high places of Creation. There, across a promontory as narrow as a whale's back, something lurched. But, rather than a man or monster, what Durand saw was the wry scrag of a tree—and a white mantle snagged upon it, lashing in the wind.

The wind hit him as he stepped out onto the rock, and he teetered like a man on the keel of an upturned ship. The mantle bore a thick collar of white fur. He knelt as the others crested the rise. Deorwen must have been right on his heels the whole way up. But Durand could only stare at the cloak. He had seen Almora nestled in it, riding her fool palfrey on the way from Wrothsilver. She had been here.

"It is her cloak," said Deorwen. "She will be cold without it. She—" Deorwen reached to put her fingers in the soft collar, but snatched her hand back. Something buzzed.

Durand got hold of the cloak, tearing it from the tree, ready to seize anything that might be hiding. But he found only a silver pendant: a bit of jewelry caught by its chain.

The amulet spread wings like slivered pennies and leapt against the end of its chain.

"It is Almora's! The little Power."

He had seen it a thousand times, flying sometimes under the vaults of the Painted Hall. Marveling despite himself, Durand reached for the tiny thing—hardly larger than a beetle. But as he touched the chain, he must have knocked it free, for the thing flew shrilling down from the precipice and off into the west, where it darted and was lost to sight.

"She was here," said Deorwen.

"Yes." The Hornbearer had carried her this far, at least. But alive or dead? Durand had the cloak still in his hand, and now, with this question in his mind, he pawed over the thing, searching for traces.

"No blood," said Doerwen. "Durand, she was alive!"

"Come," said Durand. "That little Power flew west. Who knows what such a sign may mean? But I say we must follow."

WITH RECKLESS HASTE, they scrambled down the humped back of the promontory to the floor of a stark valley, following on as it dipped and rolled westward.

After an hour of tramping in that alien place, seemingly alone under the vault of Heaven, Aliric spotted signs that men had passed this way: the sandy bank of some nameless rivulet bore the scars of many hooves.

"I had forgotten Raimer's men," said Durand.

"Aye. It could be them," said Ailric. He winced and grimaced, tilting his head to and fro. "Several horses. A line, traveling westward. Too much trampling for a certain count, and it has rained since they passed."

"If they were here too, it may be a good sign. When the trail was fresher, good men chose this route."

Ailric nodded, his face impassive. Somewhere ahead then, Raimer's squadrons were hidden in these same canyons.

Not long after, they spotted horses up a blind valley. The poor devils were wandering against a scree slope, small as insects in the distance. "They will starve," said Deorwen. "Or freeze."

"They will," said Durand. It would take a day to catch the horses on foot in this open place, but Durand was less worried about horses than riders. You did not leave horses to die in the mountains; not easily.

"Raimer will have been following some trail," said Ailric. "That might have led them from the valley. A horse cannot scale a cliff. There are slopes a man can master that no horse would try."

"Or the riders are dead," said Deorwen. "None of us are children, Ailric."

The valley died between two peaks, leaving only a dark and narrow gorge ahead. It was like stepping from the mountains into a lost temple, so narrow and thick with gloom was it.

Ailric searched the threshold and found marks upon it. "They passed here," he said.

"Then we follow."

Gone were the open winds of the wide mountains. Here, the clammy walls seemed to shut away the world.

AFTER A TIME, a strange murmur swelled between the walls. Durand looked to each of the others, but saw only the mirror of his own wary bewilderment. The sound ebbed as the wind faltered.

"It can only be the wind groaning over some hollow in the stones," said Deorwen.

Durand held his tongue and marched up the defile. Like the killing ground between castle walls, a stone rampart stretched above them before jogging right and out of sight. Durand eyed the heights, thinking of giants on the high ground and no escape for a poor fool in the gorge.

They reached the bend, climbing warily around the mighty knife of stone only to hear the voices swell once more—moaning, whispering, filling the gorge and hissing as close as lips at their ears.

Still, it was a moment before he made out the squat shapes that crowded the canyon. There were ranks and ranks of standing stones, each rudely carved. Durand made out the dark gashes of their eyes, the arrowhead blades of their beards, and the gaping sockets of their mouths. They wore miters, crowns, and helms of ancient make.

The wind in the gorge conjured aching sounds from the stones. The idols stood close, like a royal guard at attention. There was no hope of keeping distance. There must have been five hundred.

They picked their way into the groaning crowd. "This will have been some part of the wards," said Deorwen. "Coming from the south, you could not enter that whole gorge without passing through these kings."

"The patriarchs will have tried to stopper up every pass that lets into Pennons Gate," said Ailric.

A long breeze drew a rising song from the stones all around.

Deorwen looked into one stark face. "This bears an Atthian mark. He is a Patriarch, I think." She touched another. "This is a king, though I could not guess his name. How many places like these are there in these high passes?"

"Pardon, Lady. There is more." Ailric pointed beyond the crowding stones. "There has been a slide, I think. Raimer's party must have tried to skirt the stones on the high ground there."

Durand made out the heaped gravel easily enough, but, between the two-score stone heads, he thought he saw something more—a dark shape humped low at the bottom. He moved to get a glimpse between the kings.

And, with his eyes fixed on the rubble, he did not see what was at his own feet.

Something caught his leg, and the force and surprise tripped Durand to the gravel. The man's eyes blinked in Durand's face.

Ailric had his blade in his fist, but Durand said, "Raimer?"

The eyes flashed, but there was nothing like understanding in them. The clawed hands flinched tighter.

"It is only justice," said the man. And the voice—a sizzling whisper—was not Raimer's at all. *"It is justice for the burning halls, for the birthright of thousands tossed like scraps to dogs."* He thumped Durand's chest. *"They cry aloud, your people! They cry for justice, those who have sworn faith to your kin since the* Cradle's Landing." He bent low. And, without a flicker, he locked his hands around Durand's throat.

Durand wrenched himself free, startled for a moment at the iron strength in the man's limbs. "Raimer!" he barked. He was tired of mad babble. This was a man who might tell of the Hornbearer, of Almora.

With his open hand, Durand loosened a few of the man's teeth.

Raimer rolled but stopped, suddenly clinging to the ground. He drew a rib-cracking gulp of the cold air. *"Yours is the Horn. Yours to sound. Yours to call. At a stroke, your people can be free."*

The knight's head fell. All around, the idols were whispering with the stricken knight, and Durand heard them take up the same chorus. *"It is justice, it is justice, it is justice."* The whispers swelled like waves on a shingle beach.

"What is this?" said Durand. Together, he and Deorwen held the man's shoulders and kept his head from the earth.

"Like the beggars at the Banderol, Durand," said Deorwen. "Something is whispering down the wards. We are hearing echoes."

Durand spoke in a ragged undertone, as if he might wake Raimer. "This was about Leovere's horn! About the thralls!"

"I know. Here—they are speaking again!" said Deorwen.

"You have done much. And no one could fault you. Now, you must only find that same courage once more. Your task is unfinished, your foe is vulnerable. He is ready to fall. You may say she is young, but many were young who lost their birthrights in your land. And blameless? But who is blameless who lives on the proceeds of despair? You may argue all you like, but you know. At a stroke, we shall have him. At a stroke, you will have justice." The man writhed against the gravel. His back arched. Durand could see the unnatural folding of a badly broken leg as he held on. He suspected broken ribs. Maybe something wrong in his hip.

"Raimer," said Deorwen. "Raimer, we are with you."

But the man was dying now, Durand was sure. His wracked body fought to breathe. "He has fallen into this place. He'll have rolled with the horse," Durand said.

"Raimer," said Deorwen. She cupped the hard madness of his face. "It is time now. You may let go. You may seek the Bright Gates. It is time."

And Raimer sagged then. His last breath shuddered free of the strange whispers of the stone kings and into the high vault of the sky.

Durand and Deorwen paused a moment together, then she closed the dead man's eyes.

"He'll have been days lying out in these ruts," said Durand. The kings were moaning still, though the whispers had subsided. "We will get him out of this place and bury him where he can have some peace."

Deorwen was looking into the man's still face.

"This is a place of priestcraft. It is bound to the king and the wards and the patriarchs. But those whispers . . ."

"Aye. Whispers again." Durand was just standing up, offering Deorwen a hand, when he heard a scrape against the gravel at his feet, like the twitch of snake. Ailric was snatching at Deorwen's elbow, heaving her away.

Raimer's eyes were open, as blank and blind as oyster shells.

But Raimer was dead.

The man's white lips flinched and shivered. His tongue darted, a gray thing. *It is only justice. It is only justice for the burning halls, for the birthright of thousands tossed like scraps to dogs. They cry aloud, your people! They cry for justice, those who have sworn faith to your kin since the* Cradle's *Landing."*

The kings whispered too.

"It is enough!" said Durand.

He got two fistfuls of the dead man's surcoat and hauled him through the eddying hiss: *"Yours is the Horn. Yours to sound. Yours to call. At a stroke, your people can be free. . . ."* He hauled the man through the ranks of idols until, finally, they were free, and Raimer's corpse subsided once more, though Durand dragged him a hundred paces further on before the three searchers prayed the prayers and heaped the stones upon him.

"What do you think it was?" said Deorwen.

"The horn, first. Then it was her," said Durand. He would not say Almora's name where the kings might hear him; they kept up their groaning, even now.

"Echoes," said Deorwen, and Durand knew she was right. Those words, they had not been directed at him, but merely mirrors of a previous conversation, reflected back through time.

His eyes widened. "Yes. They were arguing about the girl. About her death. Pressing and pressing. And . . . Leovere's horn."

Deorwen was shaking her head.

Durand thought of the beggar king. "When last I heard the like of this, it was those Banderol madmen. But that was the king, with them."

"But these were not Ragnal's words," said Deorwen. "What cares he for Leovere and his wounded pride? What would he know of some heirloom in Penseval?"

"Nothing." Durand ground his hands into his eyes. "He has been too busy making war on his brother in Windhover and chasing old men in

Acconel." He glanced into the rows of kings. "But I would like to have a word with that hermit boy in Gowlins now."

"It does not matter," said Deorwen. "Not now. We must find her—before they convince Leovere to act!"

19
Of Ice, Death, and Stone

Beyond the gorge of the kings, they climbed rough animal tracks snaking ever higher into the mountains. These were the worming ways by which the maragrim had slipped the wards. By such high and perilous passes and lonely climbs in the dead of night, the maragrim had advanced—and in numbers unthinkable when Errest was strong.

And there were dead men in the high places.

On a scree slope at the foot of a cliff, they found three more of Raimer's party. One had been dashed to blood and rags by a stone block as large as a half-grown calf. Two others seemed to have been thrown from the heights.

Ailric stopped a moment to crouch beside the third broken body.

"They will have died on the first night, I think. We are only a few hours from the pass. They will have seen or heard it, leading them onward."

Durand nodded, still trudging upward. "The thing will have been toying with them. It could outpace any pack of riders that might have been on its heels."

"It laid in wait up there somewhere."

"Tired of its game," said Durand.

Deorwen eyed the cliff then. "Every lump I see, I am certain it is her. Every one. I have been trying to remember the color of her gown. There was the scarlet, but it might have been the other. The blue serge. For my life, I can't remember."

It was not an hour later that they saw another body. This one distant—and in blue.

Without speaking, they climbed a broad slope till they came upon the place where the body lay. Durand rolled the corpse.

He had a strong jaw and bristling brown hair. Some half-anonymous knight of Wrothsilver.

"It is some poor mother's son, but I can feel only joy," gasped Deorwen. "It is not my Almora."

At the crest of the slope, they found themselves at the foot of a great cliff. The specter of the Farrow Moon hung huge and low above it, seeming very near, almost as though the pale shell of the thing might crack upon the high sweep of the broken rock face.

Strangest, however, was the waterfall that tumbled from those impossible heights. There could be little enough water on the roof of Creation, but this spill tumbled, half cloud and half spray, fully two hundred fathoms, to shower a lake as bright as aquamarine.

The three stared up at this scene: the moon, the falls, the cliff face clapped in shimmering ice, a glassy rivulet jagging away. The wind cast veils of spray over their faces.

"Look there," said Ailric.

By the bank of the blue lake—hardly more than a pond in the gray stone shelf below the falls—Durand saw splashes of unnatural color.

Already, the Eye of Heaven burned low among the western peaks, blazing against the falls and the ice wall behind it.

They clambered to the gravel bank of the tarn, with the high falls raining down. Durand did not think it was bodies they saw. In the puddles and the stones were bundled coats of mail, saddlebags stuffed with god knows, and the bright panoply of knights. All neat. All perched on the tallest stones, the driest slabs. All shelled in ice.

The others arrived a step behind him.

Almora's silvery amulet fizzed in circles over the water.

"They have gone into the pool," said Deorwen. "They've all gone in."

Plates of glassy ice reached across the water toward the falls. Frost glittered everywhere. If Raimer's men had followed the girl to this icy loch and then leapt in, they had not come back.

"The tarn stands alone, more or less," said Ailric. "The trail goes no further. They have left everything on the bank."

Durand looked back over the roof of Creation—hundreds of leagues, mountains beyond counting. Somewhere, where the Eye of Heaven still blazed, would be Windhover, Eldinor, and the sea.

"They must have followed the Hornbearer here," said Ailric. He moved along the bank, slipping his fingertips into obscure marks in the frosty sand and gravel. "There is over-tracking. They will have gone down one at a time, one after another. It might have been daylight then, though the peaks would have put this place in shadow. They must have seen something."

"It was the Hornbearer," Durand said. "This is where it came. This is where it brought her."

The water was blue. Oddly so. And the falls stippled its face. Durand began to set his things down, unthinkingly looking for dry places. The first men here had done the same. He set his own hauberk beside the close-woven coats of steel already lying folded on the stones.

"It must have entered the pool," said Ailric.

Durand crunched to the water's edge. Pebbles glistened like beads trapped in clear glass, possibly fathoms deep. Then, toward the base of the cliff, a deep gloom shot through the water.

Stripped of his coat of mail, his scabbard and boots, he stood in the frigid sunset with only his breeches and Ouen's bare blade. The spray and breezes sent a shiver over him.

"What do you mean to do?" said Deorwen.

Durand smiled at her. The water would be devilish cold.

"I expect there will be food and some halfway fresh winter gear in these little piles," Durand said.

"Durand. . . ." She was very close to him.

"Night will come soon. Be ready to leave this place. You should not wait long."

Then Durand closed his eyes and pitched into the frigid agony of the water.

He nearly lost the sword in the first shock. He might as well have jumped in scalding oil. Through wincing eyes, he saw that the water plunged into darkness at the cliff's edge, opening like a great purple throat choked with thunder and splintered glass. Durand kicked toward this grotto of frost and left Creation behind.

The cold seared his flesh and dug hooks deep into the marrow of his bones. He kicked and kicked, blind. The black pain of the place crushed the air from his chest. He kicked and felt the hunger of his lungs forcing him to breathe. And knew that, at any moment, he would give in. Lights flashed with the pounding of his heart. But then his groping hands collided with a shattering bank of sliding needles and frozen gravel.

And he clawed himself upward and into the air.

He surfaced in an eerie, half-lit place and scrabbled onto a floor of icy rubble. He rolled on the broken rock, blinking like a maddened animal. Gasping. The pain drove every thought from his skull.

But he made no noise. He did not call out.

He forced himself to breathe. To calm himself.

He was in a cave. The ceiling was high and black. The falls must have carved a gulf from the cliff face.

Durand cursed without so much as a hiss. He felt his breath coming in spasms. But the Hornbearer might wait within inches, folded like a spider in the shadow. And so Durand forced himself to keep still and get his eyes open and working.

There were country knights who had smaller halls than that cave. One wall—the one above and behind him—was a great glowing curtain of ice, high as a steeple. That would have been where the falls had ground out the rock. He picked out signs of the others who had come before him: surcoats, a cloak, blades all strewn across the rocky floor. Here were the burdens of what must surely be dead men, all stuck to the frost.

He peered deeper into the cavern.

There was a hole, two fathoms off the floor, and a darker chamber beyond. A man would have to bend double, to crawl. But there was something else: a heap of particolored coats and a pale shape huddled in the hollow of the wall below, still as an owl.

Durand thought of all the bodies in the mountains, and he thought of the girl. But he must know.

He ventured across the rubble, cautious of Ouen's sword, afraid to let it ring from the stones. He must get closer to that owl-like face in the dark. He had to know. But every inch brought him closer to the hole just above. And, if the Hornbearer was anywhere, it must be in that black socket.

Durand crept closer until he was sure that he was looking at a human shape wrapped in woolen gear.

The face was bare—bare or clean shaven.

Then he heard a hiss, nearly like a breath from the black mouth above his head.

A voice spoke: "Durand?"

And the heap uncurled and Durand saw Almora, her hair all across her face. Surcoats in a dozen crests and colors shawled and bundled the shivering woman.

"How have you come here?" she said, very quiet.

"The thing. It is near?"

She nodded. He caught the glint of her eyes. She was looking at the opening over their heads. Durand set a finger to his lips and helped the girl to her feet. She clutched him, squeezing her face against his chest. She was very cold.

"Deorwen and Ailric are at the water's edge, by the pool. You know Ailric. We will swim."

Then a hiss issued from the mouth of the inner chamber: an unmistakable, enormous sound that filled the cavern and froze Durand's breath.

"Go!" he managed. "The water." He gave the girl a push and turned with the long war sword as the Crowned Hog unfolded from the narrow socket like a spider clambering from its lair. Long limbs splayed. The huge saddle-blank face with its black eyes and absurd crown, thrust into the twilight cavern.

Durand charged, swinging the greatsword, striking a spreading hand. For a moment, the thrall's grotesque horns caught in the entry, holding the thing like a pillory, and Durand charged, swinging at the flying limbs. But what force in Creation could stop such as the Hornbearer? And indeed, a careless, deadfall blow of the brute's huge hand sent Durand skidding across the floor.

The great bronze curl of the Horn clanged, and then the Hornbearer was free, looming against the ceiling.

The silent horror flexed and opened its long-fingered hands, finding a finger or two lopped away.

"At least I have marked you," said Durand.

The thing swiveled its head. And there was Almora, still at the water's edge.

Durand rang the heavy sword from the icy floor with frozen hands. He gave the sword a second ring.

"Come, you devil! You've had an eye on me since Fellwood. Now here I am." He rang the sword once more on the ice, and the horned face rolled toward him.

He had its eye now, and Almora might get free. She might reach daylight and Ailric and Deorwen. And they could find some patch of holy ground by nightfall and the old Crowned Hog could choke on its fury.

Durand bared his broken teeth and charged the giant. He leapt and swung, and the brute skidded like a carthorse on the icy rocks. A foot stamped down. A fist smacked a hail of skull-cracking stones down all around him.

Then a lash of the thing's splayed hand wrenched Durand into a cartwheel, sucking the air from his lungs.

He landed hard on broken rock with a flash of light jagging behind his eyes.

The thing picked him up. There was no room for air in the monster's grasp. Durand saw the damned, faceless face. And the fingers tightened, crushing. He tried to lift the sword still dangling in his fingers, but he could not. And it could not have mattered. There was no air. Only the vast dark face. The sword clanged to the floor.

And the monster stopped.

Down below, Durand saw Almora. She had pried up a blade from the ice and now wavered with the sword in both hands, its point buried in the back of the Crowned Hog.

But the monster had not died.

Durand saw that there were almost twenty paces of rocky floor between the girl and the water.

Almora ran.

Perhaps she had hoped to kill the giant. Perhaps she could not stand to see another man killed, but now she ran.

Durand fell from the Hornbearer's hand and the thing rushed, swallowing the distance with hopeless speed. Its hand snapped for the girl. Durand saw it silhouetted against the shining curtain of ice. But, as the Hornbearer reached, the thing struck sudden ice at the water's edge. And it slid.

In an instant, that giant devil of five hundred winters was crashing into the wall of green ice. Water exploded beneath it. Durand saw it twitch around, catching hold before it slid into the deep water, then the towering wall of ice gave way. The darkness shattered and the Eye of Heaven was revealed, its golden beams lancing through the falling ice and the sudden thundering roar of the waterfall beyond, and the air was full of diamonds.

As the Hornbearer exploded from the cavern, Durand found Almora safe in the curve of one wall, looking more sick and pale than any living being Durand had ever seen—but alive. She had thrown herself from the Hornbearer's path—a fact that had saved her from the thrashing giant and the falling towers of ice.

He beamed like a fool until he saw her eyes, which were wide open and seemed almost to be burning, as immovable as the mountain behind her.

Durand swam the tarn in a moment, hauling the dazed Almora out onto the bank and into the arms of a waiting Deorwen. Even Ailric, still on guard against whatever might next emerge from the ruined cavern, flashed his teeth, as giddy as a child.

"She's alive!" said Durand. "We've got her back!"

"She will need dry things. Ailric, you brought her mantle. The fur. And some of the men's things will be stout woolen stuff," said Deorwen.

She bundled the girl into rugs and cloaks, chafing her skin, forcing embraces when she could do nothing else. Almora had not uttered a word.

Deorwen took the girl by the arms, looking square in her face. "Almora, you will have to say something now. Anything at all, but I must hear you." There followed a space of heartbeats, but Almora seemed to gather herself. She straightened a fraction and her dark eyes blinked.

"I am free," she said.

And Deorwen seized her, clutching fiercely.

"You are," she said.

Durand too felt a fierce sort of joy. He must have looked mad, shaking pale and grinning like a fool. "Host of Heaven! Who would believe it?" He felt that they had torn something back from the face of doom. He was surprised to find bright blood streaming from his mouth, but a split lip seemed an impossible price to have paid for so improbable a victory.

"My father?"

"Will be in Acconel by now," said Deorwen. "Don't worry."

Durand looked into the back of the cave—now open to the Eye of Heaven where ice and stone had collapsed.

"There is no sign of the thrall," said Ailric.

"It was there," said Durand. "But I would be happier to see its carcass afloat in the tarn."

In the rear of the cave, that warren would still be there, still beyond the reach.

Despite his sodden clothes, Durand hauled on his own gear. "By rights we should have a night by a roaring fire, but I think we need to get clear of this place. And there's not much time."

"The Hornbearer lives?" said Deorwen.

"I do not see him dead, and we will soon lose the Eye of Heaven."

Almora stared into the cave from her bundle of cloaks, almost as though the Hornbearer was staring back.

"What shall we do, then?" said Deorwen.

Ailric seemed ready to carry his sword into the Hornbearer's chamber, but Durand had fought the thing and he knew that a man was too small to face the giant thrall. Only Almora's desperate attack had saved them, and there was no second wall of ice and stone to drop upon the brute.

Deorwen rounded on Ailric. "You will not stop him there, but only lay your bones in the same tomb as Raimer's men. I don't think the Powers of Heaven will grant us two such escapes in an hour."

"We must get away," said Almora. "We must all get away."

"Yes," said Durand. "We will put as many leagues between the thrall and ourselves as we may in the hour before we lose the Eye."

"Yet what good will a league or two be to us when that thing comes rushing down the passes behind us?" said Deorwen.

Durand scoured the heights, hoping for inspiration, but saw only leagues of bare rock and ice on every side.

"Why did the devil choose this place?" he wondered.

It was Almora who spoke. "It had been here before, I think. It slipped out to the lakeside when the cave was dark, staring north, its arms clasped tight."

The girl's gaze jumped to the spot where the Hornbearer must have kept its vigil.

Ailric crossed silently to the place and looked off into the northern range. "It is Yrlac there," he said. "Between the peaks, just here; you can see the hills." He squinted, shifting. "It might be the hills around Penseval, near the Banderol."

"Where Leovere's clan kept their trophy horn," said Durand. "That is what it sees?"

"So I believe," said Ailric.

"Fine. Fine. But what help is this to us now?" asked Deorwen. "Soon, the Hornbearer will climb from that hole and what will we do then?"

"The Singing Stones," said Almora. "They cannot be far. When it took me. My father's men. Some who followed. They were on a ridge above a stone valley." She blinked. Who knew what visions flashed before her mind's eye? "One man. He and his horse fell. The man rolled among— they were standing stones. There was a groan, hundreds of voices, low. The thing. It shied like a horse in a fire."

It would have been Raimer. She was talking about the stone kings.

Durand straightened. How much daylight had they left? How far was Raimer's grave and that file of stone kings?

"The wards! We must return to the kings," said Deorwen.

"Yes!" said Durand. "We may just make it!"

ONCE MORE DURAND led them in a breathless rout. This time, though, he was grinning like a thief who'd escaped with the whole treasure room.

The long mountain shadows swung over the valleys like vast shears. But this was a downhill flight and Durand's party knew every turning as they scrabbled past dead men and gravel plateaus to finally reach the moaning chorus of stone kings as the twilight ebbed from the Heavens.

They slipped among the stone figures, Durand urging Deorwen to take the girl deeper into the strange place while he stopped in the first rank, his eyes on the shadowed valley behind them. Ailric stayed at his side.

"No sign," said Durand, watching every ledge and stone of the gorge. The murk was thick and chill.

Durand had hardly spoken when both men heard something in the gorge—falling stones, a crack, a sharp report, each sound closer and closer.

"We must hope that the kings can hold it," said Durand. He drew Ouen's long blade once again and watched around the shoulder of one crude lord of stone. The Hornbearer swarmed into the gorge as quick as a spider, groping forward on limbs as long as masts and towers in the dark.

Only at the last did it check its headlong rush. Twenty paces away, the thing crawled forward, clutching the gravel. Durand saw it pass the low mound of Raimer's grave.

In the face of this breaker of hosts, there was not blood or air enough in Creation.

Durand cocked Ouen's sword, but he and his shield-bearer gave ground as the monster came nearer and nearer. It seemed wise to place a few more stone kings between them and the Hornbearer.

"We must pray there is power in the patriarchs yet," Durand said.

And then, in terrible silence, the horror of Fellwood ceased its advance, hunkering like a dog at the end of a chain. In the blank mask of its face, there wasn't any human sign.

Only pigheaded stubbornness kept Durand on his feet.

Finally, the great horror stood and, more quickly than Durand could comprehend, abandoned the gorge, stilting from the pass while the night wind breathed over the stone mouths of the idols and set them all singing.

Durand looked to Ailric. "If it had stayed there the whole night," he said, "I would have let you kill it."

"If I'd had to watch it another hour, I would have tried."

TOGETHER THEY RETREATED to the middle of the stones, where they joined the others, huddling in half-wet clothing and wishing for dry wood and a strong fire. The Hornbearer could still be seen, moving on the ridgeline.

Amid the stones, Deorwen fussed over the girl. "You have been cold and you will be hungry still. I will hold you close as you can stand under these cloaks, and you will eat what you can. We have a cheese and some cold mutton in the bags. You will eat as much as you can stomach. It's hard that we can make no fire, but stone doesn't burn. You will be thirsty as well. We must have water."

They had all seen people—after the siege at Acconel, after Ferangore—who could not shake the mortal dread of the blackest days. Deorwen's years at the head of the duke's household meant everyday almsgiving and feeding the hungry. She'd seen a lot of haunted eyes. Durand wondered if they could lose the girl.

"I had water. And those poor boys . . ." Almora checked herself. "There were woolen surcoats."

"Quite right. Wool is as warm wet or dry—or nearly," said Deorwen. "This is good sense. After you chased your father into a calends night, I wondered. Now, are you hurt anywhere and too brave or stupid to say so?" And when Almora said nothing, she glanced to the two men looking on. "And you boys? What of it?"

Ailric shook his dark head, suddenly seeming a youth of nineteen or twenty again. Durand only smiled with his broken teeth.

The kings groaned in uncanny harmony.

Deorwen pushed on. "When the Eye returns, we will make for Acconel."

"I was asleep," Almora said. "There was a shriek. The tents in tatters. The fires. I remember the spinning fires. And then I was rushing up into the night." She could not find words for a moment.

It was very dark among the kings.

"It kept to the high places. It leapt and it scrambled. Sometimes it was as still and dead as a tree, rolling that tiny crown in its hands, round and round and round. It killed those men. In the cave, it was the same. . . ." Her eyes were very still. "It rocked like a caged thing. It fondled that crown. It stared. For hours, it would stare. It dashed those poor men against the walls."

"The devil," said Durand. She should not have been able to endure it. But there was iron in the girl.

Deorwen looked into her eyes, calling her back from the place of dark memory. "Almora, we must take as much sleep as we may. Sleep is the best healer for all things."

DURAND HAD NOT planned to sleep among the stones, but weariness overcame him in the black hours and he nodded across the bounds of sleep until voices emerged from the groaning of the kings.

He heard a man's slurred mumble. *"I am not blind. I see. Oh, I see how they watch. How they whisper when my head is turned. Always the whispers! Devils everywhere."*

Durand was sure that things were circling like greyhounds at a feast.

Then, of course, he was awake. Still, even there on the mountainside, Durand was sure he had heard these things.

Uneasily, now, he found that he could still make out the wrathful mumblings as the wind ebbed and swelled among the stone kings. It was the faraway sleeper, now in the mountains.

"I am alone," the sleeper groaned. *"Every eye is upon me when my head is turning. They count every breath I draw, but I will not go! What madman counseled that I have a son? An heir between my brother and the crown? No! A devil and his whore of a mother. The boy is the tool she requires to take what is mine and hold it when she has done with me."* Whispers seethed and surged. *"It is all poisoned against me. My brother and his army. My wife. My son. Devils! I cannot sleep for the whispers."*

Durand climbed awkwardly to his feet, and the whispers swirled, voices knotted and woven beyond separation.

Unbidden, memories swam before his mind's eye. He saw the beggars by the Banderol, naked as worms, nattering of conspiracies in the mud. He saw Ragnal the king, in his jeweled robes, his crown, his great sword. He saw the black-clad functionaries of Eldinor; it the man, Hod, who'd rushed Lamoric's men from the slinking creatures of the court to a passageway below the city. And the passage that took them, past sealed doors, to the catacombs of the high sanctuary. The bones of kings. So many whispers. So much memory.

Durand set his hand on some idol's pointed head—and all the whispers were abruptly silent, like a snapped bowstring.

Durand saw the image of an iron-bound door. Black with age. Webbed over. It flickered when he closed his eyes.

He was in the mountains—and elsewhere, somewhere dark and smothering.

"Who has come?" said a voice. *"I hear you. Have you been to my door before?"*

Durand hung in the black valley of the stone kings, suddenly unable to breathe.

"You have heard my whispers, I think. Come nearer, then." It was a

parchment rasp. *"I must train my ear upon the feeblest tremblings. Come nigh."*

When Durand blinked his eyes—when his eyes flinched shut—the door was there. Rotten. Hinges of iron. Cobwebs masking it over.

Still, he could not breathe.

As the being beyond the door spoke, a voice cried out from somewhere very distant. It drew his attention from the crumbling door and the iron bands.

"You need not fear. I was once as you are."

With his eyes wide, he was in the mountains. With his eyes shut, he stood before that door.

The door crashed against its hinges.

"Come nigh, stranger! Who are you? Come nigh!" The door shook.

The shock of the violence started Durand backward, only to discover that something tangible had slipped from around the old door. Fine threads had poured from the doorframe and the wisps now coiled around his ankles, his wrists. They groped for his mouth. But he was not really there. He was in the mountains.

Still he could not breathe.

Across the leagues, across down high mountains and shadowed land, he heard his name. "Durand!"

In an instant, he knew Deorwen's voice. The stone kings were howling in the mountain wind, and then Durand was not distant, not underground. Deorwen had his face in her two hands and her eyes were the whole of the world. "Come back! Come now, Durand!"

Something struck him, knocking him away from the idol. Knocking his hand free of the mitered head.

Durand found himself on the gravel once more. He filled his lungs and rolled.

Ailric stood above him.

"Host of Heaven, Durand," said Deorwen, "you cannot leave on the night we get Almora. You cannot!"

Durand shook his head, crawling to scrabble his wits together.

All at once, he thought of poor Raimer, now buried beyond the ranks of idols.

"How long was Raimer here?" he said as the kings sung their mournful harmonies. "With all this? Cold and broken? Hells." Somehow he'd come where he could see Raimer's mound of stones.

"I know," said Deorwen. "The thrall may be wiser than all of us."

Somewhere, Durand heard a rasping voice roar its frustration. Then, it seemed, the whole valley shivered. *"Durand . . ."* said a dry and distant whisper. *"Durand."* And Durand felt the dread of hearing his name on the lips of the Powers of Hell.

"You were far away, Durand," Deorwen said.

Durand shut his eyes and the Lost filtered into the canyon—the burned, the maimed, the drowned.

"Well," he said. "They haven't got me yet."

20
A Bitter Glory

True dawn came late to the gorge. Durand watched under a bright Heaven as, one after another, the Lost slipped from Creation. The Hornbearer ceased his seething vigil in the early twilight, rearing up and stalking mountainsides toward Gireth and Errest the Old while the Heavens were the color of steel.

There was little to do but follow.

They descended from the pass, with Durand leading them at a pitiless pace. Though Almora likely needed easy stages, the mountains were no haven, and there was no place of sanctuary for leagues beyond. Mercy might have left them among the thralls at nightfall, and they could trust nothing but the Eye of Heaven to defend them.

The valley of the Banderol was empty as a bell. When they climbed to Wrothsilver on its green hilltop, they found that the whole population of Swanskin Down had slipped like a barnacle into the shell of the walled town. There was not even a dog running loose on the hillsides. But the battlements were packed with the pale faces of soldiers and plowmen. And inside, the town was crammed with people from leagues around, all kneeling in prayer. Vadir and his knights, however, had left their people. By now, they would be in Acconel.

Almora was a small joy to the people there. Many wondered to see her, alive from the mountains. Hardly thinking, people touched the parti-colored cloaks she wore with reverent fingertips.

They spent the night among the refugees in Wrothsilver. At dawn, those good people sent the party on its way again, mounted on horses nearly as steady as the poor brutes who had fed the maragrim at the

Gowlins shrine. Where they found the beasts, Durand did not know, but it meant the party would reach the walls of Acconel before the maragrim in the valley awoke again.

The Eye was dropping in the west when they rode into cool and familiar air among the hills: reed beds and wet sand. Soon they would find broad Silvermere and old Acconel, hid beyond the hills just out of sight.

"I expect that the Great Council will have scampered home," said Deorwen. "Even these fools will have sense enough to shy from the maragrim."

"They've hard heads, those Great Council fools. A man does not easily wrest a dukedom from its heirs and charters in Errest the Old," said Durand. "They might be slow to let it go."

"Well," said Deorwen, "the sight of Almora should shut their mouths. They'll look foul enough already, picking on her poor old father. But who could strike Abravanal now, with Her Ladyship home, snatched from the Blackroots? Host of Heaven! The skalds would mock them till their grandchildren would change their names."

Durand had to laugh. "We will see, I expect," he said, and they rounded a last bend of the Banderol to find Acconel standing in the forked river before them, its bridges gleaming, its walls white, and the Heavens spinning with gulls from the Mere. Less welcome, however, were the tents that teemed in the field all around the city. The war hosts of ten dukedoms had populated the open ground, and banners of half the dukes of Errest swung over campfires of laughing soldiers. These were the men King Ragnal had brought to enjoy Abravanal's hospitality, and to consider the lordship of Yrlac.

The Great Council had come ready for war.

Durand laughed. "Doubt not the pettiness of princes."

"Where are the thralls? These halfwits should be dead, camped like this," was Deorwen's appraisal.

Durand shook his head. She was right.

"They are the Host of the Hornbearer. Perhaps it was for their master that they waited."

"I'm not sure they tarried on his behalf before, and I'm not sure we caused the brute much delay," said Deorwen.

"Something has held them back."

"Aye. That's clear."

Ranks of gawkers lined the Banderol Road to Harpers Gate: sneering men-at-arms from every brothel and pigsty in Errest the Old. Leers and wolf whistles from the crowd had the women pulling their cloaks tighter.

These things had Durand snarling. But, as they reached the vault of Harpers Gate, there were worse signs waiting.

Thousands of dark birds crowded the parapet. Durand remembered the carrion crows in Radomor's days, but these were starlings again, packed like wasps in a nest. All twitching, insectile heads. It was unnatural. But every pair of eyes was on them.

"The Great Council and these things," began Deorwen. "We must bring Almora to her father, and get ourselves locked safe in Gunderic's Tower. Then we can see about talking sense to these fools about the maragrim."

They were passing under the gate, and at the first echoes of the horse's hooves, a hundred thousand starlings plunged from the battlements. The things poured from the walls and exploded through the gateway tunnel. The storm tore at Durand's cloak and maddened the horses.

Ailric caught Almora's bridle as Durand and Deorwen mastered their own terrified animals. But it was Almora whose eyes followed the birds, her chin tilted. She was watching.

"It's Gunderic's Tower," she concluded.

The dark and viscous mass was indeed surging over the citadel and wheeling then over the battlements of Gunderic's Tower.

Durand saw other birds there. Larger, laboring under the onslaught.

"Sea eagles," said Ailric. "The king's bird."

"We never want for auguries," said Deorwen. "Is everyone all right? Almora, have our little friends left you two eyes?" There were other varied nods all around. "Then I suggest we make haste for the Painted Hall!"

When they reached the castle, they found Sir Kieren the Fox shouting, "Almora! Almora!"

Even Durand could not suppress an exultant grin. Just within the gate, the girl climbed from her saddle, and the old knight clasped her in his arms. "What a thing this is! Host of Heaven, you were dead, child! As dead as old Duke Gunderic. They must have been looking for you at the Bright Gates."

"Do they know the hills are full of maragrim, Sir Kieren?" said Almora. "Do they understand?"

"Child, there is little enough they understand." Kieren shook his head. "But we must get you to His Grace, your father. You will save the old man, I think. And then we can work on their understanding. Come!"

The tiltyard between the walls was packed with people. Hundreds of knights milled, and Durand heard shouts.

"There is a thing or two you should know, I suppose," Kieren began. Then he had to grin at Almora. "It is such a wonder! The wonder of our age, child!" And he shook his head once more.

"But to business. The Council, first. You know they are here? Well, they will cast their vote at the setting of the sun." The shadows were already long. "It has been hurried. Some word of the thralls has reached us here, but some will think they're an excuse of Abravanal's, a Girethi trick. Maud of Saerdana has said as much, under her breath. Moryn Mornaway looked like he would slap her. He's your brother, is he not, Lady Deorwen?" At her nod, he pushed on. "Sunset's not long now." The man dodged past a group of outland knights, giving them a frown. "The king is set against us, and the Council's only too happy to pluck a man's wings, the devils. I'm not sure what will be left for the maragrim."

They broke through into an open space.

"And here, look." The Fox gestured. Across the yard stood Red Leovere in a knot of knights and captains. His man, Lord Morcar, blinked at Durand. Neither had expected the other. Durand wondered what it meant for the maragrim. If their master was here in Acconel—if he was waiting on the Council's vote—would the maragrim wait? If Leovere got what he wanted, would the maragrim return to Fellwood?

Durand wondered.

"Abravanal will be ahead. Come, come," said Kieren.

"The vote," said Deorwen. "What of Mornaway? Garelyn?"

"Ladyship," Kieren said, "your brother will vote with Abravanal, of course. And Garelyn. But, together, we are four votes—even if our friend here could conjure the Lady of Lost Hesperand once more, we must lose. The shadows are long. The Eye of Heaven will leave us and the Great Council will vote Abravanal down."

Yet still he smiled, despite the grim way of things. "But, Almora, it is worth a great deal to find you."

Now, Durand heard the unmistakable grunt and shuffle of single combat. It explained the mob.

"There!" said Kieren. Durand saw Abravanal through a few rows of onlookers.

Durand shoved a few of the noble audience aside, but stopped.

He'd got a good look at the swordsmen.

First was grim-faced Coensar. The other was Ragnal, King of Errest, lean and broad-shouldered under a cloak like a jeweled book. A fierce grimace split the man's black beard as he wheeled in the wake of a huge High Kingdom sword.

"Again, you dance!" King Ragnal was saying. "You are like the queen and her son. Always where I cannot lay hands on them." The king roared, launching another two-handed swing. Coensar could only skip away, letting the king lurch past. A man could not stick a blade into his king.

Ragnal smiled. He raised his eyebrows at a noblewoman and dark-haired boy at the edge of the ring. This would be Queen Engeled and Prince Reilan, Durand suspected. The boy could not be more than five years old. "This is how they all face me. They see there are teeth still in the wolf's jaw."

The king would have returned his attention to Coensar, but already people around the circle were talking. They had noticed Almora. They saw Durand.

"What's this?" said Ragnal. The crowd turned now, and every eye was upon Durand and the girl.

Ragnal seemed to have noticed Kieren. "What is it, Fox? Always the bow and the scrape. Always the sidelong look with you. Another story about bogles in the Blackroots? Boggarts in the hills? Your schemes cannot save this dukedom of yours." The king waggled the heavy sword toward the western sky. "The vote comes with nightfall, and this game is nearly finished."

"As you say, Highness," began Kieren. But the king had found Durand. "What is this now?"

Another man joined Ragnal in the circle. "Durand Col, I think, brother. He fought at Tern Gyre, though several years have passed." Slim and bearded, Prince Biedin gave Durand an apologetic glance. "This is Abravanal's Champion, sent to the Blackroots after poor Almora was taken in the mountains."

"*That* story. A lovely one, I thought," said Ragnal.

Abravanal groped forward. "Durand?"

He had not yet seen the girl. There were so many people.

"She is safe," Durand said. And Almora, cowled in a soldiers' cloak, stepped forward.

Gasps shivered through the crowd. "I had not dared to hope," breathed Abravanal.

"This is the girl?" said Ragnal.

Almora rushed forward, catching hold of her father.

"Almora!" he gasped. He looked into her face. "We are alive once more."

"What is this, Abravanal of Gireth?" the king demanded. "What are you scheming at?" He looked to Kieren. To Almora and Durand. "What tricks have you planned?"

The king still had the bare blade in his hand, and now took a step toward the old man and his daughter. Seeing the blade twitch with the king's anger, Durand shoved himself forward until they were chest to chest. They were nearly of a height, Ragnal and Durand Col. But, somehow, Durand did not doubt that the king could slay him in a moment. Something sickly flickered in the man's eyes.

Prince Biedin set his hand on his eldest brother's shoulder.

"Now, here, Brother. Good Sir Durand. This is a wonder! We must be careful, I think. The Powers are to be praised at such a time. Thanks are due. I wonder, should we be churlish with the gifts of Heaven? Such a thing should be feasted."

Tall Kandemar, the Herald of Errest, looked on, gray as marble. The king's eye found the man before he turned to his brother.

"The Council pronounces its judgment at the setting of the sun," growled Ragnal.

"Yes. But the vote might be delayed to allow for the celebration. You need but ask. No man who hopes for Heaven would say you nay. And you are king, after all, Your Highness, eh?"

Ragnal raised his bearded chin. There was something of the lion in Ragnal, but Biedin was a thoughtful man, tall and balanced.

"There are plenty who do not jump at my word, Brother," said Ragnal, "but what you say of Heaven is true: Few men are fool enough to deny the Powers what is theirs." Ragnal turned to address the company. "A feast in lieu of judgment?"

By their looks and muttering, the crowd granted a grudging approval.

Ragnal bared his teeth. "Good! Good! Then let us have our feast, you gallows birds! Let us show the Heavens that we are grateful! Go, my lords and ladies, go!

"And you, my girl," he said to Almora, setting thick fingers on her shoulder, "you will come with me."

In a storm of fluttering lackeys, the company crammed the stairs into Gunderic's Tower and poured into the Painted Hall. Starlings, too, tumbled up the stairway.

The storm bowled into the Painted Hall like a gale of leaves, with the king braying out commands for lords and serving men alike as he made his way to the high table. The starlings peered in at the windows, they flew down the hall, and Ragnal flapped his hands. "I've had my fill of these damned birds! Block up the windows, damn you!"

Abravanal scarcely noticed all of the jostling. "I have hardly seen this hall these ten winters. It is black still from the fires in the siege, and we have lived here every day. No longer, I tell you." And he smiled at his daughter.

Biedin stopped before Abravanal's high table and called together the serving men. "Here, the hall you made ready for judgment must now serve as a feasting place. The daughter of your master has returned. There must be food and wine. Wine first, I suppose. And we must make room at the high table for Her Ladyship, of course." He gave a smiling bow toward the benches at the king's right hand. "I will yield my own place at the king's side."

Ragnal scowled and planted himself in Abravanal's chair. "Bring her, but her father must keep his place. We will vote tomorrow, and I can have no favorites."

"No," said Biedin. "I see. There is justice in that."

Abravanal clutched Almora's hand, but had to leave her. The Duke of Gireth was not fit for the king's right hand. Not that day. Durand remained near the old man, certain that the Painted Hall was no safe place with Ragnal and the Great Council camped all around.

As Durand sat beside the old man, his eye was drawn to the curious noise at the arrow loops: thousands of starlings crowded out the light. Serving men lugged long shutters, but the windows gave glimpses of vast flocks surging round and round Gunderic's Tower.

Two hundred nobles settled at the boards and benches.

The servants hammered the shutters into place. Other serving men had started to bring out wine.

There was hardly a word spoken in that long hall.

"Too quiet!" said Ragnal. A gaggle of the black-robed toadies had brought the crown—Durand remembered calling the court clerks "starlings" when he'd first seen them. Ragnal snatched the crown from the fawning creatures and seated the thing on his head. The gold flashed and the fat black sapphire Evenstar glinted with its cat's-eye sliver.

The black-clad men seemed to be scurrying everywhere. A few were whispering advice in the king's ear. Ragnal pressed his massive hands to his temples.

"Musicians!" he said. "Anything." And Durand remembered the king's plague of whispers.

Durand wondered if this was the way of things in the Hall of Eagles back in Eldinor. He wondered how these people would fare when the Hornbearer was at the walls.

"Yes. Well," began Prince Biedin. "There was meant to be an entertainment, even before this evening brought us a wonder." The prince grimaced at a dozen serving men, saying, "I think that we need not wait for our little show. There is space enough between the tables, I think." And the little men rushed off, bowing and licking their chops.

Durand took note of Leovere and his men sitting stiff-necked and closed-mouthed well down the hall from the high table. Here was Leovere giving the realm a last chance, perhaps. They had, no doubt, expected great things from the Council vote. No matter what Ragnal and the rest thought, Leovere knew that the Hornbearer was nigh.

Leovere was not alone, of course. The Great Council were all around. Maud of Saerdana, lady herself of two dukedoms, sat among her people. Nearer at hand was Gireth's old friend, Alret, Duke of Garelyn, with his long mustaches. Farther away was Deorwen's brother, the austere Moryn of Mornaway. And bearded Ludegar of Beoran, who had worked hard to upturn the kingdom ten years before.

"Durand, I am ashamed," said Abravanal. "You have been in Accolnel since you were a boy, a loyal man twenty winters and more. I should have flung Leovere's accusations back in his teeth at the Lindenhall. A man's heart should know such truths when he has seen so many winters."

Ragnal curled his lip. "Now *you* are whispering, Duke Abravanal?"

The old man gripped Durand's arm, and the king sniffed.

"Where is this entertainment, Brother?"

"They must take care with it, Highness," said Biedin. "I am not sure why something simpler would not have served better."

Just then, a clamor arose from the entry stair—a rattling of chains.

Biedin raised his eyebrows. "Here we are." And a gang of handlers pulled a bear into the hall. The ragged creature moaned. Chains stretched from a broad, gilded collar, cut like a crown. The handlers tugged the animal into the midst of the company where someone had fixed a ring in the floor.

Next, it was brutish dogs for the bear and a haphazard gang of fiddlers running up the steps to the minstrel's gallery. The beasts shrieked below while the musicians sawed in the gallery above. It was no wonder that Ragnal was going mad.

Ragnal waved off the latest flock of serving men. "If we must have a feast, where are the trenchers?" griped Ragnal. It had hardly been long enough for a man to run to the kitchen.

"Here," said Biedin. "They are coming." He gave Almora a pleading glance. It seemed that he must often apologize for his brother. "Bread and butter. Claret and beer."

The bear roared and thrashed against his chain as the dogs snapped.

Plates clunked down on the high table, but Ragnal's were snatched away and set before a pair of clerks who gingerly tested each morsel.

Ragnal must have read something in Durand's glance. "You goggle at my tasters, Durand Col? Do not fool yourself. There are many who'd like to see their king dead. Our brother, Eodan in Windhover, for one. He has tried. And half the barons of our Great Council. And our darling wife and loving son, oh yes. And what of you? I have heard a line or two of your own tale." He nodded to Abravanal. "Would your master not like to see our decision deferred? A vote delayed? Have you not killed for this old man before?" He curled his lip at the tasters. "So eat, my boys, and tell me how Abravanal's cold kitchen fares!"

Down the table, beyond Almora and the giggling tasters, Queen Engeled and her young son had begun to leave the table. Durand felt that, at any moment, things around the king could go wrong. His Highness had seen his wife's attempt at slipping away.

"Oh no, no," said the king. "We are a happy family, yes. Let the people see, I say."

Prince Biedin seemed to note his brother's increasing impatience.

Having taken a place at the lower tables, he now stood, a cup of wine in his hand. "Your Highness, ladies, gentlemen. The miracle of the duke's daughter demands a word or two from us here. A toast, I think."

The dogs got hold of the bear then, and, for a moment, no man could hope to speak over the din. The bloodied creature kicked, unable to right itself as the snarling pack worried its throat and limbs. The racket was devilish.

Finally, the bear fell, thrashing its last, and the hall was silent.

"A moment, Brother," said Ragnal. The king was standing. "Let me raise *my* glass. Almora! A fine young woman. Heiress to Gireth. Heiress to Yrlac." He paused to let the crowd grumble. "Or so some say."

He gave Almora a look. "Fresh as the cherry's first flowering."

There were some few leers among the many at the long tables. A few men exchanged elbows.

Durand scowled, but Abravanal was furious, spluttering, "Villains! She is a noblewoman in her own home." Durand was sure that no one could hear him.

Between the tables, the bear was truly dead now. Handlers got hold of the dogs.

"And a word for Durand Col!" said Ragnal. "An exile! Survivor of the headsman's stroke. Battler of Kieren's monsters."

The king waited a moment as two stooped men in Eldinor black shuffled out to take hold of the bear, dragging its black carcass from the center of the hall. There was a long smear of blood, and the whining of dogs straining at their leashes.

As the whole room watched the dead beast, Durand—and Durand alone—saw the appearance of bent figures, slipping from corners and under tables. There was Euric with his bladder face, and the thorn-crowned King. Even Lady Alwen and her babe crouched at the trail's edge. Before Durand's horrified eyes, the babe scrabbled out upon the reeds—a ghastly crab-scuttle driven by a convulsive thirst.

Ragnal was still speaking.

He waved at the shabby ruin of the bear. "Where gallant and dashing knights from all Gireth could do nothing, Durand the exile, Durand the black and battered outcast, somehow found his way to the mountains and back with Abravanal's runaway girl! This is the tale we are told."

A few laughed outright, but Durand Col was as far from anger as he was from the Farrow Moon.

Suddenly, he felt a hand on his arm and Abravanal shot to his feet. Down the table, Durand saw ancient Kandemar, Herald of Errest, standing now as well. A witness, stern as a stone Power.

"It is enough!" Abravanal said to the startled company. Many smiled at his anger.

The king gave the duke a little pucker of disdain.

"No!" said Abravanal. "In the Lindenhall, I was a fool. With a good man's blood, I sought to buy peace. My steward raised Gunderic's Sword before all Creation and that old blade broke before it would strike down Durand Col. I tell you, blind steel knew what I ought to have known."

The shaking old man turned to Durand. "Durand Col, I command you, kneel before me."

Durand did not know what Abravanal intended, but as Durand looked out into that hall of Lost souls and sneering nobles, he knew that he could not shame the old man. Not before these people. He slipped from the bench and knelt, bowing low, feeling very like the scarred bear before the fond old man.

"Durand Col," said Abravanal. "I would have you repeat your oaths to me if you will."

Durand nodded deeply. He put his hands between Abravanal's.

"Swear fealty to me and mine, your hands in my hands. Love all we love, shun all we shun, and swear to defend me and mine against all creatures that live and die."

The words of the old formula were not air alone, but an incantation to bind a man to the wards and the patriarchs and the king. Durand felt each syllable closing around him, defining him, putting an end to exile and shame.

"I do swear it, Your Grace," Durand managed.

But Abravanal had not finished.

He cast a defiant glance over the company.

"And while it is yet mine—by right and by conquest—I cede to you, Durand Col, the honor and title and lands of the duchy of Yrlac!"

The crowd exploded and the king swore.

"And!" pressed the old man. "And as you are the greatest of friends to my family, I offer to you the hand of my only daughter, Almora."

Durand wavered like a starving man. Abravanal had stepped back a pace and stretched out his hand to Almora. And Durand knew that she'd come. She would no more shame the old man than would Durand. Durand tried to say something. He tried to plead a whispered, "Your Grace!" But this was Abravanal's masterstroke, and he led the girl to Durand's side and joined their hands. Almora looked up into Durand's eyes, her mouth tight. But there was no fear or frustration in her face.

A flock of starling courtiers had rushed the high table, priest-arbiters among them, for the king raged. "Can the man do this?" he shouted.

And the bobbing courtiers answered yes, unless and until judgment is passed against him, she is his daughter, lest she says nay.

"What say you, girl?" Ragnal demanded.

Durand saw Almora's face. Abravanal had done a monstrous thing, but after a moment's shock no greater than Durand's, the girl only raised her chin a resolute inch.

"We are betrothed," she said.

Durand glanced at Deorwen, but now there were leagues of distance in the woman's dark eyes.

"I am your man," said Durand. He was trapped—so far from what he wanted. "She will be my only thought."

Abravanal smiled—a broad, toothy grin. He clutched Durand's arm. "My heir now, and holder of half my dominion!"

Down the hall, Leovere and his brigand lords were, all of them, off the benches. Not a few looked ready to hack their way down the tables to Durand and the old man.

What would Leovere of Penseval do now?

"Out!" Ragnal was raging. "All of you! Out!" And Durand joined the last of the company to depart, hearing, as he left, Ragnal saying, "Where do you go, my son, my wife? You, I think, will come with me. We will find a place to have words."

21
Like a Red-Gold Coin

Y ou did not expect that, did you?" said Abravanal. "And neither did they!"

Durand and the rest had fled the Painted Hall. Abravanal could not contain his glee. He took Durand's wrist as they climbed the stair. "I foxed the lot of them. And their faces!" The old man whooped once. Durand had not seen Abravanal like this, not in all the years he'd served in the man's hall. It made it hard to remember that Leovere had the Hornbearer and his devils hidden away among the hills of Gireth.

Kieren, Coensar, and Doerwen looked less pleased. Durand was sick.

They gathered in the chamber block's passage, keeping an eye open for Ragnal's functionaries. None but Durand noticed the Lost following him up the stair.

"What will they do now, the devils?" said Abravanal. "All the writs and seals are aimed at the wrong duke!" Abravanal grinned. "Duke Durand you are now, my lad. Durand of Yrlac. Lamoric would have laughed—and you will be a fine duke too, it is sure."

His elation faltered a moment then as he remembered Almora.

"Oh, my daughter! If I'd had a moment, I would have spoken to you. But there it was. There was the chance. You are more dear to me than all the titles in Creation."

"It is fine," Almora said. "I am content." Her words, at first, seemed numb. But then she nodded sharply to herself. There had been a whole great world of hopes and fancies to be set aside in an instant. And, whatever she thought, she would not gainsay her father's masterstroke—not by word or even by a glance. "I am happy."

The Lost had now joined the circle. The beggar king peered close at Kieren's whiskers.

Durand thought that another knight should have gone for Almora to that mountain cave. Another knight would have been a better match.

He glanced from Deorwen's half-concealed glower to the young girl he'd watched grow. There she stood, looking up at a black-bearded thug little better than the Hornbearer.

He realized that she must be waiting, and that she'd had no word from him.

"It is a more joyful doom than any man could merit," Durand said. He took her small hand. "Almora, your life and happiness I set before all things."

Men would laugh. The girl and the bear. Well, he would break the engagement when the Council nonsense was done. He would set Yrlac aside—if they survived Leovere and his friends from the forest. But, with the duke at his elbow, he could not utter a word of these thoughts.

"Well," said Kieren, carefully. "I wish you joy, both of you. And you, Durand, you'll now be in the eye of the Great Council. Your Grace, I suppose I should say."

It was true. Leovere, at least, would be after his head. "I suppose."

"Ah, Durand," said Abravanal. "Once again, I have done this to you."

"I wonder," said the Fox. "It is likely that the Council will contest His Grace's right to pass the title, though it will take days to redraft the various documents. The laws must be searched. They will be an unhappy lot, but Patriarch Oredgar is out there somewhere, watching them all, so they can hardly pretend it did not happen."

"What will the boy do?" said Abravanal.

"Leovere? He's been prowling round the table like a dog at a feast since he rode in. And it's been more and more likely that the Great Council will throw the bones to him. There's not one of them who wants the others to take Yrlac. They would far sooner let it fall to a baron from Penseval. Now, the man can only wait to see how the arbiters rule."

"Yrlac was sure to be his," Deorwen said. "We must *hope* he waits. If he has any sense, he will stand by a little longer. He might yet win without a war."

Almora curled her hand around Durand's arm. "He has called upon the maragrim," she said. "How long will such a man wait? Now the maragrim are in every village and the kingdom tears at itself. What can we do?"

"We must pray," said Abravanal.

Heremund the Skald appeared in the stairs, bowing with his cap crumpled in his hands. Euric stepped aside, goggling, to let him approach. "You got up Ragnal's nose, that's certain! Um. Your Grace," said Heremund. "What do you mean to do next? I suppose our Durand has a seat at the Great Council now."

Durand spat a curse long before he could stop himself.

"His Grace has much to atone for this day," laughed Kieren.

"This is mad," said Durand.

"We will need to send riders," said Kieren. "Our loyal men in Yrlac must learn of their new lord, and the barons of Gireth must know what's been done."

Durand nodded. "They should be strong parties only. The roads are full of devils."

"And you will need to receive the oaths of your barons in Yrlac." The sound of it was strange. "That must happen quickly."

"Durand Col, Duke of Yrlac," marveled Heremund. "You remember, Durand, the road near the Col? Riding double? Your poor horse!"

Durand nodded, remembering very well the dread and hunger of those days.

"You must swear fealty now to Ragnal, then?"

"Fealty to Ragnal," Durand repeated. He had felt Creation move, lock and key, with those words. There was doom in them. He could do nothing else until he had given his oath to Ragnal.

"Ragnal was not pleased," said Kieren.

"Yet," Durand said, "if I'm to hold Yrlac, it can only be in the king's name." Though the king seemed to have been driven half-mad by his court and the whispers, Durand was a fighting man and Ragnal was king.

"I will go to the king," Durand said. "My oath is his, if he'll take it."

Deorwen frowned. "I wonder. It may do much. Appease His Highness and he may tire of this business. We may be free of the Great Council for a time."

Very suddenly, the Lost swiveled. There had been a sound.

"A scream," Almora supplied. "Down the passage, toward the Painted Hall."

Durand put the others behind him and stalked toward the sound. He thought of the maragrim. He wondered about nightfall and the Eye of Heaven beyond the walls.

"Kieren, find a room," he said. "Bar the door." There was no knowing what madness might come. Yet even as Sir Kieren nodded his assent, Queen Engeled staggered into the passage. She caught hold of his coat.

"My son!" she said. "He has my son. I have heard him. He is raging! Reilan is only a boy. Ragnal will kill him!"

"Where?" said Durand. The beggar king inclined his gory head, blood slithering down his hollow cheek.

"There," she said, gesturing down the chamber passage.

"The minstrel gallery, I suspect," said Heremund. "At the back of the hall. It's a good place to watch what's going on below."

"Please," said the queen. "He will kill our son!"

Durand nodded. "I will see the king." The beggar corpse was bowing now, torn bone and brain there above his eyes, and the queen was offering thanks.

Durand stalked toward the minstrel's door. The Lost were drawn after him, their numbers swelling and building in the passageway. Durand came to the small door and shook the handle. He could hear the king raging behind.

It squeaked open, and there was Durand in the dark loft under the ceiling of the Painted Hall, where the king held his son in his fists.

"Your Highness," said Durand, stepping out onto the creaking floor.

"Who disturbs me?" said the king. He stood at the rail.

"Durand Col."

"Aah, the new Duke of Yrlac." He laughed. The boy—the prince and Ragnal's son—met Durand's glance with wide, terrified eyes.

"Have you sons, Duke Durand? Have you?"

Durand creaked nearer. "I have not," he said.

"Very wise," said Ragnal. "A son is a perilous thing, do you know? The wise women are quiet on that score, oh, yes, but a son is a creature whose whole fortune hangs upon the death of his father. Still, nothing is said." The king drew his four-foot High Kingdom blade from its scabbard. The gilded hilt of it nearly rapped the low ceiling. The boy cowered against the rail high over the floor.

"Your Highness," said Durand, stealing closer still. Only a few steps left.

"Here he is, sniveling now. And you would not believe it, 'Duke' Durand. But this sniveling thing is to be my death." He stopped a moment, jamming the heel of one hand to his temple.

He grimaced, a kind of smile. "My wife. Without the boy, she is nothing. With me dead, she is outcast, swept aside as a new king—a new household—takes Eldinor: Biedin, lest Eodan can convince the Council he's no traitor. A beggar at my brother's table. But with a son," said Ragnal. "With a son, she may act. The smallest thing: a saddle strap, a bit of bad meat, a hunter's arrow." He twisted the dark glint of the blade an inch from his son's throat.

"Look at him. Respect is due a father, but here you see fear. She has bred this in him. Day by day since his birth, she has poured her poison words into his ear. I saw love when first I knew her, but no more. There is only dread. For she has made this thing you see before me. A weapon of flesh and blood, a living blade at my throat."

It was dark up there under the black ceiling. An iron wheel of a chandelier hanging beyond the railing gave them a weak and wobbling light. And the dead crowded the loft. Even the king seemed to feel their uncanny presence. He tottered and the lethal point swayed, nicking a fat drop of blood at the boy's chin. The king twisted his fist against his temple.

"I will be free!" He blinked, his eyes very wide. "I will be free." He spoke these words in the breathless tone of a man who had reached a decision, and, to Durand's horror, he swept back the blade.

Durand leapt.

A dozen years of tiltyard fools and battlefield brawls sent him springing into the arc of the man's swing, clashing Ouen's sword against the king's cross guard. The king roared in shock and pain; the force of it must have stung the man's hands.

For a heartbeat, they were in the worst sort of bind. A twist of the king's blade might have had Durand's guts out, but the king only leapt back.

Bare blades in shirt sleeves was madness enough.

The king's eyes flickered. He gripped the sword. "Bastard! How dare you? How dare you!" To Durand's eyes, the king and his blade were in the midst of a packed crowd of Lost onlookers. Durand wanted to lead the boy from the loft. There was an open door behind him, and the rickety stair down into the hall. But he daren't signal the boy. He knew what the king must do.

"Highness. There's no need."

"You'd lay hands on your king? This is the queen's doing! She has champions who will brawl for her babe."

The big man darted, his blade glinting in the dark loft, but Durand knocked it ringing aside.

"Highness. He's a boy—your son!"

The king lashed out once more, the blade darting slick as an adder's tongue. Durand slipped and clashed the thing aside. Fiendish point and edges scissored at his face and shins. The blade slid with sudden wet terror over Durand's jaw. And Durand was no dancer. This could not last.

"Please, Highness," Durand managed. In an instant, he must strike back. But Ragnal was the king, and all of Errest the Old was bound to the man. All the wards. Every oath. If the maragrim could fight through now, they would run free with the wards thrown away.

"I will not endure it," Ragnal panted, mashing a hand against his brow. "There are whispers within whispers within whispers. Circles and circles. The boy is the knife at my throat."

The dead were all around. The shadows lapped cheekily even at the king's sword, the old blood there. The man huffed a breath through his flared nostrils and leapt—not at Durand, but at the boy: the boy of four or five years cowering as his father raged. The sudden blade nearly struck home. But Durand half threw his sword in the king's way, crashing bodily into the man and the railing. With the top-heavy force of it all, the king's blade cracked wood and the two men pitched sickeningly over the brink. For a yawning instant, Durand felt the king's hands upon him. He snatched at a rope—something from the iron chandelier. Then the stone floor struck like the end of Creation.

Blood filled Durand's nostrils.

He could not draw a breath. There was a ringing.

A spinning flash revolved a step past his hand—the Evenstar crown of Saerdan the Voyager, rolling like a red-gold coin on the hall floor.

Above him, caught in the rope of chandelier, was the King of Errest, like a hooked fish thrashing. Durand saw the soles of the man's boots.

"Hells," gasped Durand. The flat fall had stamped the wind from him. He could do little more than gulp as the king kicked and kicked and then finally swung still.

Although the hall's narrow windows had been shuttered and stopped with rags, slivers of light still reached the floor. Then the light wavered like guttering candles and the hall went dark. This would be the Vault of Heaven above them. Above Gunderic's tower—above Errest the Old—the Heavens would bear the mark of a king's murder. Durand had seen it before—rings upon the firmament as if a stone had plunged into still waters.

The rope creaked over Durand's head—the only sound for an instant. A foot from Durand's hand lay Ragnal's High Kingdom sword. The hilt was corded with gold and studded with blobs of carnelian. The goldsmiths had made stern eagles of the cross. Durand noted this as he lay, twisting, on the floor.

A gale like a living thing was on the move over Creation, roaring over hills and forests and plowlands. It stormed around Gunderic's Tower, rattling shutters and snatching the rags and finally blasting the shutters from their frames.

Durand pressed his face against the stone and the rushes, fighting tears. He felt wild flocks churn around the tower: there were starlings, sea eagles, even rooks in the maelstrom.

He heard a scream from the loft above him: the queen in the door, certainly. Engeled rushed to her son, catching up the little boy—the uncrowned King of Errest. Lifting him to her cheek. Durand saw her gazing down in astonishment at the corpse of her husband, her king. When the wind subsided, leaving its burden of leaves and thatch and branches heaped over Acconel, the first lords tried the doors of the Painted Hall.

Durand heard the child, the mother, the storm. The doors shook. Men bellowed their indignation. Damned Ragnal must've barred the doors.

Durand blinked hard, trying to crush the stupor from his skull. The crown of Errest with its fat sapphire was within arm's reach. Then the doors were breached and the first fifty men roared through. Fighting men, priests, and clerks. They screamed at the sight of the king, his purple tongue, his pop eyes. They roared at Durand, still gulping for air. The more capable found the cleat that hung the big chandelier and lowered the royal corpse to the floor. The most direct got hold of Durand Col and, railing against all traitors, ripped him from the floor, nearly jerking limbs from their sockets in their ardor to be first to exact their revenge.

"Here!" said a voice against the clamor. "Here, what is this?"

A man stood practically on top of Durand, arms raised, even throwing men back. Biedin, the youngest brother of Ragnal, calling the mob to heel.

"My brother is dead. We can all of us see that! But there is no rage or haste of ours that can do a thing to alter it."

Men panted like hounds. Already, men had found the boy and brought him and his mother down by the little stairs. All of them saw it: the trembling child, the ashen mother.

All of them knew.

"He has not been as he should," said Biedin. "I say only what we all must know."

A knot of court functionaries bobbed in their black robes. Durand saw jowled Hod among them. In their faces, he read more glee than sorrow. Heremund Skald seemed to notice as well.

"You have all seen," Biedin continued. "This was no mere man-slaying. It is tragedy, but it is no murder. And it is finished now." Biedin looked over them all. "He is dead. There is only the boy now. And so we must get to Eldinor. The king is dead, and we must crown his son."

From somewhere in the back ranks, Leovere put himself forward. "You mean to leave things as they stand?"

"Lord Leovere, the king is dead. You cannot expect the Great Council to meet without a king. We must return to Eldinor."

"And Yrlac?"

"Without a contrary ruling, things must stand as Abravanal has left them."

Durand had not seen Oredgar the Patriarch, but before Loevere could speak, Oredgar strode into the circle of lords, daring any to meet his terrible gaze. "It is enough, Lords of Errest. Ragnal is dead, and the land is unbound. In tatters fly the Wards of the Ancient Patriarchs."

He crossed to the astonished boy; the men were only just covering the king's livid face.

There was Lady Maud of Saerdana, seemingly ready to shelter the child, till a glance from the Patriarch made her reconsider. The old man raised his hands to Heaven.

"Host of Heaven, the king is dead, but here stands his heir!" he intoned.

Beyond the windows, a great croaking chant groaned up from every quarter, trembling in against the shutters and thrumming in the bones and stones and rolling like the sea.

"Heir, I anoint him. Reilan, I name him to you, son of Ragnal. King-to-be of Errest the Old." The Patriarch stooped like a striking eagle. He marked the Eye of Heaven on the boy's brow with his long thumbs.

Durand saw the Herald of Errest, silent as ever, bow low to the boy.

"By our prayers, now, we hold the wards—every priest and monk and brother, by will and prayer alone, until the Rite in Eldinor is complete."

The Patriarch flashed fierce eyes at the Lord of Penseval.

"The wards are parting," he said. "We will sail half-blind under a ragged sky and still not see Eldinor for two days more. My brothers will not eat. They will not sleep. The boy must keep vigil of his own: three days under stone. Three days in the crypt of his fathers. Three days to test the mettle of his heart. My brothers will not take a drop to drink while they keep this vigil, while they hold the parting threads of the wards in their hands."

Leovere did not answer.

"Not in a hundred winters has our vigil been so long. And you speak of biding in this place and playing court. Not in a thousand winters have the wards been so sorely tested! And not in all the days since Saerdan

Voyager have the thralls of the Enemy stalked the roads of our realm. You would squabble till the kingdom falls.

"We must leave at once. The boy must be taken to the high sanctuary of Eldinor. The right of kingship cannot be delayed. He must be given over to the venerable Semborin the High Patriarch and keep his vigil under stone or the realm will be swept away and all your titles, lands, and jealousies with it!"

Leovere looked to Durand, then turned on his heel.

What would he do?

Biedin offered Durand his hand. "Watch Leovere. He will not wait now, but there is nothing for it. We cannot stay."

Durand looked into the prince's face. So much could have gone so badly wrong. "I thank you, Your Grace."

"My nephew is to be king. There is time for neither blame nor mourning. Eldinor is a hundred leagues, and there isn't a moment to be spared." Biedin ordered his grim cadre of fighting men to search the harbor and seize the likeliest ship for the prince. Maud of Saerdana comforted the queen and the royal heir while sending her best men to the quay to do the same. In an hour, there wouldn't be a rowboat left in Acconel.

Ragnal's court lackeys scuttled out on the heels of knights and princes. Durand saw Heremund watching his old friend, Hod, among them.

WITHIN MOMENTS, MESSENGERS on the swiftest horses were flying from the gates of Acconel. The rest roared for the strongest ships in the harbor, and the contingent from Gireth gathered Durand up.

In the Painted Hall, the time had come for a council of war. On one hand, there was the iron-wheel chandelier with its upset candles. On the other, the smeared patch where Ragnal's men had dragged the bear.

"I had no thought of killing the man," Durand began.

"Oh, of course not," said Deorwen. Two of Gireth's allies had not joined the mob heading to the harbor. Durand knew Alret, Duke of Garelyn, with his long mustaches, and the dark, lean swordsman, Moryn of Mornaway, son of the aged Duke of Mornaway—and brother to Deorwen. The two men bowed.

"The poor devil," said Kieren, "it was too much for him. Kingship. By all accounts, he was a good man. But you saw him at the end. Now, it will be the boy."

"The realm will fall if Reilan goes as his father did," said Deorwen, and they all felt the Powers in these words.

Abravanal stared into Deorwen's face, his pale blue eyes almost opaque.

Kieren intervened. "Your Grace, my men at the West Bridge tell me that our friend Leovere is over the bridge and riding for Ferangore already. You were meant to have stopped him before he left, I suspect. You'll never make a tyrant at this rate."

"The devils! We should have hung the man ten years ago!"

Kieren looked to Durand then. "I'm not sure about you either, Your Grace. It'll be your dukedom that Leovere's after, I'd guess." The man blew out his cheeks.

"We will need to muster the host," said Abravanal. "We have no priests left to us. And he has summoned God-knows from the forest. We must strike him down!"

"He might be made to cast the thralls back across the mountains," said Deorwen.

Alret of Garelyn spoke with a narrow eye. "Or they scatter when he's dead."

"Coensar, you must summon the host," said Abravanal.

"Your Grace."

Lord Moryn interrupted. "Coensar, you must do what you can. But, Abravanal, you will have no time to call them all. And half, at least, will be locked up in their halls with these maragrim thralls banging at their gates."

Durand hadn't expected the man to know so much about the maragrim. Moryn must have seen something in Durand's face.

"My sister is not mute, Durand Col," he said. "And I have with me three score men of my father's household guard. They are yours if you wish them."

Abravanal grinned, clutching the man's arm, and rawboned Alret of Garelyn winked.

"You're welcome to me and mine as well," said Garelyn. "I didn't come with the whole pack of knights back home, but I'd planned on bringing enough company with me to keep the rest of Their Graces from starting anything. Such men as might be useful now, I think."

Durand cast him a grateful look.

"Now then," continued Garelyn, "I say gather up every man who will answer today, and we will see what we have. I won't throw my lads away."

Garelyn and Mornaway bowed and took their leave.

Ships were found. Riders pelted off in a hundred directions. The queen, the prince, and the king-to-be—and all the starling functionaries of Ragnal's diseased court—left for the quay of Acconel.

Durand sat with Abravanal, Kieren, Deorwen, and Almora in dazed silence. Around the perimeter of the Hall, Durand's dead companions milled and shuffled. He saw Sir Waer from the cliffs of Tern Gyre and the moon-faced giant of Valdura.

Now, he only waited for the king.

"I know it is foolish," said Abravanal, "but I feel so damnably pleased with myself." He glanced in Durand's direction, and Durand could not guess what he saw there.

"Oh, Durand. Do not think me mad. I know all of this about the king and Leovere, but I feel so very alive now. You cannot understand because you have always been an active man. But I have sat at the high table in this black hall and let events wash over me for a good long while now. It is true and I know it. That Great Council, Maud and Beoran, and that Highshields spider, their vote would have snatched Yrlac from us." He gave his palm a fierce smack.

Then he faltered, a cloud of doubt passing over his features. "Almora, you are happy, aren't you? I did not mean to harm you."

Almora smiled. It was a very gentle thing. She reached out and took Durand's hand. "I am happy, Father. Sir Durand has cared for me since I was a child."

"I would do nothing against your will," said Abravanal. "Everything I would undo, if you should say so."

"I know, Father. I have always known it."

Durand felt the girl squeeze his fingers. He saw Deorwen looking on, her face unreadable. Here he was trapped in women's business—marriages and deaths and children.

"Your Grace," prompted Kieren. "We'll need you down to the quay, and we should round up the captains we can find. If you would join Coensar and I, we can begin assembling a host before this fleet of peers can ship anchor." Abravanal nodded. He touched Durand's shoulder, then cupped Almora's cheek. And in a swirl of bluff talk and flying cloaks, dukes and stewards left.

And there they were—Durand, Deorwen, Almora, Ailric, and the Lost. Deorwen clamped her lips tight.

Almora took Durand's hand once more. "Durand, you've no call to pity me. I am a duke's daughter, not some village girl. A match was to be made one day, and I have fared well." He felt every bit the battle-scarred bear of Ragnal's jokes, but the poor woman twinkled at him. "Really, Sir Durand. I am alive, thanks to all of you. Host of Heaven, Father thinks that you will take care of me. I suspect it will be the other way around.

No, I am well pleased. With the king dead and the south marching to war, a marriage—even my own—is scarcely a worry at all."

Durand must have frowned, but Almora swept on. "Now, Lady Deorwen, let us leave this gloomy place. I want a change of clothes before we head to the quay. Let us see if my bedchamber is where I left it."

The women left, and then it was Ailric and Durand alone among the Lost.

The youth, for all his customary intensity, looked very young and very tired—hardly more alive than Euric and the rest who muttered behind him in the rushes.

"The king is dead," Durand said.

"Aye," said Ailric. "He is that."

22

The Starlings, the Eagles, and the Crane

By torch and moonlight, the court of Abravanal took to the streets to bid farewell to the dead king and his heir. Word had it that Prince Biedin found his ship: the *Crane,* the largest vessel on the Acconel quay, which took careful handling through Silvemere's shoals and shallows.

The rush into the streets was a hasty business, and Durand disliked bundling the duke and his people into the streets so recklessly on the eve of war, so he corralled the few knights he could find into a squad as tight as tournament conroi. Townsfolk gawked from every doorway, goggling and whispering as the duke's ladies stepped through the torchlight.

Soon, they passed the crowded warrens of the city and clattered into the deep barrel vault of the Fey Gate. The air in the gate was full of reeds and the Mere. Durand thought of the Banished thing that haunted the gate and the bay: the buggane. Ten years before, Durand had swum with the reeking old devil as he tried to cross the bay to summon Abravanal's barons and break the siege. Like a bull and a giant and a drowned man, the stink of the thing was still in his nostrils. He supposed it was still out there.

They emerged from the tunnel onto the gloomy shelf of cut stone between the city's high walls and the Bay of Acconel; this was Acconel Quay. Durand spotted the *Crane,* an eighty-foot cog as broad as a bowl. As the duke's party approached, the pilot boats had hold of the broad-beamed *Crane* and were hauling its head round to face the crossing.

There was no doubt about which was the royal ship, for the whole dark length of the *Crane* shivered with the uncanny chanting of distant holy men. Here was the focus of a thousand fervent prayers from all across the kingdom. Here, the will of the singing world trembled in harmony around a young prince while the oars of the pilot boats splashed in blithe sacrilege.

On the wide aftercastle or in the ship's low waist, there was no sign of the boy, Biedin, or even the Patriarch, though Durand made out dozens of the black-clad clerks chasing about the decks, and he spotted the tall Herald of Errest staring squarely back at him across the opening slice of waves. Sailors were at work on the long main yard. In the aftercastle, others were working a windlass with handspikes.

"We have missed them," said Almora.

"By moments only," offered Sir Kieren. "Patriarch Oredgar was eager to be away."

"He was," said Abravanal. The air reverberated with prayer, and the sound shifted as the boat lolled into the bay. The water stood in rings.

"It taxes them, this prayer," said the duke. "They will not eat or drink. I remember when Bren died. And Carlomund. It will break many. It is desperate work."

And then, though the ship was only ten paces from the quay, something stirred in the water and Durand's borrowed mount shifted uneasily. A huge figure erupted from the water. Large as a shipwreck, it seemed. The putrid slime of the lake bottom streamed from the heavy, massive horned head. Here was the bull of the Mere in all its rotting glory.

No one on the quay blinked an eye.

And the brute had no time to waste upon Durand Col. It climbed onto the dark water as if it were stepping onto a stone floor, all without a glance at dukes or towers ashore. Instead, it made to follow the royal bark cowering low against the waves. Here was a slave of the *Cradle*'s landing and a Banished lord of Creation's beginnings, confronted by the very magic that held him bound.

Before Durand could voice his astonishment, there was a new turmoil. And this time in the Heavens, where the starlings were, once more, on the move. Storms of the dark birds poured from the rooftops of the city, bursting over the city's parapets like floodwaters over a dam. Durand

clung to his mount's neck as the torrent roared over the quay and gathered over the *Crane*. The broad wing of the sail caught the evening breeze,
filling in an instant.

The men and women on the quay—hundreds of sailors, townsmen,
nobles and their households—raised the Eye of Heaven and muttered
prayers.

"What good will another prayer do?" wondered Abravanal. He shifted
his cloak higher around his neck with a surly glance down the quay, where
various magnates were wrestling their belongings into the boats of various sizes. "Well, I've no intention of waiting here to wave at Maude of
Saerdana or that fool from Beoran. Let's go! There is much to do." With
an adroit twist, Abravanal ordered his horse to turn and his household
guard to reverse themselves.

As the horsemen jostled, Durand glanced back at the *Crane*. The lake-
bed stink of the buggane filled his nostrils as sharp as a decade before,
when the old specter mocked him on the Mere. Black water stretched
now between the *Crane* and the quay: ninety paces, a hundred. He
thought of the little boy on that boat.

He edged a step nearer the water. All of the horses were skittish, eyes
bulging, ears twitching. They knew.

He looked into the gloomy water, shadowed by the city and the quay.

The company was leaving, but he had swung himself down from the
saddle.

"Durand?" It was Almora's voice. The chant was ebbing with the
Crane and oarsmen.

"The duke's guard is leaving you behind, Your Ladyships," said
Durand.

"Durand, what is it?" said Deorwen.

"Ailric, watch them close."

Ailric nodded, leaving with the rest.

Durand saw that sea eagles still turned, high above.

He stared, sure that he would see some other prodigy. Instead, he
heard staggering footfalls slapping the quayside stones. It was Berchard.
He had not noticed the man since they had parted at Wrothsilver.

"Berchard?"

In a rush, the man caught Durand in a sudden embrace. He was
soaked.

"Hells!" Durand shoved himself clear. "Have you been swimming?"

"What are you doing here?"

The man planted ten fingers into Durand's chest.

"Durand. Heremund was after these creatures of the king's, these clerks. He talked of them before. Hod and all that."

Durand nodded. "And?"

"Well, each man in Gunderic's Tower was running in his own direction, but I'd heard Heremund grumbling. He lit off after the king's clerks and there was no one to follow. I don't know how he's lived this long. One of the guards saw them come this way. To the quay!"

"Here?"

"Yes, Durand. Here! I thought they'd got him on the boat, but I don't think so now. I think I found him. Come. You must come now!"

Durand abandoned the *Crane* and its prodigies and chased blind Berchard down the quay. He stumbled a dozen times as he pitched between piers and docked ships. Durand struggled past Maude of Saerdana and Ludegar of Beoran, barging straight through their households on the heels of blind Berchard.

Finally, Berchard stopped, his hands spread.

"Here," he said. "All these fools clomping around, this way and that. It's here where I heard him. Heremund? Heremund! It's old Berchard!"

They were nearly alone at a timber pier jutting from the quay where no ship was moored.

"There!" said Berchard. The man's hand shot up. "Did you hear that, Durand?"

Durand had heard nothing. The *Crane* was several hundred paces across the black waves, and Maud of Saerdana's ship had been rowed from its moorings.

"Come!" said Berchard. He tottered out along the pier. "Heremund? Is that you, mate? Heremund?"

And now, Durand heard a groan.

"There!" said Berchard. "There! There is someone." He tramped the deck with his heel.

Durand dropped to the planks, peering down, and saw a man, thrashing. And he wrestled free of his sword belt, saying to Berchard, "Hold this!" And he jumped into the murky waters.

"Gods, who is it?" spluttered a voice.

Durand fought the waves, blundering against a slimy piling. A man struggled against him. There was little light.

"Damn you, haven't you done enough?"

Loops and loops of chain belted the piling, with manacles or collars of iron clamped around the man's ankles. He was corpse-cold and upside-down—and already too weak to keep each wave from closing over his mouth. It was Heremund the Skald.

"If I meant to kill you, I would have done so before now," said Durand.

"Durand? Heaven be praised!"

"Thank Berchard."

Durand caught the spluttering man under the shoulders.

"Was those damnable clerks, Durand. See 'em? See 'em climbin' 'board the boat? Man after man crawled 'board the ship and all of 'em together, they didn't weigh that boat down. Not one sailor's step. The boat didn't sink a strake even with the whole pack aboard, the devilzzz!" The skald took a lung full of water. He thrashed. "Upside-down, they hung me."

Durand kicked around and tried to keep the man's head up. The water was deep at the pier.

"The devilzzz . . . They were thinkin' of Eldinor, with isss tides. Know nothin' of lakes, damn 'em. Gah!"

Abruptly, the man lolled back, and the water poured over his face. He would be finished in moments.

"Do not sleep," Durand said. "A few moments more." And he got his fingers into the loop of chain. All he needed was one brittle link, but no amount of hauling did any good, and while Durand pulled and twisted, the half-frozen skald swayed back, struggling to keep his face out of the waves.

The iron links bit Durand's hands to the knucklebones.

He sloshed back, thinking that chain must have a lock or the devils couldn't have looped the piling. He looked for anything that might get Heremund out of the water. A step, a rope—anything. But he saw nothing.

He would have to break the chain.

It was hard enough to keep himself above water then.

"Berchard?" Durand managed. The man was watching. "He's chained. Ankles to the piling. You'll have to drop my sword to me." It was six feet down.

"Aye, Durand."

Durand got his shoulder back under Heremund's head and watched as the blind knight scrambled and returned with the sword belt.

"Right," Berchard said, and sent the scabbarded blade swinging down. It was all Durand could do to reach it. When his finger touched the tip of the scabbard, Berchard let it go.

The thing was gone, or nearly; like a greased arrow, it shot deep. Durand lashed out and caught the loop of a buckle just as the Mere swallowed the thing. Heremund coughed. He'd slipped under again. The man was no help to himself anymore. Durand had to free him—now. There would be no hacking through the links, and he'd no leverage to hammer the tip in. The only way was to get the blade between the piling and the loop and prize till sword or chain broke. Heremund sank as Durand moved.

"For God's sake, Heremund, you must stay awake!"

But Durand had to have both hands, so there was nothing to do but let the man drown.

He left Heremund's back, ignoring the man's mindless thrashing as he stabbed the long blade of Ouen's war sword down between the loops. He felt the chain slip and then catch tight. With all his weight and the whole strength of his back and legs, he levered down, the blade still in its scabbard, edge against the chain.

Berchard was calling down. "Durand, I can hear him. He's drowning, Durand! What are you doing?"

There was an iron crack and Durand dropped into the water, but it was the chain and not the sword that had given way. Heremund swung free as the links rattled loose, and it was only by the wildest fingertip reach that Durand caught the man's collar. He heaved the choking man to the surface, fighting with the blade in one hand and the skald in the other to keep his own head out.

"A rope, Berchard! I have him. Find a rope!"

Together they managed to heave him up, and at Berchard's urging, they rushed the skald into the heat of the kitchens rather than the hall. In the kitchens, the serving men and cooks had hot cauldrons and fires. Berchard had as much sense as Deorwen. Durand would have had him dead in the Painted Hall.

The kitchens were as crowded as a brigand's cave, with ruddy faces blinking back at Durand from every corner.

Heremund mumbled his thanks, and the two old friends grinned down on him. "Berchard seemed likely to be upset if you drowned," Durand said.

The skald smiled his gap-toothed smile.

"I've a tender heart somewhere under my rough hide," said Berchard. "You ask the girls who have known me."

"Or their granddaughters," stammered Heremund.

"It is rare a man who can show proper gratitude," said Berchard.

Heremund laughed, though his teeth chattered

"I am too great a fool to have lived so long."

"You will tell us what happened," said Berchard.

"I put that Hod thing to the question—nice and friendly, mind. It crooked a finger at me. I was thinking maybe I was going to learn the truth, but you saw how that ended." His eyes focused on something beyond the kitchen. "Damn sure no one would hear me."

Berchard dug at an itch under his eye patch. "Maybe it's the blindness, but I find I'm reluctant to lose things these days. I'm always setting something down and then it's gone. But losing a whole skald? No."

"And while I'm having my little swim, you've been busy?"

Durand told him what they'd seen. "Mornaway and Garelyn brought the best part of two hundred household knights. They'll help us make up for some of the men who won't hear the call in time."

"A lot can happen while a fellow is chained under a pier," said Berchard.

"And now, what of the crown, I wonder? Was there any talk of who would play regent until Reilan is of age? The boy is very young."

"None," said Durand.

"It would have been Prince Eodan, of course, the boy's eldest uncle, but they won't have him. There were the rumors when their royal father died. Hunting accidents, though that might have passed if it weren't for this mad Windhover revolt. They could not give the kingdom to a traitor. Prince Biedin might have it, though Maud or Beoran can each swing the Council, and, together, they could choose whom they like. And you say Garelyn and Lord Moryn are here at Acconel?"

"Aye, they are."

Durand thought of how Prince Biedin had taken the reins when Ragnal lay dead. Without him, Durand might well be dead himself. The kitchen lads brought Heremund hot malmsey. It smelled sweet.

Over the smoking bowl, Heremund was thoughtful. "You can feel it, can't you? It's like watching the trees bend to a strong wind, one after another. An unseen hand, playing all these pieces: the maragrim in the south. Leovere and Abravanal. The starlings. The king."

"The Whisperer," said Durand.

"What do you mean?" said Heremund.

"In the mountains, we heard whispers. At the site of some ward: files of stone kings and patriarchs. Something like it, we heard in a shrine near Gowlins. We heard echoes of something pressing someone to call the maragrim. A whisper urging someone to stand against tyranny in Yrlac."

"A voice calling to Leovere, then, you think."

"I do." He made no mention of the Rooks and their talk of whispers tempting them northward when old Radomor was riding.

"It is just like ten years ago," said Heremund. "The sanctuaries. A revolt on the Hallow Downs. A revolt in Yrlac. Those two sorcerers. The Great Council ready to throw down the king. And then it ended." He shook his head. "I think we will not be so lucky this time."

Something popped in the fire.

Durand looked up, seeing first the faces of kitchen boys and cooks, then, beyond them, the ghoulish figures of his Lost companions. Crouched by the door was a strong man that he hardly recognized: Sir Waer, the knight he had killed on Prince Biedin's lands in the Tern Gyre tournament ten years ago. And there, slipping through the door, Ragnal: thick hands at his own throat, royal robes askew, dragging. Durand did not stay to see the bulging face.

"We will have to be ready when morning comes. And we must set watches against the maragrim tonight."

AILRIC SLEPT AT the threshold of Almora's door. Kieren was in a chair on the duke's doorstep, a bare sword across his knees.

Duke Durand of Yrlac stretched himself at the foot of Abravanal's altar and fell into darkness alone.

23

At the River

The city of Acconel stood upon an island. On a map, the island would be drawn like the head of a spear, or the leaf of a chestnut tree. Acconel's high walls and citadel towered at the heel of the island where Silvermere and the quay was. At the tip, the island split the Banderol. A village called West Bridge stood at the fork, backed by plowlands.

The West Bridge itself waited to take them into Yrlac, a bowshot away.

The War Host of Gireth crammed the streets of West Bridge village, waiting to march. Riders pelted up and down the island. Behind them, the Eye of Heaven blazed among the battlements of Acconel.

Everything was prepared. All they required was the duke himself. They would cross into Yrlac's dukedom and begin the hunt for Lord Leovere. The best part of a thousand knights jostled at the bridgehead, every man with an eye on Durand, Alret of Garelyn, Moryn of Mornaway, and the other commanders on the high deck of the bridge. Each fighting man watched for the order to ride, but the host could not move without the duke, their master.

It had been an hour since Durand sent word to Gunderic's Tower that the host was waiting.

All of this would have been hard enough on the nerves of the fighting men, but, to add to their troubles, something had gone wrong with the river they were meant to cross. Under the West Bridge, the Banderol had ebbed until only the dregs of it now gleamed in its muddy bed. Broken things—bones, barrels, and boats—jutted like the contents of an opened grave.

Durand tried not to think. His head was full of Leovere—bolting through Yrlac, opening the distance, banging on the gates of his allies, and setting the countryside alight. This he understood; he had Coensar scouting the Yrlaci side. What the river portended, however, he could not guess, and this too crowded his mind.

Worse still, he heard voices. Somewhere among the rooftops of West Bridge, the Rooks were watching. From his place on the bridge before the entire army, he dared not crane his neck to find them.

"He best get a move on, hadn't he, brother?"

"I should think so."

Durand mashed his face in his palms.

"The thralls, they have been days in Errest now."

"It will not be as it was with us. A few shrines down. A few sanctuaries aflame."

"Or befouled."

"The maragrim tear up all as they go. And now there is no king."

"And no priests."

"The priests are occupied, brother, but I take your meaning."

"What a home they will make of Yrlac!"

"The maragrim? Yes. But it will never be enough for them. It will be, what do you call it?"

"A beachhead, perhaps?"

"And, with the wards unknotted and gone, how many of the Banished will we find, do you think?"

"Under every rock, I'm sure. Bugganes. All sorts of elder spirits. Most inconvenient."

"This Leovere fellow is very brave."

The lanky duke of Garelyn favored Durand with a grin from under his elaborate mustaches. He'd loaned Durand a proper horse and was taking a perverse pleasure in Durand's sudden elevation. "You must relish this, Your Grace." He laughed and waved a rough salute to his own banners.

Durand straightened, surveying the hundreds of knights from Gireth and Yrlac. It was all he could do not to twitch. He wished he had an archer and a better idea of where the Rooks were hidden.

Garelyn laughed again. "You are no better than Mornaway, here. As grim as any two devils this side of the grave, you look."

Mornaway hardly raised an eyebrow. "You will have to be jolly for the lot of us. Leovere and his Fellwood friends distract me."

"A fighting man likes to think his lord his keen," said Garelyn.

Mornaway wriggled his fingers deeper into a black gauntlet. "Perhaps they will be distracted by the river," he said.

Just then, shouts arose from the army. There had been many messengers and latecomers, and each time, Durand expected to see the duke. This time the excitement came from sentries on the Yrlaci side of the bridge: Coensar was galloping into the caravan yard on the far bank. He passed the tollhouse with his stallion stepping high.

At least now there might be news.

The steward shouted his greetings, riding into the circle of mounted captains.

"Where is he?" said Durand. "Have our riders caught sight of him?"

Coensar glanced at the mudflat under the bridge. "First, we've seen no sign of the thralls yet, not on the Yrlac side. And there are knights heading west. Every man-at-arms for ten leagues is either with us or riding west." West was where they had chased Duke Radomor. West was the seat of the dukes of Yrlac.

"The Ferangore road?" said Durand, aware that the old name conjured black memories for them both.

"I'd wager it's Ferangore he's bound for, aye."

They had all fought in the siege at Ferangore. The fires. The tiered streets. Radomor and the Rooks and the blood.

"What men did Sir Kieren leave in Ferangore?"

"Not many, I think. Not men enough to deal with a revolt. Maybe Kieren's garrison can hold the walls a few hours. We might get Leovere in the field. He is still gathering his forces and that will slow him down." Durand remembered the dead in those streets. He remembered Lamoric and damned Beowlin.

"Time to go, I think," added Coensar.

"We have been waiting on His Grace," said Mornaway. "Sir Kieren means to bring them."

"We cannot wait long," said Coensar.

They were turning to Durand, looking for his word on the matter, when there came a clatter from the village. He heard a Rook calling, "Haw! Haw!"

"Here now," said Garelyn. "Here will be tidings of Abravanal, finally."

But it was not Kieren or Abravanal or any of the knights from the city; instead, this new commotion had arisen among the banners of Swanskin Down and, in a few moments, Baron Vadir himself had broken from his people and was riding for the bridge.

The baron could scarcely get a word out. "A rider," he said, without preamble. "One of the garrison at Wrothsilver. He says the thralls have gathered below the citadel. He cannot find words to describe what he's seen." The man would have left the hill town well before dawn.

"Then they have come," said Durand. He fixed his gaze up the muddy, half-choked Banderol. Wrothsilver was up that river.

"My castellan sent the messenger when they sighted the thralls. Hundreds or more, but dawn might have caught them. Duke Durand, you were there. You know how many shelter within those walls. We might still save Wrothsilver. A giant walks among them."

Vadir's horse tossed its head, half-wild. Every horse on the bridge looked to have been spooked by the baron's agitation.

"It'll be the Hornbearer," said Durand.

"We must turn from these fools in Yrlac and ride for Wrothsilver. We are men of Gireth. These are our people!"

But they could not let Leovere loose on Yrlac, and, for a moment, not a man knew what to say.

Even that moment's hesitation was enough to enrage Vadir, and the man's horse seemed just as wild.

"I will put it to Duke Abravanal, gentlemen! I will put it to the duke and we shall learn where our duty lies!"

The baron made to ride, but his mount fought him. It stamped with darting eyes. And then, for a moment, every man on the bridge was fighting to keep his mount under him. But it was not Vadir who had put such fear into the horses.

There was a rumble upriver, but none could see a storm cloud in that southern sky. Then the bridge trembled beneath Durand and the captains.

And into the channel of the Banderol rushed a torrent of water higher than city walls. The wave bowled down the muddy channel, heaving with spray and uprooted trees. It came on as fast as a charging battalion.

The West Bridge would be swept away.

"Ride!" Durand yelled, cleverly. But Vadir and he were last, and the flood was already upon them before they could reach the bridgehead. The wall of water exploded against the bridge in geysers twenty fathoms tall, blasting Durand from his horse's back and flinging him, breathless, against the balusters of the bridge rail. Vadir careered into the rail beside him and the two men fought against the water, pinned like fish in the teeth of a rake. Full-grown trees cartwheeled over their heads.

Pier after pier of the old bridge was beaten into the river while the deck peeled up and vanished into the flying spray. Durand got hold of Vadir's arm and roared: "Come! It must be now." He prized himself off the balusters and fought onward with the surging water tearing at his legs, battering him into the rail, flinging stones and trees past his head until finally the torrent ripped away even the last pier below the deck.

But Durand had reached the bridgehead.

He hauled Vadir from the last clutching waves. And, staggering where great gobbets of the bank were falling away, Durand understood where the river had been all that morning.

"This was the Hornbearer. Vadir, it wasn't Wrothsilver he was after. It was that bridge of yours." The long white bridge with many spans. The maragrim would have heaped cartloads of rubble against it. "They've crossed into Yrlac. Leovere's called them. His horn. And now they've come."

The two men staggered back as more of the bank slumped into the water. Durand had Vadir's arm. Coensar and the others tried to get them to safety.

"Your city's safe, Vadir. Or a ruin, maybe. Heaven help us. But it's done. There's no use for an army in Gireth. Not anymore. But these things. We cannot let them loose in Errest. We must get Leovere."

The flood was already subsiding.

Durand released the baron's arm. "When Duke Abravanal arrives, you may say what you will, but I will not let Leovere have his way."

In moments, there was nothing left of the bridge but a few broken stumps, with the bridgehead thrust out like a step to nowhere. The shocked and half-scattered host now surrounded Durand Col. He had survived the cataract. He had hauled a man from the water, and now he saw something new in their looks.

"What must we do now?" said Vadir.

It was then, of course, that word reached them from the city.

Four grave riders joined the company at the bridge. Here, at long last, were Almora, Deorwen, Kieren, and Ailric.

Durand stood, dripping at the bridgehead with his sword trailing in the mud as old Kieren bowed but said nothing. The duke was not with them.

"What has happened?" Durand said.

It was Kieren who, eventually, raised his chin and answered. "Duke Durand. His Grace, Abravanal, Duke of Gireth, is dead."

An invocation murmured through the host.

"In his sleep," said Kieren. "As I sat outside the door." He paused for a moment, then added, "Peacefully. He was an old man. The fire, I guess. And the damned Council. They were enough." He faltered into silence.

Abravanal was gone. But there they were, all of them, ready to fight for him.

To Durand, Kieren said, "We've been speaking. Lady Almora will not let the Hornbearer run loose in Errest the Old. She won't leave Lord Leovere free to fill the kingdom with nightmares. It's what she said."

Kieren stood in his stirrups.

"Men of Gireth, you have heard that Duke Abravanal has left us, but you must know that his heir is with us now." Kieren stretched his arm toward the small, sad girl on her white palfrey; both held very still. "Lady Almora would have me tell you that she means to ride in her father's place. That she will ride with you till Leovere of Penseval is hanged or brought to heel. That she has her father's sword." Almora hauled the heavy scabbard from under her riding mantle and held it over her head. Durand could hear the broken shards of the old blade rattling in the scabbard. The hilt would fall out.

Deorwen met Durand's gaze; he guessed that she'd had something to say about this. She might have lost an argument.

Gradually, as the old sword trembled before the host, the rumble of approval shivered through the knights of Gireth. Blades flashed in the Eye of Heaven, and the men shouted their defiance of Leovere and their pride at Lady Almora.

"Now," Sir Kieren said. "There is more than one bridge to Yrlac!"

And more quietly: "I hope."

EAGERLY, THE HOST set off down the spine of Acconel's island, this time bound for the Duke's Bridge by the shore of Silvermere. Banner knights offered Durand his pick of horses as he joined the march, and in the giddy tumult that followed, Kieren got close.

"An hour ago, I'd have guessed we were all as dead as poor Abravanal," said Kieren. Almora sat her palfrey a dozen paces ahead, and there were fierce smiles all around her. Without her, the host would have crumbled.

Lady Deorwen trailed behind. Her brother tried to speak with her, but she was having none of it.

"Deorwen looks none too pleased," said Durand.

"No," said Kieren. "She's not. But it's the only way. The girl saw it, and Deorwen had nothing to say. She's no fool."

"Who will watch Acconel?"

"You may safely leave the old town in my stewardship. I'll ride back as soon as I'm able." The little man glanced about, making sure there was no one near enough to hear him. "But before I go, I'm telling them a story. I mean to pass the word to every banner knight quick as I can." He pointed to the scabbard at Almora's saddle. "'The old sword broke before it would cut his neck,' I'll say. Which is true. I'll tell them that there's doom in Gunderic's blade. The sword of dukes since Gunderic and the *Cradle,* and there you were on the block in Fellwood, ready for the chop, and that blade of two thousand winters smashed to flinders before it would shed a drop of your blood."

"There was no block," said Durand.

"Or I'll tell them Coensar'd been drinking and he clipped the wall by your ear—I couldn't see any better than you could. Didn't want to, if I'm honest. We need the host to hold, Durand. It's you who's got Yrlac by gift. That's clear with the Council all but sealing it when they left without a word. But who is duke of Gireth, eh? Almora is not yet of age to inherit. She would be a ward of the crown if not for two things."

Just then an exuberant Garelyn jostled close. He thrust a lance in the air. "Fine girl there. A lucky man!" Durand smiled and nodded, taking a few openhanded blows to the shoulder before he managed to get back to Kieren once more.

"You see?" said Kieren.

"Two things you said," Durand prompted. "There's no king is one."

"Aye, and the old man betrothed the girl to you, Durand. With oaths and witnesses aplenty, and she's agreed as well! So you're her husband, and Gireth her dower lands. It'll hold the men. That, and they're boiling about Leovere. But you'll need the girl with you. Blood is blood and you are not wedded, but it will be enough for now. Your Grace." He grinned at the jostling crowd. "Look at them. We've got them."

Durand straightened in his saddle.

* * *

THREE GREAT TREES struggled against the Duke's Bridge, caught in the river, but the span held firm.

Durand rode with Almora and the rest of the commanders in the main body of the column. Coensar, riding at the head of the vanguard, cut his horse from the throng and gave Durand a look.

Durand allowed himself a grim smile. "Forward!" he called. "At them—we've given Leovere time enough." Durand would lead the main battalion himself.

Kieren, who'd been true to his word and had darted from commander to commander all through the host, trotted to Durand's side. He had a party in tow, but Durand did not spare the time to look. "A short speech, that," said Kieren. "Oredgar would have taken that chance to bless the host, or call down the Powers of Heaven with dread invocations."

Now, though, they would not find a single priest until the prince had spent his three days under stone. It seemed a tenuous way to face the maragrim. Their forbearers would have brought priests and patriarchs in plenty, Durand was certain.

"Each man will say his own words," he said.

"Kieren, old boy, that's Durand, isn't it?"

For the first time, Durand took note of the two riders straggling along behind Kieren. One was Berchard. The other was Heremund, under a heap of rugs. Somewhere they'd found a donkey.

"Maybe, together, we can talk him out of it," said Berchard. "I've had no luck on my own. He's dragged me up and down the island." The man squinted. "We're back by the Mere again, are we not?"

Kieren's mustache twitched. "My intention is to take you back, both of you. You and Heremund are more than welcome to stay with us old soldiers in Gunderic's Tower."

Every eye turned to Heremund, but, for once, the man kept his mouth shut.

"It's no good, Sir Kieren. In addition to being cold as a tomb, he's come over all closed-mouth and stubborn. Truculent, you might call him."

"Shut up, Berchard," Heremund said from his pile of blankets.

"Listen, Heremund Crookshanks, an army on the march is no place for a bowlegged old man on a damn donkey," said Kieren. "I will not chance it."

The skald clutched his blankets tighter.

Durand would not joke with the skald. "I do not know your mind, Heremund, but you know what we do. We must set a hard pace and there is no rest at the end of the ride."

Berchard could not abide it. "On my oath, Heremund the skald, I've saved your life and I won't have you cast it away so soon! If you go, I'll go with you and how's that? It nearly killed me, fishing you from that damned harbor, but there I was, the only other man alive knowing you'd vanished. I tell you, on my oath: If you go I'll follow."

"Stay," said Heremund. "I can't. Don't be a fool."

"I'll not save your life and have you lose it the next day. Who will lend me a horse? And I'll need a byrnie, at least." Berchard turned his face questioningly.

"Now, here," Kieren began.

The vanguard was across, and the twenty squadrons of the main battalion waited on Durand's word. A few hundred men watched Durand. The column could not be allowed to break up.

"Get him a horse," said Durand.

And, in moments, the blind knight had his hands on a saddle and was climbing aboard.

"Heremund?" said Berchard, "you are dog-sick and like to die. And you've more sense."

"Get down. Go with Kieren," said the skald. "They'll need more than muscle and iron."

But Berchard, obstinate, sat sightless on one of Garelyn's horses.

Durand shook his head. It was done. He called out the order to march.

THEY CROSSED THE Dukes' Bridge with many a muttered prayer. Durand saw Garelyn and a hundred others drop a coin or stone into the current where the river boiled under the bridge. As the story went, if a man left something behind, the river might call him back.

The statues of three ancient dukes stood at a crossroads just beyond the bridge. The riders passed between the old dukes: the founders of Yrlac, Gireth, and Lost Hesperand loomed, each by the road to his domain. Durand saw the likeness of Gunderic's sword carved in alabaster and taller than the door of the sanctuary. Once, the three dukedoms had been close allies. Now, two were at war and one was Lost.

The Host rode west where the Banderol forced them under the granite hills of the Warrens.

THE ROAD SWUNG south, stepping clear of the tangled Warrens. Scattered hamlets stood in the green and rolling fields. This was Yrlac, the land that Durand must take from Leovere and his thralls. Even in the midst of the army, Durand rode warily, watching the horizon from the knot of household guards that surrounded Deorwen, Almora, and some of the commanders.

At a crossroads not far from the border, the vanguard had halted. The main battalion moved toward them.

"We will need to talk strategy," said bluff Garelyn, half-turning in his saddle, "before we stumble over Lord Leovere and his friends, eh, Your Grace?"

Durand nodded. Garelyn was still having a grand time with all this.

"I would like to understand," said Almora.

Garelyn grunted his approval. "Well, Ladyship, Lord Leovere is very likely to run for Ferangore. It is the seat of the dukes of Yrlac, and we've almost no one there. He'll storm it and we'll be caught outside. That is, unless we overtake him and force him into battle. He's got a nice start on us, if he's used it, which we'd best assume he has. But he'll be gathering forces."

"You are so certain," Almora said.

"These things must be as Heaven commands, but he could do nothing with the thirty men he had at Acconel. I would have taken him then, if the king's peace allowed it."

"When do you think we will see them?" asked Deorwen.

For this, Deorwen's brother had an answer. "He left last night, twilight," said Moryn Mornaway. "That likely gave him only a few hours lead. If I were Leovere, I would have scattered my men to every ally's door in hopes of bringing together a force at Ferangore. I cannot guess what time that requires."

"And so we hope to catch him on the road."

Garelyn winked. "It would be best."

Almora tilted her head. "And there is no chance that our men will hold Ferangore?"

Garelyn shrugged, slightly abashed. "Kieren had to use what was to hand. Knights, sergeants. Some with old Yrlac ties. Some new men. My guess? The keys will be on a peg by the front gate when Leovere walks up."

"We should hurry, then," said Almora. "Already, we are too slow."

No one wanted siege, but only those who had seen the maragrim knew the danger. As Durand saw it, Leovere was their only chance. They must run him down in daylight and pray that killing the fool would scatter the maragrim he'd summoned. There was death in every other solution.

When Durand could make out Coensar and Ailric and other faces at the crossroads, he led the commanders from the column to meet Coensar.

A gibbet hung there: an iron cage that held a man long dead, like a twist of brown roots. No one paid the least attention. Ailric was pointing into the road.

"Your Grace, they've gone west."

From where they stood, the Ferangore road ran south toward the River Rushes, passing near Penseval. "Not the Ferangore road?" said Durand.

Garelyn did not believe it. "It will be some drover leading his herd, what's that way. Some market town, no doubt."

Mornaway hopped down into the road. "There is nothing that way, Duke Garelyn," he said. "No market town. Nothing. And these are shod hooves. Scores. Over tracking. Not old. No drover, unless he drives herds of warhorses." He nodded to Ailric.

"Very well," griped Garelyn. "Not Ferangore then. We will take him wherever he chooses to stand."

But Durand, looking west over the rolling country, remembered riding in that direction long ago. The Warrens like stone clouds at their shoulder, blue with distance. Then the eerie wilds of Hesperand. Coensar met his glance. "We went this way with Lamoric trying to reach the High Ashes Tournament," said Durand.

Coensar nodded. The man made the fist and fingers, a rare thing for him.

"We wound up in Hesperand," Durand confessed. "What is Leovere doing?"

Somewhere, Rooks called out above the road. "Haw! Haw!" They were as bad as the Traveler.

Durand straightened. Down the column, he could see Deorwen and Almora. Heremund would be somewhere under his blankets. "Sir Coensar, call in the outriders on the Ferangore road."

"I'll get some men riding west."

"Quick and quiet," said Durand. He liked nothing about this. "If this is some trap, we'll want to know. Whatever Leovere is up to, let's not give him time."

They followed the crooked path west. Coensar put Ailric among the outriders and, again and again, they would find the young man at a crossroads. Again and again, they trended west, until the Eye of Heaven burned high above them.

From time to time, Coensar and Durand would share a look. This was the very path they'd followed as Lamoric's Red Knight squadron. It must have been ten winters, but they knew the place. Over their right shoulders,

the gnarled hills of the Warrens gave way to the bone-pale trees of Lost
Hesperand, crowding to the horizon like a towering wall.

The wind grieved over those trees with a sound like the Winter Sea
full of ice in the distance.

"What could he be doing?" Garelyn said. "He's not running for the
duke's throne at Ferangore. And Penseval is in the south, what's left of
it. Morcar's people are in the west, but it's a backwater." And the long
arm of forest would soon bar their passage west.

AT NOONTIDE, BERCHARD left Heremund in the ranks and found his
way into Almora's company. The column came upon a hamlet where the
windows and doors were buttoned tight, and not a single eye could be
seen peeping at the shutters. Durand saw Coensar give the sanctuary a
long look as the vanguard passed.

"You came this way with my brother?" asked Almora.

"We were rushing for High Ashes," said Berchard. "It's a town in
Mornaway on the River Glass, right over the border from Hesperand.
Your brother was eager to prove himself. These were the days when he
was fighting without his name."

"The Red Knight," she said.

"Aye, but we could not reach High Ashes in time. There is a long sweep
of Hesperand's forest just south into Yrlac, and so straight into Hesper-
and we went, thinking we'd be lucky so long as we ate or drank nothing.
The idea was that we'd dart across. We found a tourney instead."

"With the Lady of Hesperand!" said Almora.

"You wouldn't smile if you'd been there. Dead men. The Lost. There
was a sort of hunt with the Lost Duke himself on our heels. Damn me."
Berchard's story faltered for a moment. "Our Durand was in the lists with
some poor boy who'd been Lost a hundred winters. It is no fit place, I'll
tell you."

Durand had killed that boy, and killed a peasant in a blue tunic. That
one had saved Coensar's honor.

In the midst of the village was a squat stone sanctuary no larger than
a wealthy yeoman's dwelling. There was a low tower, and idols poked
from under the eaves all round. An odd metal sound shimmered from
the tower—a strange echo from the bell, as though it had rung once and
the sound never died.

And Durand saw the men in the ranks ahead muttering prayers and
raising the Eye of Heaven.

"Here, what's that?" Berchard said, turning his lined face.

"Priestcraft," said Deorwen.

The townspeople had not abandoned their village. In the sanctuary yard, sixty or more men, women, and children lay prostrate, murmuring into the meadow grass. Durand could hear the village priest, likely stopped at the altar, intoning the prayers they had all heard around Prince Reilan. And, nearer still, the sculpted heads all about the eaves of the place—monsters, beasts, maidens, and holy man—they, too, prayed, their stone mouths gaping in a slow echo of the prayers. The air was thick with balsam and orris root and juniper.

Somewhere, the *Crane* would be carrying the prince north to Red Winding and Eldinor and the sacred dark of its sanctuary crypt.

24
The Vale of Ydran

When the Eye of Heaven blazed before them and finally sank below the western hills, Durand knew that they would not catch Leovere that day.

The vanguard stopped at the brink of a deep valley. At the bottom, a village stood clustered round the mound of a ring castle. There was no smell of smoke, nor light, nor sign of life of any sort. But Durand remembered the place. Ten years before, Lamoric's men had bullied Durand down into the valley to learn what was going on in the village, and its lone occupant had told him that every soul in the town had vanished into Hesperand. Now, the doors hung askew and many of the buildings had fallen under the weight of their own rotten thatch.

The road into the town—all ruts and mud ten years before—was scarcely visible as a faint depression in the grass. Ydran, they'd called it.

Ailric bore a message from the vanguard. "Leovere skirted it, Your Grace, still marching west."

Durand nodded. "Hells," he said.

Garelyn stretched his long arms. "Well," he said, "it'll be tomorrow then. In an hour we'll be blind or nearly."

Durand could not be so even tempered. Already, the maragrim would have left their hollows. He stared south over the rolling leagues of shadowed hills. Somewhere in that ocean of gloom, the maragrim were running, fighting the rills and streams of Yrlac, but on the move. Durand wanted Leovere. He wanted to save the thousand courageous fools in the ranks behind him; so much meat for the carrion birds if they do not get Leovere in time. Here were Deorwen and Almora. He wanted his hands around the man's neck. But now, they were blind, and so it must be tomorrow.

Durand did not howl.

He looked. They had the high ground: good sight lines.

"We will camp here," Durand said. "We could blunder into anything in the darkness. Set a heavy guard. Sentries deep on all sides. Ailric, make sure Ydran down there is as dead as it looks. And don't ride alone."

They encamped there upon the ridge above the Vale of Ydran. And, for an hour, Durand watched his sentries on the tops of the nearby hills vanish one after another like coins sinking into the murky depths of a pond. Men slept in stiff gambeson and coats of mail. Most kept their eyes open.

At the center of the camp, Durand sat with the commanders, and kept watch over Deorwen, Almora, and the skald.

Garelyn had found a barrel to perch upon, and the rangy duke leaned back. "The trick will be to get them turning. Old Radomor knew it on the marches, and Ragnal knew it as well. You haven't got to kill every man, just to hit one flank or another hard enough to start a man running, then it's a matter of sweeping up the rest. You'll expect a handful around the commander to play stubborn, and it's no shame. But most men? A fight with sharp blades licking and no one knowing what's what? They'll run if they feel the rest going. I don't care if it's Heithans from the Hallow Downs or belted knights from Errest the Old. There are few men who can stand when their fellows run.

"If he wants a fight, we'll try to turn his flank or cut his throat and have an end to it. But if he runs—or keeps running—we'll need to free our swiftest horsemen and get after him. He'll turn and fight if we hit hard enough. His men will make him. And the rest of us too old and slow will rush out and save who we can."

The broad Farrow Moon sailed among the ragged clouds. Durand saw traces of their host in its quicksilver touches. He thought of the maragrim swimming up the great rivers of darkness.

"We never speak of the thralls," Deorwen said, and the tall duke turned to her.

"The wards have held since the *Cradle* was floating at the quay in

Eldinor," said Garelyn. "Twice, the Sons of Heshtar raged and conquered. A thousand winters, the southlands lay in thrall, but the walls and wards barred the maragrim from Errest the Old." Durand thought he saw the man spread his hands. "It may be they aren't as many as you think, or that some old ward will yet trip them up."

Durand spoke. "Heaven help us if you are wrong."

"So then, I'm wrong. What then? Where is the skald?" He twisted around, raising an eyebrow at Heremund, who was still under his pile of blankets.

"What then, skald, eh?" said Garelyn.

"Why do men ask of such things in the dark?" said Heremund, his voice a dry rasp.

"We had better know."

"The maragrim are the dead of the battlefield, each caught up by some little secret shame. In countless battles, the Sons of Atthi died while the Beldame Weavers—ogres, they were, of a sort—swept the air, snatching men from the Gates of far Heaven. Knotting nightmares from their souls."

Garelyn thrust his chin high. "And how are they slain, then? Eh, skald?"

"They are slain already. Long ago, all of them."

"It is priestcraft," said Deorwen. "It's priestcraft that's called for."

"Of which we've none," said Garelyn.

"There is running water," added Heremund.

Garelyn laughed. "Which may be in short supply."

"And fire."

"Now that's good. Do they burst into flames then?"

"No more than you or I. But the sword can slow them."

"Slow them, you say?"

"The stroke of a blade can lame and cripple such a thing. You will find no heart in its breast or brain in its skull, but there is nothing stopping a swordsmen from hobbling the devils."

Even Garelyn could not maintain his bluff demeanor. "Well, that's something."

"And on the morrow, they rise once more, lest you turn a river over their graves or burn what's left before daylight." Heremund looked past them into the great blackness to the south. "The Sons of Atthi would walk over empty fields under the Eye of Heaven only to find legions rising up when the Eye of Heaven failed."

A night wind stirred above the hilltop, catching at cloaks and surcoats. Somewhere in the empty village, a door or shutter slammed. Heremund only turned his head.

Garelyn cleared his throat. "Well. What men have done, we can do. We'll break their legs and leave them hobbling. We'll take their heads and leave them blind. And we'll find our Leovere and see how the chicken runs without its head!"

All the while, the darkness above the hills drew every man's eye. Durand remembered the ghastly rush of the maragrim—how did a man cut the legs from under a wild leopard as it sprang from the dark? It was easily said. Durand cursed himself; he should have driven Almora back. Her father was dead. Someone should sit vigil with him. Now, she was here in the mad black with him and the devil-swarming hills.

It was easy to brave in daylight. They should have had walls between them and this nightmare. High walls and heroes all around.

"Sir Durand." It was Almora's voice. She had got to his elbow before he heard her and Deorwen was right behind.

"Ladyship, Deorwen," Durand said with a nodding bow.

He resolved to make things right. The army would march without her. A party of good knights could ride her back.

There was something in the girl's hands, clutched to her chest.

"Your Ladyship?" said Durand.

"We were thinking of you," she began, hesitating. "Lord Moryn has his blue and gold diamonds. Garelyn, the Red Wheel." Garelyn looked across, curious.

"And you are Duke of Yrlac now and Radomor's Leopard. . . . You couldn't wear that. But Lady Deorwen remembered." Durand thought he saw Deorwen make a sour face. "This," said the girl. And she held his oldest surcoat open in her hands. It had been in the bottom of the trunk in his chamber. There were three stags—the antlered heads of one over two below: Durand, his father, his brother.

Some black cloud hid the Farrow Moon and Durand could hardly see the small oval of the girl's face. Here was the anxious girl. There was Deorwen behind. Together, they had found this thing he had not worn in so many years. He reached out and took the surcoat in his hands, feeling very strange in the high black night with these two women looking on. He was to be married. It was mad. He would be the duke of two lands. If the maragrim felt like children's stories to Garelyn, these things were the same to him.

He could see no way to escape.

He could find no words to speak to these two women, and he was glad they could not see his face.

It was Deorwen who spoke next. "Durand, what is that?" she said, but she was not looking at Durand or the coat. Her eyes were on the hills.

Durand turned, the surcoat in his hands; a voice called from the western hills. With a shiver, Durand understood—it was a sentry. One of the men posted a bowshot over the hills. Someone was dead. "Arm yourselves," Durand said.

There was no time.

"To your banners!" Durand roared, hauling Ouen's sword into the night. Leovere had waited for the cloud to take the moonlight from them.

It seemed to Durand's eyes that the hill twitched before him like a horse's flank as a thousand men sprang up, scrambling for swords and shields. The men had camped near their banner knights and now they stood tight, shoulder to shoulder.

In the blind moment before the assault, Garelyn was searching the horizon. "Doubling back from the west . . . On foot, lest I'm mad. You'll have lost a few sentries, I'd guess, Duke Durand."

Moryn and Ailric had Almora and Deorwen close. "Ailric, with your life," Durand said.

"Don't get too near," Berchard was saying as he unlimbered the High Kingdom sword he carried. "I won't even know myself in the dark." Maybe he meant them to leave him to die.

Durand was mired in the midst of his battalion, and he twisted and craned to see between the helmets of his men. The gulf below the hilltop swelled with labored breathing and the footfalls of an army. At last, a gleam from the Farrow Moon flashed in the eyes of five hundred charging men.

Even twelve lines from the front, Durand felt the shock and fear as the enemy crashed into the Host of Gireth. Men braced and stumbled, creating sudden heaving crushes in the lines. Many would be pinned, helpless despite years at the pell and in the lists. But Durand could do nothing—he could scarcely see.

In ragged flashes of moonlight, Durand made out a strong wedge of Leovere's rebels, driving deeper and deeper into the jumbled line of Durand's host, cutting through the men like the prow of a ship. And Durand saw that Leovere had grasped a weakness in the Host of Gireth—in every host of Errest the Old.

This was Leovere's game. There had been just enough warning and just enough confusion that every conroi in the host had balled up around its banner. Now, Leovere's wedge shoved the conrois aside like a boar's snout in a barrel of apples. And the wedge was coming on faster than Durand would have believed.

Garelyn was roaring: "We'll have to get around him. Cut him off. Swallow him up!" Leovere's wedge pitched and jolted nearer and nearer. Durand saw wild Morcar in the spattered prow, with Leovere a step behind. And Durand knew that Leovere would not care a damn about getting out—no more than an arrow cared when it buried itself in the enemy's heart. "He comes for us," said Durand. "A few cut throats and the issue is decided, Duke Garelyn! Call your banners in. I want ten squadrons rallying here. Give every flag and pennon to Almora. Ten banners in one fist now! He comes!"

There would be no siege at Ferangore. There would be no long battle. Leovere had thrown his whole force at the heart of his enemy, striking with all of his power and all of his wiles, and it must end in an hour. If he could cut the throats of Durand and Almora, he would break the Host of Gireth and stride straight from the chaos to the Tower of Ferangore.

With Moryn Mornaway and the Duke of Garelyn, Durand launched himself into the lines of his own men, hauling banner knights and petty barons from every conroi he could reach. Any man he knew from Abravanal's court, he seized and threw behind him. "To the girl! Your banner in her hand!"

Finally, Durand turned and raised Ouen's sword as Morcar surged through the mob. Durand snarled to himself, "Let Morcar come. Let Leovere come." The whole wedge had shoved near enough to Durand that he could have spat upon them. Durand was smiling straight into the face of Morcar—when the mob of loyal swords broke around them. The cataract of blades and churning limbs knocked Leovere's wedge aside only a step from Durand and the last of Almora's guard. And there, so near, Leovere's advance staggered. In the space of heartbeats, Leovere lost his grip on the battle, for then the men of Gireth saw how small was the force of the enemy and how lost they were in the Host of Gireth and they found the courage they had lost in the confusion. Now, Leovere's men bled for the pain and shame they had brought to the Host of Gireth.

Durand, unwilling to leave Doerwen and the rest, was jostled by friendly knights crowding forward. Blades swung like cleavers and there was soon neither room to stand nor room for the dead and maimed to fall.

Durand fought for a glimpse of Leovere in the press. Now was the moment to cry for mercy. There could be neither rout nor retreat, only massacre. And the blades of Gireth were falling.

But Leovere had never been far away. Just as Durand spotted Leovere's white face and bulging eyes, someone broke through the crush and flew for Durand himself. A sudden blade hacked splinters from his shield, numbing his forearm and fingers in the shield straps. Here was Morcar. Like a beast at bay, he had broken loose from his brothers and flung himself through an instant's space. Here was Leovere's hope.

Durand smashed Morcar's face with his black shield, fast and hard. He felt blows clatter and grind over the iron rings at his shoulder and a slippery wetness at his neck, but he was fresh and Morcar had been beating steel blades in dragging armor till he could not breathe. Durand gave him a knee and skipped his fist from the man's helmet, but then he saw Leovere and an opening.

Leovere's plan might serve Durand just as well. If Morcar's blade could free Yrlac, Durand's could end a rebellion.

There was a ragged, brawling moment as Durand lunged between one body and the next. Leovere's throat was bare—just rectangle of naked skin—and Durand threw his weight behind the point of his sword, but was brought up short with his blade groping an inch from Leovere's blood. Morcar had a fistful of Durand's old black surcoat.

Stranger, Leovere's eyes were fixed on something beyond the fray, as if Durand's sharpened steel made no difference. A savage, confounding joy blazed in his face.

A groan arose from the Host of Gireth and a recoiling wave jostled through the army. The front rank had seen something on the hills. Durand imagined some reserve racing late to the fight, now taking the host in its flank, but it was not mortal men he saw when the clouds parted. Instead, he saw the maragrim. Hundreds tumbled uphill, swift as springing deer.

Lord Leovere thrust his hand at the Fellwood king and spread his arms to encompass all of Yrlac, all of Creation. And Durand knew that their doom was upon them.

A thing of stilting limbs crashed into Gireth's flank, and men became children in the face of such nightmares. Babbling, sobbing horrors pelted into the ranks. Monstrous. Vile. Impossible.

And above them all rose the Crowned Hog of Fellwood, tall as trees. Coffin narrow and spider black.

For an instant, Durand jabbed his sword at Leovere's gullet, thinking that he might still send the summoner to meet his masters Below, but the first convulsions of the mob now heaved him away. Against the mad weight of such a panic, the strength of one man was useless. Chest to chest, Durand was lifted, scrambling for balance with only one boot on the turf.

Morcar's face was a yard from Durand's fists, but neither man had space to swing or a free hand to make the attack.

For a moment then, the clouds took the moon and Creation seemed to fill with howling. A thousand men struggled in the hands of things they could not see. And Durand wondered what had become of Deorwen and Almora. He twisted against the dark and drove himself with furious elbows and pure savagery back into the mass of his own people. Every yard cost blood and snapped bones, but, when the moonlight shot through once more, Durand found himself in the final ring, where stood Garelyn, deadly Mornaway, and Ailric, flashing their blades at whomever approached. Berchard and the women stood behind. In Almora's eyes was pure bewilderment, but Deorwen knew that doom had found them.

Still, Durand could not give in.

He thought of Ydran, the town. It would mean a rout of the last standing men, but there might be a way to get a few into Yrdan and behind walls. There was a castle. He roared to Ailric, "The castle! The castle! Get them down!" and threw himself upon the knights of the household guard, spinning them at the foe. "The girl! Hold them!" And the staring animal eyes became the eyes of men as they understood that there might be a chance for someone.

The monstrous things leapt upon kinsmen and friends. Grown men were snatched from their feet while the brutes rampaged through the fight, killing mindlessly, even falling upon their allies. One thing sobbed and sobbed as its great cleaver swatted heads and hands from defending knights.

But Durand's men covered ground even as the onslaught tore their lines to pieces.

A hundred paces, two hundred—and five hundred dead. They were running through hovels. Fallen roofs. Broken walls. The castle was a bowshot below. And they fought as they fled. A pocket of men would face the enemy, holding them off as their fellows ran. But no one could stand for long. Again and again, the bravest died.

In all the tumbling chaos of the retreat, Durand lost track of Leovere and his men, but he soon found them. They had torn loose of the fight. And, as if the maragrim were not enough, now Morcar and Leovere's guard flew past a bondman's longhouse and crashed into the flank of the broken host.

Durand pitched himself into Morcar's path, knowing that soon they would be finished, and that castle was too far away.

But renewed screams drew Durand's eye. Morcar, too, was looking. And there was the Hornbearer, huge against the dark vault of Heaven, throwing the bloody wreckage of dead men.

As they watched, it seized some poor soldier and flung him, crashing into the ranks of Leovere's guard. The corpse wore the horn blazon of Leovere's own people. Only then did Durand really understand what he was seeing: the Hornbearer strode among Leovere's rebels.

Durand saw Leovere then. The lord brandished a crooked thing between himself and the Hornbearer. High in Leovere's fist was the Horn of Uluric—the battle-standard of the men of Penseval and the lure that had called the Hornbearer from his forests. The giant paused.

Creation was still. The whole night turned around the horn and the Hornbearer like some black whirlpool.

A broken man dangled, forgotten, in the Hornbearer's hand. Here were the monster and his master, frozen in the midst of the dying. Then the giant thrall seemed to shift its horned face. In its black, blank look was as little humanity as there was in the turning of cogs or gears. And, without a sound, the giant tore the man in his hands asunder.

Leovere's mouth opened as the rout stormed around him. Even Morcar seemed shaken; he'd taken a step from Durand, and Durand might have killed him then, but Ailric was calling. The boy pointed downhill, past Ydran where the vast wall of Hesperand stood—not a wall in truth, but palisade of twenty-fathom trees, old as Creation, with trunks like the long bones of the world.

Durand saw it: the thralls were running, but not in pursuit of the Atthians haring downhill. They were running toward the eaves of Hesperand.

"Stand aside! Let the devils past!" Durand waved his arms at Leovere, but the Lord of Penseval seemed lost.

Durand looked to Leovere's captain. "Morcar, damn you! Get your men out of the way!"

A scuttling thing with a man's face charged between them, mauling one soldier as the two leaders recoiled. The Hornbearer strode through with men in both fists. Something like a spider carried a horse in its mouth. They were all headed downhill. All swarming through Ydran—or the forest beyond it.

Ydran could mean nothing to them. Gireth and Yrlac meant nothing to them. Leovere had called the thralls of Heshtar into the beating heart of Errest the Old.

Morcar yanked Leovere from the path of the maragrim, and—though there were men and horses crying out upon the hillside—the maragrim left them behind. Leovere sat prostrate on the turf. His men stood, scattered and ragged as scarecrows.

Around Durand were all of Abravanal's household.

Durand still had a blade in his fist. He looked to Deorwen, Almora. Deorwen only nodded. A stone's throw downhill, the Hornbearer and its host slipped through Ydran. Maybe those lost villagers been right to flee for the uncertain, deathless trees. Durand stepped through the gap toward Leovere, sword hovering over the midnight turf.

"Leovere," he said. "Leovere of Penseval."

Morcar turned. He seemed to be the only man able to defy Durand, but he did nothing.

"I brought them," said Leovere.

"Here, Your Grace. Have a care what you say," Morcar managed.

"I called them," repeated Leovere. He squinted up at Durand. "A thousand years or more, they have been barred, and I took my grandsire's damned horn from the wall." Durand could not help think of the long watches on Pennons Gate. "I have been duped! That thing is bound for Eldinor; it can be nothing else. They have used me. My fear and wrath and pride and greed. I have been their tool. I have been the servant of whispers."

The last pack of maragrim loped into the ghostly trees, and Leovere writhed.

"What have I done?" he said. "They will come upon Eldinor unaware. That is why they had me stand in this place. It is the straight road to Eldinor. I am a fool, and worse than a fool. It is the end of everything."

Already, it was too late for a last stand, too late to send warnings to

Eldinor. There was no hope of marshaling forces at the capital. There was no king to stand against him. Only a boy, helpless in the tomb below the high sanctuary—when he reached it. The Hornbearer would throw open the portals of the high sanctuary and, in a moment, the Wards of the Ancient Patriarchs would be no more. The Banished, the Strangers, and the thralls of Heshtar would be freed upon the people.

Durand had seen the Banished cringing in the in-between places. And the Strangers, he knew, stood beyond the borders of Windhover—as terrible as anything in Hesperand—waiting to step into the ward-bound lands of Errest.

Garelyn was wild, his face white and masked with black blood. "Rightly you may call yourself a fool! Many will die for your idiocy, but, by my oath, you will not be last." Morcar blocked the marcher lord as the man thrust his sword toward Leovere.

Men in Leovere's broken party were drawing themselves to their feet. Garelyn looked hard at Morcar. "Lord Morcar, I suggest you step aside before I recall your part in this villainy."

But, before Leovere's man could answer—before Garelyn could force them—a great rushing stirred among the trees of Hesperand not a bowshot from their argument.

It was like a sudden wind. A sound like the ocean.

And the whole host of the maragrim stepped as one from the trees.

All were silent, and their great lord stood among them a moment. Then, with two balled fists like barrels of stone, the Hornbearer smote one tall tree like a man beating once upon the frame of the door that was barred to him forever.

Even Durand felt a grip of dread. Leaves fluttered down around the giant thrall and it might do anything. If the maragrim turned upon the ruined armies on the hill, not one of them could survive. And so they watched. But then, after a span of a dozen frozen breaths, the Hornbearer turned from the forest, his vast and hurried strides carrying him west. With every step, he and his host moved faster.

Durand knew the route.

"There is an arm of the forest that reaches south and west into Yrlac," he said. "They must pass around it before striking north once more."

Almora moved among them, stepping free of Deorwen and Ailric. "They mean to take Eldinor, those things?"

"Aye," said Durand. "I think so."

"With nothing standing before them?"

"There is the Host of Errest." Durand scratched the mailed back of his head.

Almora watched the retreating shadows of the host. "How will they know? The Host does not wait in Eldinor. Men must come from every corner of Errest. They have not even been called, have they? They cannot even know."

"It is so," said Durand. "I fear it is so."

A sober and broken group listened as the girl spoke, understanding that they stood at the end of the world.

"Well," said Almora. "What have you to say?"

Coensar pawed splatters from his face. "In Lamoric's day, we tried the Hesperand road. If that is barred, you must skirt the forest to reach Mornaway or Hellebore or Eldinor beyond."

"It must be ten leagues," said Deorwen.

"They have lost a night's march at least with this," said Mornaway.

"Or more. They are much delayed, it is certain," said Coensar.

Deorwen tilted her head. "And if we cross Hesperand, if we march day and night, we will catch them up and then there will be another night's work to match this one."

Heremund spoke then, from beneath his deep cowl. "Errest will not survive the Hornbearer's coming to Eldinor. Down will come the ancient wards, the armor of sanctuaries that keeps the elder spirits in their place. They have been bound too long now for sudden freedom. They hunger. They rage. They go mad."

Deorwen was not cowed. "I will speak because someone must. You must look at the thralls' work this night. What will be the result of another meeting?"

Almora turned to Deorwen, but the next voice was not from among their party

"It is of no matter." It was Morcar. His sword's point trailed in the grass. "We cannot remain." His head swiveled, taking in Leovere and the desolated broken rebels. "We meant only to take our due, but now we have set this thing loose and gained nothing. We in Leovere's party must go to Eldinor."

Durand was not sure whether Morcar worried more about the kingdom or the disgrace of being so wholly taken in. Whatever Morcar thought, Leovere was nodding now. But the rebel host scarcely numbered a hundred men—or a hundred men who might be fit for travel.

"No," said Almora. She seemed so very out of place in that ruined village. So very still and small. "None of us can remain. Not now. Not knowing. We must ride together for Eldinor, all of us."

There were dead men all around. And the dead were not strangers. Knights under one banner had slept as fosterlings on the rush-strewn floors of each other's halls. That was hard. And Leovere's men had done the killing. They had summoned the fiends. And, though Durand had little sympathy for Leovere's cause, Abravanal's lordlings still held Yrlac's lands, and Durand Col, a common knight from Gireth, was still strutting about calling himself the Duke of Yrlac.

It could not all be made right. The dead could not be raised. But there were still things a man might do while he lived.

"Leovere of Penseval," Durand said, stepping forward. The bleeding men of Yrlac looked solemnly upon him. "Before the king and Great Council, Abravanal put Yrlac in my hands, yielding his title to me and my heirs."

Leovere did not argue, though some of the old fury tightened his scowl.

"I have shed blood over Yrlac, as much as any man. And so, I say that the title and lands are mine to do with as I please." Durand pressed on into the face of Leovere's despondent fury. "And I say that they should be returned to the blood heir of the title." Men called out on both sides: outrage, disbelief, but Durand did not relent. "As they were my lands, my title, so now they are yours, Leovere of Penseval. I do this thing now before my peers on this night, and on my oath I will not be gainsaid."

All this while, Leovere had been sitting on the rutted turf. Now, a broken, wondering Leovere got to his feet, and Durand took his hand, pulling the staggered man close.

"I charge you, Duke Leovere—should any of us survive—to treat my fellows in Yrlac well. Swear it, and by Heaven I'll see it done."

"What are you, Durand Col?"

"Swear it," Durand said.

Leovere stepped back. "Here is justice, and more than justice. Men of Yrlac, men of Gireth—Sons of Atthi. Let us have peace between us, and, in time, friendship. On this field, made sacred by so much heroes' blood, I give my vow: Should my doom bring me or my heirs back to Yrlac once more, native lords and newcomers both will have an equal share of justice."

The disbelieving knights looked on. There was a ragged shout from men tired of fighting.

"Your Ladyship," said Leovere. "What will you have us do?"

The girl blinked. "Eldinor," she said. "We must ride for the king's city

and stand ready for what the Powers may give us. We can do no less."
Now the tired men were shouting. But Coensar seemed to have heard
none of all this. His eyes were on the forest.

Durand wondered, could the Hornbearer hear over the league of hills
between them? And if the monster heard, was it within its power to
sneer?

25
The Path of Ashes

They spent a dark hour sorting the able men and horses from those
too torn to travel any further. Some bleeding hundreds were left to
make their way toward Acconel or, with the help of their own people,
down the roads of Yrlac.

They could not bury the dead.

Those fit to ride gathered before the mute bounds of Hesperand, where
mist made a wall of the huge trunks.

"Hells," said Durand. The wall was high and full of memory.

Durand rode in the vanguard with Coensar, Leovere, and the women
beside him. It was not an army they were facing in Hesperand.

"If you're determined to take us into Hesperand, first or last will not
matter," Deorwen had argued. "And you'll find that these men of yours
will march in happily enough if they've seen little Almora ride in first."

Now, it was Leovere who spoke. "You have been this way before?" he
asked.

"It is ten years, but . . . Moryn and Coensar, Berchard and Lady
Deorwen have all made this journey." He thought back on those days.
He'd ridden into Hesperand as a shield-bearer and come out a red-handed
knight with two dead men to his name. He remembered throwing a villager into a river to save damned Coensar. They had burned a bridge and
killed a man for Coensar's honor.

He eyed Coensar, thinking of how he'd been struck down with the
man's chained flail and thrown from a galloping horse and ought to have
died. "It seems long ago," he said. "Hesperand is half-torn from Creation.
The Hidden Masters. They meant to fling the knights of Hesperand at
the Enemy. Now, the Enemy has come and gone and come and gone. But
Lost Hesperand's here with their lost duke and his bloody host. With
Bower Mead. And their lady."

If Leovere was uneasy because they did not know what might come, Durand was uneasy because he knew. He knew, and he dreaded.

It was worse that Almora was beside him.

With a nod and a tap of his bootheels, Durand spurred the host into Hesperand the Lost.

THE MIST WAS no mere curtain between Hesperand and the world. Among the giant trees, mist filled the lost forest. Ancient trees loomed like the shadows of giant men. No one could see ten paces, and curious sounds hung in the air between the branches.

They urged the horses forward.

"Is this how you remember it, Durand?" asked Almora.

"Near enough," he said, but, he realized, it wasn't true.

"No," he amended, for now he realized that there was a peculiar note on the air—like a bell: a bell which had tolled long ago. And the sound of chanting. "These sounds. I do not remember them."

"It is the same king's prayer, here as at that village sanctuary," Almora said.

"I'm not sure." Durand did not think so. Something else was taking place in Hesperand.

They drifted into the shallow ruts of a road that lay under an amber blanket of leaves. Durand could see only a dozen men of the hundreds behind him. It made him uneasy.

Almora pulled her cloak close, her eyes on the trees. "Who do you think turned maragrim around? There is no one here."

"Heaven knows," said Durand. "Maybe it didn't suit them, being not in Creation or out of it."

"And the maragrim are neither living nor dead. Not devil nor man," said Deorwen.

"It is a strange, chill place," said Almora.

"It is," said Durand, and, as he spoke, one of the great trees on the roadside seemed to shiver at their approach. Abruptly, the whole giant collapsed. Twenty fathoms of towering oak burst and crumbled, collapsing into a cloud of ash.

Tree after sentinel tree followed, all collapsing into gray ash and white cloud.

Among all of this ash and madness, Durand spied a row of mounted men, forty paces across the forest. In their midst sat a noblewoman, and her eyes were upon him.

"The Lady of Hesperand," Durand breathed.

But the shifting mists had cloaked the Lady before anyone else could see.

TREES CRUMBLED. CLOUDS and shadows mimicked the solid forms of watching men and beasts. And the uncanny prayer murmured on. This Hesperand was little like the one Durand remembered.

Two abreast, they followed the red road despite the voices and the bells, steeling themselves to the impossible falling of trees.

Soon, Durand realized that not all the shadow forms accompanying them through the forest were tricks of mist. Some wore shapes he knew: a limping man, furtive stooping things. There was the moon-faced giant, huge and white. There was Waer, the tournament fighter from Tern Gyre who'd fallen to his death at Durand's hands. There, Euric, Ailric's man. There, the drowned Lady of Yrlac. There, the beggar king. There, the poor villagers of Broklambe.

They appeared and disappeared between the trees, and Durand did his best to keep his back straight and his shoulders square, grateful that Deorwen and the others were preoccupied with the gulfs of mist before them. His starts and twitches passed unnoticed.

A familiar voice broke the sea-bottom stillness. "Here. Where's Sir Durand. I want a word. Pass me along forward. Is someone blocking my way?"

Berchard blundered forward, bluff and gray-bearded with his one patched eye. He had Heremund the skald in tow. The rumpled skald in his hat and cloaks and blankets looked like a heap of rugs on the donkey's back. They got themselves between Durand and Deorwen, Coensar and Almora. The dead looked on like drowned sailors.

"You should not exert yourself, Heremund," Deorwen was saying.

"I didn't like bouncing along like so much baggage—even after the Mere and the maragrim." He coughed into his fist. "Always been curious. So, I've come to learn what passes among the wise commanders of our company."

"'Wise commanders,'" Durand repeated. None of this seemed wise.

"And I've been putting my nose in among the ranks."

"You should rest," Deorwen said.

"The men are not happy," Heremund said.

"We had better say it," said Berchard. "Sometimes it takes courage to complain."

"No one would call you coward, Berchard," said Deorwen. She reached out and touched his arm.

"Not if complaining is the measure." Berchard nodded a little bow.

"Here," said Heremund. "I've heard a cross word or two about you. You know you've given away the Duchy of Yrlac? The luxury? The fawning courtiers? Feasting and high living? All gone."

"It is true," said Durand.

The strangled king of Errest, nearest of the Lost, trailed along at Heremund's shoulder, big as a bear, his coat winking with fat cornelians and lumps of sard.

Heremund quirked one thick eyebrow. "There's been some guesswork as to why, as well. . . ."

"You and Leovere have been mates since Ferangore," supplied Berchard. "That's one."

"You've gone mad," said Heremund. "That's another."

Deorwen made a disapproving noise. "With all this, they've nothing better to occupy their minds?"

"Or some say it's Leovere's thralls: they have some hold on you," said Berchard. "Or it's a stratagem. That you've some trick in store for Leovere." Leovere rode in the third row, not far behind.

"Or there's a storeroom of Radomor's silver in Penseval and it's all yours for this."

"No one said that," admonished Berchard.

Heremund shrugged from under his heap of cloaks. "The roomful of silver was one of mine."

"Not the trap?" asked Durand.

"Setting traps? Not Durand Col. You were always the straightforward type."

Berchard gave a vigorous nod. "Right at them." He smacked his fist. The sound was loud enough in that strange place that Berchard checked himself, listening for a moment. "You've a talent," he concluded.

Heremund nodded. "One way or another, Durand is a traitor, no matter how they slice it."

"And it doesn't matter, as long as you've got Her Ladyship."

"Aye," said Heremund. He gave a cramped nod to the girl. "She's a lucky stroke."

"But there's more that must be said." Berchard gestured behind him. "They are finished back there, though you'd be hard-pressed to find one to admit it. They are riding in a stupor, that lot, and this here ain't exactly the place."

"We meant to get ahead of the maragrim, to use daylight and Hesper and to outrun the devils."

"These men have just fought a battle at the end of a long day's ride," said Berchard, carefully. "Hesperand can't be crossed in one night."

"What do you say, Heremund?" said Durand.

"If the River Glass is still out there in the midst of all this, we might reach the bridge near Bower Mead tomorrow at noontide. Maybe it's eight leagues. Then another twenty to the borders of Hellebore."

"And if we ride for Eldinor, no turning?"

"Through Hesperand. Three or four days. Four days, Durand."

A whole thicket of trees collapsed then: a thousand skeletal crowns plunged into vast trunks billows of dust.

They watched on still beasts. The whole column stopped.

Durand winced into the gloom ahead, recalling the dead hounds and horses of the duke's hunt, remembering the Lady of the Bower. Her lips. Her eyes. The squadron of cold knights who rode with her to Tern Gyre. Durand felt lost then, with so many days and leagues before them. Perhaps sleep was needed.

"A little longer," he said. "There might be a better place than this."

NOT MORE THAN an hour later, Durand looked back through the murk. Leovere looked too dull to raise his eyes when an oak tree as big as the moon vanished like a smudge of ink. Berchard was no fool.

"Right," said Durand, and, when the road curved around a low hill, Coensar called a halt, ringing the high ground with sentries and sending squadrons of mounted men out to watch the road, north and south.

The hillock sat like an island in a stewpot, steam all around. Here and there, Durand could make out the vague shapes of the largest trees, looming like neighboring islands. Up they climbed, leading the horses.

On the island hill, exhausted men searched for baggage. They had lost many animals at Ydran and no one had really counted the cost. Already, there were banner knights bedding down on the spongy turf. Someone had managed to light a fire. The plain copper flames caught every eye, so normal did they seem.

Coensar took a moment to warn the company. They must not eat or drink what they found there. Not them, or their horses, though the horses would need no warning. "A shepherd and a sheep? The old ewe will wander home. But the man will have plucked an apple or supped a handful of water, and he'll be here still somewhere, snapped out of the centuries by the old sorcery." He pointed off into the mist. "Do that and you will be part of their world and Lost with them. Touch the ground in Errest the Old, and those lost winters will catch you up like those trees by the road. Dust and ashes is all you'll be."

The moonlight struck a gleam of pewter in the captain's gray hair and glinted in his tired eyes. Clouds ran like faded banners under the Farrow Moon. All of them knew the morning would arrive before long, and the thralls were marching. Men hobbled horses and settled under cloaks.

Meanwhile, the Lost mounted the hill, passing the sentries. They found brown blood here and there, knotted into surcoats and sleeves. Durand recognized the blue-coated villager from the bridge on the Glass. The first man he had killed, but Durand had more concern for the living. He saw Almora by a fire with Mornaway and Garelyn close by. Ailric had not been more than two steps from the girl since Ydran.

Leovere's men huddled like victims of a shipwreck. Hardly a hundred souls survived from his rebellion, and Leovere himself could not rest. He paced, putting his hands to his head. Morcar and the rest sat in a grim circle around their own fire.

It seemed to Durand that a great deal depended on Leovere of Penseval. If they could outrace the maragrim to Eldinor, Leovere's numbers might tell. Even crossing Hesperand, the men of Yrlac might need someone to lead them.

Durand walked the few paces between the fires.

"Duke Leovere," he said, and the man looked up. Firelight shivered in his eyes.

"You were at Ferangore," he said.

"I was," said Durand.

"You saw me at the surrender."

"I did," said Durand.

"Aye, well. It rankled, though any man could see what Radomor had been doing."

Durand nodded heavily. "The streets." The stones drank the blood of the slain. "The high sanctuary. The carrion birds."

"It was devilry. I knew it then."

Durand gave another nod.

Leovere cast his eyes on the Heavens, the trees, the fires. "Why?" he said. "You could have taken my head. Or had them string me up. Why did you do this thing, Durand Col?"

Durand touched the pommel of Ouen's sword, running his thumb over the worn knuckle of it. "It seemed right," Durand said. "What peace could we have had with an outlander in Yrlac?"

"Maybe," said Leovere. "Still, not many would have done it. You should know that. I don't know that you do." He closed his eyes. "What was that Ragnal doing? It wasn't for Yrlac that you killed him."

"It was little Reilan, the boy." Durand had no wish to say more. Ragnal was a dead man; Durand could see his shade on the periphery of camp. The pop-eyed king looked up, blindly, as though he had heard something.

"I don't know," Durand muttered.

"Whispers," said Leovere.

Now, Durand winced at the man. "What would you say of whispers?"

"I've heard them. I could see it in Ragnal. Did you see how he clasped his head."

"The pain of the realm is visited upon the king. It is in the wards."

"But I knew it. I saw the clenched teeth. It was the whispers." The man quirked his head, peering up at Durand. "But you knew it also."

Durand could only nod. "We met beggars in the Banderol Road. And in the mountains, we heard more," Durand said. "About the girl and the Hornbearer."

"Yes!" said Leovere. "The whispers, they required her death." He raised his hands as though he was holding a puzzle box before his eyes. "It was necessary. She was to die, and then Abravanal. Well, it was clear enough that without an heir, the old man could not hold Yrlac. But I could not let her die!"

Men looked. And the new Duke of Yrlac patted the air. "I could not. I'd known her since—I don't remember. A long time. She deserved—"

But here was a mystery. "Did you direct the Hornbearer then?"

"I thought so. I thought that I held it back. But then I thought it would fight under my banner at Ydran, and you saw how it obeyed me.

"Durand Col, I had kin at Penseval. Cousins. Some are here. Some died in that place when the men of Gireth came burning. But you have given me what I could not take." The man did not finish the thought; instead, he clasped his head again.

"For years, the whispers. They began by picking at my pride. They whispered of my people, and about justice and—they are silent now. The whispers have what they required now, I think. They played upon me until they had what they required. Even this battle. It pleased the whispers that we should battle at Ydran. I did not understand."

"There is something at work behind all this. It was there, too, in Ra-domor's day." Durand thought of Alwen. Of her lover. He remembered the damned Rooks and Heremund's starlings. "A strong man was un-done."

"We will stop them at Eldinor. There are knights at the capital. The barons bring more. We will stop them somehow."

"Go to your people, Duke Leovere. Soon enough, we will be back in the saddle, but we will need a week to reach the Bay of Eldinor and no man can ride seven days without sleep."

"You will not understand: what I've done, I cannot undo. But the Hornbearer is loose in the land." Durand noticed that the man had the Horn of Uluric; both his hands worked upon it. "First of all the sons of Errest the Old I have let this evil loose among our people."

Hours ago Durand would happily have sent the man to the Hells. Yet now . . .

"Leovere," he said. "Hear me. We cannot know the Creator's mind, but you are here in Hesperand, alive still. And by those fires are men who have followed your banner into a Lost land. Surely a man can read something in all this."

There were dozens of huddled fighting men in the fire-lit circles of the Yrlaci camp. "I do not know," said Leovere. "There is something here. But, in this place, I cannot see how we can stand against the maragrim or hold them even an hour. Still, there is truth in what you say. We are not the Powers of Heaven, and the Silent King will not dis-close the dooms of men. Something may yet fall in our path to cause the maragrim pain."

The new-minted Duke of Yrlac extended his hand, and Durand took it.

And, as Leovere stalked away, Durand found that Deorwen had been waiting among the plentiful shadows. "How does he fare after all of this, the fool man?"

"Well enough," Durand said. "He will lead his men to Eldinor."

"Well enough for that," said Deorwen.

They watched Leovere join the circles of his countrymen in the fire-light, touching shoulders, playing commander—a little—once more.

"The shame of this is deep," said Durand. "He has let an evil into Errest. Already, men have died, and this Hornbearer is far from fin-ished. What can a man put in the balance against such a thing?"

"But he rides for Eldinor."

"Heaven may grant him a moment to set things right."

"Or to die. He might die."

"He might." Durand smiled. "And all of us beside him, perhaps."

By Almora's fire, they could see Ailric standing guard while Garelyn snored. Even Mornaway seemed to have drifted off, his dark cloak scarcely stirring. The girl slept, surrounded by her rough court. She was pretty in the firelight, though her face and the curl of one small hand were all Durand could see. She seemed as peaceful as a child.

"She sleeps like a little girl, and we cannot close our eyes," said Deorwen. "And you, a duke for days."

Durand said nothing, and so Deorwen goaded him.

"Maybe you would have been happy in Ferangore."

"In Ferangore? All things are possible under Heaven, I suppose," Durand said, though he could not think how. Ferangore was deep in black memory: Lamoric; his sister in that tower; the burning streets; the high sanctuary full of carrion and birds. No, the more he thought of it, the happier he was without the place. If they lived, Leovere could keep it. Perhaps there had been nothing very noble in giving it up.

"You are a terrible one for blathering on."

Durand paused a moment and honestly smiled. "It is a bad habit."

Deorwen laughed despite herself, and then there was another space of time.

"What is it you wish to say?" Durand asked.

"Ah. It's just— Durand, you will be good to the girl, won't you? No sullen silences. This brooding won't do. She's young. She has a chance at happiness still. You must— You and your closed mouth and duty. It will not be enough. You have seen how the girl has lived. Locked up in that black hall, nearly as dead as her brothers."

He squeezed his eyes shut. And opened his eyes to find her staring up. He could not breathe.

"She'll stand by you. It is her father's will, and she's decent enough to see that you are a loyal man who's served her family. But that is only duty, and it won't be happiness."

It wasn't what any of them wanted. There had only ever been Deorwen and all the damned ghosts between them.

"Deorwen, it was not I who devised this." He reached out and touched her fingers, and memories choked him: of clinging together in the black siege of Acconel with the streets aflame. But she drew her hand back.

Firelight glinted over the big black depths of her eyes.

"No. There must be nothing like that. The girl deserves . . . You must be hers. Only hers."

Around the camp, the Lost roamed in great numbers, licking at blood-ied hauberks, bending like courtiers to sniff at the fingers of fighting men.

By another fire, Coensar paced. The Lost were there too, though Coen didn't notice the bent throng of charred villagers that milled as he walked.

Deorwen must have seen the direction of Durand's glance. "They are still with you, even here?" Deorwen said, her voice small.

Durand laughed. "They are." It was like market day on the little hill-top. A fair of the fallen.

She narrowed her eyes. "And there are more, aren't there?"

Durand found he had no desire to speak about them. "Aye," he man-aged, "there are. Yes."

"I have laid so many of the Lost in Acconel, I cannot count them. So many died, so suddenly in the fires. So many are Lost. But they come to me. They always have. And there is always some sign, something that tells me what I must do if I'm to help them."

Durand nodded. For these dead souls, she had no answer.

"These are mine, I think," said Durand. "Something is tangled, I don't know. Our dooms are bound somehow. Some have followed me since I fought for Coensar here in Hesperand. A man I killed for him. I had not understood."

Coensar was still walking.

"Another haunted man: Coensar," said Deorwen. "You poor boys. But it's you who's haunting the Steward, no? It was Coensar, was it not?" She gestured to the scarred right side of Durand's face. "No one has ever told me."

Durand could not find an answer for her now, but he could not think why.

"You ought to have killed him, or let him live," said Deorwen.

How Durand might have answered this he would never know, for, abruptly, Deorwen was looking elsewhere.

For a moment, Durand saw only the living and the Lost on the hill-top, but then Deorwen's hand clutched Durand's wrist, despite all she'd said before about the girl and duty.

All around the camp, soldiers were popping up from their firesides, hauling swords into the cold air.

And Durand realized that, among the Lost, a row of knights had ap-peared at the hill's edge, most in the arms of generations long past. In their midst rode a slender woman, sidesaddle. She wore green. Her eyes were clear and wide, and the thick plait of her hair was the red of new blood. The woman cast an imperious look over the Host of Gireth and

Yrlac. An invading army? Unworthy guests, blood-soaked and beaten? But before she could give voice to her disgust, she found Durand among them all.

Her glare shot him through.

In a black bolt of memory, he was thrown back to the long-ago tournament at Bower Mead and the dizzy night he had spent with this Lost woman thereafter, a dead man's blood still upon him. This was the Green Lady of Hesperand. And, in that moment upon the hilltop, she knew him, and her dread gaze flickered from Durand to Deorwen's hand upon his arm. And Durand was sure that, despite the armed host around him, death would follow.

He dropped to one knee and nodded his head low in the most abject bow. His host must pass Hesperand. So much else depended upon it.

And he stayed bent in this way for many beatings of his heart as he waited for any word from the Lady—or any blade from her men.

But, when he finally dared to look up, all sign of the Green Lady and her guard of dead knights had gone.

26

A Labyrinth of Dreams

After this grim awakening, the host gathered themselves up to leave. Leovere pulled his contingent into a vanguard for the day's march, but as Morcar led the column down the hillside, the ground gave way beneath his horse's hooves, and he and his mount plunged through the side of the hill.

After a great flap and panic, the company approached the gash in the hillock only to find Morcar staring up. The Yrlaci baron was as pop-eyed as dead King Ragnal, for he and his horse had fallen through a rooftop and landed among a family of living bondmen, all as still as idols. Under the turf of that low hill, the company found signs of a village. Roping Morcar from the peasant hovel, men found that they could perceive other houses through the windows of Morcar's hut. It seemed that they were clustered as tight as eggs in a nest, but that centuries of leaves and dust had drifted deep between them. And centuries of roots and trees had veined them all until a thousand men could sleep on the mound of it, and none the wiser.

*   *   *

AFTER THIS DELAY, the road forked, and the commanders held council. It seemed that they might travel north, up the length of Hesperand, or take a short road west and leave the Lost dukedom.

Garelyn scratched his long, red-stubbled neck. "Right," he said. "We must settle on our plan. There is a choice here." He squinted up one track. "This will be west, I think. The Mornaway Road. The quickest way out. And the other way will take us through Hesperand by the straight road to Hellebore and Eldinor beyond. Skald, what say you?"

Heremund had already peeled off his rumpled hat. The air was heavy. "The Hellebore Road will take two or more long days' riding, all of it through this sort of country. Or so I would wager. Men do not go that way in this age."

"And west?" said Garelyn.

"The Mornaway Road means turning from Eldinor and riding west to the cross the River Glass, and the Glass again on the border of Mornaway. The river swings north, then back west." He sketched an undulating path in the air. "That means finding a ford, a bridge—and we could spend seven leagues or more marching west before we can strike north again in Mornaway. But," he allowed, "we are free of Hesperand."

Leovere looked to Durand. "A day lost."

Durand only prompted Heremund.

"Aye," said the skald. "Likely enough."

"Then it cannot be," said Leovere. "We are days still from Eldinor. The Hornbearer will not wait while we tarry. There is no choice. There is but one road."

Almora had been watching all this. Listening. Now, Garelyn turned to her.

"Ladyship, it will mean more of this place. More Hesperand. Two or more days of God knows. And us without so much as a drop of water we didn't bring from Gireth—or Yrlac. We will lose good horses to the colic."

Even before Hesperand, they'd had no real baggage train. Leaving Gireth, there had been no time.

Leovere drew himself up in his saddle. "Ladyship, what we have is yours."

All along, Durand had known that it must be Hesperand and the Hellebore Road north. But, now, they were agreed. Leovere spun his charger to dart back to his men, and soon every panier was open. Laughing men of both duchies weighed out skins of wine and water and made what rough divisions they could.

It was then, as their ad hoc council broke up, that Durand thought he saw someone moving among the trees: a gray figure among the beeches, a woman, her eyes fixed on Durand across a hundred paces.

Here and there, a tree still fell into clouds.

Garelyn spoke. "Who are you?" he said. His voice was very close, and it sounded dead in his mouth. The others were about their business, climbing aboard horses, riding back to their various contingents. Durand and Garelyn were alone.

The distant figure of the Lady of Hesperand moved beyond the gray screen of trees, but it was still bluff Garelyn who spoke: "What do you want here? Was it you who did this?"

Durand glanced between Garelyn and the distant Lady, then lost her among the trunks.

Garelyn was blinking; his long mustaches jumped.

"Right, then," he said. "If we've made up our minds, there's no sense waiting."

*   *   *

THE FOG DREW closer and closer as they followed the great trails north. Uncounted leagues they trudged, up one gray warren and another, coming upon places where the tracks brawled into a broad meadow, or where walls of trees and banks fell away to leave them utterly adrift in the fog. More than once, a track died away entirely and they were forced to bull down animal trails. Heremund was often consulted, but no one truly knew their way, and the fog did not spare them even a glimpse of Heaven's Eye.

In the densest of these fogs, there was no one but Durand and Deorwen in Creation. Their two horses plodded along, side by side, as the fog swallowed trees and bushes and the riders ahead and behind, until they were alone on an island scarcely larger than a crofter's table.

He wondered if he perceived figures in the fog.

"It is eerie," said Durand.

He thought he could make out sounds. Creation was strangely close. Though there must be acres of mists and trees, Durand might have believed they rode under the heavy thatch of a bondman's cottage.

Then Deorwen spoke. "It returns to me," she said. "Your face. Your bearing. I remember these things."

Deorwen was staring at him, slack-faced. Durand searched the opaque mists all around them. Somewhere among the shadows, the Lady of the

Bower accompanied him. He heard the clink of tack and the stiff clop of hooves on the forest floor. But he could not be sure where the Lady rode.

"Let her go," he called. "She's nothing to do with you."

"I remember," said Deorwen. "You were mine. You rode in the lists at Bower Mead. I witnessed it." She paused. Durand saw Deorwen's teeth and tongue working through tangled mutterings as the Green Lady fought the confusion of centuries. That tourney, Durand knew, had been fought many times with scores and scores of lovers acting the same roles.

"Oh! And we lay together. Host of Heaven. In the very grass where you fought. I could not help myself," said Deorwen.

Durand's horse shied. And there, at his elbow, rode the Lady of Hesperand. Her hair was as red as a fresh gash across a her white brow. She gazed up into his face, avid. But there were many moods in her eyes.

"Ladyship, we only wish passage to Hellebore," Durand ventured. It was hardly a breath. "The Enemy is in the kingdom, marching on Eldinor. And our only hope to outrace them is to cross your lands."

The woman gazed, and Deorwen's voice pronounced her thoughts. "You left. I gave you my veil. What did you do?"

Just then, Durand heard a sound behind him, and the Green Lady glanced, startled.

"And who are all these? What do you mean to do here? An army?" It was as though she was only then discovering the host, as though she had only just realized that there were hundreds of riders in the fog. "You have brought an *army* into my husband's dukedom?"

As Durand made to raise a mollifying hand, there were hoofbeats. Tack and armor. Durand heard the gusty breath of a horse. And—in the instant when Durand glanced—the Lost woman vanished.

A sudden, heavy form collided with Durand: a horse and rider blundered against him. The horse's big shoulder gave Durand's leg a wrenching twist. But Durand caught at the fool, his fingers scrabbling over canvas and mail till he got hold.

The man was straining and gulping.

"What's the matter with you?" Durand snarled in the man's face. It was a knight from their own company. Others rode up, jouncing to a halt all around: the Duke of Garelyn, Coensar, Duke Leovere, some of the men who had ridden with Raimer.

"Here, I've got him," said Durand. "Lend a hand." They got their fists on the bridle of his horse, Garelyn taking a sturdy elbow in the jaw for his trouble. But, as others caught hold, they got a good look at the snarling face.

"Host of Heaven!" said Garelyn. "It's one of Baron Vadir's boys." He had come with them through the Pennons Gate without a whimper and now here he was.

"What's wrong with you, man?" demanded Durand.

One of the man's comrades spoke up. "He'd been muttering," he said. "Growling at nothing."

Now the man strained against them, twisting an arm loose and lashing out.

Almora was looking on, Deorwen's arm around her. Garelyn noticed the woman. "Here," he said, "Lady Deorwen, have you anything that might help him?"

"I . . . I am sorry. I hardly know what is happening." She was still coming around. God knew what she could recall of the Green Lady's conversation—nothing, most likely.

Garelyn nodded sharply and said to the man's comrades. "Bind him. You cannot let him get free in this place. It will be the last you see of him."

ONCE THEY HAD the poor man squared away, Durand realized that all sign of the road had vanished with the Green Lady.

They had not moved from it, but now there was not a rut or a mark anywhere among the leather-brown leaves at their feet. And the fog remained so thick that Durand could hardly believe that there could be whole battalions in the gray wastes with him. He wondered if it was the Lady's doing.

Thus, blindly, they wandered while the Lost voices chanted in the mist.

And it was not long before madness visited them again.

Soon, they discovered that ten men had gone missing—and a half dozen more were wild and unreachable, but still with the column. For these, Durand found horse litters. Durand had riders try every exhausted horseman, probing for a joke or grumble. There were men on horseback who would not answer when called and seemed not to know even their comrades.

Hours passed as more and more knights drifted away. And all the while, Durand was thinking that they were meant to have struck the River Glass by noontide. With the vault of Heaven as opaque as an oyster's shell, no man could judge the time, but he was sure that they had passed noon and ridden on toward nightfall.

Finally, Durand summoned the skald and the commanders of the host.

"We must be leagues past the River Glass," said Durand, "yet we've seen nothing."

Coensar nodded. Under his breath, he said, "We ought to have seen it by now. We cannot afford to lose so much time and so many men." It was the closest to Coensar's thoughts Durand had been in long years.

"We're walking in circles. That's what's happening," said Garelyn. "This fog has bedeviled us, and we've more men on litters every league. Actually, I think it might be a race between lame horses and madmen to see what stops us first." He pawed at his neck.

"Gives a man chills, seeing these fellows. One man pitched right out of his saddle in front of me. That Ailric of yours was wondering whether we'd be better off banning fires. Wondered whether breathing the smoke was the same as drinking the water."

"Clever lad," said Heremund.

"What of the Glass, Heremund Skald?" asked Durand. "Have we walked by the river somehow? We might be leagues north of it."

"We cannot have missed the Glass. It must be ahead. Even if we had a mind to get round it somehow, it could scarcely be managed. And we've been riding straight at the river since we stepped into Hesperand. I've had that Ailric with me and we've had an eye on the trees, the moss, the branches. Knowing that the fall of land runs east down to Silvermere, we've been cheating uphill a might. Maybe my guess at the timing was a little off. Maybe we're a wee bit slower than we think."

"We should have seen this River Glass," said Garelyn. "That is what you think. We should have seen it hours ago. Hours and hours, I'd wager."

"Hesperand is not some a one-street village, Your Grace."

"Is it not? I'd hardly noticed." Garelyn turned to Durand. At that moment, someone called out—one of the poor souls on the litters—and Garelyn winced. "What shall we do, Durand Col? Ten men we lose for every league of wandering. And, all the while, the old Hornbearer must be galloping toward Eldinor."

Durand thought of the Green Lady, and he was sure that she had taken the road from them—that she had turned them a hundred times. Still, what else could he do but drive them forward—as near to north as Ailric and Heremund could manage—and hope that the Lost woman would relent, or that she would, once more, allow him to speak with her? If someone else had led the Host of Gireth, who could know what the Lady might have done?

Still, she had sent the Hornbearer back into Yrlac and robbed the fiend of a day or more. For that, they must be grateful.

Almora was watching. Durand saw Coensar and Vadir and Garelyn and Deorwen.

"Onward," he said. "We go onward, Your Grace. What is there but to press on?"

Coensar was nodding, but his face was grim. A solution must present itself. They could not wallow aimlessly.

Garelyn gave a sudden grin. "Perhaps there is a duke in you yet, Durand Col. Onward it is."

DURAND RODE NEARER the head of the column than any wise commander would, but he had to play huntsman. He set men to range before the company on a very short tether while Heremund quested like a hunting dog, darting off into the fog and reappearing left and right. Without the Eye of Heaven they must steer by moss and dog mercury. Meanwhile, Durand was forced to call a halt twice and listen as men made up new litters. Howls and the reports of axes echoed through the trees.

Almora was the only brightness in the uncanny mist.

She chatted amiably with poor Ailric, quizzing him for hours about his priestly father, his life at the Col and at Wrothsilver. Closed-mouthed Ailric could not help but speak. The pair were even heard to laugh.

As Durand's horse clattered out onto some half-buried pavement, Heremund appeared from the gloom, grubbing about at the bottom of a broken stone idol.

"The Warders, I think, though they're as worn as an old man's teeth," said Heremund. He peered into the pocks and hollows of what might have been a pair of faces. The idols held each other arm in arm. Durand made out big staring eyes.

Almora's laughter echoed through the fog.

"A wise girl, that one," Heremund said. "If she wasn't gabbing away at that boy, all a man would hear is Hesperand chanting and our poor mad devils howling against their gags."

"She's no fool," said Durand.

"'It can't be so bad if Her Ladyship's still cheerful.' That will be in everyone's head." He jabbed a blunt finger at the face of the twin idol. "Now, there may be some power in these old stones yet, for look: We're in a bit of a clearing here. On brighter days, the Eye of Heaven must fall upon this place, for upon the cheek of our idol—if that's a cheek—is a good bloom of yellow lichen and, on his back, a good brush of moss. And so here, the stone reveals north and south, for the yellow lichen loves the Eye of Heaven. I'm told, and—"

Heremund glanced up, ready to expound upon the wind and weather, but his eyes clouded.

"Here, look," he said, for they were not alone.

Twenty paces through the mist stood a tall man in a white surcoat, his back to Durand. The man had neither moved nor made himself known as Heremund spoke. "That's one of Garelyn's riders: Bedwig, I think he calls himself," said Heremund.

"The vanguard," said Durand.

A riderless horse nodded among the trees and Durand made out two more men. These were kneeling in mist beside the first.

It would not be long before the column overtook them.

"Come," said Durand, and the two men moved slowly closer.

Heremund was wincing. "The damn chant is thick in this place." After days of the sacred litany, Durand paid the chant no heed, but Heremund was right. The air fairly buzzed with it.

Durand called to the three men in the trail. "Here, you three. What've you found? You'll need to do more than stand there." But the men made no move.

Durand now saw three horses wandering, untended and untied.

"I think this must have been a town," Heremund said. Across the clearing lumps and hummocks bulged under the leaves. "That'll be what's left of a wall over there."

Bedwig knelt beside his fellows.

Heremund was whispering—"It's three more for the litters"—as Durand reached a square-edged hump in the ground. Durand raised his foot. A step—and it was as though he had stepped on a mangonel's trigger.

Creation changed.

In an instant, the tall arch of a door swept above him into the dark. A candlelit sanctuary stood open before him, rich with the scent of wax and dead man's balsam. Durand saw knights in shining hauberks kneeling before the altar, keeping some holy vigil. Each man had laid his belted sword upon the altars.

This was the eve of the great enchantment.

Durand's mind was filled with it all. They were waiting for the coming of the dawn. Every man, woman, and child of the village stood at Durand's back, filling the yard before the sanctuary threshold. At dawn, the strength of Hesperand would be hurled in the face of the Enemy. The glory of it filled Durand's heart and he smiled a wild smile. Upon the altar, candle flame caught in the jeweled fittings of the swords like a golden twilight full of stars.

He reached for his sword belt.

And felt a hand catch his arm.

In an instant, he was jerked from the jeweled dark and back into the clammy wastes of the forest where a squat man looked up at him.

"Durand Col, where have you been?" For a long moment, he could not recall the homely face or the name it had pronounced.

Old Heremund gave Durand's ear a sharp twist.

"You'd best tell me what's been happening," Heremund said.

With his hands over his eyes, Durand told the skald of the sanctuary. Only ten paces away, Bedwig and his mates knelt in the mush where the altar step had been.

Heremund narrowed one eye. "Ah. It's the sorcery of that night, don't you see? The holy vows, the bonds of man to man, lord to lord, king to land. This is how the Hidden Masters meant to haul the Host from Hesperand. Now, the sanctuary is caught up in the old magic. Look at the floor."

Before Durand could object that there was no floor but leaves, Heremund had given him a shove over the threshold and, once again, he stood in that midnight jewel box of a shrine, waiting the fire of dawn. And, upon the floor were tiled signs: the Eye of Heaven. The Powers of Heaven. Giddy loops and lines of power.

Another tug on Durand's arm brought him back.

Heremund was speaking. "It is the Wards of the Ancient Patriarchs. It is sacred ground. Our men will have set foot on these tiles and been snatched away."

"Is there nothing we can do for them?" Durand said.

"They may be too far gone."

"All right. I won't have the column see this. We will have to move quickly."

As the vanguard of the column jingled into the clearing, Durand was snarling orders. He turned the column, sending them out among the trees to avoid the sunken village, and he grabbed a few men to throw lines around Bedwig and his comrades and add the three to the column's train of madmen. They made up litters as the column nodded past. It was hard, hurried, and dirty work, always with the threat of the column blundering into some other peril as Durand labored among the baggage to add three more knights to the scores of raving and lost men at the column's end.

Durand wiped sweat and grime from his forehead.

"This is good," said Heremund.

"You had best explain yourself. This will make twice in an hour I've thought of sending you to join the Host of Hesperand."

"Now, now. We have been worried about direction, and now we know which way we're headed. First we had the yellow lichen and the moss."

"And the idols."

"And now we have the sanctuary." He grinned his toothless grin. "Always, the altar stands in the east to greet the dawn! It is a certain sign."

Durand laughed.

"I have to tell you: this moss business is nothing but the wildest chance. You were mad to trust me. Come, Sir Durand! This is a great windfall."

And, together they rode up the length of the column. "With east planted firm, we know we're pointed north as sure as if the lodestar were before us."

At this, Heremund's donkey tramped into deep water. The animal stopped short and Heremund tumbled in upside down.

Durand reined in sharply. Heremund spat curses.

Through the shifting veils of fog, Durand made out banks of sedges and tall reeds standing in a still pool that went on as far as the fog let him see.

"Is this the river, Heremund?" he asked.

The fog stirred, opening long, gloomy caverns over dark water. It was too much water: half a league or more and no shore beyond. And so it could be no river.

"Was there a lake on your route, skald?"

Heremund cursed. "It's not a lake. There is no lake in Hesperand. There are no lakes north of Yrlac. Only the sea, leagues and leagues beyond Hesperand and Hellebore."

Yet this was freshwater.

By now, the commanders had broken from the column and ridden up.

Coensar looked out over the water. In the man's face, Durand saw the mirror of his own restless, suffocating dread. They were lost; they might be anywhere in Creation or beyond, and they did not have a moment to spare for it.

"No lake in Hesperand?" Garelyn was saying. "Not even on the high ground? Hells. You know the thralls are covering leagues every night." He glanced about for anyone who might overhear. "Who knows what chance we have, skald? We cannot afford to spend a day turning circles. We cannot lose an hour."

"Enough!" Durand swung from his saddle, helping the skald from the water. Heremund collected himself with what dignity he could muster and set about wringing the water from his garments as the main body of the column loomed and jingled from the fog. "This is some nameless pond or puddle, or it is the Silvermere. Yes, Heremund?

Heremund groused. "It's madness. If I get a mouthful of this, I'll be playing for bloody old Duke Eorcan and his Host of Hesperand for the rest of my days. I'll bet it's the same tune around and around with them."

Durand was tempted to wring the old skald's neck himself.

They must have a direction at once: there were a thousand exhausted men behind him. None had slept and all were gnawed by hunger and fear. If they knew that the company was wandering pointlessly, whatever hope remained would be lost. He had to think.

"If we've come around the Warrens somehow and butted into Silver-mere, the north will be on our left hand," he said.

Heremund's shapeless hat was still in the water. "Damn me," he said, bending back toward the water. Durand sloshed in himself, snatching the hat and slapping it in the skald's hands.

"By now, there are a hundred pairs of eyes on us, yes?" Durand said.

"Ah," said Heremund. "Ah, yes. I see now."

"We try to skirt this. We take the left-hand way. We hope to Heaven we've not been walking east since first light.

"Aye," said Hermund. "Aye, left." But the flint-brown eyes narrowed. "Heaven help us if it's the Mere. We only just saw that shrine. We *just* saw it. We can't have marched east for a day." Both men squelched back into their saddles. Durand would get more riders ranging out before the column. Whether this was Silvermere or some nameless pond, it wouldn't do to follow every twist in the shoreline.

"All decided then?"

"Aye," said Durand. "Forward!"

And, in an hour, the outriders found a break in the saw-edged reeds and the Host of Gireth was once again able to leave the shore and swing north into a delirious and shapeless gloom that seemed as broad as the open ocean.

More men fell to the madness of the accursed dukedom. Their cries piped through the fog.

And Durand wondered how long they could endure the Green Lady's wrath.

* * *

A MOMENT CAME when the last light ebbed away. The army was crumbling on the march. Coensar rode up and down the column for all the world like a shepherd's dog; the most he gave Durand was a grim shake of his head.

Heremund could no longer ride ahead. "There is no sign," he said. "Not yet, but we cannot continue this way. I think that there has never been a night so black."

"We cannot have another night waiting among the dripping trees and another day with the forest working evil upon the men," said Durand. "No."

It could not be so. He had seen pines while there had been light. The sticky scent was still on the breeze, and so Durand called a halt. "Let us see what can be done." Coensar took the men who had the field craft out among the pines. Some of the trees seemed mortal enough. And, with the homely crack of axes among the trees, Durand and many of the barons built a stubborn bonfire to get the makeshift torches going.

Coensar brought the parties in from the woods and Almora joined the stern gathering at the bonfire. She smiled around at the determined men. They were splattered with green chips and old blood as the firelight hooked deep shadows over their features. But they watched Almora, and only when she nodded did the whole group touch torches to the fire.

Fierce and giddy smiles passed among them all.

Only Durand and old Coensar looked on, grim-faced. Durand would not lead these people into this disaster and leave them. They would die on the march or they would break through.

Somewhere among the trees, he was sure, the Green Lady watched.

27

The Passage of Honor

Like some Patriarch's torch-lit procession, the company rode through that sanctuary of dark trees and they rode deep into the night by tangled ways, listening as their comrades moaned and the ghosts of Hesperand kept up their uncanny chanting. The mist retreated, but the dazzled eyes of men see little beyond the light of a torch, and, when the wind stirred in the forest, it plunged the whole column into a guttering darkness that half-stopped the hearts of the bravest among them.

Heremund drove the army through thickets. In the dark, they came upon tracks and animal trails, shrines and crossroads and ditches. The skald could only curse and guess their route. Moss smoked as he thrust pitchy splinters at the bases of trees.

Soon, of course, the merry torches winked out. An hour's light consumed three or more of the best, and so what began as a train of lights flickered and dwindled, so that in a few hours a thousand men bumbled like a string of blind beggars with only a torch here or there to show that they had not ridden right out of the world.

Durand was soon joined by a sweeping phalanx of Lost souls, limping and drifting and groveling over the forest floor.

They struck a road or ravine, their path sinking deep between root-veined walls of earth nearly the height of a mounted man; the Lost peered down. Beech trees knotted in the torchlight overhead while the horsemen jostled knee to knee in the sunken roadbed. They might have been riding in their own graves.

The eerie roadway rang louder and louder with the ceaseless chanting.

Durand became certain that they must all die, and their kingdom fall. He had mishandled the Bower Lady, and now they were, all of them, cursed to wander till madness took them. But, as he ground his teeth at these thoughts, something glinted in the dark beyond the roots and torchlight: armed men, he was sure. She was out there! Durand spurred his mount up the bank and bowled through Lost souls and into the trees.

The sudden rush battered his torch into blackness, and the baffled horse shied at the sudden gulf of dark that overwhelmed them.

"No!" Durand shouted. The glint of the knights was vanishing as he watched: The whole squadron of them slipping away like a school of minnows in some black millpond. "No! Come back!"

But there was no one to hear him.

The constellation of his army stretched behind him in their ditch. They must not hear him raving, begging at the top of his lungs for the Lady of Hesperand to free them.

Coensar and a cadre of men had found a break in the bank. They rode out.

The man looked grimly into Durand's face.

"I saw knights," said Durand. "It'll have been the Lady of Hesperand, Coen."

Coensar gave Durand a careful nod.

"It's all caught up with her," Durand explained. "All of this."

Coensar's men looked to each other. They would have seen plenty of men ride off. They had tied many more to litters, and they were likely getting set to take another, but Coensar swiveled, flashing a cautioning glance over the rest. "It's all right. We've all seen 'em. Best see if anyone else lit out while we weren't looking."

Reluctantly, Coensar's men left them.

"If that horse hadn't pulled up. . . . Maybe you'd be as lost as the rest of her lads, Durand. You know this place as well as I."

"What else could I do?" Frustration had him practically writhing. "We are melting away. We are like a sword of ice. Every day, we have fewer fighting men. Even now, if we can ever reach Eldinor, what good can we do?"

But Coensar was blinking.

Durand had hardly noticed. The Eye of Heaven was rising. The light was in Coensar's face, and Durand could see the rag-tag string of knights that he'd brought from Yrlac, rubbing their faces and staring in astonishment.

And, before Durand could open his mouth, there was a call from the vanguard. There was something in the road. Durand and Coensar set their spurs.

THERE WAS A rise just ahead of the breathless Host of Gireth. Coensar and Durand charged up. And there, spread below them, was a broad meadow where acres of open ground steamed in the morning light. In the midst of the place, Durand saw a slender bridge. This was the place where Coensar had dueled Cassonel of Algarden, where Durand had knelt and Coensar had knighted him.

Below the bridge must be the River Glass, still curling in its bed of mist and reeds. But, more importantly, they were not alone: an army stood between them and the crossing. Their grim commander, Duke Eorcan with the Peregrine Crown of Hesperand upon his brow, sat astride a black charger on the high bridgehead.

This was the wellspring of the chant that echoed through all the wastes of Hesperand. This was the Host of Hesperand, at prayer.

The men of Gireth and Yrlac were silent.

"We saw the Green Lady," said Durand.

"She has relented," said Coensar. "We've reached the river."

The prayer of the Lost host brimmed the meadow, deep and as alive in the air as bees in a hive. A thousand men or more knelt. Hundreds more stood at the bridles of motionless horses. Compared to the Host of Gireth, they gleamed like new-struck pennies. Blazons were bright with fresh paint. Burnished helmets gleamed. Durand could not help but glance back at his own men, blood-stained, exhausted and half or more lost to madness.

"Well," said Garelyn. "There is the bridge, anyway. I'd love to see our route to this place on a map. That I would truly love. We will have to pick through the lot of these old men to reach the bridge, I suppose."

Durand nodded. The Host of Hesperand neatly blocked their path. They might be moved. They might listen, if he should ride down.

Before Durand could move, Coensar spurred his charger down into the meadow.

"All right. That's settled then." Garelyn was turning to the men. "Steady," he said. "We might need to move hastily. Pass the word down the line. Be ready." Durand heard this grappling clatter of men pulling their shields from their baggage.

Coensar jounced downhill at a canter, stirring the remaining tatters of mist.

"Someone should go with him," Almora said.

Garelyn gave her a wry smile. "One is enough to lose, Ladyship. And there'd be little that two men—or two hundred—could do against those fellows."

There wasn't a twitch among the ranks of Eorcan's Host as Coensar cantered nearer and nearer. Even when the steward drew up no more than a stone's throw from the multitude, Eorcan sat like some painted statue in a city square. The wings of the Peregrine Crown might almost have been stone, except for the silver glint of the upswept wings.

Only then did Heremund join the vanguard. "What have we stumbled upon this time?"

Coensar picked along the ranks of the eerie host, his charge skittish. The men bore the long shields and tall helms of a previous age. Their coats of mail hung long. Some wore coats of burnished scales—each scale as long and narrow as the leaves of a willow.

"They're not moving. He won't be talking them around," Garelyn said. "We'll have to shoulder our way through."

There had been another bridge, upstream: a pitched wooden span. But he had put it to the torch with the help of Berchard and big Ouen. There, he had slain a bondman in a blue coat. But, even as the thought entered his mind, the torch-smoke smell of pitch and timber drifted past him and he knew that his bridge was still smoking. Just as the Lost blue-coated bondman was still in his train.

"They are gathered. This is the Host of Hesperand, and they are at prayer," Heremund was saying. "This is the day they departed. The day the Hidden Masters of old made ready to snatch their army from Hesperand to join the fight in the distant southlands. Bound by their oaths and the king and the patriarchs, they were to be plucked like one woven web and flung the leagues across Creation, to strike the Enemy and to save their kinsman beyond Fellwood."

"And here they are still," said Durand. "Lost with their duke."

"It was a fight, wasn't it?" said Garelyn. "Eorcan and some man. Something about his wife behind his back. Did Eorcan die?"

"Have a care, Your Grace," said Heremund. "They are right before us."

"Aye, well, I'd guess they aren't listening."

"They've been coming back to this place since before Uluric blew that damned horn. Before there were Iron Knights on the Pennons Gate, before Hornbearers and Lost Princes. Marching back to this day, never to ride."

Coensar was now a few steps from the nearest man. Durand could scarcely breathe.

"Thank you, skald," said Garelyn.

Coensar was picking along the lines, but he would find no way through—no way that a mounted column could pass through. Durand saw Coensar's horse, its eyes flashing, its tail tucked, and he turned to the rest.

"Right," said Durand. "We must cross the bridge. There is nothing for it, but we'll be leading the horses, I think." And he dropped from the saddle.

"Sir Durand," said Almora, her tone careful, her voice loud. "If you agree, I would walk with you at the head of the column." She smiled. "I've seen little but the rump of the horse in front of me since we set out this morning."

Durand thought a moment as she beamed for the army. If they brought the Lost Host down on them, what could it matter whether she was first or last? Deorwen said nothing. She hardly met Durand's glance.

"Fine," said Durand. He offered the girl his hand, and she climbed down.

Together they stepped down onto the field, leading the host forward, steadily approaching the Lost battalions, hand in hand. Only Durand was near enough to know that she trembled and that her hands were slab-cold.

The girl did not hesitate, chatted amiably all the while. "I suppose they cannot hear us, Sir Durand. They are lost in their rituals." But Durand could see that it was all she could do to put her feet one ahead of the other. Durand did not know what he would have done when he was her age—a boy shield-bearer for Kieren the Fox in Acconel. Now, he had seen so much, and his heart still thundered.

They passed Coensar. He was looking grimly up at what survived of their host, an arming cap like a silver bowl in his fist.

"They are following," said Almora. She wondered, but she did not look. Instead, she smiled up at Durand while he gave the army a steady glance: spread across the slope, the ragged Host of Gireth looked more like a drove of beggars than an army; they were so few and so haggard. He watched knights stumble. So many were lost. So many were stricken. How could so very few men face the Hornbearer, even if they could reach Eldinor in time? And, as Garelyn had said, they did not even know the day.

"They are brave men," Almora said. She pitched her voice to be over-heard, at least by a few. And she tugged Durand's hand.

They led their horses between a knight's long gilded shield and the pommel of a kneeling man's sword. It was like tiptoeing among sleeping adders.

And the knights were not still—not entirely—for slowly, slowly their lips intoned the words of the old chant. Durand could smell the balsam and cedar and orris of their vigils. And he knew that he would not touch these men for kingdoms.

With Deorwen, Coensar, and the rest not far behind, they worked their way through the Host of Hesperand. "I think that it might be easy to lead men," said Almora. "Which knight-at-arms will concede that a maiden girl might go where he could not?"

"Soon enough we might find out, with the way you're going," said Durand.

And she nodded a courtly bow.

Between two squadrons of knights, they found an open aisle, and, for a moment, led their mounts easily. They could see Duke Eorcan quite plainly. Almora opened her mouth to speak; one of the man's slow hands was reaching now toward the bridge, toward Bower Mead. It was clear they meant to cross—but then the Lost came to life.

Creation broke around them, full of screaming.

The Heavens were black.

A thousand men turned, their crooked hands reaching for Almora.

The dead men howled for the two thousand winters they'd lost between Heaven and the Hells.

Then it ended, and they were tottering between the silent ranks. Hesperand was as it had been: a meadow of mist and daylight. And it seemed that Durand and Almora had hardly moved. The arms of the long-lost knights were already falling, their eyes turning back to the commander on the bridge. Already, they were falling back into their dream.

"My hand," said Almora. Her fingers hovered a hair's breadth from a dead man's knuckle. For the briefest instant, she had touched bare skin to bare skin. That, it seemed, was something they must not do. "I must have touched him," she said. "But only for the briefest instant."

The Host of Gireth stood like so many startled deer. The girl blinked up into Durand's eyes, shivering. She might have been struck by lightning, but she hardly faltered now.

"Well, what a thing that was!"

"Are you well, Ladyship?" Durand said, good and loud.

"I am. Only tell them to be careful," she said. "It is better not to touch these men." She pulled a self-mocking face. "I would not do it twice."

Garelyn was weaving his way between the stiff and reaching arms.

"I thought one of the young devils had jabbed a needle into one of their backsides."

Durand swallowed. He could find nothing to say to Garelyn.

The lanky nobleman gestured to Eorcan at the bridge. "This will be our proud and mettlesome duke."

"They are about to ride for Bower Mead," said Durand.

Eorcan was a tall man. Steel and silver gleamed from his crown, his mail, and his blade. Durand remembered how the duke and the Lady of the Bower lived and relived the final days. Tournament after tournament for two thousand winters. Hesperand had turned around those few nights, always the same. "But it is changed. The whole place," Durand said. "I think the fault is mine."

"There is no point stopping here," said Garelyn, and they walked on.

"We fought in their tournament, and, by dumb luck, I was the champion. The Bower Lady gave me a token," said Durand, mostly to the girl. "A bit of green silk and promises. But I think the champion was always meant to die. It was part of the dance. Each tournament was like the first, I think. First, the tourney and a champion, then the Lady . . ." He remembered a delirious night with the Lady. "The Lady betrayed old Eorcan, and jealous Eorcan slew the champion, riding him down like a stag in the forest. Seven years, seven years, seven years. A champion. A favor. A death. Seven years. But I did not die." Only Deorwen could have saved him. She drew him back from the old dream of Hesperand. Her touch pulled him back to the world.

She did not meet his eye.

Meanwhile, Garelyn was peering into the face of one mustachioed knight: he might have been peering in a looking glass. "And these fellows are stuck in their dream, only waking from time to time to blink at the ages behind them before they step back into their places."

Garelyn smiled and left his doppelgänger behind. "It is too bad. They meant to hunt the maragrim far away. Now, the Lord of Dooms has brought maragrim aplenty to Errest the Old. They needn't risk the Otherworld." Garelyn shook his head. "Old Eorcan here, he's just ready to make some little speech and take them across to Bower Mead, thinking all the while that it's new."

Up onto the bridge they went, and led their horses past the Duke of Hesperand as easily as if the deathless man and his horse were something hanging in a butcher's window. To Durand, the strangest thing was to step once more onto the elegant bridge where Coensar had challenged Cassonel of Algarden. They had fought right on the spot while Durand had watched from a track by the river below. Coensar had been the hero then.

They crossed, army through army, until the living host assembled upon the northern bank, climbing into saddles. Garelyn gathered Almora in. There were three tracks in the offing.

"Now," said Garelyn. "We must choose our road. I, for one, have no wish to see more of this lot. Where is Sir Coensar?"

Durand had lost track of the Steward; he heard a gasp from Almora: "Oh no."

There was the man: he had been under the bridge. He was clambering up the steep bank. He had never crossed over.

Durand remembered the track there. It was the way he'd gone to burn the upstream bridge.

Coensar had the silver-bright bowl of an arming cap in his hand, brimming with water—water from the Glass, water from Hesperand. Here, Coensar had been a hero, once. Now, what would he do?

Durand sprang down from his saddle.

Someone caught his shoulders. It was Ailric first, then Berchard, and even Garelyn.

Coensar would leave the world.

"It's the water isn't it?" said Berchard. Coensar would drink the water of Hesperand. "Host of Heaven. He means to stay behind. It will be the bridge he's thinking of. Things are breaking here. He denies Eorcan the bridge: a challenge. He might prise a boon from the old ghost. It's just the thing for this place."

Sir Coensar faced them all from the bridgehead, right at the nose of Eorcan's horse. He had his old sword, Keening, trailing in his fist. Durand saw the man's eyes meet his. Then he put the metal bowl of the arming cap to his lips and drank the water of that Lost land.

"No," said Durand. But Coensar could not have heard him.

Slowly, like a man freezing, Coensar moved. He raised ancient Keening, a High Kingdom blade as old as the old duke. Already Coensar's pale eyes could not see the men he had left.

"We must leave him," Heremund said. "It may be hours. It may be years before Eorcan spies Coensar and his challenge there. He may win; he may lose."

WITH SCARCELY A further word, they left the bridge. The fog closed in once more, and after a dreary hour it was as though they had never seen the Glass. The column drifted among the unending clouds of Hesperand like a rudderless ship on the open sea. Again, men fell victim to madness. They never saw the Eye of Heaven.

They came to a place where a tumbledown heap of stones made two tracks of the way, and for a moment, Heremund hesitated, trying to determine which road to take. A pair of Rooks perched upon the pile, and as the sprawling company rode up, the two ill-omened birds lurched into the air, each choosing its own path.

"Haw! Haw!" they cried.

Durand was unamused.

"It is time we spoke once more," said Garelyn, appearing at Durand's side.

Durand squinted at the man. "What would you say?" Vadir, Moryn, and Leovere had gathered by then.

"First, Coensar took a gamble there at that bridge. I think he was mad to do it, but he made up his own mind and that's that."

"What of it, Garelyn?" said Mornaway.

"Only that it was at the River Glass."

"Aye, agreed. . . ." said Mornaway.

"On a bridge that, by rights, we should have crossed yesterday." Garelyn grimaced into the fog. "I say yesterday, but Heaven knows how such things are numbered here."

"What are you saying?" asked Durand.

"The Glass leads out of Hesperand, west."

"To Mornaway, aye. But we've spoken of this. We'd be out of Hesperand, but, maybe, behind the Hornbearer. Maybe losing the race to Eldinor."

"It's time to give it more thought. When a road forks there are more ways than two, you know. A man can always turn back."

"North is the only way to outrun the Hornbearer," said Durand.

"How did we come so late to the Glass, eh? Think on it."

The whole company looked to Durand. They should leave Hesperand by the shortest road. The place had become a maze of smoke and they were losing men every moment. But, if they retreated to the Glass, they must lose a day or more, and the thralls would reach an undefended Eldinor. If they retreated, they must fail. Only in Hesperand was there even the smallest, threadbare hope. Only in Hesperand, and only if he could solve the forest.

They were all still looking at him: the skald, the dukes, the barons. Perhaps they all knew what must be said.

"It must be north," said Durand. "North through Hesperand is our only chance. That much has not changed."

THEY RODE.

They mounted a ridge. The fog clung. They lost sight of any part of Creation. They might have ridden upon a mountaintop. They might have walked upon the moon itself.

If there was any hope at all, they would find it to the north; that was what Durand had argued. But was there any cause for hope? If it took days to travel a few leagues, there was none. If they continued to drift through the fogs of a Lost land as they had done for uncounted hours already, they would never reach Eldinor. Or they would drag their paltry few madmen to Eldinor only to find the Hornbearer brooding on the Hazelwood Throne and the kingdom ruled by monsters.

Durand scowled into the fog. What made him so certain that there was a world out there? He could see his own phalanx of dead men stealing through the trees, blithe and insane. Living men groaned. The prayers ebbed and swelled in the unseen gulfs of the Lost dukedom. They might easily march until the end of time.

Lost Hesperand was not a place of leagues and hours. When Durand fought at Bower Mead, it had been possible to believe that such rules applied even though they might be broken from time to time. Now, however, the place had come unmoored. Rivers and bridges appeared and disappeared in the fog every bit as easily as the Lady of Hesperand. There was no hope for Heremund's fieldcraft when the whole land was Lost.

Durand looked through the ranks of dead men: black-brittle villagers of Broklambe, knights and lords and even a king. Lost men in a Lost land. And he wondered. Had he been blind to the plain facts of the place? Hesperand was no living realm. Would he summon a tailor to bring his tapes and take the measure of some Lost wisp that scarcely remembered its name? Was this what they'd been doing with Hesperand? Measuring the hem of the specter's shroud?

Perhaps, here, was the way forward, the way out.

He needed Deorwen. Who knew how many Lost souls she had sent to far Heaven in Acconel?

Durand tore his horse from the line, drawing the glances of the Lost. He rode through black snares of juniper.

Ailric and Almora and Deorwen were some way back in the column, but he soon found them. Deorwen did not look up.

"Your Grace," said Ailric. He ducked near to Durand, barring passage.

"What is it, boy?" said Durand.

"We think—Lady Almora is uneasy. Lord Moryn has tried—"

Almora looked on, dismayed. Deorwen herself sat her dun palfrey, not acknowledging anyone, even as Durand urged his mount to lurch into step beside hers.

"I was sleeping," said Almora, "I should have noticed at once. I ought to have."

Deorwen had her arms clasped tightly about herself, and rode as stiffly as if she were a wooden idol in some village procession. Her eyes seemed to be fixed on her horse's black mane. Only her lips moved— mouthing quick skittering sounds. Durand reached out, catching her around the shoulders, pressing his body as close as his borrowed horse allowed.

"Deorwen? Deorwen, can you answer?" And, nearly forehead to forehead, her eyes met his. Already Mornaway, Garelyn, Almora, and Heaven knew who else were watching. Durand's hands curled tightly in her cloak.

"What is this, Deorwen?"

"They have found you, Durand?" Her eyes widened, full of he knew not what. "It is like Acconel once more. The Lost. They rave, Durand, for rest. Like the dead in Acconel, but so many more, so long!"

"No, Deorwen."

In Acconel, they had haunted her dreams in clamoring masses. Now, here she was in Hesperand, where a whole realm had been Lost.

Deorwen closed her eyes. He felt her pitching toward him, but she held on. Her hands found the saddlebow of her palfrey and her eyes sprang wide. "Durand, I tell you, I cannot. Another night, I cannot . . ."

"No," said Durand. Here was Durand's hope of finding a way from Hesperand.

Moryn, Almora, Ailric, and Garelyn were looking on as Deorwen slumped against the neck of her palfrey. Someone must've called a halt. Durand saw several ranks in the dark, watching.

"She is fighting," said Ailric, "but she won't last another night."

There were nods, but Garelyn scowled. "A hundred more are likewise on the knife's edge," he said. "We must leave this place."

Durand glowered at the man. How easy it was to know the right path when you did not have the power to choose it.

But Garelyn was not wrong: Hesperand would soon take Deorwen— and many others besides.

Durand spurred his horse and tore from the company, bowling back toward the head of the column. Coensar was gone. Deorwen would soon join him.

Durand rode past the vanguard and out into the fog, alone.

"You have us!" he shouted, up into the billows and half-visible trees. "You have us all! I don't know your mind, but you have us. You have me! I cannot escape this place."

His mount danced, uneasy at the shouting, likely in pain from the lashing branches.

"It has been you this whole time, hasn't it? You have led us round in circles. You have wrought your vengeance on me. I was meant to die, I think. I was not meant to call you from this place, to take your favor from Hesperand. But this place is death, going round and round the same story."

Despite himself, he blushed. He was shouting at the trees. Or so it seemed.

"If I have caused the end of this place, it is time. Hesperand is a living death. And you have heard our cause, I think. I have seen you shadow us, riding close beyond the branches. You have seen how these people suffer. They ride to meet their deaths. What else can come of standing against such an enemy?"

Durand faltered. He supposed that his voice might reach his men. It was possible.

What would it be like, he wondered, to ride himself off among the trees, all alone? To let Garelyn try to save them? To let it all be the problem of another man?

Then, some ways ahead, he thought he saw something motionless among the pale billows of mist.

"It is time," he said. "You know it is time. You do not need to hold us here. There is nothing left."

For an instant, Durand thought he saw the Lady of Hesperand on horseback. She sat in the midst of her household guard—dead men all. Then the mist swung shut between them and there was nothing.

"Hells," said Durand. If she did not listen, he did not know what they would do.

But, after a moment, an eye-watering light shot through the fog, penetrating from among the high branches. High over Hesperand, the Eye of Heaven blazed above the mists.

The Host of Gireth found him in only a few moments. Creation was bright and bare. There was no sign of the woman.

"Come," said Durand, and the multitude followed.

DURAND LED THE half-disbelieving host under high bright clouds.

He watched.

A thin, cold rain fell, but still they moved freely down a sloping, open country. Durand began to feel that soon he would see the rolling fields of Hesperand and ride out into some village pasture to the lasting astonishment of the plowmen there.

The road dropped once more, leaving the crowding undergrowth of the wildwood behind for an open grove where beech trees stood in a rolling pasture. Durand checked his pace on the threshold though he saw nothing to concern. The chants which had followed them since Ydran ebbed away and there was no sound but the dull rumble of horses and the jingle of tack. A few raised fingers stopped the host.

Durand and the old skald ventured alone into that place, the smallest of vanguards. Heremund favored Durand with a long look, and Durand thumbed the pommel of Ouen's old sword.

The road brought them under the branches of one enormous tree, its tangled canopy of bone-bleached branches spread just over Durand's head.

From every branch hung a knot of green cloth.

Once, he had carried just such a thing. The last time he'd tried to leave Hesperand, he'd been chased by the duke and his dogs with the Green Lady's favor knotted in his belt. He remembered falling into the old myth, into the ancient ritual of the place.

Only Deorwen had saved him.

"What is this?" said Heremund, from the back of his donkey. The tree was dead. All of its leaves were green rags. Many of the peeled limbs groped down near enough that a mounted man might touch them. Blood blackened every knot.

All but one.

Amid the blood-stiff multitude, Durand saw one bright rag, new and green, unlike any of the others. And he knew that it could only be his own: the one he'd taken from Hesperand. The Lady of the Bower had taken it from his hand in Cape Erne.

Every bit of green was another death, a rag for every man-at-arms who had won the Lady's favor—and who lay with her under the moon thereafter. And met her husband then. Durand marveled. How many men had the old duke run down, tournament after tournament? How long had Hesperand been trapped? Heremund was reaching. And, before Durand could call out, the skald had touched one hanging rag.

Durand caught the man's hand, too late.

"I suppose it was a risk. Still, a man cannot resist it." A fat drop landed on the back of the skald's hand, falling between them. Every rag on every branch—all but one—now sopped with blood, the drops falling. Rain. A downpour that brimmed the road.

A shadow passed over the Heavens.

Durand twisted. "We must get free of this place." The host was behind them.

Already the ancient trees were falling. Creation filled to the vault of Heaven with crashing branches and exploding ashes all around. The way back was lost in choking clouds.

Now, through the blood and ashes, Durand saw the Lady of the Bower and her men. She met his eye across the madness. And in her gaze was the calm of a woman trapped beyond all hope of aid.

"It is ending," Durand realized. "All of it is ending."

Like some vast living thing, a cold wind swept down from the

Heavens set to dash the entire grove from Creation. Ashes burst and boiled to the very heights of Heaven.

"Durand, we must fly!" said Heremund.

Vadir and a hundred others struggled with terrified horses. They could not remain in Hesperand.

"Ride! Hesperand's ending! We must ride or all be lost!"

Durand swung his sword in great circles. He called them on as the trees crashed one into another, falling and bursting on the storm winds. The whole of Hesperand crumbled around them, sliding before the wind. Durand roared, Ouen's blade flashing, as the host barreled past him. "Ride! And pray for Hellebore!"

When Durand saw Deorwen's half-mad palfrey blunder past him, he spurred after her. Ailric had the reins, but Durand snatched her from her saddle—he would not have her lost. He would not risk leaving her here. And as he set his spurs, he spotted the green rags too. He saw the unmarked green one, and, with a fierce lunge, he snatched it down.

And, suddenly, the world was not crashing to an end.

28
Dunnock of the Hedges

Durand followed the Host of Gireth from Hesperand into the presence of an astonished flock of sheep. The green cloth was still wrapped around his fist.

A thousand wild-eyed horsemen tore from the storms of Hesperand into the green sheepfold. In a moment, the flock had bolted—leaving an aging shepherdess standing alone, leaning on a blackthorn staff, and blinking up with a look of wounded dignity into the face of an army. The Eye of Heaven shone high and the buttercups were nodding in the grass.

As they came to a stumbling halt, men were actually laughing. Durand felt Deorwen stir: she struggled like a child waking in a strange bed, and Durand set a hand on her back.

"A moment," he said, before she could throw herself.

She twisted enough to give him a wincing look. "They have gone," she said.

Hundreds of knights were climbing stiffly from the backs of battered horses. Not a few men kissed the turf of Hellebore. Many animals dropped their heads, cropping what should have been the sheep's fodder as the horsemen argued whether green feed or nothing was best till they could turn up mashed or good old gruel.

"Durand," said Almora.

"I think Deorwen is recovered—or nearly."

Meanwhile the old shepherdess stood her ground, peering from beneath a man's shapeless hat.

Durand climbed down, taking help from Almora and Ailric to get Deorwen settled safely among the buttercups. "Where are we?" Almora asked. They were close together. "We will have to tell the men something."

Durand searched the hills for some sign of where they'd come out. The maragrim were tireless, and there were thirty leagues or more of Hellebore and Saerdana yet to cross. He knew of the monastery, Cop Alder, not far from the forest, but he saw little except hillsides and tufted trees from where he stood.

Heremund had led Berchard from the forest, and was peering about them. "Perhaps we ought to ask our host?" he said with a wink toward the old woman.

"Go, Durand," said Almora. "We will see to Deorwen."

"I don't need seeing to," said Deorwen, but she could hardly get her head from the grass no matter how she squawked.

Almora nodded, so Durand approached the woman, the skald and Berchard trailing behind.

The woman looked as though she was rooted to the meadow.

"You are Black Durand Col," she said. "Haunted man. You came to Hesperand before."

At this, Durand could not help but scowl. Hesperand had given him his fill of the uncanny.

"And this," she continued, "is Heremund Crookshanks. And with you is old Berchard of the Hag's Eye."

"I find I quite like that," declared Berchard. "I hadn't heard it before." He seemed impervious to her sour look.

The woman turned on Durand. "Betrayed and betraying, haunted man. It is a great weight of guilt and grievance you carry. Have they told you?"

Durand turned to see the forest giants of Hesperand like a sea.

"We ride for Eldinor," said Durand.

The old woman scratched at her side. "And it was you with the king too."

Durand had had more than enough of augury and prophets and far too little sleep to suffer much more of the old woman's sharp tongue. Heremund, however, could not contain his amusement.

"You are the wise woman?"

"Imma." It was probably her name.

"The horses, mother," said Heremund. "They will need water."

"It's a crime, those animals."

"She is right," said Berchard.

"Over that hill," she said, gesturing with the most meager twist of her head. "Dew pond. The water is cold. Let them take it slow."

"And we'll need to know where we are. What village is this, mother?"

"No village, skald. A steading near Hesperand."

"You never know what'll pop out of the wood, eh?" Heremund ventured. "What is the next village?"

Durand thought he had heard the name, but it was no great town, and whether it lay in Hellebore or the Fellwood Marches he could not say.

"I know it well. Where shall we find it then?"

"Take the Corpse Road north and east." She inclined her head much as before. "Over the hill."

"Corpse Road?" said Durand.

"There's hallowed ground in Dunnock, Black Durand Col. We don't lay our dead here." She crossed her hands on her stick. "It is two hours under the pall. Maybe your lot won't move so solemnly."

"As you know so much," said Heremund, "I wonder what you have heard of besides my friend here."

"The Hornbearer has come into the land. Is that what you wonder, Heremund Crookshanks? And Ragnal is hanged. The prince rides from Windhover. Young Reilan has sailed the Red Winding and lies under stone with his forbearers. The Banished are uneasy in their bonds."

Heremund nodded. "Aye. Right." He set aside his ingratiating manner. "These men here have ridden days through that old wood, and all on the heels of a battle. Have you heard where the thralls have come?"

The old woman knotted deep, her eyes shut. "Swift as wild horses, they come, but Errest teems with rivers, and the Eye of Heaven's King drives them down among the roots and stones. More than this I cannot say." She paused a moment, squinting at the thought. "There is one who hides in Dunnock. He and his kind are not what they were of old, but he may know more than we, the old fool."

Heremund nodded and turned to Durand.

"Dunnock of the Hedges. I know the man she's hinting at. As soon as we find the pond."

Berchard nodded. "The pond first."

THE KNIGHTS OF southern Errest led their horses up that hill of buttercups to a pond like a bowl of glass near the Corpse Road to Dunnock. On that hilltop of green and glass and nodding gold, not a soul glanced back into the trees behind them. Like worshipers at some high altar, they worked under the shining Eye of Heaven, and even those whom the dark journey had driven from their reason seemed to awaken in the bright light on that lofty place of wildflowers, water, and horses.

Only after he'd settled the army, did Durand seek out Deorwen. He found her sitting in the grass with her face in her hands, speaking softly to Almora.

"There were so many," she said. "It had been so long, and they were blameless, caught up and tangled and never freed. Seasons they cannot count, the ages passing."

Almora took Deorwen's hand in hers. After all of Deorwen's years settling the Lost of Acconel, this had been too much.

Durand reached out. He meant to touch her cheek.

She stopped him. The green favor he'd taken from Hesperand was still there, wrapped around his knuckles.

"What is that?" said Deorwen. "I thought she'd taken it back." And it was true. Ten years before, the Lady of Hesperand had taken her favor back with her from the Great Council vote.

Durand gripped Deorwen's hand in both fists, breathing his thanks to every Power under Heaven. They had escaped only just in time.

FAR TOO SOON, they left that hilltop over Hesperand.

By the Corpse Road, they staggered on through shuttered hamlets and wary farmsteads until Heremund spotted the sanctuary tower of Dunnock.

"How can you be sure?" said Berchard. "There will be a hundred hamlets in Hellebore."

"Not like this one."

"You sound as if it's your old mother's town."

"No. It's— Here. Picture a spire."

"Aye."

"It's jutting like the gnomon of the vast sundial of these odd fields.

They've planted great hedges, this way and that like a maze. You don't take two straight steps on the way to Dunnock, and you can't see a thing."

Berchard stretched his neck. "Good. Yes. Now, I'll ask that you tell me what a 'gnomon' is."

"The bit that stands up!"

"I'm not sure that's what the girls my way called it."

"Oh, very good," said Heremund. "Very good. And the realm in peril, too."

They took the road to the foot of the hedges. The green darkness loomed ten fathoms high, far more daunting than any wall of stone. Old oaks stood in knotted ranks, barbed with ancient blackthorns. The road led in, and then turned sharply, and sharply again.

Here and there, they could see townspeople. Plowmen and goodwives scowled at them, fingering bills and cudgels.

"Is this how the town is supposed to be?" asked Durand.

"Aye, this is Dunnock of the Hedges, all right. Left right, left right. A maze of hedges."

"Tell him about the gnomon," said Berchard.

Durand muttered a curse. "Let's see what we can do about food, water, and remounts." He looked to Vadir. "We won't have the host ride into that. We'd never get out again."

"It's not that kind of maze, to be fair," said Heremund.

"Still. I will not have us hemmed in."

"Vadir, we'll have to see about supplies. Horses, maybe. Take a strong party from your vanguard, but men with sense."

Vadir, after an affronted stare, gave up his nettlesome nobility and set about gathering some sensible men.

"Heremund, who is lord of this place? What sort of man is he?"

"A baron. One of Hellebore's, of course. Segan, I think. I remember he has thin lips."

"I hope he will understand. It'd be best if he was obliging."

Heremund laughed. "With an army in his turnip fields, he'll be happier if he's agreeable."

Durand looked back over fifty conrois of half-starved knights; they would take what they must, and, after fighting the Hornbearer, they would leave any accounting to those who might survive.

Vadir had pulled together much of the vanguard. Some had even had the sense to bring spare horses for the provisions. Durand eyed Vadir's men and the wall of thorns with a scowl, thinking that he'd seen enough unnatural greenery to last a lifetime.

"Now," said Heremund, "I'll pay a call on Mother Imma's hidden man. Someone keep an eye on Hag's Eye, here."

"We'll all ride in together, I think," said Durand. And they followed the hedgerow track into Dunnock, left and right, around and around till finally, by gaps and right angle turnings, they worked through thorny alleyways to an entirely ordinary village in the midst of the maze.

There were inns and thatched houses, shrines and wells and wary villagers looking on. Near the tower shrine was a stone building of a sort very likely to house a local lordling. Durand looked at Vadir. "Take the men. Press our case with this Segan: get what you can short of spilling blood. If Segan will come with us, he and his men are welcome."

Vadir cocked his head. "Where will you be, Sir Durand?"

"I am in Heremund's hands." And the little man grinned his gap-toothed grin.

"I see. Well, I will take these men to see Lord Segan."

"Uh. If I were you, I might let the fellow give you his name before you venture to use it, yourself," said Heremund. "I'm not sure about 'Segan.' I might have that wrong. There are many lordlings in Errest, as I'm sure you know."

"I will be guided by your wisdom," Vadir said, and he led his squadron into the town.

Heremund was already tugging at Durand's sleeve. And, in a moment, he was leading Durand from the hedges into the rutted streets of the village where shutters slammed. Their arrival conjured a gaggle of laughing children who plagued Heremund, looking to feed his donkey, wondering its name.

Finally Heremund found his destination: an alehouse not far from the sanctuary tower. The sign swinging above the door was marked with an owl and a young woman.

"Here," said Heremund, and they ducked low to enter the dark place, leaving the children giggling at the door—a place that seemed to multiply their amusement.

From the dark came a fleshy voice. "Get out of it, damn you! Misbegotten devils. I've warned you!" A shriveled apple zipped past Durand's ear, eliciting shrieks of joy from the "misbegotten devils." One of the boys offered the thing to the donkey.

Durand felt like they'd arrived at a bear's den.

"Heremund the Skald," said the voice.

"Is that you, Hagarth?" said Heremund, adding to Durand, "We've found our man, I think. Follow me." And they stepped down into a dark taproom where ruts coiled around the benches and tables.

"There he is," Heremund said, and he bowed to a squat figure hunkered in the back of the room. Durand was more worried about bending low enough to dodge the ceiling beams.

"Aye, here I am. What have you brought me, by Heaven?"

Heremund added a little flourish with his hat.

"This is Sir Durand Col, late Duke of Yrlac. Marshal of the Host of Gireth and Yrlac."

The man lifted himself from his bench. "Black Durand? The regicide is here?"

There was a mass of gray curls. A fleshy, jolly face.

"You'd best come and sit." The man called Hagarth spread thick hands. "Here, here." And they joined him. He puffed a good deal, sitting.

"You have come through Hesperand. It is so, is it not?"

"We have," said Durand. "Just about."

"An army through Hesperand."

"Aye," said Durand.

"It will be the first. Even Duke Eorcan didn't get his host from Hesperand."

Durand must have clenched his teeth, for Heremund intervened.

"It's time that concerns us, Hagarth."

"And what a time! The wards in shreds. One king dead, the next uncrowned. The maragrim loose and the priests on their knees." He sucked a big breath through his lips.

"That we know," said Durand. "What we wish to know is how far our enemy has come." Vadir would've collided with the town's little lord by now. They needed what they could get and Durand feared that it would be all too late.

"I can tell you a thing or two. Heremund was wise to bring you," said Hagarth. "You are, at this moment, some thirty leagues from the high sanctuary in Eldinor. Our maragrim friends have fought past the Banderol at Wrothsilver and stand now at the Glass, a dozen leagues west of us. They will run in twenty leagues between dusk and the dawning, though the streams give them problems." The jowled face twitched a grin at this thought.

"Thirty leagues to Eldinor." It was not enough. Thirty leagues might be two days hard riding on a fresh horse, and they had none of those. "With the maragrim covering twenty leagues in a day . . ."

"It is not impossible," said Hagarth.

"For all your wisdom, you have not seen my men. And how do you know these things? There has been no time for rumors, and I am tired of mysteries."

"Very well, then. I will say it plain: You have heard of the Hidden Masters? Well, now you have met one."

Durand looked to Heremund, who hardly shrugged at this secret. These were the men who had undone Hesperand in the mists of history.

"Here, look," said the man, climbing cumbrously to his feet. "The ceiling." He waved thick-fingered hands at the low beams. At first, Durand did not see what the man was waving at. Then he made out curving white shapes between the beams.

"What am I looking at?"

As he squinted at one such thing, he realized he was looking into the black sockets of a skull's eyes, deep and hollow as eggshells.

"Bones, Durand Col."

The skull was not a man's but, rather, a horse's long skull. Its grooved teeth bristled down.

Hagarth rose, sweeping his hand over several of the hollow hanging bones that sprung like mushrooms in the dark.

"These are my informants, Durand Col. A brass nail fixes each to its place. A thread of a maiden's hair strings one to the next."

Durand looked closely. The skulls—sparrow and mouse and fox—were strung, each to each, by half-visible lines in a web that tangled the room from wall to wall. Durand could not imagine the fingers of Hagarth stitching such a web.

"What is the meaning of this?"

Hagarth smiled. "These are the wards in miniature. Each thread. Every shrine and sanctuary from Eldinor to the marches of Garelyn. So much is broken. At every point in the larger world, I have buried my witnesses. A skull. Another skull. Graveyards and crossroads. And each is twinned with the bone in my web."

"The threads are the wards. The bones are witnesses," said Heremund.

Hagarth laughed. "And twins! That's the devil of it. They must be twins, each and all. One twin is hammered here, the other must go to its place in the larger world. I am aided in this by such things as owls and hawks which will do my bidding, but sometimes I must enlist a human confederate." He gestured toward an ox with a broad curve of horns.

"It would be an unusual hawk who could carry an ox," said Heremund.

"Or bury it," said Hagarth. He brushed past Durand, groping toward a dangling skull: a bird by its look, a gull perhaps.

"This set up dancing this morning. This skull is twin of another in a road near the River Glass." For a moment, he stood with his eyes shut and his jaw slack, two fingers jammed against the tiny skull. "I see what they see, but there is little now to witness." The man held still a moment. "Every worm and insect stands, quivering from the turf like the hairs on a dog's back, bristling over the road, the verges." He smiled. "The maragrim will be there, sunk in the mud of Creation where the Eye cannot see." Again, a smile twitched. "I think the vermin dislike their new neighbors."

The squat stranger withdrew his hand. It seemed that every skull buzzed like the strings of a lyre, and it came home to Durand that he stood right next to one of the Hidden Masters.

"Can you not do something?" said Durand.

"You have Hesperand on your mind? Oh, I understand you. But think of what you are saying. Think of what a place Hesperand has become. What a triumph that was! No. We have learned—too well, perhaps. Now, my brethren clutch their hands in fear of unsettling the natural course of events, but we are fools, of course. We have been subtle. The wards. Ill luck here or there. A word in that ear. The skalds. The wise women. The king. But we have not had the ear of the king. Not for long years. It has not been safe at the court. Men, ancient in wisdom, have vanished at the Tower of Eagles. And the wards have fallen and fallen. The patriarchs have not the knowledge anymore, and we have taken up the mantle, understanding the ancient geometries of the thing. Restoring what has been lost. But our labors have been too slow."

At the man's mention of geometry, Durand thought of the rigid hedgerows.

"The hedgerows . . ."

"You are not quite the brute you appear, I see. The hedges are an experiment of my own. They let me sleep. My own wards, you might say." The man grinned. "The baron's grandfather thought they would thwart marauders. The plowmen think they're to keep the things of Hesperand from creeping through the town by night. But the hedges were my notion. The Lost do not like corners. Neither do the Banished. So the ways to Dunnock are a maze of such turnings. And, of course, it helps with my little twin." He smiled.

"You see how small we are, Durand Col? We Masters? I have guarded

my village. I have tied my twin bones to the crossroads. You would have
me repel the Hornbearer's Host."

The old man grunted in self-mockery. "You would do better to set your
hopes in the rivers. The Hornbearer will ford the Glass at nightfall. Hellebore, they will pass by midnight tomorrow. Then they will deal with
the River Cygnet.

"You will gain some ground again in Saerdana." He waved at a region
of skulls. "The wards still hold in that part of the realm, which ought to
make the devils walk crabwise to get past them. It might mean leagues."

Durand shook his head. "You cannot help? Even a message?" His voice
was dry as anything that might have issued from the web of skulls. "Eldinor must know."

"There is no one with Biedin or the Council now. Even the Septarim
are banished; the king turned upon them and their dour counsel. Now
there is not a knight of the old order within a day's ride of Eldinor. And
no man of the Hidden Masters." He shook his head.

"Word is passing among the wise women, though none of them can
reach the court. My spies here tell me that they have carried word to Ragnal's brother in Windhover." He waved a hand into the western reaches
of the taproom. Many dark eyes stared back. "Or he has heard of Ragnal's death at least. He has taken a host from Windhover into Errest
the Old."

Heremund grunted. "A boy on the throne with no one but malevo-
lent counselors on every side? Of course Prince Eodan will come rushing in."

"Likely, he will talk of protecting the boy."

"Let the king's people wrangle over the throne if they like," Durand
put in. "Soon, it will be the plaything of the Crowned Hog."

Hagarth narrowed one eye. "The Hornbearer, even now, is almost as
near to Eldinor as we are. He will take some hours to ford the Glass. In
the west, Eodan marches from Windhover with his host. Eldinor is their
goal as well."

Durand glanced to the beaked skull by Hagarth's head. An army could
not ride twelve leagues a day—not for long. His eyes burned, full of the
hot sand of sleepless days.

"What of the king?"

"Already, he has come to Eldinor. He will be in the tomb below the high
sanctuary. Perhaps he will be awake once more when you reach the city or
soon thereafter."

* * *

Durand and a grinning Heremund extracted their animals from the gang of children and started to work their way back to the army. In Dunnock, Hagarth's maze shut out the whole of Creation. Even the Lost, said Hagarth, could not pass them. It made Durand think: a man might find a sort of peace with the Lost stuck outside. But how many people would die if he turned his back? And how thick would the dead crowds be that gathered round Dunnock if he holed up in Hagarth's inn while the Hornbearer stormed across Errest the Old?

He laughed and threw a few pennies to the children, letting them scramble.

Soon, they had managed the crisp switchbacks of the maze to find Almora waiting and the army busy tearing into packs and barrels brought by Vadir's men. There were great round loaves and slabs of hard cheese. Durand saw fresh horses—a dozen, not hundreds. And a very few volunteers.

"The maragrim have reached the Glass at the frontier of Hellebore," he told Almora. "It's only a dozen leagues from here." He glanced across the fields, past the men around Vadir's feast.

Almora straightened. "The maragrim are swift. I have seen them, don't forget."

Durand nodded.

"We are no nearer Eldinor than they." Almora paused a moment, then gave a quick nod, saying, "I will tell them."

Without another word, the girl spurred her palfrey to canter up and down the sprawled army. Though she carried no banner, soon the men looked up from the food and beer, and when she stopped, every eye was upon her.

"The thralls are at the Glass. They will cross soon after sunset. By our Hesperand road, we have kept pace with the Hornbearer, but we have many leagues yet to ride. And we know what the maragrim are. They must fear Heaven's Eye. We may ride by night and by day. They are prisoners of the darkness. And so we must not squander a moment under the Eye. We will kindle the beacon fires. We will send messengers before us. Dunnock has left us fleet horses." From around her neck, she slipped a long chain. Hanging from it was heavy ring. "They will bear my father's seal to Eldinor with word that the enemy marches—and that the Hosts of Gireth and Yrlac are riding to join the fight."

A hundred knights volunteered, and, finally, she chose two from their number.

They were all as dizzy as drunken men.

She spoke again. "There is no king in Eldinor. There are no patriarchs in Errest the Old. We must trust to hearts and to Heaven. Either they will write our names in the chronicle of our people—or there will be no one left to write at all!"

She beamed at the army. "Now, to Eldinor! To Eldinor for Errest the Old!"

And Durand roared along with the men of the company.

FROM DUNNOCK, THEY rode into the fields of Hellebore, dizzy with exhaustion. Vadir's men ranged before the column, foraging for remounts and provisions. At nightfall, the foragers were met with cheers when they returned, leading a cart of wine barrels.

Weariness snatched at them, like drowning.

Man slept in their saddles and rode the horses of dead men. And always, Durand thought of the maragrim waiting to begin their mad rush north.

Through the moonlight, under the eyes of distant sullen villagers as they juddered through country tracks and shadows, Durand found himself nodding. He had slept only in snatches since Acconel. On either side of the column, the Lost stirred in a broad phalanx among the furrows. Durand peered across the group and noticed that some of the knights he'd led to Hesperand had now joined the throng. Faces too white. Eyes too dark. Under his breath, he cursed them all.

For a moment, he closed his eyes and Creation pitched away from him.

The dead turned his way, but he could not waken.

He was falling from Creation as if he were a man stepping into a dark ocean.

This was the Otherworld, where sleepers of Creation sometimes go when they sink below the depths of their own troubles and leave themselves behind, breathless and near to dying.

In that black and drifting place, Durand heard a whisper. It ran with the echoes of the stone kings in the high mountains and chilled his marrow.

The ocean of blackness moved to the whisper, and the soul of Durand Col was drawn by it like a leaf on the surface of a river.

He plunged and spun.

He tumbled through leagues of whispering darkness till he felt himself fetch up into a dark cold place—a real place: a narrow tomb of stone where even the soul of a dreaming man could not move.

And the nebulous whispers ceased, leaving Durand in the close gloom with only the certainty that the source of the whispers was very near—very near and watching him in that lightless space.

"These threads," said a voice. Muffled. A nobleman's by its accent. Not from within the silent chamber, but as if through a heavy door. "Each thread tightens. There is Leovere in Yrlac with his jealousy and pride, the fool in Windhover, the Great Council, and our Ragnal, poor thing. Each thread strung tight. The kingdom is bound like a giant by a thousand slender threads."

Durand thought he heard laughter.

"I am better off now than I was with Radomor. All is safer with the boy. Safer. Ten years I have wasted, but the boy is like a blacksmith's iron tongs in my hands. Let him lie under stone. Let him risk Heaven! Let him hold the wards. With him, I will pluck up the crown."

There was a pause. Durand, alone in cist or grave or tomb, was sure that something crouched beside him, listening too.

"You are silent," said the voice beyond the door.

Durand was conscious of a strange ache. He had not drawn breath in the space of many heartbeats, and his living body must then be laying, drowning, leagues away through the night. In the Otherworld, a man could not draw breath.

"Perhaps I was a coward. You were wise in this, as in all things. I know that I cast much work aside. But now, it is very difficult not to smile, I tell you. They have waged wars for me, made their speeches, righted wrongs, and now our little Hornbearer is among them, and how they will beg."

"Say nothing more," said a voice: a whisper of lips nearly at Durand's throat. *"Someone has come to pay court to me after these long years and darkness."*

Durand heard the swish and click of someone planting their hand on an iron-bound door. "What is this you say?"

"A stranger."

The darkness rustled all around Durand in that gravelike chamber. Durand felt countless fleeting touches. Now Durand was addressed: *"Stranger, I know you not. Yet you have found me out in my ancient hiding place. Who are you that my doom delivers you in this late hour?"*

Durand did not answer; he could not. His teeth and tongue were leagues from that spot.

There was a savage rasp. *"So many winters undisturbed, and now . . . This is the work of the Powers. This is doom. I have lain here these long winters waiting, tending the seeds of oaks that must grow and fall to plant the seeds of my desires."*

"What would you have me do?" said the nobleman beyond the door. He had been forgotten.

Again, the darkness stirred all around Durand.

"Who are you?"

Durand felt a sensation like eyelashes against his cheek, of the drape of crawling webs across a dark passage. A thousand thousand threads were passed around his wrists, his throat, and past his lips and teeth.

"Who?" demanded the Whisperer. There was terror at the touch of this thing.

Somehow, Durand recoiled. He was not a thing of bone and blood in that chamber, but rather a dreamer's soul. The whispers burst like a nest of adders.

But now Durand was beyond the door.

He beheld a man. The figure knelt, pressed against the iron-bound door, hands splayed over rotting wood. There was a candle. Vast shadows juddered down a tunnel, black as a well. Durand could only see the man's back, and a mantle of fine, dark wool.

"He is here!" said the crouched figure, flinching from the door. Rising.

As the man stood, Durand saw faces, packed tight as white apples, crowding the narrow tunnel from floor to ceiling—men, every one as ugly and avid as the next. And worse, by their grins, Durand knew that he had been seen.

The grinning mob lunged, their touch like being speared by the tines of a rake, but Durand struggled, throwing himself from the bloodthirsty delight of the howling fiends.

"Catch him! Keep him! I would know who spies upon our conclave. Bring him!"

They were like cats upon a landed fish, but Durand lashed. He tore. And, finally, he broke free.

Durand's unmoored soul plunged into the empty darkness of the Otherworld, alone.

Then he might have been a sailor, pitched overboard on a sudden, into a calm and midnight sea. On that still, dark sea under a black and starless sky, the soul of Durand Col was without pain, without memory, with hardly a trace of duty or regret—and, almost, without thought. In that wide-eyed blindness, he thought of nothing; he was nothing and no one. The lulling power of the place took him in its gigantic grip and he closed his eyes even on the drifting void.

But a sound—it could not have been a proper sound—reached him. It reached him as if over leagues of empty sea. Something knocked, distant and echoing. *Tock.* And the still world shivered. *Tock.*

Durand opened his eyes then.

Far overhead, a light hung in the darkness: a solitary glinting thing like a burnished coin nailed to the firmament, high and huge as the Bitter Moon.

He could do nothing but stare.

The silvered disk then swelled larger and larger, until the thing—an unblinking eye—loomed as large as a world.

It was then that Durand Col heard a familiar voice, a breath over that sea that was no sea.

"Durand, no," it said.

And Durand's faraway soul felt hands on his distant flesh. He felt smooth skin against his cheek, and he was once more upon Creation, once more among those who lived and died upon the world. He lay in the broken furrows of some plowmen's acre with half an army staring down. Deorwen cradled his head in her hands.

She pressed her forehead to his, managing only to say his name as tears wet both their faces. For several heartbeats—and there *were* heartbeats—memories returned to Durand: his name, his duty. They settled upon him like coats of iron mail. Last of all, he remembered the reasons that he must not hold the woman who had summoned him back from his dream of death.

"Durand, you are very far from us." Deorwen sat up, knuckling tears from her eyes. Almora was near. Garelyn. Mornaway. Everyone. "You fell from your saddle. You did not breathe." She swallowed. "You were very far from us."

Durand shook his head. Not a soul in the field was speaking.

"I dreamed," he said, "but I can hardly say of what." He recalled much of what he'd seen: the vast unblinking eye, the narrow chambers, dark currents, and the sense that years of waiting—the plots that had brought the Rooks to Radomor, that threw down the sanctuaries, that left a king hanging in Acconel. Sieges and tragedies scattered over years. All of these things were coming to an end, and he—the landless knight from Col—

would be caught in the midst of it all. "Everything moves toward its conclusion now. Kings and starlings and traitors and whispers. We ride toward the end."

He climbed from the ground to his horse's back, conscious of the listening multitude around him in a way he had not been before.

They were watching as he nodded.

They rode at his signal.

29
Battlefields

The army reached the River Cygnet at a muddy, empty village that Heremund, in a haunted murmur, named "Wethers Bridge."

"What is the smell?" asked Berchard.

"A flood," said Heremund, "by the looks of it." The street was a mire. Doors stood empty. The stains of high water spread their traces upon the whitewash, and the army rode between silent houses full of shadow.

"And the people?" asked Berchard.

It was Durand who answered: "No sign."

The Wethers Bridge itself still stood—a covered wooden affair, quite long and full of carved Powers that beamed and glowered down upon the army as the host clattered and rumbled under the black beams and shingles.

It was like taking an army through a church, though it rumbled like a barn. But the din of their crossing did not disturb the creatures they found upon the far bank.

Ravens, rooks, crows, and brown eagles ringed a meadow. They were like moldering windrows, like dark spectators. They encircled the trampled acres like a sullen tidemark. Beyond, where thorns hedged the meadows, wolves, perhaps, or feral dogs, wove sly circles.

"Many must have died here," said the Duke of Garelyn, looking at the creatures. "But the beasts do not enter the field."

Durand rode into the trodden ground with Heremund and the men of rank, and Almora behind them. Durand hopped down with Ailric. He saw hoofprints by the score, squad after squad moving in disciplined ranks. There were banners, bloody and torn. Trappers. Broken horses. He turned to Ailric, who had his fingers in one deep track.

"Hours only," Ailric said. "No more."

Here was a host fully as large as most dukes could muster, riding across Saerdana. Who were they? Durand bent. He could see the marks of nail-heads in the clay as if the riders had scarcely gone.

"All white," said Almora.

"Hmm?" said Durand.

"The banners, the pennons. They are, all of them, white."

Ailric provided an explanation. "The Knights of Ash. The Septarim."

Berchard was nodding. "The Holy Ghosts. You remember, Marshal Conran and the rest at Acconel. The man's a giant—a one-eyed giant!"

Meanwhile, Durand stood and tried to read the sweeping patterns that the battle had left on that torn meadow.

"It would have been full dark, the Cygnet over its banks. The Farrow Moon growing old." Across the meadow, there were regular marks in the turf. Mounted men had waited in still ranks. "They watched the thralls heaping stones. They waited for the things to make the crossing." Durand could readily imagine what the Ash Knights saw. Perhaps they'd had the villagers evacuate before nightfall. Perhaps they came too late and heard the maragrim about their work in the dark lanes. "They could not squander their few knights."

Almora was looking over the field. There were lances. Here and there, a sword lay in the grass. The men upon the bridge were listening.

"Marshal Conran will have wanted a crowd—enough that a charge would tell. And then they came from the dark." In his mind's eye, Durand saw the white banners and burnished mail. He saw the ashen lances strike deep into the grotesque mobs of the thralls, ripping hundreds from their feet, impaled on razor spears. "The thralls were torn by lances. Scores went under the iron-shod hooves or were driven into the water." Flailing, screaming.

Durand walked the bank. Almora took his hand. He helped her over the rutted ground and sucking mud. In moments, he had found the high-water mark. There was a great fan of ruined earth, and he knew that he'd found the place where the maragrim had stepped into the meadow. "There were so many thralls. Even with hundreds caught on the ford, more crossed the river."

Almora did not relinquish his fingers.

Durand imagined the hideous creatures on all sides, like the waves on a hellish sea. "They were here. The knights fought." There were so many marks in the damp earth. He saw the clear prints of long-fingered, gripping hands. He saw clawed gashes and barnyard marks of pigs and goats. And then he saw the marks of the Hornbearer: huge, deep, and long-toed. Blood tinted the crooks and angles. White surcoats, stained. No men. White banners, swords and lances like half-erupted teeth. Trappers and no horses. Conran the Marshal would have made his stand here like some wild ship's master. So much blood.

Almora nodded. Her dress was marked with blood.

There was something else over the meadow, as if the mud had been scattered with white chips of wood.

Ailric, a step behind, had crouched. He did not touch the strange fragments.

"You can see here where the Hornbearer left his mark. The Knights of Ash stood before the fiend here and were struck down." All of this Durand saw before he could snatch his fingers from the mud. In a spinning instant, he had seen it all.

The Duke of Garelyn was trailing behind among the commanders. Now, he spoke. "Ragnal banned the Knights from Eldinor."

Heremund was staring into the southwest. "Not within a day's ride. That was Ragnal's command. We are not much more than that now."

Garelyn blinked. He tried a bluff grin. "Stiff-necked devils, the Knights of Ash. Many's the man who would have left the king and his kin to fend for themselves after such treatment. But they came here. And it must be confessed: the Cygnet was well-chosen. They will have stolen hours from our Hornbearer. And it might be that many of the devil's host will not rise after this bit of work."

It was Almora who spoke next. The place had clearly shocked her. "The beasts will not enter the field."

"What do you mean?" said Berchard, but no one answered.

"Perhaps, the thralls are here, even now," said Heremund. "Under the sod."

"And where are the fallen?" wondered Garelyn. There was not so much as a horse. "Maybe a sign that some fought till morning. Lived to see to their brothers."

Ailric was still crouched low, examining the ground. But now he looked up. "These chips," he said. "It is bone. Splinters of bone, tens of thousands," he said. Split for marrow.

And so the Knights of Ash had not left the field. Not a soul among the Host of Gireth spoke for a time.

Heremund had not taken his eyes from the rutted ground. "I never thought I should see the end of the Ash Knights in Errest the Old."

Half the army looked on from the covered bridge, like a host in an inn yard, and the dead were all around—men broken up for marrow bones. The House of the Knights of Ash was empty now, and open to the wind.

And the beasts of battle who bulked around the field, they would not come. Durand wondered if the maragrim were still here, trembling below their leavings.

Durand looked at the men on the bridge.

"I think the Knights of Ash have stolen hours from the Hornbearer. A night maybe." Uttering the thing's name conjured an image of that whole vast horror curled under the mud, a knot of roots and horns. "We must not squander a moment."

THEY RODE THAT day in near silence, with the Rooks flapping before them.

As the host lumbered from village to village, their advance set plowman's dogs to barking. From field to field, the dogs sounded the alarm so that every house and barn was shut up and silent when they passed, but the village shrines were a different thing. Every one rang with chanting voices while their rude idols craned from their niches. Their haunted eyes followed the company. Men counted omens in the flight of birds, a fox flushed by the horses, a deer that stood transfixed in the steaming path.

Durand wondered about the messengers Almora had sent ahead from Dunnock. Had they reached Eldinor? Would there be an army waiting for the Hornbearer?

It was nightfall when one of Almora's men galloped in. Durand joined the urgent crowd of knights surrounding the man, catching hold of his foaming horse's bridle and helping the man down. "Heremund," said Berchard. "What is it? What's he got to say?"

He was a rangy young man with down on his cheeks and a child's brown eyes.

Durand addressed him. "What have you seen, lad? Is the prince in the city?" There was much that they must know.

"Your Grace," said the young man. He could hardly breathe.

This was when Deorwen stopped them. Very deliberately, she got the man the space to breathe and a skin of wine, and even summoned a camp stool from the Garelyn baggage.

Soon, there was a polite circle of commanders waiting on the haggard boy.

It was Lady Almora who spoke.

"Now," she said, "Lady Deorwen has saved you a moment to recover. They'll have questions. We all will. I suggest you tell the story."

The messenger nodded. "Aye, Ladyship. We rode out from Dunnock as you bid us, and made good time. A man alone, you understand. Not an army. We made Eldinor." He winced. "It was this morning, but— We hired a boat at Scrivensands and rowed across. The place was empty. Or nearly—the city itself. All the Council knights had ridden out, but the city was thick with those birds. Starlings, like the things in Acconel before the king. . . . Anyway, there was something. I don't know. Kenard, he went in—took the ring to the Castle, the Mount of Eagles. We thought one of us had best wait. I was to give him an hour or two." He frowned. "Kenard never came back. And those black-robed devils, court clerks or the like, I saw them sniffing about. I thought sure they were looking for me.

"Someone had holed our boat," he said. "They were waiting. I stole another, or I should not be here."

Garelyn laughed wryly. "We'll hang you when you're finished."

"Also, the ring. Your Ladyship. They'll have your ring. The seal."

"Don't think about that now," said Almora.

Durand scowled. "What of the Council Host? They could not have been in Eldinor long, and already they had left?"

"They'd only just gone. In Scrivensands, the man we had the boat from, he said the knights had ridden to meet Eodan's Host of Windhover.

Heremund chose this moment to grumble. "Eodan's host? The fool man. What a time for such games!"

"Prince Eodan was coming from the southwest. Maybe he was in Cape Erne already. But he's crossed Mornaway and the Glass, and he's in Saerdana. The Scrivensands man, he thought there would be a battle."

"Mighty soothsayers, these sailors," said Garelyn.

"Who knows more than a ferryman?" Berchard said. "Ain't much they don't hear."

Durand did not say, "There will be no army in Eldinor."

He looked up into the Vault of far Heaven. Already, the maragrim would be awake, rising from that bloody meadow at Wether Bridge, stalking the dark, gobbling up the ground at Durand's back. And now the whole army of Gireth was off to fight Prince Eodan. A day's march, it sounded like, and they would have left Prince Reilan in that cist below the high sanctuary with none but priests to defend him when the Horn-bearer came.

Cool night breezes moved among them all.

"We are in your debt," said Almora. "Heaven willing, we will see Eldinor before long."

"Aye." The man nodded. He planted his knee on the road. "Aye, Ladyship."

Almora smiled. "In any case, I am afraid that we can offer you little rest." And there was no safety for a man left behind in the path of the maragrim.

The man nodded a sharp bow. "I would not be left behind."

It was foolish, but Durand wanted to cry for the poor man. Maybe for all the poor men behind them as well. Deorwen stood very near, and Durand found her hand in his, unnoticed in the moonlight. Durand squeezed, but then let go.

"We will ride for Eldinor," Durand commanded. "Let us see how soon we can reach it."

IN THE NIGHT, they heard uncanny sounds. Eerie shrieks and calls echoed from the distance. Soon, though, the whole of Saerdana rang to the barking of plowmen's dogs. From the terror of these beasts, the army knew that the Enemy was there in the dark and not far away.

But, despite their certainties, the Eye of Heaven rose before the Horn-bearer could overtake them. The Eye split the horizon. A few men sang out with Dawn Thanksgiving.

"Dawn, is it?" said Berchard, wincing. "I'm not sure I expected to see it."

Durand was about to answer when hoofbeats caused him to turn.

A rider broke from the low hills to the west. Maybe it was the light, but he galloped as though there were no army before him, careering into their long shadows without so much as checking his pace. Duke Leovere spurred a dozen Yrlaci knights into the man's path, ready to strike him down.

At the last, however, the stranger seemed to understand what was before him.

"Beware of ambush! Watch the hills!" Durand roared, and he charged out to meet the stranger with Garelyn at his side.

Duke Leovere had a fist in the man's bridle, fighting to manage both man and mount. The man wore a knight's gear. He was bloody, terribly slashed over the face and shoulders. Through the clotted mess, it looked like even the riveted mail was torn. He was small for a knight with a beard that might have been red and eyes like flint buttons. He strained at Leovere's hand.

"Let me go! Let me go!"

He jerked his reins and must have driven his spurs deep, for his charger nearly lunged free.

"Here, you fool," snapped Garelyn. "Open your eyes! There are a thousand men watching. Do you think they'll all run at your say-so?"

The man boggled and twisted, but finally mastered himself enough to say, "Who are you? What are you doing here?"

Garelyn swung his horse in close, knee to knee with the man; he was a good head taller. "Me, I am the Duke of Garelyn. Behind me, you'll find the Host of Gireth. What do you mean by all this? Who are you, eh? That's a better question!"

Durand watched the man try once more to master himself. There were clean white edges upon the cuts in the man's face and neck. His hair hung in gummy coils.

"I was with Beoran." He swallowed, not speaking his own name or titles. "The Hells have opened and devils walk the earth. They are behind me, I swear it."

"Ah," said Garelyn. "So you have met our thralls, then."

The man gaped at them. "Thralls? Aye, thralls. We rode to meet Eodan's Host. They'd made good time. They couldn't have come all the way from Windhover. Maybe from Mornaway or Cape Erne. We were guessing.

"At nightfall, we camped. Our scouts: they'd seen him. Maybe half a league, at Merecrop. We had pickets out. Then, it was madness. Something fell upon the Host of Windhover—God knows what."

"You saw this?" asked Durand.

"Our scouts came in screaming, but our prince, he hardly blinked." The man's mouse-dark eyes glistened, clearly brim-full of memories. "He'd been keeping a vigil, all in iron. And he was in his saddle before the riders could tell their tale. We were all Sons of Atthi, he said, then we were off into the dark, men hiking mail coats over their heads." He looked down. There were no boots on the man's feet.

"Biedin rode to free his brother?" asked Garelyn.

The little knight mashed his eyes shut. "And then we were on them. Such things, all blood. Giants, stunted things, beasts and vermin like men. I—" His hand, seemingly of its own will, scrabbled at his shoulders, the bloody mass of his face. "Something— It landed on my back, clawing, its lips in my ear, shrieking like a child on fire. I could not think for pain and—I rode, trying—trying to outrace it. I—"

Garelyn was shocked. "What are you saying?"

But Durand needed to hear what the man had seen. He needed to know what was left of the Atthians. "Here," he said, jostling between Leovere and the knight, trying to look the man in the face. "The Eye of Heaven has driven the thing away." He put both hands on the slick sides of the stranger's head. "The Host of the Great Council? The men of Windhover? How many have survived?" In the man's answer could be the doom of Errest the Old. The doom of them all.

"I do not know," the man spluttered. "The thing on my back, it—"

Garelyn straightened. "You left those men? You left them alive in the face of the enemy?" No one could deny the truth they saw in the man's wide-eyed stammer. "You do not know their doom because you fled and saw nothing."

Durand dropped his hands. He was about to protest; they'd all seen too much.

But the Duke of Garelyn had drawn his sword, and in one dread stroke he took the craven knight's head—and the forefinger from one of the man's warding hands.

The corpse slid from its saddle.

"Has there not been enough?" Leovere snarled. His face was a bloody mask.

"No," said Garelyn. He slid his sword through a pinch of his cloak to clean it. "He could not live. Not with better men dead behind him."

Leovere's mouth was a tight line. "I see."

Durand clenched his teeth. Here was another man dead at his account. Thousands, maybe. "Hells," he said. "Enough of this!"

He looked into the west. This was the direction from which the dead man had come. Already, kites and crows hung in the air, circling in their hundreds. Durand even spotted his own Rooks, much nearer, but perched by the same track.

So close had the enemy come. In the night, the Hornbearer had struck across the fields and fallen upon the princes.

He was surprised to see Almora practically at his elbow; Garelyn's barbaric stroke had adorned her cloak with spots of red.

"Durand Col," she said. "We must learn what has become of Prince Biedin and his brother. Of the Host of Errest." And she was right. A ride of half a league would tell them the fate of Errest the Old. There would be survivors, or there would not. A chance still existed.

IN NO TIME, they reached a rise that stormed with kites and crows.

"We are near to Merecrop Well," said Heremund. "There's a story about an abbey round a spring. Meant to be holy. Or the opposite. There will be a new tale of Merecrop now."

Almora nodded Durand onward. And he, with the grim Duke Leovere and a few of the vanguard, mounted the rise.

In a muddy field, he beheld five acres of slaughter. Living men sat among corpses and floundering horses. Some knights were dragging torn comrades into grisly windrows. Some prayed Dawn Thanksgiving. Others wandered, unseeing, while the carrion birds spun crazily overhead.

"There is Prince Biedin, I think," said Durand, and Leovere nodded. The prince stood in the midst of an armed knot of men. It hadn't been an hour since the Eye of Heaven would have driven the maragrim into the ground, and every man stood in the posture of a last stand.

Durand and his party rode, wallowing down into a battlefield where the living looked as witless as Durand's Lost followers, and there were so many surcoats and banners, cloaks and pennons plastered in the mud that it seemed like a whole kingdom had sunk into the mire.

Leovere was pale.

They came to the ring of Biedin's last knights; Durand bowed low as he reined in before the prince.

Biedin, however, only stared.

"Your Grace," prompted Durand, as gently as he could.

In time, the gaunt prince rubbed the hollows of his cheeks. His dull eyes swiveled.

"Who are you?" he said.

"Your Grace, I am Durand Col." He chose not to remind the man of Acconel.

"Durand Col . . ." He stared at Durand, then winced. There was a hopeless twitch, nothing like a smile.

"They are under our feet, even now," said Biedin. His men had hardly let their blades sag. Durand looked over the torn earth, the thousand curls of muck and shadow where the maragrim would be teeming. "Cracks in the ground. Fissures. Shadows under stones." Biedin twitched a glance eastward. "It was the Eye of Heaven. Nothing else."

"No, Your Grace." Durand knew the dull stupor that this man must feel. So many had died on his orders. He had saved lives, perhaps, but his men had paid. Still, Durand saw that many men had survived. Hundreds, at least. And he had need of soldiers.

"Your Grace, does your brother yet live?"

Biedin frowned in irritation, but pointed to a spot where, a stone's throw from them, a smaller island of last-standers watched from a rampart of corpses. A tall blond man had stepped from these men and was reeling toward Biedin's men; dozens of his own men straggled after. On the blond man's chest, he bore the clenched arrows of Windhover. And, though he was blond, Durand saw in his face a reflection of Ragnal and Biedin.

"Who are they, Biedin?" said the newcomer.

By way of answer, Biedin glanced sharply at Durand.

"Your Grace." Durand nodded. "We are Yrlac and Gireth. Household guard from Mornaway and Garelyn. The Dukes of Garelyn and Yrlac. And Lady Almora, heiress of Gireth."

Eodan shook his head. Up close, he resembled Ragnal. He wore a heavy mustache that gave him some of Ragnal's leonine expression.

"This is some joke of the Powers," he said. "An hour ago, these men prayed for someone like you. Now we want to dig graves." Durand could not help but think of the thralls under the earth and the distance to Eldinor.

"No," Durand said. "There is not time."

"Who the devil are you, sir, exactly?" bristled Eodan though few of his men had strength enough to lift their blades.

In the east, then, Durand's own people were cresting the rise. Shadows scissored over the battlefield, over Biedin, over Eodan and his men. It seemed to wake the prince.

"I am Durand Col, of Gireth, Your Grace. I brought men from Gireth, Mornaway, Garelyn, and Yrlac. All under arms."

"Yrlac?" The big man lifted his chin. "Four dukedoms? You would've been welcome." He glanced to the lines of Biedin's force. "As was my brother when he came riding."

Durand nodded cautiously.

"Now, all that is left is to set fires on this ground. To turn a river. To bury the thralls under ten fathoms of stone!" Eodan clutched his face. "I brought so many. Now so many are—" He looked around at his followers. The limbs of men and horses jutted from the ground for acres in all directions. Eodan had brought them to this place, these hunters and knights and yeoman of Windhover.

"Prince Eodan," said Durand, looking down upon the man from his saddle. "We are many. We have seen the Hornbearer. We have faced his thralls. Your Grace, we have crossed Hesperand. Night and day we have ridden, and lost men every league. But it is to Eldinor we ride. Reilan is waiting his vigil under stone with none but priests and serving men to defend him."

"Eldinor," said Eodan as though the idea had only dawned on him. "They will rise from this torn earth and rush the last leagues to Eldinor."

"We will meet them there," said Durand.

"The boy's in Eldinor. Three days under stone," said Eodan. A brigand's grin split the prince's beard and he turned to the few dozen men behind him. "We will go to Eldinor. We will go to Eldinor and await the Hornbearer."

Prince Eodan turned back, ready to speak to his brother, but the man was gone.

"What is this?"

Duke Leovere pointed: The army of the south was parting for the solitary prince, though he neither spoke a word nor raised his hand. Biedin was riding to Eldinor without a sound. With this example of courage, all of the magnates who had survived from the Council Host—Beoran, Highshields, Cape Erne—bullied their men to their feet.

Eodan laughed with astonishment. "It seems that my brother is riding to Eldinor whether we join him or not. And I, for one, will not be left behind!"

With that, the survivors staggered to their feet and set off on Biedin's heels, leaving the Host of Fellwood slavering in the cracked earth behind them.

30
The Bay of Eldinor

Biedin rode in grim and resolute silence; he seemed a hero from another age, and no man dared to offer him company at the head of the column. The four hosts followed without a word, drawn by the solitary prince.

It was after Noontide Lauds that dread began to settle upon them, as men still in the blood-stiffened clothing of the night's battle realized that darkness must return. From time to time, a man would step from the column and settle at the roadside, accepting the death that must come when the Hornbearer overtook him. Slowly, the War Host of Errest the Old became a long and straggling thing with Prince Biedin farther and farther before them.

Durand and the rest of the commanders watched Biedin's cloak flapping. The thing moved as if it were a fitful sleeper.

Durand took a deep breath and squinted back over the host. "At this rate, Biedin will reach Eldinor alone." And strung out like beads, the Sons of Atthi would be gobbled up by the Hornbearer's thralls.

"We are afraid, I think. Nothing more," said Eodan. "I cannot fathom how so many have agreed to march into the Hornbearer's path again today. I'm not sure how we'll bear the dark again. We should all have been mauled to death in that field. And I find that I cannot quiet my hands." He checked to see that the nearest soldiers were looking elsewhere, and then held up a trembling hand.

Durand blinked at the unwanted images that flickered before his mind's eye, and swallowed hard to quiet the fluttering in his guts. "This pace will kill them all, brave or not—and without the least hope of victory. The last man in the column will be the first to meet the maragrim. A man who drags his feet might as well be riding headlong at the Hornbearer. If we cannot reach Eldinor, we should send the men into the hills."

Berchard still rode with Heremund. The one-eyed knight smiled. "Heremund, you're meant to be a skald, are you not? D'ye know that hunting song? The one with the horns?"

"The Hellebore song? It's meant for dawn, ain't it?"

"I can hardly tell the difference, and our foes've little love for the Eye of Heaven. Let's have it!"

Heremund smiled up at dukes and princes, and sang out from the back of his donkey:

> *The bright horn it calls us a-hunting to ride*
> *we'll rest us at evening by the cool water side.*
> *O merry the hunter and merry the horn*
> *That calls us a-riding and brings us this morn.*

There were chuckles all around. Garelyn sang out and then his men and soon all of Gireth and Yrlac and even the Hosts of Windhover and the Great Council were singing too. That song and then

another and another rolled around the company. Songs from Windhover vied with songs from Beoran and Yrlac, and even gloomy Highshields had a grim song about the spearing of a ram that had the men
laughing.

The War Host of Errest the Old half-swaggered for an hour while the
Eye of Heaven was still high.

THE AFTERNOON PASSED, and near sunset, Durand sent Vadir forward
with Ailric and a hundred men to search out the Bay of Eldinor. They
needed to know how far off the city lay and whether the tide was in or
out. In Durand's heart, he had been certain that they would see the
towers of Eldinor and the waves of the bay glinting before nightfall, but
darkness would soon overtake them on the road, and there was Biedin
still riding ahead with no sign of the holy city.

They prayed the Plea of Sunset on the march. And soon, the last light
was ebbing from the Vault of Heaven.

Berchard cast about. "It *is* growing dark, isn't it? It is not my old eye?
Those men, they are singing the Last Twilight."

"With an especial passion, yes," said Heremund.

Soon, they began to hear screeches in the leagues behind them. Once,
a flight of night birds shot over the company. Somewhere a dog started
barking.

"Where are we now?" Durand demanded of anyone listening. The
whole circle of commanders, lords, and ladies rode nearby.

Prince Eodan spoke. "We are some three leagues from Scrivensands
and the bay. Many years have passed since I was welcome in my father's
city, but still I know the lands where I rode as a youth, I think. I take
that smudge of shadow yonder for Haychat Wood, where there are red
deer. And that dark village across the fields west is likely Ashwells, where
there is a good alehouse all year long. I would be sure if the Eye of Heaven
was yet with us."

"Vadir and the rest have been gone hours." Eldinor must be somewhere up the road. He remembered the city in its broad bay. At high
tide, Eldinor was unassailable, floating like a diadem upon the waves. At
low tide, an army could simply cross the flats and pluck the city from
the mud. The tide would make all the difference.

Durand tried to set frustration aside. "If the tide is in," he said, "we
will need every boat on the bay ready when we reach the shore." He tried
to fix the distance across the bay in his mind's eye. It would take time
to row it, and probably too much time at that. "We will want to get

everyone off in one go if we can. We want no one waiting on the shore when the thralls come."

"That is true enough," allowed Prince Eodan.

The prince tilted his head. "Here is something else to think of. It might be wise to pass the word to the banner knights that we are very near to Eldinor now. The men will be glad to hear it, and it might even be true."

"What use can these men be if they are weary to the point of death?" said Deorwen.

"We must pray for high tide," said Durand. "If the tide is in, we might hope to rest. If the bay is full, we will cross to the city while the Horn-bearer paces on the shore. It may be that dawn arrives before the mara-grim can make their crossing."

"A night's sleep and then a stout wall to fight behind!" said Eodan. He gave a smile to Almora. "We might hold out until the patriarchs are finished with my nephew, and that would serve the Hornbearer right!"

But Deorwen was not comforted. "And if the tide is out, Your Graces?"

Before anyone could find the words to answer, Almora spoke. "If the tide is out when we reach the bay, then we will have no need to bother with the silly boats, will we?"

It was then that they finally heard the beating of hooves in the road ahead and Ailric appeared, jouncing out of the dark.

"Your Graces, Lords and Ladies," he managed.

"The city?" said Eodan. "By Heaven, tell us, boy!"

"It is a league to the shore."

Eodan was smiling then. "If these devils do not trip us up too badly, we might see the city in an hour's time!"

"Thank the Powers!" said Berchard.

"And the tide?" said Durand.

"It was out, Sir Durand; I do not know when. But the bay was empty."

"'Empty,'" echoed the Duke of Garelyn. "And likely still when we reach it."

Ailric made no answer. He was as much a landsman as Durand, after all.

"Hells," said Berchard.

"No need of boats then," murmured Durand.

"Vadir and the rest are right behind," Ailric said. Anyone could see that the youth had been riding hard.

Before Durand could thank him, an alarm rose up from the rear of the company, and something huge let out a whoop that froze their blood.

"The maragrim!" cried Durand. He spurred his mount flying through the crowds toward the rear of the column, where he met the sound of screaming men and horses. They were fighting off a giant of the maragrim host: the thing Durand saw was a skeleton—a gaping man made from the branches of a bleached tree, all full of nails. It stood in the midst of the rear guard, swatting men from their saddles and screeching back at them in weird mimicry of their cries.

Durand joined the battle, spurring his warhorse at the brute with Eodan and Leovere in tow. Together, they struck like a scythe, hacking its long legs. In a wheeling instant, the thrall smacked the earth and the men of Errest were upon it from every side, chopping its beating limbs and catching talons with every blade they could reach.

In the moments after, Durand stood in the twitching wreckage of the thing, and he heard further whoops and cries from the vague fields and forests to the south. The wind moved in the dark leaves like breathing.

"This is the first of them," said Eodan. His hands were shaking so hard now that he must clutch his shoulders to stop it. "They will not come like a host of men, but like a pack of dogs, running us down. The Hornbearer has let them off the leash and set them upon us. They are coming, and the swiftest first."

Another strange wail rang out from beyond the fields. Somewhere a farm dog began barking—and another.

"Double the rear guard," said Durand. "The best men. The freshest. We must hurry."

THEY RODE FOR Eldinor with the quickest fiends of the Hornbearer's company flinging themselves upon the rear guard, striking again and again in ever-greater numbers. Durand steeled himself against the shrieks of men and monsters. There might come a moment when he must abandon Eldinor and turn the army upon their attackers, but that would mean the end. So although every new scream demanded that Durand turn and fight, he instead abandoned squadron after squadron of the rear guard to battle in the dark and win or lose alone in the faint hope that they were at last close to the city.

Finally, as the Host of Errest trailed Biedin onto a high bluff where sedges blew in the night breezes, Durand smelled mud and rotting weed. And he saw Eldinor, its windows glittering across the empty bay, with Biedin all alone like a single brushstroke upon the Vault of Heaven.

Part of Durand wondered if the man was mad, but he had little time to ponder, for then, with the city in sight, a clamor arose from the rear guard.

This was no solitary outrider hurling itself against a squadron; a great groan rose from the back ranks. Thousands of voices gabbled and shrieked and brayed from the road and woods behind them. Half in despair, Durand cast a glance at the wide bay, thinking that they would not now be able to reach it. But he saw something in the vast glistening expanse: half a league from the city and the cliff there were waves flashing along a shoal of clay. He remembered how the tide came in at Eldinor. He remembered walking on the flats with the Rooks taunting him and the tide roaring back to drown the false land in moments. From that high bank, he could see the brimming waters waiting to flood the Bay of Eldinor. But when?

Behind him, men were screaming.

They must get to the bay. If they could reach the walls somehow—if they could reach the city as the tide came in—they might hold out long enough to drown the Hornbearer and his fiends. Even if they could draw the Hornbearer into the bay and not save themselves, they would have done better than throwing their lives away on the bluff. It was maddening not to know how long the tide had been out or when it would come rushing back. Minutes could matter.

Durand was ready to howl the order and send them down the bank when he realized that Prince Biedin had already vanished from the promontory, still unrelenting and already leading them down.

Durand turned to the others. "We must hope for the tide! We will drown the devils! All is lost on this shore. We must reach the city and give Heaven its chance!"

The vanguard had made a half-circle around Durand and the commanders. No one had quite called a halt, and the army was jostled now between the cliff and the sounds of the approaching enemy. Leovere's horse had caught the terror in the air and was spinning under him as he spurred into the circle, saying, "Durand Col, already my men have seen the Hornbearer in the trees to the south. His thralls are upon us. It is too late to avoid him. But you must go to Eldinor. You must reach the wall with as many men as Heaven spares. Save the boy who must be king, and the men of Yrlac will hold the Hornbearer as long as the Host of Heaven allows."

Leovere had, perhaps, two hundred men. Already, they were dismounting and hauling weapons and shields from their saddles. Grim Morcar of Downcastle was unfurling Leovere's banner of the round horn.

With a glance to Almora and Prince Eodan, Durand bowed to Leovere and his man.

"Pass the word," Durand said. "Duke Leovere will hold the Horn-bearer at the cliff top. The rest of us, we race for Eldinor!"

The army fought their way down the bluff and, in a broad crescent, pelted over shoals of weed and out across acres of rippling sand in the moonlight. Somewhere in the midst of that scything mass, Durand spotted Almora and Deorwen, riding swiftly. For a moment, Durand felt that they all must reach the city before even one of the maragrim could touch them. He even wondered, for an instant, if he had squandered Leovere's men on the bluff.

But then, the smooth sand gave out.

The fastest struck first. Then Durand's mount was stumbling under-neath him, and Durand hit the mud, splashing into the mire with a force that nearly buried him. The firm sand had given way to a great penin-sula of slime. Durand's poor horse lashed and flopped against the evil-smelling stuff and could not rise.

Behind them, the thralls had mounted the bluffs, clearly visible, thou-sands strong against Leovere's force. For a moment, the thralls checked their advance. Rain began to fall. Durand saw the new-minted Duke of Yrlac take Uluric's old horn from his shoulder. In the face of the mara-grim host, he winded the ancient trumpet—and he was still blowing the long note when the maragrim exploded forward, flashing through the poor men of Yrlac like a broken dam.

In the muck below, every trapped soul remembered the terrible fleet-ness of the maragrim thralls. Durand saw Biedin, now leading his horse, picking his way toward Eldinor.

They could not stay. "The Powers will not aid us if we lie down!" roared Durand. He pulled men from the sucking mud, and the broad crescent of desperate men struggled on toward the city. Ten paces, twenty paces. Men lost boots. Their hearts were bursting. Crippled horses lol-loped around them, and the fear was like a sickness. There were Ber-chard and Heremund. Durand got his hand in Deorwen's, heaving her forward. She caught him when he stumbled.

"It is now we need Coensar!" said Deorwen.

"Aye," was all he could manage.

"Have you thought of him and the Host of Hesperand?"

But it must be too late for Coensar now. The thralls would soon be among the stragglers. He wondered what had become of Coensar and the Lost Duke.

"Have you still got that rag from Hesperand?" Deorwen asked.

"What?" he began, but then he remembered the favor of the lady of that Lost land: the one he had snatched from the tree. Now, he groped at his belt and found the mud-clotted bit of veil; once again, he had taken something from that place. Leovere's men were tumbling from the bluff. Durand felt a queasy punch of shame at having led them all to this disaster. Leovere had bought them only the smallest fraction of an hour. Durand squeezed the Hesperand rag. Once it had stood for a favor he might call upon. Now, he did not know what was left of Hesperand—or its lady.

He shut his eyes upon the first, loping maragrim to reach the sand.

The rain pelted harder.

"If you're coming, Coen, then it had best be now," he said.

A hundred maragrim had boiled onto the sand. Durand saw Leovere's standard still flying on the bluff, though the flagstaff jerked in the hands of its stricken defenders. Man after man fell as the surge of maragrim overwhelmed them, and soon the standard was carried off, spinning in the claws of the multitude. The fiends leapt over each other like tumblers as they climbed from the bluff. Durand turned to those around him. All the desperate faces. Deorwen, Almora, Ailric; the prince and the commanders. He knew himself to be a fool there in the mud, playing duke and knight and hero when Creation was so full of horrors. But he had resolved that he would, at least, stand to meet his killers with a bare blade, when a new trumpet called out over the Bay of Eldinor.

"Damnit, Coensar," he murmured. "Please."

Something moved upon the heights—not near the maragrim—the flash of banners. Heremund was calling out: "The cliff! The cliff! He has done it!"

With astonishment, Durand saw moonlight ripple upon ranks of antique banners, arms like silver, flesh like pearl.

The Host of Hesperand had crested the cliff top, and now their ancient squadrons stood row upon row, as neat as needlework. And at their head rode the Lost Duke—and Durand's onetime captain. Over all of them was the glow of a moon from another age.

They were very far away.

"It is a chance," said Durand, and he urged his people thrashing onward.

Already, the bulk of the Hornbearer's crowd had made the scramble onto the sand. Such a writhing multitude, no man could count, but Durand knew that they must number in the thousands, and as the Host of Hesperand plunged onto the flat, anyone could see that even Duke Eorcan's squadrons were hopelessly outnumbered. For a cold heartbeat then,

Durand held the maragrim and the Lost in his eye. And he thought that if he turned the Host of Errest, the two forces might strike at once. But, even then, their numbers were few.

Across the mudflat somewhere, the tide was rising against that dark clay shoal. Soon the sea would overflow that bank and come thundering in, faster than horses over the bay.

At that moment, the Hornbearer itself strode onto the bluff, its army flowing around its ankles. The giant's spider-like claws unslung the horn from around its neck, and the maragrim everywhere checked their rush to cringe toward their master. The Crowned Hog brought the great trumpet into its face, and the great horn groaned. Its shaking note filled Creation from the floor of Eldinor Bay to the vault of Heaven itself. Here was the long-delayed end of a thousand campaigns from the ancient south. Every twisted throat of the maragrim howled in answer, and as the Crowned Hog leapt in a high arc from the cliff top, its legions rushed forward. The thralls of Heshtar were in sight of sacred Eldinor.

With every eye drawn to the Hornbearer, the Host of Hesperand had left the heights.

Durand swept the bay, a thousand thoughts in his head. Had they fled? Had the dread horn worked some banishment?

But Duke Eorcan was upon the flats, and with the thralls so intent on Eldinor, none of the devils saw the fey lancers swinging down upon their flank. The knights of Hesperand rolled across the mire in perfect order until finally they brought their lances to bear on the half-blind enemy. The shock punched scores of hideous thralls into the air. Dozens more were torn down or mutilated in that first instant. And the perfect conrois of Hesperand shot through the ragged mob, tracing a long arc, as elegant as something sketched with a draftsman's compass.

As the knights of Hesperand tore free, the maragrim forgot Eldinor, and many of the brutes gave chase, lurching pointlessly over the mud in the wake of the fleet, fey horses. All in all, the charge of the thralls collapsed in confusion, and they had not reformed when the squadrons of Hesperand cantered round, as elegant as a pendulum's swing, and struck once more, their blades flashing in the dark as they tore through the maddened throng.

Durand saw Coensar among the streaming, ancient banners.

Men, despite themselves, had stopped to marvel.

"Hurry!" said Durand. "This is what Coensar has bought us! We must run for Eldinor!"

And the army of Errest ran and wallowed and staggered over the floor of the bay, hardly able to glance backward while the knights of Hesperand swung in great curving arcs, swooping like sparrows on a crow's back.

The striding Hornbearer seemed undeceived. The giant had set its ancient eyes upon Eldinor and the goading charges of a few score horsemen could not turn it aside. The Hornbearer raged over its host, driving them with sweeping mortal blows as the knights of Hesperand sleeted through their numbers. The knights rode over mud or sand with equal speed. Always the hooves flashed and water flew. No part of Creation seemed to check their stride, but Durand saw what happened when one of their number fell: in an instant, the touch of Creation sent every year of the Lost eternities rushing back upon the man and he was less than dust. Flesh and bone splattered like ash on the mud.

All the while, the living men of the Atthias ran and tripped and sprawled. Many had kept their horses and caught people up to ride double. Five hundred paces became five dozen. The walls came nearer as Coensar lashed the maragrim with his splintering squadrons. Durand saw Eldinor on its plinth of rock with its walls looming fathoms high. And, as the ground rose, he hauled scores of stragglers onto the higher ground, shouting "Up! Up!" as the Hornbearer roared, only a bowshot away.

In the frenzy, he gave his hand to the next Atthian, only to see that he had got hold of gleaming limb of a living corpse. A blue-pale face gabbled at him.

Eodan struck the thing down. "Now, Durand!" he roared. "They are upon us."

"Aye!" said Durand. The maragrim were bounding through the ranks. It was turn now or be destroyed. "Lines! Lines now. Shields! We must have a wall of our own!" He found Berchard. The man had his old sword drawn. And Durand ran from man to man, heaving banner knights and common soldiers into order. They would stand where the ground rose. A few squadrons would turn that the rest might reach the walls. Almora led the rest. "Close as you can!" shouted Durand. "Spears if you have them."

The Host, hideous in their innumerable deformities, bore down upon Durand's rear guard. They could hear shouts from some few guardsmen in the high parapets behind them. They might be close enough.

Eodan's hand caught Durand's shoulder. "Quick!" he said, and a shadow flickered between Durand and the moon, for the Hornbearer—a hundred paces through the dark—had torn a broken ship from the muck.

The thing crashed down upon the Atthian phalanx, men and timbers exploding.

The braying maragrim surged forward and crashed into the slope below the Atthians. Durand and the rest lifted their shields. And the things climbed from the mud, their hands and claws and God-knows slapped and scrabbled. And the Atthian blades flashed down, lopping limbs and heads and kicking the thralls back onto the necks of their comrades.

Every horror imaginable slavered in that mob. The maragrim were nightmares or things from the Hells; they were not a people. In a heartbeat, Durand faced a grotesquely laughing thing whose straining hands wrenched its own face bone-breakingly wide. Beside it, a gibbering thing clutched huge flat sacks that shed pennies; it swatted with these with flinching gestures as sudden as the wing-beats of a fly. There were crockery men. Men caught in machinery. Bloated men in peasants' garb, monks and priests. A woman on all fours like a crab. The most common expression on any face in the mob was terror. They were in hell.

Durand and his comrades flailed down on a sea of snatching limbs. Every thrall was driven by the strength of madness, and some were far larger than a man.

The press was fantastic. The thralls flew against them, and every man swung his sword or axe, mace or maul. The rear guard gave ground, falling back step by step. Soon they were all below the wall with a bank behind them. The crush trapped Durand's shield. It threatened to bowl him over. But, always, he kept his feet and worked his sword arm. Every man could feel his doom upon him.

Now, it was the king they defended. Now, though they were lost, they might still hold the maragrim on the flat. The tide might yet strike. Their kingdom might yet endure.

In the midst of this mortal chaos, a black shape darted past Durand's face. There was a scattering lice and feathers. Durand did not even have a hand to clear his eyes.

The Rooks were spinning overhead.

"Col! Durand Col! So glamorous a final stand. Yrlac. Lost Hesperand. That skald of yours will tell it! Should he live of course— Oh!"

The bird darted as a naked maragrim like a hairless bull tore past. Durand's shield nearly broke, along with the forearm behind it, but a Mornaway man put a blade in his brute's eyes, and they leapt on, chopping madly.

"*So near*," said a Rook. "*So tragic!*"

Durand managed a wincing glance at the birds circling his head.

"*So near, and the battle is without purpose.*"

In the thick of the fight, Durand had no time for thought. The Rooks could say what they would.

"*Biedin will end it all, and there will be nothing.*"

"*Days for a new king. Days, at least—and the wards breaking and the priests past praying, and our Fellwood friend camped in the Mount of Eagles.*"

"*There he goes!*"

At this, Durand risked a glance toward the city, and there he saw Prince Biedin. The man had climbed the rocky bank to the city wall and found a small door—a sally port—in the ancient stones. He had a bare sword in his hand.

In the next instant, Durand's eyes were back on his work as another thrall surged forward; it tried to clamber over Durand before he and his comrades could pitchfork the thing to the mud.

"*He will be through the streets in moments, and then it is the high sanctuary and the little Prince. Have you not seen him? In his eyes there is murder enough for an army of nephews.*"

"*All alone, bar the priests.*"

"*And they can do nothing, brother.*"

"*He is the boy's uncle.*"

The prince had indeed gone on. Biedin's cloak flapped once as he darted through the sally port and left the battlefield.

The Atthians were dying.

The maragrim drove deep into the Atthian line, leaving men cut off, breaking up the heavy phalanx. But then the knights of Hesperand struck once more, harrying the flanks of the nightmare mob. Even the Lost could not hammer a horse into such a solid mass. What would become of them all?

In the midst of this chaos, something rippled over the moon. Thinking to see another shipwreck sailing down, Durand glanced, but to his astonishment, he found, not some monster of the Hornbearer's flock, but instead, the naked eye of the Traveler staring down upon him. The flat glint of that silver coin and, black against the Heavens, the bare suggestion of the black disc and socket of the other eye.

Creation was still and silent under that expressionless gaze.

And, in that instant, Durand saw a beckoning figure at Biedin's secret door. There was the Herald of Errest extending his hand.

Eodan stumbled into Durand at that moment, and the world crashed back into tumult. "Durand, what are you gaping at, man?"

"The boy," said Durand. "I think he's gone for the boy—"

Now Eodan gaped.

Durand stared at the door. He heard the battle around him. They were fighting for nothing, and death must take them all before long.

But then he seemed to see the door anew.

Durand turned to Eodan.

"The door!" He gestured. The thing looked very small. A tall man must stoop to pass.

"A door?" The army heaving all around them seemed like an enormous thing.

Almora and Deorwen were nearby. The land held by the Host of Gireth amounted to a few dozen yards.

"What are you saying?" asked Almora.

"We pass the door." Durand swept his hand across the parapets. Only here and there could they see a defender in the gapped teeth of the parapets.

"Durand," Eodan was saying. "Perhaps the women . . ."

"No," said Durand. "I cannot argue. I must go."

"We will die like a rabbit in a snare."

"No," said Almora. She could see it. She strode forward, calling to the commanders: Garelyn, Mornaway. "We will take the wall! The door! The sally port." Her father's man, Vadir, was listening.

"Baron Vadir, make ready to take a squadron to the battlements. We must have the wall! Archers if you find them."

Eodan said to Durand, "And what will you do?" There were rear guards and counter charges and harrying attacks to mount, but Durand had seen the Herald and the surreptitious escape of Prince Biedin.

"Your brother has gone armed into the city." The boy-king's tomb was there. He was helpless. "Alone."

Eodan raised his eyes to the city and the Mount of Eagles somewhere within. "No," he began, but faltered. "He would not." Doubt passed over his face. And there was nothing like time for explanations.

Durand turned from the fight. Berchard was there, and Heremund—like a boy with a bulldog on a lead.

"My Windhover men will shield the retreat!" Eodan was shouting.

And Durand ran, scrambling toward the door.

31
Lost Princes

The Herald stood in the sally port under the wall, as uncanny as the damned Traveler in the sky.

"Durand?" Deorwen called after him. As Durand slid and squeezed for the sally port, she chased him. He scrambled up the bank. The Rooks he might doubt, but the Traveler gave him pause. The Powers of Heaven told a man damned little before he must make up his mind.

The Herald handed him up.

"It cannot have the boy," said the Herald. "Errest the Old cannot fall." The tall man darted into an alleyway.

"You have spoken!" Deorwen said. This was no royal message. It had been two centuries. He must pay a price, surely.

The tall man broke into a street beyond.

"'It.' What do you mean, 'it'?" Durand called.

The Herald's broad brow furrowed for a moment and he gripped Durand's shoulder.

"It was a cruel mercy, Durand Col, and many have paid who were blameless. Onward, please. He will not wait."

The man was off again, almost running. His hands slapped the walls.

"What is he talking about?" Deorwen demanded, but Durand knew no more than she.

"Make haste," said the Herald, "or it will not end!"

The huge man was stalking into the city, leaving Durand and Deorwen no choice but to scamper.

"The truth is not easily buried! It rots. It rises."

The Herald spoke in backward snatches as he walked with his towering strides, covering ground so swiftly that Deorwen could only run to stay with him.

"They did not know what to do with it, when it came!"

"What is all this supposed to mean?" said Deorwen.

Durand was scurrying like a child. "You must speak plainly, Herald!"

They were running toward the high sanctuary. "It was found in the South of Errest. Coming from the passes of the Blackroots."

"Name this thing, Herald!" said Durand.

Durand had a glimpse of the man's ashen face. "They brought it to Eldinor, Heaven help us. Bound in a coffer of oak and iron. They rowed it to the sally port and carried him by night through these very streets."

"'Him,'" said Durand. Men talked of the maragrim this way, always "it" and "him." "Kandemar. Who did they bring here?"

"Willan Blind knew him at once. Perhaps his blindness let him see. So many would not."

They jagged through the abandoned reaches of the city, every street uncannily silent after the wild brawling at the wall. A man might have thought that Eldinor had fallen a century before.

"King Willan, he meant to redeem it. Or heart-sickness stayed his hand. Or perhaps it was the crown. Willan Blind was third-born."

"Who did they find? Who did they bring to Eldinor?" said Durand, though now Deorwen tried to restrain him.

The great Herald stopped, fetching up against a lime-washed wall. They were nearing the high sanctuary. He hung his head and did not turn. The wall was support.

"A vassal knight. He carried it from Gireth. Bound in a chest of oak and iron, between two files of priests. It had passed the mountains. Such things sometimes did. But the wards had caught it. King Willan was no longer young. The thing must have been creeping north fifty winters or more." The man straightened a fraction. "Coming home."

Durand hung back with Deorwen. "Who was it, Herald?" she said.

"We ought to have destroyed it. The High Patriarch of that time, he demanded we should. A thrall of the Enemy. But Willan, he bade every man depart. All but the Patriarch and me, who could not speak. Alone, Willan Blind came to the black chest, and something hissed within, like snakes.

"Willan spoke to the thing in the box. 'This is no place for thee now. Thy time to work good or ill upon this world has ended. Thy long home awaiteth thee.' But from within the box came only hatred.

"The Patriarch commanded that Willan bring the thing to its end.

"'We will prepare a room for him,' was Willan's answer.

"'There can be no homecoming for such a thing as this.'

"But the king managed only, 'He is home.'"

Without warning, the Herald lurched off once again, covering ground so swiftly that even Durand must run to keep pace with the limping man. His hand fumbled on alley walls to keep him upright.

Durand saw blood.

"What does all this mean?" said Durand.

The big man pitched against the corner post of some shop. "Willan, he caused the box to be carried. No guest chamber. No high tower. But under the city. Below the Mount of Eagles. A strong room where Willan and the Patriarch both could keep watch.

"And it was not mercy, but a wound."

The Herald faced them. For the first time, they could see a gruesome darkness spreading down the front of his surcoat. A neat wet hole glistened a finger's breadth below the man's breastbone. He had been stabbed. The Herald dropped to one knee. Deorwen, with better presence of mind, caught him and was suddenly his only support. She slowed his fall as Durand snatched at his arm like a fool. A man could not stop the working of such an ancient doom.

"The prince," the Herald gasped. "Caught up in all this. Fool boy." The Herald must have known what Biedin intended. Here was proof of Biedin's madness, if any was needed.

"You will need care," Deorwen said. "We might still find a surgeon." But they had an entire city to search.

The Herald planted both hands and pitched himself onto his side. "The young king. Biedin will kill him," said the Herald, and he set his temple on the flagstones. He shut his eyes. And, his life's breath, he freed upon the air.

Durand looked up and found the square of the high sanctuary lying empty under the Vault of Heaven. Kandemar had brought them to the threshold.

"Come, Durand," said Deorwen. "The boy is in the sanctuary." And they left the Herald, running too quickly for conversation.

They raced into the high sanctuary's square. On one hand, beyond the broad plain of cobbles, the hundred rooms of the Mount of Eagles soared. Directly above them, however, the high sanctuary of Errest the Old towered. Its steps rose like a mountain.

They vaulted the stairs and found themselves in a cavernous, candlelit dark where five hundred holy men prayed in perfect unison. The air shivered with their voices. Every eye was shut. Overhead, windows of colored glass hung like curtains of black scales. And, down the whole length of the sanctuary, the wet footprints of the prince gleamed.

Durand spotted the altar, a bowshot down the columned aisle. He pointed. "The crypt is there. I see the tracks. They tend that way."

"He means to do it," Deorwen concluded.

And so the two pelted between the files of priests and sacred murmurs, splashing in the prince's wake, and sliding to the dark portal where the valves of the royal crypt lay open like a codex of gilded bronze. Here was tall Patriarch Oredgar of Acconel and a stooped ancient who could only be High Patriarch Semborin of Eldinor. Neither opened his eyes.

There were no stairs, and the floor was two fathoms down.

Durand called Biedin's name. And then he leapt—a heartbeat of falling—before he struck the floor, mashing candles in a scalding collision with the sacred stone.

From a war and a battlefield, Durand had come through a silent city and a praying sanctuary to this strange, quiet chamber at the heart of it all. This was a place where the crowned prince was meant to lie alone. The wards swirled in their sacred glyphs and curls, a mandala around the cist where the would-be king must keep his vigil. Even the Patriarch of Errest had not lingered. The priests had simply lowered Prince Reilan into the coffin hole, said their words, and left him to his delirium among the sigils and the dead.

Biedin peered up. The mud-plastered prince dangled his feet in the cist like a fisherman at a dock. It felt strange to see this great nobleman here, by himself. All around him candles burned. Their flames caught and glittered in the curves and arcs that the patriarchs had incised in the marble tiles. Ragnal's Evenstar Crown gleamed at the head of the cist where a thousand arcs met.

It was Biedin, Durand, and the secret boy, all alone at the heart of Creation.

Biedin had a yard of honed steel in his hand.

Durand got to his feet. From his new vantage, he could see down into the man-shaped hole. He could see the boy sleeping there with his father's heavy sword on his breast, like something from a knight's tomb. In the bay, so many were dying to keep this boy from harm.

And the point of Biedin's long blade glinted at the child's throat.

It was only then that Biedin took note of Durand.

"Durand Col," he said.

The man's blade winked in the candlelight.

"He is only a child," Durand said.

The prince blinked. "You will not understand, of course." He showed his teeth in a far-from-charming grin. "Though, you are a second son, are you not?"

"It would be better if you got back from the boy, Your Grace."

A small movement of the prince's hand caused the candlelight to spark and slither down the honed edges of his blade. The point cast reflections over the child's chin.

"I have been third since I was born. Ragnal was the Crowned Prince, and Eodan behind him."

Deorwen called down from among the murmuring priests. "Durand?" But Durand did not dare to glance.

"Your Grace," said Durand, "you are a prince of Errest the Old. A hero, perhaps." An army had followed him to Eldinor.

"Yes, I do see what you are saying, but it is too late now. You see, I was promised a secret way, and I listened."

Durand edged nearer. "The Whisperer."

"Ah! Yes. I suppose. 'Whisperer' is as good a name as any. He gave no name to me and I dared not ask. But I listened: I deserved more than I got. My brothers were unfit. Errest should be mine. That sort of thing."

He made another parody of a smile. His left hand flipped. A shrug, almost.

"We shot roots down among the foundation stones of my brother's power. My father died with Eodan blamed. The marches rebelled. We caused a great man to turn traitor." He chuckled. "And debts piled high till the Great Council howled for Ragnal's crown. You will remember all of that." He glanced at the glinting crown on the floor beside him. He might have touched it, but he did not.

Durand marveled. This was the man who had saved Durand's life in Acconel. Durand was stealing another inch closer when the man looked up.

"Ten years, I have considered, and here, I think, here is the issue. You must cast your mind back. Our games with the king and Radomor had upended the kingdom, and I was ready to slay my idiot brother. But the Heavens raged! I shock you with this business of murder. You would not have known. But do you remember the skies, Durand Col? The Banished and the Lost were howling at their bonds. I saw it all! Without a king, Errest must be torn apart." Biedin sucked a breath through his nostrils. "Errest must have a true king. But how could I lie in this place? I saw it at once: I had gone too far in darkness ever to lie in this tomb. If *I* seized the kingdom, I could not hold it for an hour."

With every small distraction, Durand inched toward the man.

"Had my Whisperer failed me? Was I betrayed?" Biedin stopped for an instant, saying, finally, "I did not speak to my Whisperer for many moons thereafter."

His lips were a hard, gray crease.

"I let Ragnal live, and the Banished were still, and I took myself back to Tern Gyre and suffered my Whisperer to call me craven.

"This next—I am only just now seeing all of this. This is new, you understand? I should not have heeded that thing! But it wheedled. It cajoled. And I began to wonder. What if I had been wrong?" He tapped his skull with the heel of his free hand. "Such a fool! But perhaps I *had* been a coward. What if I'd let a kingdom fall through my fingers? What if the kingdom had been too much for the Banished and the Lost?" He rubbed his face. "But I had seen the Vault of Heaven. I had heard the Banished raging. I knew better, but I listened!"

He panted through an inward smile, and Durand stole another inch.

He looked into the cist. "Then there came this boy, like a gift from the Powers. Little Reilan would be like a rag around a pot handle. He could stand the rite. An innocent! Through him, I could lift the crown.

"My Whisperer, he could arrange events in such a way that Ragnal's boy would have the crown, and I would rule." He looked at Durand. "We would handle the Great Council to ensure they named me regent, of course: Eodan would be a red-handed rebel. Abravanal, as well-liked and unthreatening as he was, needed care."

How many had Biedin killed? "Why the Hornbearer?" Durand said, despite himself.

"A hero must have a villain!" Biedin laughed. "I was to face the old devil down. There I'd be at the head of the host. My brother might die, try as I might to save him. But the Great Council? That old tortoise Patriarch Semborin? What could they do but proclaim me regent?"

He made the sword flash over Reilan in the cist. "Regent, and king in all but name. No rite. No tomb. And, perhaps, a few thralls of my own to help me manage the barons and the Council and the marches." He twitched a few teeth at Durand. "This is what I imagined. The Hornbearer at my command. The king in a cell. This is what we had arranged, my Whisperer and I. But the Whisperer, he wants neither king nor kingdom." He finished very quietly. "I know this now."

Durand had inched forward, handspan after handspan until he was almost in sword's reach. Biedin's blade touched the boy's throat. The point pressed a small pale triangle in the skin.

"Do you know that they call me the Lost Prince from time to time?"

"I have heard it, Your Grace."

"I slipped away from my tutors and found a passage underground. It was there that I first heard the voice." Durand had seen the man there.

He had dreamt it. "You know the Hornbearer did not heed me? I commanded; it did as it pleased.

"Ragnal, Leovere, Radomor, Eodan—each of us another dupe, another tool. What will the Whisperer do with a boy on my throne? Do you know I was lost three days before anyone found me?"

They were alone: two men and a sleeping child. "Leave the boy, Your Grace."

"Three days under stone. Three days not far from here. A very different vigil! Now it would be this boy?"

The man's nostrils flared. Durand saw his knuckles go white on the sword's hilt.

But for all that Biedin was full of devilry, Durand was faster. The broad point of Durand's blade found the prince's gullet.

Then, with a striding wrench, he pitchforked the scrabbling prince from the cist. The shrieking man's jaw took his weight. Durand jerked the point free—but before the prince could gather himself, he swung the blade back around, swiping the prince's head from his shoulders.

The corpse sprawled across gleaming glyphs and toppled candles, and Durand balanced, one foot on either side of Reilan's cist.

He could see the prince asleep at the intersection of every woven sign. Shoveling the madman off had seemed like the only thing to do.

Now, it was over. Now, there might still be a kingdom. There might be some reasons for all of the dying outside: Coensar and Leovere and all the rest, it might not all be wasted.

"It is done!" Durand called to Deorwen. "Now, the fight!" He tried to spot a ladder. There would be men dying every heartbeat, but he didn't like the idea of leaving Reilan unattended after all this. "Would you stay with the boy, Deorwen?"

Deorwen had found a plain wooden ladder and was already skidding the thing down into the sacred hole and following it down.

There was a quick hug. "Oh, Durand."

Durand felt tears.

The dead man's body was still half-heartedly groping at the floor.

"The rite would have roasted him," Durand said, but Deorwen was looking down at the boy.

"I'll have the priests down as soon as they finish their vigil. Host of Heaven, he looks so small in this tomb for grown kings. I'm not sure he's warm enough. Old Oredgar should know better. And that Semborin! And here he's still asleep despite his uncle. I feel we've all something to be ashamed of . . . priests and everyone. The crown seems big as a barrel."

Durand could not suppress a huge, brigand's grin. He had his hands on the ladder when he thought he saw something moving in the spiraling sigils, like a thread tugged down one of the gilded channels.

The Powers give a man no more warning than this. He should've moved at once.

The prince dropped from the hole, straight into blackness.

Gray webs jumped in every line of the ancient sigils. The boy was smothered, cocooned—and then torn right through the floor of the stone cist, beyond Durand's reaching fingers in an instant.

Ragnal's sword clanged, out of sight.

With hardly a glance at Deorwen, Durand plunged headlong into that black void in the floor, catching at skeins of gray web. He tumbled down the broken stone into the dark, crashing to a stop in a corridor, with a bloody jaw and torn hands.

From the corner of his eye, he spotted something alive in that space—a man-like thing had been watching, as still as a spider. Now, it crabbed backward and Durand was upon it. The webs fouled his blade, but Durand launched his weight against the apparition. In an instant, the thing's brittle fingers struck out. It cracked Durand against the ceiling and down upon the floor, lashing him about like a rabbit in the jaws of a hound.

In the very same instant, Durand's head exploded with whispers. Here was the voice of the mountains. The voice that had summoned Leovere of Yrlac and drawn the Rooks from beyond the Sea of Darkness. Thousands of thoughts spun through his head. The thing had been knotted around the very heart of Errest.

He could not think.

But, in the faint traces of candlelight that found them through the broken cist, he saw. A wizened thing hung there in the maelstrom of its own gray hair, its beard plastered against the ceiling. Durand stared up at the Whisperer.

The voices were still.

"You are the thing that Whispers!"

Durand saw images. They burst before his mind's eye. The Blackroot Mountains. The rotten forests of Fellwood. Battles far away. The Rooks. Radomor of Yrlac brooding in Ferangore. Radomor hanged.

"It has been you!"

Now, he saw different images. Errest the Old in ancient times. Banners on the ramparts of Eldinor. The Mount of Eagles full of light. A king's face and priests. Years in the dark. A wooden door.

The Whisperer writhed, hardly larger than a child. A dry curl of a thing.

"Who are you?"

The thing tugged and Durand was off the ground once again, smacking the ceiling, the floor. A maelstrom of images poured over and through him while he was still stupid with the blows. He saw war in a desert land. The banners of Errest and stranger arms from across the Atthias. He saw princes, giants, thralls, and maragrim in all their nightmare shapes.

Finally, he was blinking up at the death's-head pucker of the Whisperer's grimace.

At that moment, something clattered back where the ceiling had come down.

Deorwen had come to gather up poor Reilan. And Durand wondered if, just perhaps, she might get free.

Durand drew the Whisperer's eye.

"I saw you. In my dream, I saw you. You were happy to whisper then, but not now. Now, I see you as you are."

The shriveled maw opened wider. The claws twitched.

"You are the one who dragged himself home from the wars. The one Willan buried."

Durand hoped that Deorwen could get clear.

For now, a scream stabbed through Durand and the whole of that dark place. Durand closed his hand upon the hilt of his blade. The tunnel might have been a torrent then. And Durand flew from wall to wall. He got a fist on the old corpse's neck. The baleful cold of the thing jabbed through his knucklebones, twisting and prying at his joints. Coils of hair lashed around and around him, binding his jaw shut. Choking his mouth and nostrils.

Then the scream stopped.

Ouen's sword was trapped against Durand's ribs. Ragnal's blade was paces—leagues, they might have been—across the floor. And Durand was nearly finished. He hoped Deorwen had got the boy away, but then, with the last guttering flickers of awareness, he spotted Deorwen and the boy. Already, the tendrils were coiling about them. The sleeping boy. The last woman in Creation that Durand would have allowed to see harmed.

As the coils flinched tight around Durand, something clinked from the floor. Maybe a bit of silver from Durand's purse . . .

But the Whisperer twitched back.

Deorwen was no fool. She had seen the creature shrink, and she snatched a red glinting thing from the floor.

"Was it this?" she said. In her fingers was a gold and garnet ring, the one from the Lindenhall. The same garnet, the same serpents. . . .

The Whisperer shuddered backward.

"Just who are you then, you old devil?" Deorwen breathed. She had the ring held high. "The old ring stirs something in you." She twisted the thing. It winked.

"Shut away by Willan Blind—a mercy. Came up from the war. That's you? Kandemar has been talking."

She stepped free of the gray webs.

"Who would be so trapped by shame that the Enemy could bind him three hundred winters? Who would see the ring and remember shame? Kin to Willan Blind. A Prince, then. Shamed by the ring. Not Calamund the elder. Not the heir. Was it the second brother, then? Is that who you were? The second brother. You loved the girl too, didn't you? Is that what this was?"

The Whisperer watched, as still in his gray mane as a dead lamb in a whorl of dry grass. The bare holes of his eyes stared.

"But you gave your brother the ring. Did you not? And in the fighting far from home. Across the sea. Did something happen?"

She watched the dead thing, gauging its discomfort. "In the riot of battle, did you slay him?" A hiss. "No . . . a smaller treason. A hesitation. A warning unspoken."

The thing twisted.

"You loved that girl and you held your tongue or stayed your hand—just a moment—and he died, your brother," she said. "And thus, they had you. You are Heraric. The Lost Prince, buried alive. And you've been here. Lifetimes passing in the city above. Wars and kings and princes. Your kin entombed beyond your door while you whispered here, a maragrim prince."

The truth of Deorwen's assertions flashed past Durand's mind's eye. He saw a battlefield. He saw a stalking thing and a warning too late, and it was enough: this prince of maragrim broke his frozen silence and sprang for Deorwen, forgetting everything but hate.

And Durand had an instant of freedom.

Durand tore Ouen's old sword free and flashed the blade at the fiend's back. The wild swipe had caught the neck bones, and the devil's head was off.

The tunnel erupted. The Lost Prince lashed out in all directions, but the dry hollow of its skull had come adrift. Durand sprang upon the thing, driving the blade home—digging and tearing and gouging at the bony torso, the head, the clutching hands, till finally the storm subsided.

Deorwen had the boy prince and was hauling him away.

Durand found himself crouching upon a shriveled curl as dead and as dry as sticks in a hearth. Had this been the man, the prince? Near three hundred winters since his dying day. Untombed.

One of the Lost Princes, found now.

Durand looked about them. And realized he knew where they were— or he knew the door, at any rate.

"When Hod brought us below the palace, when the king and the starlings were out for our blood, he led us to this secret way. Me and poor Lamoric. A choked tunnel led to the crypt below the high sanctuary, but there was a locked door between. It was this door." The Whisperer's door hung open. Durand reached toward the doorframe. "He was here, even then. Right at the heart of the wards, a canker in the very bones of Errest the Old, whispering like a spider on the wards. And Lamoric and I walked by."

Durand looked down the tunnel, thinking of the proud Mount of Eagles, remembering as Hod guided them to the narrow entrance to the tunnel. "He said this was where he found young Biedin, lost three days. He was here." The notion chilled him. "A boy, running off. A boy's fears and pride and jealousy—and he found this thing. This Whisperer. What poison did that devil pour in the boy's heart?" He thought of the twitching corpse among the candles.

In a few moments, scores of priests were scrambling down the broken hole. They seemed hardly to notice Biedin's twitching remains or the husk of Heraric. Instead, they fought for a place before the boy and put their foreheads to the floor.

Durand found Patriarch Oredgar. Old Semborin could not have made the climb.

"Father. What—"

"He is king."

For a moment, Durand blinked.

"The rite is ended," Oredgar continued. "He is King of Errest the Old, and the Wards of the Ancient Patriarchs rest upon his shoulders. Semborin has said it."

So the king was a child, and only now blearily waking.

Beyond the wall, however, the battle was still raging. And now there was a king to fight for. A king—and perhaps the wards bound the kingdom a little tighter.

Durand stepped between the priests and caught the boy up. "Your Highness—lad—they need a king at the wall."

The boy blinked into Durand's face, and Durand felt like another of the monsters who harassed the child.

"You should decide," he concluded.

Deorwen gave Durand a look, but Durand only waited.

"Let us go," Reilan said.

DURAND LED THE whole company into the streets. Deorwen had the boy, and Oredgar of Acconel strode at the head of a hundred priests of Eldinor. Durand noted a backstreet shrine of the Traveler, real pennies nailed up for eyes. Durand had little idea what he was doing. He knew only that the Whisperer and all the rest had wanted kings and clergy out of their way. Now, he would bring every king and clergyman he could lay his hands on.

They ran.

"A breach!" said Oredgar.

Durand caught hold of King Reilan's little hand and the fighting was right before the wall. Three hundred men had reached the street. Biedin's door could never have admitted so many men. Things screamed in the breach. A towering rent stood in the old wall, seeming to hang like a jagged bit of sky.

Something larger than a wagon shot through the gap, exploding above the crowd in a rain of timber and plaster. They covered their faces.

The Atthians had fallen back—had been driven back—into the gap. They would have been dead without the breach as a bolt-hole. The thralls could not be allowed to reach the safety of the streets.

"What do you mean to do?" said Deorwen.

"We must get a look at the enemy," Durand said. "Come!"

Durand bulled into the crowd. He saw Berchard flailing, and Heremund with him. In twenty paces, Durand found Almora with her father's broken sword held high like a talisman.

"The tide!" she cried. "A moment longer! We must hold them!" as the Atthians fought hard to keep the enemy beyond the breach. Already, the maragrim were leaping onto the backs of the Atthians. Two hundred men held the jagged opening. The maragrim surged wildly against the Atthian lines, and all courage and loyalty in Creation would not hold the thralls back.

The press jostled Durand and the breach itself. He saw the broad tidal flat—and the half light then beginning to touch the Heavens glinted on the broad green of the tide. So near.

"Host of Heaven, it is true," he said.

Something long-limbed with a peasant woman's face rolled over him. He struck. The massive obscenities climbed into the breach. The Atthian line was scrabbling back. Thralls spidered up and around the broken wall. Mad things lashing fists and talons, driving men back. Hauling them down. Too slow, the spreading ripple of the onrushing tide crossed the flat.

Durand spotted the nearest tower in the curtain wall. The collapse of the wall had torn a ragged gash in its side. This might be a place to rally.

"Come!" said Durand, "or there can be no kingdom!"

He led the boy, tearing toward the flank of the ruined tower, hauling him up into the cleft and then stumbling higher into a half-ruined stair that shot them in and out of moonlight, with the priests upon their heels.

Durand thrust his head into a moonlit gap where the wall had tumbled away. Over the broad sea of dull mud and eelgrass, he made out a slender arc of silver spreading over the flats, rushing onward, spreading. Below, he saw the fight. A few hundred men tried to hold the Hornbearer's Host. He could see the waves coming—too late.

He heard Almora's defiant screams. He saw Coensar's Hesperand Knights, and Leovere's last Yrlacies. Eodan and his rear guard were overwhelmed. The fighting men of Gireth and Beoran and Garelyn were all scrabbling backward, with the thralls swarming over them. The wave was coming, but it would be too late. The maragrim would be in the streets.

There was the Hornbearer, flinging stones.

Durand turned to the boy. "Maybe there is a place for a king here," he said.

And Reilan climbed into that notch of moonlight. He must've seen the wild battle below them—the Hornbearer, and the dead men torn across acres of mud.

But the little boy pushed himself into the gap. He reached back, and somehow fearsome Oredgar knew to pass him the jeweled hilt of old Ragnal's sword. The glistening crescent of the tide swept nearer.

Durand helped the boy out onto the broken flank of the tower. And, as Durand looked on, the thousands of horrors in the field staggered. They gaped up: twisted men, monsters in human clothes, babes, beasts, and fishes.

All paused as that child tottered for a moment on the ruinous tower and thrust Ragnal's blade at the pale Heavens. There was the King of Errest, the crowned child, the first knot of the patriarchs' wards, and the whole web snapping tight. And, above the ancient city, his blade transected the first ray of dawn.

The thralls were spellbound. A glint from Reilan's blade flashed over a thousand wide eyes.

The deep had unleashed the tide of Eldinor and the great wave rolled nearer and nearer, its hiss and roar shivering in the tower. Not one of the maragrim stirred. The froth of the expanding wave hissed in the twilight while the Atthians scrambled ashore. The wave was rushing through and not a thrall of the Fellwood Host was moving. The king and his royal blade had transfixed them all.

The Hornbearer turned its hideous eyes upon the young king. Somewhere in that dark mind, the thrall must have understood that the hopes of Errest the Old hung completely on the child atop the tower.

The Hornbearer plucked a massive stone from the slime. And, even before Durand could seize the boy to throw him clear, the Hornbearer had flung the stone through the battlements like a spear through a man's teeth. On the tower, everything was blood and splinters. Priests had become a mess of rags. But Reilan tore free of Durand's hands and raised his sword yet higher. The tide was rushing over the flats, and the Hornbearer knew its peril. It charged.

In midstride, the giant snatched up a stone like a cowshed. Beside the king, Durand could only wince as the monster wheeled its arm and struck the tower again. They felt the heavy shock in their knees. Then, a dull thunder rose from the hollow bowels of the old turret. "Host of Heaven," Durand snarled, and he felt his stomach roll as the whole top of the tower pitched like the bow of some ship plunging over the end of Creation. Oredgar called upon half the Powers of Heaven.

The tower fell, and they rode it into the bay. Men screamed on its stairs and thralls were in the water all around. Durand had the boy by the wrist.

The tower exploded into drowning mountains of water.

Durand got hold of the boy's tunic and hauled him up as the rubble of the tower subsided into the salt waves.

HE MUST HAVE taken a knock.

He woke, blinking at the silver crescent of the Farrow Moon, full of bruises. The rush of water at his ears brought him round.

The thralls were drowning. And Durand lay on a new and painful spit of land. The rubble had made a new jetty beyond the wall, where the tide swirled the last of the thralls from Creation. He saw a hand, a helmet, a long beetle-back. And they were gone.

Closer to hand, he beheld a mystery of broad yellow petals thrusting up through the rubble. Only slowly did he understand that these were hanks of priestly cassock and that there was much blood. He saw the battered soldiers of Errest scrabbling at the bank, hauling stricken comrades from the waves, letting the maragrim lash against their fate.

But, over all this, he heard the *tock* of the Traveler's staff, and knew with a chill that it was, none of it, over.

The sudden clench of a small cold hand reminded Durand of the king. The little boy lived still. There was blood here and there, but the worst of it seemed to be where a long wedge of a stone stair had landed on the writhing boy's knee; there wouldn't be much left of the thing.

Durand flipped the stone away. "It is done, Highness," he said, but the Traveler's staff rapped again beyond Creation: *Tock*. And Durand knew that he was lying.

Durand got to his knees, sure that something must come.

His glance searched the shore. He saw Almora cradling her father's broken sword, with Ailric watching over her. He saw Coensar with the last of the Host of Hesperand. There were three or four men of Leovere's host still mounted—even Leovere, himself. Deorwen, looking aghast, was tottering over the rubble toward him. From her face, he wasn't sure if she meant to embrace him or slap him witless.

He might have smiled, but the staff rapped once more—*tock*—and Durand turned back to the broad expanse of water behind him. From the tower to the black smudge of the far shore, he could see nothing alive. "There is something more to be seen, or the Traveler would have left us," Durand muttered.

Then the stones lurched beneath his elbows.

"Ah," said Durand. "Here we are." He had the king by the wrist.

A great brown hand like a wheel clacked down upon the rubble only a pace from Durand's chin, then the giant Hornbearer was hauling himself from the waves and stone.

Durand hoisted the broken boy as the Hornbearer drew itself up. Water streamed from the giant, raining down all around Durand as the knight twisted onto his feet.

Durand resolved that he would not die staring. He tried to run, the boy on his back, but the stones flung them down. He could not get free. And the Hornbearer loomed.

For an instant, he could only hope that Deorwen would get clear.

Then something flashed overhead. Durand covered the king and twisted as four knights crashed into the thrall.

There were only a few men still mounted, and Durand saw, with amazement, his old captain and the accursed Duke of Hesperand. They had charged, on their Lost horses, over the shallows and struck the great brute with force enough to knock it flat. One knight crashed in the snap-boned tangle of his warhorse. He touched Creation at Durand's elbow and burst into wet clots of dust.

The others met the lashing savagery of the capsized giant: a riot of catapults and windmills. In that moment, Durand saw Duke Eorcan of Lost Hesperand, after an age of Lost wandering, dashed from Creation. And only Coensar fought on.

Durand got hold of the king, hauling him desperately toward the walls. Coensar's heirloom blade darted, flashing scratches over the giant devil's face and warding limbs. But, finally, the monster righted itself and turned a power that had wasted armies upon a solitary man of Errest. One blow smacked the jaw of Coen's horse to the stones. The rider followed.

Already, Leovere was stilting past.

"Go!" he said. "Get the boy from here!" and he struck at the Hornbearer with a clattering mortal sword. It was hopeless. As Leovere of Yrlac made to wind the Horn of Uluric one last time, the Hornbearer swatted both man and horn, and he flew in a boneless cartwheel to land, dead, in rocks at Durand's left hand. The blood and breath of the Duke of Yrlac spattered Durand and the boy as he landed with a clang of the old horn.

It rang, just a little, like the Traveler's staff.

Now, Durand alone stood between the thrall and the king. There were no more Lost horses. No one could dart across forty paces of jagged rock to yank him away. Deorwen was stealing forward, trying to reach the king. And three fathoms over Durand's head was a crown among the horns and tusks, like a ring in a hog's ear. The dripping saddle face tilted and Durand saw himself, very small, in the flint-glass bowls of the monster's eyes. He saw the great blackened curl of the horn around the thrall's neck, for all the world like a horse collar around the neck of a fool.

And he heard the rap of the Traveler's staff a last time.

He glanced to the horn in dead Leovere's fist. It had been dashed half-flat by the fall. The Hornbearer was raising one massive fist, but Durand could not look from Leovere's horn. He saw a hunting scene—a stag of branching antlers, a squadron of riders in pursuit. He saw the very same scene, black and bulging, in the arc of the great horn.

"Here," said Durand. "Who were you?" Who had they decked with the blasted trophies of Aubairn of the Forest?

The fiend held its fist poised, straightening itself to its full impossible height.

This Hornbearer had been someone out of the ordinary before the Beldame Weavers got their hands on him. "A great man to make so great a thrall," concluded Durand.

The giant brought its fist down, while Durand tried a tumbler's leap over the ragged rock. He caught Leovere's horn—the horn of Uluric, the horn that summoned the King of Aubairn, the horn that had cried for aid and got no answer of the king who had sworn to help.

Durand took the horn in his fist, and the fiend checked its next blow.

Again, Durand saw himself in the glistening bowls of the fiend's eyes. He got his feet under him, raising the horn, holding it before the brute like a talisman.

"A great man. A great shame. That horn round your neck, it was never meant to mock the men of Aubairn. It is *your* horn, and *your* crown. All this time. It is you they are meant to shame."

Durand stood no higher than the knees of this ancient thing, the horn held high. He still had Ouen's sword.

He hoped to Heaven that Deorwen had got the king out of the rubble.

"They were there at Pennons Gate, the Beldame Weavers, when the Enemy overran the Host of Aubairn." Durand's head swam at the thought of the thousand winters and countless battles seen by the wretch before him. He remembered the name: Aidmar, last King of Aubairn of the Forests. And here he stood, bound five centuries by a shame older than half the kingdoms in Creation. Aidmar had sworn to ride at Uluric's call, but he had let Uluric die betrayed rather than turning back with his people in tow.

Mightiest of Atthians in the west, yet caught by shame in that hopeless time as the Iron Knights held their Gates and he—with all of his people—died, Uluric and all the rest dead and betrayed for nothing.

"You could do nothing else. Aidmar, king. You could not know." Durand held the horn between them. "And now they've called you here, but your wars are long ended. You are Lost. I wonder. Can you remember what caught you?" The thing clutched its head. The horns. "Free yourself," said Durand. "The man you wronged? He'll have been walking the Halls of Heaven these hundreds of years. Where is the shame in such a thing? How can you be bound by such a knot?"

The giant was still. Durand threw the horn to the stones. He did not blow the note which sounded through Aubairn of the Forests when Uluric held the horn and so many died.

The giant swayed there like a hanged man, and then it lapped its hands on its narrow breast in such a way that one spot no larger than a man's heart was laid bare between thumbs and long fingers.

With this, the Hornbearer reared up, throwing arms wide as a mainsail yard, tipping its hideous face toward the Vault of Heaven. And Durand knew that there was a moment. The great chest was a fathom over his head, but there were stumps of the old tower still standing and Durand vaulted these, Ouen's blade like a spear in his fists. The point bit and he drove it home. He could feel the greasy squeeze of his own blood where his chain gauntlet gapped, but the blow shivered through the giant.

Durand remembered the pale ogre of Benewith and the meager scrap of jaw bone. He fell. But he saw the blackness blazing up from the point of Ouen's blade. It shot like a torn seam, opening a canker in the thing's hide—a mouth spilling roots like gnarled hair, bursting with gravel and stones. Living things pattered down. Scorpions flipped and twisted. Beetles. Worms and writhing centipedes rained upon Durand's face.

Aidmar the King struggled to keep his face full upon the Heavens, his arms still wide while the vermin and the worst horrors tumbled from the giant's breast.

Finally, then, the blade came free, and the Hornbearer folded over the crater of its heart. The vast saddle face crashed on the stones with the horse collar of the mocking horn, and the Hornbearer was no more.

A few dozen of the maragrim had reached shore and now shrieked and fought alone, surrounded by the men of Errest.

Durand got to his feet, seeing Leovere sprawled on the rocks. He spotted Almora with Ailric at her side. The Hornbearer was gone. Biedin was dead. And the Whisperer, the Prince—his tongue was still from now till the world ended.

32

The Mount of Eagles

Durand . . ." It was Deorwen speaking. She had the young king in her lap. She sat in the rubble, the boy's head cradled in her arms.

"Durand, Host of Heaven. I think he needs the priests."

"Oredgar. Where is Oredgar?" he said.

Deorwen's hollow glance told him everything. The terrible Patriarch of Acconel lay across the stones, one attendant at his hip. And Durand thought of the long body of the Herald. Oredgar was very still. He would be no help to Reilan.

"Semborin!" Durand said. "The high sanctuary."

He plucked the boy from Deorwen's lap and staggered from the wreckage of the Hornbearer.

He saw the face of his onetime captain. The man was broken a few steps from Leovere. He had ridden with the Host of Hesperand. He had bullied the Lost Duke to take his host into Errest once more. Durand saw not a single rider of the duke's company now alive—none save Coensar, whose chest still rose and fell.

"Durand . . ." pressed Deorwen.

The old knight was fading now. Death had drained his color, but he met Durand's stare. Once, Durand had hated the man, but now he knew a little of the fear that had moved the man all those years ago.

"It must be now, Durand," Deorwen pressed. There were Ailric and Almora, looking on.

Coensar gave Durand a curt nod and, with an answer, Durand gathered up the young and broken king.

Heremund had found them. "Old Semborin will know what can be done, if anyone does. He has been priest and Patriarch since the days of Ragnal's father." They set off, a ragged crowd pulling itself together to follow.

The boy bobbled limply in Durand's arms. The collapse of the tower had done no good. There would be bones smashed, organs ruptured, or blood pumping free somewhere within. Durand had seen any number of men broken this way.

"The boy will be well," Heremund was saying.

"Enough, Heremund," Berchard said.

Durand might have thought that Reilan's injuries were their greatest threat, but events had made him forgetful. Long before the Host of Fellwood ever marched upon the city, there had been evil within the walls.

Durand entered a square, and, from the inky gloom of an alley, there poured a dozen black-clad men, their heads bobbing like bladders. The monkish starlings padded out on splayed feet with a tittering show of ingratiating sympathy. First among them was Hod—the man who'd slipped them through the tunnels from the Mount of Eagles. Or his ghost.

"No further!" said Durand. He had the boy in both arms.

"Hod," said Heremund grimly.

"What is it?" Berchard demanded. "Who is there?" The man had his broadsword bare.

Hod bowed a step or two closer. "No, Lordship. No," he said. "No, of course." And, in that instant, the devils darted.

Though there were seventy men behind Durand, for a mortal few heartbeats he was very nearly alone with two dozen fiends. Needle claws snagged at his arms and jaw. Mannish faces twisted into ghastly masks of teeth.

Only a desperate wrenching twist pulled the boy away.

"Ailric!" Durand called. Durand thrust the king at Ailric even as two hundredweight of fiend crashed down on Durand's back. Its teeth and talons seared and spattered fresh blood before Durand could throw it down and wrest Ouen's sword from his scabbard.

Though they wore the shapes of swag-bellied scribes and courtiers, the starlings now sprang with feline lethality. Talons snatched red spray from Durand's face. Awful mouths gaped a foot wide, baring jaws crammed with slim teeth, longer than fingers.

Durand came up with Ouen's sword, striking off a head and warding hand, and whipping the razor blade through another distorted face before three more of the devils leapt upon him, beating him to the ground as he twisted and clawed.

Hod's wild, distorted visage stretched jaw-breakingly in Durand's face. The teeth, row on row, trembled with blood already. The jaws clapped and the Hod-thing smiled—then they were both struck.

The crowd behind Durand had come alive at last.

Durand felt one fiend torn from his back. Men from ten dukedoms fell upon the starlings, hacking like a butchers.

The Hod-thing pulled Durand's head down toward its mouth like some fiendish mockery of lovemaking. It was too mad to flee, and too strong to resist. Durand had an elbow jammed in the thing's chin, but his arm was breaking. In an instant, the thing must have him—even if the king was saved.

The devil smiled.

Then a blow fell.

Ailric had broken free. He must have seen and understood—and left the boy. The youth's sword flashed like a whaler's lance past Durand's cheek to shiver against the cobbles at the back of Hod's head.

Hod's iron grip gave way and his face sagged. Then the whole hide of the thrall went slack and Durand was sitting upon a boneless, bursting sack of stinking offal. From the staring eyes, the open mouth, erupted a slurry of reeking stuff as dark as claret and thick with indescribable matter.

Sick, Durand rolled free of the mess and sprang away. Almora and Deorwen crouched by the king. The crowd was chasing the last of the devils back into the streets. Ailric got his arm, but Durand waved him off.

"I think it's only blood." And, saying so, he saw that his hands were red, and that black blood spread over the green surcoat Deorwen had given him.

"Has any harm come to His Highness?" said Durand.

"He has taken no new hurt," said Deorwen.

Durand turned to Ailric. "Tell them we'll have a vanguard and a rear guard this time, with these things loose in the streets. I want armed men on every side, and a few fearless whoresons down the alleys." He bent, getting his hands under the boy. "They may guess we're heading for the high sanctuary. We must hurry."

Durand was bundling the king back into his arms, but the boy was saying something. "No! No. Not the sanctuary."

"Now, Your Highness," said Durand, "you needn't worry. Old Semborin will see you right in no time. . . ."

The boy was hardly awake. "Eagles . . ." he managed. "My mother. She is there. She's there with *them*."

And with the last word, Durand understood. The Mount of Eagles had been heaving with starlings when Durand had last set eyes on the place. The boy's mother would be somewhere in that hive of devils. He thought of the poor woman, so powerless and alone. She would likely be dead already. He could say nothing.

"We must hurry," said the king.

Heremund tried to speak. "She will want you safe, child."

"We must find her!"

"We'll send some men, Highness," Durand said. "We must get you to the high sanctuary."

"No. My mother. My mother first."

"Highness, you'd best hear this: we fear for your life."

The boy looked solemnly up into Durand's face. "If I am king, then you will take me to the Mount of Eagles. The Host of Heaven will watch over me if they will, but I can't leave my mother to those things."

"Highness . . ." Durand looked into the boy's face, wanting to tell him that he must forget his mother, that too many men had died to save him. He could say none of these things.

"Am I king?" said the boy.

"All right, boy. You are king."

"My mother, then. Your word on it."

"The Mount of Eagles. You have my word."

A good hundred men were looking at him and the limp boy. Baron Vadir was the foremost. "Take a conroi for the damned Patriarch, Baron. You'll have to run the old man across the square."

THEY JOGGED A new route, listening to the shrieks and clatter ahead as the vanguard and patrols flushed maragrim and turnskin thralls.

Every lurch stabbed a groan from the king.

Durand could not stop to examine the boy, but he'd seen men bleeding into their guts flinch the same way around the pain in their bellies. And it was no good when a young man could not rouse himself. Vadir had better be quick with the Patriarch.

The gates of the Mount of Eagles hung unlocked and unattended. Strong men pushed the doors wide and the company stepped inside. The place stank and hummed with flies beyond counting. Men turned to Durand.

"We will bring the boy to the throne room. Post a squadron at the gate, and send Semborin to us with a strong party. I cannot guess what we will find inside."

Ailric took Almora's hand. "Let us see," she said.

In the first black anteroom, they found mortal serving men by the dozen lying torn and strewn all about the place. The walls dripped like a meat market. Durand slipped and skidded in clotted stuff while Ailric pointed to the smears of splayed toes.

In the gloomy corner of a barrack room, something had heaped a score of dead men. As the newcomers forced themselves closer, they perceived a grinning court toady atop the pile like some mad hen. It blinked and averted its eyes. Without a word from Durand, ten hard men closed with the thing. It flayed the face and throat of one man into bloody white ribbons before his comrades could hack the devil to pieces. The maimed man did not live.

"Throw the shutters wide," said Durand, hoarse. The garrison of the Mount of Eagles had stacked many hundred pikes and bills in that place. "Break the doors. Pull down the roofs if you must. Lay it bare to the Eye of Heaven."

Every room that they entered, every passageway, men threw themselves upon the shutters and doors with axes and iron bars. And the dawn broke through. Bright planes and blades shot through the gloom, driving thralls cringing before them.

THE HALL OF the Hazelwood Throne was a vast place, nearly as lofty as a sanctuary and treed with columns in glittering rows. Gems bulged in the twilight, glinting like uncountable mute and lidless eyes as Durand brought the boy onto the bare patch of floor before the dais of the throne itself.

Durand paused while half a dozen black-clad men flapped down a side passage.

Almora stood tall.

Heremund explained. "Turnskins, men call them, not maragrim. The turnskins went among the Sons of Atthi as brothers and sons and children. Bulging in dead men's skin."

As the last starling vanished, Durand scowled. "They are not like the maragrim when they see the Eye of Heaven."

"But neither do they care for its touch," said Heremund.

Deorwen had her hand on the child's forehead. "He is not dead yet. This will set old Semborin running."

"Now we must see about the boy's mother."

Deorwen caught her lip in her teeth.

Durand could feel the old throne above them. Under garnet, gold, and beryl were timbers felled upon the Shattered Isle, before the *Cradle* landed in Errest the Old. Undaunted, Deorwen commandeered one of the old feasting tables and some of the least unsavory pallets. She probed the king's stiff abdomen and worried over the heat of his brow as Durand laid him down.

Durand knew himself to be no nurse, and so he looked to the defense of the boy in that half-haunted old hall. "Men at the doorways, Ailric," Durand said. There were many doorways in that gloomy forest of pillars. Two hundred men would not be enough to guard them all, and he did not have half so many.

Durand thought of the boy king's order. He had sworn to find the boy's mother, so he could see only one way forward. He took hold of Ailric's arm.

"Nothing must harm His Highness, Ailric. If the Patriarch cannot reach him or priestcraft cannot prevail, that is doom. But no thrall will touch him while any of you lives."

Ailric nodded. He must have seen how Durand eyed the passageway to the royal chambers; how he filled his lungs and set his teeth.

Almora was no fool. "Let us send men with you."

Deorwen shook her head. There were tears in her eyes. "There are not men enough, and he will not unspeak his word to this boy. He will not let his king die for being a boy and loving his mother." Very pointedly, she did not look up. Her lips were a stiff line. "He will go."

Durand wished he could do or say more, but there was the boy king dying, and there was the Lady of Gireth, his betrothed, looking on with poor Ailric. Ailric was still holding her hand.

Durand left the Hall of the Hazelwood Throne and took the stair to the lady's chamber with whispered directions from men who knew the Mount of Eagles better than he.

WITH OUEN'S SWORD in his fist, he climbed a corkscrew stair with his shield between him and whatever might come barreling down. Soon, though, he was putting his head into a broad passageway. Mail made it hard to hear. He saw slashes of light slipping between shutters here and there. He twisted his neck, thinking that the last devil had nearly torn his head off. The royal apartments were along the passage. There were meant to be stools at either side of the doors to that apartment. Durand stepped out.

At one shadowed door, he saw two stools. And, when nothing leapt on his back, he moved closer still. The door was set deep. What he saw was unbroken, but scarred. How long would the thralls have been loose in this place? Till the Whisperer died, the things had been on a leash.

Durand moved through a curtain of light.

He wondered if the thralls had given up. The door was stout and there must have been easier pickings among all the passages and storerooms and kitchens of the palace. Then three lumpish men uncoiled themselves from the shadows of the deep doorway. All three smiled, but every one was spattered with the grim evidence of their ravenings. In their eyes, Durand saw nothing more human than a bit of glass.

"Ah," said the closest one. It winced nearsightedly. "What a night it has been! Yes. Quite a night. With these . . . things . . . at liberty . . . in the Mount of Eagles." The thing managed a shaky bow. There was something familiar about the face; the black-robed creature seemed to feel likewise. It tilted its head.

"It is Sir Durand, is it not?" The thrall pawed a drop of something from his upper lip. Embarrassing. "You came to this place. Lamoric and the hostages. You were his man. Ten winters, or nearly. Hod took charge of you."

Durand remembered the creature. "The Master of Tapers," it had called itself. Boiling tallow somewhere beneath the palace. And it had not changed, though its hesitant progress left a heron's splayed track every second or third step. The Master of Tapers was absentminded.

Durand felt the grip of Ouen's sword through the mail and leather palm of his gauntlet. Tapers was not alone. And three of the things would be too many for Durand. He thanked the Powers that door had held.

The Master of Tapers cringed low as it bobbed nearer: three paces now. Durand was desperate to find an advantage.

"Her Ladyship is within, we believe," said Tapers, "but we cannot know. She will not answer. The door is barred. Or there is a barricade. . . ." The fiend's eyes glinted blankly. "Perhaps some harm has befallen her." It remembered to blink and took another step. "We must know."

With these final words, Tapers was near enough to strike. Its jaws flashed wide—belt to brow in an instant—and its clawed hands sprang.

But Durand was not fooled. He bulled straight at the thing, knowing that few would have dared such an act before. He drove hard behind his shield, jamming the cover into the scrabble of teeth and claws till he had the devil on its back.

Durand spun then and swung in a new direction. A second thrall, not ready, pitched into the rising arc of the blade. Its face and shoulder flew free, the bilious flesh bursting.

From the floor, the Master of Tapers caught Durand's mailed leg in its teeth and talons. Nearly, Durand fell, but rage and terror kept him upright. He drove his blade down. And the devil dodged free, yielding the leg for a moment.

Two remained. One tall and baggy, the other, old Tapers. They watched him.

Durand staggered past a window. The thing had been painted black, but there were flaws. Durand's shadow flitted across the face of the tall one and it winced.

Durand backed a stepped into the alcove where the window hung.

Meanwhile, the tall turnskin stepped forward. He was all jowls and a high gray skull. His jaw lolled, and a tongue like a skinned serpent jumped among the knife-blade fangs all up and down.

As Durand stepped before the blackened glass, the thrall leapt.

And Durand collapsed at its first touch, making a fulcrum of braced arms. The monster was airborne, levered high in a wrestler's throw that sent it crashing through the black glass.

Though Durand had struck his head, the devil was done, and now the passageway blazed with the Eye of Heaven.

But before Durand could clear his head, the Master of Tapers was leaping left and right, bounding like a jungle cat through the blades of light, impossibly quick and strong. More sudden than an adder, it snatched the long sword from Durand's fist. Another slap from the shadows cracked Durand against the window frame, cartwheeling him into the passageway. For good measure, the floor stamped his mouth full of blood.

Tapers swarmed forward while Durand gulped at the air. It flung Durand onto his feet and thrashed him from wall to wall. He broke one of the queen's stools. He tumbled into the alcove by the door. Then he saw it gathering itself. The vast mouth dropped once, then its lips—as long as a fat man's girdle—twitched in a big slack grin. It leapt.

In the same instant, Durand's head and spine struck the queen's door, and the old door broke. He landed with the broken door slapped flat beneath him and then the thrall's fingers were in his lips, hard as iron hooks, wrenching while the warped face slathered above him, full of stink and teeth.

Durand caught at the thrall's arms, at the black eyes, at the slack and rippling features—at the raw gory thing now only half-hidden by its stolen skin. This creature could not prevail.

The thing's eyes crackled with glee.

In that moment, Durand caught a glimpse of Queen Engeled herself as she looked on. Her room had tall, deep windows, all shuttered. Things shone in the gilded walls. She had been trapped with the devils wheedling and beating on the door. They would have her next.

He thought that she should jump for it. Choose a window. It did not matter. There might be drain pipe.

And, as if answering his prayer, Engeled threw the shutter wide.

The thing on Durand's chest hissed.

The woman should have jumped. He saw her foot on the windowsill. But she had seen the devil react and suddenly she was on the move.

With a bound, she crossed to the next window, darting up and throwing the shutters open. Plane after plane of bright dawn fell across the room, and the thrall writhed in the face of it. The Eye of Heaven blazed on every gilded wall.

The thrall crabbed backward and Durand could do nothing more than blink at the image repeated in gold leaf and polished stone: there was the thrall cringing before the Eye of Heaven, dragging itself from the room and into the safety of the passageway.

There was a swirl of skirts through the light and the queen was before him. She had one long shutter. It flashed like a sail high over her head, and she drove it axing down on the thrall.

Again and again.

Even to find her son, the Queen of Errest did not leave Durand, though he could not blink the fog from his aching head.

"Years I have lived in this place, surrounded by these leering devils." She clutched herself. "I find that I am shaking." The bright walls of her chamber shone upon them. "You will take me to my son, Durand Col. You will wake up and take me to my son. He is alive or you would not be here."

Durand's tongue would not answer, but he allowed himself to be helped to his feet and let the Queen of Errest nursemaid him down the many damnable stairs of the Mount of Eagles.

Deorwen and Almora ushered the queen close to the unconscious boy while Durand supported himself on a pillar nearby.

He peered up and down the ancient hall, seeing doorway after doorway, each with some poor solitary knight standing guard—as if any man could stop a thrall who meant to do the king harm. Breathing deep cost him a spasm of pain. They must find a bolt-hole somewhere. Somewhere they could defend.

Deorwen looked into his face. Her glance skittered over him, seeing torn seams, bruises, blood, and nails uprooted.

"The king'll have a shrine," Durand said. "We should take the boy to the king's shrine."

It was the queen who answered. "There is such a place. It is not far. Follow me!"

THEY LAID THE boy before an altar with the breeze from the Bay of Eldinor spinning in the vaults and broken windows. Almora and Deorwen brought water, making useful rags of an altar cloth. Durand packed the shrine's two doors with fighting men and stood watch with a drawn blade. Soon, Patriarch Semborin appeared, bringing a better healer: a lean man who had worked in city hospices. Long fingers probed the boy's ribs. And the knee was viewed with winces.

When he could not help himself, he watched the boy breathe.

All the while, Reilan's mother held his head in a delirium of hope and dread, and hours of prayer and watchfulness passed while the doom of the realm waited upon a small boy.

He was not well.

THREE HOURS AFTER Dawn Thanksgiving, Heremund stepped out to learn what had become of the city and the host.

Two hours after Semborin muttered the Noontide Lauds, the Duke of Garelyn appeared at the sanctuary door with Maud of Saerdana and the Duke of Beoran in tow.

Very nearly, Durand ordered them to wait, but, nose-to-nose with Maud of Saerdana, he relented. Despite long nights of perilous flight and battle, she looked every bit the ruler of two dukedoms. Beoran, following after, now seemed nothing more than a beard and sunken eyes.

"Look whom I've found," said Garelyn. "Spent the night in a stout oak wardrobe, it seems. And I've led them past some nice bright windows to see if they flinch or shrivel."

There was a flutter of offense from Beoran; Maud merely peered past Durand, her eyes on Reilan.

"Sir Durand," said Maud, "will he . . . how is His Highness?"

With the child's mother so near, Durand would say only, "We are watching."

"Of course," allowed Maud. "Of course, Sir Durand. The poor child." The woman slipped past Durand and descended upon the boy. The queen had to give her space. "The poor thing. So brave. His father would have been so proud."

Durand blinked deeply. "If I had not hanged him," he refrained from saying. "I am sure," he said, instead.

"Of course, poor boy," said Maud. "He will need someone to look after him."

"He will," said Beoran. "He will need his interests protected."

Garelyn snorted. It was the loudest sound they'd heard for hours.

Durand closed his eyes. His head ached from the thralls' beatings. Here was the injured boy lying on the very threshold of the Gates of far Heaven, with his grieving mother at his side, and already these fools were wrangling over influence. They were, very nearly, worse than the turn-skin thralls. He took a big breath through his nose.

Almora stepped between him, Maud, and the Duke of Beoran.

"Perhaps we should let the boy rest," she said. "These are important matters, but he is not well."

"Wise words," said Garelyn.

"I think that nothing is finished," said Maud. "We all saw the tide and the Eye of Heaven. But who knows what has survived of this host from the Fellwood, and the king has only a few hundred fighting men remaining to him. The Host of Hesperand is no more. The Duke of Yrlac died upon the tower ruin, if we can grant Lord Leovere that title."

"I think we'd better," said Garelyn.

"And Eodan of Windover," said Maud. "No one knows what has become of him."

"For now," amended Beoran.

"And there is the young king to consider," said Maud. "He is only a boy, after all."

Durand felt his fists tighten. In an hour, the boy might be dead and Engeled a grieving mother only.

"Come," Almora said. "There is a chamber, a vestry, just beyond the door." The highborn fools seemed to think this reasonable.

Durand had not moved.

In the carved doorposts, the stone Powers of Heaven shifted at his glance, stone eyes rolling in their carven sockets. This old Mount of Eagles was a place of uncountable warrens, and the maragrim prince had been casting his whispers upon the dark for three hundred winters, drawing the devils down.

"Sir Durand," said Almora. She had likely expected Durand's support. Maybe for him to do the speaking.

"You must go, Almora. You are daughter of the Duke of Gireth. Ailric can advise you."

The girl blinked a moment, but then nodded.

Lady Maud had opened her long mouth to announce her approval, when Heremund appeared.

"They've found the boy's uncle."

People turned, about to exclaim with joy, but the skald flapped his hands. "Ah, no. Sorry, no. They found a number of men at the tide's ebb. The waves had been at them, but hauberks and helms moored them fast to the bottom. They had a time making out faces."

Without a word, the men and women in the dim shrine turned to the boy near the altar. There was no king but Reilan. None of Ragnal's line survived.

"Now," said Garelyn, "we must talk."

33
The King's Watch

The king did not heal.

Hours passed in the sanctuary. Soon, night winds breathed through the tall windows. Somewhere, beyond the Mount of Eagles and the streets of Eldinor, the bay flooded with the cold, deep salt of the Westering Sea and drained away once more.

Semborin's priests and wise women hovered about the boy and his mother, and the prayers were never ending. Deorwen worked. Durand watched near the sanctuary door, far from the altar. And it was not long before he realized that the Lost were standing among the columns, keeping a mute vigil of their own as they crowded the sanctuary.

One breath from the window across the aisle carried something rank in it. Durand was not surprised to see the Rooks settle in, peering over the dark blades of broken glass still trapped in the frame.

"Oh," said a whisper. "Such a time we've all had."

"It has been a long night for the poor boy."

"Aye. Though others have had it worse, I fear. The tide is a sudden thing about the walls of Eldinor. So many wounded men. The wild struggles. And then the silent hours . . . brave men bobbing against the weight of iron rings."

Bits of broken glass crackled under their claws.

"And then, of course, the sea drew back its coverlet and laid bare their graves."

"For the curious."

"And the brothers and lords and fathers and sons of the slain."

"And those gulls, of course."

"The black-backed gull can yelp just like a man!"

"It had not occurred to me until this day."

"It is a most disconcerting effect when a fellow is tripping and stumbling among the corpses, to be sure."

"And I had not thought to see eagles picking among the slain."

"The king's bird, they say."

"But here is the poor boy, struggling now."

"The issue is very much in doubt."

"With Eodan crawling with rag worms and crabs."

"What will become of Errest the Old after so much bloodshed?"

"The Banished and the Lost, they will be listening, watching, waiting. The very air of this night trembles with it. There is not a beast or bird asleep this night. They all keep watch."

"And the denizens of the Still Kingdom teem upon the Bourne of Jade."

"And the Thurser Lords of the Halls of Silence. They will be gazing from the eaves of their forests."

"The Sons of Atthi may cast their minds back upon the Hornbearer's days with fond hearts."

"And to think that our Durand fought till his bones cracked."

"And threw a dukedom away."

"It is a hollow prize."

Durand watched the boy breathing.

As Durand stared through the crowd of scorched and mangled specters, with the Rooks taunting and the poor king slowly dying, he realized: the sanctuary ought to have been barred to such things, yet here were the Rooks picking their way along the broken edges of the windows, in and out of the consecrated space.

Durand was moving, stepping through the eerie crowd.

The Broklambe children clutched at ankles, clung to pillars. Some, he saw, were worrying at the tiles with brittle fingers.

"They have hidden something in this place," said Durand.

Semborin turned. It was his whole hunched body that moved, like a beehive. "What do you say?"

Already, Durand had his knife at the edge of one square tile. The Broklambe dead crowded eagerly.

He blinked at a cough of reeking air. There was a hole.

Inside, he saw something. A putrid something, as slick as a pot of boiled apples. An infant, maybe. There were coarse stitches. The stiff fan of a black wing grafted. This would have been the Whisperer or the turn-skin thralls or mad Prince Biedin. He wondered how much evil these men had done. He wondered whether thrones or vengeance or any of it could be worth even one such horror.

"Look not, Durand Col." Semborin had lowered himself. "But much is explained." He looked to the boy king. "We will set this right, and then we will see about His Highness."

The Broklambe children worried hungrily at tiles here and tiles there. A spot near the king. Another high on the wall where a bit of molding had their attention.

Semborin pressed a finger to his temple, and, by his glance, Durand guessed that the Patriarch could then perceive the Lost or the hiding places or both. "A tidy bit of desecration," pronounced Semborin. He gave Durand a rheumy squint, but did not ask how Durand knew. "Now, let us see what can be done."

Semborin summoned the priests to work. "This is matter for priests," he told Durand. "You have seen enough."

Durand pushed through the guards in the doorway, thinking that he had, in fact, seen too much. For guilt. For jealousy. For greed. For power. Too many horrors. Maybe they would put the Mount of Eagles to the torch. Maybe they would drag the old throne into the square. There could not be soap or sunlight enough to make the place clean.

In this mood, he nearly stumbled over Almora.

She stood before him with Ailric at her shoulder.

"Almora," Durand managed. He had the presence of mind to say, "Do not go in." And he thought to add a few words to say that the king was in no greater danger.

But the girl only nodded. This had not been her errand.

"We are taking a moment to think," said Almora. He could see Maud stalking off with Beoran on her heels. "Sir Durand, there were others who might have watched over the king, yet you had me go alone. You had me go alone to argue over the doom of the realm. Or rather, you had me go with Ailric when you, you were battle commander of all Errest."

Ailric, knowing an awkwardness when he saw it, attempted a shallow bow. "I have no place here—"

But the girl raised a few fingers, and he was silent.

"You might have seen Ailric and me. How he is with me. You might have been thinking of that. It's this I was wondering about. Whether you thought I'd keep faith."

Had he been thinking of this? The boy watched over her. He recalled their long talk under the trees of Hesperand.

"You've done nothing," he said.

"You must know, there is no question. We are bound to marry. I have agreed. Everything that has been promised, you will have. You need not fear."

Behind him, they were digging up the rotten things. Clinks and scrapes reached them, while, at the same time, the bewildered dead abandoned the sanctuary, passing all around until Almora spoke from a silent crowd of mindless faces: Euric, Ragnal, Gol. The black Broklambe creatures huddled. Sometimes, Durand could not even see Ailric's consternation through the throng.

The priests were singing.

Not a death song. Not a song of reverent dread.

They raised their voices in a building harmony, high, bright, and wild. Like washerwomen pounding at the river. The old priest threw life at the death of the Host Below.

At once, Durand knew what he must say.

"You are not bound, Ladyship. I kept out of their talk to watch the boy, or because I needed to rest a while and let my mind work." Where the marketplace bickering of the boy's supposed liegemen could not be heard. "You are not bound to me. Ailric is a fine boy, though I'm sure he will have a job to win your hand. For my part, he is free to try."

Almora blinked. "What do you mean?"

"I make no claim upon you or your father's domains. I claim no one and nothing." Dead faces turned, but he only smiled. Maybe the guards had heard him too. "If you wish, we might keep it secret till things can be arranged for you. I'm not sure you'd wish to be ward of the king or some king's regent. You will decide." How that would end, no man could say. Durand could only hope.

Ailric was still looking on, clearly astonished behind his accustomed reserve.

"And Ailric, if Heaven will hear me, you have what blessings I can give."

The girl clapped before talking hold of Ailric's hand.

"Your Grace," said Ailric, bowing.

"You need not style me 'Grace' or 'Lord,' my friend." Durand smiled. "Good luck to you both," he said, and left.

He should have felt fear at this. Fear for his future, now uncertain. But, in his heart, he found only gladness.

*   *   *

DURAND WALKED OUT into the holy gloom of the Hall of the Hazelwood
Throne, his Lost followers trailing him among the orchard of columns.
He stopped before the reliquary throne. Blacked by time, here were the
very bones of the ship that carried the Sons of Atthi from their shattered
home across the seas: black framed in gold and precious stones.

In recent years, the broad window above the throne had been smothered up in black curtains. Now, already, the twilight before dawn glowed
in the web of colored glass. Scenes came to life in the glass: heroes,
castles, ships, and a sea full of childish kings and sailors.

The Lost trailed Durand across the tiles, and now Durand even
grinned at his collection of monsters. Almora and the boy had gone back
into the Council meeting.

Durand marveled that between all the rooftops bristling upon the
Mount of Eagles, there was room for the Eye to shine upon that window. There would have been generations fighting the builders over such
a thing, Durand was sure.

The light had the Lost clinging to the backs of the various columns.
But Durand, duke of nothing, rounded on the things. And, for the first
time in God-knows, he spoke.

"Here," he said. "It'll be dawn in a moment's time, you know. The bells
will ring, if the Patriarch's lads remember. And you are free."

He peered into the staring faces: the bloodied, the burned. And he
raised a hand to the round window full of light.

"What use is there in trailing after me? Here is the Gate of far Heaven,
beckoning. Here is your chance and hope of better than grubbing at shadows and pestering a fool. Here," he pressed. "Go, I tell you."

The dead stared from their hiding places, and Durand could not have
said they understood. "If it's me that's holding you, I say go. I have seen
maragrim thralls beyond counting. The Hornbearer. Heraric, the Prince.
Biedin, even. None of them could drop the greed or guilt or pain they
hung on to. But I must take their lesson. I've been a fighting man. I've
slain men for countless causes, but mostly to keep my people from harm.
I've been no monster."

The dead watched him. It seemed their faces turned toward him. It
was hard.

"I will not turn from you. Not now. And I confess there was wrath
and cowardice and greed in my dealings with you. But I will come to
the Bright Gates in time and try my fortune there, and so ought you all.
By our Creator," Durand implored, "by his Queen, by the Warders of the
Bright Gates, by the Champion, the Maiden, the Nine Sleepers, by the

whole Court of Heaven, I say go now. Seek the Bright Gates. If some madness of mine has bound you, let me break your fetters and cast them away."

Some ray of the Eye of Heaven burst between the rooftops and pinnacles of that old palace then, kindling the east window with a new fire and painting the throne room with color.

This time, the dead did not cower. This time, they stood, half-wondering in the slanting column of light that poured through the window and glittered in the candle smoke. The beggar king, Ragnal himself, the one-eyed giant, the Lady of Yrlac, the blue-clad plowman of Hesperand; one after another, they turned their eyes from Durand Col to face the great Eye of Heaven. One by one, the great company of them, faint then as shadows, walked into the light and out of Creation, all vanishing like shade at noontide.

Durand heard, just then, the rap of a brass-shod staff on the stone.

"Not you too, now," he said.

But, with all that had been going on, it seemed that he had not been listening—or not to the commonplace sounds of Creation. Now he heard a clamor of voices echoing in the high hall, like a mob beyond a sanctuary's windows, though he could not have guessed a direction.

As Durand wavered before the throne, a portal swung open, filling the vaults with voices. And there was Baron Vadir of the Swanskin Down, a bowshot down the orchard of columns. He had been commanding the guard.

The man stalked into the hall with an eye on the door.

He called down the hall. "Lord Durand, the people have come. Hundreds from the city. They have heard many tales. There is a new king in the Mount of Eagles. The king is dead. The king lives."

The voices rang in the passageways of the palace. "It is too late to tell you 'Bar the gate,' I think."

"They boiled up like mice from burning house, Sir Durand. There must be half a thousand gates to this palace for those who know them."

"Your men must hold the throne room, Vadir, but I will not shed Atthian blood."

"Nor I," called Vadir, but a ring of knights tumbled backward, overborn by the throng of common people pouring into the hall, filling the long aisles and crowding the broad nave. Yet just as the mob seemed ready to overwhelm them, the spell cast by the Hazelwood Throne, and the glass that shone like garnets and emeralds, and the pillars studded with gems seemed to cow the multitude. People goggled at the windows and then looked up into the gilded vaults over their heads. The ancients had worked traceries of gold wire into winding designs that flew up each column. They met and wove in liquid patterns in the dusky archways above, like the patterns in the cellars of the High Sanctuary. Most would never in their lives have seen the Hazelwood Throne.

Vadir and two dozen baffled knights had fetched up at the foot of the dais with Durand. The whole of the surviving Great Council rushed into the room and stopped also. In a moment or two, the mob would wake up. God knew what they might do.

"Durand," called a whispered voice, and Durand turned. Deorwen had appeared between the columns where the little sanctuary was hidden. The sight of her made Durand smile, despite it all. He wondered if she'd been there long enough to hear his great speech; he supposed he'd said it all aloud.

Deorwen was beaming.

"Well? What is it?" said Durand.

Rather than making an answer, Deorwen stepped to one side. And there, tottering on a very plain crutch, appeared the boy king himself, with Patriarch Semborin a respectful two paces behind.

"Your Highness!" said Durand.

Two hundred people flopped to their knees in a dull thunder, as quick as if they'd been cut down by a scythe. Sobs of thanksgiving erupted here and there, but the majority pressed their faces to the floor. They'd come to the Hall of the Hazelwood Throne and now, in their marrowbones, they knew it.

Durand, however, saw the trembling boy. The queen and the Patriarch had let him walk. They stood among the columns, watching him totter like a foal. The lad's eyes blinked from shadows as gray as the pale bowls of mussel shells. Durand caught the boy's arm and got an abashed look.

"They should stand," Reilan said.

"You tell them, Highness," said Durand, and nodded to urge him on.

"Rise!" Reilan said. "It is no time for the Sons of Atthi to kneel."

The crowd, half of it, got to their feet.

"Throne or bed, Highness?"

Heremund the Skald bandied alongside like a shepherd's dog, watching Almora, Ailric, Moryn Mornaway, a grinning Alret of Garelyn, old Maud of Saerdana, Ludegar of Beoran, sly Highshields, fat Hellebore, and one or two more of the Great Council. None but Garelyn looked cheerful. With Patriarch Semborin, they created a procession.

"Throne," Reilan said, so Durand helped the king to the dais. The

Hazelwood Throne was up a few marble steps from the rest of the hall, and the boy was on one leg for now.

Garelyn ducked close. "Sir Durand," he said, "we reached an agreement. If the boy lived." He nodded a bow to the king as Durand helped him across to the throne. "Ludegar and old Maude have got men enough to guard the boy till he's of age, but neither one will bend their neck to the other."

The crowd sang, paeans of praise.

Heremund happened to catch Durand's eye. The man wore a big, doltish grin.

Garelyn tilted his head. "Eodan's dead, Highshields is crooked as an adder, and Almora's a girl. It was Heremund's idea—though each of them think they devised it. They none of them trusted me."

Durand helped the boy up one step and then another. Really, he should have carried the boy, but there were too many eyes on him. He hadn't the heart.

"I don't understand," Durand said.

"Nothing else would satisfy," said Garelyn, but, by then, they'd reached the broad dais and Durand was walking the boy to the Hazelwood Throne. The populace looked on, and the barons of the Council ringed the throne a respectful few paces from the boy. The Patriarch and his men had found the Evenstar Crown. Someone had even brought up old Ragnal's sword with its gilt eagle cross guard.

As Durand settled the boy into the seat—thinking that the crowd might have waited a day or two to see the king enthroned, considering all he'd been through—he found himself at the king's right hand with the queen opposite. There would be greater oaths and greater rites to come, but the High Patriarch of Eldinor was no fool. Ancient Semborin raised the Evenstar Crown over the boy's head and spoke in a voice that made even Lady Maude blink.

"Barons of the Great Council, people of Errest the Old, before you sits Reilan, son of Ragnal, your undoubted king by blood and rite to whom it is your duty to do your homage and service. Are you willing to do the same now before the Eye of Heaven?"

The assembled people knelt low and rumbled their consent. "I swear it." Few were the common people who had sworn such an oath before. None spoke the words lightly.

Next, the barons, every one, came forward, knelt, and swore terrible oaths with their hands between the boy's small hands as the Patriarch held the Evenstar over the boy's small head. Their lands were his lands. Their lives and their treasure they pledged to his service against all creatures who can live and die.

As Duke Alret of Garelyn took his turn, he gave Durand a winking look, and Durand too came round and swore his oath, though he had no land or titles to owe the boy.

As he stood, every eye of the barons was upon him, and the High Patriarch had come from around the throne bearing Ragnal's gilded sword with its eagles and precious stones. The king's jeweled belt was wrapped around the scabbard.

"Durand Col, you have sworn to serve your king, and now His Great Council bids you stand."

Durand looked into the faces of the barons on that high step. He saw Heremund grinning from the rows beyond, and Deorwen at the queen's side.

The rough Patriarch clapped the rattling High Kingdom sword into Durand's hands—the sword which had so nearly slain him in Acconel.

"Durand of the Col, as you are held in high honor by the magnates of the Great Council, the lords and banner knights of the kingdom, and are known by all to have bled much on the king's behalf, we call you to stand as the Regent of Errest and Lord Protector in the minority of His Highness, Reilan, King of Errest."

Durand took a deep breath, gulping, he was sure, like a fat pike in the bottom of some fisherman's boat.

"I— What?"

"Will you, Durand, serve as Regent and Protector?"

For a dizzy moment, Durand looked over the crowd of them. Here was the prize that all of Biedin's machinations had tried to conjure, now dropped in Durand's hands, unbidden. And, looking at Maude and Garelyn and Beoran and the rest, he was sure that it would be a devil of a thing, but he must do it. They were right. There was no one else.

And so Durand nodded then and swore his oath.

He turned to the people in the great hall, and raised his hand toward the boy upon the Hazelwood Throne.

"Long live the king!"

The people of Eldinor shouted the dust down from every corner of the Mount of Eagles, and ten thousand birds took to the air.

*   *   *

WITH THE KING finally ensconced in the royal apartments, Durand found an anteroom where he could sit and think a moment. His life would change now. It would no longer be enough for him to stand behind his master and growl. Already, men sought him out with a petitions beyond counting. There was, for example, hardly a serving man left alive in the Mount of Eagles. Durand would be cook, laundryman, and regent all at once if he could not find the men.

Durand blinked, eyes sandy and raw.

The little room he'd chosen must have been of use to some clerk or scribe. There was a good table and a large window, now empty of glass and free of shutters. Durand could not have guessed the hour, though some light slipped down between the buildings outside. Maybe it was evening already. He guessed that it was noon at least.

Inevitably then, Durand heard the Traveler's staff. *Tock. Tock.* And it seemed to him that a shadow, something broad as a sail, swept over the wall beyond his window.

In the next moment, something crackled on the sill's broken glass. Durand saw the Rooks hop there, but now Durand did not shrink from the devils. He only stood for them and smiled. They were great ones for working at the cracks in a man's heart, like the whispering prince had pried at vanity and jealousy and greed and all of that nonsense.

"Why don't you trouble someone else?" said Durand. "I think we're finished with each other."

There were bits of broken shutter here and there, and Durand shied a good-sized one spinning through the pair of them, and off they went.

Durand turned to find Deorwen standing in the only door.

"What were you saying?" she asked.

"Ah. I was just bidding some old friends good-bye."

"I will speak to the Patriarch about those two, whether you give me leave or not."

"I didn't know you'd noticed them."

"You are not the most observant of men."

Durand laughed a little. It was a very small room. Deorwen of Mornaway took a step closer.

"We'll need a glazier as well," Durand managed. "That's another man I'll have to find."

Deorwen made a small sound. It might have been a laugh. "I was with Heremund," she said. "Almora has other things to worry her. Did you know that Berchard knows the High Patriarch?"

"How is that?"

"If I understood correctly, Berchard and the good father spent a summer guarding a ship on the River Greyroad. It will have been forty winters. He knew all about Berchard's eye."

"A hag got the eye, he said."

"Just so. Father Semborin joked that the hag likely regretted the quarrel now. Berchard said she'd got plenty of use from the eye and had no right to complain. They had Heremund in tears."

They stood together in the small room. Durand was sure that the Traveler's great shadow still lay upon the wall, that Heaven was not done with him. Not yet.

"Deorwen," he said, "I have been laying things aside lately."

She stepped nearer.

"Dukedoms. Wives. I've noticed."

"Aye, well, I'd been lugging a lot of old foolishness with me, I find."

"I think I'd told you as much."

"But it's left me to wonder if I'd been carrying all the wrong things. All this nonsense. Coensar. Lamoric. All the rest. What if, all this time, I'd left something behind that I was meant to have kept?"

She stepped closer once more.

There was enough light in the old room for him to see her face, tilted up. She was so small. Always, this fact amazed him.

"You will have to make your meaning plain," she said, and Durand's ears caught the slightest falter. "I am going to hold you to that much, Durand Col." He thought he saw her dark eyes swimming a bit, but the dim light kept her confidences.

"Why can we not be happy too?" said Durand.

"That is not enough. You have not said it yet."

And, as nervous as a bridegroom, he put his hands on her arms. He hadn't done as much in ten winters, and even that little made him catch his breath. It was worse than the dizzy moment by the Hazelwood Throne.

"I've loved you since before I knew your name. Since Red Winding all those years ago. I think I would have killed Lamoric for you." Lamoric had left her behind, left her to run after him as he played Red Knight. Maybe he had not known her. "And then there he was, dead. And there was I, his man, and I'd betrayed him. But I could do nothing else."

"You did none of this alone," she said.

"But he is gone now," Durand said. "All this time. You know, he has never been among my Lost friends. Maybe he was too good for the Bright Gates to let free. But I think he has been very much with me. In my thoughts. He was a good man, but I think it is time. We must try. Perhaps there is a way to be happy."

Beyond the window, Durand heard the Traveler's staff. The brass ferule was rapping, now farther away. He was sure that the long shadow had left them.

Durand looked down into the woman's shining eyes. "I love you," he said.

She seized him as though she were a little girl, and Durand plucked her up and kissed her while her toes kicked the air.